"Delbanco's book of narrative riffs and meditations is a wonder. He may know more than just about anyone about the serious play that it literary life, and he writes of it with great spirit and flair." —Lorrie Moore

"Delbanco, like Malraux, has extended his method to explore a different context; a sensibility of enormous sophistication stretches itself to take in both the private and public domains . . . An excellent writer is among us, and if we neglect him . . .we shall have to apologize to posterity." —John Leonard, *New York Times*

"The wisdom of a superb, experienced writer and inspired teacher is here distilled for our pleasure. We have much to learn from Delbanco's maturity, broad perspective and erudition, his devotion to literature and to all those who struggle to achieve it." —Philip Lopate

"In its classic yet unmannered cadences, in its fidelity to the beauty of land and seascape and to the ambiguity of mind and heart, it is a true work of imagination." —Virgilia Peterson, *New York Times Book Review*

"A book of rare beauty, feeling, sensibility, art . . . We must support writers like Delbanco. And if we don't we don't deserve them." —Margaret Manning, *Boston Globe*

"Let a writer loose in his own vineyard and he'll make astonishing wine! . . . This is a book that tells many kinds of truths with accuracy, and often with pain, about the many kinds of people who spend their lives making novels." —Rosellen Brown, *Before and After*

"From where else but the panoramic cultural erudition of Nicholas Delbanco could such a tour de force of artistic sensitivity have come? This book is an engaging course in twentieth century Western humanities and a literary gift for its readers." —Sherwin Nuland, *How We Die*

OTHER BOOKS BY NICHOLAS DELBANCO

Fiction

It Is Enough
The Years
Sherbrookes (The Trilogy)
The Count of Concord
Spring and Fall
The Vagabonds
What Remains
Old Scores
In the Name of Mercy
The Writers' Trade, & Other Stories
About My Table, & Other Stories
Stillness
Sherbrookes
Possession
Small Rain
Fathering
In the Middle Distance
News
Consider Sappho Burning
Grasse 3/23/66
The Martlet's Tale

Nonfiction

Still Life at Eighty
Why Writing Matters
Curiouser and Curiouser: Essays
The Art of Youth: Crane, Carrington, Gershwin & the Nature of First Acts
Lastingness: The Art of Old Age
Anywhere Out of the World: Travel, Writing, Death

The Countess of Stanlein Restored: A History of the Countess of Stanlein
ex-Paganini Stradivarius Violoncello of 1707
The Lost Suitcase: Reflections on the Literary Life
Running in Place: Scenes from the South of France
The Beaux Arts Trio: A Portrait
Group Portrait: Conrad, Crane, Ford, James, & Wells

Books Edited

Dear Wizard: The Letters of Nicholas Delbanco & Jon Manchip White
Literature: Craft & Form (with A. Cheuse)
The Hopwood Lectures: Sixth Series
The Hopwood Awards: 75 Years of Prized Writing
The Sincerest Form: Writing Fiction by Imitation
The Writing Life: the Hopwood Lectures, Fifth Series
Talking Horse: Bernard Malamud on Life and Work (with A. Cheuse)
Speaking of Writing: Selected Hopwood Lectures
Writers and their Craft: Short Stories and Essays on the Narrative
(with L. Goldstein)
Stillness and Shadows (two novels by John Gardner)

REPRISE AND OTHER STORIES:

THE COLLECTED STORIES OF NICHOLAS DELBANCO

About My Table
The Writers' Trade
Reprise and Other Stories

DALKEY ARCHIVE PRESS
Dallas, TX / Rochester, NY

Deep Vellum | Dalkey Archive Press
3000 Commerce Street
Dallas, Texas 75226

WWW.DALKEYARCHIVE.COM

Support for this publication has been provided in part by grants from the National Endowment for the Arts, the Texas Commission on the Arts, the City of Dallas Office of Arts and Culture, the Communities Foundation of Texas, and the Addy Foundation.

 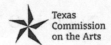

Library of Congress Cataloging-in-Publication Data

Names: Delbanco, Nicholas, author.
Title: Reprise : the collected stories of Nicholas Delbanco.
Description: First Essentials edition. | Dallas, TX : Dalkey Archive Press,
2025.
Identifiers: LCCN 2024044513 (print) | LCCN 2024044514 (ebook) | ISBN
9781628975642 (trade paperback) | ISBN 9781628976144 (epub)
Subjects: LCGFT: Short stories.
Classification: LCC PS3554.E442 R47 2025 (print) | LCC PS3554.E442
(ebook) | DDC 813/.54--dc23/eng/20241002
LC record available at https://lccn.loc.gov/2024044513
LC ebook record available at https://lccn.loc.gov/2024044514

Cover design by Daniel Benneworth-Gray
Interior design by Douglas Suttle

Printed in Canada

ABOUT MY TABLE

For Elena

Contents

What You Carry

H IS DAUGHTER TAKES after his mother, they say; the two would have gotten along. But there are few who can make the connection, and he avoids it. Kenneth Perrera had prized independence when young; he thought of himself as self-made. Yet he had also been family-proud, able to convey—with just the necessary negligence, the offhand remark that established what it seemed to deprecate—his ancient honored name. Sephardim, his ancestors were bankers. A sixteenth-century Venetian merchant had been famous for his charities. "I've been busily compounding thirty thousand ducats," Kenneth would say, "at seven percent per annum for four hundred years. He gave away my patrimony, trying to buy Christian. It didn't work."

The Perreras came from Portugal and went to Italy, then to Germany and several points in South America. They prospered and were persecuted. His own branch of the family had been entrenched in Hamburg till Hitler caught and slaughtered them. His parents fled to London, where Kenneth was born in the Blitz. He was an only child. When Hitler turned on Russia—or so his mother later claimed—she turned to her husband and asked to get pregnant; it seemed like a gamble worth taking. The odds on survival had never been long, but they had improved.

In 1952 they settled in America; he remembered hiding on the day the *Queen Mary* sailed. On the third day of the voyage out, his parents gave him full-length flannel trousers. He threw his shorts overboard. They ordered caviar each night in the cabin, as if it would be unavailable in the New World.

"Why did we come here?" he asked his mother, later.

Her answer was deliberate. "A country where it doesn't matter what country you come from," she said. "Or which religion. Where everybody's equal and a refugee . . ."

Kenneth did well. He attended Harvard College and Columbia Medical School. He became an internist, with a sub-specialty in pulmonary disease. When in the army he worked—as a major, and in exchange for the years of deferred draft status—at Fitzsimons General Hospital. Denver proved a revelation; he had not traveled west of the Hudson before. But he learned to love the mountains, the air so pure in the pinewoods it felt as if he inhaled clarity with the automatic act of breathing. He began to rock-climb and ski. After the first winter, he met a girl from Colorado Springs. She was a lapsed Catholic and not at all concerned with Kenneth's own lapsed Judaism; they were married by a justice of the peace.

Their honeymoon trip was on horseback. "Let's just disappear," Susan said. "Let's just let the horses find the way." They camped together three miles north of Estes Park. She tethered and curried and fed the horses carefully; she told him that she'd spent her adolescence in a stable. She'd bought the whole mystique, she said, she'd been so fixated on that Palomino of hers she never noticed boys.

Susan wore her blond hair long. She was exactly his height. For years thereafter his favorite photo remained the one he took that afternoon: his bride emerging from a sun-shot grove of aspens, the horses' heads behind her, tack draped across her shoulder like a scarf. She wore a paisley cowgirl shirt with mother-of-pearl buttons, and her riding boots accentuated the length of her slim legs.

His mother, too, had been photogenic; he had a leather album showing stages of her age. At first she was a German schoolgirl, carrying a purse and hat and satchel, her hair festooned with ribbons and her walking shoes laced tight. The white of the photograph had faded to ocher, and the black to brown. Her eyes were therefore accurate: large, focused on a spot above the photographer's left shoulder. Some years later, dressed in a fur-trimmed floor-length coat and a karakul cap, she posed in front of a painted backdrop of the Matterhorn. She sported sabots. The next was a full-face portrait of a woman in full bloom: a large-brimmed hat slanted softly from her forehead to high cheek. The lips were Clara-Bow-perfect, their expression both imperious and shy. The throat was bare, the blouse scoop-necked. The one eye not in shadow was astonishing: it fixed the photographer with what Kenneth recognized as disapproval. Perhaps the man behind the box, his head swaddled in black fabric, had been insufficiently respectful when urging her to smile.

She demanded such respect. She was polite in a fashion that unnerved his friends. Through all his adolescence and young manhood this was constant: a continual sense that the woman in an armchair, her reading glasses on and a martini in a water glass on the coaster on the rosewood table at her side, her black hair going gray, her ability to beat him at chess less certain, her German accent decreasing, her roses more splendid each spring—a sense that his mother was someone to reckon with and serve. He was, she said, the apple of her eye. He brought his girlfriends home for her approval and brought his laundry home till he was twenty-three. She had a massive coronary six months after his marriage to Susan, and they flew east.

His father met them at Logan. Kenneth had been wearing his army uniform. "You'd better take that off," his father said, "once we get to the hospital."

"All right."

"It does help with traveling," Susan said. "And we thought she might be proud."

"No." Simon Perrera was courtly. His gray hair had been barbered, and he wore driving gloves. "She doesn't like to be reminded. War. It's not what you should think about when you've had a heart attack."

"How is she today?" Kenneth asked. "I've talked to Blodgett. And Wiesenthal. I mean, how is she feeling?"

His father made a left turn, slowing as he always did and drifting too far to the right. "What did they tell you, the doctors?"

"Nothing you don't know already," Kenneth said. "It's serious."

"She'll be grateful you came," Simon said. "I mean it, both of you. I know how tired you must be." Simon patted Susan's knee. "She's been so happy, lately, having a daughter-in-law. Someone to confide in . . ."

"Someone to complain to," Kenneth said. "About the god-awful men of the house."

His levity was forced, however, and his father did not laugh. They parked, and Kenneth extracted a tweed coat from the carryall. Beth Israel was familiar to him, and the business of dying had come to seem routine. He took Susan's arm in the hall.

She lay flat, her face to the window. Her breathing was shallow, her pulse weak; he kissed her cheek, then wrist. She greeted him with no surprise, as if his arrival were normal, as if he had come home from school and not from Colorado two thousand miles away. She had been vain about her skin, its youthful resilience; before bed she had coated it with Elizabeth Arden night cream.

Now it felt dry beneath his fingers. More than any other fact—the charts he read, the consultation with Dr. Wiesenthal in the nurses' station—this desiccation taught him her mortality. His father cranked her upright, and Susan fluffed the pillows. "I want a grandchild," she said.

"There's no rush," Simon told her.

"Not for you. For me."

They spoke in German then, as they had done before he came to understand the language; it had been their stratagem for privacy in public. They had argued, always, with a shared unspoken pleasure in the argument, as though marriage meant continual debate. Susan said she'd like a cigarette, and he took her to the waiting room to smoke. "How do you feel?" Kenneth asked.

"This isn't easy for you, is it?"

"No."

"You said she'll recover. On the plane you said the critical time with a coronary was just after it happened." Susan exhaled. Her eyes were slate-gray and her cheekbones pronounced. The smoke that wreathed her billowed in a downdraft. Her lean shape seemed to thicken, as though with child; he shut his eyes and recognized how much he hoped for just that soft addition to their lives. "Are you all right?" she asked.

"Yes. Let's get back." In Belmont, that night, in his bedroom and the single bed, he made such urgent love to her she worried for his father's sake—that Simon, down the hall alone, would hear her cries. He told her not to worry, that his father would snore through an earthquake. When they were finally finished, he went to sleep on the floor.

Susan had a difficult pregnancy; her morning sickness was severe. She had headaches and anxiety dreams; her lower back gave her great pain. Kenneth told her the adjustments were normal, typical, a question of hormones, not fate. She said it didn't matter why she felt so terrible, but it mattered that she did; they drove together to the Garden of the Gods. This was a favorite outing, a day's drive from Denver with a stop-off at Pikes Peak. But she was out of sorts; she shifted position continually and complained about the altitude; she said that four months more of this were more than she could bear. Her family had moved to Honolulu; she wished that she could visit them and lie beneath the palm trees, drinking rum.

When he turned off the car's air-conditioner, the heat became intense. Susan could not walk. The rock formations greeted them, soaring astonishingly up and out, and all she saw were shapes that boring water made. The multicolored sand seemed garish as a postcard, and she'd seen it once too often anyway. What made them think the Gods would plant a garden in such godforsaken country; why wouldn't they have picked the lowlands where it's green? "Your mother's dying," Susan said. "I'm certain. I dreamed it all night."

"We spoke to her two days ago."

"I know."

"She's fine. She was. You're being superstitious."

"Yes."

Their child was an alien presence as yet, a pillow on her stomach tied by flesh-cords that they could not cut. "I know I'm sounding crazy," Susan said. "I don't mean to be like this. I hate it."

"What?"

She waved at the vista around them, the rocks and scrub and light so white it seemed fluorescent, the tourist buses at the Coca-Cola stand. "This being so far from them. Not only your mother. My parents. Everybody. Our baby. . . ."

"I'll call when we get back," he said.

"No. Now."

So it was from a phone booth in the Garden of the Gods that Kenneth learned of the second, fatal heart attack; his mother had collapsed that morning in the kitchen, cleaning up. "She drank too much coffee. I warned her," Simon said. His voice was reedy, static-riddled. "I said it twenty times a day. 'Don't smoke. Don't drink so much coffee.' She was standing there, Kenny, the pot in her hand. She looked so, so"—his father paused—"surprised."

"I'm coming home."

"We'll be all right. I will be. You don't have to come."

"I'm not sure Susan ought to travel. We're out of town is why you couldn't reach me. But I'll be there as soon as I can." He watched her through the phone-booth door: a leggy figure with her back to him, wasp-waisted still, their child invisible.

"Surprised," Simon repeated. "That's how she looked. Even with the warnings, Kenny, even when you know you're sick you just can't get prepared. You don't believe you're dying but you die. *Furchtbar*," he said. "It's a terrible business."

"Yes. I'll call the airlines, okay? I'll make a reservation and then call to let you know."

"Perreras," said his father. "There's only the two of us left."

This time he flew from Denver alone and rented a car on arrival. It was August 25. He spent the trip attempting to marshal statistics on the populace of Leadville, and the influence of altitude on blood volume and pulmonary function. This failed to distract him, however. All through the flight, or drinking gin and tonic at the airport bar, smiling at the Avis girl who told him his smile was contagious, driving, taking two right turns, then a left at the fork by his house—through all the business of travel Kenneth felt himself her boy, behaving. "Punctuality," she used to say, "is the politeness of kings."

She had lived in three countries, she said, and had believed each one would prove her lifelong home. When they take everything away from you, they can't steal what you carry in your head; they can burn the books and confiscate the paintings, or display them in the city museums and not offer compensation—they can strip you of your freedom but not your dignity. She had cousins and uncles who knew the whole of Goethe's *Faust* by heart, or at least all of Part I; they survived Bergen-Belsen and Dachau by reciting Goethe's *Faust*. There had been no copies available, of course, but cousin Arthur Lehrmann had a photographic memory, and his recitation had saved dozens of inmates from death. She had letters assuring her this. For her own part, unhappily, she could remember nothing but the chorus of the spinning song; she recited poor Gretchen's lament:

Meine Ruh' ist hin,
mein Herz ist schwer;
ich finde sie nimmer
und nimmermehr.

Kenneth's German had been poor. He knew the girl was hunting peace, was heavy-hearted since her lover left; he knew that Gretchen's misery was nonetheless in rhyme. He remembered his unkindnesses; he parked. He stood and stretched. When twelve and troubled by their dinner guests' attentions to his mother, having been excluded from their after-dinner coffee and Cognac—though they called it "excused"—Kenneth had offered a toast. "I know a sentence," he said. "Doesn't anyone here want to hear it? I know a German sentence."

"Not now, darling," she said. "Now you can watch TV."

"*Muttie hat dicke Schenkel,*" Kenneth pronounced. "Mommy has fat legs. That's a German sentence, isn't it?"

"It is," she said, her face so dark he could not determine if it flushed with shame or rage. "You can go now. Thank you." He remembered her ten years later, in a hotel in Nantucket. His parents had been on a summer vacation, and he joined them there one weekend after exams. He had taken the long ferry ride, head still stuffed with physiology and jokes about cadavers when the janitor locks up. Gulls cavorted in the wake. He walked to the hotel, jaunty in the bright sea air and feeling like a foreigner; his mother waited for him on the wide veranda. The steps had been sluiced down and scrubbed.

She was sitting in a rattan rocker and, for the only time he can remember, drunk; there were two glasses and an upturned empty bottle of Asti Spumante in an ice bucket. "Well, hello," she said. She waved a hand out at the sea. "*Finalmente.*" She tried to rise. Kenneth sat.

"I got tired of waiting," she said. "Your father's somewhere playing golf."

"The ferry was late."

"*Si.* It's sweet."

He lit a pipe. He would give it up that year without reluctance, but the paraphernalia pleased him. He sucked at the pipe stem and puffed.

"I always forget," she said, "just how sweet is Asti Spumante. It's better than Champagne. I mean, if you like sweetness."

"Yes."

"We could have another bottle. I ordered this one for you."

"No, thanks. I'd like a drink, though."

The waiter appeared. Kenneth ordered a Singapore sling. It was his summer for Singapore slings; he had been introduced to them by a girl at the Four Seasons. "Imagine," said his mother. "I can drink Asti Spumante and you can drink Singapore slings. It's as if we were in Italy, for example."

"Have you been swimming?"

"No."

"Is there a tennis court?"

She smiled. "In Portofino, for example, there wouldn't be a golf course. Or they wouldn't let him on, he's such a—what's the expression—'duffer'? What is it you dig up—'divots'? In Genoa, Rapallo, Padua, Siena, Piacenza . . ."

She continued naming cities, ticking them off on her fingers, citing every town in Italy that would not have a golf course. She smiled at her own slurred mispronunciation, saying Fear-*Enz*i for Florence and *Roam*er for Rome. He drank. He put his feet on the porch railing and he also rocked. "You're looking well," she said. "It looks like you're the one who's having a vacation. But you've lost weight."

"The Cherry Heering in this drink has vitamins," he said. "And so does lemon juice."

"I'm glad I don't have daughters."

"Why?"

"The trouble they would be . . ." She sighed. "The only reason to get married is to have children. I mean it. Don't even *think* about marriage until you want a son."

"I'm not thinking about it."

She smacked her lips, appreciative. "My son who loves ladies," she said. "Thank God that I didn't have girls."

In those next minutes, sitting, watching the sea tilt and rise, waiting for his father and some sense of what to expect, smoking, looking at a family with plastic rafts, a beach umbrella and a Styrofoam container straggle up the stairwell, he came to see his mother the way a stranger might: a drunken, plump old lady at a beach resort. She was flirtatious, nearly; she waved at the waiter and asked for some peanuts or cheese. She giggled; she sawed at the air while she spoke. Her fingers flashed with rings. Kenneth put dark glasses on; sun glinted off a truck. He saw her in the hospital, then dead.

Simon was in the kitchen when Kenneth arrived; he barely looked up from his work. He had his toolkit open and was testing the connections on a toaster oven. These things are firetraps, he said, you could burn the house down just by heating up a roll. It's gotten so bad, Simon said, insurance companies won't pay you for the fire damage if you leave your toaster plugged in; they call it negligence. He himself unplugged the toaster oven every time he used it, and Kenny better learn to do the same. "Your poor mother," Simon said. He indicated the Formica tabletop, the oil and screws and battery, his wrenches wrapped in cloth. "She'd never forgive me. This mess. But I can't work in the basement, with the phone ringing every five minutes. . . ."

He stood. He wiped his hand across his face, then wiped his palms on his pants legs. "I'm glad you managed," Simon said. "I know it wasn't easy."

"How are you, Dad?"

"Don't ask." He turned to the toaster, sheepishly. "This thing is keeping me busy. It does do that."

Kenneth put his kit bag on the pantry steps. The house was airless, and its smells familiar.

"The funeral's tomorrow morning," Simon said. "No formal service, no flowers. Just us." He latched the toaster-oven door, then pushed to release it. "And Susan—how's she feeling?"

"Unhappy," Kenneth said. "I mean, about not being here. We so much wanted Mom to know her grandchild."

"Grandchildren she hoped for," said Simon. "But she knew this was coming—your baby."

"Elizabeth. We'll call her that. We agreed last night to name her after Mom. If she's a girl. . . ."

They sat together for some time, in companionable silence. There was something soothing, always, in his father's painstaking formality. The phone rang but Simon ignored it. "She'll be a girl," he said. "Elizabeth Perrera. And may she make you proud."

Elizabeth did make him proud, in the years to come. She was precocious, an early talker; she walked on her first birthday and memorized whole books by two. She recited what the pictures said, then turned the pages earnestly, so that strangers were persuaded she could read. Her eyes were light blue, flecked with brown; her hair had Susan's texture. They called her Liz, then Lizzie, then Elizabeth; she had been born by Cesarean section, and he stayed out of the room.

He would have been welcome, of course; the doctor invited him in. But Kenneth had asked Susan how she felt about his presence there, and she said she'd rather he waited outside. She hated to think of herself under anesthesia, a slab of meat just waiting to be butchered, and she didn't want her husband to think of her like that. "I don't," Kenneth told her. "I wouldn't. That's not what it looks like at all."

"Still," she said. "You're a doctor. You've been through this before."

"Not with my own wife. Not my baby."

"That's the point."

He offered once more anyhow to be there at her side; she turned her face from him, panting, taking shallow breaths. When the contraction ended, Susan turned to him again; he dabbed at her white face with a wet cloth. "Everything's fine," he assured her. "You're terrific."

"A heroine." She took his hand. He had had enough of hospitals, he told himself, of knowing what the risks might be and what the procedure entailed.

"Just don't hold your breath," he said. "Remember your breathing."

"Yes, sir."

"Yes, Doctor."

"Yes, darling," she said. Her smile was a rictus, however; he had had enough of women in his family in pain. They wheeled her away. He prepared himself in any case, putting on a gown and cap and scrubbing at his hands and wrists and forearms till they shone. He used pumice stone and a nail brush; he repeated this procedure several times. A resident recognized him. They discussed the Broncos' season, then the price of town houses in Aurora; the resident liked ponds. Where he came from, he said, there was so much water in the hills you could rent a dozer for a day and make yourself a swimming hole; a weekend's work and you could dig a lake. "Where do you come from?" the resident asked.

"I was born in England," Kenneth said. "If that's what you're asking." He inspected his fingers, and then he turned back to the sink.

Elizabeth at four years old is complicated, inward; she will not go to other children's houses and spends much time alone. She has two pet cats and goldfish and a collection of dolls; she tells them lengthy stories but does not want him to listen. Once he overhears her telling the goldfish that sharks are a problem, and that the cats will cremate them, which is the final game. He asks her if she knows what "cremate" means, and she says of course but will not tell him; it is a secret, she says. She colors things for hours but will not draw freehand; she is meticulous and expert at filling in the blanks. Her favorite books illustrate ballet, and she colors every ribbon of the costumes for *Swan Lake*. "It's anal," Susan says. "It's so tight I can't stand to watch it. One button out of place and she wants to start all over."

Elizabeth likes magazines also; she leafs through them intently. This afternoon she finds a photograph of Henry the Navigator of Portugal. There is a brief biography attached. She points to it. "Daddy, this is God."

"What?"

"This is what God looks like. This is His picture."

It is Sunday afternoon; he has been watching football. There are leaves to rake and bills to pay and phone calls to return, but it is his partner's turn to be on call this weekend; Kenneth feels at ease. He takes the glossy journal. "It's a statue, darling. It's not God."

"It's what He looks like."

"Have you seen other pictures?"

She nods.

"What do you know about Him? God, I mean."

"He's the most important person," Elizabeth says. "Because when you're sick He makes you all better, and when you're dead He fixes you."

Henry the Navigator of Portugal is stern-visaged. He rises from the pedestal as if balanced on a bowsprit, his cape wind-tossed, his arm outflung. Sea-spray from the harbor soaks his beard. Kenneth cannot determine, however, if the statue is of bronze or stone. "I'm not sure I believe in God."

"I do. I pray to Him."

She finishes her apple juice and repositions her Peter Rabbit cup. It has its own saucer and soup bowl and plate. "Who taught you how to pray?" he asks.

"Oh, everybody. Marian."

"And what do you pray for?"

"Peace on earth. Goodwill to men."

He drops the subject, and she asks what time it is. He tells her, and she asks, politely, if he's finished watching football could she watch Disney's *Wonderful World*? "It's not on yet," he says, and she says, "Yes, it is." He turns on the set to disprove her, and Disney's *Wonderful World* is indeed in progress; she says, "I told you so." He pours himself a drink. When Susan returns from her afternoon ride, she sits on the couch while he pulls off her boots. The second one works free with a queer popping sound. "What's the matter?" Susan asks.

He indicates Elizabeth. She is watching alligators, rapt. The living room is large, high-ceilinged; he need not fear she'll hear him, but he drops his voice. "Religion."

"What?"

"She's convinced of it. A convert. She's certain there's a God."

"And Santa Claus too," Susan says. "It doesn't matter."

"Yes, it does. It does to me."

She stands. She pokes at the fire he's built. "Since when?" A section of cardboard flares, fades.

"Since fifteen minutes ago. Since I learned she's on her knees at night. Who's Marian?"

"A friend of hers from play group. Why?"

"I'm Jewish," Kenneth says. "My family was exterminated, remember? This little house painter called Adolf sprayed roach powder all over the ghetto. I want her to know where she comes from. I don't want her forgetting that."

Susan wears a turtleneck. She lights a cigarette. "You haven't done much to remind her."

"All right. But there's a difference."

"Why?"

He will not be deflected. "No daughter of mine is going to worship Henry the Navigator of Portugal."

She points to Elizabeth, restive now. "Let's discuss it later. All right?"

"All right."

But, later, things are not all right, are disturbing to him still. They eat dinner by the fireplace; it is November 18. He consults his calendar; it displays a picture of the Grand Canyon at sunset. He thinks perhaps

November 18 might be his parents' wedding anniversary but has made no record of the date; he dials his father just in case, but Simon does not answer. It is neither his mother's birthday nor the date of her death, and his failure to identify the meaning of November 18 becomes significant. He thinks of the Battle of Britain, or D-Day, or Election Day, but none of these apply. It is as if he, Kenneth, has lost all sense of ceremony and how the past pertains; he empties the bottle of wine.

"Relax," says Susan. "You're overtired."

"Yes."

"We could go to bed," she says.

He looks at the framed portrait of his mother on the mantelpiece. Simon took it years before. This photo is in color, one of the few he possesses; it shows Elizabeth outside. His mother is wearing a windbreaker, smiling at the sun. The sky is of a bright whiteness, and she wears dark glasses. There is what might be a boat in the background, or a structure that evokes one; water blends with the horizon so that he is not certain if she stands by an inlet, a river, or the sea. There is a brown shingled wall to the left.

It is her smile he examines, however, the mouth both expansive and pinched. She is smiling at Simon—from the pleasure of the occasion, perhaps, or the beauty of place, or because of something someone said. It would not have been Simon, however; this is a smile of assent at something more amusing than a request that she smile. Kenneth grows certain, suddenly, that there was a third party present—someone at the edge of things, beyond the lens or range of his remembrance, some business associate of Simon's with a camera, or someone passing through who made his mother laugh. A gull preens on a railing by the wall.

Then Susan yawns and says, "I'm going upstairs, anyhow." He will have to leave for work at seven, she reminds him, he ought to get some rest; the weekend has passed like a day. He arranges the fire and fastens the grate. He lifts Elizabeth from the couch where she prefers to fall asleep. Holding her yellow blanket, she puts her arms around his neck; her breath is hot. He will take her to visit his father on their next vacation, he promises himself; he will invite Simon west. Her legs feel thick where they grapple his waist. "I love you," Kenneth says. "I'm sorry. I so much wanted you to meet."

The Consolation
of Philosophy

WHEN HE HEARD his first lover was getting divorced, Robert Lewin panicked. He had not seen her in ten years; they had not been together for fifteen. They had few friends in common; her world was not his world. She was an actress of sufficient fame for her private life to seem public; she smiled at him from newsstands or in the supermarket checkout display. He read about her husband's drinking problem, her near-fatal car crash in Topanga Canyon and their second son's kidney malfunction. The photographs in gossip magazines had captions like "Sally Smiles to Hide the Tears," or "Tragedy Offstage!"

Robert disapproved. But in a way that was not casual he had loved her all his life; he dreamed that they grew old together, laughing in their sixties at the passion they shared when eighteen. He was thirty-eight years old, an architect; he, his wife and daughter lived on the Connecticut and Massachusetts border. Sally would purchase a house near their village. Knowing that he lived there, she would hire him to remodel her country retreat. She would want the silo to have two bedrooms and a bathroom, and the barn to be a studio. She would dam the stream and have him build a sauna and a free-form swimming pool. All this would be accomplished at long distance, and via intermediaries. She would buy the property sight unseen, and with all its furniture; Samantha, his wife, would not know. One bright autumn morning, Sally would fly in from the Coast to check on her dream's progress. He would receive her smiling, wearing dark glasses, not old. She would fold herself into his arms. She would say nothing, since nothing could improve the silence they shared.

At other times he gave her lines. "I never loved another man," she said. "Not the way that I loved you. It never does happen again."

"I know."

"It happens differently," she said. "I won't pretend I didn't love Bill. Our marriage was—well, workable. But no other man in my life . . ."

"We don't have to discuss it."

"We do. No other man in my life was ever quite as—what shall I call it, *protective* as you were. Considerate. You *did* take me under your wing."

Her diction had grown formal. "Is this a performance?" he asked.

"No. You took care of me. You helped with my homework, remember?"

At this point inventiveness stopped. Robert pictured them in bed but using their twenty-year-previous bodies; he had not seen her in the flesh to judge how flesh had changed. His own had thickened, some; his hair had thinned. Her consorts were the beautiful people, and he would not fit. His clothes were out of date. He passed for fashionable in the Berkshires, still, but felt less and less at ease in cities or with the gaudy young. He designed doctors' offices and banks. His clients all distrusted what they called the avant-garde. They wanted renovation work and, where possible, restoration. They wanted contemporary styling with a Colonial theme.

He worked alone. He had a large, illuminated globe on a teak stand by his desk. When drinking coffee, or in the intervals when concentration failed, his habit was to spin the globe and shut his eyes and stop its spinning with his finger. There, where the rotation ceased, he would embark on a new life. He landed in Afghanistan and northern Italy and the Atlantic Ocean and near Singapore. With disconcerting frequency, he landed on the Yucatán peninsula; once he pinpointed Mérida four times in a row.

The phone rang. "Are you coming home for lunch?" Samantha asked.

"I wasn't planning to."

"All right."

"Has something happened?"

"No. It's just I've got some errands, and you said you might come home this morning. And I wanted to be here if you did."

"If you're coming into town," he offered, "we could meet."

"No, darling, really. I've got forty things to do and might as well start doing them."

"I'll work right through," said Robert. "And I'll be home by five. Five-thirty at the latest."

"See you then."

Something in her manner troubled him, as if she called to know his plans rather than meet him for lunch. He lifted the receiver in order to return the call, to find her at the house and tell her he was coming home; his plans had changed. It was eleven o'clock. He did not dial. The prospect of a day without appointments was satisfying, nearly; he shut his eyes and spun and landed in Zagreb.

As the years passed, his years with Sally grew abstract; they both had been beginners, he would say. He forgot the reasons why they grew apart, the bitterness and boredom, and remembered only love. His memory was made up of amorous scenes. He remembered singing with her on a moonlit night in Tanglewood, standing by their blanket in the intermission, drinking rum from his initialed flask and harmonizing on the chorus of "Old Devil Moon." It was 1963; they both played the guitar. Their parents approved. She told him her last boyfriend drove a Thunderbird and wanted to be an astronaut; he probably would be, she said, he understood machines and thought the human body was just another machine. He didn't understand the finer things, spiritual things; by comparison with her last boyfriend—by comparison with everybody—Robert was a prince. Each night when he left her she whispered, "'Goodnight, sweet prince.'" He said, "And flights of angels sing thee to thy rest." She said, "Drive carefully," and he walked backward to the car so as not to lose the imprint of her face. She blinked the house lights three times in farewell; he flashed his car lights also and, for her sake, did drive carefully.

Sally wore her dark hair long. She had a Roman nose and large brown eyes. He called her "almond-eyes" and "beauty" and "love." They took each other's virginity. He remembered how she came to him in her parents' house in Weston, wearing a white negligee and carrying a towel. They spent their college weekends together; he attended Amherst and she, Smith. They embraced in pine lots and in barns and on the rear seat of his Impala and, later, in hotels. They intended to marry as soon as he got his degree. A hollowed-out tree trunk, he said, with a view of the sky would be plenty; it doesn't matter what we do so long as we do it together.

While Robert studied architecture, she applied to and was accepted by the Yale Drama School. They shared an apartment in New Haven, but her schedule and his schedule did not coincide. She performed when he came home from class, and he could not rouse her in the mornings. She dressed in black. They struggled with fidelity; she said she was attracted to Mercutio in her scene-study class. He did not confess to it but slept with a girl in Design; their afternoon encounters increased his passion for Sally at night. When she discovered his affair, she broke their stoneware plates and slammed the cutting board so hard against the counter that it broke.

He could remember how he watched her in rehearsal and saw a gifted stranger. Even then she had the quality of apartness, that silent holding-back the critics came to praise. Her first reviews were raves. They called it "presence," "power in reserve," and when she went to Hollywood, they said that Broadway lost a rising star. Robert lost control. All that fall he called her nightly, running up a telephone bill he had to borrow to pay. He drank too much and worked too little and flew round trip to Los Angeles just to have a cup of coffee with her at the airport. She was living with another man, she said, and would not take him home.

He completed architecture school and elected to practice in Stockbridge, not Manhattan. At twenty-six he married a girl from Springfield; they bought property southwest of town. He modernized the farmhouse and converted the barns. Samantha played the violin and formed a local string quartet; on their sixth anniversary, Helen, their daughter, was born. He prospered; they spent summers on the Cape.

He could have been an actor, people said; his voice was so mellifluous. He could have been associated with such men as I. M. Pei or Edward Larrabee Barnes. Once a friend had said to him, "Don't sweat the small stuff. I see you with a beggar's cup. Saffron robes. That's the kind of change you ought to contemplate, that's the way to get in touch with universal flux. I see it. . . ." Robert failed to, but he had been flattered. He carried with him, always, a sense of alternative possibility; his dreams were of escape.

"What's wrong?" Samantha asked.

"Nothing. Why?"

"You're sure?"

He had been splitting wood. He brought in an armload of logs. "It's cold out there," he said. "It feels like snow."

"Is something bothering you?"

"No."

"Do you want to talk about it?"

"I told you," Robert said. "It's only I'm restless. That's all."

"Would you rather I take her?"

"No."

Helen studied ballet. She was plump and unenthusiastic; he had promised to drive her, that afternoon, to see *The Nutcracker* in Springfield. Helen had wanted to go with a friend. "Why can't we take Jessie?" she asked.

"There aren't any seats left."

"How do you know?"

"It's sold out," he said. "I heard it on the radio."

"Jessie's busy anyhow," Samantha said. "Her grandparents are visiting."

"Would *you* come, Mommy?"

Samantha looked at Robert, and he shook his head. He would have liked nothing better than an afternoon of silence, but he had committed himself. He showered and shaved; the forecast was for flurries, so he took the Jeep. "Be careful," said Samantha.

"Yes."

He called her Sam. They were happily married, he said; she had the kind of resilience he lacked. She lived in the present, he said; if she had an emotion she showed it. If she was angry she expressed it, and the anger disappeared; when she was happy she sang. Helen slept beside him, her seat belt cinching her coat. Beleaguered by desire, he watched the women in the cars he passed, and in oncoming cars. He was, he told himself, just facing middle age, the loss of prowess and mobility that torments every-man. This did not help.

He had last seen Sally at a party in Hyannis Port. They had been eating baked stuffed clams and drinking spritzers; his host was saying that he never ate an uncooked clam these days. There had been a hepatitis scare. "It's not as if," his host admitted, "cooking makes a difference. But I feel safer, understand, as if the odds are better when it's cooked." He offered Robert the tray. "It's a kind of roulette we play with our bellies," he said. "It's the bourgeois way of risking things." He discoursed on the difference between littlenecks and cherrystones and quahogs; they were standing on a lawn that sloped down to the shore. "Littlenecks grow up to be cherrystones," said his host. "You understand that, I suppose. And cherrystones to quahogs; it's just a question of when you harvest them. As Marx observes, a sufficient change in quantity means a qualitative change." He lit a pipe. "I always ask myself at what point such change is enforced."

"Enforced?"

"Yes. Decided on. Agreed on, if you'd prefer. When does someone somewhere say, 'Enough. Thou shalt be no more Mr. Littleneck. I dub thee Cherrystone'?" His host laughed and flourished the pipe. "The trial by fire. Sir Clam."

Sally approached. She was wearing white. He felt his stomach tighten and release. "Ah," said his host. "The guest of honor. How *are* you, my darling? Do you know each other? This is Robert . . ."

"Lewin," Robert said. "Yes. We've met."

She had been as shocked as he, she confessed, but had seen him from the patio. She had been in the area for summer stock, a one-week stint, and was leaving; why is it always like this, she asked, why do we have to go just when we want to remain? He was looking wonderful; his beard made him look like a badger. Was his marriage working out; was his wife at the party?

They made their way to the beach. A rowboat and a Sunfish were pulled up past the tide line, and she settled in the rowboat. He also sat, facing her, facing the house.

"I miss you," Sally said.

"Yes."

"It doesn't change, does it?"

"Not really. No."

"This is horrible," she said. "I wish you wouldn't look like that. I wish I'd come here by myself."

"Who's with you?"

"Everybody. I hide it better, that's all. You should have seen your face—oh, Robert, when that man said, 'Do you know each other?' How are you, anyway?"

He scanned the lawn, then patio, then porch.

"All right."

"You mean it?"

He nodded.

"We've wrecked each other's lives, you know."

"No."

"Yes."

"That's overstating it."

With one of those reversals that had made her, always, his equal adversary, Sally said, "Of course. I know I'm overstating it. I'm being theatrical, darling. That's what I do best."

"Other things also," he said.

"But I'm not lying. You lied. You said you were all right." She shifted weight in the boat. In a movement he could picture clearly, ten years thereafter, she stripped off her white tights. It was a practiced motion, neither suggestive nor coy; she crossed her long, bare legs. She leaned back on her seat. He asked himself—and would, repeatedly—if she were proposing sex or getting ready to walk on the sand. Her clothing was intact, her sandals and her tights placed neatly by her side. He looked away. Samantha appeared on the porch. Men stood with her, gesticulating. He could hear her laughter. "I hate this," Robert said. He rose; the rowboat rocked. He put one foot over the gunwale. "I want what's best for you," he lied. "And that was never me."

"I'll stay here, thanks," she said. "Goodnight."

"How did it go?" Samantha asked, when he and Helen returned. He hung up his coat. He kicked off his boots. "Terrific," Robert said. "Twenty dollars so she gets to see the bottom of the chair. The part you look at from the floor."

"I closed my eyes, Mommy," she said.

"But what about the Christmas tree? The celebration?"

"I liked *that* part," said Helen.

"And the dance of the Sugar Plum Fairy?"

"He was horrible," she said. "He had big teeth and this enormous tail and his sword was all bloody. He looked like a *rat*."

"The Nutcracker kills him," Robert said. "You should have watched that part."

"I *told* you," she said, stamping. She turned from him.

"Well, maybe next year," offered Samantha. "Maybe this year was too early for you."

"Let's have a drink," Robert said. "Two vodka Martinis and one hot chocolate for our famous ballerina here."

"All right."

"You do the hot chocolate," he said. "And I'll do the vodka."

They entered the kitchen. Light from the kitchen fireplace played off the copper pots. "Next year," Helen asserted, "I'll be the Sugar Plum Fairy. I will be. You'll see."

Outside, the first snow continued. He had spotlights in the tamarack and maple trees; he turned them on. The garden appeared to leap forward and the kitchen's cage recede. He watched with genuine attention while the snow increased. The grass above the septic tank retained a warmth that melted flakes, making a rectangle of bare land on the lawn; it looked like a lap rug thrown over a sheet.

"I don't know what you want from me," Samantha said. "It feels like it's never enough. No matter how much I give, it feels like there's always this one thing left over—this way that we fail you."

"What is it now?" Robert asked.

"She's scared of the Mouse King." Helen was drinking her cocoa in the television room. "So you make it seem *my* fault . . ."

"It isn't your fault."

"I'm not saying that. I'm saying you *think* so; I'm saying you've blamed me all day. As if no child of yours could ever hide under a chair." Samantha exhaled. "As if her sensitivity is something we should apologize for—as if there's something, oh, shameful in a child who has feelings."

"It isn't shameful," he said. He set himself to placate her; he poured another drink. "Control yourself" had been his mother's injunction. Whenever he was greedy, loud or frightened, she would say, "Control yourself. A gentleman has self-control. He doesn't make a fuss about the things he doesn't understand. And if he understands them, there's no need to fuss."

"I love you," Sally said again. She would have purchased Sevenoaks Farm; they would be forty-five. "These barns, that view of the mountains."

"And I love you," he said.

"What have you been up to, baby?" She lit a cigarette. She offered him one; he declined.

"I didn't know you smoked," he said.

"Only when I'm happy. This house makes me happy. And how's your family?"

"They're good," he said. "We live a quiet life."

"You have a daughter, don't you?"

"Helen. Yes."

Sally examined the bay window. "Will you move in with me?" she asked.

"Right now?"

"No. Tomorrow," she said.

His most recent client had been a family therapy center. They had wanted picture windows in the waiting rooms. This had violated Robert's sense of decorum. He said so; they disagreed. There was a village grave-yard in the adjoining lot, and he situated the pentagonal structure so the picture windows overlooked the graveyard. "It's tempting," Robert said.

"Be tempted."

"You're serious?"

"Yes. Never more so."

"We've got twenty years," he said. "With luck. Twenty good years, anyhow."

"I'm ready to quit," Sally said. She was emphatic. "I've done enough acting."

"You'll miss it."

"No way. Not for a minute."

He knew enough to know this was not likely. "It's a hard habit to kick," Robert said. "I'm sure it must be difficult. All that applause."

"Those flowers," she would tease him. "Those parties at Sardi's, those feet in Grauman's Theater. Baby, it's nothing like that. It's sons of bitches, ego trips and cameos from here on in."

"You're sure?"

"I'm sure. I've never been more certain in my life."

They would sit in peaceable silence; there were no telephones. They would not bicker as they'd bickered when young; they understood the value of a gentle reticence. The sunset would be doubled by the clear reflecting mirror in the pond and, beneath it, the pool. He dreamed of this in winter while he sluiced down his own pond and scraped it for skating; he dreamed of it that early spring while the ice cracked and thawed. He filled the pool in May. Brian Dennis, after his annual checkup and the lab results, pronounced Robert fit. He redesigned the railroad station, making it a restaurant. Samantha started to jog. She was a natural athlete and soon attained four miles a day. She looked radiant; he wondered what she pictured as she ran.

Their village had a harpsichord maker. He had a shop in West Street, with a sign saying "Master Craftsman" in the window and a harpsichord-in-progress on display. There were marble steps and lintels in the shop, and ornamental hand-carved treble clefs on the door. Samantha knew him, apparently; she mentioned him in passing as a person Robert might enjoy, an adequate instrument maker. He sometimes joined their string quartet to add a piano part. The shop had an apartment on the second floor. Robert, walking to the bank or on his way from lunch or driving home from work, would slow down at the door. He was prepared to ask the price of harpsichords and, perhaps, to commission a lute. The door was never open. There were signs of life, however—fresh piles of sawdust at the workbench, or coffee mugs, or a wastepaper basket filled with what he recognized as that week's Sunday *Times*.

The upstairs apartment, too, seemed untenanted. One day Robert noticed its windows were open, and a woman with her back to him was brushing her brown hair. He stopped. He stood on the opposite side of the street, staring up. There were white lace curtains that obscured his view. He half crouched by a pickup truck; he put his feet on the bumper, one after the other, and pretended to adjust the laces of his boots. He felt exposed, aroused, but could not leave. Her body was supple. She wore a white brassiere that emphasized the pallor of her back. The light was on. She brushed her hair with metronomic regularity, stopping to shift angles every twenty strokes. She was looking at a mirror; he could not see her face. He wondered, was there someone in the room? Her attitude suggested readiness, a knowledge that she might be watched, a sense of self-display. She was familiar, somehow, yet he thought he did not know her: the mistress of the man who made the harpsichords. Her arms were lean. Robert shook his head to clear it, and in that unfocused instant the woman in the window disappeared. Yet he thought he heard her voice. He waited for some minutes, then continued home. Samantha was not there.

He turned thirty-nine in March, and they invited friends for dinner. There were jokes about Jack Benny and the wheelchair he would get next year. "If you think *this* one was bad," said Brian Dennis, "wait till you're forty."

Richard Beale had been studying Baba Ram Dass. "'Doing your own being,'" he said. "That's what it's all about, really. Just being here in the here and now. Your health, amigo," he said. "May you be here with joy."

Samantha served poached salmon, and then a rack of lamb. This repeated the menu they shared on their first night as man and wife; Robert was touched. "It's better now," he told her. "You're a better cook than those restaurant chefs."

"You're paying more attention to your food these days."

"All right. I meant it as a compliment."

"I take it that way."

"I'm grateful," he said. "When I said things were better, I didn't mean only the food."

"Happy birthday. Many happy returns of the day."

"'After forty,'" Ellen Dennis said, "'I hold a man's face against him.' Who said that, anyway? I think it was Abraham Lincoln."

"Winston Churchill," Brian said. "It must have been Churchill, not Lincoln."

So they argued over eloquence, and whether Lincoln or Churchill had been the better native speaker, more in touch with the language and times. Jim and Patty Rosenfield had just returned from England, from his sabbatical semester; they contended that the English had a greater native eloquence. "The problem is, however," Jim said, "they all speak so well that you never know who's *saying* something. And who's just making sentences. Even the dumb ones sound smart."

"Another thing," said Patty. "Inflation. You can't imagine how bad it is over there. How expensive everything has gotten. We entertained a little less. Maybe we ate out more often. But at the end of every week we filled two garbage cans."

Richard drank. "What does all this have to do with Lincoln or with Churchill?"

"Waste," she said. "That's what I'm discussing. We throw away more food than all Australia eats."

"I'll drink to that," Robert said. He shut his eyes. The image of Sally assailed him again—some taste or word or smell or sight inciting memory. They were near a sandbar in a saltwater inlet, making love. He lay on his back in the warm shallows, and she sat on top of him. There was a thick fog. Sailors glided in the distance; he propped himself up on his elbows so as not to swallow salt. It was the start of the fall. The cranberries were purple already, and the beach-heather was brown. Gulls watched, incurious. She bounced and settled on him, smiling, her eyes wide. They rented a bungalow called Peony; it stood in a strip of bungalows named after flowers; their neighbors were Tulip and Rose. The fog felt palpable. He saw himself the sailor now, seeing from the channel how the complicated obscure shape of youth is jointed at the waist; he watched how fleetingly they fused and broke apart. He toasted his guests and his wife.

They kept in touch, but distantly; a friend of friends said, "Sally sends regards." Her telephone number was unlisted; she sent it to him in April and wrote, "Hope to hear from you." By the time he did call, from his office, a recorded voice pronounced, "We're sorry. We cannot complete your call as dialed." He was not sorry, he decided, he would not have known what to say. Panic is the fear engendered by the great god Pan. He comes to the party unannounced and overturns the chairs and spills his drink on the rug. He will attempt his magic trick with the tablecloth. He scratches his beard, paws the floor.

Promising the cutlery and plate and crystal will remain in place, he whisks the white linen away. He is clumsy, however; things crash and tumble all over. The girl at the head of the table gets wine on her jumpsuit. She scrambles to her feet and scampers down the hall. He follows her, apologetic. There are remedies. They huddle together. There are dry cleaners, other parties, prospects of the sea. There is time.

Wind rattled at the pantry door when his wife opened the door to the mud room. She settled her handbag and two paper bags on the bench.

"You're having an affair," he said.

Samantha took off her gloves. She placed them on the shelf. "Was that a question?"

"No."

"Good." She shrugged out of her coat. "It didn't sound like a question."

"Are you having an affair?"

"In any case"—she selected a hook—"I don't think I'll bother to answer."

"His harpsichord. How quickly can he build one?"

"That depends," she said.

"He's careful?"

"Yes."

"Attentive?"

"Very."

"A master craftsman," Robert said.

"I've been downtown, master. Shopping." She opened the mud-room door again. "In case you're curious."

"Yes."

"Be careful with the eggs," she said. "They're in the bag in the Jeep."

In June the local ballet school offered a performance. It ran for three successive nights, and each was sold out in advance; the children came home from rehearsal with their allocated tickets. Helen was in the school's youngest class, but there were students all the way through high school. The program was immense. Its theme was that of "The Magic Garden," and children were divided, according to age and experience, into several units: there were butterflies and inchworms, bumblebees and bunny rabbits, a group of birds and flowers and scarecrows. The soloists were labeled Spring, Summer, Autumn, Winter; there were twelve such soloists, with four to perform on each night. The owner of the ballet school was, as she put it, *bouleversée*; she made a speech before the performance and said she was just so excitable because of these wonderful wonderful students that *bouleversée* was her only expression; we are enraptured to see you all here.

Helen was a Black-Eyed Susan; she wore a bright green tutu and brown leotard and fitted orange cap. There were twenty other Black-Eyed Susans, and they skipped onstage, then curtsied and circled and whirled. Helen did so by herself. Then they all joined hands and did what looked like the Virginia Reel; fathers filled the aisles and, using flash attachments, photographed their girls. Robert had not brought his camera. He had had a long afternoon. He had come directly from the office to the auditorium; there were problems with the railroad ties he'd used for decorative beams.

During intermission, he could not find Samantha in the sea of women and daughters waiting in the hall. He pushed through swinging doors to what would be backstage; the Rhododendrons and the Owls were doing warm-ups by the barre. There were belly dancers also, waiting for their turn in "The Magic Garden"; they wore veils and diaphanous skirts. Mothers were removing rouge and lipstick from their daughters' upturned faces. Helen said, "Hi, Daddy."

He looked for her.

"Hi. Here we are."

Samantha closed her makeup kit. She stood.

"Well, look at you," said Robert. "You look beautiful."

"Thank you, Daddy." Helen pursed her lips, demure.

"Doesn't she?" Samantha said. "How do you like these sequins?"

"Very much," he said.

"The ponytail?" asked Helen.

"Yes. You'll be a star."

All around him, Robert knew, fathers were thinking the same of their daughters; all around him the girls were transformed. She was, he said, his precious ballerina, his precocious soloist. A belly dancer brushed past. "Do you want to watch the second half?" he asked.

"I'm tired, Daddy."

"You?" he asked Samantha.

"I'll tell the Cartwrights we're leaving. We got a ride down here with them, so we could all go home together."

She was, he told Samantha, wonderful. Helen wore eyeliner and mascara and had not smudged her lipstick or her rouge. Samantha turned and, bending, began to scrub at the upturned face. "Leave it," he said to his ladies. Helen wore her tutu to the car.

The Executor

IT HAD BEEN snowing. This was the season's first storm, and the tamaracks were brown, not bare; oak leaves lay on top of the snow. Edward
built a fire, then made himself a drink and settled to read. The letters were
a jumble—thrown into a cardboard box that crumbled at the edges. Bits
of paper came loose in his fingers, and he inhaled decay.

He had had trouble driving home; the weatherman used phrases like
"snow alert" and "traveler's advisory." He had lived in Massachusetts for
ten years. Yet every year, at the first snow, Edward felt just such a shrinking
fear—as if he had to hibernate but would be unprepared. The certificate of
death for Jason Simpson was a photostatic copy, black, reduced. Category
6a of the personal particulars read: "Usual Occupation (Kind of Work
Done During Most of Working Life, Even If Retired.)" The examiner
had typed in "Artist." Category 6b read: "Kind of Business or Industry in
Which This Work Was Done." This space was blank.

"You remember the Simpsons," his father had said.

"Barely."

"It wasn't all that long ago. They died in—let me see—1966."

"That's long enough," Edward said. "I was just finishing college."

"Yes. But you do remember them."

"A little," he admitted. His father's nostalgia was its own system:
the stories he told seemed pointless, self-regarding. Edward (home for
Thanksgiving, slicing the overlarge turkey, ignoring their questions about

the pending separation and where Marcia might be this holiday weekend, telling his cousin, "The truth is we woke up one morning and turned to each other and said the same thing: 'Does it have to be this way? Do we have to go on for the next forty years?'...") bent to his plate.

"They loved *you*, apparently. Jason *and* Nadia," his father said. "They wanted you to have this packet. I'm the executor."

Edward was preoccupied. He tried to scan the pattern of his father's emphases. His wife had flourished in such celebrations; she liked the bustle and clatter.

"*When* you're thirty-five years old. It's a stipulation," his father finished. "Which you are now. So that's *their* life story, this box."

"All right," he said. "What do I do with it?"

"Take the thing home. Sell it. Burn it. Whatever you want; it's *your* business, Eddy, not mine."

Driving north the next afternoon, as rain turned to sleet then snow, he summoned up the Simpsons' images again. They had been his father's friends—thin elderly people, the man in a wheelchair, the woman's skin translucent. Even as a child, when the distinction in age mattered little, Edward knew his father's friends were a generation older: family dependents somehow, on the dole. He remembered an apartment cluttered with canvas, vaporizers, and a blown-glass antelope they gave him that he broke. Edward was examining it—pleased beyond caution by the intricate fretwork—and shifting it from hand to hand when the pink creature fell. He remembered the small shattering (a tinkle more than crash, a little set of splinters at his feet) and the horror of having to sweep the thing up. Old Jason Simpson told him not to worry, never mind, but he picked every shard from the rug.

Edward came from Scottish stock. He used Scottish expressions with frequency and made much of his ancestors' "deportment." They were sheep-stealers, he claimed, and had been deported for taking one North country Cheviot too many through one stile too few. "I like to think of Philip," Edward said, "my great-great uncle's great-great-uncle. Caught in the midst of bogs or fens or wherever it is the laird does the catching. With a sheep stuffed up his kilt in imitation of Gammer Gurton's needle. 'What's that you're hiding, Philip?' the laird on horseback asks. He asks this not unkindly, for there's humor in the scene. The sun is westering; we have echoes of the drum and bagpipes, lewd music mostly. 'Nothing, milord,' Philip answers. 'Nothing but what any man who has it has to cover.'

"'A fair thought, nothing,' answers the literate laird. 'To lie between maids' legs.'

"'Milord?' inquires Philip—whose bumpkin learning has not embraced *Hamlet*.

"'Ah, maun ye mock me?' inquires our laird—a collateral cousin to poor Bobbie Burns. 'There's not a lassie lying ten miles aboot who'd let that beastie baa at her.'

"For indeed the North country Cheviot bleats. In vain my cornered ancestor attempts to call it broken wind; in vain he claims himself full-fleeced around his parts. The laird ups with his kilt and outs with his guilt and away goes the clan to America . . ."

And Edward would tender his glass. He told the story better on his second drink than third. Then he included border dogs and made reference to "wool gathering" in *The Second Shepherd's Play*. On his third drink, also, he would speculate about the tall tale's "thread" and "darn good yarn"; he told the story often and, he was persuaded, well.

Some letters were in envelopes, some torn. His father's generosity was real. There were postcards and letters and offers of help, then the legal structures of support. His father sent them a small monthly check, arranging that ten other patrons do the same. His efforts on their behalf (with museums, with the landlord who had tried to raise the rent, with the City of New York when they required nursing care) were, it seemed to Edward, ceaseless.

Then he discovered his own scrawled thank-yous from twenty years before. If the Simpsons sent him an Indian headdress, he sent them a poem about it; when they congratulated him on his acceptance at Yale, he sent them a self-deprecating cartoon. Edward drew "a bulldog leading meek me by the leash," and, half his life later, feeling the tug of propriety, recognized the truth in his cartoon. When they sent him a book about Joseph and the Nez Perce—the last gift; he'd turned twenty-one—Edward responded politely, saying that he had a waning interest in these matters and they were kind to remind him. Later he had come to realize that the warrior-chief was emblematic to the crippled Simpson: the admirable outlaw in him had been shot.

"Why are you giving me these?"

"They're yours," his father repeated.

"They're valuable."

"I wouldn't know. It's your *business*, Eddy; you're the curator."

He said "curator" as others might say "doctor"; Edward changed the subject. "How are you feeling?"

"All right. I've been to Meyrowitz." His father shrugged. "I'll live."

"What about the holidays? If you'd like to come . . ."

"Eddy, I can't keep this with me any longer. There's only so much I can keep in the closet. You follow? What'll happen to these things? I ask myself; someone should make sense of them. Not me."

His father coughed. It had taken him years to propose that Edward's life was wanting. He had not been reproachful. They rarely met; his father carried independence to the point of indifference, Edward complained.

"That's reciprocity. His way of getting even," Marcia said. "It's how you used to behave."

"With whom?"

"With everybody," Marcia said.

"You flatter me," he said.

Edward spent his life at art: handling and appreciating and assessing and paying the freight. He bought and sold and owned and restored it, always respectful, curatorial—always, he told himself, bored. Why should a man as sane and sweet as Jason Simpson seemed—why should a figure so compounded of decency, ambition and a stubborn sense of making—make no difference finally? There's no madness, Edward thought, like that of the gambler in art; the horseplayer, lottery addict, the lady at the one-armed bandit dawn by dawn in Vegas, all have better odds. Now he handled the receptacle of some long-dead adept's efforts, and he had to read it through.

There were letters from men who went to Pamplona in the wake of Hemingway and girls who learned to cook with Alice Toklas. In the thirties the notes were trilingual—spiced with German phrasing, laced with Italian or French; notes from England in the forties made no mention of the war. There were thank-you letters, Christmas cards, apologetic letters for "the length of time we've been apart" and promising to write more often soon. There were lawyers' letters, bills, receipts, the leavings of the fifty years that Simpson had spent scrambling for a toehold and safe perch. His wife received few letters; he was the family scribe. There was a packet of his correspondence when her breakdown kept them separate, or when he worked in California making murals for three months.

John Marin sent a map to where they spent the summer. Someone had scrawled in the margin, "Hope you'll find it possible to visit. Dew Drop Inn!" e. e. cummings thanked the Simpsons for their birthday gift, and Stieglitz, answering a request for assistance, countered with needs of his own. Girls Edward had never heard of sent back impressions of Paris; a woman on an ocean liner sent them sketches of the waves. The language was formal or tub-thumping; the writing meticulous—Marianne Moore's—or barely legible—E. Walsh's. There was such a sense of energy, of time forever on their side, of the instant's immortality for all that generation: Thomas Hart Benton hoped Jason would feel better after his damned stroke.

Wind forced the cat-door open; Marcia had taken the cats. When he closed the door again, the latch proved inadequate, so Edward propped a log against the door. Wind found its perimeter and blew past the four sides. He imagined the chill rectangle advancing till it shaped itself, intact, upon the room's far wall.

He himself had hoped to be an artist, once. He'd bought, as he told Marcia, the great American dream. This consisted of paint-spotted tweeds, an unlit pipe, unruly hair, the wild-eyed glint behind sunglasses that signified a man could see. Write in water, paint in sand; scan *The New York Times* each Christmas for some mention of your year's accomplishment, and year by year accept oblivion because Picasso and ten others reap rewards.

But he'd always known himself, he claimed, you had to give him that. Even at twenty he had suspected what his twenties proved: that art was a necessity for others, luxury for him. He painted an acrylic version of "The Rape of the Sabines." He conceived a three-act theater piece about the life of Byron, entitled "Curious George," to be performed in drag. It's what to do when the dishes are done; it's not flourishing in China where they force-feed equality.

So Edward painted as an avocation, not vocation, but quite well. His degree was in art history, and he took a job, when twenty-eight, as assistant to the Curator of Prints and Drawings in a museum in the Berkshires that was privately endowed. His reticence seemed pleasing; his ignorance had been construed as modesty by the dowager who hired him. She owned a Jason Simpson drawing of the Statue of Liberty in rags; it was inscribed to his father, and she recognized the name.

The work was undemanding, and he settled in. Edward organized the files, reorganized the cabinets and had the Flemish collection uniformly framed. He rented a small white clapboard farmhouse on the edge of town and, once assured of permanence, he bought. The last time we changed staff, his secretary said, was after the *Titanic* sank. At a black-tie testimonial dinner in honor of the donor of a set of Goya etchings and a portrait by Franz Hals, he met his future wife. Marcia was the director's niece, up for the fall foliage, she said, just mad about the oaks. When he realized that she said this with the edge of mockery, not meaning "mad about the oaks" but to establish that she thought the phrase was foolish, and the celebration, and the solemn, owl-eyed scrutiny of "Los Caprichos," Edward asked her to come home with him for a postprandial snort.

"If you mean coke," she said, "no, thanks."

"I didn't mean that," Edward said.

She also noted mockery and, noting this, accepted him; they shared a bottle of Remy Martin.

That night he built a fire, heralding the fall. "I usually don't drink this much," she said.

"Say 'usually' five times," he said. "If you get the last one right you're sober."

"Usually, usually, usually, usually"—she paused for breath and laughed. He watched her red hair glinting in the firelight, the coppery tones and lips and cheekbones and said, "All right. You've proved it. You're the perfect figure of sobriety."

"Picture of sobriety," she said. "That's what you mean. Not figure."

They kissed. They fell against each other on the hearth like warriors. Her body surprised him—the lean conformation under what he first had noticed, her breasts. "I thought there was more meat on you," he said. She laughed and told him that she always felt too cold up here and therefore wore too many clothes, an extra layer to keep men like him away. "I'm glad it didn't," Edward said, and she raked her fingernails along the inside of his leg.

Three months later, when they married, Edward said he'd found a home at last; Marcia said she knew exactly what he meant. His job was secure; they owned the house and two cars. Saturdays he set up his easel in the garage and painted still lifes there, and a portrait of his bride with coconuts. She encouraged him; she said she liked his sense of line, the dark and cutting range of the palette.

Simpson made rag dolls; he collected kachinas. He had an eye for horses and did variations on a circus theme. He was a colorist whose cityscapes and seascapes used the same shade of blue. "What do you think of this painting?" he asked.

Edward had studied it, shy.

"Don't be embarrassed," said Simpson. "Just tell me what you see."

"See?" He squinted at the riot of color and shape.

"Don't *read* it. Don't tell me what you want to see. Just describe what's there."

Nadia nodded, encouraging. She had a plate of sugar cookies and she gave him two. He chewed one; it tasted of oil.

"I mean *literally*, boy."

"There's a dancer," he said. "There's what looks like a camel he's leading."

Simpson took a cookie also, and he held it poised. With his left hand he turned the wheelchair full circle.

"Maybe that's a tower, I can't tell," said Edward. "The green thing sticking up back there. Maybe a windmill. Or trees?"

"You're just pretending." Simpson licked his lips. "You've lost the gift of sight, my boy. It's not your fault. It's how they've taught you, everything you've learned for all these years."

"It *is* a windmill," Edward said.

"You were closer the last time. 'That green thing sticking up back there.' That's what you saw."

Nadia patted his arm. "Don't worry," she offered. "We all forget what we knew. What do you see, for instance, when you look at Jason?"

"A man about sixty. With white hair. A painter. Your husband."

"No," Simpson said. "Wrong again. You were right about the white—the rest of it, though, is invention. Accurate invention, as it happens, I grant you. Sixty-seven. But what you saw was this green shape you're thinking should be 'sweater'; what you see is orange here, and a blue mass above it, then two brown things that, for the sake of convenience, we'll call pants. You've got to make up the world, boy, see it as you saw it when you only saw the undersides of sinks." He threw out his arms, theatrical. "The day you decided those pipes and that bowl meant 'toilet'—function, not form—that was the day you went blind."

Edward added ice. Suddenly he understood the reason for their gift. The old man must have seen him as a caretaker, curatorial even then. So this bequest had been self-serving also, not selfless or random. Edward knew he'd seemed the logical successor to his father's stewardship—the next supporter, Jason might have said, by right of bourgeois birth. They'd predicted his career. If he hadn't ended up in the back offices of some Berkshire museum, he'd nonetheless have access to the place. Jason might have guessed as much—had been responsible, even, in the course of that first interview for Edward's very hiring and would expect compensatory thanks.

He poured a second scotch. He stretched, switched off the reading lamp. That he should be predictable—who'd lived his professional life in order to encourage and justify just such prediction—irritated him. He drank. He said aloud, testing the phrase, "They've left me holding the box." He thought the substitution amusing, mildly; he bit the rim of his glass.

Then the irritation passed and he stared at the fireplace. It was deserved, after all, and there'd been value in the gift; he could sell the notes by cummings and the map Marin had drawn. He could turn their loss to profit, judiciously, then pay his father back. Edward felt his concentration slacken and release. Whatever problem he'd been set to solve was slipping from him cozily. He shifted his weight, stretched again. And in the succeeding instant he felt rage—shock after shock of it, jolting. He stood. His adult life held no such anger; he was a child again, biting the bedspread, kicking at whatever he could kick. He tore at his nails with his teeth. Out there beyond the bedroom there was expectation's tyranny: he was nothing original, nobody, never had been or would be.

Edward threw on a birch log. It came to him—alone, in his well-appointed house in the foothills, standing by the fieldstone fireplace, with its oak mantel bearing Tibetan woodblocks (four of them, acquired from the Victoria and Albert, of elephants with maidens on their jewel-encrusted tusks, the great-limbed heroes dancing)—that he would leave.

He pressed his nose to the living room window and peered out. The tamaracks were dark.

Marcia would be with her lover now in Roland Park. She'd acquired children—three from his first marriage—and would, Edward imagined, be making turkey soup out of their supper's leavings. Thanksgiving must have been a shock to her. The size of the turkey, the number of portions of yams and chestnut puree and bowls of cranberry and rice and gravy and relish, and cornbread—all this evidence of family might give her pause. There would be traditions in which she had no part; the weight of the wineglass felt wrong.

"What you don't understand," she had insisted to Edward, "is ambition. It's wanting to count in this world."

"No."

"Yes. To make a difference. To be able to say, when you walk in a room, 'I matter. I'm here. This is me.'"

"That's vanity," said Edward. "Or arithmetic. You're only talking addition."

"Ambition."

"*Count*," he repeated. "A *difference*. Assertiveness training, that's all."

Then she seemed deflected by his parrying agility, and they made peace. She wanted a shower, she said. They agreed that they each had been wrong. She would stand at the counter he had never seen, wearing the apron he'd bought her (or maybe something with oysters and lobster on it, since she'd moved to Maryland, some chef's hat over pastry shells that spelled: "Welcome to Chesapeake!"), ladling soup. He could imagine it precisely: the size of the carrots she sliced, the stalks of celery she'd wash with brisk inattention.

"I'm leaving you," she said that night.

"When?"

"As soon as possible."

"And who are you going to?"

"Edward . . ." she began.

"Notice I didn't ask *where*. Notice I know that it's someone, not somewhere." He focused on her ear. There was a turquoise pendant he could hook his finger in.

"Harrison."

"In Baltimore?"

"Roland Park," she said. "There's a difference."

"He's the one with all those brats?"

"They're not brats."

"I'm only saying what you said. You called them brats, remember? Why'd you pick that one?"

She sighed and spread her hands. She said, "You flatter me. I didn't have that much choice."

Marcia had the gift of prophecy. She saw things when she shut her eyes. She saw jessamine and wisteria and azalea blooming in the courtyard or in winter sleet. She could tell, the night before, what color the baker's wife's apron would be when she changed it next day. She had never seen an orange grove, but she knew the way an orange grove in California looked—a certainty not based on but attested by the postcards she'd received. Someone could describe the Isenheimer altarpiece—and Marcia shut her eyes and *saw* Mathias Grünewald in a frenzy of invention, and she saw what he had had to eat and the paint stain on his index finger and the way he chose to rectify his first version of the foot. She had pictured Edward standing in their house.

That was before they met. He was standing in the kitchen; she had recognized the gas stove right away. He was wearing blue work clothes but the sun poured in so brightly from the window by the pantry that she could not see his face. He had been waiting for water to boil; he whistled but she could not hear the tune. That first evening at the banquet—did he remember the watercress soup?—she had seen the menu by the time they reached the door.

Edward had been dubious. He made up explanations or ascribed it to coincidence if she reached to take the phone before it rang. She would press her head and hold it at the instant of a car crash miles away. Four-leaf clovers fairly leaped at her from roadsides and in meadows. He asked her how she found them, and she shrugged and said she never looked, just something about the pattern forced itself on her attention.

Edward heard two village churches where he sat. Their clock towers did not agree. One chimed the hour three minutes earlier than the other, and the half- and quarter-hour chimes were discordant also. That three-minute interval became the stuff of anxiety, an emblem of exactitude that had turned inexact. One of the clocks was correct, but he could not identify which. His own watch halved the interval, so possibly they both were wrong and he should have heard a third chime.

It was ludicrous, he knew, to squander his attention on the clocks. He thought of crepes suzette, of Caravaggio, of every woman he had ever slept with and whether the initials of their names comprised the alphabet. He reached "I" with no trouble, and he had two candidates—Zoe and Zara—for "Z." But he ended up unable to provide a woman who began with "I" or "Q" or "X." He assumed that this was commonplace, that women with those first initials would be, by comparison, rare. Edward took comfort in his memories, their unsurprising result. Then the first clock started in.

Was it possible, he asked himself, that he in this entire kingdom of the one-eyed would prove blind? Everywhere he saw the visible world intensely: a blade of grass sheeted with moisture, a cloud whose billowing edge was strange shapes, a wall that needed paint. Yet those who looked at him saw nothing, a translucency. Marcia saw him as a man to be dismissed.

"Drive carefully," his father had urged him.

"I will. I'm sorry," Edward said. "I've been preoccupied." His father was an earnest man—tall, stern. He wrote letters to the editor and to his congressman about the shameful way this nation treats the elderly. He himself was fortunate to have both health and a modest retirement income, but everywhere he turned he found people were less fortunate than he. "I'm glad you came," he said. "Thanksgiving is for the family. It's a family *occasion*, and that's right."

"Can I ask you a question?"

"Of course."

"Tell me why you did it."

His father adjusted his glasses, quizzical. They were standing at the door.

"Took care of the Simpsons, I mean."

"*Did* it?"

"Yes."

His father touched the box. "It isn't something to do," he said. "It's a way of being. A way to be."

"'They also serve who only stand and wait,'" said Edward. "Is that what you mean?"

"Not at all."

Nadia had something to tell him, she said, something she ought to explain. Jason got excited by visits, so nervous he should have a rest—she patted Jason on the head and told him she'd take Eddy to the store because Eddy could bring back the bags. Those steps, she said, were getting steeper; she could use the help. Did Jason want to close his eyes while they were at the hardware?; she'd return in a jiffy with linseed oil and light bulbs and toilet paper and, if he behaved himself, some of Gristede's corned beef.

Her excitement was transparent. She clattered down the steps like a schoolgirl, string bag slung from her wrist. She took his arm at the corner, saying, "Guess what, Eddy? I wanted to tell you. It'll be such a surprise." He piloted her across the street; she stared at taxis and the halted, idling cars. "The museum called yesterday," she said. "Mr. Moneybags. He didn't say so, of course, they're far too cautious, curators, but what they were asking—I can tell, I haven't been with Jason all those years for nothing— what they were asking was would we sell those charcoals he did on our visit to Scotland? You remember, don't you, the Glasgow mills at dawn? You remember the pictures, I mean. Those great big blokes—is that what they call them?—all covered with coal dust, their eyes like whitecaps on a positive black *wave* of faces, Eddy, the dogs, the grass that he managed to make look wet so you just knew it was raining . . ."

Nadia paused. What she needed to tell him was not this, she said; she needed to say something else. She had been planning ever since Edward arrived to get him outside on some sort of errand and tell him that Jason was dead. She could smell it in the room. He must have noticed, hadn't he, the stink on the wheelchair when Jason wheeled up? He was dying even if the doctors couldn't see it, and their prescriptions and advice and optimistic machinery were helpless. Nadia blew her nose. She lived with him, was there each day and every moment of each day, she knew how his breathing had changed. What will I do, she asked, how can I go on without him, how will I ever continue?

They walked the aisles. He helped her gather nails and flashbulbs and turpentine and paper towels. At the plumbing fixtures section, Nadia extended her hand. She fingered a display of faucets, smudging the sheen.

"My life is his," she said. "His life is me. I can't live without him, I haven't the skill. It's what I told the man who called, the one from the museum: I haven't the skill or desire to live while my Jason is dead."

Therefore he piled the sheets—precisely, using paper clips, then rubber bands for decades. He filled the box again. The folder for the forties bulked the least large. The fire snapped and crackled at him, and he fed it with a pine bough that flared. "It is my wish that I be cremated. Please take care of this matter." Edward knew the indicated gesture was now to feed this fire with the ranked packets before him. The flame was picture-perfect, the length of the log: high, hot. He rearranged the box. He pictured its consumption: first brown, then black, then crepitant, a shapeliness adhering to itself.

For several minutes he conjured the Simpsons. Their death had been a release. He studied the certificate and its grim declension: of natural causes, attested in triplicate. They had lived together fifty years, and he was separated after four. He found a postcard addressed to the hospital in East Islip, where Nadia had been sent in 1932. "Sweetheart," the legend read. "I send you all my love, and hope things improve for us always." There was a watercolor of a man on a horse, doing a handstand with a beach ball on his upraised foot; the sweep of the balancing act carried across to the stamp.

He would not, at any rate, burn the letters. He rose and took the box—through the kitchen door, then the storm porch and down the stone steps. There was ice on the trees. He wore no coat or gloves and shivered, inhaling. Edward smelled his own fire's downdraft; the sky had cleared. His wife had planted tulips in abundance just before she left him, saying, "Why not, after all, what else would we do with these bulbs?" He'd helped her make a flowerbed beneath the western wall. That ground was open—protected from the blowing snow, and warm enough so that what landed was melting. He placed the carton, carefully, in the center of this wet dark strip. It would weather the winter, then shred.

Traction

WHEN ALEXANDER WAS informed his daughter had a dislocated hip, he had no clear image of the operation involved. He had visited his dying mother, friends in pain and wife in childbirth, but disease had always been at a remove. He imagined traction, then the knife. He nodded sagely at the doctor, seriously, his mind a cartoon-riot of shapeless things in plaster, their Ace bandages raveling, legs hiked high. There is always a one-line tag, but Alexander could not read it. The doctor was saying, "Ten days."

"Ten days at the most?"

"For traction, yes. On the average, Mr. Cullinan. We'll have to keep testing and see."

"It could be less?"

"Could be." The doctor sounded dubious. His hair was long, coat white; he was in training for the marathon and had been trained at Massachusetts General. He was an expert, they said, an excellent orthopedic surgeon, the best in this town. Jane was with their elder daughter at ballet; therefore Alexander had brought Gillian alone. She lay in her snowsuit, eyes wide.

"How do you test for it?"

"By X-ray. Ten days is a ballpark figure. We'd hoped the Pavlik harness would have done the trick."

"We'd hoped so too," said Alexander. When their baby had been fitted for the harness, six months before and six months old, they'd thought it cruel confinement; now it seemed like freedom by comparison with what would come. Freedom's a comparative, he thought; the sling was of an airy lightness and had not hampered her. She had been learning to crawl.

"You understand," the doctor said. "It's not so early anymore. It's frankly dislocated now. We can't afford to wait."

"I understand that. But a second opinion . . ."

"Of course. You should take her to Boston."

"Yes."

"Take the X-rays with you and let's hope they disagree." The doctor smiled, not meaning it. "I'll set up the admission here for Tuesday."

"Is there any chance the traction will be adequate? I mean, just traction? That you won't have to operate?"

Her X-rays filled the envelope. They were encased in cardboard but felt leaden nonetheless. "No. I'm afraid not. None."

"Thank you, Doctor."

"You're welcome."

"I'm sorry to have taken so much time."

"That's what we're here for."

"It does surprise me," Alexander said again. "We had such faith in the harness."

They stood. They were of the same age and height. Gillian opened her arms, and he hoisted her up from the table. His authority, however, had been relinquished in the waiting room. The doctor took some seeming relish in bringing the lawyer to book. "We've got to make the best of it," he said. "It won't bother the child if it doesn't bother the parents. You'll be surprised at how adaptable they are. She doesn't know what walking's like, remember; she won't miss it. And in any case we've got no choice—we've waited as long as we can."

He drove to Boston the next day, with his three women on the back seat of the Jeep. His wife was drinking heavily. She had periodic bouts with what she called her first lover, Jack Daniel's, though she had had affairs with George Dickel and Jim Beam and Ezra Brooks. She cradled a fifth of Jack; their four-year-old, Suzanne, was sleeping in her lap. The Cherokee had poor suspension, and the approach roads to the turnpike were riddled with frost-heaves and potholes and ice. The winter had been hard. "It's like a goddam washboard," Jane said. Her voice was whiskey-thick, and he strained to hear her over the engine. "Like a roller coaster, Alex, can't you be careful for once?"

"I'm trying."

"Try harder," she said.

Suzanne slept, her blanket with its frayed silk edging up against her mouth. He saw all this in the rearview mirror—the threads responding to her breath, the rings on Jane's fingers and lace at her wrists, the golden cluster of his daughter's curls beneath her parka's hood. But he could not see the car seat; it was directly behind him. He could not turn sufficiently to see how Gillian fared. She made no sound, however; he collected his ticket at the turnpike entrance and turned east.

"I don't believe him," Jane announced.

"Why not?"

When drinking, she reverted to the insults of their youth. "He can't tell his ass from his elbow."

"Except he's the best we have. He himself suggested we go for a second opinion."

"To Mecca," she said. "Just because he trained there—Boston. The hell with it. He can't tell his ass from his elbow."

Alexander humored her. "Must make it hard for a surgeon."

"Ha ha," Jane said. "Mecca. The lame and the halt heading home."

Their families both hailed from Lexington, and therefore Boston did seem home; they would stay with her parents that night. Gillian had been an amiable infant—she stared and ate and slept as if at peace. At six months old, however, the pediatrician warned them that something was wrong with her legs. After consultation, she was placed in a Pavlik harness—trussed up like a portly frog so the ball would fit the socket of her dislocated hip. This had been difficult. They had had an anxious week till the buckles and straps became manageable; the Velcro tapes were urine-soaked, and Gillian complained. Soon enough, however, she learned to compensate; she crawled limp-legged across the flooring of their renovated barn. "'Man is born, he suffers and he dies,'" said Alexander, quoting Buddhist precepts that he did not deeply feel. "'There's worse to come as long as you can say that life's not over yet.'"

"That's chitchat," Jane said. "Just elegant chitchat. As long as they tell us our baby's all right . . ." She tilted the bottle toward him and left the phrase unfinished; Suzanne stirred in her sleep.

*

In Children's Hospital, however, the diagnosis was confirmed. Gillian would require an operation, and the sooner the better; she would wear a spica cast for six months at least.

This doctor was a woman; black-haired, wearing glasses. Her waiting room was full, and she had small interest in or patience with the Cullinans. "It's congenital," she said. "In ninety percent of the cases. And ninety percent of those affected are female. Did you"—she turned to Jane—"or did your mother have a dislocated hip?"

"Not that I know of," said Jane. "No one in our family."

"Well, there we have it then. The recessive gene." She took the X-rays once again and slapped them on a lighted screen. "We could admit her here," she said. "Or you could do it in Vermont. Go to the sixth floor and look at the ward. There's a baby there who's just been operated on, and the nurse will show you what it looks like. Good luck."

Dismissed, they rose. The baby on the sixth floor was stretched on a steel frame. She was encased in plaster from the armpits to the toes; the problem, the nurse said, was keeping the cast clean. Jane sat; she put her head down. "I'm dizzy," she said. "I may faint." There were rocking chairs and mobiles and stuffed animals on the ward; there were cuckoo clocks with sprung works on the walls. The child on the bed was logy from the anesthetic, said the nurse; she repeated the word "logy" as if, once alert, the child would have no cast. A plastic bag protruded, and there was a basin underneath the frame. "For her evacuations," the nurse said. She touched Alexander's arm, proprietary. "When she voids."

"We have to go now," Jane said.

Alexander held Gillian. She clutched her blanket, flush-faced, with the line of bone beneath her eyebrow pink from recent crying. "I have to have air," Jane said. "Thanks for the demonstration. We have to leave."

It was rush hour, and their retreat to Lexington was slow. In the car Jane keened; she rocked in her seat, saying, "Baby, my baby," and "Why did this happen to us?"

"It happened to her," he said. "It'll be better. She'll do the high jump."

"I want to die."

"You don't mean that."

"I do. I want this pain to end."

"It will."

"Six months. Six whole months in that cast. Just when she ought to be learning to walk. A toddler."

"She'll talk instead. I didn't walk, apparently, till I was two years old."

"You don't have to comfort me, Alex. You have a right to your own pain."

He braked. The traffic on Route 2 was heavy. "We'll make it."

"Of course. It takes two adults to turn her—that's what the nurse said." With her free hand she reached for his own. "It's torture, Alex. That cast."

"We'll manage," he assured her. "It could have been far worse."

In the days that followed, such assurance fled. The temperature dropped; he had to thaw their pipes one morning with a propane torch. It was minus thirty Fahrenheit, the worst cold snap on record for that week in February, and they huddled by the heat vents as if under siege. Alexander stayed home from the office and prepared his briefs under the eaves. Jane drank; he thought of himself as afflicted. Suzanne returned from the Early Childhood Center at two each afternoon, trudging in the tracks she'd made the week before; the snow was too heavy to shift. Alexander read fairy tales aloud. He fashioned paper crowns for her, and she danced to *The Nutcracker Suite*. Gillian would watch enchanted, banging her spoon on the tabletop. He fondled her continually, squeezing the flesh of her legs. On Tuesday she was admitted to the hospital, and Alexander drove to Albany, then flew through O'Hare to Moline; he had a claim to settle out of court. The John Deere company was willing to indemnify his client; their tractor's electrical system had exploded on ignition, and Sam Reed lost a leg.

"Mr. Cullinan," the farmer said, "they could give me five million. I'd take it, I ain't pretending I wouldn't. Between you and I. But they can't give me my leg."

Sam Reed was bald, with a white beard, and had provided maple syrup to the Cullinans for years. For Suzanne's first birthday, he had sent them a bushel of peas. He called up Alexander from a pay phone at the hospital, saying he could use help from an educated person in the law like you are, Mr. Cullinan. I know it's not the usual thing, but how would you feel with one foot on the pedal and one in the spreader all covered with shit; if he'd been alone that time he'd have bled to death in minutes. But they were putting him back together, Sam said, with pins and wire and plastic and soon enough he'd walk again, so what he wondered was what chance did a person stand of getting back at corporation presidents that never sat a tractor in their lives? Alexander said he'd help, and in the months that followed filed for damages. He deplaned in Moline in the snow.

"Can't you postpone it?" Jane had asked. "It's been dragging on for years."

"A year and a half. They're in a hurry."

"But can't you finish it by telephone? Of all the days we need you here . . ."

"I'll be back tomorrow, love. It's what Sam Reed's been dreaming of; it's not fair to ask him to wait."

"He's used to it. You're doing this for free, correct? So you want to get it over with; it's not like you're paid by the hour."

"Expenses," Alexander said. "We've got momentum now. Give them a change of venue or delay and they might change their minds."

He was proved right. The officials were conciliatory, generous; the facts of Mr. Reed's case having been ascertained, the depositions received, the faulty grounding located and the guarantee applicable because the intake-valve malfunction was not something they cared to make public, the John Deere company having a reputation to protect, and Mr. Reed having been unable to obtain redress from dealer or distributor, it devolved upon the company as such to compensate him for his leg. They were prepared so to do. They met Alexander at the airport and drove him to the offices and, over coffee, attained an agreement; by five o'clock the letters of intent were typed and signed.

He wanted to return. There was no plane, however, and the connection out of Cedar Rapids would be as efficient next morning; a company official who lived near Cedar Rapids offered to drive him there. Ned Sampson was insistent. It was the wrong way for Chicago but the right way for a drink; why not come home and eat with us, he asked, then book yourself out on the 7:05? Alexander had attended Columbia Law School while Ned was an undergraduate, and Ned thought the face looked familiar; the wife would love to meet you and we'll talk about old times.

Alexander refused. He said he was tired and needed some sleep; he explained about his daughter in the hospital. This excited Ned's strong sympathy; his secretary changed the booking and he would not hear of Alex having to eat out alone. They drove to Davenport, then Iowa City, in fog. The conversation flagged. There was a single lane carved out of the snow on I-80, and there were drifts. Ned Sampson lived on Summit Street; his driveway had been plowed. "Cost me thirty-five dollars this morning," he said. "For thirty yards and a turnaround. Should have bought a snowblower instead."

"Isn't it a long commute?"

"Mm-mn. But this town has some action in it, understand—a college town. It's where Alice comes from, besides."

Alice Sampson received them expansively. "I'm so glad you could come," she said. "I know what motel dinners must be like. And when Ned travels he's always so grateful for someone to talk to at night." Her palm was warm; she pressed his hand and held it, then turned as if in a square dance and, addressing the first partner, kissed her husband on the cheek. Her legs were good. "Where's Billy?" Ned asked.

"At the Parkers'," she said. "He wanted to sleep over, and I thought— when Sally called and said you'd be bringing Mr. Cullinan on down—I thought we might as well have us an evening alone." Her laugh was girlish, high. "And eat an adult supper for once. I do so want to hear about Ned's escapades in New York City way back when."

Alexander called the hospital. He reached Jane on the Pediatrics Ward. It was an hour later there, and Gillian had cried herself to sleep. "The traction's not so bad," she said. "It's a kind of stirrup, really, with weights. It's not so terrible. But everyone wears white in here, and every time she sees somebody wearing white she starts to cry."

"I don't blame her."

"They've taken blood. They take her temperature all the time. Suzy's all right. Dot's staying at the house, and they watched the Muppets. It's the cast that frightens me. I wish you were here."

"I will be tomorrow. We won. Sam Reed won't get five million, but he's got enough."

"Yes. Hurry."

"I'm taking the first plane," he said. "I'll be back just as soon as I can."

Ned brought him bourbon in a water glass. He took it soundlessly and drank. The walls of the study had photographs of Alice naked in a swimming pool, the water just under her breasts. Her eyes were closed, her hair was down; the breasts appeared to float. "Goodnight," he said to Jane. "I love you."

"Yes," she said. "I'm at the desk. The nurses here are friendly. Like riding a horse on your back."

"What?"

"The stirrups. It's one week in traction at least."

"I'll sleep there tomorrow. Warm up that bed."

"Yes. Goodnight."

"Kiss Gillian for me when she wakes up. Goodnight." He replaced the phone, stretched and drank. In the living room the lights were dim; James Galway played flute favorites, including "Annie's Song." Alice had her eyes closed and her head thrown back, as in the photographs; within the loose white blouse she wore, her breasts appeared less full. The couch was Naugahyde.

"You want to hear a story. You'll never believe this," said Ned. "When Lyndon Johnson quit—the night after his announcement—I was at a party. And I knew that we'd get Nixon then, somehow I knew it that night. So I was in a funk, understand, a real flat-out depression. And I went for a walk in Riverside Park, I mean nobody walks now in Riverside Park; it's dangerous at night. But things were different then, or maybe I just didn't care. And there was this yellow-haired thing, this midwestern beauty walking by the water too. Corn-fed. We didn't get busted or mugged, understand, I took her back to the party. Well, it's a simple story but the complicated thing, the part that makes it interesting and why I'm telling you, is this midwestern lady is my wife."

"Have another drink," she said.

The telephone rang. It was United Airlines calling to tell him his flight had been canceled; Ned's secretary had provided his home number. The fog was increasing; Cedar Rapids was shut and the equipment had been overflown. The storm had not yet reached Chicago, but snow was predicted; they could change his reservation for the day after; he had to decide. There would be surface transport available from Cedar Rapids to O'Hare at seven the next morning, but he would have to miss the flight for Albany, and the storm was heading east. Alexander tried to route himself through Minneapolis or Denver, but the computer denied him; he could not leave from Iowa except along the ground. Moline was also closed. If he could reach O'Hare, United Airlines said, his morning flight was listed routine, and Albany was clear. He said that he would try to drive; the lady in Chicago advised him to drive carefully. He thanked her and hung up.

"A problem?" Ned inquired.

"Yes. Are there car rentals in this town?"

"Out at the airport, maybe. Not in this village at night." He called and got no answer. Alice brought him cheese. The cheese was bite-size, with toothpicks protruding. She loosened his tie for him, smiling. Her fingernails were pink. "What about buses?" he asked. "Is there a Greyhound to Chicago?"

"It's a local," Alice said. "You don't have to hurry."

"I do."

She studied him. "I'd like it if you stayed."

"I'd like it too. But there's a daughter in a hospital."

"Ned told me. I know."

"I've got to get home."

"Home." She repeated this without inflection, as if home were a word that failed to signify. He did not know, and would not, what her wide-armed welcome was intended to convey; he imagined Gillian in fitful sleep, Jane drinking beside her, and put down his glass.

"Where's the station?"

"Just around the corner," Ned announced. "Two rights, the first left."

"I should have headed back this afternoon."

"I'm sorry."

"No. It's not your fault. You were being generous."

"I'll drive you to Chicago. Hell . . ."

Alexander wanted credit for his good behavior. He did not wish to share or apportion such credit. "Just point me to the bus."

The terminal was empty. There was a bearded man asleep on a back bench, and a counter with a clock behind it, reading 8:15. There was bright fluorescent lighting, and the walls of the room displayed framed posters of Biarritz. He had an hour to wait. He settled down to do so, consigned to that limbo where the traveler goes nameless and unrecognized, where no one who knew him knew where they might find him. The paving was slick. He had nearly fallen in the terminal's front lot.

When finally the bus arrived, it was eleven o'clock. The driver took his money, said, "Them roads are like a skating rink," and told him to go get a seat. There were none, it appeared. Then a black man on the aisle stirred in his sleep from the sprawl that had taken two places, and Alexander sat. He had, he realized, never ridden a long-distance bus in America; he had done so with some frequency in Italy and Switzerland and India and France. The dark shapes all around him seemed inured to such slow passage; they were asleep, or talking softly or staring out windows at Iowa City in fog. Smoking was forbidden; he would have welcomed a smoke. The bus, with its windows sealed shut, felt overheated; he transferred his briefcase and satchel to the rack. Standing, he took off his overcoat also; the bags were from a matched set Jane had given him on his thirty-fifth birthday, with his initials underneath the MC from Mark Cross. He felt embarrassed by such luxury and grateful for the dark; the black man beside him shifted again, his head shaved and skull like a mask. The eyebrows had a ridge of bone, and Alexander spent some minutes trying to identify the face; his father had instructed him in the distinguishing marks of masks. The phrase "Yoruba, Ibo, Dan" became the litany of remembrance, and he decided that his neighbor derived from Ibo stock.

His father had had a collection of masks, and Alexander used to brandish shields and spears and daggers in the living room. His favorite mask was Ekoi and trimmed with human skin. "It's possible," his father said. "The skin here could be antelope. But that's thicker, usually, and not so mottled. These teeth are monkey teeth."

They stopped at a motel in order to change drivers, then stopped at Davenport. He closed his eyes but could not sleep, saw Gillian encased in plaster, Sam Reed blown apart. The fog was thick; the turnpike lights had a soft yellow nimbus, and he heard the trucks they passed before he saw them looming. The driver wiped his windshield often, but there was no snow.

Alexander read signs to Wisconsin and to Indiana; they reached the outskirts of Chicago before dawn. Then the traffic increased. At six o'clock the sky had not cleared, and he commenced to worry that O'Hare would also close. Arrived at the Greyhound Terminal, he called United Airlines, and the operator said the equipment was in Chicago, but that the decision to fly would be taken at departure time; he confirmed his booking, and she said, "Good luck." He drank from a child's water fountain, then took the escalator up to find a taxi for O'Hare.

At the top of the escalator, a crate with wire strapping blocked his path. It occupied the width of the platform. He hurdled the thing and fell free.

The act of leaping gave him pleasure, he walked with loose-legged jaun-tiness past the janitor who watched. A policeman waved his nightstick at a woman wearing hot pants and yellow platform shoes; there were rows of travelers watching TV. At seven o'clock the outside air had a wet chill; he breathed this with relief. Two men approached him and lunged for his bags, crying, "Airport, sir?"

"All right," he said. "How much?"

The younger one was jumpy; his taxi was the first in line. "Get in, get in."

"How much to O'Hare?"

"I'll drive you, sir." He wrenched open the passenger door and revealed a body; he pulled the man out by the feet. His speech shifted accent; he came from the islands. "Out wid you, mon, out I say." The man within unfolded. He was staggering-drunk, six foot six at least. His eyes were yellow; his forehead was cut and there was dried blood on the wound. He steadied himself on Alexander's shoulder, then spun off. "Get in, get in. Twenty dollars."

Alexander turned. The elder driver smiled at him, retreating to the second car. He did not know the proper price but felt compelled to bar-gain. "Twenty dollars is too much."

"The book, the book! That's what it say in the book for the airport."

"Show me."

The driver flipped through pages and produced a suburb called Des Plaines. "Twenty dollars to Des Plaines, that's what it cost. It the rules."

"O'Hare," said Alexander. "I don't want to go to Des Plaines." He entered the second cab, hearing cries of "Fifteen dollars! Twelve! I take you, sir," and settled in. The second driver laughed. "He tried to fool you, see, it don't take twenty dollars. Not to O'Hare. Fifteen's more like it, sir. He look in the book and you look in the book, and there's no airport where he looking. You a person who travels, correct?"

"Correct."

"That boy he don't know nothing. He thought he could fool you. Des Plaines!"

The fog was palpable. Alexander closed his eyes. The driver was solicitous; he lectured Alexander on the need to get some rest. He him-self came from Natchez but worked in Chicago and had his children and grandchildren in Chicago also; that was what was keeping him when he could go home. He had a pension from the railroad and he drove this taxi for diversion and because the times were tight; just to keep busy, understand, keeping out of his wife's hair. He asked where Alexander was going, and when Alexander said Albany, he asked if Alexander lived near the Rockefeller ranch. They discussed the death of Nelson Rockefeller, and the driver speculated on the role of Nelson's wife and brothers, how much money they would get and what he himself would have done with the money; he reminded Alexander that Joe Kennedy left more behind than Rockefeller, four hundred million to sixty-six about, and he wondered whether maybe someone could be holding something back; he wasn't a fisherman himself but he could smell something fishy like that a mile off and driving a cab. He asked what was Alexander doing in this town, and whether he had family, and when he learned the reason for the trip he said, God bless your daughter and don't worry she'll be fine. They drove in silence then. The airport was crowded; he had forty minutes to spare before his scheduled flight. When Alexander proffered a five-dollar tip, the cabbie repeated, "God bless you. I'll pray for your daughter. Good luck."

He called his home. Suzanne answered. "Who is it?"

"Hi, darling."

"*Hi*, Daddy."

"How are you?"

"Fine." She said this with an intonation she reserved for phones—languorous and sweetly thoughtful. "I miss you."

"I miss you."

"When will you be coming back?"

"As soon as possible. I'm on my way. Almost there. How were the Muppets?"

"Fine." She would not be deflected. "Tonight? Tomorrow?"

"Today, I hope. Is Mommy at the hospital?"

"Yes. Do you want to speak to Dot?"

"I just called to wish you good morning. You're off to school now?"

"Yes."

"I'm glad to hear your voice," he said. "I'm bringing you a present."

She hugged the phone. She told him she was hugging it, then promised she would build a snowman after school. It would be at the top of the driveway, she said, it would be the first thing he would see.

His plane was late. O'Hare had one functional runway for arrivals and one for departures; the problem was not fog so much as ice. He bought a motorized Snoopy for Suzanne, perfume for Jane and a tin of cigars for himself. He bought a newspaper and tried to read; he consulted the departure screen frequently and drank two Bloody Marys at the stand-up bar. The Midwest was an obstacle course he was trying to negotiate; his skills were those of motion and not immobility. The man beside him serviced a high-speed paper counter, and he said the competition was seeking an injunction—in eighteen months he had them running scared. He'd worked for a firm out of England until just eighteen months ago when he'd started up his own. He'd quit when he was good and ready and not because some candyass English assholes asked him to cease and desist.

The captain welcomed them. He said the field conditions in Albany were such that the decision to land there would be taken on approach. He apologized for the delay and hoped they'd have a pleasant flight. The flight attendants would be bringing breakfast as soon as they were airborne, and he'd announce their destination just as soon as possible; they were number seven on the runway for departure.

The plane rumbled forward. He watched the processional—planes at right angles rolling to position, then the sudden check and halt and accelerating release. He studied his hands. The plane roared, immobile. He remembered his first flight—to Washington, with his father who took him along for the sheer sport and spectacle, the cloud bank beneath them seeming like swansdown, the tilt and rise of it and his stomach lurching with each updraft and descent. He thought of Robin Templeton in college, and his army training plane; the best thing for a hangover, Robin used to claim, the only way to clear your brain is try a few maneuvers. So they would go up in the morning after parties, boasting of the night before or the anticipated night to come, and Alexander would strap himself in, his head a riot of panicky pride, the taste of metal in his mouth while Robin looped the loop.

His mother's dying wish had been to have her ashes spread on some loved stretch of countryside. She had been cremated, and Alexander took the urn. He chartered a Comanche out of the Bennington airport, and the pilot flew for half an hour over the Green Mountains till the fields beneath them seemed mere shape and the hills and lakes and villages went unrecognized. Then Alexander opened the door, working the urn cap loose and scattering ash. He had not anticipated the force of the wind, or the door's resistance, and much of the bone and ash flew back inside the plane. He held the urn, however, letting air empty it out. Much of the ash, he told himself, would surely have been coffin-ash, and the bone had been transformed to the size and consistency of cat litter. He took a shower later, washing this substance out of his hair, until the hot water was gone.

"We're number two in line now, folks," the pilot said. "Will flight attendants take their positions."

Alexander thought of how he'd learned to ride, to set his horse at a canter by pulling back on the reins, then kicking at the instant of release. Jane was the better rider, on the more spirited horse, and she would bolt in front of him, raising dust or mud. They lifted free. He felt the now familiar tilt and rise. The flight was smooth. They could not land at Albany, however, and landed at Plattsburgh instead. He had been traveling now for twenty-seven hours, and the airline bus to Albany would take him too far south. He went to the information counter and asked, "You got a boat?"

"Sir?"

"I've been in a car," he said. "And bus and taxi and plane. I require a boat now."

"Sir?"

"To bring this trip full circle. My car's locked anyhow. It's in the long-term parking lot at Albany. I'll leave it there. My daughter's in the hospital."

"I'm sorry, sir." The woman at the information counter assessed him, uncertain. "Where were you planning to go?"

He told her. She suggested Amtrak, and he took a taxi to the Amtrak station. The subsequent hours unreeled in slow motion, and all he would retain were frames: blurred, indistinct, himself jolting backward through snow. His baby lay in a hospital bed; he would tell her on arrival, though she would not comprehend him, how the world is in an orbit and all things are therefore circular.

At Saratoga Springs he disembarked. There were no taxis waiting, and he watched the train head south. Here the cold was absolute, and he waited by the train tracks for a taxi to arrive. There was a work crew on a siding, spreading calcium to clear the track. They dug and shoveled and ladled the stuff thickly on a single rail. Alexander raised his collar and watched his breath condense. He faced the four directions, turning slowly and counting to ten; he tried to imagine himself as a compass, the fixed point where Gillian lay conjoined to all such circling. She would improve. They would manage. The three men leaned on their shovels. They watched him till he turned their way and then returned to work.

Ostinato

Dear Mr. Bentham:

*I hope you and Mrs. Bentham are having a pleasant winter in Truro. How
I wish to be there with you to spend summer the same way I spent it in the past
with both of you. For when I think about you and your place I always get a
special feeling, the feeling you get for special places and people you have loved
and trusted and found happiness with once, just like the feeling I get toward
my home in Japan and to my family.*

*I just come back from the concert hall. I give exact information about your
performance to the all of my friends because it gives me a sheer pleasure, Mr.
Bentham, of being your friend that I always feel so proud of. Yes to tell the truth
I wanted ticket to send Jon as a gift. It's sound romantic, isn't it? And I think I
am, as I were sometimes. Anyway I have already invited him for your concert
because I wanted him to meet you and I wanted you to meet him because I like
him a lot and I like you a lot. Also, to me it is the only chance to ask him openly
to be with me and it is the only chance he can accept the concert in a casual way.
So would you please meet him for me? I met him at the Pub Club where he was
playing piano as a member of the young music band. And there was no special
relationship between us except he as a music player and singer and I as a one
of fan among the many of his fan, at least I made it clear to him and myself.
And I think he understand it.*

But it's me who failed again in a game of love. Problem is that when I become to like someone I could not play it as I should. I play it too seriously, I think. That's why it hurts me now when we see each other like stranger again though my feeling toward him are still same. It is foolish to feel hurt when I know the reason why I was attracted to him is only that he is so beautiful and charming and young, 26 years old, and although he care for me enough to come up to my table on a recess whenever I go there sometimes, half of it are out of courtesy. And I wish we were once lovers and strangers again the next morning rather than purely platonic. And worse of all we are not even in platonic love either. Yet I can't ignore him.

Anyway, he will be gone again soon and we might not see each other anymore. So I would like to make a last chance of togetherness with him and first reunion in five years with you to be a perfect one. So please help me make it wonderful one for three of us. That means I would like to have pleasant night with most smile and laughter that is only possible between true friends if we can only see you for a few moment at the backstage after concert. But I wish we could find some time to talk. He is young but not like hippies although he has a long hair but it is beautiful so he won't make you feel any embarrassment. That's I can promise about him.

By the way what time will you arrive here on Monday? If you are not tired and don't mind to listen to the music they play which I am afraid you might say that it is not music but loud noise unless you find it something personally attractive, and personally I think they play pretty well, I am mostly happy to come to his place with you. In any case please write me as how I can see you if you have still got a time but if not please call as soon as you are in Halifax. And please leave a message if I was not in. Although I will be careful not to miss your telephone all day.

I wish you safe trip. Again I wish Mrs. Bentham will be here too so you will help me with my trouble and then everything will be settled in nicest way.

See you soon. P S. I enclose telephone and address. In hastly.

Mishiko

"Well?"

"Well what?"

"Are you going to see her?"

"What do you want me to do?"

"How long has it been?" Helen asked. She gave the letter back to him, and he left it on the table.

"Five years," Richard said. "I would have thought she'd be in Tokyo again."

"Nara."

"Tokyo was where she worked, remember?"

"I wouldn't remember."

"Come off it, Helen. You do."

"Yes. I suppose so. There's so much to remember."

He paused. "Her visa—working papers. They must have been renewed."

"She found some other happy family. Some other cultural exchange program."

"I don't have to see her," Richard said.

"She'll find you, anyhow. Those hands of yours will be caressing keys on every lamppost in Halifax. Has she written before?"

"No."

"'*Mr.* Bentham,' it says. Only 'Mr. Bentham.' She could have included us both."

"I'm the one who's going, right? She's got another pianist."

"Younger this time."

He looked at his hands. "Not so famous."

"No. Not yet, at any rate. That's why she wants you to meet him."

"A rock 'n' roll band? She wants me to listen to some third-rate pianist at the, what's it called . . . ?"

"The Pub Club," Helen said.

"Yes. Why don't you come with me?"

"No."

"Please. I could use the protection."

"You're dying to meet them. Her. Anyhow, it's the most beautiful month here."

He pocketed the letter. "Why don't you join me for once?"

"No."

"Just overnight? There's a darling little pub club."

"Please. I don't want to talk about it. You know I can't come."

He changed his tone. "I never really know, now do I? What's so marvelous about December here alone?"

"The privacy," she said.

"We'll miss Christmas together. You wouldn't have to leave the hotel."

"It isn't overnight. It's the first in a series of concerts—two weeks."

"You could come back." He raised his hands. "But have it your way, Helen."

"Don't wheedle. *You're* the one who booked this tour." She said this with the intonation he had used before—a practiced self-pity soliciting praise. "It's your way too. Ours."

"She was a good gardener. You said so yourself."

"Snow peas," Helen said. "On those tender little knees of hers, picking up the weeds with her fingers like tweezers. One by one. So terribly attractive."

"She did help with the house."

"She's crazy if she thinks I'll have her back."

"She doesn't think that."

"So find out what she does think. What she's after. Go to her."

"I'm going to Halifax, remember? Not to her."

"The Oriental mysteries. A massage parlor for the maestro's fingers. 'Oh, please, Mr. Bentham,'" she mimicked, "'let me chop the callots. Don't hurt your hands.'"

"All right."

"It's not all right."

"I can't cancel."

"No, I know that, darling. You couldn't help it, could you?"

"If she wants to come," he said, "I'll see her. But I won't try to find her."

"It's a flee countly," said Helen. "You do what's best to do."

That week he drove to Boston, trying to assess the winter colors of the Cape. His windshield was tinted, and the sky's blue had depth. The pine trees were less green than in the summertime, and the sand less brilliant at the edges of Route 6. He wondered, as often before, if Mishiko had been truly displaced or would seem at home in Tokyo. There, he imagined, she'd know her directions—knowing in the signless streets which way to turn for the theater or where to purchase fish. He made the plane at Logan with little time to spare, carrying his music in his briefcase. His itinerary looked this month, he'd joked, like a primer course in foolishness: name sixteen towns you've never heard of, and Richard Bentham will be there, introducing Eskimos to Bach.

It had been more disconcerting than he'd dared acknowledge. He had not seen her handwriting in years. The perfectly wielded pen, the black precision of her script stood in such startling contrast to the mutilated language as to appear nearly purposive—as if she mocked his exactness by both aping and burlesquing it. Or as if she'd wanted, after all this time away, to show that she'd learned nothing since she departed their house. Or as if she wrote him in an agreed-on code—but one that he'd forgotten how to read.

Yet there remained her habitual grace. He'd not been wrong in urging her to make a career of transcribing; there were few enough by now that you could trust with scores. Instead—what was she doing?—receiving unemployment, probably, in some backwater street in some town in Nova Scotia. He ordered bourbon, neat, and sat back and kicked off his shoes.

More and more successful, he'd been less and less at home these years. A performing career has its own sort of logic, he'd say; you play until they stop inviting you. At first, and even when they could barely afford it, Helen traveled with him. She delighted in the bustle and applause. While he practiced in the windy halls, gauging the piano's action, she would roam whatever place they'd come to, finding the museums or shopping arcades or bistros or fountains that later, alone, he would never quite manage to find. She would acquire scarves or catalogues or pastry or the region's wine. Then they'd meet at the hotel at three. They would shower and nap and make love, his mind empty of all but that preparatory hush he needed for the sounding silence of the concert yet to come.

Things changed. Helen grew more needy but appeared to need him less. They bought a summer house in Truro and had it winterized. They kept their rent-controlled apartment in New York, and she began referring to it as their West Side *pied-à-terre*. She painted—badly, he thought. She took Yoga and dance and recorder lessons. Impatient with any but demonstrated expertise or professional ambitions, Richard found himself humoring her. They had no children. In what they agreed was a predictable seven-year crisis, Helen said, "It's just too much. Keeping the home fires burning. I do need help with the place."

So he found the thirty-year-old cousin of the daughter of his recording engineer: a Japanese. They sponsored her arrival and guaranteed employment. They fetched her at Logan—a pale, mute person wearing jeans, with two straw suitcases she'd tied together at the handles. That summer, he had promised Helen, he would stay at home. And with the exception of a master class or two, with the exception of recording dates in Amsterdam and the festival at Bath, he did remain in Truro. He was, he told himself, attempting to shore up collapse.

They painted the house. He heard somewhere that Jung had cured a patient by telling him to stop analysis and purchase an acre of land. So he had truckloads of topsoil delivered, and they staked out a garden on the southern slope. City people, the Benthams were clumsy at first, but he reveled in the amateurish frenzy of it—cutting stakes for fence posts and digging and forking and hoeing with such glad abandon that Helen feared for his hands.

The flight was rough; Richard stared at the clouds. Mishiko had been patient, practiced, and she tended the garden with care. She liked to do the marketing, and she cleaned their spattered paint. They gave her a portable radio for her birthday. She acquired a broad-brimmed straw hat also, and would accompany them to the beach, sitting in her own created shade with earphones, nodding. For her sojourn in the garden, she would turn the volume up. "It frightens the rabbits," she said. Later, when he pictured her, it was always in that hat, on her knees in front of the pole beans or corn, being crooned at by some caterwauling indecipherable Englishmen, rapt.

He would emerge from his day's practice, blinking in the sun. The two of them would greet him—Helen dark and seeming heavy by comparison. He would propose a sail or swim, and they would proffer the harvest, and Mishiko would turn down the sound. She seemed like some ancient retainer or serving woman to him then—three steps behind him where they walked, a gliding presence perfectly located in their lives. When Helen left for New York—to see her doctor, she said, and to deal with the rubble that the upstairs tenant's overflowing bathtub had made of their dining room ceiling—it seemed merely proper that he enter the guest room bed.

Mishiko accepted him. A woman, he maintained, should take off modesty with her clothes. Yet she was clothed in passionate demureness for the nights that they made love. In the morning she served him tea and buttered toast, the radio already on, as if nothing could have altered the pattern set up that June. She left the following week. He acquiesced in her departure with relief. Though she'd become his mistress, she attempted to explain, Helen was still mistress of the house.

December 22

Dear Mrs. Bentham:

I can't tell you enough how glad and happy I was to seeing Mr. Bentham again. On Monday we had few hours to talk and laugh together as we used to did and I can't believe that there is five years between us to meet again. I can picture it clearly when Mr. Bentham says that "everything is same in Truro," even though I have heard all news, including the some of sad news that had happened to the people I knew of. But back to the first night I must tell you that, in spite of Mr. Bentham's busy schedule, it was so nice to accept my wish to come and see my "wish-to-be-my-boyfriend" and I was so happy with seeing two man friend I like so much talking together. However, in spite of Mr. Bentham's cooperation, it was I think the night I had really put Jon into difficult situation and made him really hate me. If I hadn't a pleasant time with Mr. Bentham I would have been so unhappy and depressed for the result of coming to the concert with Dave instead of Jon. Yet I am glad whole situation seems turned out very nicely for every one. The concert was beautiful as always, and Dave, my former employer who gave me the first job in Canada to do airbrushing on T-shirt and I still work for him occasionally when he needs, enjoyed it immensely and Grace, who was my roommate and nice friend, enjoyed it too.

There was another enjoyable time when Mr. Bentham took me to the Japanese restaurant. It was a restaurant I worked as a cashier for four weeks in September. There it was snowing. I must thank you again for most pleasant time. One thing I regret myself is I failed to call Mr. Bentham this morning to say one more time "Thank, you" and "Good-bye" and "Wishing you a nice trip," etc. I called all right but it was too late. Hotel-man said that he left five minutes ago. I called two airline to find out if . . . but by the time I find out right airline I give up to call because I thought it might give Mr. Bentham a only trouble to get it if he was not nearby telephone.

I do hope Mr. Bentham will be continuing safe trip with successful musical performance. And I do hope you will not be too lonely while Mr. Bentham is away and not be too tired or bored. Love.

Mishiko

The mystery, of course, was how she had stood it at all—not how she had withstood it for so long. Her grandmother had turned one hundred in

November. Helen journeyed to the nursing home and attended a party the other inmates—she couldn't help it, she thought of them as inmates—put on. They had ice cream and cake and party hats and favors, and her grandmother wore a corsage. When the singing was over her grandmother stood and clattered on her water glass for attention. She looked so prim but nervous that Helen by her side had straightened also, straining. Then she delivered a speech. In her singsong, high-pitched whisper, the celebrant said, "Life is not what you make it. Life is how you take it," and fell back to her chair as if released.

This jingle stayed with Helen through the holidays. She found herself repeating it in front of the news, or while drinking coffee, or in the intervals she paced by her easel, considering a Wyeth-like series of gulls. She heard no music those weeks. Richard's records bulked beneath the stereo system like a dusty, pinched reproach; he'd made so many lately that the space she allocated to her husband could scarcely contain him. She put out suet and sunflower seed. The chickadees and jays and grosbeaks clustered to her feeders, and she watched them through the picture windows, unafraid. When Mishiko's letter arrived on December 24, she called Bill up to wish him Merry Christmas, and to ask if there were some sort of party she might attend or make. He said, "But gladly, gladly," and came down from Provincetown that night with a bottle of Old Bushmills. She had had trouble with the fireplace, and he pointed out to her—gently, not making it a joke or an occasion for scorn—that first she had to open the flue. Then he built a fire, mixing in pitch pine and oak and warming the living room so that they elected to lie down in front of it, no other lights on in the house.

Bill stroked her back. He blundered on about the possibility of change, how she could come with him to Provincetown and maybe San Miguel de Allende, where he taught in the Art Institute, and he'd show her turkey buzzards to sketch instead of gulls. "*Xopilotes*," Bill said. "That's what they call them there." The mystery was how to make the world of art and privilege seem anything but grown-up games, be born again, was how to pry free his fingers as they closed upon her arm. Bill said she kindled flame in him, but Helen fell asleep. She heard the language of seduction go up the chimney, weightless, incorporeal as smoke.

When Richard called the next morning, she told him that a family of pheasants had settled by the junipers beyond the porch. That seemed the most important thing; she had nothing to ask or report. He said, "It's hard to be apart," and she agreed. He said, "I wish you'd come with me," and she answered, "Yes. That would be nice." He told her that he'd be back home the following Sunday by eight.

She read the Sunday *Times*. She left *The Tale of Genji* with a bookmark in it by their bed. She wondered if the nastiness that had invaded her these months (the word for it *was* nastiness, this chill propriety and prejudice she'd thought of as her mother's curse) might dissipate and lift. She made a New Year's resolution that such brittle rigor would go. The problem was just how to make it go. The issue was where to locate that shivering delight she'd known at twenty or thirty or even last year when listening to Richard perform the *Schubert Impromptus*. Or in some tavern with him, dancing in a circle dance with sweaty men with handkerchiefs; the question was where pleasure fled and hid.

Helen studied herself in the mirror. It was not unkind. The flesh that had been soft was firm, the planes of her face more pronounced. She dressed herself attentively, pulled out but did not play his record of the *Goldberg Variations*, and settled in to wait. She made canapés. The few cars passing by their house seemed self-propelled and pilotless; their headlights lit the pine trees at the driveway's end.

Then Richard arrived. He rumbled down the driveway and she heard his brakes complain. She listened to him, motionless, hearing the engine roar and cease, hearing him open the car door, then the trunk. She heard him stamp and shuffle up the steps she had remembered to light, and opened the front door in for him as he opened the storm door out. The mystery was how he did not notice, as she greeted and embraced him and took off his overcoat, how she'd traveled so far to return.

"Welcome, world traveler," she said. He said the house looked lovely, and so did its mistress, his wife.

After he'd unpacked, given her the perfume and a Hudson's Bay blanket (blue, with a dark blue stripe, and doubling the size of his luggage and anyhow not as good as blubber for igloos, he said), after she'd told him that seals were in the harbor here, and asked about the audience in Montreal, the cousin who came to Toronto to hear him, told about the New Year's celebration where they'd gotten so falling-down drunk that William pretended the dunes were a ski slope, and said the Witherecks were sweet, had been utterly insistent that she dine with them, two times, and that she'd therefore asked them to dinner on Monday, tomorrow, and hoped he didn't mind; after she'd asked for and seen his reviews, complimented his haircut, asked about the weather in Vancouver and said they did have snow for Christmas but it didn't last, she brought out cheese and rum and said, "I got her letter."

"Whose?"

"Hers. About the nights in Halifax."

"Oh. Mishiko's."

"Yes. Mishiko's."

"And what did she tell you?" he asked.

Then Helen stretched and watched him watching her; her breasts rose with the motion and she locked her hands behind her head, leaned back.

"Do you want to see the letter?"

"Not especially. Not yet."

"Her grammar's no better," she said. "It must have been some scene."

"What?"

"The nightclub. The boyfriend. The three of you wrestling."

"Do we have to discuss this?"

"No."

"I'll have another drink, then."

She covered her glass with her palm. "No, thanks. Not yet. I want to discuss it."

"Oh, Helen . . ."

"Oh, Helen, what?"

Richard sighed. He topped his drink and watched the liquid rise above the level of the glass. It adhered to itself, and he hunted the word for such molecular adherence.

"Oh, Helen, *what*?" she repeated.

Meniscus—that was it; he drank, pleased. "Oh, Helen, I've just gotten here. So let's not squabble over lunatics, all right?"

"Like who?"

"Like those two. Cheers. Your health."

"To us," she said. "Someone cut a blue spruce from the driveway. I'd been to Provincetown shopping, and I'd anyhow decided not to buy a tree this year. But up there by the parking lot I noticed something missing. And

I knew it right away—the spruce that you planted, the middle one—the best. We've got a wreath on the door. It doesn't seem fair."

"I'll talk to the police."

"For what? Because they cut a Christmas tree? He never made your concert, did he?"

"Jon? No. But Dave did, and the airbrush gang."

"You spent *two* nights with her."

"The first at the nightclub, the second at the concert hall. We called."

"Not very often."

"Often enough. You weren't home."

"Look, is this some sort of inquisition?"

"I rather thought it was," said Richard.

She stretched again. He had the menace of strangeness about him, always, after such trips. She set herself to elicit his threatless familiarity. "I do like that haircut," she said. "Where did you get it?"

"The airport. I can't remember which one now. Somewhere we had to wait."

"I did cry, darling. About that tree. I stood there with my groceries, watching the place where the sap still leaked, just feeling so sorry for us . . ."

"There are enough trees," he said.

"I'll go with you next tour, maybe. To France?"

"Yes. And Italy. It would be fine."

"Yes."

"I'll tell you what her letter said," he said. "If there's anything else then she lied. I got to Halifax that evening, and got to the hotel. She was there; she'd been waiting by the desk all day, she told me, but it didn't matter, she was pleased to find the right one. Grinning, speechless. She wondered if I'd go to the Pub Club—hear her little rinky-dink ragtime pianist, Jon. I think they called themselves the Wolverines. Yes. Bishop and the Wolverines. That's what they called themselves. Jon Bishop. From Ireland, can you beat it? A Bishop?"

"They're Catholic there," Helen said.

"Well, anyway, we went."

"You don't have to tell me."

"I know. That's why I'm doing it. He must have been appalled to see me—this ancient, earnest person come to check on his intentions. Stride piano, that's what he played. Not all that badly either, I have to give him that. And Mishiko just sat there, nodding, beaming, drinking milk, and he joined us between sets. We talked about Rachmaninoff. He'd learned the name to impress me, I think, but he said he always thought Rachmaninoff was the nuts."

"He didn't!" Helen laughed.

"Yes. He used that expression—the nuts. So I agreed with him but said that I believed Fats Waller was just the nuts also, and Willie Smith, and we discussed the respective merits of Rachmaninoff and Waller and Willie 'The Lion' Smith. Then I paid and said I had to get some sleep and thanked him. Said I hoped he'd come to my concert tomorrow, and left them there, and left."

"We're being condescending."

"Yes."

"He didn't come."

"No."

"What did he look like?"

"Red-headed," Richard said. "A Vandyke beard, more or less. Short and thick and wearing sequins and one earring. Just her type."

"It doesn't matter."

"There's more."

"No more. You're home again and have a haircut and it's the New Year. Later you can tell me," Helen said.

"Next day I took her out to lunch. To the restaurant she'd worked at—a kind of Horn and Hardart's, where you could eat *sashimi*. Rice. *Sukyaki* for a dollar; it was awful."

"Is she happy?" Helen asked.

"I wouldn't be."

"That's not my question. Is she?"

"Would you be? With so little?"

Richard gestured at the tasseled rugs, and at the marsh outside. He turned on the floodlights and it seemed as if they saw the bay, down beyond the flagstone path: boats raised on blocks at the edge of the visible, all they surveyed and owned. She spread out their thick new blanket.

"I want to be happy," said Helen. "It's my New Year's resolution."

"Yes."

"Do please take your shoes off. I'm trying."

"Yes."

He did, and she embraced him and felt him rise against her. The contours of their flesh fused in practiced opposition. Richard lay on top of her, and she on the Hudson's Bay blanket. But as their bodies meshed she felt such unslaked hunger for some further kind of fusion that she wept; she could not halt the crying that he took as love's approval and excited him; he plunged inside her fiercely while she formulated words like "condescension"; "Murasaki"; "sea." She tried to make a pattern of them, but they would not scan; she tried to find a rhythm in them, but they did not fit. Her husband's weight was as an anchor; it kept them together yet kept them apart. He stood. He said, "I love you," and transferred his clothes to the hamper. She was not endangered, not adrift.

January 8

Dear Mr. and Mrs. Bentham:

I have finally got the photograph to be developed and enlarged, and I am very happy to be sending you now. I hope you would love it as much as I do. You and Jon looks so gorgeous in the picture. This is the first time in my life I get complete satisfaction out of pictures I have ever possessed. I would cherish it and admire it always and every time I look at it I will remember all the beautiful memories those beautiful people, you and Jon, have brought to me.

I regret to say that the pictures taken at the backstage on the night of your concert has been all come out black which I was half suspected since the flashlight did not work, normally then. For that picture I hope there will be another chance again, possibly next year when you are here?

There is one more thought for which I also need your help for securing a job. I would like work as stagehand or paint stage props at a theater. What I am hoping for is your influential assistance to get some steady connections with people in theater management. Since you are performing I thought you have access to the people even though yours is a musical society. I was tempted to apply for it here but I dare not try because I know the results before start. If I apply for it all by myself because I would never get the job when at mere sight of me the interviewer will say that it is not a woman's job. I do hope you have someone in mind who can help.

By the way I would like to tell about the letter I had received from Jon. It was a letter of apology and he explained in it that he sent his apologies to the theater to you backstage about 8 o'clock on concert night. I don't know if you really receive it or not.

Whether what he is saying is true or not please forgive him for what he meant to. He has left for his home country after his last performance. He will be coming back in April and will be playing 6 weeks from 5th of April and maybe in May too. Ever since he left to his home in Ireland he has sending me nice letter explaining why he had to acted with me like he had been. I think, we will remain as a best friend for each other for the rest of our life since it is the best and only way we could find our happiness. I think we both know there will be no other way. Now he says he is going to send me a record which will be released soon. That is all we are now at the moment. I am also sending him a picture, and I am happy.

Mishiko

Marching Through Georgia

H<small>E ARRIVED IN</small> Knoxville half asleep, having left for Albany at five. The trip was uneventful though prolonged. There was rain at the Albany airport, then rain at Islip and Washington; the skies cleared while he waited for his connecting flight. His lecture was scheduled for four.

George Allison liked travel; it gave him some sense of expanse. But he had done enough of it these months, he told his wife, to last a year. She had kissed him sleepily. "Be careful." Allyn stood at the door. "Don't step on any alligators."

"No. Go back to bed."

"Wish you were here," Allyn said.

His taxi driver had been garrulous. "I'm glad you asked me, Professor. I wouldn't want you driving down yourself. The way they keep the airport parking lot. It ain't safe. I hate to think of you leaving that sports car behind."

"I'll just be gone three days," George said. "But it isn't worth the hubcaps."

"Hubcaps, hell," said Billy Peck. "They'd take the tires too."

George made no answer. The autumn dawn was cold. They were driving in the limousine that Billy Peck used for funerals. The road was slick; they saw few cars. "I got to do a burial later," Peck said. "How's the family?"

"They're fine."

"The twins. I see them on the way to school."

"They're growing up," said George. In his raincoat, he shifted. It came as no surprise to know how much the driver knew, but it embarrassed him that he could not reciprocate. He did not know, for instance, if Billy Peck had married and had children of his own; it seemed too late to ask.

"I remember," Billy said, "when every night before we'd dig we'd burn a tire to draw up the frost. Speaking of tires. Just douse and light them is all. Sucks it right out of the ground. The supervisor used to tell us, save your tires, boys. Six foot of frost. They all used to do it . . ."

"What happened?"

"The way rubber smells. Pollution." In the light from the dashboard he examined his finger. "Outlaw this and outlaw that and now you dig graves you get a jackhammer to do it. Like working your way through concrete. You leave your car at airports and it's wrecked. Welfare benefits. But burn your own leaves and you're risking a fine." Billy chewed a cuticle. "A field full of tires, smoking," he said. "It's twenty years since I seen tires like that."

At the luncheon that they gave for him, George fought the desire to sleep. They discussed the inflation rate; the Chairman of the History Department sent regrets. His wife was in the hospital, they said; he would have been here otherwise, he'll be sorry to have missed it and he wants to hear the tape. They ate at the Faculty Club. His host, Sam Hall, was a previous acquaintance; as far back as college, Sam told the others, the two of them agreed to disagree. As far as he, Sam, was concerned it did a person honor to have George as his adversary. They discussed the siege of Vicksburg at some length.

The waiter brought him coffee. "Thank you very much," George said. The waiter seemed surprised. It would come at some point on the trip, it always did, and George accepted it now. Not so specific as shame, it nonetheless afflicted him—this sense of being welcome under false pretense. He was a fake, he told himself, not the smiling soft-voiced notable they waited for at airports and advanced on, threatless, hands held out. The hospitality was real. The local newspaper would have carried a three-year-previous photograph and a caption announcing his attainments; the campus radio station would have done the same. They did not know his work. They would misspell his name. But the intention was there, and the attention flattered him; Sam Hall had made his students read George's monograph on Grant. "I believe this summer we'll be heading north," Sam announced. "If they're still racing horses, we'll visit your part of the world."

The talk was a success. He presented his reading of Sherman: that the methodology of pacification derived from Caesar and presaged Ho Chi Minh. "A house divided against itself" is more a metaphor than faulty building technique; we may give Lincoln marks for diction but Sherman penned the deeper truth that "War is hell." In the discussion period, later, he displayed what was by now a characteristic blend of erudition and modesty; he lingered with the graduate students; he asked for permission to light his pipe. In the rest-room mirror he saw a stranger smiling back at him: the visitor, half drunk with lack of sleep and dizzy with recurrence. He called his home. The phone was busy; he told the operator he would try again.

They ate supper at a warehouse transformed into a restaurant; George had invited the Halls. The decor was a cross between Gay Nineties, Gashouse, and French Brothel; a red lantern hung above their table. Ginny Hall was pink and plump, excited by her first night out in what she said was weeks. The conversation was desultory; George wondered if the crab bisque was fresh. The prices on the wine list had been inked out and raised. A bottle of 1973 Chateau Margaux sold for a hundred and thirty dollars. He realized he might order it; there was nothing on the menu, no matter how pretentious, that he could not afford. This recognition troubled him. When he had first arrived in Saratoga Springs, his apartment cost less than a hundred and thirty dollars per month; he spent two months in Barbados, once, on what he would earn from this trip.

"Let's hear some country music," Sam said. "If you're up to it. There's the best little band in Knoxville playing at Buddy's tonight."

"All right."

"If you'd like to hear that band before they get away. . . ."

"Up north, he means," said Ginny. "Or to Nashville."

George paid. They drove to Buddy's, but could not find a parking space; they parked two streets east. The night air was wet and warm. It felt, he told the Halls, like New England in July; girls in T-shirts jostled for position, and boys weaved past, waving beer. The tables at Buddy's were full. They stood in the back of the hall and listened to the group; they were playing "Foggy Mountain Break Down" laboriously. Then the lead singer said he would imitate Elvis; he performed a hip-grinding version of "You

Ain't Nothin' But A Hound Dog." Next he imitated Tennessee Ernie Ford, and his voice changed timbre and range: he sang "Sixteen Tons." Then the bass player joined him, and they harmonized on "Do, Lord, Remember Me," and then the whole group sang "Carry Me Back To Ol' Virginny."

George, listening, looked at the crowd. There were few blacks there, and nearly no one of his age; they rocked and clapped and waved their arms with pleasure. He felt none. The noise was jangling, discordant, and the spirituals were offered in the spirit of a barbershop quartet. He asked for coffee, not beer. He excused himself again; this time he reached his wife.

"How is it going?" she asked.

"It's going."

"You don't sound too happy."

"I miss you," he said. "I'm calling from a bluegrass bar with fifty thousand children."

"There's been an accident here," Allyn said. "Betsy Sigurdsen and three of her friends were in a car crash last night."

His first reaction was relief: the twins were safe. He covered his left ear. The band was resting between sets; he blocked out the noise at the bar. Allyn had been notified by the Dean of Students; she apologized for telling him but knew he'd want to know. Four students, carousing at midnight, had wrapped a car around a tree and been hospitalized. The two boys were not badly hurt; they had been wearing seat belts. The driver had a broken arm; his car was wrecked. One girl was in serious condition, with a lung full of blood and both legs broken; she would recover, Allyn said. The prognosis was good. She named those three. "But Betsy is in Albany. They took her there; it's serious. They've been operating all day long."

"What's wrong? Do you know?"

"Her skull was fractured, George. They say the brain pan was exposed; she'll lose an eye at least. The optic nerve was severed."

"Christ."

"She may survive it. She's young. Her vital signs are excellent. I know all this because they're keeping us informed from the Medical Center."

"Christ knows how fast they were going," he said. "Drunk, I imagine. Or stoned."

After some time the conversation shifted. The twins had gone to Sally

Rifkin's birthday party and were so tired afterward they fell asleep on the couch; Allyn had been reading Simenon. "Next time you come along," he said. "I've had enough of motel rooms without you."

"My darling carpetbagger," Allyn said. "Just come on back."

Thirty-eight years old, a professor of American history at Skidmore College in Saratoga Springs, George stood in what he liked to think of as an ambiguous relation to undergraduates. He had been a senior when his present freshmen were born. Too old to share his life with them, he nonetheless claimed to prefer their values to his colleagues'. In the sixties he had considered politics; he led the college deputations to Washington, D.C., and felt joyful solidarity when teargassed with his class. At twenty-nine, he married a student. Allyn produced an essay on the *Federalist Papers* that he still considered a model of its kind. Her view of Alexander Hamilton was perhaps a touch overly critical—but otherwise, he wrote, her reading seemed acute. The research had been thorough and the language expressive; the essay was fully first-rate. He hoped she would continue in the field.

She came to his office to contest his opinion of Hamilton, wearing cutoff jeans and a shirt tied up under her breasts. It was October, the height of leaf season; he said he'd just as soon continue this discussion in fresh air. She suggested they go for a drive. She led him to a waterfall she said she wanted him to see, and took his hand approaching the cascade. They found a bower underneath a split-leaf maple flaming in the pines; cows grazed in a meadow beyond a low ridge. Her diaphragm, she told him when he asked, was already in.

They were married the following June. He had a small inheritance and she too had some money; after Allyn's graduation, they spent nine months in France. He revised his dissertation, and it became a book. His analysis of Sherman's march through Georgia, with particular reference to Special Field Order No. 15, and the present relevance of "Forty acres and a mule" earned him some attention. His work thereafter on Tunis G. Campbell and the separatist enclave on the Georgia Sea Islands brought him renown; when he was offered tenure, they decided to accept.

"I worry," Allyn sometimes said, "about your students. Trying to seduce you. Coming on in hallways."

"Don't worry," he would tease her. "It can't happen here."

"If it happened before it can happen again."

"There's a difference," George said. "Remember?"

"What's the difference?"

"You. And the difference is that I get older, but they stay the same."

Their daughters were born in 1974, and Saratoga seemed a safe place to raise them; they purchased a house on the edge of the campus and he sometimes skied to work. In his sabbatical year the family returned to France; he wrote on the range of French reaction to the Civil War. Allyn was happy in the Vaucluse. "I could live here forever," she said. Retentive, he maintained the Alfa Romeo that she gave him as a wedding gift; for her birthday two years later he gave her a Jeep Wagoneer.

From Knoxville he traveled to Shreveport. This conference was called "Fort Humbug," and George gave the keynote address. According to local legend, the town had been saved from assault by pine trees painted black. The fort's commander had ordered them felled and mounted overlooking the Red River. He had had no ammunition; these trees were "humbug" guns. The flagship of the Northern fleet, however, had panicked and retreated; the town remained untouched. The legend was instructive but untrue. George spoke of the varieties of siege, using "Fort Humbug" as an instance of the illusory objective and diversionary assault. This applied to the South as well as the North. In the drama of the Civil War, he said, as with the ancient Greeks—and note the expression "theater of war," notice how historians employ the rhetoric of theater—the consequential actions were taking place offstage.

A lawyer and a doctor and their wives took him to supper that night. He deserved a change of scene, they said; they drove to a nearby lake. Bob Bevis was expansive; he had beer and white wine in the cooler. He was passionate, he said, about good beer—he went to England every summer just to bone up on the dark. He was chief attorney for a local oil consortium and a distribution planning board; big business, Bob said, was about the only place you got serious planning these days. They know those pipelines will be sitting in the ground when there's no oil or gas left to pipe, and they're thinking hard and long about it; they entertain reality scenarios. Those pipelines have got to hold *something*, he said, and that's what we're discussing. "I take my hat off"—he uncapped a beer—"those companies plan in advance."

Horses grazed, and there were squatters' shacks. The woods increased. Then they came to a clearing at lakeside, with houseboats huddled
to a dock; an ancient black man hauled jerry cans of gas. "How's things,
Brownie?" Bob Bevis asked. The doctor parked his station wagon and
locked the four doors. Brownie put down his gas cans and straightened,
wiped his hands on his shirt and grinned. His gums were pink; he had
no teeth. Bob laughed. He turned to George and said, "You know what
I asked him? I asked if there's been any changes 'round here. And he
tells me, 'No, not unless you've changed.'" They loaded the hampers and
cooler and coats on a pink houseboat; the doctor started the motor. Bob
laughed again, with proprietary fondness: "'Not unless you've changed,'"
he said.

There was duckweed in the lake. Cypress trees rose from the water
as if it would recede again; ducks scooted ahead. The Spanish moss
hung thickly from trees he could not name, and the rising moon was
full. The women complained of the cold. Bob distributed drinks. "We
could drive to Mermaid Tavern," said his wife, Lucille. "There's a road
right up to it. But this is more fun, don't you think? Especially on the
way back."

The Mermaid Tavern had electric lanterns on the dock and a stuffed
alligator at the entrance door. They drank their wine in paper cups and
kept the bottle underneath the table; the tavern had no liquor license.
There were murals of mermaids; the kitchen had a carved sign reading,
"Davy Jones' Lock-Up!" George ordered boiled shrimp; his bowl was
heaped high. The others ordered catfish or combination plates and made
him taste their several dishes. "Got to keep your strength up," said Lucille.
"That's what I always say."

"Wild nights," said Lynda-Kay across the table. "When the moon
gets full like this . . ."

"What's the full moon got to do with it?" her husband asked. "Why
wait for the moon?"

George peeled his shrimp and piled the shells on his empty salad plate.
He thanked his hosts and, for the moment, meant it: how gracious and
hospitable, how open-handed they seemed. The wine was abundant and
good. His tongue felt furred. This is a variety of deathlessness, he said, a
truce with time. He proposed a toast to Master Death and how they had
outwitted him this night, how paper cups are goblets when newfound

friends agree. His hosts agreed. They said, "Your health," and drank, but his speech had been discordant. Death and immortality were not proper topics to raise.

Allyn and the twins collected him on Sunday. He brought back Confederate flags, breakfast grits and a miniature bale of cotton. Patty and Sarah told him their news, how they played musical chairs and blindman's buff and could see right through the blindfold at Sally Rifkin's party, and how much they missed him every night. He drove. Allyn took his hand and pressed it to the inside of her knee.

That night he called the Sigurdsens; they said he would be welcome whenever he could come. Betsy was still in danger, and blind in her right eye—but miracle of miracles, her mother said over the phone, there seemed to be no damage to the brain. The doctors had been wonderful; they had had to throw away six pieces of the skull. "No one seems to understand," her mother said, "how Betsy made it through that operation. Or the crash. Of course we've prayed and prayed, and now we have to keep our fingers crossed."

He went south the following Friday, after his ten o'clock class. The day was overcast but warm; he drove with the Alfa's top down. It was Indian summer, the end of October, and he packed jogging clothes in the trunk. On the way back, he told Allyn, he'd stop off somewhere for a quick run. "I can taste it already," he said. "The smell of that hospital room. The stink of machinery"—he clucked his tongue—"you know how I hate hospitals."

"Drive carefully," she said. "Send Betsy all our love."

He kissed her. "Yes. When's their ballet lesson over—five? I'll be back before that. Soon."

The car responded well. They had purchased it in Milano and shipped it home from Marseilles; he had had it rust-proofed and repainted. On the Northway and in Albany the Alfa drew attention; he closed and locked it in the hospital parking lot. At the entrance he bought roses from a woman in a wheelchair. "Bless you and yours," she said.

Betsy Sigurdsen was in room 752. "Relatives only," they said at the desk.

"I'm her professor," George said. "Her parents asked me to come."

He walked down the hall, knocked and hesitated. "Her mother's inside," said a nurse. She lay on the bed, white hospital sheet at her hips, head shaved, her eyes like a raccoon's. There were black crescents under them, then a white arc of flesh. "Hello," she said.

"Hello." His throat was dry; he cleared it. "How are you, Betsy?"

"Tip-top," she said. "Look who's here." She shrugged, then winced at the gesture and put out her hand. He showed her the flowers and bent down to kiss her; she shrank at the touch of his lips. "Yow," Betsy said. "Don't mind me. It's just I hurt all over."

She rearranged her shift. The pattern on her skull seemed familiar, and he shut his eyes and saw a piece of cloth with stitches while Allyn taught the twins. Her sewing machine was black; the cloth would be cross-hatched and stippled with thread. He turned to Betsy's mother and said, "Mrs. Sigurdsen?"

"Yes. We've heard so much about you."

"Some of it good, I hope."

"Oh, all of it. Those flowers. I'd best get a vase for them. Water."

"Don't bother. They can wait."

"I'll do it now. I know just where the vases are. I'll be right back."

She hurried out; there were flowers all over the room.

"How are you really?" George asked.

"She's scared of you." Betsy lifted her arm. "She's been wonderful, though. I hurt all over."

"Do you want to talk about it?"

"No. It wasn't Bill's fault. He wasn't drunk. We'd all been studying and stayed up late and had just one beer maybe, and he fell asleep at the wheel."

"You don't have to protect him."

"I know. Three beers, maybe."

"What matters is you made it. You're alive."

"My nose is my best feature, don't you think? And that hasn't been broken. And I haven't eaten so I'll lose a lot of weight." She put her hand up to her head. "Do I look awful?"

"No."

"I do. You never saw my ears before."

"You look beautiful," he said. And it was true, absurdly, as she lay before him, her skull that had been masked by hair now naked, egg-shaped, the whole of her face jarred loose from its bone-struts and smashed. The left side of her head seemed lower than the right; symmetry had gone. She had been rearranged. She worked an eyepatch into place over the blind right eye. "You mean that?" Betsy asked.

Her mother returned. "There"—she placed the roses on the window-sill—"we'll give them the place of honor. Long-stemmed roses, Betsy—aren't we fortunate?"

"My father left. I wish you could have met him," said the girl.

"He'll be back," said Mrs. Sigurdsen. "We've never been to Albany before."

Then they conversed about the airplane trip from Raleigh-Durham through Atlanta to Albany and the relative merits of Atlanta and O'Hare. The Sigurdsens had moved to Chapel Hill. Mrs. Sigurdsen said everybody at the hospital was wonderful; you couldn't beat this hospital for kindness, the Women's Auxiliary Club had an apartment for visiting parents, and she'd brought her needlepoint and was snug as a bug in a rug. Of course, she hoped that they'd be home by Thanksgiving, but there's so much to be thankful for she wouldn't mind it in the slightest if they had to stay till Christmas and eat their turkey dinner sitting by this bed. You get used to things, she said, there's no use complaining, if you've got to make do you make do. You get out of the woods if you wait.

A nurse arrived with pills. "Now swallow these, dearie," she said.

Betsy made a face at him; he studied the curtainless window. His roses seemed crimson, and wax. The problem is, said Mrs. Sigurdsen, there's all this spinal fluid coming from her nose; if it doesn't stop leaking they'll operate again. He told Betsy not to worry about course work or credit or reading; she said she worried, anyhow. He asked if there were messages she'd like to send, or people she would like to see, and she said, "No. Just you again. You've been so kind. And I know how terrifically busy you must be. He's the busiest teacher on campus, Mom, he's so sought after. You wouldn't believe it."

"I believe it, dear. From everything I've heard."

George sat at the bed's edge. He felt prized beyond his value, and hot in his tweed coat.

"You have two lovely daughters, Betsy says. How old would they be?"

"Six," George told her. "They're twins."

"And your wife's name?"

"Allyn." He made his old joke. "She's got a man's first name, so she married a man with a woman's name last."

Mrs. Sigurdsen smiled. "Allyn Allison. She must be beautiful."

"She is, Mom," Betsy said.

He recited Sarah's poem. That morning, eating her soft-boiled egg and English muffin, mouth full, she had announced, "I wrote a poem, Daddy. Want to hear it?" He told her to finish her muffin and then he would listen. She swallowed and said:

> Day chases morning,
> Evening chases day;
> Night chases evening,
> And all fades away.

"How wonderful!" said Mrs. Sigurdsen.

"I told you," Betsy said. "Didn't I tell you? Too much." She settled back, breasts bobbing, as if the achievement were hers. She smiled at him, raising her legs. The swelling underneath her eyes increased at this angle; he stood.

"I ought to be going. The nurse said not to tire you."

"You only just got here."

"I'll be back."

"How's the Dred Scott decision?" she wanted to know. "Is that what you're doing in class?"

"It's fine. Yes. You'll be released in no time and come to the house for a drink."

"Oh, George," she wailed, "I'm not allowed to. The doctors won't let me. Nothing to drink. Or smoke. Or anything."

He kissed her hand. "Be patient. See you soon."

"A patient patient, that's our girl." Mrs. Sigurdsen ushered him out. In the corridor she said, "She wouldn't want me saying this, but your visit has made Betsy's day. Thank you so much for the flowers."

"Take care," George said. "Be well."

"I hope you never know, Professor—I hope you never have to feel what we're feeling today. Those beautiful daughters of yours, those marvelous bright children . . ." She took his sleeve, detaining him. The hall seemed improbably dark. "I hope by the time they grow up, when they are Betsy's age, I pray there's no more cars in America."

"It wasn't her fault," he offered.

"No. It never is. It's always someone else's fault, it's always some drunken lunatic coming at you in the wrong lane. Or falling asleep at the wheel. It's always somebody else's problem when your life gets wrecked."

"I'm sorry."

"Yes. I have to have someone to talk to. That passage in the Bible, do you know it, 'Absalom'?" She closed her eyes; her voice changed register. "It's just exactly how I feel, it's just what I keep saying: 'Oh Absalom my son.' Would to God I had died for you. Would to God I had died for you, my son . . ."

He kissed her cheek. When he turned at the elevator and looked back, she was still standing there, her eyes squeezed shut like fists.

Returning, he took secondary roads. He drove past barge canals and bridges, past feed corn being cut and the fair ground standing empty now, its placards proclaiming last month's county fair. He had been more stirred by such bruised nakedness than he could reveal. Betsy Sigurdsen had been his student for three years. She was pretty enough, and pert, full of an avid anxiousness to learn, with an appetite for facts. Her ankles were thick, shoulders broad. While others in his seminar would shake their heads and frown at documents or use his carefully amassed files of microfilm only at term-paper time, Betsy would swallow whole volumes of data and spew forth dates as if they signified: she saw the decline in Sea Island long-staple cotton in 1856, she would say, like the shirt off a gentleman's back.

She often stopped him in the halls and asked for an appointment; she came to office hours every week. So he grew familiar with her history, the rigor of her background and her skill at horseback riding, the decision to come north from Chapel Hill; she was the only student in her high school class, she told him, who studied in New York State. Her elder sister had left home and worked for American Airlines; she traveled all around the world and sent back postcards always ending, "Wish you could be here!" She had boyfriends and she blushed but talked about them, anyhow: the way she could outlast them if they took on a bottle, or tennis, how Robert or Philip could dance. He knew about her trouble with her jaw, the way it would lock open in what she called intimate acts.

He knew her aspirations too: she dreamed of graduate school. He himself had gone to Brown and promised a recommendation; he saw no reason why she shouldn't persevere. Her particular cluster of aptitudes,

George said, could well make a historian; she had been preparing for the Graduate Record Exams.

The sky was gray. He listened to the weather forecast, after the three o'clock news. He loosened his tie and, at a traffic light, pulled off his shoes. What troubled him was how his visit had eradicated distance, as if their teacher-student stance had been a sham for years. She had displayed herself as if to a suitor, not a friend. Her ankles had been hidden in the blanket-tangle underneath his hand. He thought of her with love.

George shook his head. He consulted his watch; he had time for a run. He slowed and made a detour to the right. It was farm country here, hilly, and he concentrated on the drive: unpainted barns and silos and corncribs and a stock pond in the rain. The road had been recently tarred. He passed a sign saying "Windy Hill Farm. Maple Syrup. Eggs." and remembered having been this way before: The town of Schuylerville lay beneath and if he went due east he'd come to the river. He mapped out his run.

She'd said, "Or smoke. Or anything," and shifted in the sheets as if to a rhythm they shared. Death had embraced her one week before, and now she understood more of mortality than he. He double-clutched, advancing into fourth.

Directions: he had lived his life by them. What signs he read he followed; what turns he made he made with adequate warning and judiciously. He had been faithful to his wife, despite her half-serious fears; his career was going well. And he adored his daughters; had Mrs. Sigurdsen asked to see their photographs he would gladly have pulled out his wallet. He had taken the girls to Woolworth's for a set of pictures. The visiting photographer had placed them on a table, instructing them to hold hands and how to smile and when to smile and how to hold their positions. He changed the backdrop poster several times. They sat first before a sylvan scene, then by a snowy mountain, then in front of a picket fence. The Allisons would get a complimentary eight-by-ten, he said; they could select the poses they preferred.

George found the session bizarre. The photographer insisted on making the twins laugh. He put a beanbag Snoopy on his head, then let it fall; he tried to eat a handkerchief, saying, "Whoopsiedoodle"; he asked them to call him "Potatohead" or "Cabbagemouth." They did not dare, and he urged them. "Call me Cabbagemouth," he said. "I promise,

I don't mind." So, tentative, politely, they pronounced "Potatohead" and "Cabbagemouth."

"Louder," he said. "I didn't quite hear."

"Po*tato*head," said Sarah. "Cabbagemouth," said Patty.

"*What* did you call me?" the photographer roared. The twins giggled, and he pressed the buttons for the flash.

So George possessed wallet-size photos of the girls embracing before a picket fence. He hoped that they might stay that way: intimate yet separable. He thought of taking Betsy in, of asking her to spend her convalescence in their house. He saw a car nose out beneath him on a dirt road to his right. He braked and swerved and honked his horn, but the car continued. It blocked the intersection, then it stopped. He screamed. In the instant of collision, George saw several things: the raw, shocked face of the boy behind the wheel, the way the others in the car—a brown Chevy with a red rear fender—had waved the driver forward till he froze in the T. With three feet more he might have made it, but there was no chance, no choice; George headed for the right rear fender, then the ditch. The shock of impact swung him back; he hit again, this time less solidly, with his left rear panel on the Chevy's driver's door. There was much broken glass. His radiator steamed. The engine continued to run; he switched it off. He felt for injuries, felt none. "You've done it; now you've really gone and done it," he said aloud, several times.

The boy in the other car rolled down his window. "Are you all right?" he asked. His voice was high-pitched.

"I think so. You?"

The boy nodded. George counted slowly, carefully: there were five others in the car. "Is anybody hurt?" he asked.

"No."

There was blood on his cheek from a small shard of glass, and his stomach ached where the seat belt cinched him; he released the belt. Methodically, moving with a thoroughness that imitated calm, George put on his shoes and tightened his tie and stepped out. His elegant indulgence had crumpled in the crash. There was chrome and glass and rubber all around him, and a stream of water. He bent and sniffed for gas. The cars stood alongside each other companionably, like animals—hissing, snuffling, snout to tail.

"You might have waited."

"I know," the boy said. "They told me to try it. They *told* me."

"This your car?"

"My dad's. He'll have a shit fit." The boy was close to tears, was just past driving age and in the kind of trouble he would have sworn that morning to avoid.

The Alfa did not move. George wrenched the wheel back from the fender that braked it. He peered into the Chevrolet and saw three girls, three boys, a six-pack. "Bury that beer," he advised.

"I wasn't drinking."

"The sheriff's going to ask you that . . ."

"I could have made it," the boy said. "If only I'd stepped on the gas."

"You could have done a lot of things. You could have stayed at the stop sign, for instance. Just stopped there, like it says. You could have tried reverse. You could have accelerated straight across the road and up that driveway, maybe. The only thing you couldn't do was what you did do, friend, take the whole road . . . He straightened, exhaling. "I hope you're insured."

"Yes."

"Because this car's expensive. They don't make them anymore." He had the odd sensation, standing while the children sat, that he was in some lecture hall. There was a farm to his left. A woman advanced with a broom in her hand. "It's a bad corner," she said, commencing to sweep off the glass.

"We ought to make some calls," said George. "Would you have a phone in the house?"

She nodded, pointed to the kitchen door, and he and the boy walked in. Bob Folsom and he exchanged names. Then George produced his driver's license, registration and insurance card, and the boy did likewise and they copied numbers; they called the state police and a local wrecker, and Bob called his parents and they said they'd come to get him. George called Allyn last.

"Hello?"

"Hello. Not to worry," he said. He attempted to steady his voice.

"What's wrong?"

"I'm all right. Nothing's wrong."

"George, what's the matter? Where are you?"

"On Windy Hill Road," he said. "At some no-name intersection on the way to Victory Mills. Off of Johnson Hill. Near Schuylerville, you know. Route Twenty-nine. The bitch of it is that if I'd been driving at something like speed I'd have been long past that T."

"What T? What are you talking about?"

"I had an accident," he said. "I'm all right, though. I am. Nobody's hurt. The car's a wreck."

"Darling . . ."

"Maybe we can fix it. Maybe there's replacement parts. It wasn't my fault, Allyn. I haven't been so law-abiding in that car for *years*."

"The car doesn't matter," she said. "I'm coming to get you."

"Yes. Have someone pick up the kids, will you, from ballet? Ask Eloise. I wouldn't want them to see this."

"No."

"You know the directions?"

"I do."

The taste of tin was in his mouth; he rubbed his hands for heat. He had a headache; his neck hurt. Outside, the state police had arrived and were directing traffic, taking measurements of tire marks and consulting with the riders in the Chevy. He approached.

"That your car?" the sheriff asked.

"It is."

"Afternoon, Professor," someone said. He turned. "A shame," said Billy Peck. "About this car."

"Yes. No one's hurt, though. That's what counts."

"They'll ticket him," Billy confided. "For failure to stop at a stop sign. I happened to be passing through."

"Yes."

"You got some scratches, Professor. I could call the ambulance."

"No. Thank you. My wife's on the way."

"Go check in at the hospital," Billy said. "The emergency room—takes ten minutes. I got a radio, I'll let them know you're coming. Just have them look you over, just in case." He lowered his voice, respectful. "It's better for insurance claims. If you plan to file them . . ."

"I was going jogging," George explained. "You won't believe it, but I've just come from the hospital. Not this one, not the one in Saratoga. The Medical Center. I was down in Albany. I was visiting . . ." His voice trailed off. They were not listening, had turned to greet the wrecker. Rain was falling steadily, but to the west sun shone. Bob Folsom's father had appeared and was shouting at his son. They waved their arms like pinwheels; Mrs. Folsom intervened. "The main thing is nobody's hurt," she said. "Let's thank our lucky stars."

Crows gleaned in the corn stubble, and there were penned turkeys and hogs. The wrecker whistled, studying the Alfa. "A collector's item, this one is. Knocked the Chevy clean off its frame. You wouldn't think it, but that baby's totaled." He jerked his head over his shoulder. "Now this one here, we'll see."

George walked in circles, waiting. The farmer's wife invited him to have some coffee if he wanted, and he thanked her but refused. She said he could wait in the kitchen; he told her he needed the air. He gave his deposition. They treated him with courtesy, with the attentive deference due to rank and age. He watched the sports car being hooked up, hauled away. He remembered, as the tow truck lumbered past, that his jogging gear was in the trunk; he signaled the wrecker to stop and extracted the brown paper bag. The sheriff watched him distantly. He pulled his sweatshirt from the bag so the man would not suspect a bottle and, holding it, walked down the road in order to intercept Allyn. A dog appeared and menaced him. She would be driving south.

Some in Their Body's Force

I N THE SPRING of his junior year at college, Peter Danto fell, as he put it, in lust. It was 1962, and he had turned nineteen; he was trying on his attitudes like clothes. That spring he wanted a life in the theater. He played supporting roles in *Major Barbara* and *Othello* and Jean-Paul Sartre's *The Flies*. In this last play he portrayed King Aegisthus—jaded, motivated not so much by desire as reason.

Clytemnestra's name was Inger; she was attending Radcliffe for a year. He had heard rumors about her. She had that glacial blond beauty supposed to be characteristic of Swedes, and she was rich. Her father was variously reported as a prince, a chancellor of the university, the designer of Volvos and a shipping magnate. She was the Ping-Pong champion of Europe, the youngest of seven sisters. She carried a gun in her purse, it was whispered, and when she went home she was slated to marry a duke.

The director said he wanted her for Clytemnestra because of her accent. The director was of the opinion that the cast should know why they had been chosen; he went around the table, discussing attributes. According to his, the director's, opinion, the queen should be an alien presence in Argos. It was a play about pretension and unpretentiousness; Inger had the latter quality, he said. The director wanted *The Flies* to be about estrangement, and he repeated this often.

Her face was round and soft, her feet were bare. She was high-breasted and slim-hipped; she wore a green striped tank top and white skirt. Her laugh came easily. They read through their parts without stopping, and

Peter focused—in the intervals when Aegisthus was silent—on Inger's legs: the way they tapered to her ankles, the muscularity, the hint of less firm flesh above the knee. He invited her for coffee; she said yes.

There was a coffee shop nearby called Casablanca; photographs of Bogart, Ingrid Bergman and Sidney Greenstreet lined the bar. Boccherini emerged from the walls. Peter and Inger selected a table in a green bower of plants. He discoursed on the Oresteia, its relevance to the Vichy government and Nazi-occupied France. Sartre's text belonged, he said, to the literature of resistance: it was an inquiry into power, a parable of usage and abuse.

They ordered *cappuccino*. She watched while the coffee was made. He would remember the components of that instant: lamplight, music, the Danish pastry, the speculative intensity with which they disagreed. When she shook her head for emphasis, her yellow hair cascaded. Reaching for the sugar, he grazed her hand with his hand. "*Du schwarzer Zigeuner,*" she said.

"What does that mean?"

"You dark gypsy. '*Ach,*'"—she hummed a phrase—"'*du schwarzer Zigeuner.*'"

"Tell me about Uppsala."

"There's little to tell," Inger said. "We have a house like you'd imagine: many windows with flowerpots. Fir trees by the balcony."

"Do you miss it?"

"A little."

"Right now?"

"My father's very serious," she said. "You, Peter, are you serious?"

"I'm a bad actor," he said.

She disconcerted him by taking this at face value; he had assumed she'd smile. "Then why do you do it?" she asked.

He drank. "I don't know, really."

"For fun," said Inger. "To show you're not my father."

She smiled. Her front teeth were uneven. They talked about their roles. Peter said that killing Agamemnon had been, in Clytemnestra's case, not so much a matter of sexual passion or envy as an *acte gratuit*. It all hinged, he maintained, on whether Agamemnon had slept with Clytemnestra before his ritual cleansing in the bath. If she killed him after sex, there might indeed have been a passionate revulsion. But if she killed her husband while he washed, the knife thrust was dispassionate, a mating dance enacted for the audience. The text suggested this was so: Agamemnon's feet were smelly, his hair unclean. So he was prinking up for purity—getting ready, making certain not to mess the carpets. Offstage, Cassandra was being gang-banged by the palace guard.

Inger swallowed. Foam from the *cappuccino* flecked her upper lip. He was making it all up, of course, aroused by her attention. He felt reckless and inventive; he asked about her sisters and she told him she had none. When they parted for the evening, she pressed against him briefly—and they agreed to meet again after rehearsal that week.

Peter lived in Adams House. His room had bay windows that gave on a courtyard, a sleeping alcove and a bathroom lined with tile. There was what once had been a functioning fireplace; the walls were wood-paneled. He could pretend to independence once inside the door, but the foyer of his entry was a trial. She printed her name in block letters on the sign-in sheet. Laundry was being delivered on the second floor. Inside, he kissed her several times. Inger was, suddenly, shy. He fumbled with her buttons while she sat on the bed.

"Be careful," Inger said.

Her body was thin, her breasts small. She said, "I want some music," and he played *Leon Bibb Sings Love Songs* on his new stereo set. At "The Water Is Wide" he took off his shoes and, during "Down In The Valley," he removed his shirt. He was self-conscious about this, since he had many pimples on his back. When she closed her eyes, he closed his also, in gratitude. They kissed again and, some seconds later, he opened his eyes to find her watching him. They smiled. When he pulled back her hair, her face had a baby's smooth roundness, and the small hairs at her neck were white. He said, "I want to be with you," and tugged off her skirt. He took off his pants and lay down.

Leon Bibb completed "Dance To Your Daddy" and began again. His voice was high. Peter penetrated Inger; she was unresistant. She was not helpful, however, and seemed to be in pain. He asked her if she was worried, and she shook her head; he asked her, was it safe for him to be inside her, and she said she took the Pill. He asked her, was she happy being on his casting couch, and she tried to smile. He pretended expertise.

When they finished, she was bleeding. She said, "I thought I was no virgin," and covered herself with the sheets. He assured her that she could be bleeding because he touched some part that had not previously been reached. She said, "You think so, Peter?" and he said he hoped so, yes. He felt triumphal, huge. He produced a towel and she said, "I want to shower."

"I'll join you," Peter said.

In the shower she sang to him, softly. Her high spirits had returned. She soaped him, and they pressed up against each other, and he said Aegisthus had a better time than Agamemnon in his bath. "It'll be better next time," he said.

"What will?"

"The sex. It's always an improvement the second time."

This was not a statement he could verify. Inger placed the soap back in the soap dish, rinsed herself off and stepped out of the stall. By the time he too emerged, she was dry and collecting her clothes.

"Is something wrong?" he asked.

"No."

"What is it?"

"'It'll be better the next time,'" she said.

"I'm sorry."

"You make me feel foolish."

"No."

"Could you please turn off that record?" Inger asked.

He could not bring himself to say the line was borrowed, that he'd read it in a book. "We have to get to rehearsal," he said.

"Yes."

"Are you hungry?"

She shook her head.

"Will I see you again?"

"At rehearsal," she said.

His daughter went to school in Arizona. They had argued lengthily as to whether she should go that far, whether she was old enough or really had to leave. The local school system, said Judy, was so destructive they had no choice; peer pressure to fail was too great. She had been learning nothing but the names of drugs and cars. "One more year like this," said Judy, "and our little darling will have her own little darlings. We've got to get her out."

So they sent her to a boarding school in the suburbs of Tucson. The admissions officer admired Lucinda. "She's one tough cookie, isn't she?" he asked. Peter felt forced to agree. She was thick-tongued and torpid, who had been his quicksilver child. She fell in love, that first semester, with a horse named Bill. She wrote detailed descriptions, with photography enclosed, of Bill at rest and eating, of Bill in his stall or by the river, in the mountains, with the ribbons that she won for riding him in novice class.

By spring she was no novice, and Peter purchased a thousand-dollar saddle. He bought her boots and a coat and cap and tack; he sent her books on *dressage*. Judy said he was being extravagant, doting from a distance, and Peter agreed. But he preferred to picture her in stalls than on the back seats of cars; he'd rather that she mucked about with horses than with punks. Lucinda called on his birthday and said, "Bill loves you too."

"We haven't met," said Peter.

"No. But you should see him, Daddy. With that saddle."

"Yes."

"He's got you to thank. So we both wish you happy birthday."

"Thank you, darling."

"I'm going to buy him," she said. "Right now he belongs to the whole school."

"I'm on the upstairs phone," said Judy. "Buy *who*?"

"With the money Nanno left me. I can do what I want with it, right?"

He shifted the receiver. "I'm not sure Nanno meant it that way."

"Bill's mine," she said. "He knows it too. He just despises it if any other girl gets on. That Missy Tief, for instance."

"It's your father's birthday," Judy said. "Not yours. We'll discuss this later."

"Happy birthday, Daddy."

"Yes."

"I'll see you in three weeks."

"We miss you," Peter said.

He had broken his ankle; he walked with a cane. He had fallen down the office stairs. Since he was vice-president of an insurance agency, this called forth humor from friends. "How about your coverage?" they asked. "Does it cover your own office? What's the policy on sliding down a banister instead?"

The stairs were wide and smooth, no obstacle. He traveled them ten times a day. Later he would ask himself what had been the distraction, what whiff of springtime in the air or birdsong or engine caused him to fall. He landed unevenly; his right ankle buckled and he heard a single, popping sound. He lay there, then built himself back to his feet. He could not put weight on the foot. He stood, leaning against the wall of the building, feeling the brick, balancing, waiting for what seemed a rainstorm to subside. There was no rainstorm, but there was a roaring in his ears, and the air went cold. He sat. His head dropped to his knees. He spent some time deciding if his head dropped to his knees involuntarily or whether he had lowered it on purpose. Blood coursed through his head. It felt palpable, a liquid he could see with his eyes closed.

The village of Sandgate, their home, celebrated Memorial Day. Peter took his son to the parade. Sam was nine, excited. They had an invitation to Mrs. Welling's porch. They walked together from West Street to Main Street, slowly. "Do you miss your sister?" Peter asked.

Sam shrugged.

"Having someone to go to the pool with?"

"No."

"Why not?"

"She never takes me."

"This summer she will," Peter promised. "And she'll teach you tennis too."

"I bet."

"She plans to," Peter said.

"Do you think you'll play tennis again?"

His cane was ebony, with a steel tip, and intricately carved. He flourished it. "Of course."

"I want *you* to teach me," said Sam.

"I'll come along. I'll be coach."

"She'll probably go horseback riding."

"Well, I want to see her."

"I don't."

Larry Welling, Jr., waited on the porch. Larry was fifty, a bachelor. "How's the leg?"

"It's mending," Peter said. He settled himself on a chaise longue. "They've cut me out of the cast."

Larry was a large man, blockish, fond of fishing; his hair was white. Sandgate perched on the Cold River, along the Mohawk Trail.

Mrs. Welling appeared. "You handsome man," she said. "You sit right there."

He put a hand on Sam's neck. "The boys' day out," he said. "We're giving Judy a rest."

"Good morning," Mrs. Welling said to Sam. She poured lemonade. "Could I interest you in this?"

"Say 'thank you,'" Peter said.

"Thank you."

She was seventy-seven years old, she told anyone who asked, and just as much inclined to dance as way back when; if you asked her to go waltzing she'd be happy to accept.

Sarah Beame closed the screen door. The porch required paint. "How's Judy?"

"She's on a diet."

"Oh? Which one?"

"The Scarsdale one," said Sam. He perched himself on Peter's chair. "The one where the doctor got killed."

The adults laughed. Volunteer firemen assembled. The bowling team captain was Sam's teacher, and he noticed Sam and waved. It had rained that morning, and the lawns were wet. The sidewalk glistened, and Main Street was washed, expectant.

Mrs. Welling offered pie. "I'll cut a piece for Judy too. You take it back to her."

"Lemon meringue," Peter said. "She'd shoot me."

Fred Peaslee walked up the steps. He stretched, then took a seat. "How'd you do last night?" asked Larry.

"Well, hello," Fred said. "Everybody."

"There was birds last night," said Larry. The sun angled into the porch.

Fred drew his index finger sharply past his throat. "Birds," he said. "I never did like to bet birds."

"Dogs, though. Now that's another thing."

"Not me. I got no stomach for it." Fred sighed. "I take a lady to the track, and if they're racing dogs, why then I'll sit on my hands."

Mrs. Welling turned to Sam. "You eat this piece we saved for your mother, okay? Or have some gingersnaps."

Sam took two. A Labrador barked in its sleep. A girl walked by in white thong sandals; the light outlined her legs. Sam went, "Oompah, oompapah" and leaned out over the rail. Peter felt a spasm of excitement, a sudden lifting. The girl smiled—at him, possibly, or at the tableau on the porch. They were at home here; this was home; he accepted coffee in dead Mr. Welling's own cup.

Peter and Inger went walking together one Thursday; it was a fine spring day. They walked through Cambridge streets and then the Mt. Auburn cemetery; there were fresh flowers everywhere, and many people visiting. They looked at marble griffins and studied the inscriptions on the more imposing crypts. Inger was familiar with the creed of Christian Scientists. Mary Baker Eddy was supposedly not dead, she said, but just asleep; a telephone was supposed to be kept near the grave. When Mary Baker Eddy woke up and wanted something, the only thing she had to do was make her wishes known.

They found themselves in streets he did not recognize, with family grocery stores and plumbing shops and bars. They continued. The sun was hot. He was wearing old, torn clothes, and his hair was long; the crowd looked at him with disdain. Men stared at Inger openly, and some of them whistled and snickered. He heard a drumroll down the street, the sound of trumpets and then a band playing.

"Where are we?" Inger asked.

"Watertown, I think."

"So many people here," she said. "For lunch."

Men sold balloons and ice cream; there were crepe-paper garlands on the lampposts. Men waved flags. "I just remembered," Peter said. "It's Memorial Day."

The sound increased. There were floats and police cars and, in the nearing distance, the sound of piccolos. She clapped her hands delightedly. "Let's watch."

They took positions by a fire hydrant. Policemen on motorcycles rolled past. The queen of the parade was draped in red, white, and blue. Her float was flower-strewn. She twirled a baton in her left hand and blew kisses with her right; she switched hands as she drove by Peter and Inger and, for a moment, lost the beat. There were horses and firemen and men from the Rotary Club walking in business suits; there were Boy Scouts in uniform, and Little Leaguers with the legend of their sponsors on their backs. Men held banners and wore sashes reading "United Way."

"Do you want a hot dog?" Peter asked.

"A what?"

"A frankfurter," he said. "A little sausage in a bun."

She laughed. "I know what a hot dog is, silly. I didn't hear your question."

"Well, do you want one?"

"Yes."

He tried to attract the vendor's attention but failed. The man pushed on, clanging his bell. Then the sky went dark. It was without significance, a single shadow, yet the scene in front of Peter darkened in aspect also. Something triggered a storefront alarm. Inger wore a white dress that buttoned to the waist, with mother-of-pearl buttons and a ruff of eyelet lace. He was with a foreign woman while the Veterans of Foreign Wars paraded down Main Street. He himself was alien, a make-believe gypsy whose pockets were full. He took Inger by the elbow and stepped back.

"How was it?" Judy asked them.

"Fine."

"Did you enjoy yourself?" She took Sam's coat.

"Mm-mn. I'm hungry."

"Didn't Daddy get you anything?"

"Just pie."

"And gingersnaps," said Peter. "And lemonade. Potato chips."

"I'm *still* hungry."

"Yogurt," Judy said. "That's what we're having for lunch."

"With honey and raisins?"

"With raisins," she said.

Judy was polishing silver. She did this when dieting in order to keep out of the kitchen and still keep her hand in, she said. Today she was so hungry she could eat the knife.

"'I eat my peas with honey,'" Peter said. "'I've done so all my life. It might taste kind of funny, but it keeps them on the knife.'"

"Did you thank Mrs. Welling?" she asked.

"We did."

"And how was the parade?"

"Fine."

"Not long enough," said Peter.

Judy turned back to the spoons. She had demitasse spoons and soup spoons and teaspoons and serving spoons on the table in the dining alcove; she had completed the forks. "Can we go swimming?" Sam asked.

"Not now."

"But Tony's going swimming."

"I can't take you," Peter said. "And your mother's busy."

"How's the leg?" she asked him.

"All right. I sat and watched things, mostly."

Tony Neff appeared. They can't go to the pool, his parents have decided, but could they go in the woods? Peter cored an apple, offered a portion to each of the boys—giving his son, scrupulously, the smaller piece—and said yes. They ran to their fort in the woods. Peter watched them as they cartwheeled down the slope: motion unrestricted. He moved to where his wife was sitting, leaned down and kissed her hair. "How was your morning?"

Judy set the rag and polish on a serving tray. "I have a headache," she said.

"Maybe it's the silver polish."

"No. This diet."

"You look terrific," he said.

"Five more pounds. Five more and I'll weigh what I weighed when we married."

"Five *less* pounds."

"You know what I'm saying."

"I love you."

"Yes."

He lowered himself to a chair. "Let's take a trip."

"Where?"

"Anywhere," he said. "Sweden, maybe. Or Norway. I've never seen a fjord."

His failure to have seen a fjord seemed, for an instant, serious. Peter closed his eyes. Mrs. Welling had been affable, solicitous. She walked them to the intersection at the bank.

The family went to Prince Island in July. They rented a house on the north shore; theirs was a private beach. Judy had spent summers on the island in her childhood, and she said the place was magic still, a panacea for each ailment of the soul. She meant that sentiment, she said, although it might sound overwrought. They have proven lately that sunshine makes a person cheerful, whereas clinical depression can be induced by the dark.

Who's proved that? Peter asked, and she said psychologists. Sociologists, he said, or physiologists maybe, but it sounded wishful to him—the kind of attitude induced by skillful advertising, a tourist bureau somewhere that needed to drum up new trade. Well, anyway, she said, this island is my magic place, it's everything I need. It's long days lazing on the beach, and fish, and gin and tonics on the porch at sunset, a chance to play Scrabble and dream.

Helicopters buzzed the coast. Peter listened to the radio. He ate and swam without urgency. Men stood by the wharf, surfcasting. They had waders on, or bathing suits; they had Styrofoam coolers, and beer. Where fish broke the water, or birds gathered, or where there was a sudden darkness, men cast; they stood for hours, smoking, catching nothing he could see. Sometimes a rod would stiffen and bend; there would be a flurry of adjustments, a palpable attention. Then the line would part or the rod go slack, the fisherman would bring in a piece of dripping wool or wood.

Peter watched. He himself was thick-fingered; he had no desire to fish. But something in the manner of the men at the tide line compelled him; they had an equilibrium and a purpose he lacked. They were hunting something and it did not matter if they caught it, yet it mattered how they caught it and how they passed the time. They focused on procedure with the passion of initiates. He lay and drank and dozed. He was healing, he assured himself; he had been more tired than he knew.

On Saturday evening there was a dance at the Grange. Lucinda did not want to go; she was grossed out by square dancing, she said. It was definitely not copacetic, all those boys with cowboy hats and gum. So Judy drove Sam to the hall and Peter returned to collect him. A woman approached his parked car.

"Peter Danto?"

He recognized her vaguely. "Yes?"

"I'm Janice Esterman. You knew me as Saxe. Janice Saxe."

"Of course." He opened the car door, embarrassed.

"You haven't changed," she said. He stood. She offered him her hand. "It's lovely to see you."

"I mean it. You look just the same."

"Our eyes get older," he pronounced, "along with the object perceived."

She smiled. Her breasts were fuller than he remembered, her ankles more substantial. She wore expensive, casual clothes: white pants with a drawstring, a silk shirt. Her sandals were gold, her skin dark. They made conversation about what he was doing here, about coincidence and how long it had been since they last met.

"Are you married?" she asked.

"Yes. With two children."

"Your first wife?"

He nodded. "And you?"

"Congratulations," Janice said. "That's some kind of record, I think. I'm in the process myself."

"Of marriage?"

"Divorce. We've been divorcing since we got married. Sometimes it seems like"—she laughed—"since *before* we got married. But this time there's lawyers involved."

The square dance was over. Children jostled out of the Grange, some with their arms still crossed or do-si-do-ing with their partners. Doors slammed. Mothers started their car radios and turned on their lights. "Are these two yours?" he asked.

"Lydia. Bill. Meet Peter Danto."

"I knew your mother long ago." He coughed, then cleared his throat. "It's nice to meet her children."

Sam appeared. He came to Peter shyly. They repeated introductions, and Lydia said, "We met inside. At the Virginia Reel."

Janice was scanning the crowd; she gave him her profile. He watched. The memory of sex, he thought, can be as powerful as its expectation; their one previous encounter compelled him now again. He remembered it in detail and with clarity. They had gone to the movies together in August in Manhattan; it was a wet night. She wore dungarees and a wool shirt, and the shapelessness of her apparel made her seem all the more shapely by contrast. He invited her back for a drink. When she accepted he had known she would accept him also; she put her arm around his waist as they waited for the light.

"I have to go now," Janice said. "It was a real pleasure seeing you."

"Good-bye." The children nodded, and she offered her right cheek to him. He kissed it lingeringly. She had been just getting over her period, she said. She rarely had an orgasm the first time with a partner, and she never did during her period; he shouldn't mind about that. She would take her pleasure by helping him have his. This phrase remained with Peter eighteen years thereafter, and he wanted to recite it in the parking lot. Their children were at their elbows, however, and there was confusion at the exit ramp. "I remember you," he said.

"Do call." She smiled and was gone.

"Who was that?" Sam asked.

"An old friend," Peter said. "Did you enjoy yourself?"

"No."

"Not even the Virginia Reel?"

"I couldn't hear. I don't know the directions and everybody was talking."

"I'm sorry."

Magnanimous, Sam said, "It isn't your fault, Daddy."

"No," he said. "Let's go."

His daughter had grown beautiful. He had been prepared for this but not for its sudden coming, the transformation in one summer from pudgy child to clean-limbed grace. It took him by surprise. In the grocery store or post office he watched men watching her—their sidelong glances or open admiration, the space they gave her where she walked or banter at the checkout line. She wore shorts and a halter; her breasts were unbound. The length of her legs and the way that they tapered, the ridge of her pelvis and the hooded stare she offered when he asked her for more coffee—all of this, he told himself, had altered overnight. The telephone rang incessantly. "Ma Bell's best customer," he said. "'Reach out and touch someone.'"

"They all go through it," Judy said.

"Miss Yellow Pages, 1981. The model for the Princess phone."

"We could get her a separate number at home."

"Yes."

Lucinda took up water skiing with the absolute attentiveness she had shown to Bill. She was out on the bay every morning. She learned to ski backward, and also with one slalom ski. She would criss-cross her wake, leap and glide. He watched her from the porch. She would emerge from the water, dripping, shaking her head, her tank suit the color of flesh. Wind-surfers angled past their house in what he came to think of as a purposeful display. The sun unrolled a golden carpet in the waters where she swam. "Our Venus on the half shell," Peter said.

She also went swimming at night. She said she loved the freedom of it, chilly black water and phosphor and not knowing when you shut your eyes where you were in the water or why, not knowing if the thing that bit you was your buddy or a crab. "Be careful, Lucy," he said. She said she was being careful, and under the influence of the Crab it didn't matter anyway what bit you in the night. What was really copacetic was celestial navigation. It meant learning how to tell the signs up in the zodiac, to know the difference, say, between Orion and Sagittarius. She bet he'd never know the difference between Sagittarius and Orion if he was forced to steer by them, if Orion came right down and slapped him in the face.

"Orion's not likely to do that," he said.

"There's shooting stars."

"They don't exactly slap you in the face."

"They do me. Every night when shooting stars come this direction, I feel it," said his daughter. "Just like a signal."

"From light years away?"

She nodded.

"Henny Penny thought so too," he said. "And Chicken Little."

"It's a matter of timing. They might have been right."

The speed of her retort alarmed him. "'Live every day,'" he said, "'as though that day will be your last. Someday you're bound to be right.'"

"That's from *Breaker Morant*," Lucinda said. "That's his line, isn't it?"

"You saw *Breaker Morant*?"

"Last Thursday, remember? At the Community Center."

She was escaping him, he knew, her memories and knowledge no longer his to control. "I worry anyhow," said Peter, "about this nighttime swimming."

"I'll be careful."

"Promise?"

"Yes." She was placatory, dismissive; her horoscope instructed her to go with the flow.

"Can I come too?"

Lucinda turned to him with Judy's tolerance. "It's a free ocean," she said.

His most recent passion was for a photograph. He had been leafing through the autobiography of a movie star. The man was a great and advertised rake; he had squired leading ladies since the thirties and was—or so the flap copy claimed—"baring all." He told about his love affair with a figure skater and what she did with him one afternoon in the practice rink; he told about his walk-on roles in pornographic films. He had worn a fake beard and wig. One underground classic kept the camera focused "between navel and knee"; he said he had been widely recognized nevertheless. He told about the hiring system in Hollywood's heyday and the degree of business acumen in starlets who start on the couch. He had a chapter called "3-D: Drink, Dogs, and Drugs." He listed blondes, brunettes, and redheads in terms of their competency on horseback and in bed; he had been married six times.

One woman, however, commanded the author's respect. Peter saw her photograph. She had been reading a book. The other women in the photo section were wearing bikinis or low-cut gowns; they were smiling at the camera or brandishing pistols and whips. But Isabella Morris was attending to the text. Her brow was lightly furrowed, her posture upright yet relaxed; she sat in a white deck chair on what seemed to be a porch. Her dress was white; it buttoned to her throat. Peter recognized this woman as a woman he had known.

Her last name when he met her was D'Augremont, not Morris; she had been sixty, and frail. She was the aging mother of a briefly famous singer he had dated in New York. She had called him Mr. Danto with formality that felt unforced; he had been their houseguest in Katonah. She discussed Camus and Gaston Bachelard with him at breakfast, after he had spent the night disporting in her daughter's arms. He needed sleep. He crept back to his quarters at dawn, and at seven she sounded the gong. It rang in the hallway outside. He would wake and wash and shave, anxious to cover the night's fierce tumult, the way Betty raked her fingernails across his back and bruised his neck. He would drag himself to breakfast where Isabella quartered oranges and offered toast with no crust.

The actor mourned Isabella. She had been the one pure lady in his impure life. He said as much. He said she had no public name and did not belong in a rogues' gallery. They met and courted in Manhattan in the

Second World War, and he had been the happiest man, the most entirely blessed on leave. They stayed together at the Plaza, and everything was champagne and violets and declarations of fidelity forever and ever; she had been—here he borrowed a phrase from a script—"a pearl among white peas." He had gone to Hollywood after the war. He spent the first three days just waiting for her call, for Isabella to join him and to share his life. She did not call. Her telephone conversation, when he called, was brief. He accepted an invitation to a yachting party, and there he met a pretty girl and they started dating each other. One night at a restaurant she told him she was pregnant, and he woke up the next morning married, with a whiskey hangover and a telegram slipped under his door that read: DARLING I'LL BE OUT TO JOIN YOU NEXT WEDNESDAY STOP ALL BUSINESS FINISHED BACK EAST STOP I HATE THE PHONE STOP ALL MY LOVE FOREVER ISABELLA.

The actor reproduced this telegram in his book. He berated himself for one whole paragraph, saying he had missed the opportunity of marriage to a splendid woman because he was impatient. He would never forgive himself ever; he counseled those who read this text or saw that photograph to pause a moment for love. Her face was lean. Her nose was patrician, her eyes downcast. She had dark lipstick on and what looked like a white wave in her short hair. Since the photograph was black and white, Peter could not tell for certain—but Isabella appeared pale, almost unwell. She wore a strand of beads, a bracelet, and no ring. The photograph was dated 1943. She was to marry someone who later died in the Alps. As a young and wealthy widow she did not lack for suitors but chose to live alone. She raised her daughters to be intellectual and athletic and polite. His girlfriend, Betty, had such enthusiastic orgasms the instant he entered her that Peter felt irrelevant. She sang torch songs at The Dugout, then folk-rock, then tried scat-singing. She strained her vocal chords, however, and was told to rest. She told him that she did not miss the life of a nightclub singer, not in the slightest, and would rather be in France. He did not wish to go to France and they separated without rancor. He missed his toast and marmalade and morning conversation more than he missed her at night.

Peter turned to this photograph often. He had known Isabella well, and had known her daughter intimately. He admired her good works, her charitable enterprise and uhnflagging determination to aid the deaf. She was fluent in sign language, and her servants all were deaf. They would clear the table and offer wine mutely, politely, nodding as he thanked them until Peter nodded back.

Yet her love affair with the actor had the force of revelation. It was common knowledge once, he read, and made the gossip columns. The actor's ghostwriter might have written for permission for the photograph and, perhaps, to ask if she had anything to say. She would have had nothing to say. She had told him, Peter, nothing. The image of this society lady as a supple beauty once, not desiccate and severe but nakedly embracing her lover in the Plaza—this image haunted him. It was a reproach. It argued lost youth, transience, the irretrievable past.

One night he did decide to join Lucinda for a swim. There was a bright three-quarter moon; he looked down from the dune's height at two heads bobbing in the waves. He heard what he could have sworn was laughter; the heads appeared then disappeared together. He shouted from the stairwell's crest, "Lucy, are you all right?" When he started down, however, he had to watch his footing; his ankle hindered him. The stairs were steep. For a moment he lost sight of her among the waves and rocks. By the time he reached the cliff's base she was standing at the waterline, wrapped in a white towel and holding a dry suit. "I could have sworn you were in trouble," Peter said.

"No, Daddy."

"Was there someone with you?"

"I was diving."

"I saw two heads. I heard you laughing."

"What makes you say that?"

"I was worried," Peter said.

"Don't be. I can swim."

They ascended. She had not answered his question, he knew, and knew not to ask it again. Next morning, she said, "Sagittarius. Ted's a Sagittarius. That's why we get along."

"Who's Ted?" he asked her at breakfast.

"A friend."

"Does he live here?"

"Not all year round," she said. "He comes from Arizona too."

"You go to school in Arizona, remember? You come from Massachusetts."

"Anyway," she said. She helped herself to beach plum jelly. Peter waited. He could hear her eat her toast.

"Anyway what?"

"Anyway nothing. You asked."

"Does he go swimming with you?"

"Yes."

"On the buddy system?"

She looked around the table, sighing. "Why such a federal case? You're making a federal case out of nothing, you know."

"I myself," he said, "was once a Sagittarius. I used to go swimming with girls."

"Big deal."

Peter finished his juice. "The beginning of wisdom," he said, "is knowing when to quit. I never was a Sagittarius. I never went swimming. I'd like to meet Ted."

"Fine," she said. "I'll invite him over."

"Tonight?"

"You're a Taurus," she said. "People don't go around changing their signs."

"I suppose not."

"The leopard his spots," Judy said. She had been frying eggs.

"Will you buy Bill?" he asked.

"I don't know." Lucinda turned to her mother. "I haven't thought about it much."

"Then don't. Bill's doing fine without you, right?" Judy said. "You shouldn't buy a horse unless you want it worse than anything."

"*Passata la commedia*," said Peter. "Now it's Ted."

Inger left for a tour of America after the last class. She would not return in the fall. They sat, legs touching, in the last row of the lecture hall; she took the seat by the door. *The Flies* had been a success. Their pictures appeared in the *Crimson* together. The portly bespectacled French professor wiped his lectern before every session, then used a separate handkerchief for his hands and mouth. His specialty was Baudelaire and the "voyage motif." He sported a bowtie and unwrinkled suits. He wore pink shirts, always, and had a moustache.

She wanted Peter to accompany her; they could visit the Grand Canyon together, she said, and San Francisco. There were cars and relatives and rooms available everywhere; they could be each other's traveling companion. This proved impossible. He had a summer job, and his parents would not have approved. Her parents would certainly not have approved, and she was planning to visit friends of her parents in Chicago and Aspen.

She called him every night of the first week they were apart. She sent him letters from the Grand Canyon and Taos and Yellowstone Park. He loved, he wrote, her circumlocutions and her funny, twisted English, and he thought about the hand that wrote it and the wrist and elbows and arm and shoulder and everything connected to the shoulder.

By degrees, however, Inger's letters grew less frequent and her language less ardent. He turned his attention elsewhere, and, the last time she called, he was in bed with a girl from summer school. "This isn't a good time to talk," he said. When he called back later she told him she would fly to Sweden from New York, not Boston. He could meet her at the airport if he wished.

He did wish, and he tried to get to New York but could not find a car and had been planning to attend the Red Sox game that night. He pictured himself at the airport with Inger, wrapping his arms around her and declaring with intensity that they were star-crossed lovers whose paths would cross again. The picture faded. He knew he could not persuade her of his vivid passion; it was unpersuasive.

In the years that followed, Peter heard of Inger often. She became rumor's subject once more. Rumor had it that she slept with Ingmar Bergman and bore his child but stayed married to an Italian industrialist nevertheless. The industrialist was sterile, and she therefore had his sanction to sleep with men of superior qualities and blood. She worked with refugees in Kenya and Thailand; she renounced her singing career but made pornographic films. She became a surgeon in Brazil.

Peter heard one story he did believe to be true. He encountered the director of *The Flies*. The director had prospered; he was returning from the festival at Cannes. "*Les Mouches,*" he said. "Can you believe it? All those years ago . . ."

In Cannes, he said to Peter, he had met that Swede again; they were driven in the same car to the village of Valbonne. Ike and Tina Turner were playing in Valbonne, and celebrants from the festival drove up for the last show. He would have known her anywhere, he claimed; she had the same wild accent and green eyes.

The road from Cannes was narrow, and traffic slow. Someone in the party produced cocaine. When it was passed to Inger, she inhaled deeply and started to laugh. She said she had powdered her nose. She called Cannes the end of the world. The director described this with precision, and the image grew actual to Peter. Her long neck was arched, her body taut; she seemed convulsed with mirth. The limousine negotiated a hairpin turn; Inger fell to the floor. She spread her hands and crossed her legs and extended herself as if on a cross. He could not tell if this was a seizure or pose. She lay there, twisted, grinning, till the car reached Club Valbonne—then gathered herself from the floor and walked off.

She had been crazy, the director said. She had absolutely refused to acknowledge him. She had been so spacy it was like the Hayden Planetarium right there in that car, in her eyes. Whatever she was into, she was into absolutely and he, Peter, should be grateful he'd got out.

He picked his way along the beach. Theirs was a rocky shore, with much litter and weed and many points where boulders made the going difficult. There were clay cliffs and freshwater streams. He walked for a full hour, heading east. The tide had washed away all traces of previous passage; he saw no footprints but his own. He did see Clorox bottles and beer cans, a torn beach sandal on the dunes, charred stumps and rocks in a circle.

Peter favored his ankle, testing footholds, anxious not to hurt himself so far from help. Sweating, he pulled off his shirt. He tied it to the branch of a fallen scrub oak where he could collect it on the journey back. The cliffs behind him had huckleberry, gorse and beach plum; there was poison ivy in abundance also. At his feet was a tangle of skate cases and mussel and horseshoe-crab shells. He came upon the object of his walk.

Two freshwater streams formed a cove. There were clay cliffs on either side, and a brickworks facing north. He had not been there in years. The place was familiar, however, its slope to the shoreline unaltered. Fog increased. Someone had tied a ladder to the scree-strewn dunes, and he clambered up it gratefully. A single brick chimney remained. There was a waterwheel and a network of pulleys and gears. The iron rail had rusted and the sluice had been clogged and silted in. Wooden archways gave on nothing. The struts had sprung and the structure collapsed. Whole timbers lay at his feet. Initials had been carved in them, and hearts, and telephone numbers.

Yet the kiln he had come to was massive, its height intact. Small sea-birds fled his approach. They fluttered past him noisily. He pictured the brickworks at work. He saw men shaping clay, then firing it, then stacking and loading the brick on barges and floating them off with the favoring tide. Peter sat. He closed his eyes. Horses would be grazing where men cleared off timber to burn. The waterwheel powered the bellows. It was hot. It was noontime, possibly, and time for lunch; a gong would sound three times. Men lay beneath the smokestacks or took their ease on the beach. Some chewed tobacco; some had cigarettes and pipes. They adjusted their caps. They talked about old Norton and his skinflint ways, the Mosler safe he had, the carriage, the daughter too who'd just as soon see you struck dead as smile, the big-mouthed bass at the head of the creek, the herring run that week. There would be a chopping contest at the fair next Thursday, and Norton's white Belgian by himself would pull more weight than Brady's team. The prize at ringtoss was to get to dunk the fireman; it had been a good year.

He had few friends. He had been a "ladies' man" and now was a "family man." He had acquaintances, of course, and men he could consult in need; he was sociable. But on the shore he felt himself abandoned, distinguished from the sea-wrack only by his sentient alertness to the distinction as such. And for an instant even this faded, even that self-consciousness was washed into transparency. A buoy clanked out in the channel. In the nearing distance, he heard horns. The dream of fair women was with him, his daughter taking pride of place; she frolicked in the waves. The stream had not yet silted in nor production on the mainland proved more efficient. The barges had not grounded or been sunk. He pictured three such chimneys while yet the brickworks thrived. Demand for brick was at its height; there were many who sat watching from the cove. Some sat slack-jawed, dozing, toying with their food or pipes; some boasted of their prowess or offered their opinion on the merits of a dog. Some gloried in their birth, some in their horse. Hope and fuel seemed inexhaustible, the future that is now the past still flaring, fiery bright.

She twirled and floated, oblivious. She and all her company swam by as though in thrall. The water was his arms. She was wearing a snorkel and therefore kept her face submerged; her hair fanned out around her like thick weed. He loved her unreservedly. Beauty decomposed. Had she been able or willing to listen, he would have told her so. She whistled in the spume.

Peter is thirty-eight years old and an insurance broker in the Berkshires. He plans to build a windmill as an alternative energy source. Now that their daughter is away at school, and Sam so often busy, his wife considers buying into or establishing a business. She is sure-fingered, with a taste for children's clothes; she is gifted at and interested in puppetry also. They do amateur theatricals and pageants for the holidays at home.

The Dantos are a three-car family. He drives a Saab and a Buick sedan and a yellow Datsun pickup truck; his ankle heals more slowly than he hoped. He is afflicted with nostalgia for imagined opportunity that had not been, when offered, opportune.

Judy does the crossword puzzle. "What's eight letters for traitor?" she asks. "Beginning with *q-u*."

"Quisling."

"That doesn't mean traitor."

"Close enough."

"I looked it up," she says. "It means collaborationist."

"Fellow traveler," he says.

She fills in the letters with pencil, provisionally. When she is certain of a word, she writes the letters with pen.

"Imagine," Peter says, "getting your name known for that. Imagine Mr. Quisling's children, and his cousins and his aunts."

"What was that Frenchman called? The man who ran Vichy?"

"Pierre Laval," he says. "Or *le Maréchal* Pétain. There are a whole host of quislings. But they all have his name."

She lights a cigarette. Her hands, she says, indicate most clearly that she is no longer young. You cannot counterfeit youth with your hands. "What's twelve letters starting with *c*," Judy asks, "that means both beginning and end?"

"Commencement."

The long reach before him looks calm. Cliffs and thick spruce entanglements rise on either side; the finger of water he follows seems an extension of flesh. It is slate-gray, however, then black when the moon goes down. He has taken on provisions at the head of the fjord, at a harbor he cannot pronounce. There are herring, flatbread, ice, and akvavit.

Northiam Hall

MARTIN ROTHER WENT to England on a research trip. Following the journey that the poet Harold Emmett made—though his began where Emmett's ended—Martin reached Sussex in August. Emmett had died there on March 23, seventy-one years earlier; this August marked his birth's centennial. It had not gone unnoticed. Martin was approached by an editor in Boston; they ate lunch. The time was ripe, the editor suggested, for a reappraisal.

He liked the suggestion. A modest little book, he thought, to suit the modest talent and the little span of Emmett's life—a cautionary tale about the way success goes hand in glove with failure. There had been a movie, once, based on the poet's career. From cub reporter to war correspondent to barroom lover to the tubercular genius scribbling deathbed verse—all this took ninety minutes from the first frame to the last. There had been armies, flamenco guitarists, pale women wearing black. Greyhounds sported at the poet's heels while he walked to Winchelsea, his brow contracted in thought.

Martin planned the biography he would write. It would have to be conscious, of course, of the irony in overstatement. By the very use of cliché, the chapter headings that would trumpet their own stereotype ("A Wand'ring Minstrel," "Paradise Lost"), he could undermine the notion that such passion was original. Emmett had read in schoolbooks how the bareheaded artist must run out to drink in the rain. Friedrich Hölderlin, his model, had come from a walking tour in Switzerland, saying only, saying always, "*Apollon hat mich geschlagen.*"

"Apollo has struck me"—was this the blight of sunstroke or searing inspiration; did the phrase signal genius or idiocy? It had been the epigraph for Emmett's first collection, and it became a kind of motto for his behavior thereafter. Hölderlin had died old, mad and happy. He spent his final decades composing children's rhymes. But "Apollo" meant enlightenment; it made of Emmett's indifference to doctors a romantic repudiation that defied not merely common sense but fate.

"I'd write about him warts-and-all," Martin told the editor.

"Certainly. I expect so."

They were lunching in Mulberry Street, on baked stuffed shrimp. "I'm not even sure I admire him," said Martin. "It will take a while before I'm sure of that."

The editor drank. He wiped his lips. "*The Quest for Como*," he said. "Symons wasn't certain what he thought of Rolfe. Have you reread it lately?"

This flattery—"Have you *re*read it?"—was not displeasing to Martin. There were, he thought, points of comparison. Though Emmett was no Frederick Rolfe and he himself no Symons, the notion of a quest for an elusive character had its appeal. He was between projects. The advance would last a year—eighteen months if he were careful—and he could apply for further research funds. It had been decades, after all, since Emmett was considered major, and Martin was a recognized expert. He had annotated the poet's war and travel verse. His *Selected Letters* had done well.

The wine was Pouilly Fumé, and the editor proposed they risk a second bottle. "Friday." He signaled the waiter. "The office shuts at four. Every secretary in the place has weekend plans for the Vineyard. We could conduct our business far better on route three in a traffic jam on Friday afternoons. That's where you find the world."

"It might be," Martin admitted, "time to reconsider."

"Let's hope so," said the editor. "*I'm* not going to spend my weekend waiting for a ferry. Let's drink to that."

They raised their glasses and touched rims. Then the editor recited, at accurate length, Emmett's poem on the virtues of good friends and bread and wine. Called "Cumpany," it extolled just such celebrations as these, the breaking of bread—*cum pane*—as a ritual partaking of God's body since well before Christ.

"You've done your homework."

"No. I learned that one in school. And I've known Emmett's verse for more years than I care to remember. That's why we're meeting, of course. It's a labor of love and not profit for us. It's something that *ought* to be done."

That *ought* remained with Martin for the next few weeks. The editor's sense of urgency and the veiled imperative gave him a degree of confidence. Elsewhere, he had lost it. A love affair that promised much delivered little; his apartment needed painting and his car needed a drive shaft. Lightning struck his stove one night, inflicting damage only on the stewpot left to simmer and on the element beneath. Yet it seemed a signal: *Apollon.*

Vaguely, Martin envisioned casting the book in retrospect, beginning with the deathbed scenes and working back to birth. His own interest had been captured by the overt necrophilia of Emmett's final volume; he assumed the reader too might wish to start with death-in-life. He himself was thirty-nine—ten years older than Emmett when he died—and self-professedly a beginner. He enjoyed, he said, three cs: cigars, carpentry, and companionable women who would let him leave at night. Of the former he had a supply; of the last, at this moment, none. He spent July in the Maine woods, in a cabin he had built, adding a screened porch and deck. The business of buying lumber and the business of composition came to seem related, as if the structure of his book had to be preplanned.

One morning he woke with a toothache. He had trouble with his teeth and did not want to trust himself to a stranger. So he made an appointment—on an emergency basis—with his own dentist in Boston. He drove the whole distance in pain. His dentist pulled the tooth. "You made the right decision," he told Martin. "I could have tried to save it, but there's just too large an abscess. It would have bothered you sooner or later. *Bon voyage.*"

Returning, he again felt pain; the novocaine wore off. He promised himself a jam jar filled with bourbon, and no ice; he solaced himself with images of dreamless sleep in the hammock he'd slung between pines. He'd wake to rhythmic rocking; Susanna would be back again and clothed in sunlight only, the lead-rope to the hammock coiled around her waist. Smoke poured out from under the hood. He slowed down; smoke increased. Martin coasted to a stop on the road's shoulder; he was fifty miles from Boston and eighty from his home.

He stepped out and opened the hood. The radiator was a geyser; it spewed forth green water and steam. A truck pulled up behind him and a bearded man in overalls approached. He leaned over, considered the engine, then smiled at Martin mirthlessly. "Cain't fix that with no Silver Seal," he said.

"Thank you for stopping."

"No problem. This is your problem." The mechanic pointed to the radiator. "We'll go up and get us another."

He ran a junkyard, it turned out; his name was Thomas Larrabee. He produced a toolbox. "Thirty-five bucks plus the old one," he announced. "That's what it'll cost you. Labor too."

Martin nodded. His mouth was aflame. He watched while Thomas Larrabee extracted the old radiator from its casing. They drove together through the back roads of York Corners to a clearing by a quarry where cars huddled, discarded, like the shells of shellfish. There were pyramids of tires. Larrabee stopped in front of the twin to Martin's car. "Ass-end's stove in," he said. "This baby's off its frame. Except the front end ain't been touched. Wait here."

Guard dogs circled. Martin sat. A plastic go-go dancer dangled from the rearview mirror in the truck; her hair was orange and her hip boots purple. Pain clarifies. He made his bed in other beds, his books about the books of other authors. He planned a final feast of steamer clams and lobster and felt ceremonial, aggrieved, at the fact he would eat it alone.

In London he spent several days on Emmett's faded trail. The poet's rooms had been destroyed by a direct hit in the Blitz; those restaurants he patronized were long since closed or changed. His friends had died. This did not trouble Martin; he conceived of Emmett as a solitary. True, the man went to parties and loved riotous assembly and celebrated in his verse the solidarity of men at war. But he moved from place to place displacing, it seemed, nothing. He left no mark on any life but that of his one daughter—whom he marked for life. Had Martin stumbled on a cache of papers or a vivid firsthand recollection, he would have been nonplussed. He told himself his poet loved oblivion; he rented a car and drove south.

The Old Rectory in Northiam had been transformed into a bed-and-breakfast establishment. Martin stayed there, on the upper green behind the church. The first night he went walking and approached the church as bells were rung; he entered silently. Five women hung from ropes.

They pulled in sequence, watching one old woman in a shawl who seemed to be the leader and familiar with the beat. If they hesitated pulling, she would count out their numbers: *one* and two and *three* and four *and* five.

Martin's last name, Rother, was the name of the river that divided Kent from Sussex in these parts; his family had once come from the region. He felt no sense of homecoming, however. The closely clipped lawns and the fields of hops and apple orchards had the feel of strangeness, not familiarity. When he said in the Old Rectory that he'd come to study Emmett, they told him that an Emmett lived in town. "Granny Emmett," his landlady said. "And she wouldn't mind your calling, she lives just across the way. With Charley Walters, he's her lodger. In that weatherboard cottage just there." She winked. "Not the way *you're* a lodger, if you take my meaning. He's been living in that house ever since Emmett passed on."

Martin was greeted at the door by the principal bell ringer; she wore the same fringed shawl. She had never heard of Harold Emmett, and her husband's family—"him as is dead" was how she referred to him—came from Manchester. She did not read poetry herself. But as long as he was visiting she'd like to show him through the house, and here was Charley to help. Charley Walters shook his hand. Unwillingly, he entered.

"Look at this," said Granny Emmett. "This used to be the pantry. And he makes a downstairs bathroom, isn't he a clever man?" She turned the bath taps and water came out; she left them running for a moment, then turned the taps back tightly. "Linoleum," she said. "Until he fixed this flooring it was just cement."

She showed Martin the linen closet and the cupboard's several drawers. She slid out each drawer as if for inspection, then pushed them back flush. "Rollers," Granny Emmett said. "And every single one of them faced with Formica. Such a clever man."

Charley Walters opened doors. He showed where he removed what used to be a closet and how he fixed the kitchen so you'd never notice when you looked it used to be two rooms. Martin admired the white wallpaper and the red-and-blue checked pattern with Beagles playing checkers. "Seven coats of wax," said Granny Emmett. "That's how many coats are on this floor."

She wore a pink housecoat and slippers to match; her shawl had beads on the fringe. She was, she told him proudly, eighty-three. "He's been living here"—she indicated Charley—"since him as is dead passed away. Eleven years." She shook her head. "You'd never know to look at this house the shape it was in when he came."

"It's wonderful," said Martin. "Thank you so much."

"Just a minute," she said. "You mustn't miss upstairs."

"I didn't mean to disturb you."

"This staircase too." She led the way. "Watch your head. This banister. Charley found it down by Hurlbird Close when they were redecorating. So he brings it home in sections and says, 'Bess, we'll have a staircase like the Hurlbirds used to have.'" On the landing, panting, she smiled at Charley fondly. "What a piece of luck."

"Eleven years," said Charley. "We've been busy all that time."

"Look at this closet, for instance," she said. He made it too. Made everything." She opened the white deal doors. Charley's coats hung like a troupe of bodiless gray privates on parade; a second door disclosed his trousers and shoes. The drawer beneath it held underpants. "Isn't he a tidy man?" she asked.

"Yes."

She reached up and patted his cheek. "It's such a pleasure to show somebody how much Charley's done for me."

"For us," said Charley.

"He takes pleasure in it too," she said. "He's not above the occasional compliment."

"It's a lovely house you live in."

"We thank you," Granny Emmett said. "For taking so much time out of your busy schedule for a pair of old people like us."

Her words were not ironic. He felt shamed by their sincerity, the mock they made of his own inward mocking and impatience to be free. A plane above them banked, descending for Gatwick. "Nice weather you've had for your visit," said Charley.

"Yes," he said. "It's wonderful. I'll come again. Goodbye."

That June Martin had delivered his high school's commencement address. It had been more than twenty years since Martin had graduated from the school; he retained few pleasant memories and had not been back. He did not send money or a list of his accomplishments to the *Alumni News*; he attended no reunions. It came as a surprise, therefore, when a letter from the principal invited him to speak; his book on Heinrich Schliemann's Troy had been an inspiration to the eighth-grade class. Their spring-term project was "Hellas," and his biography—here the principal quoted a teacher—had "taught my students more than the *Odyssey* and *Iliad* combined."

Martin composed a speech. He admitted to inadequacy in front of such an audience; only grown-ups were supposed to address the assembly. How had this happened, he asked; how did he make it from the third row to the podium? He claimed the track had been contracted, though it still was a fifth of a mile. He evoked his adolescence, praised his teachers and the love of learning they instilled. He practiced his speech in front of the mirror and the tape recorder, perorating on the word "commencement" as an endlessly valent beginning. He felt a fraud. He remembered, mainly, his chubby, competitive, short-legged self afraid to do a somersault; he remembered his yearnings and boastfulness, his acne, the jostling at lunch.

The private school was well situated. It nestled in the hillocks of an expensive suburb; the approach roads had thank-you-ma'ams to cut down on driving speed. He arrived an hour early and walked the campus grounds. No one paid attention; he slung his coat over his shoulder. He qualified, he knew, to be some student's uncle or the only slightly youthful father of a graduating senior. Sauntering toward the tennis court, he felt as self-conscious as ever in his high school days: the windblown intellectual, alone.

A pine branch brushed his face. A bush he had not recollected blocked his climbing path. The breeze was warm. He stood where he kissed his first girlfriend, sweat pouring from him after tennis, the Slazenger upright between them like a sword. She pressed against him briefly, saying, "Don't." They were fifteen. She wore a tennis sweater with crossed rackets on her breast. Where had he gone wrong, he asked himself, what turning taken on the way from youth to citizen that left him in this thicket unaccompanied? He moved among the shapes of other people's memories and made them shapely, literate. He would revise his speech.

Martin buttoned his cuffs. He adjusted his tie. He would say how it seemed natural to Schliemann once to scrutinize the sand and locate Troy. There Helen lay with Paris while Hector paced the town walls; this is the rock where great Achilles grieved. You have to look closely enough. You have to adhere to the text. He would ask his ancient instructors to explain it if they could: how have I come to this pass?

The next house he visited was a bungalow named Nautilus. Reginald Hurlbird invited Martin over for Friday at eleven. "It's the second smallest place in town," he said when Martin called. His voice was reedy, high. His family owned Northiam Hall; his uncle had leased it to Emmett. "Just beyond the Esso station," Hurlbird said. "Look to your left at the station, and you'll be at my gate."

The directions were precise, and Martin arrived ten minutes early. An old man wearing a vest and leather gardening gloves was weeding by the holly hedge. He straightened and took off his gloves. "Do come in," said Reginald Hurlbird. "I live alone here now, so please excuse the mess."

There was no mess. The bungalow was trim as a ship's cabin, and the photographs and paintings hung on a level, like portholes. They depicted the sea. A chandelier in the shape of an anchor had two electric candles. Reginald Hurlbird turned on the switch, and the chandelier candles blinked alternately. "Make yourself at home," he said, and indicated a red leather chair. "What are you drinking? A gin and tonic? Wine? Sherry?"

"Thank you."

They sat. They talked about the weather and inflation. Hurlbird remembered having shared a barber with Emmett in 1908. He had been agog, he said, at meeting so famous a figure. Emmett's boots were brown, and shone; he had been extraordinarily polite. That was the sum total of his firsthand recollection, however. "I always say," he said, "that the great man—the *truly* great, I mean—has time for little children. And for animals. I was only a boy, understand. And I've never forgotten how kind he was, how absolutely attentive. People say he was a snob, and I couldn't speak to that. But I *can* speak most emphatically to the way his boots gleamed, and his American accent. . . ."

Reginald Hurlbird had white eyebrows and a white fringe of hair; his clothes sat loosely on his frame, as if he had lost weight. He did not drink. The sherry was acid; Martin consumed it in small sips. He asked about the manor house, and whether he might visit.

"Dear boy, there's nothing to see," Hurlbird said. "I thought you knew."

"Knew what?"

"They never could determine just what caused the blaze. It's such a pity, isn't it, the house stands for five hundred years *without* wiring, and no sooner do they put it in than"—he snapped his fingers—"pop!"

Martin shifted in his seat. He had counted on permission to explore the fabled house. It had figured largely in the poet's work. By all accounts the place had suited him; he liked to take his morning ride on one of two white horses and gallop down the entrance drive to greet arriving guests.

"They plan to fix it up again," said Hurlbird. "I'm dubious. You should see for yourself—quite a job."

"I will." Afflicted by the sense of his intrusiveness, he smiled. He drained his glass.

"That's all I can tell you, I'm afraid. Your poet was—how shall I put it—a bird of passage, wasn't he?" The corner clock chimed the half hour. "He spent so relatively little time in this area. We've been here for six hundred years." He spread his hands. "'From darkness into darkness,' says Alcuin of York. One hears so many stories and remembers so very few."

"Were you a sailor?" Martin asked.

"Yes."

"Emmett also loved the sea."

His host's conviviality had been exhausted, however. He stood, an old man in need of his lunch. "I couldn't bring myself to go back to the place. They kept on telling me, 'It's not so bad, Reggie, do visit.' So one day I went and, let me assure you, I turned right round again."

Martin found the manor house. It lay in a valley, at the bottom of a basin the Kent Ditch had shaped. Fog shrouded it, though the surrounding hillside slopes were greenly brilliant. Sheep grazed. He thought he saw a horse. Tall trees he could not name rose from the mist around the roof; there were signs instructing him that this was Private Property, Unauthorized Persons Keep Out.

He entered cautiously. A tractor turned in a far field and then was lost to sight. The drive was graveled, rutted, and it curved. His motion along it seemed stasis; the drive itself appeared to guide the car's four wheels and therefore the fifth in his hands. When he came upon the ruin, he was unprepared.

The garage was intact. It could have contained a fleet of carriages. Martin parked in front of what had been the servants' entrance, possibly; a bathtub blocked the door. There was a disconnected toilet in the anteroom behind, and piles of rubble and brick. A hanging beam triangulated what would have been a passageway; he picked his way forward, came around a standing chimney and found himself in open space that had been Northiam Hall.

There were shards of roofing at his feet. The staircase held. But where the landing should have been there was nothing now: a floorboard like a spear lodged in the earth. Birds scolded him from the black eaves, and something scuttled away in the rubble. He pivoted. The medieval fireplace where the poet roasted lamb and pigs seemed unimpaired. Everywhere beyond was wreckage, the chapel in the northwest tower gone, its stained-glass windows burst. Emmett would have welcomed this, perhaps; Martin cleared himself a place on the lintel. He lit a Schimmelpenninck and he sat.

"Maiden, war is your lover," Emmett had written. "The house watches over / what you yearningly call cover / Night, the windhover / His uncle. What tower / Like a mote in wind, our / Own resistance proving power / In th'assaulting hour / Might withstand...." He could not remember the rest. Those tortured rhymes, brief stanzas, had been Emmett's hallmark for the time he spent in Northiam; the romantic figure of the virgin on the parapet was transformed in its urgency to a whore awaiting customers. When he moved closer to the sea he would write his lighthouse poems— and the martello-tower series anticipated these. "Bright thrust of lance / And parrying glance / The mating dance / She wants" was the refrain.

Martin thought him overrated. The excellence of even his best work was more a matter of bombast than style. And compared to those two poets with whom he was most frequently compared—Hopkins on the one hand, Wilfred Owen on the other—his intricate arrangements of sonority seemed simple. But there was a residue in Emmett, a kind of drained truth waiting at the bottom of his verse like dregs—and to this bitter residue Martin found himself responsive. A phrase like "Home again, the garroting wire, love's stump" was as acidic—or, as Martin had put it earlier, as "subject to accidie"—as Owen at his bleakest or Hopkins when most desolate. His last book was his best. Underneath the posturing—the pomp and silly circumstance—there could be heard the accents of conviction; given time, Martin believed, he might have produced major verse.

Emmett's life, however, was more celebrated than his art. His amorous exploits were legend, as was his fondness for gin. His narrow escape on the slopes of Mont Blanc made headlines all over the world. His heroism under fire, when a correspondent in the Boer War, the *bon mot* with which he greeted those who watched him row across the Golden Horn—these became the touchstones of a minor cult. He was handsome, young, not poor. He left his native Newark without a backward glance; only three sonnets evoke the New Jersey of his birth. And Emmett traveled widely. At twenty-two he'd been around the world; at twenty-six he settled in this structure; at twenty-nine he was dead. For those final years he cultivated the role of the *poète maudit*, half in love with easeful death; friends who told him to consult a doctor were told in no uncertain terms to leave their friend alone. Those who counseled rest cures elsewhere were told the poet knows no rest: "I had rather sleep in Bedlam's bed / Than chew this hospice bread."

So when he died of tuberculosis there were many who had warned him—many who had held a blood-stained handkerchief while he was wracked and coughing. "Northiam Hall" became a posthumous success. Martin knew the poem well and therefore knew the space he sat in as the banquet hall; he could half persuade himself that Emmett sat beyond the lintel, drinking, dropping scraps from the table for dogs. The dogs were called Alfred and Chips. He held a silver tankard with a glass bottom; he could see his adversary once he drained the glass. The poet raised and emptied it, and his eye was veined with foam; his hand held steady, however, and he did not blink.

Martin lit a second cigar. A photograph of Emmett taken days before he died showed what a friend at bedside called that "level, inward gaze." His black moustache obscured his upper lip. He lay against a pillow, staring straight at the camera lens. This seemed the great conundrum of the life; if Martin came to terms with Emmett's curious willingness to lie in a sickbed with no help from doctors, to give up with no struggle what he'd struggled so to gain—if he could understand the ending, then the middle and beginning might come clear. The biographer, he thought, must be the retina, the glass, the lens; he must see what his subject once saw. Pigeons settled on the chimney. Martin focused on a dropping where his foot approached a brick; a skeletal mouse lay encased. It would have been digested by an owl.

"'Alcuin was my name. / I was always in love with wisdom. / Say a prayer for me that you mean / When you read this writing. . . .'"

Emmett too had quoted from Alcuin of York. The writer has one privilege, he wrote—that of formulating his own epitaph. Martin asked himself, returning, if those who die senescent in a well-warmed bed know something that the youthful poet imagines only chancily. Granny Emmett's house was lit; her shadow flitted past the window. He wondered had she told the truth when telling him her husband came from another town. "Looks go. They go. Yours will go as mine did," Alcuin had warned. Music drifted on the green: a tune he knew but could not name. Martin stood a moment, listening; there were stringed instruments. Then he made for the Old Rectory and his evening meal.

They served him in the dining room. He ate alone. Susanna studied modern dance. She would have teased him into playfulness, he knew, or roused him from his lethargy; she would have made him celebrate their bodies' fleet union and skill. Yet this dark space and meager serving appeared his rightful portion. Martin lingered over coffee. He drank a second cup. Blood and flesh and bone compacted intricately everywhere; he tapped the ash from his cigar and marveled at his fingers that, five minutes earlier, had manipulated a knife.

He visited Dennisport next. Emmett's final home, it overlooked the coast. Here his friends had gathered while the poet died. His wife and daughter stayed on, however, and when his wife remarried she left Dennisport in care of her daughter; Julie Emmett lived there all her life. She too was briefly married and had one daughter, Sylvia; Sylvia retained her grandfather's family name. Martin knew the lineage, and that Julie spent her life as her father's votary. She treated the house as a shrine. The ill-kept secret of her lesbian entourage added luster, somehow, to the memory of that rampaging masculine presence snuffed out when she was three. She was as gifted as she was reclusive, and she'd filled the house—according to report—with plaster casts and paintings of her father's face.

Sylvia, the granddaughter, would be fifty-three. She answered his letter politely. If he would care to call on Wednesday afternoon at two, she would be at home. She had read his monograph on her grandfather's "Ballads" and the Introduction to *Selected Letters*. She would be pleased to meet its author and show him Dennisport; she referred to Dennisport as though it were some other someone's home. She looked forward to meeting him soon.

This house was unimpressive. It squatted in a grove of leafless elms. Its outer walls were gray unpainted stucco, its roof slate. There was a central chimney with several chimney vents. The windows had neither curtains nor shutters; a latticework of ivy straggled by the door. He waited in the driveway, then advanced. Emmett had written, "We are happy here / In this small space / The place would appear / To erase place / Giving instead on queer / Confinements, the sheer Drop and cliff face / of Fear. . . ."

Sylvia Emmett appeared in the doorway. "Mr. Rother?"

"Miss Emmett."

"So good of you to come." She offered a strong hand. She was as tall as he, sharp-visaged, wearing a painter's smock. She had wound a scarf around her forehead and hidden what he guessed was clipped gray hair. Her eyes reminded him of Emmett's own: protuberant, large-pupiled, dark.

"Welcome to Dennisport." She moved aside to let him enter.

"Thank you. How long have you lived here?" he asked. "Oh, all through my childhood. Then lately, when Julie required it." She made a vague, dismissive gesture. "And I've not been much good, I'm afraid, at keeping things trim."

The entrance hallway stank of cats. It was damp and dark, with photographs of Emmett on the near wall and an umbrella stand that held what Sylvia told him were the poet's walking sticks. "That hat too." She pointed. "It's what he wore when it rained. Though mostly he went bareheaded, Julie used to say. Used to say it was the death of him."

The ceiling was discolored, the plaster veined with age. Areas of plaster had buckled altogether. In the dining room he made out a mural—clumsily drawn, faded—of a satyr eating grapes and holding what appeared to be a chicken in its fist. The sky contained both zeppelins and bombs.

"Your mother stayed here during the war?"

"They all did."

"All?"

"Violet, Samantha, Alison." She smiled again and spread her hands. "It was one of Julie's rules that we used each other's first names only. She objected to surnames, you see."

"Is that a portrait of her father?"

"The satyr? Yes."

"She painted him repeatedly, I'm told."

"We must remember, mustn't we, that grandfather died when she was three. So none of these likenesses are, how shall I put it? remembered.

Not done from life. One of my own earliest memories is how she studied photographs. With a magnifying glass. . . ."

Sylvia managed to appear both candid and rehearsed. This was not the first time she had conjured up such memories, and it would not be the last. He played the part of the polite inquiring stranger, and she the role of guide. She showed him where the poet slept and how her mother kept the curtains drawn thereafter; this was the one room of the house, Sylvia said, with curtains. That way air could enter while the room remained dark. She said her mother recollected sitting in a darkened room, hearing the poet cough out fairy tales to keep her amused. He whispered stanza after stanza of what sounded like a nonsense poem. Emmett was working, she knew; he was always working. He could not have produced so many volumes otherwise in such a short time; he was working when he climbed Mont Blanc or in the oarless rowboat he memorialized in "Spindrift."

His washstand stood untouched. The silver-backed brushes and combs had strands of what she assured him was her grandfather's hair. The mirror lay face downward on the tabletop. "All this may seem a little silly to you," Sylvia said. "But I tell myself I'm honoring my mother's wishes. And her memory." She hesitated. "Devotion. That doesn't seem so silly, does it?"

Martin had no answer. He picked up a book. It was leather-bound, a copy of *Transvaal and Other Purgatories*. "Devotion," Sylvia said again. "That's what this room represents. And why I want to maintain it. Not because of who lived here or how he died, but because my mother desired a father. . . ."

She stood so close to him he smelled the staleness of her breath. Her clothes gave off an odor also: turpentine. "You're a painter?" Martin asked.

"I paint a little. Yes."

"Is your studio here?"

"Not here," she said. "I wouldn't want to paint in this place. Not with Julie over my shoulder. All those witnesses."

She led him through the house. There were storage rooms and bedrooms and bathrooms, each decorated with the same lean face and goggle eyes. The portraits were in oil. They had been executed over a period of time sufficient for the style to change; they varied both in attitude and mood. At times the face was shown as that of a young celebrant, at times with the green pallor of age.

One portrait held his attention. It showed the poet in the likeness of a troubadour, wearing motley and plucking what appeared to be a man-dolin. The landscape was obscured by mist, but two trees—a cypress and an olive—grew together in the top right quadrant of the composition. A horse was suggested there also, tethered, grazing. The whole was eclectic, thick-fingered, but something in the wash of light evoked a courtly clarity, a man who saw the comedy in posturing yet nonetheless wore costumes.

So Julie had painted her father's face in many variations. What Martin could not tell and wanted to discover was if she had seen the comedy in things. If not, he thought, these paintings were the markers of a lifelong grief, a girl so blighted by her early loss that nothing thereafter could be transformed into gain. She did a series of portraits of Emmett at a cobbler's bench, with lightning in the window of the doorway at the left.

His sunburst of notoriety had soon enough been eclipsed; his name was no household's word but her own. Yet she painted him exclusively; she worked at nothing else. Her imagination had been hobbled as surely as if with a rope.

Sylvia offered him tea. He said, "With pleasure," and she said, "We could take it in the garden, if you'd like."

The garden was enclosed. There were straggling apple trees, rose beds and dahlias; mimosa grew through windows of what was once a potting shed. Beyond, in the hazy distance, he could make out a gray line of sea. There was a green ironwork table with a glass top. She conducted him to a chair, swiped at a bench with the hem of her smock and asked him, "Sugar, cream?"

"Please."

She poured from a dark green pot. His cup was chipped. He had an image, suddenly, of the editor in Boston who knew Emmett's toast to "Cumpany" by heart. The conjunction of this garden and that restaurant seemed fitting, like paired parentheses or an arc that comes full circle.

"You remain"—Sylvia paused—"compelled by my grand-father also."

"Yes." He tasted the tea.

"You suggested in your letter that your visit here was motivated by something more than curiosity. . . ."

He nodded. There was a small sunken pool, with lilies, and a bronze frog squatting in its center. We never quite end where we planned, he thought; the corner post is two degrees off true.

"An article?"

"A book," he said. "I'd thought of a biography."

"Yes."

"But you're against it, aren't you?"

"Biography." She watched him. "It's all so very long ago."

"One doesn't feel that in this house."

"Perhaps not. No."

"You *are* against it, aren't you?"

"Yes."

Martin drank. "If you'd permit me," he said, "I'd like to buy a portrait."

"Which?"

"The troubadour in the workroom."

"There was a film," she said. "You know it, surely: Harold Emmett inventing sonnets in the sunset."

"I've seen it," Martin said.

"It bothered Julie very much. The terms of her will were so stringent. She thought it, oh, an invasion of privacy."

"Hers?"

"His too, I imagine. I'm so sorry." She placed her hand on his. Her fingernails were bitten, broken. "The pictures aren't for sale."

They sat for some moments in silence. A cat emerged and made for Sylvia; it rubbed against her legs. She fed it cream from her saucer. The cat was large, long-haired. "What do you call it?" Martin asked.

"Artemis." She stirred the sugar in her cup, added cream and did not drink. "She used to have a brother, but now we're both alone."

That night in the Old Rectory, he tried to see a pattern in the houses he had seen. There was a weatherboard cottage, a bungalow that emulated a ship's cabin, a ruin, a shrine. There was his cabin by the Allagash and his apartment on Fresh Pond—subleased to a lawyer now who would be unwilling to leave. Martin lit a Davidoff cigarillo; he sat in the upholstered chair. His bedroom had a lithograph of Rye as envisioned in medieval times. The harbor beneath the walled port was crowded with vessels; it was market day. There were cows and pigs and women hawking bread. Above, on the last parapet, there was pageantry. A lady with a flowing scarf leaned forward to gaze at her knight.

Emmett was committed to the forms of chivalry, and he used them often. His "Virelay on the Whippet" urged the heraldic mode. "Winchelsea" was populated by ladies whose bright eyes reflected the sails of an incoming fleet. "A proper man," he wrote, "is one who has fathered a son, built a house and completed a book."

Martin raised the window. Outside, a light rain fell. He felt again, in the rented room, how much he was a trespasser. It had not been intentional. He had hoped to be a witness. But he had witnessed nothing pertinent, no scene that seemed to require him. The lamplight from his window illuminated air. Emmett's teaching had been suicide; he was better left alone. We each must learn to die; exampling helps only a little. Of the three accomplishments of manhood, Martin had managed two—and if he had not fathered a child, that was a function less of chastity than prophylaxis.

He heard the bells of Northiam Church. He shut his eyes and saw again how Granny Emmett hung from ropes, jumping in sequence, her slight weight suspended. He would not remain. He would pack and return in the morning. He would tell the editor that Emmett was a bird of passage and had flown from dark to dark. Those warming themselves by the fire had shivered for an instant only. "Christ," they said, "the wind turns ugly." Then they huddled to the hearth again and held out their hands.

About My Table

TO THE MEMORY OF JOHN GARDNER

DEATH VISITED HIM daily. He did what he could to deny it but could not avert his eyes. Headlines blazoned and newscasters announced it: bombs and strangulations and cancer were the news. Arson increased. The alarm in his smoke detectors at home whistled at him shrilly for no apparent reason in the night.

The engines of war were well oiled. Animals were slaughtered, and the slaughter was called business or a by-product of progress or sport. His Golden retriever, deaf in the right ear, failed to notice a Toyota Celica and was crushed. Torture was a commonplace, and terror; the models in the toothpaste ads grinned at him mirthlessly. What he saw behind the rictus was the skull.

Daniel was thirty-eight. He was not by nature meditative and not, his doctor assured him, ill. "You're under the weather, that's all. Stop pushing. Get more exercise." His doctor, Chester Allen, was a paddle-tennis buff; paddle tennis helped him mightily, he said.

"All right."

"It's the weather," Chester said again. "It's those revolutions. How long have you been back from—where was it—Nicaragua?"

"Fifteen months."

As if that were the appropriate answer, Chester nodded and told him to dress.

The winter had been brutal; pipes froze. For the first twenty days of the year, the temperature failed to reach zero; it was thirty below every night. In cold like that, he told himself, all things must wither and shrivel. The weather bureau reported it as the second coldest January since the start of record-keeping; the pattern of upper-air currents had changed. The frost went six feet deep. The slope of his wife's shoulders had lost its youthful buoyancy; his breath was stale. Rats scuttled in the basement; he found their corpses in the disused cistern by the pump. These he fished out with a trout net and, holding the net at its full extent, walked them to the woods behind the house.

Adriana, their daughter, turned four years old on Sunday, March 8. They gave a birthday party. She had friends from day-care and the neighborhood; nine little girls arrived. She was passionate for tootsie rolls; therefore Ann had baked a cake in the shape of a tootsie roll. Two feet long, a roulage with fudge icing and a red design that followed the tootsie roll pattern, the cake was a success. He took photographs. Adriana could scarcely contain herself; she climbed the chair at the head of the table before they were ready to eat.

He offered Bloody Marys to the mothers. They praised his special secret ingredient, and he said it was no secret, just horseradish. Sun slanted through the picture window, illuminating everything so that he needed no flash. The woodstove was hot. Adriana said, "You're the best daddy in the world."

He felt both charmed and flattered, though he knew the phrase had been designed to please him. Her voice rose; she announced this to her company. "My daddy's the best daddy in the world." The women smiled; their daughters appeared unconcerned. Ann put on a record, and they played "Pass the Apple" till the music stopped and whoever held the apple lost. They then played musical chairs.

This was not easy with four-year-olds; Daniel slowed the pace. The girls would clamber to their chairs and sit there for a moment, as if ascent was what mattered, and location. They switched seats reluctantly. Ann had decorated the room with streamers and balloons and a paper cutout, hung from rafters, with Adriana's name. Each letter was a different color, except for the three yellow A's. He smiled at Ann. "You're the best mommy," he said, "in the whole wide world."

"Darling," she said.

He stopped the music. There were three girls standing in the center of the circle, and two empty chairs. Adriana, rapt, was watching her tootsie roll cake. "This isn't working," he said.

"No."

"Let's let them all be winners."

"Fine." Ann clapped her hands to get the girls' attention. She said that everyone would get a prize, that musical chairs was a silly game anyhow— who wanted to be the winner, if winning meant you were the only one left? "Let's get these chairs back to the table," she said. "Let's eat cake."

She lit the candles. They sang, "Happy birthday, Adriana." The fifth candle, Daniel saw, was a trick candle; it could not be blown out. It sat apart from the four candles signifying her age, and when she blew it guttered down, then sprang back into flame again. "That means good luck," he told her. "That's a good-luck sign."

So then Ann sliced the tootsie roll, and he added ice cream and passed around the plates. There was pizza for the adults, and Champagne. Pouring, Daniel realized that there were sixteen women in the room. He took no pleasure in this but instead felt out of place, as if his chosen comrades had left him for a meeting of some consequence. They were making for a battlefield; he alone was left behind. They were wounded; they were playing poker; they were inspecting ships. The mothers laughed and chatted and emptied their glasses and threw back their hair.

"What's the matter?" Ann approached.

"Nothing."

"What is it?"

"These children," he said. "These beautiful, clean children." He indicated where they sat. "I wish that this could last."

"It lasts," she said. "In memory." She touched his arm. "In those photographs you're forgetting to take." She moved off to the table, dispensing Coca-Cola and apple juice and chocolate milk; Adriana wanted all three.

Yet death comes unannounced, he knew, and holds dominion everywhere. The news next day included a memorial to a lyricist Daniel had interviewed once. They played his songs. They said he had been a committed civil libertarian, a spokesman for the underdog who cried out against repression and the power structure. Daniel remembered, mostly, a spry old man in yellow slacks who wrote about the rural poor—coal miners, apple pickers—for Broadway and for Hollywood. He played nine holes of golf every day. He confided to Daniel that he—like everybody of his generation, like anybody who cared about language and wasn't a plain fool—had started out a poet. He'd intended to outlast John Keats. But Keats died in his twenties, a pauper, and he was in his seventies and rich. There's ways and ways, he'd said; I turn out a good limerick from time to time these mornings. I find my satisfaction where I can.

They were drinking by the swimming pool; Daniel had stayed for the night. The lyricist's new wife said, "You don't mind," not making it a question, and removed her bikini top. "I wrote one good song anyhow," his host announced. "Back in the McCarthy days. You're too young to remember what it was really like."

"I watched the hearings," Daniel said. "I admired Joseph Welch."

"But it was just a TV show. If you never met McCarthy, if you never knew the man . . ." His voice trailed off. He was watching his wife do a back dive, then a steady Australian crawl. She flipped again at the pool's near end and commenced the backstroke for a length.

"Which song was that?" Daniel asked.

"They cut it from the show. 'Too risky,' my producer told me. 'Too much a matter of taste.'" He sighed; he rubbed his legs. "It doesn't matter, really, it's all about that fascist and what he did to *Robert's Rules*. That's what I called it, '*Robert's Rules*.' You know, the 'point of order' stuff, the 'point of information, Mr. Chairman,' while you ruin a man's life." He sang, in a thin tenor, "'Do you still beat your wife?'"

She was emerging from the pool, dripping, glistening. She returned to the board and did a front half gainer.

"Tell me," Daniel asked, "why you let them cut it out. If it was a political statement, I mean, and if you knew it was good?"

"It wasn't. Who'd fall for that old gag?" The songwriter finished his drink. "Besides, we didn't need it."

"No?"

"McCarthy croaked," he said. "A week before we opened in New York."

The profile wrote itself. He was an amiable person, with the desire to please. His wife was provocative, he sprightly; they made an impressive pair. Daniel presented it that way anyhow, though he had had his doubts. The dapper little millionaire, with his vegetable extracts and exercise machines, seemed more fearful of extinction than he had cared to admit. He died, the radio announcer said, in his home in Beverly Hills; we all will miss his lyrics and the dream of a community he urged us all to share. Children in every town in America sing his songs of hope. The tribute ended with a chorus from his famous "Goodnight, Gus." They played the original cast version: "Goodnight You and Me and Us."

Thursday morning he read of a death that touched him far more deeply. Theodore Hatch died "after a brief illness" in New York. He was survived by his wife, the former Elizabeth Cummings, two sons and four grandchildren. For twenty years he had been editor in chief of the magazine that offered Daniel his first job. A memorial service was to be conducted at the Princeton Club that Saturday; in lieu of flowers, contributions could be made to the Heart Fund.

"Look at this," he said to Ann.

"At what?"

He tore the page across and handed her the article. She looked at Hatch's picture, dated 1968. "Oh, *no* . . ." She bent her head.

"Heart trouble, I imagine. I didn't know he'd been ill."

"You should go to New York for the service."

"Yes. We all could, if you'd like."

They reminisced at breakfast about the editor's brusque integrity. Daniel had been wary of the man. Then one summer Ann and he went for a week to Martha's Vineyard; they found themselves on an adjacent tennis court to Mr. and Mrs. Hatch's. When the younger couple's court time had elapsed, they were invited for mixed doubles. In tennis clothes, Hatch proved less prepossessing; he had a paunch and knobby knees and trouble at the net. Daniel's first serve was too strong; he therefore used his second serve continually. He worried as to whether this could be construed a compliment or insult, a breach of etiquette. Later, they had cocktails.

"I noticed," said the editor, "you've been holding back a bit."

"No. Why?"

"That serve. You didn't have to slice it every time."

Daniel made no answer. The silence that followed, however, was comfortable, as if the elder man took pleasure in the junior's prowess—a pleasure laced with pride at his own acumen in hiring and ability to see through what was after all a gesture of respect. When he and Ann left the Vineyard, Daniel received instructions as to the best way back, and that autumn he received his first feature assignment. It was a cover story on the underground railway to Canada, the draft resisters' network and a clearing house for Vietnam deserters.

When they moved to New Hampshire in 1977, Daniel made a living as a freelance journalist. Yet Hatch retained a shaping hand, a sure assessment of intention. They would meet for lunch. Daniel listened to tales about Virginia, the first time Hatch had seen the sea and what that illimitable blue vista had appeared to promise. It was a promise, Hatch confessed, undelivered by his stint in the Pacific in the war. He still looked for gun emplacements on each beach. Those day sailors out of Edgartown got on his nerves; the outboard motors were worse. Every time he saw some idiot with a gin and tonic on a stinkpot, Hatch hoped the thing would sink.

He grew increasingly cranky. His sons were in Australia, doing God knew what. He complained that all this hoopla about "investigative journalism" was new dogs up to old tricks. He himself, he said, had been born with a hatred of grand-standing; he couldn't help it, it was like an extra thumb. Hatch told Daniel of his disagreements with the publisher, his concern for his wife's health—she had one kidney and one lung. He offered rambling anecdotes about Puerto Ricans and Irishmen and Poles and Jews and Canucks. But at the end of every lunch, Daniel felt as if he—not his companion—had been loose-tongued and too talkative; he felt unburdened, always, as they puffed at their cigars.

"I wish we'd known," said Ann. "We could have visited."

"I'll call Elizabeth," he said. "I'll tell her how sorry we are."

"Yes. I wish he'd wanted company."

"'Of a brief illness,'" Daniel said. "That means it wasn't cancer. Or not a long one anyhow."

"You ought to go," she said. "On Saturday, I mean."

That afternoon the weather changed; the breeze bore the mild hints of spring. The sky was blue; the ground yielded under his feet. The shadows in the valley sported highlights of deep green. It was sugaring weather, and the sugarhouse at the base of the mountain was sending white plumes skyward. Adriana, back from day-care, asked him why did maples bleed.

"A tree's blood is called sap," he said. "It doesn't hurt the tree."

"Blood isn't always red," she told him.

"No?"

"Blue. It's blue inside you till it gets outside. And that's when it turns colors."

"What a lot you learned today."

"I learned it from Mommy," she said. "Mommy says a tree feels better to know it gets put on pancakes."

"Would you like to see them sugaring?"

She nodded.

"When?"

"Tomorrow, Mommy promised. Or the day that you go to New York."

"Let's all go tomorrow," he said.

She turned from him to enter the house, and he had a vision of her mangled, bullet-riddled body after an attack. He shut his eyes. The indiscriminate killing, the chemical spraying, detention camp, assassination—all the menace and brutality he'd reported on elsewhere seemed come to this valley to haunt him. His daughter, his precious four-year-old hostage to fortune, his sweet and trustful witness—Daniel shook his head to clear it. He exhaled and touched his toes. He picked up fallen branches and made a pile of kindling and carried kindling to the door. He carried two-foot lengths of oak and ash from the stacked wood by the parking lot to the breezeway by the mud room. He was hot from his exertions when at last he went inside.

The third death came next day. Robert Entemann and he had met in college, and the friendship had endured. They kept in touch by letter and the phone. Robert worked for public television out of Boston; he had volunteered for Vietnam. Like Daniel and the others of their graduating class, he had been against the war. But Robert came from military stock and was even more opposed to letting poor blacks fight the battles of the generals and congressmen. He served with the marines until Khe Sanh. He was released with shrapnel in his prostate gland, a knife scar on the right side of his neck that missed the windpipe by two inches, and, he said to Daniel, more information than he wanted about how to make things explode. That can of kerosene, for instance, and that garden fertilizer there—Robert clicked his tongue. They'd kept him for five months in Walter Reed. He still had trouble sleeping, and he hated it when helicopters buzzed the beach.

In the fall of 1980, Daniel wrote on the campaign. He visited Marietta,

Ohio, where Candidate Reagan was giving a speech. He was booked into the Lafayette Hotel—a brick pile at the confluence of the Ohio and Muskingum rivers. The town had been named, he learned, in honor of Marie Antoinette. Lafayette had landed on the banks of the Muskingum, thereby instituting tourism from France. This was the place the Northwest Territory called its capital, a place to be proud to call home. Daniel was invited to admire the gun rack in the lobby and the authentic relics of the steamboat days. He was shown the high-water mark on the stairwell, from the year of the great flood.

It was Reagan country, Daniel knew; the circumstance and pageantry left no doubt of that. He had heard the speech before and would hear it again in the morning; he decided to take the night off. He walked down Front Street to an establishment named *The Becky Thatcher*. A paddle-wheeler, it rode in the brown water, with a gangway for the customers to cross. *The Becky Thatcher* had been painted blue and gold and white; there were gaslights in the bar.

He sat on a red leather stool. He ordered a J & B, double. Robert entered. "I can't believe it, Dan," he said. They embraced. "It's been too long," they said. Robert said, let's just not leave this tub, let's have our dinner right here. Where are you staying? Daniel asked, and he said, down the road a bit, in that awful motor inn. They laughed; they were registered for the same floor. I need a friend, said Robert, I couldn't take another night with forty thousand cheerleaders. He's going to win, you know.

All through the meal, the shock of having met in this strange place remained. They took a corner table; Robert took the corner seat. They joked that it was neither coincidence nor fate but only the same travel agent. The food was surprisingly good. They talked about their college years and agreed to go together to the next reunion. Robert was tired, he said; he was either on expense account or eating out of cans.

He drew his hand across his eyes; he'd fallen for a married woman once again. She was a real estate broker from Ipswich, and he ought to have his head examined. How was Daniel's family? he asked; he would like to visit sometime soon and see what a real family was like. Ann and Adriana, Daniel, said, were fine, When Adriana had been born, Robert sent two dozen long-stemmed roses to the hospital The note read, "May she have her mother's looks, and her mother's brains."

"You're welcome," Daniel said. "Whenever."

"Thanks."

"I mean it. Deer season. Whenever. If you like to ski . . ."

"There's Harvey and Judy," Robert said. "I ought to see them too. Mostly they just come to the big city and watch me at the studio and wish it was a quiz show so they'd get to be contestants."

"And win prizes," Daniel said. Judy, Robert's sister, had married Harvey Williams, the CPA in town. When he and Ann had first arrived, Daniel looked them up. "My crazy kid brother," said Judy. "And his crazy friends."

A tug maneuvered past. It blew its whistle several times. *The Becky Thatcher* rocked.

"I heard a funny thing today. They send more coal and limestone down this river," Robert said, "more tonnage every year than travels the Suez Canal. Or possibly the Panama Canal. I can't remember which."

They would not meet again.

Ann and Daniel married on a clear September morning in Vermont. They were married by a justice of the peace, beneath an elm tree at Ann's parents' country house. Then there was a scheduled reception at an inn two miles away. He was twenty-eight, she twenty-six; they both had been giddy with need. He drove her to the party but they detoured down an unpaved lane and parked in a small turning and made love. He kissed her fingers, then the ring. She pulled her wedding dress above her hips and sat on top of him in the front seat, so as not to appear, later, too badly disarrayed. While she rocked above him and the car rocked to their motion, he noticed, he felt, everything: the perfect square of beauty marks on her arching neck, the color of the maples, the scent of pine and of her perfume, and the startled songbirds disrupted into flight. She was heart-stoppingly his darling, and he told her so. She held him when they finished with a calm unyieldingness; she never ever wanted this to end. She rearranged her stockings, he his pants. They were married, they assured each other, in sickness and in health, and they could be a little late to the receiving line.

When they visited her parents the next year, Daniel drove to see the place. It was not there. He tried again, and with the same result. He became superstitious about it; he knew absolutely where they'd turned and how far they had had to go and where the deer had leaped the puddle, skittering away. He remembered how she looked at him when he proposed they park, how he switched off the ignition and the engine's tick-tock cooling while his own breath quickened, as did hers. But he could not find the spot. He hunted it repeatedly; there was no exit from the road between the house and inn. In time he came to see this as a compliment to Ann: without her, he was lost.

Tonight, Daniel promised in the morning, he would make a lucky Friday of this Friday the thirteenth; dinner was to be his treat. He wanted to make Ann a romantic and excellent meal. They staved off boredom that way, sometimes, taking turns as chef.

So after the fish store in town received its shipment, he bought oysters and lobster and shrimp. He next went to the health food shop for fresh asparagus. He then went to the Gourmet Shoppe and ranged along its aisles, looking for the bread and cheese and ladyfingers and lemons and cherries he required. It was raining, a chill, solid rain. The wheels on his shopping cart squealed.

His accountant stood by the cereal shelf. "Hey, buddy," Harvey Williams said. "Have you ever eaten this stuff? What's it like?"

He held out a carton of Swiss Familia—Müsli—for inspection. Daniel told him it was excellent with fruit.

"Judy's gone to Boston," Harvey said. "Or yours truly wouldn't be here. I can't tell Post Toasties from Hostess Twinkies now. It's all a rip-off anyway: you pay more for the product with fewer additives."

Daniel agreed. "What's Judy doing in Boston?"

Harvey positioned the Familia in his cart. "I thought you'd heard."

"No. What?"

"I'm sorry." Harvey looked at him. "I just assumed you knew."

"Knew?"

"Robert," Harvey said. "He was blown up by a package Wednesday night."

He straightened.

"Some son of a bitch," Harvey said. "Some absolutely total stranger sends him a *plastique*. He opens it and . . ." The accountant raised his arm, then made a fist. "I hope they catch the bastard. I hope the bastard dies."

He did not trust his voice. "They know it's a stranger?" he asked.

"I've got to run." The accountant consulted his watch. "When Judy gets back, come on over. She'll tell you what she can."

"I'd be grateful," Daniel said.

They wheeled their purchases to the cash register, Harvey first. He paid and left. Then Daniel did the same and sprinted to the car. On the front seat, a lobster had worked loose from its wet bag. It waved its hammer claw at him, but the claw was pegged and threatless and he shoved the lobster back.

Storm clouds masked the sugarhouse; he drove the final mile in snow. A spasm of revulsion seized him at the fork before his home. He had been jailed once, hungry once, and shot at from a distance several times. This did not make him a hero. He had political convictions that were eroding steadily, and a sense of outrage that was mere plaintiveness now. Three people he had known had died within the week. Yet his reactions had been self-regarding, self-obsessed—as if he, Daniel, and not they had been confronted with mortality. He took the whole thing personally, privately, as though he alone in all this land might mourn. He gripped the wheel. Two men had died in the fullness of time, and he thought about the widow of the one, the failure of the other to invite a deathbed talk. A friend who had reported on the increment of violence became an additional victim; Daniel wondered if they'd failed each other, when and how and where.

He thought about the lives they lived, this business of reportage, until they themselves were news. He had written, lately, on a football game in Tennessee where the players soaked the field beforehand so as to make certain it was mud. Then they used a piglet for the ball. He had written on a helium balloon race, a cockfighting syndicate, settlers in the desert who called themselves survivalists and were stockpiling arms. Robert had reported on the danger to the aquifers, the high-school boy from Newton who was blinded by a bear, Atlanta, outmoded radar systems, and an outbreak of plague in the hills. A tow truck, downshifting, roared past.

At home, he told Ann what he'd learned. He went into no details since he had none to tell. Adriana was watching TV. Ernie and the Cookie Monster were capering for joy. Someone spoke to them in Spanish, which they were delighted to acquire. Munitions makers thrived. Ann held him, and they stood together in the kitchen. What he saved out for the compost heap would keep a tribe from starving. "Someone called," she said. "From *Esquire*. They wondered if you'd like to do a story on El Salvador. I told them you'd call back."

"I'll call," he said. "But the answer is no."

"It's all around us, isn't it?"

He nodded. He set about preparing the asparagus and shrimp. "I'll go to New York in the morning," he said. "And come home via Boston."

"Yes."

"Let's have a drink." He opened a bottle of wine.

"Please."

Something scurried in the walls. "Your health," he said.

"And yours."

"Should we get another dog?"

"Not yet," she said. "I don't think I could handle it."

Big Bird appeared. He was cajoling a puppet in a garbage can. He danced with the garbage can lid. The roll of photographs he'd taken at Adriana's party had been developed, Ann said. The shots were wonderful. There was one of Adriana with her mouth so stuffed with cake it looked like she'd swallowed the tootsie roll whole. There was one with her cheeks puckered, ready to blow out the candles, that made her look like a chipmunk, adorable.

He looked up to see her crying. "It's awful," Ann said. "It's so awful."

"Not everything."

"It is."

He set himself to comfort her. Death visited him nightly. It comes when it will come. It could be a furnace malfunction, allergic reaction, rabid bat, oncoming drunk in a van in his lane, suicide, undiagnosed leukemia, handgun in a shopping mall, pilot error, stroke, the purposive assault of some unrecognized opponent, earth, air, water, flame.

THE WRITERS' TRADE

For Willard Boepple

Contents

The Writers' Trade

M ARK FUSCO SOLD his novel when he was twenty-two. "You're a very fortunate young man," Bill Winterton proclaimed. They met in the editor's office, on the sixteenth floor. The walls were lined with photographs, book jackets, and caricatures. "You should be pleased with yourself."

He was. He had moved from apprentice to author with scarcely a hitch in his stride. It was 1967, and crucial to be young. One of the caricatures showed Hawthorne on a polo pony, meeting Henry James; their mallets were quill pens. They were swinging with controlled abandon at the letter A.

Bill Winterton took him to lunch. They ate at L'Armorique. The editor discoursed on luck; the luck of the draw, he maintained, comes to those who read their cards. He returned the first bottle of wine, a Pouilly Fumé. The sommelier deferred, but the second bottle also tasted faintly of garlic; the sommelier disagreed. They had words. "There's someone cooking near your glassware," Winterton declared. "Or you've got your glasses drying near the garlic pan."

He was proved correct. The maître d'hôtel apologized and congratulated him on his discerning nose. The meal was on the restaurant; they were grateful for Winterton's help. This pleased him appreciably; he preened. He spoke about the care and nurturing of talent, the ability to locate and preserve it. Attention to detail and standards—these were the tools of his trade. This was the be-all and end-all, the alpha and omega of publishing, he said.

Mark began his book in college, in a writing class. His father came from Florence and told tales about the family—the Barone P. P. who thought he had swallowed a sofa, the passion for clocks his aunt indulged obsessively, the apartment in Catania where they sent the younger sons. Of these characters he made his story, fashioning a treasure hunt: the grandmother from Agrigento whom the northern cousins spurned, the legacy she failed to leave but set her children hunting. He borrowed his father's inflections; his ear was good, eye accurate, and the book had pace. He completed a draft in six months. Then the work of revision began.

Bill Winterton was forty-five and given to hyperbole. He had been a black belt in karate in Korea; he had known Tallulah Bankhead well, and Blossom Dearie; he had heard Sam Beckett discourse on Jimmy Joyce. He drank and lived in Rhinecliff and was working on a novel of his own. Mark's book was slated to appear the second Sunday of July. "That's the first novelist season," Winterton informed him. "Coming out time for the debs. We want to get attention while the big boys are off at the beach. Not to worry . . ." He flourished his spoon.

Mark worked that summer in Wellfleet, at a bicycle rental garage by the harbor; he also served ice cream. He spent long hours clamming at low tide. He liked the brief defined conviviality of work, the casual commerce with strangers. He rented the upstairs apartment of what had been a captain's house. "Everybody was in whaling," said his landlady, Mrs. Newcombe. "All the men in Wellfleet." She meant, he learned later, in 1700. Her house had a large widow's walk, and furniture and ornaments from the China trade.

He was sleeping with the daughter of a real estate agent in town. Bonnie returned from her sophomore year at Simmons to find the local boys inadequate; they whistled and hooted at tourists, and lounged on the Town Office steps. They made peace signs and shouted "Flower Power!" and wore ponytails. They went drag racing on the sand and passed out drinking beer. She was small and blonde and sweetly submissive and had hazel eyes. Her father would kill her, she said.

Mark had read that writers lived along the ponds. He saw them on Main Street, buying papers or fish, sporting beards. He watched them strolling on the dock, wearing caps at jaunty angles, smoking pipes. He heard them at The Lighthouse, conversing over coffee, and at the public library, where they donated books. He told himself he too would be a man with a mission, aloof.

His room had a view of the dock. He had a double bed with a board beneath the mattress and brass bars painted white; he had a chest of drawers and a rolltop desk beneath the window. He organized the pigeon-holes, the stacks of twenty-weight paper, the marmalade jar full of pens. The paraphernalia of habit codified, that summer, into ritual observance. He made himself strong coffee on a hot plate; he bought a blue tin cup. He played solitaire. This permitted him, he felt, to stay at his desk without restlessness; it engaged his hands but not attention. He could sit for hours, dealing cards.

He wrote his pages rapidly, then rewrote at length. The little ecstasy of correction, the page reworked if a syllable seemed inexact, or missing, the change of a comma that felt consequential, the tinkering and achieved finality: all this was new to Mark. He recited paragraphs aloud. He read chapters to the mirror, conscious of inflection, rhythm, emphasis. He blackened the blank pages with a sense of discovered delight.

Mrs. Newcombe's parlor shelf had Roger Tory Peterson and *Songs the Whalemen Sang*. An ancestor had figured in Thoreau's *Cape Cod*. She owned *The House of the Seven Gables* in a leather-bound edition; she had instruction books on quilting and *Just So Stories for Little Children* and *The Fountainhead*. He loved the smell and heft of books, the look of endpapers, the crackle of pages and literal flavor of print. He loved the way words edged against each other, the clashing, jangling sounds they made, the bulk of paragraphs and linear austerity of speech. He recited lines while driving or at Fort Hill gathering mussels; they formed his shoreline certainties while he watched the tide. A phrase like "shoreline certainties," for instance, seemed luminous with meaning; it served as his companion while he shuffled cards.

At Columbia he argued philosophy and baseball with his suite mates; he ate spareribs at midnight and went to double features at the Thalia and New Yorker and took his laundry home. His thesis had been focused on Karenin and Casaubon—the stiff unyielding husbands in *Anna Karenina* and *Middlemarch*. There were parallels, also, between Vronsky and Ladis-law, those weak romancing men. The question most urgently posed, he wrote, is how to live a life alone when urged by a secular power to succeed, a secular temptation to accede—or, as Lewis Carroll put it, "Will you, won't you join the dance?"

We each have known conviction, the sudden flush of rightness; Mark came to feel it then. His book had a blue cover and its title was handsomely lettered. A bird ascended—framed by temple columns—from the sea. The stages of production grew familiar. But that his work would be transformed—that strangers in another town would take his words and reproduce them—this careful rendering in multiples provided his first sense of public presence, the work existing elsewhere also. We grow used to the private response. When someone speaks our name we assume we are nearby to hear. We answer questions asked; we find ourselves aroused by provocation, flattered by flattery, angered by insult—part of a nexus of action and talk. But his career, he understood, was in the hands of strangers—someone who might read the book to whom he had not handed it, someone who might help or hinder from an indifferent distance. The recognition startled Mark. He was the master of his soul, perhaps, but not the captain of his fate. He was reading Joseph Conrad and could recite Henley's "Invictus"; such comparatives came readily to mind.

"I don't know you," Bonnie said.

"Of course you do."

"No. Not any longer."

"I haven't changed," he said.

"You're changing. Yes, you are."

She turned her back to him. It was beautiful, unblemished; he traced the white ridge of her spine. She shivered.

"I'll only be away three days."

"You won't come back."

"Of course I will."

"I mean you won't come back to me." She fingered the pillow.

"Make up something for your parents. That way you could come along."

"No."

"We'll figure something out."

"I wanted to be at the party. I'm so proud of you. A publication party. I did want to celebrate."

"You'll be there anyhow," he lied. "You go with me where I go."

"Parting is sweet sorrow . . .'"

"'Such sweet sorrow,'" he corrected her. Mark flushed at his involuntary pedantry and—to counteract the rightness of her accusation—pressed her back down in the bed. She was all the more exciting when she cried.

His parents had scheduled a party. They were proud of his achievement and would celebrate on publication day. They lived in Rye, New York. His father took the train to Manhattan, working for an import-export firm. He dealt in bristles, hides, and furs; he placed orders for Kolinski, Chunking 21/4, Arctic fox, and seal. They were moderately prosperous and happy, they told him, to help. His job at the bicycle shop was therefore part time, a gesture; he drove an MG. It was British Racing Green, a graduation gift. "From here on," he promised his mother, "I'm enrolled in the school of real life."

She thought this phrase enchanting. Much of what he said enchanted her—his pronouncements on fashion, for instance, his sense of the cartographer as artist, mapping the imagined world from its available features. She had two vodka martinis every afternoon at five; he joined her on the porch.

"My son the poet," she said.

"Except it's fiction, Mom."

"You'll always be a poet." She swallowed the olive intact.

His mother liked occasions. She was not sociable and did not attend parties herself. But she welcomed the caterers' bustle at home, the porch festooned with lanterns, the garden sprouting tables and white plastic chairs. She gave birthday and anniversary parties, graduation parties, wedding parties. The house was large. She felt less lonely entertaining, she explained; they should put the place to use. She asked him for a guest list six weeks in advance.

He listed friends from Columbia, his editor, the publicity woman, his cousin, a classmate from high school who was an all-night D.J. His father invited business associates; his mother included the children or parents of friends. She disliked a party at which everyone knew everyone; a party ought to take you by surprise.

She made a habit of pronouncements, and then repeated them. One such repeated assertion had to do with variety, the spice of life, the way ingredients invariably vary. He humored her. He had come to recognize his parents needed humoring; his father's politics, for instance, had to be avoided when they met. His father admired Judge Julius Hoffman. He wished the judge had thrown the book at those impertinent Chicago-based conspirators; he was afraid of Hoffman's leniency, he said. He trusted Mark. He knew his son refused to bite the feeding hand.

On the Sunday of the party, he drove from Wellfleet to Rye. Trucks rumbled past at speed. He reached the Sagamore Bridge in a sudden cloudburst and pulled off the road to raise the convertible top. Tugs whistled in the canal; Mark saw the line squall receding. His book was coming out that day; he would celebrate that night. He opened his shirt to the rain.

There was much weekend traffic; he made New London by ten. He wondered if the tollbooth tenders worked eight-hour shifts. They would take coffee breaks. They would bring a heater with them in winter, soft drinks in Styrofoam cups; they would have portable radios for music and the news. They would have a grandson in Spokane. This grandson played the drums. Mark was learning to provide corroborative detail for his characters: birthday parties, a distaste for lima beans, a preference in socks. "Make a catalogue," his writing teacher had advised. "Make it on three-by-five cards. Know everything you can. Tell yourself the person despises lima beans. Try to decide if she likes snow peas or string beans better, and if she wears a girdle, and if she sleeps soundly at night."

He took the turnoff after Playland and reached his house by two. It was a sprawling half-timbered slate-roofed structure; there was a three-car garage. His mother met him at the kitchen door. "Congratulations," she said.

"I made it," Mark said, stretching. "Six hours on the nose."

"It's a wonderful review."

"What is?"

"You didn't know?"

He shook his head.

"A beautiful review," she said. "In this morning's Sunday *Times*. I thought they would have told you."

"No."

"They must have planned to make it a surprise. It's wonderful. You'll see."

The pantry was filled with salads. There were trays of deviled eggs. The review was prominent, and generous; he had heard of the reviewer, and she made much of his book. "Classic and unmannered cadences," she wrote. "Fidelity of mind and spirit, a tale told with economy and grace."

The novel avoided those pitfalls young writers so rarely avoid; she hailed "an auspicious debut." His mother clapped her hands. "They've been calling all day long," she said. "We tried you up in Wellfleet but you'd gone already. Everyone who's anyone reads the Sunday *Times*."

We all have been assessed in public, whether by report card, hiring, or review. Our system incorporates rank. We are used to reading how we've done, what we are doing, and in which percentile. But this was new and newly exciting—far more so than the notice in trade journals earlier. He had never heard of the *Library Journal* or *The Kirkus Reviews* prior to their praise. To read himself described as "brilliantly inventive," "persuasively original," was a "heady, yet heartfelt experience"; he took his duffel to his room, and then he showered and changed.

His parents knew an author who wrote children's books. Ernest the dog was anything but earnest—was, in fact, mischief itself. Ernest got into and barely escaped from trouble; he was a cross between a dachshund and Dalmatian—known as a dachmatian to his friends. Mark, nine, disliked the books. His parents thought them cute, however, and gave him *Ernest in the Monkeyhouse*, *Ernest Goes to Boarding School*, *Ernest and the Alligator Swamp*. There were elaborate inscriptions from the author for his birthday, for Christmas, or when he was sick. Ernest had a pal called Busy Bee. They helped each other out—when Ernest was being chased by the men from the dog pound, for instance, Busy Bee distracted them; when Busy Bee was slated for the honeymill, Ernest picked the lock.

One day the author came to lunch. His name was Harold Weber, and he had a big white beard and was completely bald. Like one of his own characters, he wore a blue velvet vest. His wife, who died three years before, had been Mark's mother's cousin; they kept distantly in touch. Harold Weber drove a Lancia; his father admired the car. "This is your biggest fan," he said, presenting Mark. "He knows *Ernest Goes to Boarding School* by heart. And *The Frying Pan and Fire*. It's his favorite."

That November had been blustery; the last dark leaves of the Japanese maple beat at the bay window. Branches blew past. His father said, "Let's have a fire," and a voice from the chimney said, "Wait!" "What's that?" his father asked. "Wait, won't you?" called the voice. "I have to get my family out first. We fell asleep."

Mark approached the fireplace and put his ear to the wall. "Hello, little boy; what's your name?" He turned to his parents, shocked. "I've got it—you must be Mark. Ernest told me all about you. You're his favorite person on all Echo Lane." Then the voice changed register, grew gruff. "Hello, Mark. How've you been? Tell them not to start that fire till I get Busy Bee out."

Harold Weber leaned against the mantelpiece. He was smiling; his mouth moved slightly, and his Adam's apple worked. Yet the voice came from the chimney, not where he stood beneath it. Mark said, "You're doing that," and Harold Weber bent, shaking his bald head, raking his beard with his fingers, looking up the fireplace and saying from what seemed like the window, "He's not."

Then there were drinks. There were cheese biscuits and shrimp with plastic toothpicks impaling them on a cabbage, so it looked as if the cabbage grew multicolored quills. "Don't poke me," said the cabbage. "I get ticklish if you poke." Then the cabbage giggled, and Harold Weber laughed. "I guess we'll have that fire," he said to Mark's father. "I guess Ernest helped old Busy Bee to get his family out." "I guess," agreed Mark's father, and they laughed and swallowed shrimp.

That day he knew he'd witnessed magic—not the poor ventriloquy but the invented voice. A creature from a page had spoken to him, Mark, from a familiar place. He adored Harold Weber through lunch.

The party started at six. His father's business partners, his uncle from Arezzo, his neighbors arrived. They congratulated him. They offered wine and a leather-bound notebook and a subscription to *The New York Review of Books* and champagne. His sister's plane was late. She took a taxi from La Guardia and clattered in, exuberant, embracing him. "I knew you could do it," she said. She told him that Johns Hopkins was a prison, and medical school like some sort of boot camp or jail; she hadn't slept in weeks, and then just for an hour with the surgeon on the cot. She laughed with the open-mouthed braying hilarity that meant she did not mean it. "I love the place," she said. "Seriously, kid."

The caterers served drinks. They set out food. There were several pâtés and salmon mousse and sliced roast beef and a whole ham and veal in aspic and caviar and water chestnuts and vegetable dip. Bill Winterton drove down from Rhinecliff. He accepted scotch. "It's quite a spread," he said. Mark was uncertain if he referred to the tables piled with food or to the house itself. "It's a question of proportion," Winterton observed. "Your folks are spending more for this than we paid for the book."

His friends appeared. They drove from Manhattan and Riverdale and Westport and Larchmont and Barnegat Light. They arrived in pairs or carloads and three of them came on the train. Betty Allentuck traveled alone. She had been living with Sam Harwood, his close friend; she and Sam had broken up that spring. Sam was on a Fulbright in Brazil.

Betty had thick chestnut hair, long legs and high wide hips. Her breasts were full. She smoked and drank and swore with what he thought of as erotic frankness; he had envied Sam. They brushed against each other in the foyer, and she kissed him happily. "Your big night," she said.

"I'm glad you're here."

She kissed him again. "Later," she promised, and they went out on the porch.

That promise hovered where she stood in the gathering dark on the lawn. Spotlights in the oak trees lit the far stone wall. There were lanterns and torches as well. There were aromatic candles in glass jars. His father moved among the guests, wearing a pinstriped blazer, looking like a politician, pumping hands. The punch was good.

His friends attended him. They asked about the Cape, they praised his tan, they asked for free copies or where they could buy one or if he would sign books they brought. They talked about themselves. They were in law school and business school and advertising agencies; they were moving to Los Angeles and Spain. There was a rope hammock, slung between two maples; Betty lay inside it, swinging, sandals off. His father's accountant said, "Mazeltov," pointing in what seemed to be her direction; his uncle asked about his plans, what he was planning next. There were checkered tablecloths and helium balloons in clusters anchored by his book. The balloons were blue and white.

Then there were toasts. Bill Winterton said he was pleased, and Mark should get to work. He hoped and trusted this was the beginning of a long career. There was applause. Mark's sister said, I want to tell you, everyone, his handwriting is rotten. Scribble, scribble, scribble, Mr. Gibbon. People laughed. There was a toast to the reviewer for the *Times*: may her judgment be repeated. I'm proud of you, Mark's father said, I'm grateful you folks came. Imagine what this food will look like in the morning, said his mother; please everybody take seconds. Help yourselves.

By the time dessert arrived, he had grown impatient. A party in your honor is supposed to be more fun than this, he told Betty in the hammock; it was nine o'clock. Dessert was cake. His mother said, "You cut it, dear," and led him to the serving table. They made space. The cake was large, rectangular, its icing fashioned in a perfect likeness of the cover of his novel. The blue sky and the bird outstretched against it and the pillars with his name inscribed—all were reproduced. He was embarrassed. "Beautiful," they chorused. "It's magnificent." "The word made sugar," said Billy the D.J. "Take of my body. Eat, eat."

There were photographs. Flashbulbs popped repeatedly while he smiled and blinked. His mother provided a knife. "You cut the first slice, author."

"I can't."

"It's the book's birthday. We made it a cake."

"I don't want to."

"Please," she said.

He took the knife and flourished it, then stabbed the air. He wielded it as if it were a saber, impaling, conducting. In the angle of his vision he saw his mother's face, shocked. He advanced as might a fencer, left arm curled above the shoulder, wrist cocked, thrusting. She would construct indulgence yet again. There were a hundred portions, and he hacked.

"You were wonderful," said Betty.

"When?"

"With the cake. I loved it."

"You're in the minority."

She put her hand on his arm. "When the party's over would you take me home?"

"Is that a proposition?"

"Yes."

The guests dispersed. They took their leave of him as if he were a host. There were pots of coffee for those who had to drive. The caterers cleaned up. His parents and his sister rocked companionably on the porch. "You'd never make a surgeon, Mark," she said. "Look what you did to that cake."

He told them he was taking Betty to New York. He claimed a bottle of champagne, said thank you to his parents, and promised to return by dawn. "Drive carefully," they said. "To the victor," said his sister, and they laughed.

The MG's top was down. The seats were wet. He dried them with his handkerchief, and Betty leaned against him, and they kissed. Headlights from a turning car illuminated their embrace; she did not turn away.

What followed was delight. They drove into Manhattan in their own created wind; she rested her hand on his thigh. The city spread beneath them like a neon maze through which he knew the track, a necklace suspended from the dark neck of the river. At the Triboro Bridge toll booth the attendant said, "Fine night." He found a parking space in front of her apartment, and they closed the car. "I've wanted this all year," she said. "Haven't we been virtuous? It seems like I've waited all spring."

The sex was a promise delivered. Betty took him into her with a high keening wail, a fierce enfolding heat; she flailed against him in the bed, repeating to his rhythm, "God, my God, my God." He was proving something, celebrating, displacing his friend in her flesh; he battered at her till she cried, "I love you, Mark." He wondered, was that true. They drank champagne. The ache in his knees, in his back, the plenitude of travel and arrival and release, the long day waning, the radio's jazz, the whites of her eyes rolling back—all this was bounty, a gift. Each time he entered her she begged him, "Stop. Don't stop."

On Tuesday he and Winterton met again for lunch. This time they ate at Lutece. "Word is the *Newsweek* is good. And *The Saturday Review*." He handed Mark *The Saturday Review*. There was his photograph, and a review entitled "Timeless Parable." Again he had heard of the critic; again the assessment was kind. "I wish I could have written a book this good at twenty-two. I could not, and very few do. There's a major talent here. Hats off."

"Publicity is ringing off the hook," said Winterton. "Don't let it go to your head."

The bumblebee, he said, is by all scientific measure too slow and fat to fly. Cheerfully ignorant of this, however, and to the dismay of scientists, the bumblebee just flies. Winterton flapped his arms. He drank. You've got to learn, he said, to be like that bumblebee flying: just go ahead and buzz.

"I'm working on a story," Mark announced.

"Good."

"It's about discovery. Self-discovery. A boy who sleeps with his best friend's girlfriend, then finds out she's the Muse."

"Don't spoil it by analysis."

"I'm not. I'm only telling you."

"Well, don't." He pressed his palms to his temples and then extracted glasses from his coat. He had not worn glasses before in Mark's presence; he studied the menu with care. "There's nothing that can happen now," he said, "that's anything but a distraction to your work. If the praise continues, if it dies down or changes or stops. All of this"—he waved his hand—"it's beside the point. The point is to keep working, to not stop."

He said this with bitterness, smiling. The first course arrived. Thereafter the mood lightened, and Winterton grew expansive. Ernest Hemingway drank rum, and Scott drank French 75's, and Bill Faulkner drank Jack Daniel's; he emulated them all. You can tell a writer's models by which drink he orders, at which bar.

His tennis game was off. He had lost his backhand and his overhead. His marriage was a warring truce, his boy a diabetic, and his secretary couldn't tell the difference between Tolstoy and Mickey Spillane if her raise depended on it; his eyes hurt. No one read Galsworthy now. No book buyer in this room—he raised his arm, inclusive—could tell him, he was certain, where "The apple tree, the singing and the gold," came from, and what was its original.

Mark too recited a verse. "Samuel Smith he sells good beer / His company will please. / The way is lit and very near / It's just beyond the trees."

"What's that?" asked Winterton, incurious, and Mark said he read it in Wellfleet. It was a tavern motto from a tavern washed away. The whalers weighed anchor off Jeremy Point—but all they found was pewter now, a bowl or two, some spoons.

"Mine's Sophocles," said Winterton, "in the Gilbert Murray translation. 'Apples and singing and gold . . .'"

The garden room was full. Light slanted through the windows; women laughed. Mark had taken the train to Manhattan and would take it home again; his car was being serviced in the garage at Rye. They drank Italian wines, to honor what Bill Winterton described as his true provenance; it seemed important, somehow, to pretend they were in Italy. This went against the decor's grain; the waiters spoke in French. "You know where Napoleon comes from? It's a riddle." Winterton coughed. "The question is what nationality was Napoleon at birth? I ask you, 'Can you answer?,' and the answer's, 'Cors-I-can.'"

This seemed uproarious to Mark—witty, learned, apt. They celebrated lengthily, and there was nothing he could not attain, no prospect unattainable. Walking to Grand Central he breathed deeply, weaving. He made the 4:18.

Between self-pity and aggrandizement, there is little room to maneuver. His stomach churned; his shirt felt rank. The train was old. Mark wandered to the forward car; the conductor waved him in. The gray seats were unoccupied, the windows dark. He sat sprawling in the window seat while the train filled up.

A woman with two shopping bags settled beside him. She wore a pink knit suit and had a purple handbag and white hair. He made space. She produced *The Saturday Review*. The train lurched and rumbled forward, and he told himself his father made this trip five hundred times a year. They stopped at 125th Street, and then they gathered speed.

He needed water. He wanted to sleep. His neighbor read the magazine with absorbed attention and came, on page 23, to his photograph. He was sitting on a rock in front of Long Island Sound. His tie had blown over his shoulder, his hair was engagingly tousled by the propitious breeze. He wanted to tell her, "That's me." He wanted her to know that she was sitting next to Mark Fusco, novelist, whose first book earned such praise. He imagined her shocked disbelief, then recognition. She would tell her husband, when she got off the train at Pelham or Greenwich or wherever she was getting off, "Guess who I sat next to, guess who I met on the train?"

Mark was on the verge of telling her, clearing his throat to begin, when the train braked. Momentum threw him forward; he jerked back. They had no scheduled stop. His neighbor had her handbag open, and its contents spilled. "What was that?" she asked. The whistle shrieked. He bent to help her gather pens, a tube of lipstick, Kleenex, keys. "What was that?" she asked again, as if he might have known.

They remained there without explanation. The train lights flickered, dimmed. He tried to open his window, but it had been sealed shut. Brown grime adhered to his hands. His head hurt. He excused himself to drink from the water dispenser, but there were no paper cups. He pressed the lever nonetheless, and water trickled out. In the space between the cars conductors huddled, conferring. They looked at their logbooks, their watches. The next stop was Larchmont, he knew. He tried to see the Larchmont station down along the track; he saw the New England Thruway and apartment buildings and gas stations and what looked like a supermarket and a lumberyard. The train had been stopped in its tracks. He understood, of a sudden, the force of that expression; he returned to his seat and repeated it. "The train has been stopped in its tracks."

Then there were rumors. The train had hit a dog. It had hit a car. It had narrowly avoided a collision with a freight; the switching devices failed. The President was on his way to New Rochelle, and traffic had therefore been halted. There was trouble ahead with the switches, and they would wait it out here. There were work slowdowns, strikes. The woman to his right protested the delay. Her husband would be worried silly; he was a worrier. He liked to feed the cat and canary just so, in sequence, and if there was some change in the schedule, some reason to feed the canary first, he worried for the cat.

Her husband would be waiting at Mamaroneck. He would keep the motor running and fret about the wasted gas and fret about the timer oven since this was the maid's Tuesday off; since her husband had retired, she called him worrywart. She went to New York once a week. It wasn't for the shopping, really, it was to escape—a freedom spree, she called it, not a shopping spree.

Mark drifted, nodding, sweating. They would know him at Lutece. He would buy a pipe and captain's hat and lounge along the dock.

The grandmother from Agrigento buried donkey bones. She told her children there was treasure at the temple site, and they ought to dig. They were greedy; they vied for attention. She lay dying by the seawall, seeing her progeny fight, watching them swing shovels and threaten each other with picks.

Her favorite nephew watched too. He had flown to Sicily on a visit from the north; he was torn between two women—a big city sophisticate and the girl next door. The grandmother stretched out a finger like a claw. He mopped her brow with flannel soaked in lemon water; he ground rosemary and garlic and fed her moistened mouthfuls of bread and olive oil. Her house was bright with broken glass embedded in cement. Barbed wire clung to the doorframe like a climbing rose.

"Giovanni?" she said.

"Grandmother?"

Her voice was as the sea on gravel. "When there's treasure, *stupido,* you look for it here." She scratched at her ribcage, then nodded. "You understand, *caro*, the heart?"

He understood, he said. Dolphins played in the white surf. This teetered on the verge of sentiment, said Winterton, but it might be profound.

Then the conductor appeared. His hair was brown, and he wore a handlebar moustache. He stood at the front of the car, expectant, gathering an audience. They quieted. "We're sorry to inform you"—he cleared his throat, repeated it—"I'm sorry to inform you of the cause of our delay. There has been an accident. A person or persons unknown has been discovered on the track. That's all I can reliably report." His voice was high. He relished the attention, clearly, and refused to answer questions. "That's the statement, folks."

Police appeared beneath the window, with leashed dogs. There were stretcher-bearers and photographers; it was beginning to rain. He said to the woman beside him, "I need air." Then he followed the conductor to the space between the cars. "Can I get out and walk?" he asked. "I'm late. I know the way." They would not let him leave. "I might be sick," he said. They pointed to the bathroom door, unlocked.

The bathroom reeked of urine; the toilet would not flush. He held his nose and gagged. He braced himself upon the sink and stared at his reflection—hawking, blear-eyed, pinched. "'The apple tree . . .'" he mouthed. What was out there on the track found him irrelevant; it proceeded at its chosen pace, and Mark was not a witness they would call.

In the next two hours, waiting, he learned what he could of the story. He heard it in bits and fragments, the narrative disjunct. A body was found on the tracks. It had been covered with branches and pine boughs and leaves. It had been a suicide, perhaps, or murder. It was female and, judging by hair color, young. The engineer had noticed the leaf pile ahead and slowed but failed to stop. By the time he identified clothing underneath the branches, and what looked like a reaching hand, he could not halt the train. No blame attached to his action. The body had been crushed. There were few identifying marks. Bone and flesh and clothing shreds were scattered on the engine, spattered on the crossties and beneath the first two cars. If the act were suicide imagine the anticipation, the self-control awaiting death; if murder, the disposal of the corpse. Forensic experts had arrived to gather evidence. Police were searching the approach roads to the overpass, and all nearby foliage. Traffic was delayed in both directions, therefore, while they combed the tracks.

"I'm leaving tomorrow," he said to his parents that night.

"For the Cape?" his father asked.

"So soon?" his mother asked.

"I need to get to work again."

"We wouldn't bother you," she said. "We'd leave a tray at the door."

"We'd screen your calls," his father said. "We'd say, 'No interviews.'"

"I didn't mean it that way. I left my work in Wellfleet."

"Coffee?"

"Please."

They settled in the living room. He tried to tell them, and could not, what had happened on the train—how his blithe assumption of the primacy of art was made to seem ridiculous by fact. It was flesh and not Karenina that spread across the track. It was rumor, not a cry for help, he heard. What impressed itself upon him was his picture in a magazine, and Betty's lush compliance in, enactment of his fantasy, was how much money they might spend for lunch. Mrs. Newcombe's ancestor spat in the coal grate. Bonnie will not take him back, will work in the Town Library; she runs off with the drummer from Spokane.

He would write it down, of course. Mark made notes. It would become his subject; he would squeeze and absorb and digest it—as might have, once, the Barone P. P. He would throw his voice. It would take him time, of course, but if it took him twenty years he'd balance the account. He would feed the canary, then cat.

And With Advantages

IN THE FLUSH of his first manhood, he found himself courting old men. They wrote books. They looked less robust than in their photographs, but he had seen their photographs—less jowly, thicker-haired. They clapped him on the back. They inclined their heads toward him, shaking hands. They liked to see young people; it made them feel young, they declared. Old people need young people as the younger need the old.

This was not a proposition Ben believed in, though he seemed to—nodding, smiling, volunteering help with the woodpile or the canapés. He wanted their help, not advice. He flattered them by imitation, stroking his girlfriend's long thigh. He wanted them to know he would supplant them soon.

He was twenty-six years old. He had published his first book. It had been successful and, in some quarters, acclaimed. His present project, therefore, was the story of his life. It would be cast in fictive terms, but it was nonetheless and recognizably his own—the childhood in Alaska, the mother's early death, the series of surrogate mothers who either ignored or adored him, the loss of his virginity in Rome.

Ben admitted influence. Like Daedalus, he planned to forge the uncreated conscience of his race. Joyce mattered to him greatly, and he called the stockpot "Stately, plump Mulligan Stew." He liked to cook. Once a recipe for escargots worked on three successive nights with three successive partners; he made garlic butter in advance, and kept the white wine chilled. Women came to see him on the weekends, or while their husbands worked in town, or after a day's shopping spree. Often, making love, he considered the distinction between the colon, semicolon, and the serial comma; he had read that others, in order to postpone ejaculation, conjugated Latin verbs. "*Introit ad altare tei*," he whispered in their ears. They called him elusive, allusive, charming; he did not disagree.

His father knew a lawyer with a client with a carriage house in Yorktown Heights. Ben settled there. He paid only for the telephone and heat—exchanging his weeklong presence and a kind of informal caretaking attention for rent. The manor house (it was one, really, in meticulous and detailed imitation of a Cotswold cottage) stood empty all week. On Friday night the bustle of arrival (heralded by headlights, the horn amicably blaring, the smell of woodsmoke on the wind, and, on mild evenings, the conversational clatter, laughter and music and ice) distracted him. On Sundays they would leave. Late afternoon departures (two or three cars often, in summer the convertibles, cars rented at the airport, a limousine with tinted windows) left him, inexplicably—half-glimpsing guests, half-hearing, waving—bereft. Of all the signs of speech, he wrote, the worst is the parenthesis; it heralded and then confirmed its own irrelevance.

The owner of the manor house was a writer too. He was seventy-seven years old. In his twenties he had known Kerensky, Trotsky, Lenin; he had consorted, briefly, with Eastman, Dell, and Reed. He had dabbled in the theater and in publishing; his most recent project was titled *Naming Names*. The first volume had to do with boyhood and young love, the second with his various adventures in the war. He was imposing, and knew it; his white mane of hair and thick-limbed bulk were leonine. This was a word he used. "Leonine" his belly laugh, his satisfied rumble at supper, his confident assumption that the guests about his table were enthralled. His habit of possession declared itself by pronouns. "My Chagall"—he pointed—"my memory of Einstein playing chess, my favorite spinach soufflé . . ."

Ben met him three weeks after having settled in. The afternoon was hot. He lay in the hammock, shirt-less, reading Thomas Mann. The book was black-bound, heavy, and he had trouble focusing; *The Magic Mountain* seemed remote from all such buzzing plenitude, the summer's lazy passing. He heard dogs. He had heard them before and did not raise his head.

"Herr Settembrini, I presume."

Ben jerked awake.

"Herr Settembrini," said his landlord. "My name's Slote."

The trick of where he waited backlit him gaudily; sun enlarged him where he stood. "I've got some people up the hill. Why don't you join us for drinks?"

"Thank you very much."

"Six-thirty? See you then."

This conferral offered, he moved back through the trees. The golden retrievers rolled and tumbled noisily ahead. Slote wore a madras jacket and a shirt with pineapples and crimson slacks; the regalia did not seem absurd. It flattered, rather, the austerity of the white hair and head, the inward-facing melancholy of his face at rest. He walked with a slight, shoulder-rolling limp.

Ben showered, shaved, and dressed. He appeared at the agreed-on time; there were others on the porch. He knew the actress's name. He knew the television commentator in the rocking chair, the publisher with a cigar. He felt the dependent independence of a man who knows his worth but knows it not yet known. "Gin and tonic?" offered Slote. Ben set himself to politeness, a deferential attention. He had arrived where he wanted, and would stay.

"What will you do in September?" they asked.

"I'm hoping to be here."

"You've finished school?"

"I have."

"And what will you be doing in ten years?"

"I can't imagine. I know I'll be writing."

"You do?"

He nodded, solemn. "Yes. But where or how or with what success I can't imagine, I just couldn't say."

He passed whatever test the invitation signified; he was charming, proclaimed Mrs. Slote. He must come and visit, he shouldn't feel confined to that sad cottage down the hill. "It's a beautiful place," he protested. "Isn't it," she said. He brought a presentation copy of his novel, *Widowswalk*. The inscription read "Please keep me on the shelf."

In the next weeks Ben came to grow familiar with the house. He offered to walk the retrievers; he collected groceries and mail. As summer waned he waited more and more for Friday night, its companionable summons from the hill. He wanted to be welcome where they reminisced, to sit in the firelit circle where they laughed and drank. He wanted to play Anagrams with members of the Grolier Club and men who earned a Pulitzer and critics for the *Times*. It was not so much their prominence he courted as the sense of past attainment. He was sucking up to history, said his visitor that weekend, Jane; you shouldn't judge a life by liver spots.

"Why not?" he asked. "What better measure is there?"

"He's trying to screw me," she said.

"Who?"

"Slote."

"I don't believe it."

"Have it your own way." She shook her hair free.

The thought that the old man had propositioned her excited him; he took it as a compliment. "What did he do?"

"Licked his lips. Sent flowers. What do you want me to tell you?"

"Everything."

She watched him. "Jesus Christ."

"We're tenants in this house." Ben raised his arms, inclusive. "We can't insult the host."

"I thought it worked the other way. I thought the host gives up his chair. I thought he offers his wife."

"It's you I want," he said.

He bent above her then, and she received him greedily, lifting her knees to his neck.

Gretchen Slote was tall and spare and what Ben imagined as horsey; she would have been devoted to horses when young. Her hair was streaked with gray. She wore it to her shoulders—defiantly, he thought—and often she wore riding boots when tending to the garden. She told him, when he asked her, that no, she had never liked horses, it was the one obsession she had managed to avoid.

"How long have you been coming here? To Yorktown Heights," he asked.

"Oh, always. I was born here."

She gestured at the valley and the hospital, whose slate roof crested the opposing hill, whose chimneys matched her own. "You thought Slote bought it, didn't you?"

He watched her hands.

"They all think that. Slote wants them to. He married well," she said.

One night he stayed for dinner with three men. They were old and honored, longtime friends: a painter, a theatrical agent, and a judge. The painter kept an unlit pipe clamped between his teeth; he had thick tufts of hair in his ears. Hair sprouted from his nostrils also; capillaries mapped the delta of his cheeks. The agent wore a turtleneck and tweeds, the judge a leisure suit. He stammered; the others seemed deaf. At ten Gretchen excused herself and left them to their brandy. "It's been a long day," she said.

They spat; they shook with glee. They shouted and pounded the table and laughed great raucous laughs. They told stories about women, other nights, themselves when young; they told the one about the chandelier, and poker with that blonde. "You filled the inside straight, remember?" said the judge. The painter—Quentin Wallace—took a red and black Pentel from the marmalade jar by the phone. He took a piece of paper also and sketched a naked woman with pendulous breasts, long red hair. He did this rapidly, frowning. Then he drew the four of them naked, on their knees, their penises engorged and ruby-tipped. A deck of cards emerged from her spread legs.

"Remember Sally?" asked the judge.

Slote laughed. "I carried her memory right to the doctor."

"What a night," said Wallace. "What a night."

They talked in this manner at length. Ben waited for the spark of wit, some proof of eminence earned. They swallowed cashews and chocolate-covered almonds; they told elephant jokes. "How do you fit five elephants in a Volkswagen?" asked the judge. "Two in the front and three in the back," Slote answered. They chortled and nodded and drank.

What of the larger life?—Ben asked himself, pouring—what of politics and art, the impersonal issues of state? They spat into their handkerchiefs; they laughed and shook and blew.

"You sonofabitch," said Alfred Wasserstrom. "You cocksucking sonofabitch!"

"An inside straight!" said Slote.

"Come off it, Alfie," Wallace said. "You never took her home."

This struck them as uproarious. "What happened to her anyhow? She married, I remember that—some lawyer from Atlanta."

"Coke, I think."

"He means Coca-Cola," Slote explained, "the Coca-Cola fortune, am I right?"

They would tell him how careers are made, how their own were fashioned; they could speak of the late great. They might describe Manhattan when it was an easy town, when Harlem was a friendly place to visit after dark. They had known Theodore Dreiser, Babe Ruth, Thomas Hart Benton, Josephine Baker, Chaplin, Chaliapin, Pound. They could explain the usages of smoke-filled rooms, the proper measure of ambition with mete modesty, the secrets of longevity and growth.

"Can't drink like I used to," Slote said.

"No."

"You never could," said Wallace, and they laughed.

They had watched the rise and fall of fortunes, tidelines, hula hoops, and wigs. The spinning wheel, they might confide, was Sally's little counterweight, and when she rolled her hips the fix was in. They would define the wheel of fortune in the age of the computer, missiles, and the laser beam; they could show him how Arabia—its boundaries, the price of oil—was rigged.

One Friday Gretchen came to him. "I have a favor to ask."

He stood.

"I've got to be away." She handed him tomatoes. "It would make me happy—make us all more comfortable, really—if you'd stay up at the house. Slote's been having trouble, and I hate to leave him alone."

"Of course. What kind of trouble?"

"Nothing serious. What they used to call the vapors." Gretchen smiled. "Only that was way back when, and woman's sickness, wasn't it? Now it's *petit mal*. He gets a little dizzy, and I don't like leaving ..."

"Has he seen a doctor?"

"Yes." she spread her hands. "They've got him on so many drugs it's hard to remember how much to take. And what's for what, and which counteracts which, and what are only side effects. Don't ever grow old," Gretchen said.

"When are you going?"

"Tomorrow. Normally he'd stay in town, but this is the season he loves it out here—and if you wouldn't mind?"

She was wearing mascara, he noticed, and had not before. Her eyes were green. He could not tell if she were flirting with, flattering, or condescending to him; these were the relations his experience encompassed. She pivoted on her boot's heel and, looking back over her shoulder, said, "Come for drinks. We'll talk about the details then," and left.

That afternoon he read no more. He balanced his checkbook instead.

She was going to Virginia, she told him over cocktails; her sister needed help. She would be gone for four days. Her kid sister had married a golf pro, and he was off on tour. Juliet had a hysterectomy scheduled for Tuesday, but the son of a bitch was in Hawaii and not coming back; this was his first season with the big boys, and he'd ironed out his swing. Gretchen had offered to pay for the flight, but he'd said, no thank you, not a chance.

They were drinking gin and tonics on the porch. Slote had his feet up—thick woolen socks and sandals—and his glasses off. He rested in the chaise longue, half-attentive, drifting. The sun set. Gretchen said her sister loved athletes and was a glutton for punishment; she never learned, not Juliet. She was the cheerleader who believes the quarterback is wonderful, the girl outside the locker room who could never get over being cute. So now they'd scrape it out of her, and her golfer husband was chasing the caddy through sand traps, underneath the palms.

She apologized. She offered cheese. She didn't mean to bore him with her troubles or her sister's troubles. But Ben should know where she was going and where she could be reached. Fleetingly he wondered if she spoke to him in code; she stared at him unreadably while he'r husband slept.

When Gretchen left that Saturday (taking the Mercedes, leaving him the Wagoneer, clattering down the driveway as if she might be late, promising to call from Kennedy and then again from Richmond, kissing her husband, then him on the cheek), he felt his own incompetence, the size of the space she filled. "Well," said Slote. "What's on TV?"

"It's news' time, isn't it?"

"Yes. Cronkite. The sickness. Do you know what *Krankheit* means?"

"Sickness in German?"

Slote cackled. "He knows." The laugh he gave was high-pitched, false, theatrical—as if there were an audience and the scene were written in advance.

"Can I make you a drink?"

"A fire. Make my fire first."

There was kindling by the hearth; he crisscrossed it in the ash. He crumpled newspaper also and went for logs; a wind arose. The first stars had appeared. A dog barked in the valley, accentuating silence. When he came back in with wood, Slote was in the wing chair, facing not the television but the wall. He had turned off the light. His hair above the headrest seemed dissevered somehow, a white aureole. He snored. Ben knelt to place wood in the grate, and the paper rustled and Slote woke.

"About time-lapse photography. That's what I've been dreaming . . ."

Ben checked the flue. He lit the ash, then paper. "You know the way they show a crocus pushing up through frozen ground." Slote's speech was thick, laborious. "Then opening, then dying, all in the space of ten seconds. Or what we looked like when young." The fire took. His face grew ruddy, watching it. "The sphincter valve, for instance. What a triumph of control." His mouth went slack; he slept. Ben poured himself a bourbon, neat, and wondered what he had agreed to. Slote's proprietary power had vanished with his wife. When he jerked awake at nine o'clock, he wanted frozen pizza. They boiled soup.

As the days wore on, however, he improved. Slote seemed alert at breakfast, high-spirited when working. He sat at his desk in the morning, rummaging through files and reading his old journals, making notes. The retrievers hovered, tails thumping, at his feet. He was compiling memories for Volume Three of *Naming Names*. Ben came down from where he woke to find Slote dressed, the coffee cold, the tabletop covered with sheets and the wastepaper basket full. He had assembled his notebooks, articles, and albums; he had photographs of friends. There were photographs of previous houses also, and naked women on the beach. He slid them across the green baize desk top as if for approval, their breasts emerging from the waves, their laughter-loving mouths displaying teeth. Or they wore jewelry. Or they stood with him, smoking, on dance floors, or waved from the railings of ships. On the back of every photograph, in pencil, he had written their names and the date.

"Gretchen doesn't like it," Slote confided. "Not that I blame her, of course. I used to have this photograph"—he pointed to a blonde in lederhosen, with a German shepherd puppy nipping at her heels—"there on the bulletin board. Christina, my first wife."

"She was German, was she?"

"Yes."

"She's beautiful."

"'*Das Ewig-Weibliche*,' yes. I've been writing how we met and how we married—in Karlsruhe. Long before Hitler, of course. *Habe nun, ach! Philosophie*—you understand German?"

"Not really."

"I'm making a bad joke by Faust. We were very young, we fell in love, we moved to this country, and then she went home." He stepped to the window and stood looking out. "It's the oldest story of them all."

He did not elaborate. He placed the picture carefully back in the file marked "C." "My recollections will be shocking only in their innocence, their pitiable fervor. You're older already, your whole generation is old."

"We were born after Hitler."

"Of course. That has something to do with it also. But during the Weimar Republic there was no such thing as hopelessness. We affected it, naturally. We smoked cigars and drank schnapps and stayed in bed till noon. But everything seemed hopeful, everything was grounds for hope." He laughed. "It's easier to be romantic when you don't know the language. The accent of untruth . . ."

They moved outside. "How's Gretchen?"

"Fine. She's fine. She sends her best."

"And how's her sister doing?"

"We recuperate so quickly when we're young. They're talking of a trip. Gretchen always wants to see Uxmal; I tell her it's too hot for me, and so she takes her sister."

This was at odds with the story she had offered Ben. The tamaracks were yellowing, the Japanese maple crimson, and the wind was high. Slote walked with a black burnished cane, its handle shiny from use. He decapitated goldenrod and slashed Indian paintbrush and grass.

"When do you expect her back?"

"Who? Gretchen? I don't really know. I should have gone with her, of course."

"She's going to the Yucatan?"

"She might."

Consciously, Ben changed the subject. He was planning dinner and wanted to know what to cook. He wanted to show Slote his work. The dogs chased squirrels fruitlessly. He needed an imprimatur, a proof of merited attention. He hoped for what he thought of as a laying-on of hands. When he thought of those hands, however, they were Gretchen's, and smoothing his shirt.

Then Gretchen did return. She was back the next Wednesday, grateful, full of information about hospitals in Richmond. "They're so *polite*," she said. "The doctors there. Unless you're Edgar Poe."

In the kitchen, privately, she asked him how Slote seemed.

"Well. A little tired, maybe."

"Did he show you all his pictures?"

"Some."

"We never had children, you see. I wanted to. He didn't."

"We've been working hard," Ben said.

He was going to discuss the problem with the fictive life, the difficulty of completion when you know where you are coming from but not where you will go. His imagination faltered at the prospect of finality; *Widowswalk* had ended with its closure incomplete. He was planning a scene with a skater, an ice-clogged estuary and the seals in bellowing alarm.

Gretchen said, "It's lonely here. He needs the city's stimulus. It's time to shut up shop."

The woman skating backward on the ice was wearing gray. He could see it, was trying to write it. Snow would be falling; she let the flakes melt in her hair.

"What about the photographs?" Ben asked.

"When he starts speaking German, it's time to go back to New York."

"Will you come weekends?"

"Yes."

"*Frisch weht der Wind*" sang Slote in the dining room. "*Der Heimat zu . . .*"

"You see what I'm saying," said Gretchen, and rested her hand on Ben's cheek.

That winter they flew to Bermuda. There were available doctors, but not excessive heat. The Slotes rented a house in Tucker's Town—and there was room, Gretchen said. They would welcome Ben's visit and help. They had established a beachhead on the beach; he should join them for a week.

He had a cold; his throat hurt. On the flight south from Kennedy he tried to read, to sleep; his imaginings were fretful. He saw himself behind Slote's wheelchair, with the old man naked and the wheels locked irretrievably; when he bent to free them, Gretchen laughed. She who did not smoke was wielding a cigarette holder; ash glowed and fluttered at the tip. He took a taxi at the airport; it was a dark, brief ride. The smell of salt assaulted him, and sweet fermenting rot on the night breeze.

"We're glad you're here," said Slote.

"Welcome," Gretchen said.

They stood in the doorway together.

"How was your trip?"

"You've eaten?"

He nodded. "Airplane food."

"Your room is back behind the kitchen," Gretchen said. "It's closest to the water and the bar."

"But we've had such terrible weather. Monsoon season." Slote coughed. "Maybe you'll change our luck."

"He beats me every night. At Anagrams, I mean."

"This house looks huge," said Ben.

"It is. It was built for a Grace liner Grace."

The walls were pink. There were candles in hurricane lamps. The floor was terracotta tile, and it extended to a patio with palms. In the dark beyond the railing, he could see the sea.

"How's your sister?"

"Better. She was here last week." Gretchen took a lemon and sliced it in quarters, then eighths. "Someday you should meet her. But she left."

"She's recovering," said Slote. "You should see her in that pink bikini. A delightful sight."

"He's recovered too," said Gretchen. "Can't you tell?"

She offered him a rum called Gosling's—local, dark. He excused himself to change and did so, swiftly, emptying his single suitcase into the bureau by the bed, setting up his typewriter on the desk provided. He was grateful for their welcome and glad to be a part of even this declining. His ears cleared. *Widowswalk* was on the coffee table. "I've been reading it," said Gretchen. "I haven't finished yet."

It rained. There was a fire in the study fireplace. They sat and talked and he would not later remember—though he tried to, though it would matter—what it was they spoke about and how Slote had behaved.

There had been nothing remarkable; he shifted in his seat. They played a game of Anagrams, and Gretchen lost. He and Slote seemed equal till Slote formed "cubeb" with his final letters; a cubeb, he explained, was what you smoked behind the barn in the days when cigarettes were scarce.

This archaism pleased him. He told Ben the language was conservative; it kept old words around in order to remind itself of youth. It did not so much relinquish as accrete. The phrase "relinquish as accrete," for instance, would signify, for Ben, a stuccoed room with cedar paneling, a gaunt woman crossing her ankles and scratching where she said she had a spider bite, the taste of rum and lemon and that inward drifting of the traveler at rest. It was the last phrase he remembered—and the white head wagging, the cuticle he bit that bled, the blur of his tilt toward sleep.

He woke to find Gretchen beside him. She was shaking his shoulder, not gently. "Wake up," she said. "He's dead." He knew he was dreaming; he rose to her breast. "He's dead," she said again. "He isn't breathing, Ben. You have to help him. Help."

Then he was wide awake but panicky; she handed him his clothes. "Dead," she said. "There's no pulse, nothing. I know he's dead."

And it was true, was manifest as soon as he saw Slote, though Ben had seen no corpse before—the eyes rolled back, tongue disengaged, pulse unrecoverable in the stiff chill wrist. He tried to take it anyhow; he kept his fingers there. "Forget it," Gretchen said. Her voice was shrill. "Get a blanket. Cover him."

He did. The body bulked beneath the pink twill clumsily. He opened the window. Outside, it was dark. "Are you all right?" he asked.

"Yes."

"What happened?"

"I woke up. I heard, it was almost like, gargling. Like clearing his throat." She made a vague, dismissive gesture. "Then he tried to stand, I think, tried to get out of the bed. And then he just fell back. Like this...."

She wilted; he held out his arms.

So it became a matter of arrangements, of calling the police, the doctor, the funeral home. They were efficient; they offered their condolences and their expertise. Through the long day that followed he felt himself an actor, acting, emulating attitude—the play of grief and shock. But in truth he felt embarrassed, cheated of the sun outside, the intimacy he had anticipated, flying south—embarrassed by his ignorance of what she felt, or how to offer comfort beyond the managerial: attentiveness to doctors, certificates, the albino travel agent who would help ready the corpse.

He signed and countersigned and called and reserved and confirmed. The officials were polite. They commiserated with him, nicely allocating sympathy—in part for his unfortunate loss, in part for his bad luck. They spoke about the methodology of death in Tucker's Town, and how much Slote had meant to him; they asked if he had known the history of heart disease and if the deceased were regular with pills.

"He had a long, full life," said Ben. "He lived each day with the conviction it could be his last." This phrase appeared, with attribution, in the morning paper; Ben was described as a "close family friend."

Gretchen sat dry-eyed throughout the procedures, drinking quantities of tea. She regarded him, he thought, as though he had been summoned for just such an occasion. She had made him welcome for her husband's sake, but he would be dismissed. He had failed her, he was certain, but he was uncertain how. When the body was released and the authorities withdrew, Ben asked her if she wanted dinner, and she told him no. He asked if she were tired, and she said, not really, no; he asked her what she wanted and she said to be alone.

Aggrieved, he sought his room. There, in the increasing silence (a map of Bermuda on the wall, a photograph of a koala bear in eucalyptus leaves, his bed unmade, the closet full of scuba gear—a wetsuit, flippers, oxygen, a mask) he knew he would fly north. "'Who once flew north . . .'" he said aloud, and misted the mirror, saying it. Sea wrack festooned the rock beyond the window, and a stunted palm. It rained.

The memorial service was scheduled for Frank J. Campbell's. Ben arrived at two. By two-thirty a crowd had assembled, and there were no seats; he relinquished his to a white-haired lady who smiled at him, bobbing. "You're very kind," she said.

Gretchen wore dark glasses and a hat. She listened to the music, marking time.

"My name is Sally Donat. Thank you very much, young man."

He recognized faces: Belinda and Frank Simmons, Bobby Morris, Etta Sloane. Alfred Wasserstrom was there, sporting a velvet bow tie, and

Quentin Wallace with an eye patch and a cane. There were faces out of magazines and television news.

The program was succinct. There was music, there were speeches, there were readings from Slote's work. He saw Jane enter, draped in black. She stared at him, or seemed to, and half-raised her hand. He thought of her bruised acquiescence in his earlier withdrawal; he had not seen her in weeks.

They spoke of Slote's embrace of life, the pleasures of his conversation. "There's no point," said Wallace, "no point pretending he's a plaster saint. We should honor what he was. A man with clay feet to his eyebrows, and all the more noble for that." He coughed. "A glutton for life's what Slote was. And a voracious eater at the feast."

"How are you?" he asked Jane.

"I thought you might be here."

"I was with them in Bermuda. When he died." They stood in the foyer. She wore a black skirt and black boots. "It must have been sudden."

"I don't really know."

"How's Gretchen? How's she taking it?"

He raised his hands, uncertain. "You look well."

"Was it sunny in Bermuda? You didn't get much sun."

"We turned around. I went for a walk once. That's all."

"Are you working?"

"No."

"It's good to see you too," she said.

Alfred Wasserstrom kissed Sally Donat on the cheek. There were limousines waiting outside.

"Are you busy? Later?"

"Tonight I might be." Then she smiled. "But not this afternoon."

She took him back to her apartment, and they opened wine. The rooms were familiar, not strange. The bear rug by the bricked-in fireplace, the Indian clubs and basket of dried flowers, the Miro prints and picture of the swimming team at Smith, the Marimekko bedspread and the rubber tree, the Exercycle by the dressing room and mirror on the mantel—all these remained in place. She said that she would quit the advertising business, it wasn't going anywhere, *she* wasn't going anywhere, she was thinking of production work instead. She was going on location to Nepal. All those sexy little Sherpas, all those Lhasa apsos; wasn't it just typical? Jane asked;

I tell them that I'm quitting and they send me to Nepal. Kathmandu or bust, that's me, I wonder if Slote would approve.

"He approved of you," Ben said.

"He was a randy old bastard."

"Yes."

"He loved to celebrate. The idea of celebration, anyhow."

"Let's celebrate," he said.

She moved toward him teasingly. "You want to come to Kathmandu?"

"I've missed you."

"Don't say that."

"It's true."

"You're a randy young bastard."

He bowed. "At your service, ma'am."

"Well, aren't you?"

He placed his hand on her neck.

"Well, aren't you?" she repeated.

"From time to time," he said.

In the country of the blind the one-eyed man is king. He can follow trails that would be trackless to the populace; he may scale a battlement by watching where to climb. He need not be fine-fingered or surefooted to succeed; he need only keep the claw at a safe distance, and avoid conjunctivitis and the fistful of flung lye. Jane lay with her eyes shut. Without her clothes on, beneath him, she seemed nonetheless aloof.

It is, he wanted to tell her, not always or predictably the fittest who survive. They had made love often, months before; she said, "I'd know you anywhere," and he said the same. They knew each other's rhythm, and kept pace. On the cosmetics shelf behind the bed he saw Slote's photograph—at fifty, windswept, cuddling a goat—inscribed "To Darling Jane." There were violets there also, and a jar of facial cream.

In the morning he drove north. There was ice by the side of the highway, and brown snow heaped at the crossings; the air was thick and gray. His heater was fitful. He would organize the files. He would learn what could be made of *Naming Names*. "How often did you see each other?" he had asked her, leaving.

She drew her bathrobe tight. "Not often."

"'The randy old bastard.' Is that what you called him?"

"Correct."

He studied her. "Do you want to come with me?"

"To Yorktown Heights?"

"Are you all right?"

She shook her head. The glare of the overhead fixture was ungenerous. He kissed her cheek. She shrank from him. He left.

There was sleet when he arrived. It coagulated on his windshield thickly; the wipers grew ice-lined. His cottage was cold, unlit. The lights did not respond. He stood in the dark foyer, and sleet rattled at the window like a drum. He called the power company and was told that lines were down, were being fixed; the problem had been located, and he should just hold tight. "Hold tight?" he asked, and the woman at the switchboard said, "That's what we're saying. What we're telling everyone. It'll all be over soon."

Ben walked up the hill to the house. He wore a yellow slicker and a pair of stiff gardener's gloves. Where first he had seen Slote in full possession, glorying, where women lay in bathing suits and men of consequence, attended by retainers, laughed, and the lawns were carefully attended to, and the swimming pool, and ivy trained to trellises—where all had been immaculate was wreckage now, hail-pocked. A Coleman lantern hung hissing at the entryway, its light intense. He knocked. The lion on the door, he noticed now, was snoutless. "It's open," Gretchen said.

"Hello."

"You're back."

"I came to see if I could help. If there's anything or any . . ."

"There isn't. But how kind."

She was sitting in the dark, in what had been Slote's chair. She made no move to greet him, and it took time before his eyes adjusted. The lantern seemed to dance suspended in the air. She was alone. She wore sweatpants and an overcoat and thick ski socks and had a bowl of popcorn at her side.

"I got so used to taking care of him," said Gretchen. "And now there's nothing to do."

"You did so much."

"That's what they mean by comfort. Those are words of comfort, am I right? That's what you say when there's someone in mourning. That's what they mean by condolence."

"I'm sorry."

"Yes."

"You shouldn't be alone," he said.

"I shouldn't? I'll get used to it."

"I wanted to tell you I'm sorry."

"Yes. You offered me words of condolence."

"I'll be leaving."

"Yes, you will."

He rose and said, "The power's out. In my house also, I mean. I didn't mean to bother you . . ."

But she was lost to him, oblivious, her left hand in the popcorn bowl, her right across her mouth.

The path was dark. He descended cautiously; the rutted clay grew slick. He understood nothing, he knew. He had not understood the usage Slote had made of him, the service he performed or what Gretchen knew of Jane. He did not know, for instance, if he should remain. Why should he feel so canceled, derided by vanity; how share in the general loss?

The lights of his cottage switched on as if tripped by a wire; the furnace clicked in. Behind him, on the pond, Ben heard the susurrus of skates. He stretched his hands in front of him as if to break a fall. He could hear the chimney hum. He could see it, thickening, cylindrical, a vertical column of air. What deeds he did that day.

You Can Use My Name

"I'LL CALL YOU tomorrow, OK?"

"OK."

"I'll be in touch, I promise."

"Fine."

"Wait just a minute, will you? Let me get rid of that call. The other goddam line."

"All right."

"I'll be right back, OK?"

"I'll wait."

"Terrific. Great."

So Adam Friedberg waited until the phone went dead. He had expected it; he expected nothing now except such interruption. He had known Richard since Iowa, and they kept in touch. It was important, they said; it mattered to them both.

Yet Richard seemed to thrive on discontinuity; there were other calls to take. There was always someone waiting, something urgent from the coast. There were always conflicting engagements, a party later on. He called at midnight, two o'clock; he seemed to need no sleep. Since Richard had grown famous, his ability to pay attention—provisional, erratic—had wholly disappeared.

That was what his old friends said; that was how they dealt with it when he drifted off. "He's changed," they said. "He's not himself."

Adam disagreed. To prepare for disappointment is to lessen its effect.

"Oh yes he is. Completely himself."

"It's cocaine," they argued. "It's because he's hooked on drugs."

"No," Adam said. "It isn't. He just tries them on for size."

"He's too rich," they said. "Too famous. It's too much too soon. The only calls he answers are from gossip columnists."

"How different would you be?" he asked. "How else would we behave?"

In Iowa City, in 1979, Adam and Richard shared a house: a dilapidated clapboard structure with a wraparound screen porch. They were first-year students in the writers' program—a two-year course of study for the M.F.A. The rental notice had been posted on the Department Office bulletin board. "Writers Preferred," it said. "John Irving lived next door!"

The house was small, steep-roofed, with eyebrow windows on the second floor; the trim had been painted pale blue. The owner was Rutherford Greene. He sold insurance for a living but liked graduate student writers; he understood, he said, what they were going through. He supervised the furnace installation when the furnace broke and had to be replaced. He dropped by to check on things and brought along a six-pack and told long, disjointed anecdotes about his clientele.

Adam and Richard grew close. It was a two-minute drive or six-minute bike ride to campus; on clear days, they walked. They took the same fiction workshop and admired the same books. All that fall they argued principles of narrative, dialogue, anachrony, synesthesia, parataxis, the fallacy of imitative form. "The eighth type of ambiguity," Richard would declare. "That's what we're after, isn't it? The one Empson never dreamed of is the one we're living out. Enacting."

"Which one's that?"

Richard dropped his head and lowered his glasses and assumed his mock-professorial accent. "The eighth variety of ambiguity. Dot's simple, *boychik*, don't you know nuzzink? It's when the writer doesn't know what in hell he's up to. Why he's writing, or who for."

"For *whom*."

Richard had an ear for accent and Adam an eye for grammar; between the two of them they licked the platter clean. Syntax is the art of subjugation, they agreed; it's knowing what depends on, is subordinate to what.

That first winter they spent time, together, with a girl called Marian.

She was a second-year student and had been published already and was an optimist. "If you're good enough," she said, "they'll notice you. They will."

"What they notice her for, *boychik*," Richard said, "ain't going to help the two of us. No way."

They discussed their prospects. "With this information explosion," Marian maintained, "there's much less chance that great work goes unpublished."

"How can you tell?" asked Adam.

"We can't. Except all editors depend on making discoveries. And there's so much talent out there now, and so much competition. They've got to find new blood."

"'Son of The Scarlet Letter.'" Adam laughed. "I've got this book I'm writing."

Richard leered and pulled imaginary postcards from his raincoat pocket. "*Feelthy* pictures stressing togetherness. You like, Miss Miss? You buy?"

She had freckles and thick, springy hair and a swimmer's body; she came from California and wrote poetry. She was twenty-three. She had the kind of exuberance Adam at first believed feigned. He had noticed her that fall, at the "Welcome to the Workshop, Don't be Bashful Bash." She wore a Cedar Rapids Miss Wet T-Shirt Contest First Prize T-shirt; the fabric appeared to be wet. The shirt was pink and red.

Marian was having an affair with a member of the wrestling team; only when it ended did she make herself available. She would sit drinking coffee at The Mocha Cow or wine at The Brown Jug, and call him over and produce the current issue of *Lachesis* or *The Running Dog* and say, "Can you believe this?"—jabbing her finger at the page. There she would be listed as a contributor, and sometimes her photo was also included—wide-eyed, large-mouthed, smiling at the camera and sun.

One of the professors gave a party at his farm. He lived five miles outside of town, and owned thirty acres. The idea of the party was that poetry and prose should mix; the second-year students played host. "Welcome to Iowa," said Marian. "We're number one in corn."

She was wearing a yellow parka and tight Gore-Tex pants. The sun was bright and cold. It had snowed the night before, and the driveway to the farm was being used as a toboggan run. There were two-person toboggans, and cross-country skis. "Want to try it?" Marian inquired. She smiled at Richard and Adam, proprietary. "Both of you. One at a time."

Adam joined her, lying down, and they pushed off together and she squealed and clung to him, shouting, as they gathered speed. At the bottom of the hill they lay an instant, tangled, panting. Then they climbed the driveway and she lay down again and Richard lay beside her and they did the same.

There were kegs of beer and lamb chops on a grill that the professor supervised, and baked potatoes and cider and bourbon and an open fire, later, under the full moon. "It always makes me crazy," she confessed to Adam.

"What does?"

'That ol' devil moon. When it's full."

"What are you doing, later?"

"Going home with you," said Marian. "They say that story you workshopped last week was really something."

"Oh?"

'The one about the circus barker and the dancing pony. You'll show it to me, right?"

She never slept with poets, she told Adam the next day. It would be too confusing. She loved his prose and his cute little ass and his use of dialogue and that scene on the trapeze.

Marian drew the line at poets, but Richard wrote prose, and the three of them spent happy times together, reading work-in-progress and discussing their shared present and their separate futures. They took a trip to Cozumel, leaving Cedar Rapids in the dank, chill morning and flying through Chicago to Cancun. In Cozumel, however, Adam got food poisoning, and he stayed in the hotel while his companions went to the beach, telling him to rest up, not to worry. They returned that evening, laughing, sunburned, regaling each other with stories of turtles and the astonishing fish. Adam understood that they had slept together and asked—with the lucid, self-pitying clarity of fever—if Marian's choice of Richard meant things were over between them, or if they would continue, and she said of course not and of course.

Later he would wonder if this was a form of betrayal. But at the time it seemed an extension of friendship, an enlargement even. They had shared their work, its pain, and now they added pleasure; this was an additional experience to share.

They spent five days in Cozumel. Adam recovered quickly and ate turtle steak on their last night with no trace of revulsion. Richard's story,

"Coral Reef"—in which he wrote about the double-dealing pilot of a glass-bottom boat, and his twin brother the client—was taken six weeks later by *The Iowa Review*.

"I brought him luck," said Marian. "I brought you luck, now didn't I?"

"My muse," declared Richard. "My inspiration."

"Our mistress of fine arts," said Adam.

"*Nous nous amusons*," she said.

When they separated late next spring, it was without regret. Adam went to Kennebunkport, where he found a job with the local newspaper; he wrote obituary notices and covered the courthouse and tried to write feature stories about tourism in Maine and fishing and unemployment and management procedures at L. L. Bean. Marian drove to Arizona and wrote long, romantic letters about the integrity of landscape and a group of potters who were living off the land. Her poetry became a ritual observance; she composed it, naked, after meditation and a pot of tea at sunset; she missed the taste of Adam, the feel of him, and urged him to come visiting and write her every week. He did write her, often, and said he missed her very much and was finding it hard to make friends. Richard had moved to New York.

"How goes it?" he would call to ask.

"It's raining," Adam said.

"And the inner weather?"

"Wet. What's up with you?"

"I'm working," Richard told him. "I'm getting down to it."

"The novel?"

"Yeah. 'Move over, Moby Dick.' How's 'Son of Scarlet Letter'?"

"Slow. I can't seem to get to B. The letter B, I mean."

"This connection's terrible. Is it ship-to-shore, or what? Don't they have telephones up there?"

"SOS," said Adam. "Buddy, I wish you were here."

The professor with the farm had introduced them to his editor. "This guy can help," he said. The editor had curly hair and wore leather clothes and smoked cigarillos. He and the professor talked about duck hunting and a buck they'd stalked with bow and arrow and how the steelhead ran that season up in Michigan. The editor had offered, "When you have a manuscript, when you're pleased with something, show me. Really pleased, I mean."

Adam had no manuscript, but Richard completed a draft of *Isle of Women* and did send it on and, miracle of miracles, he called to say, wonder of wonders, the book had been bought. It was accepted, no ifs ands or buts. They were bringing it out in the fall. The scene with the shark and the glass-bottom boat was on the cover mock-up; he wanted Adam to see.

"What shark and boat?"

"The one where she gets off on the air hose, remember?"

"Air hose?"

"Well, anyway, I want you here. I want you to come to the party."

"When?"

"Next Thursday. Don't be late."

"That's New Year's Eve!"

"You got it. The start of a new era, *boychik*. Ours."

"Congratulations," Adam said.

"There's movie-talk already. Ryan O'Neal. Michael Caine."

"That's wonderful," he said.

"So get your act together, baby. Get yourself in gear."

Of the graduating M.F.A.s, Richard was the first to sell a book. He would not, however, be the only. Billy Benton wrote a novel about baseball, and Karen Adelman published a collection of short stories about life in Hudson Bay. Eric Thurlow won the George Schmidt Poetry Award, and Gillian McDermott produced an account of growing up her father's daughter, hooked on heroin in the fashionable suburb where he ran a clinic for substance abusers. In the two years after Iowa, a dozen of the students made their debut—modestly, in magazines—in print.

Richard proved the success. His book became a movie, and he commuted from New York to Hollywood. He made the best-seller list in Italy. His second novel went up for auction with "a high six-figure floor." The critics despised him; their insults sold books. He displayed a kind of genius for publicity; his new friends all were famous, and he was mentioned at the parties where rock stars and politicians and movie stars would congregate. He modeled clothes for *Esquire* and *G.Q.* Armani sent him suits. Photographs of blondes in strapless dresses, passionate and thin-armed, festooned his bulletin board. Their cheekbones were pronounced.

Adam watched. With decreasing irony, he described himself as one of the "crowd." What he came to understand was that Richard flourished in

a ruckus of attention; his subject, he claimed, was "the scene." He planned
to chronicle the eighties as Fitzgerald had the Jazz Age and Salinger the
fifties. He became a corporation; he appeared on David Letterman and
Good Morning America and MTV and *Donahue*. He was gathering
material for a comedy of manners, a modern-day *Satyricon*. The artist
ought to party until the party's over, he told Adam on the phone, since
everything's grist to the mill. The pressure of celebrity is a topic too. Burn
the candle at both ends; there's double the wax and flame.

"I worry for you."

"Don't."

"I mean, about your health," said Adam.

"No."

"I mean, that stuff they say you take."

"It's good for the digestion, *boychik*. It's called a reality pill."

Adam married Carol in 1982. They had met in Boston, in a Chinese restaurant, when the man that she was sitting with passed out from eating
fish. "That's what he calls it," she said. "Really, it's bourbon." Adam assisted
them with coats. "I wonder, are you busy?" Carol asked.

He had not been busy, had been nursing his spareribs and soup through
the hour till the movie—a romantic triangle, French—began. He told her
this. "I've just provided you with plans," she said. "It's lucky, isn't it?" Her
escort slumped against the doorjamb, a purple silk scarf wound around
his mouth. She wondered if Adam very much minded seeing the two of
them home. She looked at him without embarrassment, with what even
then he recognized as impersonal desire. It had been compounded by
disdain. He did not mind, he told her, although he should have minded,
although in time to come he minded very much.

They put Alexander to bed. She was visiting, she said, and had only
just arrived. Alexander was her cousin and a problem drinker and a bore.
He lived on the outskirts of Concord, in a white frame house too large for
him alone. So he had invited Carol to visit, to help with the shopping and
furnishing and redecorating and such. "Brandy," she asked, not making it a
question. Then she produced snifters and poured. "What else do you help
with?" Adam asked. She laughed. "That's for me to know"—she spread
her arms—"and you to find out, cousin."

Those were the years when he pretended kinship with the rich, when he "dabbled in the market" or was "involved in real estate." So the names she dropped were names he knew, and her need to confer lineage on any man she slept with was one he understood. Her anti-Semitism, for instance, did not emerge until Antigua and their honeymoon. He had taken as self-evident her distrust of blacks. Her mother tended graveyards where they buried members of the D.A.R.; her father was a barber in Dubuque. She said he had abused her until she was fifteen. "He used to shave me," Carol said. "He liked the lather hot."

At eighteen she set off alone. She became a model in Chicago, briefly, then a buyer for Hudsons, and then a designer for Field's. She lived with the floor manager, then left him for a lawyer she met in a delicatessen; they each reached for the same can of soup. It was Campbell's split pea and ham. Through this man she met other lawyers, commodity brokers, the upwardly mobile and the already entrenched. So she invented a history of boarding school, a childhood love of horses, a proficiency at tennis until her ankle shattered. And distant claim sufficed for Carol; "Blood's thicker than water," she said. She was the second cousin of Alexander's ex-wife. Cousin Beatrice had had the Mayflower people empty the whole house. They came to Concord one morning and packed up all the furniture—the carpets, plate, and pictures—and drove away that night.

Then Carol (with her expertise in furniture, her decorator's eye) moved in. Alexander had money; she, glinting allure. She was twenty-five years old, with a close-fitting cap of curls, high cheekbones, bright blue eyes. Alexander collected his gentleman callers from every streetcorner in town. And as diversion, sometimes—although he called it "variety"—he wanted someone to bring in the boys. She complied. That had been why they accosted Adam, she told him, except Alexander was drunk. He had been on a weeklong bender, and the MSG and bourbon did not mix. She had thought maybe rice and fish would help, and all that lukewarm taste-less tea. She had been growing tired of her role as consort, her position as decoy and hostess. And because she was tired of sleeping alone, while Alexander squealed in the adjacent bedroom, she invited Adam to drive them both back home.

Carol was expert in bed. He left her at three in the morning, and they promised to meet the next night. Three weeks later they were married; it seemed the thing to do. She said Sedgewicks and Channings and Brad-fords would celebrate when they returned. He did not believe her, but it made no difference; he was trying out the random act, the unconsidered response.

His parents were in Europe. Her parents sent flowers to Concord and a telegram that offered "Many Happy Returns of the Day." "It's the wrong holiday," said Adam, and she said, "That's my family. There you have them. Clowns." Alexander owned a summer place in Truro, and he offered them a long-term lease on condition that they winterize, with a purchase option in two years. This seemed as good a way as any to settle into marriage and what Carol persisted in calling connubial bliss.

That had been seven years ago; they did not last the year. What it took him time to see was that all of this was fleeting, fraud—an impersonation like others she would have tried before. Carol's passion for pedigreed status, when he confronted it, ebbed. "This too will pass," she said. Connubial bliss is a lie, she maintained, it's only playacting, it's just playing house.

His wife changed characters, it seemed to him, constructing a new history. She decked herself in thrift-shop shawls and gypsy skirts; she wore a barber's razor on a chain around her neck. She called him Daddy Adam and started smoking pipes. She stared into the fire nightly, rapt, arms around her knees. Her women's support group in Provincetown turned out to be a macrobiotic coven with connections to Tibet.

Their leader, Sara Wigglesworth, had not in fact been to Tibet. She had been turned back at the border, but had received there, Carol said, an illumination—an experience of light. The mountain passes of Nepal were not unlike the hills of Wales or, come to that, Big Sur. Kashmir was ineluctably related to Plymouth, and Bradford's plantation could still be accomplished; Srinagar and Eastham were as one. The point was, Carol said, to recognize the similarities in seeming opposition, the constant contrariety, the body's single map and country of the mind. Her sisters, Swami Sara taught, were the permeable membrane through which life-liquid poured.

"You don't mean that."

"We do."

"Osmosis?" Adam asked. "That's what you've been studying?"

"Plasmolysis," said Carol. "You've got it turned around. Swami Sara knows much more about molecular transference than you do. She studied it in flounder, for your information, she worked three whole years in Woods Hole. The point is not to take in liquid but to yield it up."

"To whom?"

"To the receptacle," she said. "To the deserving sisterhood."

"That's snobbery again."

She presented her white back to him, the perfect shoulder blades. "You wouldn't understand," she said. "You've never understood. Go back where you came from. Get out."

Where he went was to Manhattan and Richard's apartment on West Eleventh Street. Richard made him welcome. Their reunion was enthusiastic; they had not seen each other in a year. They would have a chance to talk. "A port in a storm," Adam said. "It's exactly what I need."

The apartment had eight rooms. The ceilings had been decorated with plaster pineapples from which were suspended Tiffany lamps; the drapes were in the pattern of the Bayeux tapestry. Framed copies of advertisements for Richard's books (in French, Italian, German, Japanese) filled the entrance hall.

It was elk season, however. Richard apologized; he had forgotten all about a promise to go hunting, a trip he was committed—contracted, really—to make. A magazine was sending him; he hoped Adam understood. He knew Adam wouldn't mind. He repeated his welcome and left for Montana next morning, leaving the key. He would return in two weeks.

There was a study facing south, and Adam sat for hours in the bay window, looking down, watching the pattern of traffic and the sideways scuttling motion of the heads beneath his feet. He was writing stories in the manner of Chekhov and John Cheever; he was influenced, too, by Paul Bowles. So he made Greenwich Village into a kind of marketplace, and what they sold there were the wares of fleshly commerce: influence, survival, a body for the night.

The stories did not work. While Richard moved seemingly-effortlessly from *dojo* to disco to pup tent to castle (his English editor had a "country place" in Scotland, and now the refrigerator was covered with photos of the writer and his editor and wolfhounds and long, pale girls with riding boots, staring; "Have you noticed" Richard asked, "how amateur photography shows everybody smiling? The family album's all smiles. But professionals just glare at you, nobody grins at the camera—right?"), Adam felt adrift. His writing was unearned. The clothes in the cedar-lined closets fit another man. The phone rang frequently but did not ring for him. When he finished the Beefeater and Remy Martin and Laphroaig, he used Richard's charge account to stock the shelves again. "Success, like water," Adam wrote, "seeks its own level. Except it runs uphill."

This was the single sentence he retained; he threw the rest away. He took baths. He thought of Marian often, and attempted to locate her. She had moved from Arizona and left no forwarding address with the Iowa Writers' Workshop and there were forty-seven entries with her parents' last name in the L.A. telephone directory and in any case, he told himself, he would not have known what to say. Then Richard called to announce he would be home tomorrow. He was bringing company, a lady he'd met in Missoula, and they really needed to be alone together and hoped Adam wouldn't mind; he hoped New York had worked for him and how was the weather and how goes the work? "It was splendid," Adam said. "Terrific. You've been the perfect host."

In 1986 he married Esther Mermelstein. She was small and dark and earnest, a potter. She worked at The Left Bank, a gallery in Chatham, and tried to sell to Cape Cod tourists what she produced off-season. She had been born in Riverdale and spent her junior year in Paris and then dropped out of Smith. Esther wanted to travel before settling down; the two sets of parents agreed. She said, whither thou goest I'll follow, I've been in the boonies too long.

The wedding reception took place at Tavern-on-the-Green. She danced the hora with him, and at some point in the evening he pulled out his handkerchief and danced a Greek handkerchief dance. Richard arrived at the party late, wearing dark glasses and a double-breasted white silk suit. He sat at a table, smiling, signing autographs, doing a star turn for strangers, and so entirely vacant Adam feared he might pass out. "Are you all right?"

"I'm fine. Just fine." His speech was thick. "Introduce me to the bride."

"We're glad you came."

"Wouldn't miss it"—Richard pronounced each syllable. "Wouldn't miss this party. Not for the world."

The bride and bridegroom flew to Istanbul, then Sicily, and then the south of France. They rented a house in the Lubéron range; there Esther studied Vasarely and Brancusi and Cézanne. He drank. She had her third miscarriage in Pertuis and came back from the clinic whey-faced, inconsolable. "This isn't working," she said. "It wasn't meant to work."

The Café Ollier was where he drank—its bright beaded curtains clicking in the constant wind. Men in blue coveralls played cards and read the papers carefully; cats foraged by the bar. Sitting in his corner on the day that Esther told him, insisting she had to go back to America and would do so by herself if he preferred to remain (the pastis suspended in water, the hard-boiled egg and bread a stay against confusion, the Cavaillon melons in crates at the door, the flyers for the dog show coming to Cadenet on Tuesday, the mechanic next to him explaining what he could not translate, why their secondhand Renault needed a valve job, was losing its oil), Adam saw—so clearly the vision was tactile; he could close his eyes and taste it—that he had to get to work and that he worked better alone.

They flew to Boston from Paris. The flight was difficult; she cried soundlessly for hours. He drank her splits of wine and every cocktail he could get the stewardess to serve. "I'm empty," Esther said. "I'm drained. I'm all used up."

"It wasn't so awful," said Adam.

"Pertuis." She spat out the word.

"Our marriage, I mean."

"Not for you."

"You said you wanted to travel."

"That's true," she conceded. "But not to Pertuis."

"I liked it there," he said.

It might have been like this, he felt—the random act, the gratuitous choice—when Noah picked out animals to double in his ark. They barely knew each other and would have to learn to share. You two will do, the captain says, you can use the stateroom for your pleasure; you two we'll save from the flood. This is natural selection, folks; this is the pairing I want. But it did not mean the gates must close or gangway draw up on the deck; it need not mean that others are excluded from the ark. You could not close it off. You could not draw the bridge.

And there had been pleasure in the coupling, he tried to tell her at Logan; the two years of their journey had brought him much delight. He had made brothers whose names he forgot and fashioned a goat's likeness out of *chèvre* from their landlord's farm. He learned the names of the thirty-two winds of Provence. He had named them from the parapet of the Pont du Gard, and in Ialova Spa watched a brother called Ufuk swallow raki upside down. In Palermo he had seen three men machine-gunned in the street, and in Catania watched a car blow up. He had admired Cézanne. He was glad she went along with him and glad to say good-bye.

Esther shook his hand at Customs and walked, formally, quickly, away. His own bags—the steamer trunk tied shut with rope, the leather pack, the duffel—were searched with meticulous care. He needed to go to the bathroom, and an agent accompanied him, saying, "Don't mind me. I'll wait." They made him empty his pockets; they studied his notebook and emptied his bottles of aspirin, making certain of the brand.

But there was nothing to discover, nothing he wanted to hide. He had been well past thirty then, with a list of professions too long for the passport—and none of them serious, none of them what he would claim. As a pilgrim he had failed to find salvation, and the very word *sannyasin* seemed disjunct from *mokska*. He did not find instruction in the thirty-two winds of Provence. He would embrace sobriety, drinking only beer. He grew a beard, then shaved it, then shaved his head completely, then grew a beard again.

Richard was in trouble, he told Adam when he called. He'd lost it, whatever it was. "You remember how we used to argue over Empson?"

"Yes."

"What the hell did we argue about?"

"Ambiguity," said Adam. "Its various guises, remember?"

"No."

"Anachrony and parataxis. Stuff like that."

'There's another call," said Richard. "Hold on. Just stay there."

"Fine."

"I'll be right back, OK?"

"OK."

"Parataxis. Christ."

This time he came back on the line and said he needed company. They met in his apartment; it was eleven o'clock. The lights were dim. The air smelled rank, and Adam—who did not shock easily—was shocked. Richard's grip felt slack; he had lost weight. His breath was acetone. You name it, he'd had it, he said; it had been a bitch of a year. He'd lost his confidence. He'd lost the moves. You know how when you start to walk you think about it, practicing, and then you know how to do it—like riding a bicycle, swimming—and don't think about it and get good. But maybe something happens like you break a leg or wreck your inner ear and lose your equilibrium and therefore have to start again and suddenly it's hard, hell, it's impossible, a miracle of balance just to stand. It used to be so simple, it used to be—remember Iowa? Maid Marian?—that all you had to do was ask and the answer would be yes.

"What happened to her?" Adam asked.

"Who?"

"Marian. Any idea?"

"She's in town, she left a message. The world comes to Manhattan."

"I'd like to see her."

"Right. It's class reunion time."

Richard subsided. He sat. Then it was Adam's turn. The sound of sirens in the street, the radiator clanking, the fitful music from next door—all these made him expansive. He spoke about the novelist as nomad—a rootlessness, a restlessness—and how it became second nature. He loved, he said, the traveler's oblivion: the sense that no one knows your name and nobody who knows it knows where to locate you. There are ways to wander that do not entail first class; he had gone unrecognized for years.

"You can use mine," Richard said. "My name, I mean. For all the good it does you. Or did me."

Then he grew animated. He asked Adam how he planned to earn a living, where, and what he had been up to after all. What if he and Adam traded lives, replaced each other for a day, a week, a month—Richard was pacing, gesticulating—hell, a year! They knew enough about each other's pasts to pull it off. He thought it might just work. He'd made so much money he ought to be rich, but somehow—here his voice went shrill—he was spending more than that cocksucking accountant of his allowed. He, Richard, would go underground and Adam could go to the parties. They could trade their clothes and habits and bank accounts and bills. They could do a book together, in alternating chapters, about the way it felt to be an alter ego, to eat each other's breakfasts and write each other's books. He was sweating, urgent, laughing, giddy at the prospect of escape.

They met at *The Right Stuff*. Marian gave him her hand: an elegant, tall woman, with close-cropped curly hair. She carried a red leather briefcase and was wearing heels. "At last," she said. "At last."

"It's been too long," said Adam.

"Hasn't it?"

She took his arm. "I'm so glad I reached you," Adam said. She ordered cappuccino and strawberries; she was in town for a week. She was using the apartment of her in-laws—ex. The only good thing about Harry—that son of a bitch in Chicago—was his parents, Roz and Irv. She loved them like her own actual parents, and better than their son. Harry had his virtues, but all of them were obvious and none of them lasted the month.

Marian was talkative; she ordered a glass of red wine. She complained to Adam about the terms of her separation agreement; she was thirty-three years old and part of the workforce at last. This was a business trip. She had given up on poetry and given up on pottery and her experiment in holy matrimony was a holy mess. Except she wanted children. She wanted them a lot. They'd lost track of each other, hadn't they, after Arizona; was he married now? Did he worry about Richard and didn't it make sense for him to enter a detox clinic and did Adam remember Cozumel, that enormous anaconda outside their hotel? She had given up toboggans and sonnets and suchlike; she smiled at him indulgently. Did he remember that Wet T-Shirt Contest and his attitude of perfect outrage even though she won? With her napkin, she patted her lips. Their old professor was dead. Adam was looking wonderful; was he writing and what was he writing and where did he live now?

"No place special. I'm not sure. I'm trying to decide."

"Decide?"

"Richard wants me to move in."

"You're not serious."

"*À la recherche*, or something. I think he thinks I'll keep the creditors away."

"Those demented children."

"Who?"

"The clones, the look-alikes. The ones who want to be him."

"So you've discussed it with Richard?"

"He's using you," she said. "He's got this, this *pathological* need to be admired. Don't you see?"

He had traveled here to find—what?—a body touched as his had been by the quickening blood-beat of grief. He shook his head to clear it; consciously, he blinked. It was not so much her presence that disturbed him—one chatty woman, spooning fruit—as the vivid tactile certainty that they had been intimate once. He saw as if already enacted the way he would approach her, the processional to her borrowed apartment, the keys, the double lock. He imagined as if actual the way she would receive him, the comfort in mourning, the candlelit dark. Marian would hunt in him as he in her the trace of their shared passion, how they were abandoned together. "Excuse me," he said, leaving. "I've got to make a call."

His Masquerade

THIS HAPPENED AT Clint's farm. You know the place. Cossayuna is a village twenty miles from Saratoga Springs; it waited, with a kind of grim gentility, for the prediction of real estate agents ("Can't miss," the agents promised—"Just look at this beaming, this vista, do the demographics . . .") to come true. Clint bought the farm before he married Kathryn, in 1978. He would sell it four years later, at a loss. He had a small inheritance and large ambitions then—and the place approximated a gentleman's retreat. He called it "Farm and Content," and, sometimes, "Symbolic Farm."

He was hoping for tenure at Skidmore, and working on a book. He wanted to combine the poem and the essay; they married in the spring. The house was brick, with a central chimney and slate roof. There were three outbuildings: one used as a garage and two for storing hay. There were sixty acres, "more or less," according to the deed; the land had been measured in chains.

His wife came from Chicago. She had been raised with horses in the summer, and she wanted to fix the small barn. They intended to add a corral. That winter the pipes froze, and the barn's east-facing roof buckled under ice. He and Kathryn sat huddled in the kitchen; he was certain the windows would crack. How can glass be so warm on the inside, he asked her, and be so bitter out? This house has stood two hundred years, she told him; it will last one more.

He doubted it. His work was going poorly. He had been teaching

Melville, and the power of darkness compelled him. He said, "November in my soul" at intervals, aloud. Between Bartleby and Billy Budd there's not much margin for hope; between the tongue-tied and the resolutely silent, how to stake out speech?

"You've got what they call writer's block," said Kathryn. "That's the trouble, isn't it?"

"No."

"So what's the trouble? What do you need?"

"Something to write for. About."

"The world is full of instances." She was admonitory this way often, possessed of a kind of conviction he both envied and disliked. She could dismiss in a minute what it took him months to accept.

He added wood to the Resolute. "I'm trying to find one. One instance, I mean."

Kathryn had been baking bread. She cleaned the marble slab.

"Like what happens to this window when it's twenty below and eighty degrees by the stove. Why it freezes, why it melts."

"It's time to order seeds."

"I love you very much," said Clint. "Except I wonder why we're here."

"The spring list came from Burpee's." She pointed to the catalogue. "That's one good reason, isn't it?"

"Is this the asparagus year?"

"It's a commitment," she said.

Asparagus beds take three years to establish, and he doubted if they would be there to eat the first result. It was an act of faith in continuity that rendered him uncertain. Belgian endive is a two-year proposition; he proposed endive instead. Their own third anniversary would come on April 10.

"Let's have some music," she said.

The dark outside was palpable. He saw ripples in the window glass. No matter how he misted it, the asparagus fern turned brown. He played Fats Waller and then the Mendelssohn octet and added wood at intervals to the hissing stove. He would speak next afternoon on the undercutting irony of Melville's title *The Confidence Man*. All confidence had fled. There were raisins and walnuts and honey in Kathryn's rising loaf; he did not know how to proceed.

That Wednesday night they gave a party for the poet passing through.

He was coming to Skidmore to read. His name was Samuel Tench Hazeltine—and, as they would come to learn, he called himself by all three names at whim. He came to dinner with Clint's chairman, and their wives. It snowed.

Kathryn prepared boeuf en daube. She used the recipe from *To the Lighthouse*, and looked—distracted, fine-boned, inward—just like Virginia Woolf. Clint told her this while they were setting the table. She smiled. "Have you made salad dressing?"

"No. I will."

"Eloise Macallister's a bore." She produced the garlic and the garlic press. "I feel as if she's judging us. As if she thinks *she's* chairman, and the question of your tenure rides on the dessert . . ."

"What's for dessert?" he asked.

"I'm serious. She's so *judgmental*. Coeur à la crème. Mousse torte."

He smacked his lips. "My favorite."

"Who is this poet anyhow?"

"Hazeltine. He's good, I think. He comes from upper Michigan and writes complicated rhyming things about bears and sleeping with his leman in the snow."

"Leman?"

"Darling. It's an early word for darling."

"Christ," she said. "I bet Eloise just loves him."

"No," said Clint. "I mean it. He *is* good."

They worked, then, in companionable silence—setting out the candles, her family's silver, letting the wine breathe. Outside, the snow had slackened; a plow passed. The moon appeared. He was responsible for college functions of this sort—the reader's series, the symposium on Caribbean literature, the memorial lecture endowed by the widow of the previous department chairman, having to do with myth.

Hazeltine, however, had not been Clint's idea. He had been sponsored the previous year by the senior poet at Skidmore. Then the poet—intensely anxious, ferrety, with a red wisp of beard—took a leave of absence. He claimed he needed drying out, but Clint maintained the preposition was wrong; he needed drying up. He was not missed. His skin had flaked in patches. He went to Florence with his lover, the quattrocento art historian "big in Botticelli"; they adored Italian cooking and called each other *caro* in the halls.

Hazeltine's *Selected Poems* had recently appeared. Clint stocked six at the college bookstore, and bought one. He read "Caribou and Booster Chair," "Both Beautiful, One a Gazebo," and "Pica's Pique" with irritation; they were too clever by half. They preened. Yet something contrary struck him in the formulaic punning, the wordplay and formal invention—some undercurrent to the verse he wanted to call bardic: a dark demented chanting held in check by wit. It was as if the poet, knowing his own power, declined or was fearful to use it—"growing grim about the mouth."

"What about his wife?" she asked. "Do I take her shopping? Or is that part up to Eloise?"

"Don't be angry. I'm grateful. You know that."

"Of course." She went into the downstairs bathroom to apply her face.

They arrived two hours late. Frank Macallister, the chairman, came in first. "Whooeee!" He clapped his hands. "Not fit outside for man nor beast." He did his imitation of W. C. Fields. "We've got to be crazy," he said.

Dark shapes surged behind him, slapping at the air. Kim Hazeltine was blond. She was, he knew from jacket copy, born on the same day as Samuel; they were forty-six. There was much bustling apology—the plane was late at Albany, the roads bad, the luggage lost—not lost exactly but delayed, the change in Pittsburgh, the weather advisory, and having made the wrong turn at that intersection three miles back; how did you ever find this place? how about a little privacy? are all those cows your neighbors? I could use a drink. . . . It took him some time, therefore, to disentangle his guests from each other, their coats. The mudroom was cold. He closed his eyes an instant, tilting up against his own blue parka ("The Down Syndrome," Kathryn called it), making space.

"I'm glad you're here," he said. "We're very glad you made it. Welcome, all."

"I know your work," said Hazeltine.

His hand was limp. He was taller than Clint, potbellied, oddly awry—as if he had gained weight or lost it recently. His cheek twitched. He produced a pipe. "What can I get you to drink?" Clint asked. Macallister was pouring.

"You're good," said Hazeltine. "That's the reason I came. I'm here to teach you everything you don't already know."

"He means it," said his wife. "He wants to save you. Scotch."

She had a wide engaging smile that he thought insincere. He found the J & B. "They're real," she said. "These emeralds." She lifted her chin at him, arching her neck. "I know you're asking, are they real? They are."

Kathryn offered cheese.

"What are you working on?" the poet asked. "What have you been up to, lately?" He filled and lit his pipe.

Eloise Macallister had substituted heels for boots. "These winters. I don't understand how we manage. Every year I tell myself it's positively final, it can't go on like this . . ."

"Are you hungry?" Kathryn asked.

Macallister gazed at her greedily. "I am, my dear. I am."

They moved toward the Resolute, its spreading warmth. "We never see you anymore," Eloise complained. "Hiding out here, just you two. Rusticating."

"Is that what they call it?" asked Kim.

Hazeltine held out his glass. "What are you working on?" he asked again.

Then Kim was at his side. "Poor darling. No convert in *weeks*."

"Her husband's keeper. Call me Sam." He jangled ice. "It's scotch."

Clint poured. "Not much," he said. "Old Herman."

"Your poem on 'His Masquerade.'" They drank. "It's good, you know. You're good."

"This food won't wait," said Kathryn. "I *am* sorry."

"It's our fault," pronounced Macallister. "We're starved."

"The trouble with poems," said Eloise, "is nobody remembers them. It's impossible these days to remember poetry. Because it doesn't rhyme. The poems, I mean."

"His do." Clint raised his glass to their guest. There was salmon soufflé, and dill sauce. There were Kathryn's own baguettes.

"'In Flanders Fields,'" Eloise persisted. "I was forced to learn that one. I forget who wrote it, even, but I learned it all in second grade. I stood up in front of the class. 'In Flanders fields the poppies blow . . .'"

"'Between the crosses, row on row,' her husband joined in, and they both recited. "'If ye break faith with us that die, we shall not sleep, though poppies lie . . .'"

"It's 'us that go,'" said Kim. "And then 'the poppies blow.'"

"Well anyway," said Eloise. "You get what I'm trying to say."

"This soufflé is terrific," said Clint. He made a point of praising Kathryn's cooking, and it did deserve the praise. "Anyone ready for seconds?" Hazeltine held out his glass.

In this fashion the evening proceeded. The poet drank great quantities of scotch. He spoke in high, staccato bursts about the town of Charlevoix, the Indians, the French, the lilac bushes that the voyagers there planted, and the indiscriminate screwing—Excuse me, he turned to Eloise, but there's nothing else to say—they're not like the English, not fastidious or racist, they left lilacs and babies all over northern Michigan, but they weren't what you'd have to call settlers, not the Jesuits, not Père Marquette. The inward exploration, westward ho!, synecdoche, the part representing the whole . . . Synecdoche, said Kim, isn't that a town near this one, the one catercorner to Troy? They laughed. They spoke rapidly, shrilly, of life on the road, the woodpecker nattering jargon of praise, the strangers with their hands held out—not you, of course, he turned to Clint: you're exempted, brother, *ego te absolvo*—for healing and reference letters and book jacket blurbs and advice.

The boeuf en daube was a success. Macallister said "*Encantado*" to Kathryn, and he kissed the fork. Clint wondered what she thought. Her composure was glacial and subject to cracks. He asked her, "Can I help?"

"What you don't understand," Hazeltine continued, "is coming up short at the fence. Is just simply losing your nerve. Is figuring that all the games aren't worth the candle. Help?"

"He means with the dishes," said Kim. "I'm sure that's what he means."

"Our Clint is always helpful," said Macallister. "He's always there in the department pinch." Then he leaned across the table and pinched Kathryn's cheek. She drew back.

"Like when the Dean was cutting your budget, remember?" Eloise appeared not to notice; she turned to Clint, benign. "When he took a head count at that reading last November, and came to the conclusion poetry's not popular."

"Cost-efficient, was how he put it. It was the yardstick he used."

"We'll pack 'em in tomorrow."

Clint went to the kitchen for salad.

"Of course. Now Tench is back in town." Kim said this with a high, bright laugh.

"Scotch," the poet said.

There were reserves in their abandon, assessments of inconsequence Clint shared. He was gratified to think they were in league. They drank their way through salad and dessert. "If someone asked me," Eloise declared, "what tree I'd be—we play that game—I'd answer the Dutch elm. There are so few examples of them left."

"What *twee* are you?" asked Hazeltine, making his voice shrill. "What twee are you, fwiend Clinton?"

"Elm," asked Kathryn. "Why elm? They're blighted mostly, aren't they?"

"Maybe that explains it," said Macallister, sententious. "The noble elm at risk."

And suddenly the six of them were busily assessing trees—the kinds of tree or bush they'd be, the varieties of weather, scent, time, taste. He himself was willow, Hazeltine proclaimed. Large and spreading and yellow in springtime and sucking up liquid and sentimental and trash: a trash tree, willow is . . .

"What's all this got to do with poetry readings?" asked Eloise. There was strawberry sauce on her cheek. "'In Flanders Fields,' remember? That's what we were discussing."

"You were, darling," said her husband. "Only you discussed it."

"I prefer not to," said Clint.

They left at two. He and Kathryn carried in the dishes; there was much stumbling about in the snow. The car lights flickered, blazed. He watched them through the pantry window, wreathed in the white smoke of the exhaust. They seemed ceremonial, wiping windshields with attention, meticulous about the doors. Snow was falling lightly, noiselessly; he watched the car drift down the hill. "What did you think of them?" he asked.

She scraped plates. "We don't need to do this. We can leave it for the morning."

"Just the food." Clint produced Saran Wrap, flourished and tore it. "I'll put the cheese away."

"He seemed desperate."

"Hazeltine?"

"Yes. He was talking to himself. He was making connections like crazy, but they made no sense."

"I'm not sure I agree with that."

"You heard him better, maybe. I was in the kitchen, being pawed at by Macallister." Kathryn shook her head. "What sort of sense did he make?"

"Huck Finn and Mickey Mouse. Don't laugh: there's the problem of how to approach them. Do we read them the same way? Arguably they're masterworks, creatures of inspired inventiveness, right?"

"Right."

"And they both give pleasure, both engage our interest and make us laugh or cry." He stretched. "So what's the difference, really; why should we as readers think the one must be taught and the other ignored?"

"He can take care of himself." She pondered this. "He doesn't need the sponsoring. Mickey Mouse, I mean."

Clint wrapped the mousse torte carefully. "Why is *Moby-Dick* a better book than *Jaws*?"

"Did you notice?" Kathryn asked, "how Eloise pricked up her ears? When he was praising you."

"The argument from weakness. My enemy's enemy can't be all bad—so too with my friend's friend."

"If that's what happens to success, I'd rather be a . . ."

"Failure?"

"Let's get some sleep," she said.

Next morning he drove to the school. He followed a snow plow on Route 29, and trucks spewing sand. Hazeltine was in his office, holding forth. There were students at his feet: Betsy with the long black hair, Jill the tennis player, the twins from New Orleans. They wore sweaters and high leather boots. They had their notebooks open and were taking notes. "Hey, buddy," said the poet. "We're using your office, OK?" They were asking Hazeltine whom they should read; they asked him how he wrote—if he used a typewriter or pen. They asked him what hours he worked, and how he first got published, and when he discovered he wanted to write, and what he was working on now.

Hazeltine wore the same clothes as on the night before; he had not shaved. He chewed his pipe; his eyes were red. "Bright kids here," he wagged his head. "Except they don't know shit from Shinola. What have you been teaching them?"

"The usual."

"Apollonius of Rhodes," he said. "That's who they ought to be reading."

He swept his hand dismissively across the shelf. "Not this anthology shit."

Outside, the wind was high. The pines by Palamountain Hall were snapping, shaking, sprung. Snow cascaded whitely. "'Pied beauty,'" Clint announced. "Until I knew you'd come to class, we had Hopkins scheduled. He's up for discussion today."

"Let's talk about *your* book."

Betsy with the long black hair leaned forward, showing cleavage.

"Let's find out why you're writing it," said Hazeltine. "Or not."

The twins from New Orleans—Kiki and Kay Kay, though he never could be certain which was which—turned to him, expectant. "Oh please," they urged him. "Do."

"Let's talk about your work instead," Clint said. "We've been reading 'Quahaug Chowdown.' 'The Sunrise Downer.'" He smiled. "The ones in the anthology."

"I asked first," said Hazeltine.

"You never tell us what you're writing," said the tennis player. "*Please.*"

Trapped by all their emphases, cornered in his office, Clint began. He wanted to write the chapter on whaling from the whale's point of view. He knew that sounded hopeless. He knew it smacked of good intentions, bumper-sticker pap like "Save the Whales." Remember, he asked them, that great blue plastic whale in the Museum of Natural History—its enormous hanging shell? Well, imagine what it feels like to be polishing the eye, suspended with a feather duster and a mop, snouting up through impossible watery bone-crushing weight after air, then diving again, blowhole full. Imagine the bottoms of boats. That was what—he warmed to this—a whale would see, or sense, inconsequential timber preparing to be jetsam where it yawed. There would be wood. The chapter would splinter to stanzas. There would be metal, no more than a pinprick but lasting. There would be rope, the pilot fish, the plankton; the school in its tail's wake would scatter. Down, down, down it sounded: blubber, blood, and hemp.

He stopped, surprised. He did not usually permit himself such language, the intricate echo of lies. Hazeltine was grinning, lighting up his pipe. "It's fine insofar as it goes."

"But?"

"But it goes insufficiently far."

They looked at each other in pure opposition. "Professor talk," said Clint.

His students closed their notebooks. It was time for class. They apologized. They stood.

Confidence, Clint told them, is the mutuality of trust. That is its root meaning, the force of the term; we confide in each other, we grow confidential. A man who trusts himself is confident, as if the body knows the mind, the mind the spirit, the right hand the left. Yet a "confidence man" is not to be trusted, though he engenders confidence—being of respectable appearance and address.

We have all had the experience of dislocation, a sudden ringing in our ears or floaters in our sight. Vertigo and masquerade and the question of identity are commonplace in film and fact; what do we know and how do we know it and when do we make up our minds? Imagine for a moment that a stranger comes toward you, smiling, affable, rolling up his sleeves as if to demonstrate that there is nothing hidden there. He praises you; he if full of high-flown flattery because you volunteer. His hat has a rabbit, however, and his handkerchiefs are knotted and his rings ring hollow; he says he can cause you to levitate, to rise in the air on a chair.

There is something pleasing about his assurance, his smug conviction he can manage because he has managed before. He takes your weight into account. He places your hands on your knees; he tells you to relax. He waves his hand near the slats of the chair in order to prove there are no wires; he avoids the filaments attached to the headrest and legs. Throughout his patter and performance, he glances into the wings.

Why confide in strangers when we keep silent with friends? Why give ourselves to lovers when their files are confidential, their health histories unknown? Melville's book is "Dedicated to Victims of Auto Da Fe." Are we not all such victims; do we not walk through doors routinely, or drive into enclosing darkness, or dive into clear water of uncertain depth? We speak of chance encounters or an accident narrowly missed. What we mean is we are confident of gravity: the chair will not rise up unaided. Confidence is not the spurious confession, the revelation opaque in its false clarity, the card up the dealer's rolled sleeve. It is knowing what you will accomplish, what you won't; it is knowing what you know and what you don't.

Kim and Eloise and Kathryn had been shopping. They met at Mrs. London's

Restaurant and displayed to the men what they had bought. The table seemed too small. There were angora sweaters and a photograph of Saratoga Water being sold from a horse-drawn wagon. Kim loved to shop, she said. She confessed she was compulsive but could always give it back. Or to the Salvation Army, or we can have a tag sale; I've spent your check already, dear, she said. Whenever we're too crowded we just buy a bigger house . . .

There were garnet cuff links; there was a box of chocolates; there were coral beads, a pair of gloves, black ankle boots, a hat. Eloise, too, was talkative. She had bought an espresso machine. "After last night's feast," she said, "we decided we just had to have one. We need it, don't we; it's a business expense. You can go a lifetime not knowing what you need." She put her hand on Kathryn's wrist. "You'll show me how to use it, won't you, the proportion of coffee exactly?"

Kathryn promised. Samuel—he was referring to himself in the third person now—said they must come to Michigan and visit Tench and Kim. The dogs, the horses, whitefish, the dunes, the anapestic trimeter of town names, their involuntary wisdom: Betty Groeze. It means *Bête Grise*, he said, a place where bear roamed freely once, or something tameable only by pronunciation, ignorance, and guns. He studied Clint. "But you're suspicious, aren't you? You wonder what Samuel's after."

"Yes."

"Greatness."

"He's joking," Kim said. "Pay no attention."

"He has never been more serious," said Hazeltine. "Not ever in his life."

"He means it," Kim told the others. "He does."

"Either you come back with us or Sam's staying here."

In the motel, after lunch, he expatiated on art. It was not a luxury but a necessity, not only light but air. When they made shelter in the caves they started painting walls. In the long winter nights we whittle shape. We whistle when alone. Why then should this be just a pastime or sport, a casual encounter for the weekend or on Wednesday night; why should we let jealousy distract us, or petty envy, ambition's shrunk shank? "Don't piss away your life." He rubbed his low belly; he yawned. "Don't get suckered in by this, by what you think you're working for." He waved at the boxes in front of the closet, piled about the bureau: Kim's booty for the day. "A nice place you got here. A nice place to visit." He sat on the complaining bed, then threw himself backward and slept.

Clint and Kathryn, the previous summer, had gone to Nova Scotia; they talked about it as a way to live. It was cheap and manageable, protected by the Cabot Trail and beyond the reach of academe; if they had to leave Cossayuna, this could be a refuge and escape. The sea was cold. The lobsters, however, were plentiful; on Cape Breton they made camp. They joked about life lived among subarctic flora, the edible tundra for lunch. "Let's have some edible tundra," Clint would say, and make camp coffee and Spam. They spent ten days on the Cabot Trail, clambering on rock.

In Dingwall, near Meat Cove, they found a house for sale. The schoolteacher, Mrs. Helen Borden, was planning to retire. Her husband had recently died. She showed them through the rooms and pointed to the bay, a neck of rocks where the property line ended, a garden, a toolshed glazed with rain.

The price was low. "There's a carpenter," she said. "His name is Alec Moore. He'd like to have a go at it. He'd live here when you don't." She regaled him with the virtues of the neighborhood, the value of the property, the pleasurable prospect of a future in the Maritimes; there would be positions in the school system for literate persons; Clint could have her job. The post office, too, needed help. "Alec lost an arm," she said, "when he was a fisherman. But you should see the things he manages with just the one he's got."

The afternoon wore on. Her enthusiasm wearied them. The more she praised the place, the more they grew suspicious of her decision to sell. "Real oak," she said, "this flooring. And we've never had a leak. Not since he patched the roofing in, let's see now, '64." They met Moore in the driveway, his sleeve pinned to his shirt. He had close-cropped hair, a sailor's lurch, advancing. He reeked. "This is Alec Moore," she said. "How nice he happened by." Alec proffered his good right hand. His nose was bulbous, red. He said they'd find it dull in winter unless they had a hobby; he had a hobby, himself. He was interested in model planes and fashioned them from balsa wood; there's nothing like a helicopter made of balsa wood to help you pass the time. He lifted his sleeve at Kathryn, smiling. He'd gotten used to making do, to doing without, he wasn't complaining, but eighteen foot of snow could make a person impatient, he hoped they had hobbies to help pass the winter, young marrieds like you are, you two.

Mrs. Borden said, "Come out of the rain, would you kindly?"

Beer bottles littered the shingle. Gulls preened. "Excuse me," Alec said. "I need to get on with it, Helen." He bowed. "Good afternoon to you both." His courtesy was drunken, his deference excessive. The thin band of light on the western horizon shut off as if with a switch.

Later, at the lodge, they talked about a winter with eighteen feet of snow. "No wonder they drink," Clint said. "No wonder it's so cheap."

"This too will pass," Kathryn said.

They both used that expression. It gave a kind of certainty to progress, the promise of endurance before anything endured.

The hall was full. Clint thanked the audience for coming, the department for its sponsorship, the memory of that deceased chairman who made this evening possible. He tried to be yet parody the smiling public man. He shifted tone, however, when introducing Hazeltine; he borrowed phraseology from our guest tonight. The arc of the intelligence, the vector of the metric drive, the circumference of reference, the radical radius squared—all these figure in what I would like to call the geometry of love. Whatever we might mean by this has something to do with poetry also, the feel of the moss underfoot while you wait, the way the black bear and steelhead conspire, or, in that memorable stanza, copulate in foam that is not sea spume but sludge, the industrial park of the soul. He ended with a flourish, to applause.

What followed was astonishing. Hazeltine wore black. He had brought a mandolin and flute. He strummed and blew and spoke with a high, keening wail; he stamped his foot for emphasis and overstated rhyme. "Howl," and "Who'll," for instance, and "gravid" and "beloved" were matched pairs. His voice was thin, his music mediocre, his attitude both self-effacing and pretentious; he kept his eyes closed. Clint laughed, or wanted to; he did not look at Kathryn, for fear she would laugh too. Macallister coughed, shifting in his seat. "Whatever you were ever," chanted Hazeltine, "come over here, come near; whatever you wear never, don; come *on*." This rhythmic burble soothed him, seemingly; he swayed and rocked and sang.

His body *was* the language, his thick throat the flute. "Bear, bear, bear," he chanted, cuffing the microphone as if it were salmon, pawing the stage like a rock. "The showman, the shaman." He danced. His face went slick with sweat. He had the long poems by heart. He looked at the twins, reciting, as if it were to them he spoke, for them he wrote; he worked his way—in the second stanza of "Victus"—up to fever pitch. "In the transept of the birch cathedral / they rise above us, tetrahedral / reeking where / there once was bear / the spoor / of you, locked leman, poor / bloody remnant"—here he flourished the mandolin—"of the scrotal, fetal sack / come back!"

Clint, listening, dreamed Arrowhead, that dark expanse of wood, the meadow behind him, the sun on the poplars, the tree pollen drifting, Melville with a waistcoat and gray beard and tankard and great anxious intelligence declining—saw further how the whole of what he had been working for was represented as burlesque by the man above him strutting, his wife in the audience twisting her rings, the flower child gone weedy, the bard with nothing consequent to sing, codified in self-indulgence by the indulgence of just such admiring acolytes as he, Clint, had become (and what of his colleague in Italy now, the fifty-five-year-old with black shoes and dungarees and a leather vest and boy that he brought to the Piazza della Signoria, hoping to impress on him the marmoreal grace of David, the dispassionate homage a witness must pay to that most potent curving thigh, the way that the boy, if sufficiently urged, might return with the poet to their pensione, hear how he was misunderstood in Saratoga Springs by Philistines, how his companion, the Botticelli expert, had decamped for Siena with Angelo, and therefore they might share a grappa, an evening, a bed—this too in the service of art, the crease of the bedsheet, the pillow, the cry, the curvature of clothesline at the window, *et in Arcadia ego, ego, ego*), the dream of the hunter, the long line baited, the perception fading, fading Clint's sense of resolve, of the thick-bearded failure in Pittsfield—and as the reading tilted to completion, as Hazeltine wound down, hoarse now, wrung by effort, the associate professor of European history asleep, the composition teacher correcting texts, dealing with serial commas, and Betsy with her skirt hiked up, a scar on her knee he had not noticed, and all of this predictable—applause, the books to sign, his self-revulsion at the prospect of security, small daring, and large scorn—this was the candle, not game; the process, not result—saw the reception afterward, with cheese and apple slices and white wine and cider and doughnuts and beer, and then they would repair to someone's house for drinks, the die-hard remnant and the recently divorced—where Hazeltine was holding forth, backed against the counter, saying "In my opinion," often, discoursing on renegade verse, the notion of the "sacred fire," the *vates*, the poet possessed, talking rapidly, coherently, his eyes blear, blank ("I'm tired," he would say to Clint, "whipped." "It takes it out of you, right?" "It does. I need a drink." "Scotch?" He nodded.)—Kathryn in the corner, inattentive, patient, discussing asparagus still in the kitchen until they might withdraw, offering apologies, their explanations and farewells and the promise, absolutely, to remain in touch, to get to work, the long cold drive to Cossayuna, the chance still of snow, their escape.

In bed that night he turned to her. "We can't stay here."

Kathryn feigned sleep, or was sleeping.

"We've got to go."

"To Michigan?"

"No. And not to Dingwall either."

"It's one o'clock," she said. "Let's sleep on it, darling."

"I can't."

She gathered herself in the pillows, then heaved upright. He watched her breasts.

"This sucking up to college students. Jockeying for tenure. Wondering if Melville merits the attention. Christ," he said. "I quit."

"It will come your way."

"I doubt it."

"Those are actual emeralds," said Kathryn. She was reaching for a cigarette. She liked to smoke in bed.

"Whose? Kim's?"

She nodded and inhaled. "That's why he can rail at the academy. That's how they afford such scorn."

"You wanted a horse barn," he said.

"I want a child." She knocked out ash. She had not said this before.

"What changed your mind?"

She dropped the sheet and would not say. He bent above her, rapt.

The night was clear and cold. A crescent moon hung framed by the top left-hand pane, its edges iced. Tomorrow it might snow again; the moon

seemed sheathed in light. "'In Flanders Fields,'" he found himself repeating, as silent inward litany, "'In Flanders Fields.'" The Morgan in his
neighbor's stall stirred in its sleep. He had been moved by Hazeltine,
impelled by the great thrashing malice of the invocation, invitation to the
dance: here's a doubloon for him who finds the fish. Everywhere about
him they were singing whaling songs, they were doling out a tot of rum
and doffing their caps to the breeze. The wind stood fair. While Kathryn
moved beneath him, her white breasts roiling, spume at her neck, he
studied The Book of the Quick.

The Day's Catch

I

EVERYWHERE THEY TOLD him stories; all of them wanted to talk. Everyone confided in him elaborately. It was not so much his reaction they wanted as his respectful attention; let me tell you, they would say, the story of my life.

David listened. He told himself this was useful, a lesson, the way a writer works. The difference, for example, between someone who would get the car and someone who would fetch it was a difference to record. It was not so obvious as "trunk" and "boot," or "let" and "rent"—but it did signify; someone who would "fetch" the car had spent his childhood in England, or New England, or tried to make it seem so. Appearances deceived. The glitter of surface, the glimmering sheen of the harbor at night, the focused diffusion of light—these were their subjects, therefore his. He made notes.

Why do we distrust those men who will not talk to others, those women who talk to themselves? Some poke their way through garbage continually muttering; others keep mute. If eyes be called the window of the soul, then surely the mouth is the hallway, the ear the door. What he heard was confident or confidential, full of mock or true humility; he heard it in diners and restaurants and cabs.

Voice, he came to understand, is the play of utterance—its registered timbre and range. It may confound or confirm expectation: so deep a sound from so small a throat, so nasal a twang from such elegant lips. Who has not been astonished by the barrel-chested athlete in the tenor section, the sultry alto burble from a child next door? Voice amplifies the eye; it travels as slowly as sound.

At any rate he listened. He watched the smile belying anger, the gesture of evasion, the passionate avowal or pretense of indifference, the sharp rushing intake of breath. The way it all happened, they said, the way it used to be, you'll never believe this, you'll never, the story of my life. He wrote it down every day.

In 1968 David Lewin moved to Martha's Vineyard. His parents approved. He was twenty-two years old, a Harvard graduate, and classified 4-F; he arrived in May. He rented a shack at the edge of Quitsa Pond—a shack that would be sold, ten years later, for four hundred thousand dollars. It sat on two acres of land and had been the schoolhouse privy. A black kerosene stove offered heat. The plumbing was erratic; the roof leaked in a northeast rain. He knew the leaks' locations and could gather the water in pails; he rigged himself a shower stall outside. He had been trying to write.

He believed, that season, in a return to ancient techniques. He wrote fables, parables. He had completed three. He felt invaded by the beauty of the scene—the heather and spear grass at his doorstep, the soft slope to the pond and glimpse of dunes and the south shore beyond, the ocean a distant, deep blur. Gulls wheeled above him, then dove. A great blue heron nested nearby; often, in the mornings, he would watch it preen. He had no lock on his door. The shack was one large room, with partitions for the kitchen and the toilet and the bed.

He had many visitors. He was young and single and heterosexual, and there weren't enough of those, they told him, to go around. Their fathers or their boyfriends or their husbands wouldn't mind; they were divorcing anyhow, or separated, or on vacation. He was in demand. They liked his car or hair or laughter or paragraphs or hut. He had no telephone, and therefore they dropped by. They came to take him sailing or to dinner; they brought him wine and peyote, and one woman brought her own sheets. His bed was double, with tarnished brass bars. Its mattress was thin, its frame sagged. He had nailed a reading light to the beam above. Once he returned to find a garter snake coiled to the lamp, hunting heat; he did not recognize the snake as harmless and, panicky, cut off its head.

David held two part-time jobs. He drove a delivery truck for the Menemsha fish market seven mornings a week. He rose at dawn and dressed in rubber boots and army surplus khakis; he arrived at six. The owner was there before him, an unlit pipe clamped in his teeth; he had been bringing in the boats and buying fish and putting up orders since four. On slow mornings they had coffee; then the fish cutters arrived. The market had holding tanks for lobster and an ice room for the larger fish; it opened on a retail basis at nine-thirty every day. By then he had loaded the truck. He delivered swordfish and lobster and bushels of quahaugs to the island restaurants and to the Vineyard Haven ferry slip.

David liked the work. Thick slabs of swordfish bulked gleaming in the truck bed, and he would carry two or three whole fish. The wooden lobster crates leaked. Their weight when loaded was greater than their delivered weight; the lobsters were packed in seaweed, and they yielded water. He needed help unloading; there was camaraderie in the delivery bays. He learned the island gossip, learned the backroads and shortcuts between the towns and, on his return trip, if he ran ahead of schedule, could stop for a swim or cigar.

Part of David's salary was fish. He collected fish scraps from the cutting table, or a ragged fillet, or lobsters with no claws. He learned to shuck shellfish expertly, and at cocktail parties he was called upon to open oysters and clams. He was back at his shack before noon, and he had the afternoon to write. On clear days he took his typewriter outside. He set up a table beneath the shingled overhang and kept his carbon copies in a doorless Kelvinator by the western wall.

He also worked twice weekly as the paid companion to a twelve-year-old blind boy. Anton Longley Mackin, Jr., was fatherless. His cousin had gone to college with David and asked him as a favor if he'd be a friend to Tony, a pair of male eyes. It would be worth his while. The kid was surrounded by women, he said; he needed to go bowling or talk about baseball instead. "Where would we go bowling?"

"He should get out of the house. Mom-mom wants to meet you. It's arranged."

So David drove to a great gabled home beside the bay and was ushered in while Tony waited, docile, in the hall. The boy loved jazz. He had been blind from birth, and his aural memory was extensive and exact. They played a game called "Blind Man's Bluff"; Tony proposed the name.

David selected a record, selected a side and a cut. If Tony failed to identify the song and the performance within five seconds, he lost. He rarely lost. Once he confused a Jelly Roll Morton solo in terms of the date of the recording; once he could not place a Muggsy Spanier performance until twelve seconds had passed.

"Mom-mom" was rich. She wore flowing caftans and used a cigarette holder and said "*Dah*ling" as if she'd studied for the part. This turned out to be the case. She had been an actress, David learned, acquired in Cleveland by Mr. Mackin when Mr. Mackin was drunk. He had been drunk for years. He had wanted, she told David, to be the youngest of his set to succumb to cirrhosis; he thought cirrhosis of the liver had cachet. There was no distinction to a heart attack, or cancer; it took a special kind of perseverance to die of alcohol. That was a distinction, she said, conferred upon the very poor and rich; that was the reason opposites attract.

She had been sufficiently his opposite, she said, and attractive. There was a prosy, truth-telling side of her that David came to trust. Anton Mackin had spirited her from backstage at the Cleveland Playhouse like the seducer of showgirls in some melodrama or farce. He plied her with champagne and telegrams and roses; his great black car purred in the alley. Only there was such studied nonchalance in the gestures he made that she spotted them as studied; she learned to see the parody behind the high romance. There had been more self-mockery than mockery about him; there had been a cold-eyed calculation in the operatic ardor and the fistful of rings that he asked her to wear once engaged. She did want David to understand—as her husband had once wanted her to understand—that money was a means, not end; it was a shared illusion, a conventional acceptance of what was merely scrip. Why should a check mean money? Why should a broker call one day to say we've made a thousand dollars or a hundred thousand dollars or five hundred thousand dollars, since the takeover bid? It was a dream people dreamed. It was a God more persuasive than God; whole societies were organized by the convention of wealth.

For those with wealth, however, and no capacity for dreaming, it also was a joke. It divided and multiplied and reproduced itself like cells. There were men in Wall Street and Chicago and Cleveland who were working overtime so Anton need not work. Slowly she too came to see the comedy in things; there was nothing they could buy that would not increase their purchasing power, no expenditure so great it would not be recouped. Did David know the Billie Holiday refrain—"'Them that's got shall get, them that's not shall lose. So the Bible says, and it still is news . . .'"

Therefore he made random gestures, and one of those gestures was marriage when he knew he was going to die. He told her this, in San Francisco, almost as an afterthought. "By the way," he said, "I ought to tell you. I've got six months to live." She had not believed him, of course. They were staying at the Fairmont, dressing for dinner; he was tying his tie at the window, looking out. His back was to her, and she asked him to repeat it, and he said he had cirrhosis and did not choose to die a bachelor; he hoped she understood. She would remember forever the way he tied his tie. His fingers seemed translucent and the brown stains at his fingertips looked suddenly like blood. The tie was a bow tie, dark blue. She came and stood beside him, and he put his hand on her shoulder and said, "I want a child."

Anton Jr. had been born with his father still alive. But they had been on different floors of the same hospital, and when she brought the mewling blinded premature bundle down for inspection, her husband had not known his son; he kept his eyes closed also, and failed to acknowledge their presence. He died when Tony was seven weeks old; she had been bereaved. That *was* the word, said Mom-mom, even if bereaved was foolish, the kind of word you read in newspapers or flower shops. Yet it was how she felt. She told her story to David in twenty-minute segments, drinking tea. It all happened years ago, but years ago was yesterday, since every day she lived with the abiding presence of the past. She could not help it; she minded; she had been bereft.

One month she had been living in a third-floor walk-up in Cleveland, hoping to play Ado Annie in the *Oklahoma* revival. She had been offered the Janis Paige part in a bus-and-truck company version of *The Pajama Game*. Next month she was in Venice, at the Gritti Palace, with a man she barely knew whose last name had become her own legal name, whose fingers were translucent and who bought her whatever she paused to admire. She fell in love with him then. She had not married for love. She had not married for money, precisely, although the money helped. There was no point pretending it did not help. It was the collective dream; it made her own dreams come true.

Yet what she elected to marry was the clear-eyed chilly assessment in Anton, his gambler's sense of risk. She would have liked to know him better; he had surprised her, as she surprised him. She had surprised him, for instance, with her knowledge of the Tiepolo ceilings and how they used perspective. She had had what Anton called more than a pretty face. Mom-mom laughed. He, David, mustn't pay attention; she had been fishing for praise. It was a bad habit. No man could walk into her home without arousing in her what she recognized as sorrow, a passionate nostalgia for her own lithe youth. They had had a gondolier to escort them everywhere. Her memory of Venice was a wash of marble and green water, the wine Anton ordered for lunch, the lanterns, Torcello, the pastry, the light. In Venice her true love was born, and what is born must die.

So when he told her, some weeks later in their suite at the Fairmont, that the doctors could not save him, that it was irreversible—when he said he was dying and wanted a child she took that as a general truth: we all die, we desire children to strew flowers on our grave. And it had not seemed specific, had not meant his liver would quit. Cirrhosis meant nothing particular; it did not mean him lying sweating, shaking, unable to swallow; it had not meant she'd continue with a child born blind.

Mom-mom was thirty-eight now and not reconciled. She had had too little of her husband; it was a brief, waking dream. She had married a stranger dead twelve years ago, and now she was nearly his age. He had been thirty-nine, so possibly he had not been the youngest of his circle to die of cirrhosis—but from her newfound vantage he had been young enough. She and Tony summered on the Vineyard and wintered in Manhattan and Londonderry; they traveled to Barbados every March. She was not complaining. She had little to complain of; she could have a private performance of *Oklahoma* if she chose. She could give so large a sum in memory of her husband that the Cleveland Playhouse would build a Mackin Wing; she was considering that. And Tony did not seem unhappy—he too was content with his lot. He had a shy sweetness like his father's, Mom-mom thought—only it had not yet hardened into nonchalance.

"You'll like him," she finished.

"I do already."

She smiled. "He's sensitive to strangers. He notices more than you think."

David stood.

"It's like a dog," she said. "I don't mean to compare him to a dog, of course. But he can sense immediately if you're frightened of him, or pretending interest. He knows by someone's footsteps if that someone is a friend."

As if on cue, Tony entered. They walked together to the beach. "You didn't take a shower," Tony said. "What's that I smell on you—swordfish?"

"Three of them this morning," David said. "I brought you a present."

"What?"

"This." He handed Tony a dried swordfish sword. Nearly three feet long, and grainy, it seemed capable of skewering a rowboat. The boy was grateful. He veered between civility and childishness; he kicked off his shoes and waved the sword. They charged the surf. Tony galloped, whooping, and was both horse and rider. "Cavalree!"

They had many such routines. On clear days they would walk the shore or go horseback riding on the bridle trail behind the golf course. Tony owned a bicycle built for two, and he enjoyed tandem bicycle trips. "Two eyes and four feet and two seats," he would say. "What kind of animal do you suppose we make?"

He joked about his blindness. It was a running patter, a continual allusion. "You should have seen Mom-mom last night," he said. "I swear she was blind drunk. And that old bag across the street, Mrs. Tillotson. She came over with Jenny, you know? They couldn't walk a straight line. They all needed blinders last night."

On rainy days they listened to music, or David read *The Last of the Mohicans*, *Kim*, or *Oliver Twist*. Once he collected Tony and took him on the fish run. Tony enjoyed it, he said. But the way he traced the dashboard with his fingertips seemed fretful; he scratched at the blue vinyl seat. He positioned the radio buttons and the treble knob. He inclined his head, absorbed, and his attention to the banter of the men at the ferry loading slip felt excessive. "What's a portagee?" he asked.

"Portagee?" David reversed the truck.

"They were mentioning a portagee. They said it couldn't add."

He swung into traffic. "Portuguese. They were joking about Johnny over in Woods Hole. His daughter kept the books. And apparently she's pregnant now so Johnny's going broke."

Tony laughed. He slapped at his knee. Yet the laughter had been dutiful; they both knew the joke was not funny. He did not ask to join in the fish run again, but he always inquired after the men in the market or at the restaurants or dock. "How's Ted?" he'd ask. "How's Bill? How's Johnny Portagee?"

One Thursday it rained and they followed Mom-mom to Vineyard Haven. She had some errands, she said, and they might as well have a soda or something; they could poke around the Goodwill store while she assessed the breakfront Harrison had found. You couldn't trust him, naturally; he'd claim a piece was Chippendale before the varnish dried. But Harrison did have an eye and knew what she wanted and claimed to have found it, and therefore it was worth a look since tennis was out of the question.

The rain was warm. David lingered for an instant at the Goodwill door. He held it open. Later he would ask himself, if it had not been raining, if Mom-mom had not dropped them there, if Tony were not blind—if any single one of all the things that were the case was not the case, would he and Alice have met?

She had been looking at clothes. She stood in the rear of the long, littered room. There was a rack of children's clothes, a rack of women's dresses, an aisle of men's trousers and coats. She emerged from this last. Hooked rugs showed deer on the wall. The shoes were dingy, the appliances secondhand; there were glass plates and used blenders and a chess game with one knight missing. Tony hunted records beneath the paperbacks. He would insist on extracting the disks—running his fine fingers along the countertops, rummaging in cartons. Then David read out the titles and Tony said, "There, that one. Yes," or shook his head.

Alice approached. She was looking for a mirror; she held a man's hunting jacket with red and black woolen checks. There was no mirror. She worked herself into the coat, then belted the belt. "It looks terrific," he said.

"What does?" Tony asked. He held a selection of Fred Waring 78's.

"The jacket. Tell her that you think so too."

"Which one is this?" David read the titles and the girl moved away, comprehending that Tony was blind.

They met again at the register. "Did you decide?" he asked.

She nodded.

"My name is David. Lewin."

"Alice." She held out her hand.

"And this is Mr. Jazz," he said. "Tony. We come here for records."

"I see that." Alice colored. Tony touched his arm. "You should have bought a raincoat," David said. Mom-mom would reimburse him for the records. The lady at the register cracked open a brown paper bag.

"We could give you a ride?" Tony asked.

She refused him, gravely. "I work across the street. I work at the jewelry shop. It's the end of my lunch break, you see."

Later he would tell her that she'd told him to return. She said, "Don't flatter yourself." Later still, in his arms, she whispered she was glad he listened, glad she told him where she worked. "Imagine," Alice said, "how close I came to missing you. Imagine how that would have been."

He could not imagine it. He tried to, in the years to come, but failed. Her hair was thick and blond; it fell to the small of her back. Her nose was aquiline. She smiled at him at six o'clock, when he entered the jewelry shop, saying without surprise, "It's you." He said, "It isn't raining. Would you like to take a walk?" She switched off the light at her work desk. She made a pile of shavings, arranged the necklaces—turquoise and coral, on thin silver strands—and asked him, "Where's your brother?" The display case had a scallop-shell motif. He told her that he had no brother, Tony Mackin was a friend. "I have a car," he said. "We could go up-island, if you'd like."

They drove to Indian Hill. He followed the road through the woods, then parked where the path ended at the forest ranger station; there were tracks in the sand. There was no one in the fire tower, however, and they climbed in silence. An Indian burial ground and a replica of Reverend Thomas Mayhew's chapel lay to the west; they climbed above the trees. The stair slats were wet. At every landing stage they paused; the farms assumed dimension, and the shore appeared. He pointed out the visible landmarks; he knew the island well. She wore the hunting jacket he had seen her buy that afternoon. Wind took her hair. "I'm glad you're showing me this," Alice said. "I get so sick of beaches. Everybody and his brother has a favorite beach."

They reached the ranger's cabin, but the trapdoor at the entrance had been padlocked shut. The sun was roseate. It was August 14, 1968. Later he and Alice would disagree over the date; she thought it had been August 12. He remembered standing with her on the topmost platform, the sun descending, sea birds beneath, and telling her this whole display was for her benefit.

"You've been to Versailles?" Alice asked. He said, yes, he had been to Versailles. Somehow their shared knowledge of that royal pleasure-perch, how queens and princes could survey from balcony or window what those watching from ground level had to gape to see—the possibility that they had been together at Versailles, had glimpsed each other in the halls or down a green allée, had stood in the same ticket line or heard the same interpreter or admired identical portraits—that shared invented meeting made this seem a second chance. "A third," said David, "if you count this morning."

They remained on the tower, not touching. A ferry made for Cuttyhunk, and day sailors beat before the wind to Lambert's Cove. A chimney on the mainland gave out smoke like a white fan. "I have to go now," Alice said. "I do want to see you again."

They saw each other daily, and on Labor Day she moved into his shack. Things changed for David, were transfigured; the jeweler closed down for the season. The days grew briefer, the light more clear. He whistled love songs while he worked and relinquished his cigars. He started a novella about life at the fish market, the tall tales he heard. Her skin was fair, her body lean; she was not adept at sex. The first time he entered her she seemed to be in pain. She lay beneath him, eyes wide, resistant, staring at the ceiling. He asked her, was he hurting her, and she shook her head. He asked, did she want him to stop, and again she shook her head.

Alice came from Chapel Hill. Her father was a lawyer, and her parents had divorced. She had two sisters—one still at home. Her mother had once trained to be a pianist; she married on a whim. Then the whim became a household full of squalling argumentative children, and she couldn't concentrate or go to auditions or, when the opportunity came to perform, remember the music. She always used to remember instead—so she told her daughter—that she'd left the right rear burner on or maybe the porch door unlocked; she'd failed to feed the dogs or get the guestroom ready. She drank. She grew partial to pink gin. A pink-gin fizz at lunch helped make the world acceptable; without pink gin at hand, Estelle found it unacceptable—the way we maim and slaughter animals, for instance, the inequity of wealth.

Her father had been in the air force during the Korean War. His family was army, and his decision to join the air force had been greeted not so much with disapproval as shock: why trust yourself, they asked him, to all that untested machinery? His answer had been speed. A pilot got involved in combat more quickly than did combat troops; he had a stronger, swifter sense of purpose in the air. He was sent to the Pacific, and he came back changed. Alice could not remember him before he left; she had been a baby, and her mother was pregnant with Beth. But she did remember how he came back pole-thin, bald, impassive, not smiling at their mother or his children or their "Welcome Home Daddy Hero" sign, not wanting to be touched. He allowed himself to be handled, but there was no answering pressure, no sense of quickening warmth. If he mentioned aircraft carriers or landing or the enemy, that was all he ever said, not answering her questions about the bamboo cage. She had heard he spent a year in China in a bamboo cage. "I can't talk about it," her father said. "Not yet."

He dreamed about it, however, and Alice could remember waking in the dark because she heard him shouting, screaming, "No!" He would launch into unintelligible speeches in what she guessed was Chinese; he would jump out of bed or cover his eyes while they tried fruitlessly to wake him; he had been engaged, for years, in a tortured private wrangling they were powerless to halt. Her mother helped, at first. At first she sat by his side for as long as it took, holding his hand, stroking his forehead, speaking with that soothing croon she used when the children were sick. She had been the picture of compassionate patience for years.

Then imperceptibly—or by so slow a gradation and shift that Alice barely noticed—her father improved. He composed himself at mealtimes; he took an interest in the paper and the television news. He tended their garden with skill. He pruned the shrubbery around the walk. Alice returned from school one morning to find her father at the hedge, a neat, boxed section behind him and an overgrown straggle to tend to ahead. He was trimming things, setting things straight.

Then as if all Chapel Hill waited on his recovery, his neighbors and associates welcomed him back to the fold. They made as much of his return as if he had been Lazarus. He could have gotten the keys to the city, if Chapel Hill had a key. He resumed law practice, and cases came his way. He sported a moustache. He still had a reserve about him, but it seemed appropriate; it was civil, *civilian*, and often someone in the streets would remark to Alice how lucky and proud she must be.

That was when her mother started in to drink. Alice had it all muddled;

her childhood was a muddle just like everybody else's, and she couldn't say this happened and then that happened and then that. You don't get over shellshock overnight. Neither do you go from sober to sodden, from painstaking nurse to failed musician in a nightgown, drinking gin at noon, sweeping the coffee cups into the sink, showing more leg to the gardener than the gardener thought proper—neither did her mother go from support to burden overnight.

So there might have been a moment when the prisoner of war believed his wife angelic and thought himself beloved. Florence Nightingale had syphilis; she wondered if David knew that? She died in the Crimea, having ministered to soldiers there a little too particularly; that's what her mother said. Her father took business trips. He acquired from his wife what she was visibly losing, and there might have been a month or year when they met as equals in the house and bed.

But Alice could remember no such time. She remembered only imbalance, the way the walls would seem to tilt, the argument between them that was spoken or unspoken, and the way the doors would slam or be closed so gently, precisely, as to constitute reproach. She and her sisters would huddle in the playroom, playing Monopoly or Crazy Eights or with their grandmother's dollhouse, the one that had real marble pillars on the porch. It was a white plantation house, with antebellum furnishings and pickaninnies in the kitchen and a stately entrance hall. The whole stood four feet high. She remembered playing with the fervor of belief: everything could be adjusted, perfect; all the cups and saucers would be put back on the shelf.

In springtime they would flee outside, and there too the world was in order. They had a pony and chickens and, when their father returned to his guns, bluetick hounds. He refurbished the cinderblock privy by the chicken run. It became her playhouse, with curtains on the windows, whitewash, and a screen door. She and Beth—Mary Kate had grown too old for this—would sit for hours on the window seat that had been the three-holer and play "Who Do You Like Better?" or "Sleeping Beauty" or, later, with the portable radio, sing along with that week's hit parade. She knew the hit parade from 1958 through 1963 by heart. She could remember the first time she heard Elvis Presley, for instance. She had been taking a bath. He sang "Heartbreak Hotel," and his voice warbled as though there were water in her ear; she wasn't certain, till she heard it several times, that she was hearing right.

Later she headed for Memphis just to see his house. Bobby McKelroy from U.N.C. said he knew Colonel Parker, and all they'd have to do was go to the front door and knock. He came for her one Saturday morning on his Harley; he called it a hog. They had pretended they were going swimming, and she packed a picnic and bikini and, for when she would be introduced to Elvis, a makeup kit and her see-through crocheted top. They rode for hours on the Interstate, and it was hot and boring and he had a blowout at eighty miles an hour on a curve. She would never forget the way it sounded, the tearing roar beneath her and the jolting skid and rubber screaming on concrete. She knew she was going to die. She closed her eyes and held to Bobby like salvation, like her father's dream of Chapel Hill when he was nose down, diving, metal shearing everywhere; they bounced and teetered and bucked. Impossibly they stayed upright; impossibly the cycle slowed; he shouted "Jump!" and they landed in the grass.

Bobby was sick. He stayed on all fours, retching, while she felt for broken bones. Her wrists were skinned, her hair a mess, but she was otherwise unhurt. Alice tried to pray. All she seemed able to remember was the grace beginning, "Give us this day our daily bread," and the Twenty-third Psalm. She began to recite these and stopped. Her father too had faced a green oblivion when landing on the terrace by the riverbed that, from his plummeting distance, might well have looked like grass. He too refused to pray. Bobby came to her, wan-faced, stinking, and said, "I ain't never met no Colonel Parker. I just wanted to get you to Memphis. Just you and me in Memphis, off alone."

He looked so hangdog, standing there, she hadn't the heart to be angry. Mostly she had felt embarrassed for him, and ashamed. She collected his toolkit and wiped his bloody nose with her bikini top. He blew his nose in it, crying, "I'm no good. I'm shit." She did not contradict him, but she did not tell the trooper, either, that he had spirited this minor, her, across state lines. They were in Tennessee, and he could have been arrested, but instead they fixed the tire and made their way back home. She could never hear Elvis again without that rush inside that meant they were exploding and would crash; she watched him gyrate on TV and saw the state troopers above her, Bobby on his knees.

David lay beside her in the dark. Her breathy voice, her series of secrets, made him hold his breath. "You don't want to know this," she said, and he told her yes he did. "You don't have to listen," she said, and he rubbed her back and shoulders while she talked. Her elder sister married when Alice was fifteen. They had had the most beautiful wedding, all silk and lilies and champagne, and when the bridal couple left her father called his three remaining women to the den. "Take off your shoes," he said to Beth and Alice. "Make yourselves comfortable."

Their mother had done so, ostentatiously, kicking off her heels and stretching and sitting with her legs splayed on the ottoman. The girls sat in the black leather chairs in a room that, without being precisely off limits, was so clearly his haven that they seldom entered. It reeked of pipe tobacco, leather-bound law texts, and oil. Alice faced his gun rack, she remembered. He poured them flat champagne. "Your mother and I have something to tell you," he said. "Something you should know."

The scene that followed was banal. She had guessed it in advance, had understood recrimination and control and tears not quite spilled and shock not quite genuine would be the order of the day. "Your father is leaving," their mother announced. "Mary Kate has gone her way and he'll be going his."

"I've taken a house at the Kerr's. It's not as if I'm leaving. Think of it," their father said, "as if we bought an extra home."

She had had too much to drink. She had french-kissed Geoffrey Williams in the TV room; he said her tongue was like solid champagne. She wasn't sure she heard him right, like the time she wasn't sure she heard Elvis sing "Heartbreak Hotel" on purpose as if he were gargling—but by the time she had had an answer Geoffrey was gone. That Saturday she stopped him, saying, "What a peculiar thing to say," and it was clear from his open-faced puzzlement he hadn't known what she meant. "Solid champagne," she reminded him, and still his expression stayed blank. Yet in her father's den, respectful, trying not to hiccough, all she could think of was "solid champagne" and the feel of his tongue on her tongue and if she would be sick; she could not listen to the hackneyed consolation they offered her and Beth.

It wasn't, she wanted to say, as if they were in need of consoling; it was water spilled so long ago you couldn't find the bridge. Alice laughed: there were proverbs somewhere struggling to be free. You cried over spilled milk but shouldn't, while water spilled under the bridge. You took a stitch in time, and birds in hand were worth two in the bush. She was his bird in the hand. You made your bed to lie in, but stitches in time would save nine; she muddled the proverbs and hiccoughed and, sitting in her father's chair, curled and uncurled her toes.

David too wiggled his toes. Had he noticed how his toes curled back when he came? Each time he had an orgasm his toes turned in and pressed. She knew his breath would quicken and his pulse increase and muscles tense; she watched him carefully. She loved to watch him come. He coiled in the bed like a spring. She came to take such pleasure in sex that she felt like a kid with a first set of skates or some long-desired doll; she examined him minutely, asking, "How does this feel? How does *this* make you feel, how does *this*?" Alice shifted in his arms. "If everybody stayed in bed, the world would have no problems."

"Population," David said.

"OK. If everybody stayed in bed and used birth control."

"And lived on an island like this one," he said.

"You're making fun of me."

"Yes."

In retrospect it all seemed fun, loud childish fits of laughter in the middle of the night. They wrestled; they had pillow fights; they tickled each other exuberantly. "Let's go to bed," she said, and he said, "No, I'm tired. Let's play three sets of tennis instead." She left him notes beneath the pillow, or in the sugar bowl or above the soda shelf in the refrigerator; they read, "Darling, I adore you." Or, "You have such a great big juicy beautiful"— and then, beneath the fold—"ear." "Don't ever leave me," she lettered, and pinned to his fish clothes where they flapped drying on the line. Once, after an argument, Alice wrote, "I love you very much. And that makes me very happy." He could not remember what they argued over, what lilt of voice or lift of chin or topic had occasioned disagreement—but he remembered with no trouble the trouble she took with that note: the pen she used, the open blue print, the lined yellow paper, and the curling initial in the lower right-hand corner with which she signed off: A.

He was her first love, she said. He was her first and only love and would remain that way. She had had other lovers, of course. She ran through men about as frequently as he did women, though what it meant in her case had been something very different: a baseball saved, or dance card, or ticket to the double feature where she had had her first kiss. She had, she said, a promiscuous imagination: she watched each man who passed her by—or those who watched her passing—as if he could be stripped. Did David find that shocking? Did he behave the same way? Only he could act on it, had acted in the Goodwill store and later at her jewelry desk and later in his hut.

She could think and feel the same, of course, but couldn't let him know. She'd have to smile and bat her eyes and cross her legs and look away. It was amazing, really, it came from the Pleistocene epoch. It was—what was the word? she ran her hand around his knee—antediluvian. Her first boyfriend, Henry, had spouted a jingle. He was very proud of it, it expressed his whole theory of life. "Higamus, hogamus, woman's monogamous. Hogamus, higamus, man is polygamous." He had flexed his muscles, smiled, and posed in front of what he thought to be the admiring mirror of her eyes. "That's the difference," he proclaimed. "We men just can't be tied down."

Alice had not needed him. She was learning about freedom, and one of the principal freedoms was to learn to say no thanks. She had said no thanks to Henry, as she said no to most of those who gave her baseballs or orchids or wolf whistles at the swimming pool or from the front seats of cars. And if she said yes instead, yes why not, that too was freedom; she would not be cajoled. She refused the second baseman. He was all puffed up with his picture in the papers and his charley horse from headfirst sliding and the rumor that the Cubs had sent a scout. She told him she would rather take the bat boy home, or that gangly left fielder with acne. So she dispensed her favors—Alice giggled at the phrase: "These are my favors," she said, "what a way to describe them," placing his hands on her breasts—with the mindlessness of fate. That was how she liked to think of it and what she liked to say. When Henry announced, "Higamus, hogamus, woman's monogamous," she quoted Augustine to him instead. "'Do not despair,'" she said, "'one of the thieves was saved. Do not presume; one of the thieves was damned.'"

He stared at her, wide-eyed, and she said, "Don't worry, Henry, it's the doctrine of election. There's nothing you can do about it. The answer is no." The way he had looked at her was indescribable, as if a cautious swimmer had discovered the sandbar drops off. There are fish and coral and riptides in the water; everything's precarious, at risk. And what you took for granted you cannot take for granted; your beauty, youth, and prowess each will go. If there's anything to take for granted, Alice said, take that. She didn't want to worry him; it wasn't something, really, there was any point in worrying about, but what Henry took for granted—her—was not his to take. The gift had been bestowed and now would be withdrawn. It had meant nothing, would mean nothing: one of them was saved and one was damned.

She laughed. There's nothing like Saint Augustine to take the wind out of a man. He can strut past, full of beer and pumped-up-cock-of-the-roost boastfulness, and all you have to do is turn away. All you have to point to is the dunghill where he struts. She had been prepared to do so in the Goodwill store. She had seen David coming, had gauged him from across the room behind the coats. Then he took that blind boy by the hand. They were reading record labels, and he read them carefully aloud. She watched him for some time.

"You sleeping enough?" Mathew asked. Mathew ran the grocery store. He worked twenty-hour days in summer and drank all winter long.

"Mm-mn. Why?"

"Just asking," Mathew said.

"I sleep."

"A beauty sleep," said Mathew. "Right?" He opened a carton of Nestle's Crunch and stacked them on the shelf.

David selected corn.

"That girl. That Alice who's moved in. You two on separate accounts?"

"No."

"Mostly she pays cash." He tore a Nestle's Crunch in two. "Just asking," Mathew said.

He paid. He was cultivating reticence. A customer entered and gathered tonic water bottles, two to each hand. "Might rain," said David.

"Not till tomorrow."

"Is that what they're predicting?"

"Well fedded and well bedded," Mathew said. "Don't take it personal."

She had dropped out of college that June. She spent two years at Hollins, playing tennis, riding her roommate's Morgan, and wavering between majors in psychology or French. All the girls had crushes on the French professor, she told David; he managed to be both devilish and cuddly.

He was better dressed than anyone and even when she sat at the foot of the French table and he sat at the head, she could inhale Old Spice. But her psychology professor played tennis; she liked the way he toyed with her at net.

He had a beard. He also had three daughters and a wife who brought iced tea and cookies to the courts. The students called her "How you doin', darling?" because that was what she asked. She always asked it, and he always answered, "Fine." He threw a pass at Alice one morning by the stables; he asked her if she knew what cathexis entailed. She said she thought so, yes, it was a series of emotions, a whole set of connections. He said, yes, there's emotional cathexis and sensory cathexis and he felt them both that morning and wondered if she felt the same.

His beard was sweat-soaked. He wiped his neck. She said maybe they should go off campus to discuss it, because she couldn't handle a cathexis while her roommate saddled up. He complied. He brought his station wagon to the stable, and she knew without his asking to meet him at the gate. She got in and pulled her cap down over her eyes and turned toward him, averting her face from the window. He seemed pleased. He drove into the mountains, telling her that Roanoke was not the town it used to be, that when he first arrived at Hollins College there were farms all around. Now you have to drive for twenty miles to be alone—that's progress, he supposed.

"Do you do this often?" Alice asked.

"Not often," he answered. "Do you?"

She had wanted to provoke him then; it all seemed so routine to him, and foreordained. "Not since I got VD."

He tightened his hands on the wheel. "You're serious?"

"Yes."

He drove for some minutes in silence. "What did you want to talk about?" she said. "About sensory cathexis, I mean."

The joke had been on her, however, when she told him it had only been a joke. He had been so sweaty, panicky, so fearful of contamination that he couldn't get aroused. She told him not to worry and he lay there by the stream they'd found, being ravaged by mosquitoes while he said this never happened, not to him. She said she was into Abraham Maslow and self-actualizing personality; did he think a person could acquire the power of self-actualization, or was it already too late? He squeezed and poked her, kneading her nipples, and she squeezed and prodded him. He pulled away. She said, "This isn't working," and he slapped at a mosquito on his thigh so hard his fingers were imprinted there pinkly. She laughed; they looked like pricks. He asked her why she was laughing, and she couldn't tell him, wouldn't tell him when he urged her, and he put his pants back on and buckled his belt.

Then she knew she'd have to leave. Hollins College was not home to her and offered no cathexis; his lectures on Freud, Jung, and Erikson would be too hard to take. She had had to take them, of course. She sat in his class while he spoke about Jung, the collective unconscious, and the deep drive driving us all; she copied, with no conscious malice, what he said about the stages of men's growth. He called her to his office. He said she disconcerted him, he wished she'd stop giggling in class. She said she didn't giggle, and he said, well maybe not out loud. She said to give her love to "How you doin', darling?" and that she was going to leave.

Her suite mates were not shocked. Rather, they seemed envious; they asked her to describe how his penis hung limply, what color it was, how he explained himself to her while pulling off his pants. He had not been exploitative, she said. He knew what he was up to, psychologically, and how to go about it; he made it clear she could choose. Yet Alice felt exploited anyhow—exploited by his age and position and weight, the tennis courts, the black men mowing and raking and sweeping, the campus police, the circumstance of college while our air force strafed and burned. We were bombing villages while her teachers talked of foreign policy; we made craters out of mountain peaks, defoliating forests while she attended lectures on the Civil War. She read "On Civil Disobedience," and then was told that protest permits had to be denied.

On the final day of spring semester she took Tracy—her roommate's Morgan—for a ride. The bridle path was overgrown in what seemed overnight. Everywhere things sprouted; every fruit tree was in flower; the sky was a blue canopy above a lush green bed. She couldn't help it, she told David, that was the way to describe it: everything at peace. Tracy trotted easily. She reined in, however. They stopped.

What happened to her next was hard to tell. She had an illumination, an experience of light. It was what she'd read of and they talked about in class. Had her psychology professor been along with her that morning, she'd have asked him for advice. But he was home washing the car; he was home taking out garbage, or dealing with his wife or scrubbing down the patio or helping his kids with New Math.

Tracy breathed in unison with every living thing; Alice saw the lung. The world was a lung, pumping, and she was a cell in the infinite cluster of cells. Leaves had no perimeter that marked them off from air. She felt the leaves, their veins and sides and indentations and microscopic particles, could see with perfect clarity how they were formed yet formless, how they inhabited air. Alice laughed. She knew it was hard to explain. She had not felt that way before and did not expect to again. The earth and sun and leaves were of a piece, she told him, and she too was of that wholeness, constituent, her body a membrane like his.

He touched her leg. "How long did this last?"

"I can't tell. It felt like—oh, I can't explain it—my body was a membrane and everything inside of me and everything outside was a balanced solution, perfect, so it didn't make any difference if I was inside or outside, or if the horse could talk. I know it sounds silly. You have to accept that. I saw the bombing, saw the Mekong Delta in a branch of dogwood. Tracy was a plane. We were intruders, we didn't belong. Not on this planet, I mean."

"I understand."

"You don't. You can't."

It was in this fashion that he entered what he came to think of as his outlaw state. Alice joined him. They took mescaline and psilocybin and LSD and hashish and cocaine together. She wanted to try heroin, but he said, let's wait. They read the first page of *Finnegans Wake*, convinced it held the key to everything that followed; if they understood that page, he said, they wouldn't have to read the rest. They pored over her catalogue of "Treasures from the Louvre." The Louvre was the place, she said, where wolves ran freely in the periods of plague.

"Did they teach you that at Hollins?"

"No."

"Imagine," David said, "wolves on the rampage in Paris."

"When are you leaving the island?"

"I haven't decided. You?"

So they stayed on for the fall. He had had enough of schooling, he told his parents on the phone; he needed a little more time. His work had begun to make sense; he was listening to stories and filling the refrigerator with his second sheets. "Are you finding yourself?" asked his mother. "Is that what they call it these days?"

It was a halcyon time for him; he woke up each morning replete. If he had to drive the fish truck, he crept out of bed without waking Alice and left. On those mornings when he did not need to work—and these increased as the autumn wore on; he met the noon ferry; the restaurants closed—David rose at dawn nevertheless. He stood on the front step a moment, letting the air wake him, watching the color soak into the sky. Then he brewed their coffee, poured himself a small black cup, and let the pot stand on the stove.

In November the days darkened early, and rain rinsed the pond. The wind was, continually, north northeast; the scrub oak trunks turned black. He and Alice took turns with the buckets, and if they went down-island for a movie or provisions they came back to water on the floor. They added their two sleeping bags to the nest of blankets. Squirrels scuttled in the eaves. He said, "Indian summer. It's got to come soon." But the tour buses ceased, and the old man who sat at Gay Head in his headdress departed. The tennis court nets at the Community Center were removed; houses sprouted shutters and driveways were blocked off with chains. The parking lots were empty; there was no line for groceries or mail.

And something wintry entered also; Alice bought a radio and lay each evening listening to news. It was rarely good. She grew restless. She said she had no occupation, and fashioning trinkets for tourists was not work she wished to continue. Her peers were getting married or preparing for law school or graduate school; her friends were in the streets. This emerald glimmering place, this retreat for the famous and rich, this tourist brochure aimed at those who choose privacy—Alice laughed. The blacks in Oak Bluffs were all gingerbread blacks, cute enough to eat. They trimmed their houses neatly; they were glad to cut those lawns with power tools and keep on painting curlicues for the front porch. The local men were getting drunk, they were lying in the cranberries and watching the celebrities and stars. Again she laughed. The sound was not mirthful; she sucked in her breath. It's one hell of a place, Alice said, it's good manners and ex-Cabinet members and the cunning little surf lapping at the cunning little beach. We're killing villagers in Vietnam so that you can write your fantasies at leisure.

"What do you want me to do?" David asked.

"I don't know."

"What do you want?"

"If you hadn't been 4-F," she asked, "would you have gone to Canada?"

"Irrelevant," he said. The army had rejected him, and it did not therefore matter if he would have rejected the army in turn. There had been no choice to make.

"Yes, but what *if* . . . ?"

"The assumption is false." They were unpacking groceries. The paper bags had torn. "So the conclusion will be faulty."

"Every draftee in America didn't have rheumatic fever. Some of them are going. Some are getting killed."

"The categorical imperative," David countered, "fails to apply. If my behavior were the behavior of each potential inductee, there'd be no army. No war."

They argued this way often. They discoursed on civil disobedience, the effective forms of protest, and where to stake one's claim. Alice favored the Black Panthers, a group on the West Coast. She said Huey Newton, their jailed leader, had a real chance to be free. The Alameda County Courthouse would prove a testing ground. She said Bobby Seale and Eldridge Cleaver and the rest were showing white men what manhood could mean; if Angela Davis said "Shove it," she knew what she was saying and what her audience wanted to hear. Men like H. Rap Brown and Stokely Carmichael had this in common also: they knew which way the wind blew, and which camera was working. They were media creations who would bite the feeding hand, but not so hard that toothmarks marred the palm.

Mom-mom sent a letter, saying, "You don't answer at the market now. We'll be there this weekend and would love to have you visit. Just Tony and me and some friends."

"And our little blind archer?" she asked. "Our wealthy musical Cupid. Will he be there?"

"Others too."

"Just you and me and Mom-mom make thirty-three," she said. "Will she mind if I come with you? Tag along?"

That night he dreamed of banishment, the sense that he would come to see as augury that something evil entered, and their isolation could not be preserved. What walked abroad would stalk them too; it could not be avoided, Alice said. He had no talent for language; when he offered this opinion she did not disagree. "I'm leaving," Alice said. "I've got to get off this island."

"When?"

"Not the next ferry. But soon."

Call it boredom, they agreed, belief or the conviction of inequity that ought to be addressed—for where Fred Hampton slept and woke to hear the Chicago police was by extension their bed also. A nation that permitted this would not permit them privacy. They were, in the already hackneyed phrase, for the revolution or against it, part of the solution or the problem—not happily aloof no matter how protected by birth chance or choice.

When the rain came south southeast it streamed in through the window casings; shingling on the northern wall looked black. The nights were bleak. They found a book on constellations and tried to identify stars. He was proud of his ability to spot Orion's belt. Some mornings she remained in bed; some afternoons it seemed too much trouble to dress. She said he should learn to relax. At times when he lay next to her, the pattern on the wall—crosspieces of the rocking chair, the paper sporting a motif of a captain with a beard and pea jacket, smoking a pipe, holding a ship's wheel in one hand, a threatless whale spouting to starboard—appeared instructive. There was locution in the mist if only he could follow it, a message in the wind, some cipher cawed by starlings at the chimney. He felt on the verge of clarity, the brink of change; she cupped her hand to his neck.

In the morning, however, the weather cleared, and they spent the day on the beach. They walked to where the dunes began and took off their clothes. He spread their towels on the slope of the first of Zack's Cliffs. They faced Squibnocket Pond. Unbroken sand stretched west and east; there was water before and behind them. Geese rested there, and gulls. "I love you," Alice said.

"It makes a difference, doesn't it, this sun?"

She laughed. He said turn over, and she turned. There was no wind. He kissed her breasts, then stomach, then the slight rise of her abdomen. "I'm getting fat," she said. He shook his head. He worked his tongue along the inside of her legs the fluttering way that she liked it, lightly, from her ankle to her thigh to the lips of her cunt. She placed her hands on his hair. She burrowed a declivity by shifting weight in the sand. That scooping motion moved him—the sideways swing of her buttocks, weak sun on his back—and when he rose to enter her he felt completed, unafraid, the twinned half embracing, made whole.

II

Yet voice changes pitch over time. Strain and training alter it; so do cigarettes, whiskey, and age. Compare early Billie Holiday with late, the first recorded Armstrong vocals with the last. Mr. Jelly Roll gets hard to hear, the needle going blunt.

David wrote a story about a deaf boy who lip-read at speed. So rapid was "Allan," in fact, that he finished the phrase a stranger began, completing conversations by himself. In this way dialogue proved monologue, and the voices in his head were a chorale. Then he wrote a novella called *Wolf.* A philandering bass player discovers the "wolf" in his instrument, that dead space where vibrations cancel out. In the end he dies of lupus, dreaming himself back on stage.

Ventriloquy next engaged his attention. He wrote a piece about a Charlie McCarthy-like dummy who could throw his voice. The puppet imagined himself his own master, and that he went on TV. This happened. The puppet became, briefly, a celebrity—with T-shirts and beach towels and thermos bottles and lunch boxes emblazoned with his face. David, promoting his work, felt like just such a puppet on talk shows—given two minutes' air time only, and someone else's script. Through the years of his professional attainment (the job at Sarah Lawrence, the job with *The New Republic,* the television work, the time in Hollywood authoring the screenplay of *The Hut*) he felt himself a mouthpiece, not so much a writer as someone being written. His agent got pregnant and quit. His parents died. He edited anthologies. He met Mom-mom and Tony once, by accident, on location in Barbados; there was a strained silence between them. They were delighted, they said, they had so much in common and so much talking to do. It was terrible the way time flew, but aren't we looking well.

Voice is a function and aspect of speech. Yet it predates utterance; a child will voice complaint or pleasure with no language. Nor is language irreplaceable. The cries of love, of anger, the ululations of the hunter and the haunted—these too are voice. They resound. We are the sum of others' stories, and they the sum of others, and so on in a kind of chorus: a round, a catch, a half-heard snatch of song. Everywhere he went they told him, story of my life. . . .

The family flew to Tortola in 1983. It was their son Billy's school vacation. It would be, said Alice, a second honeymoon or—she raised her hands—that's that.

"That's what?" he asked.

"The end."

"Is this an ultimatum?"

"Yes." She had called the travel agent, made the reservations, and presented him with tickets. "Let's see if there's anything left."

"Why Tortola?" David asked.

She handed him a folder: British Virgin Islands, the *Welcome Tourist* guide. There was a cloudless sky, a seascape with islands, and a boat whose spinnaker looked like the Union Jack.

"A quiet place," said Alice. "Where there won't be many distractions. Just sun and sea, the two of us."

"And Billy. He can keep score."

"I can cancel," Alice said. "If you don't want to give it a try."

She was wearing her navy-blue jumpsuit, and her hair in ringlets. "What the hell," he offered. "At least it isn't Virgin Gorda. All those Rockefeller intimates staying decent for each other's sake. Someone just came back from Little Dix."

"Who?"

"And they said it was so *comme il faut* you wanted to break plates."

"Who said that?"

"I can't remember." For the moment he honestly could not remember, and his irritation at forgetting flared. "It doesn't matter anyway. She wasn't pretty, if that's what you mean."

"I mean," said Alice, "everything we talk about turns into an argument. It did again, just now. I want to try to have a family vacation, to see if it can work again. That isn't too much to ask."

"No." He raised his hands, in conscious imitation of her previous gesture. "It isn't, is it? Let's see."

*

The flight was full. American Airlines had overbooked, and they offered cash to passengers who would be willing to wait. There were few of these, however, and the amount increased. Finally, prior to boarding, nine hundred dollars in travel vouchers were offered to three ticket holders, and seats on the next open flight. "What do you think?" David asked. "This flight's certain," Alice said. "The connecting flight's certain, the one from San Juan. I think we should do what we promised we'd do." Billy nodded, solemn, sleepy. She stubbed out her cigarette and stood.

It aggrieved him that she seemed so resolute—unwilling to take chances on a future trip. He compiled a list of grievances while they took their seats; he nursed them during takeoff and through dry martinis that seemed a single swallow in his clear plastic cup. Billy hated lunch. He said the chicken tasted yucky and he tore the salad dressing packet; it spilled across his cake. "Can I have yours?" Billy asked, and David told him no.

"You can have mine," Alice said. "But try to be more careful, darling." Billy spilled his Coke.

The air in San Juan was palpable; he felt as if he had walked into a steam bath wearing clothes. Men in shorts brandished cigars; a woman in a sari tried to sell him pamphlets on the peace that comes from bliss. There was no one at the counter for Air British Virgin Islands; they proceeded to the gate. The woman in the sari drifted through the terminal, soliciting. He thought of her as someone's daughter, lost and far from home; would her parents know her, passing through San Juan?

The second flight, however, had about it something celebratory—a sense of actual distance traveled and, therefore, impending release. The sun set as they flew. They passed through Customs easily and walked out under palm fronds in an evening breeze. Billy found a shell. He held it up, delighted, and the taxi driver was too.

They rattled over a one-lane bridge. "The Queen Elizabeth Bridge," their driver said. "This connects Beef Island to Tortola. Queen Elizabeth herself arrived to open it in 1966." He had been to England for three months three years before; he said it was too cold. He drove his aging Mercury on the left side of the road. They passed goats and Land-Rovers and trucks alarmingly. Every quarter mile or so, the driver slowed and rocked across a ridge. "We call them sleeping policemen. It keep you from driving too quick."

Their hotel fronted the water. Long-fluked fans beat at the air above them, and a piano player adapted Beatles songs. By the time they had unpacked, a saxophonist arrived, and he played "Yesterday." Then they played stately Calypso, stressing "Island in the Sun." David had purchased rum at the airport. He poured drinks. They had a double bed and rollaway bed in addition; there was a balcony. Sailboats clustered thickly to the jetty at their left. "Your health," he said, and Alice said, "To us."

Billy fell asleep without his dinner. They sat on the balcony, shoeless. "I'm glad we came," she offered. "I'm glad we didn't trade our tickets for a later flight."

He sniffed the air for sugarcane and listened for the sound of a steel band. "What's that dance they do, the limbo?"

"You're thinking of Jamaica," Alice said.

What he was thinking of was youth—the glittering discovery of prowess, the future envisioned that now was their past. They used to dance. They used to make love on the floor; then they thought of middle age as their present age. He could remember couples on Squibnocket Beach, with picnic hampers and beach chairs and plastic inflatable boats and buckets and shovels and children on Donald Duck towels. He threaded his way past them once but would take his place there now. Billy muttered in his sleep. It was like those fairy tales in which the granted wish came all too literally true. When was the last time, he asked her, that they did the unexpected—took off all their clothes, for instance, and went for a midnight swim?

"Don't go getting maudlin," Alice said.

"See what I mean? I suggest we go for a swim, and you call it a midlife crisis."

"I didn't say that. Billy's sleeping."

"Wake him up. Or let him sleep."

"It's our first night here," she said. "He's seven years old. We can't just leave him sleeping in a strange hotel."

"Q.E.D." He finished his drink. "That which was about to be proven has been proved."

Next day they did go swimming; after breakfast they walked to the pool. There was an exercise class in the water, and a tape deck producing music; an instructor in a bathing cap smiled up at them expansively. David felt white and bloated and, even in dark glasses, forced to squint. Alice rubbed Billy with sunblock and made him wear a hat. He counted seven women in the pool. They wore water wings on their arms. "Why can't they swim?" asked Billy, and Alice said, "They can."

"Why are they wearing floaters, then?"

"It makes them move more slowly. It's like an added weight."

David lowered his chaise longue and lay in the sun. "One and two and three," the women chanted, bobbing. "Four and five and six." The song proclaimed the singer's intention to do it all night long. The women in the pool were plump and elderly; water lapped at their waists. It blurred their bending legs. "Ex*tend*," the teacher chanted. "Back and *two* and three."

"Can we go swimming, Daddy?"

"In a minute."

"Can we, Mommy?"

"Soon," she said.

"I'm hot. I'm boiling."

"You can go in by yourself."

"Can I, Mommy?"

"Daddy will take you," she said.

He let the sun invade him; he tried to hear nothing but music. "And *up* and down and *three* and four and up and *six* and hold!" There were palm trees by the guardrail, and an empty kiddy pool whose blue cement had cracked. In the fork of the palm trees fruit hung; he tried to distinguish if that which soared brightly above him was coconut or breadfruit. He tried to remember, also, the names of such tropical trees. There were trees called woman's tongue with long, rattling pods that clattered in the breeze; there were tulip and flamboyant trees, and many flowering bushes that he could not name. "I'm boiling," Billy said again, and David said, "Let's swim."

What he was hoping for, he wanted to tell them, was peace: no clamorous expectancy or bills. He wanted to sleep in the sun. He stood in the shallow end, helping his son do the dead man's float; he applauded the distance that Billy could swim. Alice read. The women in the exercise session smiled at him approvingly; a frigate bird flew past.

Alice praised his books. She did so, however, with a certain caution and what he thought was reserve. He resented this. He feared her pride in him masked disappointment, her flattery disdain. She said, "I'm sorry, he's working," when the phone rang in the morning and he was not yet at work. She said, "You *have* to read this. It's terrific," about the latest pan-flash, the coffee-table talent of the month. He thought this a betrayal. Her enthusiasm for the work of others should be tempered, he believed, by greater admiration of his own. That she never voiced a criticism—she who could be so severely critical of how he drank, or talked, or dressed—made him the more suspicious: she was holding back. Her silence had enlarged—the praise ringing hollow, the compliments false—to become an echo of David's own self-doubt.

"You're projecting," Alice said.

"No."

"What do you want me to tell you?"

"The truth."

"The whole truth." Alice raised her hand. "And nothing but the truth."

"So help you, God," he said.

"I mean it. I just love the story."

"Except?"

"Except I don't just love an inquisition. And you don't want my criticism, and it's simpler all around if we just leave it alone."

He pondered this. He had given her the galleys, not the typescript of *The Hut*. Some part of him had surely known she would not take it well. The story of their courtship had been tailored to his hero's past, then butchered for the benefit of plot. She said he was dishonest, and that art required honesty; he said the problem is that honesty needs art.

That afternoon they took a taxi on a tour. The roads were steep. A road called Joe's Hill led to the crest of the island; the switchbacks were continual and the climb abrupt. Billy had wanted to stay in the pool. "You don't want too much sun," said Alice. "Not our first day out . . ."

Their driver was thick-armed, affable. He wore a red cloth cap, an earring in his right ear, and a goatee. "Mac's my name," he said. "They call me Mac the Knife." He drove them to a restaurant at the island's highest point, from which they could survey Drake's Channel and the multicolored sea. "You got this only boy?" he asked. "You just beginning, Missus?"

"No. How many do you have?"

"The ones I know about?" Mac the Knife winked broadly. "Eight at the table and one in the oven."

He recited the names of his children, their ages, the name of his wife, the place they lived, how many brothers he himself was raised with—and this singsong litany, half-comprehensible, became a kind of counterweight to David's own attempt at measure: what had he accumulated and what was it worth? He was a member of the PEN Club, the Century Association, and the Writers Guild; his third book was translated into seven languages. Mac said, "I come back in an hour. Maybe two."

A cement truck blew its horn. Mac turned on the radio, made a U-turn, and rattled away. Clouds massed above the bay, and the wind was easterly. At the restaurant entrance, Alice smiled. "It's beautiful here. That island"—she pointed—"it's named for a pirate. Van Dyke."

The sun was hot. They stood together at the guardrail, watching the few whitecaps and the sailboats and the ferryboats and what looked like a tanker in the distance. "Jost Van Dyke," he said aloud. "What happened to us, do you think?"

Billy shouted from the observation deck above them. "A *big* boat, Mommy."

"Happened to us?"

"Yes," he said. "The romance of the trade winds. Galleons. All those one-eyed buccaneers, and maidens walking the plank." He gestured at the horizon. "The way it used to be."

A waiter said, "Your table, sir," and they ordered rum. "The difference between us," said Alice, "is that you refuse to grow up. You think the world owes you attention, and I think we owe attention to the world."

This had the ring of rehearsal. "A fine phrase," he said.

"I mean it. You've got to grow up."

Billy clattered down the stairs. "Your mother thinks I'm selfish," David said. "But she's wrong. Watch this. You can order ice cream—or a piece of that huge chocolate cake on the table there. And I won't take one bite."

Billy grinned, expectant. He went to examine the cake. "How could you call me selfish?" David asked.

Alice lit a cigarette. She did this in moments of anger, or concentration; she would not be deflected. "My hero." She stubbed out the match.

"Are you seeing someone else?" he asked.

"That's not the point."

"But are you?"

"Would it matter? No."

He studied her. In the bright light she looked pale. A sense of their shared history assaulted him, and its physical concomitant—Billy, the lines at her mouth, the weight of the flesh at her chin. "You're a beautiful woman," he said. His throat thickened at the waning of such beauty, and he took her hand. "I've been paying too little attention. I'm sorry."

Billy came back. "I want cake."

They ordered cake. He ate it, and David started whistling "Mac the Knife."

Alvin Prendergast had sparse white hair, a moustache stained by nicotine, and a stomach that seemed larger each time he and David met. They had known each other since Harvard, where Alvin studied architecture; by coincidence they moved into the same apartment building on West End Avenue and Ninety-seventh Street. Alvin loved David's novel, he said, and made him sign a dozen copies of *The Hut*; they would make Christmas gifts. He praised the second book lavishly also, and bought six copies of the collection *Reality Principle: Tales*. In 1976, however—and before the publication of David's most successful book, *Orison*—Alvin said he had had it with climate control, the rat race, and nuclear threat; he would rather build with cane and thatch than reinforced concrete.

He announced this, the writer remembered, at lunch. They ate together often, or the families had drinks. Alice and Carrie were friends. The women played tennis on Wednesdays and took the same aerobics class. Sometimes David thought of them, towel-swaddled, gleaming in the sauna, interchangeable. They would raise their legs from the hot cedar bench and open their four arms.

The Prendergasts' marriage went bad. Carrie said he was smothering her. He came back home and sprawled on the couch, she complained, and shed all over everything like a Great Pyrenees. If she wanted a lapdog, she said, it shouldn't have to be two hundred pounds and give her no personal space. "I'm an architect," he said to David, "right? The one thing I know is personal space. A room with a view, Christ, a room of her own . . ." Alvin twisted his napkin. He made distracted motions with his knife. "Does Alice give you that?"

He chewed carrots and celery sticks. He had been sailing that winter and come to a decision; he'd said to himself, Alvin, old boy, you're not getting any younger, there's nobody who needs you and precious little you need. Three of the things you need are right here: a steady breeze, manageable anchorage, and cheap abundant rum. He could live five times as well in Road Town for one fifth the price.

So he had moved to Tortola. He was one of the two licensed architects in town. Did David remember the Babar books; had he seen them lately? The town of Celesteville was Road Town; Alvin thought of it that way. The palm trees and the coconuts and pastel stucco houses and porches and light green shutters; that had been his first impression of the place. He expected to see elephants in costume on the dock. Your standards of beauty can change, he said, your expectations of what houses and women should look like. He, David, should come down. He could do a travel piece, or maybe one of those "far-flung correspondent" numbers for *The New Yorker*, or just let his typewriter rest. Alvin built a house from time to time, or helped with a government building, or provided a hotel with a patio and pool; it wasn't full-time work. He wanted it that way. He had "personal space" in the channel, and no disapproving first mate. He sent the Lewins postcards—of sunsets, beaches, girls in bikinis, and men wrestling game fish or standing proudly beside them. He always printed, in block letters, WISH YOU COULD BE HERE. When Alice came home with the tickets, and they looked at the hotel brochure, David said, "He's there."

"Who?"

"Alvin. You remember."

"That will be nice," Alice said.

When she was eleven, her family went to the Yukon. It was their first shared vacation, and it would be the last. Their father had wanted to camp past the tree line, where everything is visible. What comes at you comes from a distance, he said—you see elk miles away. Yet the ground got softer, springy, and she remembered walking in a kind of marsh, sinking to her knees each step and asking him if moss could freeze, if the Arctic was just frozen mud.

Her sisters complained. Her mother refused to complain, spreading out the picnic cloth and taking sandwich meats from the hamper and pouring milk and cold tea from the thermos with the kind of scrupulous attention that meant she was furious, resigned, not about to quarrel but past compromise already, totaling each day's discomfort in the ledger labeled Grievance that their marriage had become. Her mother had been a good sport. She could go anywhere, uncomplaining; she could rock-climb and fry ham with the best of them, or serve tea in a marsh. But there was nothing yielding in the gesture, no complicity; she sat apart.

Alice had a horror of sitting in that fashion; she saw it these years in herself. Her father, for instance, could never remember if she took milk in her tea. It was silly to complain—but somehow his forgetfulness had mattered a great deal to her. It stood for all his years away, his conclaves with the Hunt Club or lawyers or district attorney while she waited in the hall. She had thought that fathers were supposed to do the waiting; they were proud to come and get you after ballet school. They smoked a pipe outside the stable while you worked the jumps. They waited, checking the clock, for you to return from the prom. But it hadn't seemed that way in Chapel Hill. She was the one who waited. He would come out from the bowling league twenty minutes late; he'd emerge from a meeting to wink at her, saying, "Just a second, honey, I'll be right along." He'd cover the telephone receiver while she sat across the desk, and look up and whisper "Soon."

Once she asked him, "Daddy, why'd you keep me waiting?" It had not been easy, asking. Her manners rebelled, and her habit of obedience; she had smiled and asked offhandedly, as if the question just occurred to her and the answer didn't matter and was just a point of interest. He had ignored her, hands in his pockets, studying the floor. Bravely she repeated it; she knew he had some sense of time that was not hers, not theirs, not anyone's in Chapel Hill. "'They also serve who only stand and wait,'" he said at last. "That's worth remembering."

Alice pondered this injunction—for it had been one, clearly, a way of checkreining her rush. He spoke of the virtues of patience. He was patient himself, explaining it, saying time that hurtles when you're young becomes all you ever have to deal with, dying of starvation in a prison camp. You die of boredom, really. It's no accident, he said, that another word for patience is the game of solitaire. It's what you learn when solitary, and it doesn't hurt in public either; patience is a game we all must learn to play.

She remembered her own childhood rhyme. "Patience is a virtue, virtue is a grace. Grace is a naughty girl who wouldn't wash her face." Patience wouldn't wash her face, she could remember cackling; patience was a naughty girl—and virtue didn't enter into it, or if it came it did so slantways, twenty yards from center stripe in the hockey field, whispered by Marsha Prentiss who had been french-kissed already and had seen Tommy Altschulter's thing.

Her father had no patience with anyone's imperatives but those he made his own. He preached silence and exile and cunning, chattily, from the screen porch.

He would freshen up her Shirley Temple with a sprig of mint. He had been born in their house; the house had belonged to his family since the first brick was fired: exile is easy to preach.

Two days after their arrival, Alvin came to the hotel. He drove an ancient Jaguar sedan with a bright blue right rear fender; he had acquired a limp. His white shirt sported pineapples and grapes, and the legend *Welcome to Daiquiri Country* on his chest. He had not shaved. "Davey boy," he said, and embraced Alice lingeringly. Then he held her at arm's length. "A sight for sore eyes, sweetie. You look terrific. Why don't you leave this bum and stay down here with me?"

She laughed. "You've got a lunch date, remember?"

"I'll leave the bum at lunch and we can sail away."

"Meet Billy," Alice said.

Billy presented himself. They shook hands.

"Well, all right then," said Alvin. "So what's-his-name and me will go to Rotary instead. Don't say I didn't ask you."

"When you're finished . . ." David said.

Alvin licked at a cigar. In the car he continued his banter. "Did you hear the one about the Irishman and Mexican? The Mexican asks the Irishman, 'In your language do you have a word for *mañana?*' 'Yes,' says Paddy. 'But it has less urgency.'" He repeated this, delighted. "*Mañana's* too urgent, you see."

"How are you, really?"

"I'm good." He waved at a man in a doorway. "I like this way of living."

"You live alone?"

"With visitors." He pointed out the governor's house, and the hospital. A cruise ship had arrived and was disgorging passengers; taxis crowded to the pier. "I'm not in touch with Carrie, if that's what you mean. We parted, as the lawyers say, amicably. She sold the apartment, of course. She costs only half what I make."

"Is she still living in New York?"

"That's where the checks go," said Alvin. He made a left turn, and they started climbing. Schoolchildren idled past. He pulled into a hotel parking lot. "We meet here once a week. It's the one appointment I do try to keep."

The bar was full. A man sat at the door, with a checklist for members and guests. David gave his name, and the recording secretary—an Englishman in a beige linen suit—filled out a lapel card. "Alvin's guest," he said. "Well, we can't help that, can we?" The Englishman beamed, showing teeth. "You're welcome anyway. What brings you to us, Dave?"

"Pleasure," Alvin said. "This is an important man. This is the great writer. I'm buying. What's your drink?" There was a swimming pool outside, and a view of the bay. Rotarians came up to Prendergast and clapped him on the back or took him by the elbow and then shook David's hand. The majority were black. They spoke about the weather and the question of beach rights on Virgin Gorda and the proposed hospital addition. They discussed Prince Charles and whether he was as good as Prince Philip with horses.

"*Philippos*," someone said. "That means 'lover of horses' in Greek." This was the minister. He was being transferred to Nevis in a week. Alvin said to David that the minister was being censured; he had answered the telephone, "Planned Parenthood; can we help you?" once too often. There was laughter at the bar. They asked him how long he would stay on the island, how long he had known Prendergast, and what kind of novels he wrote and if he liked to fish.

David tried to listen. He thought of Alice by the pool, and Billy with his flippers on. The recording secretary was assessing fines. One Rotarian had gotten in line before his guest; one brother had failed to maintain silence during grace; one had said there were an "awful lot" of visitors. This insult drew a fine of fifty cents. You should not call your visitors an "awful lot." There was laughter, then applause. There was a raffle. There was a speech about providing for the anticipated increase of tourism attendant on completion of Marina Cay. There was a round of applause for the minister, and best wishes from the membership of the Tortola chapter for his continued health, prosperity, and happiness.

The minister stood. He took small, cautious steps to the microphone; he wheezed at it, clearing his throat. He then made the sign of the cross. "You forget," he said, "my own immortal soul." He handed the microphone to the presiding officer, returned to his seat, and sat down. There was a moment's silence. Then the presiding officer—a black man with high sloping shoulders and white muttonchop whiskers—said, "That's your department, Father. We don't interfere."

Again there was laughter and prolonged applause. "Great bunch," said Alvin, "right? You always know just where you stand, this is a great bunch of guys." They left. The afternoon was bright; the leather seats of Alvin's car retained and gave off heat.

Orison is a novel, David explained, about voice. He gave interviews. Remember how Claudius, kneeling, says prayers rise to heaven while his thoughts remain below? Remember Hamlet saying, "Nymph, in thy orisons, be all my sins remember'd"? It is not clear, however—and staging must take this into account—if the prince intends this as a question or imperative, if he says so in her hearing or when she cannot hear.

Much of what we learn is voiceless—the body language of a friend or enemy, the caressing motions of bereavement or maternity or sex. When we say we "change our voice," we mean it changes pitch. But how does this relate, the interviewer asked, to that scene where Jack almost drowns in his kayak, off by Noman's Land? If you have to ask, said David, the scene just doesn't work; what I wrote is what I meant. Did you always know, they asked him, that you would be a writer; when did you first start writing, what are your favorite books? Do you use a pen, they asked; what are your work habits; what hours do you work?

We throw the reader "plot," he said, as the dog trainer throws a bone: first to engage attention and second to reward it—but not because the bone as such matters in the telling trick. If we are the sum of other stories, others' stories, then the game is zero sum. Thanks so much, they said, this has been very interesting. We're not sure we can run it, we'll see how much we can print.

That night Alvin joined the Lewins for dinner at The Pub. It was, he said, the place for *tout* Tortola. His exaggerated courtliness continued through the meal. He referred to himself as Alice's ardent admirer; he said he hadn't been so happy since the last time they met. They should quit the rat race—all of them—and come to the island to stay. There were no tax problems; as a resident alien David could pay nickels on the dollar; that's what Alvin did. His whole tax bite—he clicked his tongue, demonstrating "bite" for Billy's sake—had been one hundred twenty-seven dollars this last year. You couldn't beat it, he said; he, Alvin, couldn't beat it and he doubted others could. They should try the tuna or the dolphin steak—he clicked his tongue again—grilled.

Men clustered to the bar. They played a game called "foosball"—with wooden soccer players on a rotating stick. They scored goals with golf balls when the goalie failed to block; there were seven balls. Billy went over to watch. Alice sat with her back to the water, the moonlight behind her, wearing a white shawl. "Two days of this," said David, "and I feel I've shed two weeks of winter." His skin felt pleasantly puckered by sun; he tasted the salt on his lips.

"You know why we came down here?" Alice asked.

"To see me," Alvin said.

"I'm being serious. Has David told you?"

"No."

He looked for his son at foosball.

"I want a divorce," Alice said.

Billy was standing, his head at table level, his back to them, absorbed.

"He's practicing avoidance," Alice said. "He could have mentioned it."

"I wanted to give you the pleasure. I knew you'd want the fun of making the announcement."

"I'm sorry," Alvin said.

"For what?"

He spread his hands. "Your trouble."

"It isn't your fault, Alvin. Don't apologize."

"It's nobody's fault," Alice said. "It's something that happens, that's all."

"I didn't know. I'm sorry."

The waitress appeared, checking drinks. "Another round?" she said.

"I've been through this, remember? I know what you kids feel."

"You don't know," Alice said. "You don't have any idea." She put her hand on David's forearm, not lightly. "I just thought I'd sound it out. I don't like the way it sounds."

Billy returned. "Can *I* play, Daddy? When they're finished." His hamburger arrived, and there were home fries and pickles.

Alvin leaned back on the bench. He locked his hands behind his head, stretching the pink shirt. "You two amaze me. You do. I'd forgotten how much fun it is to yank at the short hairs, correct?"

"Correct," said Alice. "As you so elegantly put it."

"Can I have another Shirley Temple?" Billy asked.

"Love," said David, in the intonation he knew his wife hated, "love is a spectator sport." Their waitress brought the dolphin, and he concentrated on that. By the cheesecake there was peace between them, camaraderie again, and they agreed to meet next morning to sail to Peter Island on Alvin's catamaran.

That night he dreamed of sailing, and the drone of the fan above him seemed like the sound of the surf. It was irregular, off-center, and the shift into rotation invaded his light sleep. They were on that blue-green water he could see beyond the bedroom, but it might equally have signified the Aegean or South China Sea. Natives pranced along the shore. He could not tell, however, if they welcomed or warned him away.

David woke. His wife was breathing heavily, her face slack. This made him tender toward her. He got out of bed and cracked open the balcony screen and sat on the balcony, smoking. In holding on, he asked himself, what was he holding on to, what attempting to retain that was not past retention, and would not memory go with him where he went? He was enacting, dutiful, his own imagined scene. He felt precisely centered, in an equilibrium not so much the consequence of balance as inertia self-opposed.

The last time Alice saw her father, he visited New York. He called to say he was in town and explained he was there on a case. He had depositions to take. Yet something in the timbre of his explanation—some pause to light a cigarette, the exhalation signaling not intimacy but pride, an after-dinner chattiness with brandy and unloosened tie—told her her father wasn't alone, was there on business not business as such. He asked her to meet him, by herself, at Jack's. The table was reserved for three—and she had been, if not prepared, unsurprised.

The maître d'hôtel bowed her in. Jack's was a good choice: the room well-lit but private, the decor unassuming to the point of ostentation. She ordered Dubonnet. She saw her father enter behind an Oriental wo-man—short and thick and gray, so absolutely not what she expected that Alice thought they were entering separately, strangers, and maybe she was wrong. Then the pair approached. The woman smiled at her, showing gold teeth. Alice rose. "I'd like to introduce you," said her father. "Wa-Lee, this is Alice. Alice, Wa-Lee." Wa-Lee did not giggle but seemed to. They sat.

That night a tale unfolded—decorous, oblique, but unmistakably a tale of passion. Alice heard it out. Her father did most of the talking; Wa-Lee nodded for emphasis. When he came out of prison camp he had been sent, for the first stage of his debriefing and recovery, to Honolulu. There she attended him. Wa-Lee was a hospital orderly. "Not so much a nurse," she said, "as 'Assistant Nurse.'" At night she cleaned the ward. One night he beckoned her to talk, begging for companionship, unable to sleep in the bright dormitory light. In halting English she conveyed to him that blindness was best, that what you see is horror and better to keep your eyes closed. She massaged him skillfully. He shut his eyes and did not mind that he remained awake, that nothing induced him to dream.

She had seven sisters who worked in Maui, on a coffee plantation. One had married an overseer, and the other six were therefore also employed. The overseer, however, had made improper advances to her—Wa-Lee dimpled, giggling, as her father said "improper advances"—and she fled. Heaven only knew what the other six sisters were thinking, or what their response had been; heaven knew whether or not they responded to his provocation in the fields. Kau-ling had surely responded, for her twins had cauliflower ears and the same peculiar shade of red hair on their heads. She preferred the hospital; she did not think if you married one member of a family this entitled you to sleep with the sisters as well.

Wa-Lee had been nineteen and unused to the way of the world. That was her expression, said Alice's father, "unused to the way of the world." When this tall, silent stranger—her father smiled, apologetic at this way of describing himself—asked her please to talk to him, to remain at night so he could sleep, she thought there need be neither gossip nor recrimination on the ward. She lost her job. The supervisor made rounds while she, Wa-Lee, was dozing, catnapping, her cheek on the pillow beside him and hand on his bare back. No matter how he explained, how she protested she was helping him to rest and must have fallen asleep, briefly, by his side, not intending to, not having any reason for exhaustion or having gotten underneath the covers as the supervisor could plainly observe—no matter how they argued, Wa-Lee was dismissed.

Jack greeted them. He hoped everything was to their satisfaction and they would try the soufflé. They ordered the crabmeat soufflé. They ordered a bottle of wine. It was only after the firing, her father confessed, that he awoke to responsibility; they released him for a weekend on the town. He walked out of the hospital whistling, a citizen on his own. He had never planned to talk about those months. He apologized to Alice. He had never felt the need or the ability before. But now she, Alice, was a wife and mother, and they were in this town together and this restaurant, and she should know that Wa-Lee was an angel, that her ministration brought this patient back to life. That night on the plantation (a driver had taken him there, had known the address and the place from the piece of paper she had scribbled, leaving, and wound out of town and into the hills and up beyond the smoke into the startling trees) was paradise on earth. He came for what he failed to claim while on the ward. For all those weeks of comfort there had been nothing sexual, nothing but her hand between his shoulder blades, her palm on his eyes till he slept.

And then the world's suspicion made it plausible to act. Then they might as well be damned for wolves as sheep. He took her for a walk. Then he took her, in the recommended fashion, to a hut overlooking the valley where the workers kept a Primus stove and mattress should they need to stay the night. She took off her clothes without shame. He would spare Alice the details but assured her it was paradise on earth.

Throughout this long recital Wa-Lee remained attentive. She too appeared to hear the story as if for the first time. She smiled at the end of it widely, showing her gold teeth. "Why are you telling me this?" Alice asked, and her father answered it was time she knew. For all those years in Chapel Hill he had been a man without allegiance, remembering the hut and sweet odors of the hillside and what sounded like a nightingale beyond the open window. It was time to make amends. It was long since overdue. He had lingered in Hawaii for two months. He had been no hero, had extended his sick leave and recuperation period, and returned only halfheartedly to his wife and family—you—still hearing the nightingale, hearing Wa-Lee.

He brought her to Chicago. She was a chiropodist; he saw her whenever he could. Did Alice remember *South Pacific*; did she remember their trip to the City Center to see the revival, how the whole family—her sisters complaining, playing "Booey" on the trip and singing "Three Little Maids from School Are We"—drove north and stayed at the Biltmore; did she recollect the original cast album, with Ezio Pinza and Mary Martin, the planter singing "This Nearly Was Mine"? That was their story too. She could have seen the stranger across a crowded room, but the stranger was Wa-Lee—so their story really was the story of the flier and Bloody Mary's daughter and prejudice. It was in *The King and I*. There they sang "We Kiss in a Shadow," and there too the tale was familiar: prejudice, unyieldingness, a cross burned on the lawn. Rodgers and Hammerstein knew all about it; it was everywhere you looked the second you went looking, and took no skill to find: intolerance, indifference, the leering supervisor on the plantation or ward.

He wanted to marry, of course. But Alice's mother had not offered a divorce. She knew this part of the story, the years in Chapel Hill while they snapped at each other or were polite, the warring neighborliness and his drinking problem, then hers. Then, when they were separated, when the divorce came through—the very same week—he had flown to Chicago and, as he had promised, proposed. They were no longer in the flush of youth, the blush of it—he smiled—but this was a promise delivered. Wa-Lee said no. She had made a life of her own in Chicago and she had relatives there. Chiropody was both an ancient and an honorable trade. They knew that in Illinois.

Wa-Lee had an acrid odor, a sharp perfume unfamiliar to Alice; her laugh was loud. Her father's tale wore on. Wa-Lee had been the moon and stars to him, the life raft for a drowning man. Alice could not remember ever having heard him talk so much, or with such sentiment. Each time he addressed a convention, or argued a case out of town, each chance he found they met and solaced each other like castaways. "Like castaways?" she asked, and he nodded solemnly. He was tired of legalistic distinctions, sicker than she'd ever guess of dotting the i's crossing t's. Life is a tempest-tossed ocean, he said, on which you are a shipwrecked sailor and you dream of shore. He proposed a toast. He hadn't had this much to drink or drunk it with two people he loved more since heaven knew when. He wanted them to understand how much this evening mattered. Wa-Lee's English is far better than you think, he said, she knows what I'm trying to say. She's been in Chicago since 1961 and has heard it all.

Wa-Lee ordered zabaglione for dessert. The waiter slipped, approaching them, and in a caricature-frantic attempt at a save, hurled the zabaglione into her lap. She shrieked. There were apologies. The maître d'hôtel bestirred himself to wipe her, but she drew back from him, dripping. They stood. Alice thought about the songs from *South Pacific* and *The King and I*, her father in the prison camp, then hospital, and then receiving comfort from a limber Wa-Lee in the hut.

He had lost, if not his birthright or familial pride in Chapel Hill, at least all sense of home there, homecoming, the center of things come unstuck. She thought about her father's baffled payment for the privilege

of declaration, a confidence exchanged (though till that moment there had
been no countervailing equivalent, no "Dad, I knew it all along, we all did,
I'm so glad you're happy, I don't know what went wrong . . ."), showing
his daughter a gap-toothed fat Hawaiian masseuse in this place aswarm
now with waiters, an apron produced, Jack insisting that they send the
bill to his personal attention, and if dry cleaning failed then buy a dress
on him—thought maybe it was true and Wa-Lee had saved her father's
life, saved anyhow his sense of possibility, thought therefore her own
childhood had been shaped by something she herself had till then known
nothing about, no name to call it but absence, no face to give it but blank.

Alvin came at nine. He had a picnic hamper on the backseat of the Jaguar,
and an extra life preserver. He was apologetic. "I rode you pretty hard last
night," he said. "This morning I'll behave myself, I promise. Hey, Billy,
you know why a lawyer can swim in this water without fear of sharks?"

"No," said Billy. "Why?"

"Professional courtesy." Alvin guffawed. "He's got professional
courtesy, see?"

David explained to his son what professional courtesy meant; Billy
laughed. There were whitecaps on the water, and the wind was high. "We'll
motor out," said Alvin. "Then raise sail."

On water he seemed less of a buffoon. He positioned them expertly,
readied the craft, and cast off. There was no waste motion in him now; he
worked without talking. Ferry boats roared past. Tacking, he told Billy
to hold on. When the harbor receded, however, and they held a straight
course in Drake's Channel and the jib was set to Alvin's satisfaction, he
opened a beer. He offered one to Alice, who declined. He told them he
had fishing gear, if anyone wanted to fish. "You look like a pirate," she said.

"I don't feel well," said Billy.

"What's the matter, darling?"

He shrugged. "I just don't feel well, Mommy."

"Does your stomach hurt you?"

He nodded.

"Badly?"

"I need to upchuck," he said.

David laughed.

She turned on him. "I'm glad you find it funny."

"I don't," he said. "Just typical."

"Terrific." She bent over Billy.

"He'll get used to it," said Alvin. "Won't you, sport?"

Billy nodded, his face green.

"Take deep breaths," David advised. The catamaran pitched and rolled. "Lean over the side, if you have to. We're almost halfway there."

"Think of it like Popeye," Alvin said. "Like Popeye the Sailor Man." He grimaced, squinted, did a two-step. "I loves me spinach, yum-yum."

Billy did not love spinach. He buried his head in his hands. His mother rocked him cautiously, embracing the orange preserver, one hand on his neck. "Breathe deeply," David said again. Billy's shoulders shook. A pelican Immelmanned past.

"Think of Columbus," Alvin said. "Discovering America. These are the waters he sailed."

Billy was sick. He gagged and retched. Alice held his waist. Alvin brought the boat into the wind, and they made their way in silence for what seemed like a long time. Then Billy collapsed back into place and David asked, "Feel better now?" and he nodded. "Seasickness," Alvin said. "It happens to everyone once."

Peter Island had a newly built resort. It was of brown wood, with roofs painted blindingly white, and a central structure with restaurants and gift shops and a swimming pool. The manager emerged. He knew Alvin from the Rotary Club, and David from the day before, and he made much of Billy and gave him a white golf cap with *Peter Island* on the bill. They had ice cream on the patio, and Billy said he felt much better. They boarded a golf cart and drove to the beach. These are vacation rituals, David said to Alice, this is what a family is supposed to do by way of enjoyment.

She lay in the shade of a palm tree, while the men lay in the sun. There was a raft in the water, and sunfish and paddle-wheelers for rent. There was an open-air bar, and David brought her rum and tonic in a plastic cup. The swizzle stick had a pink parasol on top. She smiled at him, accepting it. "It's beautiful here," Alice said.

"Yes."

"I've been imagining nuns. Dreaming of"—she smiled again—"the Holy Orders. Don't they renew their vows?"

"Something like that," David said.

"I don't know much about it. But I think that's what we're doing."

He put his hand on her knee. She did not move away. She was watching Billy as he shaped a sand castle with moats.

Alvin had a yellow pail. Big-bellied, absorbed, he was pouring water on the turrets of the structure. He was making stucco, he said, sand-driblets like Gaudi's best. "It's worth it?" David asked.

That night, however, it wasn't worth it; he knew this on the balcony and, later, in their bed. It hadn't been worth it for years. There was nothing between them but Billy, and habit, and the self-affrighting solace of pressing on a bruise. She knew it too. She had known it all along. He had been raised with the conviction that marriage lasts, and family, and that you married once only till death did you part. Yet there were little daily deaths, and the carapace of good behavior cracked to birth a corpse. He had fashioned a career. He had written three books and was completing a fourth. He had used up their story. He was nothing on his own. He spent the next week swimming, watching Billy learn to surface dive and stand on his hands in the pool.

Panic

IT SEEMED TO be the season for marriages again. Robert Potter was forty-three. In his twenties the weddings took place in September; this year, unaccountably, they filled every weekend in June. He was invited to six. Two of the couples were children of friends—romantic striplings fresh from college or completing business school. More of them were second marriages, or third—with complicated etiquette as to who invited whom. In one case the woman was pregnant and, in one case, blind. What interested Robert was the month: the late-spring sense of possibility and risk. He went to the weddings alone. Marriage represented—as someone said, making a toast—the triumph of hope over experience.

"I've heard that before," he told his partner at lunch.

"Yes."

"Who said it?"

She was tall, black-haired. He tried to read her place card.

"Dr. Johnson." She had put on glasses to watch the round of toasts.

"'The triumph of hope over experience,'" he repeated. "Lovely, isn't it?"

"It's lovely, yes," the woman said. She pursed her lips to drink.

The groom's name was Shem. His best man made a jingle: Shem would marry the *crème de la crème*. Robert barely knew the happy couple, but the bride's father was a college friend as well as neighbor, and he explained this to those who asked. The wedding luncheon was salmon and veal; the wines were good.

"What do you do?" the woman to his right inquired.

"I'm in real estate," he lied. "And you?"

"Photographer." She smiled at him. "And a philanthropist."

Shem and Katy make a team that will be the cream of the cream. A long and happy life was proposed, a marvelous honeymoon trip, and all the trips thereafter—this occasioned laughter from the ushers' table—a great day for the parents and grandmother of the bride. A bald man with a handlebar moustache toasted her dead grandfather. "He would have been so proud of you. He always called you his jewel. Ladies and gentlemen, friends, I speak for the elder generation when I call this girl a jewel."

The reception took place at the Explorers Club. There were plaques and photographs and maps and books about travel downstairs. Upstairs, on the landing, a polar bear loomed placidly above the receiving line; someone draped a scarf across his paw. "He should be holding the bridal bouquet," Robert said. The day was hot. A group that called themselves The Separate but Equal Circuit came to play. The girl who sang wore an electric green Oriental-style sheath with side slits high up her legs. He was offered, and accepted, a cigar. He could not understand the lyrics, and the band was loud. At three o'clock he excused himself, saying "Congratulations" several times. The groom, gyrating, bumped Robert as he left. "Sorry, old man," the groom said.

He had been staying, since April, on the Connecticut coast. This weekend was the weekend he could not have Jimmy; Jimmy and his mother were going to Nahant. They were opening the house, she said, and Jimmy at eleven was old enough to help. She and Robert had been divorced for two years. She could use a man around the place—all that opening and closing, with no one to carry the shutters or take down the storms. Robert had offered to help. Janet hesitated briefly before she refused. He could picture her, speculative, tapping a pencil, at the other end of the line. "You can have him next weekend instead," she said. "I'm sorry if it complicates your plans."

So he had gone to the wedding, arriving in time. The minister intoned the service lengthily; the pews were full. That Wednesday, in Old Lyme, he had attended The Burial of the Dead; the son of his first agent had come home after school and gone to the attic and taken his father's service revolver and shot himself in the mouth. The memorial service was brief.

"I'll miss you, Dad," said Jimmy.

"I'll miss you."

"I want a wet suit."

"Now?"

"For my birthday, OK?"

"We'll see."

"We'll see," in their negotiations, meant "yes."

"If I had it now," said Jimmy, "I could go swimming this weekend."

"No."

"Why not?"

"You're helping your mother, remember?"

"Not *all* the time."

"All the time she needs you."

"OK."

Robert smiled. He coiled the cord; he would give his son the wet suit when they met. "I want to be there when you put it on," he said. "To show you how to move in it."

"OK."

"What color do you want?"

"What colors are there?"

"Yellow," he said. "Red, I think. Mostly black."

"Black like frogmen wear?"

"That's right."

"It's what I want," Jimmy said.

The wedding one week earlier had taken place in Water Mill. Robert used the ferry from Bridgeport to Port Jefferson, then crossed Long Island in the late morning. He drove against the flow of traffic, unimpeded. The justice of the peace was garrulous; he had lost more weight sweating, he said, than he'd gained all winter. He and Robert waited for the happy couple on the porch. The bride and bridegroom gave themselves a party. The bridegroom was a novelist; he had just sold movie rights to *The Bronx Book of the Dead*. Their families were warring—the father and mother of the bride had not spoken for years, and it proved difficult to locate a city that would not be "taking sides." They had dismissed Winnetka, Asheville, and Grosse Point. So they rented a house in Water Mill and invited friends. There was a tent with a yellow and white striped awning, in case of rain. It rained. There would be a juggler and magician and steel band from Jamaica. There would be a clambake on the beach.

This wedding, said the J.P., put him fourteen short of six hundred; he'd seen all kinds. Last week, for example, at the Yacht Club there were two hours of cocktails and they had to prop up the groom. His talk, he said, would last four minutes exactly. "The first part's mine. And then I'll ask the groom a question, and his answer is 'I will.' Then the bride answers, 'I will,' then you as witness"—he nodded—"give him the ring and he gives it to her and then the last part's mine again, the legal bit."

He was planning to retire after one more term. He and the wife had a piece of land in Florida, and they figured six months here and six months there was one whole year of paradise; between you and I and the lamppost, he said, this burg gets dull in winter. What with the parking tickets, the felony charges, and the D.W.I., it's hopping all July.

"Ceremony," the groom told Robert. "I hate it. I hate it for *me*, understand." They stood alone in the hall. "I feel like a trained seal. I really should get back to work."

"You're working?"

"No. Are you?"

The house had been recently shingled; the wedding took place on the porch. Behind the swimming pool three horses grazed, switching their tails. There were cherrystones and littlenecks waiting in abundance, and champagne. "Ceremony," the groom repeated. "Not my cup of tea."

There had also been a christening that week. At ten-thirty Robert drove to St. Peter's—a white stone pile near the center of Mystic—but the doors were locked. A man with a flower bouquet met him at the steps. "It says ten-thirty," he said. "I'm to deliver this—Pratt? You're with the Pratt party, correct? I hate to leave them sitting here," and he handed Robert the vase.

So he waited in front of St. Peter's, holding a stranger's bouquet. During the service his attention wandered, and he scanned the walls and pews. Then he joined in the responses and complimented the mother of the child. They said how brave a boy he'd be, how strong a swimmer, happy in water, how much like his mother he looked. The child was wearing, they said, his grandfather's chemise. He thought of how that other boy, eighteen years old, came home from school and looked in the kitchen, looked in the living room maybe, found nobody home and went up to the attic—the walls lined with photographs of his own father holding up bear, up antlers, up fish, with hunting knives and rod and tackle and Spanish shotguns and the pistol his great-great uncle used at Shiloh—thought how he turned on the radio loud enough to drown out nòt the result of his procedure but the noise of preparation, to make it seem routine when he inserted the cartridge and released the safety and, with grace, because he always had been an athlete, moving with deliberation that nonetheless felt practiced, raised it to his mouth and licked the barrel and squeezed.

His marriage had collapsed not out of restlessness or boredom but of its own weight. He met Janet in graduate school, and they married and moved to Manhattan in 1972. They found an apartment on Riverside Drive and, three years later, bought at the insider's price. He placed their bed against the window and, rising, saw New Jersey, the Palisades jutting above the tame rush of the river. They went to Chinese restaurants and late-night double features and The Frick Collection and the Guggenheim. He worked in what had been the maid's room, a cubicle glutted with books. They would be faithful forever, until death did them part; they needed nothing in their lives but each other forever and ever; they were a sufficiency together and incomplete apart. He would remember those phrases: the litany of love breathed into his neck, his ear, on pillows, in the shower stall.

"I believe there are three things," she said. "Three concentric circles, if you like. Sex, consciousness, and history. Sex and history are polar opposites, and when you fuse them you get consciousness. That's what I've been working on." Janet said this, not joking, with consequential earnestness, tracing—with her fingernail—the concentric circles on his thigh. "This one is consciousness," she said. "And here's history. And then a little higher, here, it's the dialectic—sex."

Increasingly he thought it comic—her scrutiny of self. Their marriage consisted of talk. Janet believed in intense, continual articulation; she accused him of dropping off to sleep or changing the subject or refusing to give her the credit of an answer. She said he listened harder to the radio than to her, and her opinion of his work mattered less to him, apparently, than the opinion of that illiterate high-heeled groupie from the publicity department, or those darling children he taught at The New School. He said that wasn't true, she was his toughest critic. What's that supposed to mean? she asked, and he said what I said.

Increasingly he gave readings in cities a plane trip away, and it was easy afterward to take what he thought of as solace. There were ambitious girls in graduate programs, with novels of their own. They read him their first chapters and wanted his response; they kept the work-in-progress in boxes by their beds. He took a Visiting Professor job in a writing program in Baltimore, and then one in Syracuse, and then a position at Princeton in order to commute. When he returned at night Janet met him at the door; she couldn't sleep without him, she had been waiting up.

"I missed you," he would say.

"I missed *you*."

"What did you do all day?"

"Do?"

"I mean, did you have fun? Did anything happen to tell me about?"

"Nothing important," she said.

He took off his raincoat. "Mail? Calls? *Un*important?"

"To you." Her sketchbook lay open, face down.

"When this job is over," he said, "let's take a vacation. Somewhere hot."

"When this job is over you'll get another."

"Not right away."

"Right away."

He could find no answer. She said this with a voice so expressionless as to seem feigned. They embraced.

In September he went to his high-school reunion. There was to be a cocktail party and, the invitation promised, frolicsome remembrance of things past. There was a questionnaire entitled: "Twenty-fifth Reunion Test: What Vegetable do you think you were and what have you become? Will you bring your Spouse or Significant Other? Name? Can you (check one) still do the quadratic equation? Five laps around the track? Remember Smitty's Dog?"

He had not intended to go. The questionnaire evoked that self-congratulatory coyness that had marked his high-school years—the sense of inherited merit and car pools with chauffeurs. He had been a member of the second most popular clique. The world divided, said Janet, into those for whom high school meant the best years of their lives, and those for whom it represented the worst. Robert disagreed. For him it meant a staging process, a wash of expectation through which girls moved wearing cashmere, and he conjugated Latin verbs and jostled in the lunch line or the locker room.

The class secretary called. "We haven't heard from you," she said.

"I know. I'm sorry."

"They're coming from all over." Her voice was reedy, soft; he tried to remember her face. "Two from California, one from Oregon, and three from Atlanta."

"Congratulations."

"You're coming, aren't you? Author, author . . ."

"I'll try."

"We've got the highest percentage," she said, "of any reunion class in the last eleven years. If I can get seven more people we'll have the highest percentage ever."

So he had promised to come. It was not a promise he felt obliged to keep. That Saturday morning dawned brightly, however, and he was restless, headache prone; he had no other plans. He drove approach roads to the campus knowing when to brake and where to turn, with the kind of body knowledge that outlasted time. The school was slate-roofed, turreted, with iron entrance gates. The classroom buildings were fieldstone, and the library and auditorium and gym and dining halls were brick.

He had been successful at school. The caption to his yearbook photo read BORN TO SUCCESS HE SEEMS. Yet he carried with him, dormant, the seeds of that first forced growth—the conviction of showiness, merely, that his was a talent more rumored than real, and his adult gesturing still adolescent strut.

Arriving, he first saw his teachers. They had not changed. The Japanese mathematics teacher was as sprightly as when she tried to teach him calculus; the physics teacher had retained a horseman's swagger to his walk. They formed a welcoming committee. "Bobby Potter," they exclaimed. "How are you? Welcome back!"

The woman who taught French, whose breath was tinged with caraway, stepped forward, offering her cheek, and said, "*Je t'embrasse.*"

"*J'entre dans la salle de classe,*" he pronounced. They laughed.

His history teacher, bearded now and using a cane, labored up. They had been his elders, always, and therefore exempt from the arbitration of time. Behind them in the quadrangle a herd of strangers clustered to long trestle tables where there were hors d'oeuvres and a bar.

Helen Applebaum Morris embraced him. They had played strip poker in eleventh grade; he read the name at her neck. She said she had three children, was about to send her eldest off to college; he's six foot two, she said, he looks at me, this bruiser, and says, Mom, I'm hungry, wash this shirt. Can you believe it, Bob?

Then he was surrounded. Those he sat next to in eighth grade, those he played basketball with, those he sang with in *Iolanthe* when they made a chorus of peers—they gathered near him, chortling, pointing to their name tags, lifting glasses, and swallowing shrimp. Jim from California had flown in that afternoon. He mentioned Burt Bacharach's name: yesterday Burt Bacharach had been playing tennis on the adjacent court. Jim from Colorado arrived from Italy. He was into Buddhism, very deeply into Buddhism, and there was a guru near Montecatini he planned to study with. Those baths, those healing waters—he pursed his lips and narrowed his eyes and softly kissed the air. He spoke the guru's name. Then he handed Robert a card. "If you're ever in Boulder," he said.

Peter from Seattle loved it there. You get used to the weather, he said, there's no more rainfall than New York, it's just it comes more steadily. He was a labor lawyer. Now he went canoeing every weekend, and sometimes after work, and the salmon jumped straight for his freezer. They had a second drink. Black women in uniform tended the bar. Eric, a Gestalt therapist, lived in Baltimore. He introduced his wife; she was pert and freckle-faced. She knew one of Robert's books. They had met at Esalen while doing primal scream.

The secretary approached. A redhead grown gray, she wore a jockey's cap, backward. She handed him his namecard. "Bobby Potter. Welcome back."

"How do you attach this thing?"

She showed him, peeling tape. A wind came, threatening rain. "I knew it," Eric said. "I could smell the rain, I always can. Ask Janey about it, ask her if I'm ever wrong."

"Yes," said Janey. "Often. But he's right about the rain."

They laughed together happily, as if this perception were shared.

Then they moved into the auditorium for slides. They shouted out their classmates' names, applauding. The token Negro had been photographed most frequently. He was shown with the basketball, the football, a protractor, his arms around his teammates, with a carnation in his buttonhole, and sporting a beret. There were pictures of the senior year drama production, *Caesar and Cleopatra*. The boy who played Apollodorus had died in a car crash; there was a moment of silence when his photograph appeared. Caesar wrote homoerotic verse and lived in Los Angeles now.

Ralph Atcheson who played the ukulele was cajoled to play again. He happened to have brought it with him, just in case. They all said how much fun this was, how they should keep in touch. They pressed business cards on Robert and wrote in their home phones; they said they couldn't wait to read the story he would write about this day. "You travel," Helen said. "Come see me in Washington soon."

The class secretary read off the results of the questionnaire. The most frequently named vegetable was eggplant, the most frequently named animal the koala bear. Sixty-two members of the graduating class of 1962 were present; forty had responded to the data sheet. It was not too late, the secretary said; she pointed to a corner table piled with questionnaires. "If you've been inspired by this inspiring occasion," she said, "please tell us how you feel."

Robert coughed. He blew his nose. At a certain point, he told himself, foreknowledge is as actual as event.

The last Sunday of September, he left Jimmy at what used to be their home. Janet, entertaining, was not pleased to see him. "My former husband," she said. She introduced Robert to the Kappelmans and Cravens and to a man named Magid. Robert said, "I can't stay," and she accepted this. "I've got to get back," he told the Cravens, who smiled.

Janet wore white. She inclined her cheek to Jimmy, embracing him, and said, "There, there."

"Thank you, Daddy."

"See you next week."

"Did you have fun?" she asked, offering her profile to Magid. The image of youthful maternity, she bent to Jimmy, concerned.

He nodded.

"Good," she said. "Has he fed you?"

"Bread and water," Robert said. "And eel soup for breakfast this morning."

Magid had a wrestler's thick neck. His hair was close-cropped, graying, and he sported tasseled loafers and brown tweeds. Robert appealed to him, leaving. "It's a wonder the kid eats at all."

"Nonsense," said Janet. "I asked if he'd had lunch."

"I did," said Jimmy. "I ate."

He hated the end of the visit, their ritual bickering. It happened this way, always, an aggrieved politeness edging up to argument. But he could not bring himself to leave Jimmy in the lobby; he made a point each Sunday of arriving at the door.

They had gone, the day before, to the Yankee doubleheader. Robert had had visions of camaraderie, of hot dogs and heroics and the two of them hoarse with shouting, the game a thriller till the final pitch. At the entrance to the stadium, he bought them both programs and hats. They hurried up the ramp. Jimmy brought along his mitt, in case of a foul pop. Their seats were good; he explained to Jimmy why this was the house that Ruth built. There were records and percentages he remembered with no trouble—names like Miller Huggins and Joe McCarthy and Tommy Henrich and Lou Gehrig. He knew about Lefty Gomez and Red Ruffing, even if he had not seen them pitch; he had seen Allie Reynolds on TV, Vic Raschi, and Joe Page.

"I started coming here," he said, "after DiMaggio retired. Then of course there were the Mantle years."

"When was that, Daddy?"

"The fifties," he said. "And the early sixties too. We called them the Bronx Bombers. Men like Gil McDougald. Yogi Berra. Casey Stengel."

"I've heard of him," Jimmy said.

"And 'the crow.' Frankie Crosetti." Robert looked in vain for Frankie "The Crow" Crosetti in the coaching box. "And Phil Rizzuto. That guy on TV. Hank Bauer. They used to be my idols."

"Can I have a hot dog?"

"You may."

They admired how the vendor snapped his dollar bills together, and the way he balanced, teetering, to hold out a hot dog and roll. The men around them wore windbreakers and carried radio sets. There was much shrill laughter in the box across the aisle. He pointed to the bullpen and its plaques. "That's where they honor the great ones," he said. "That's better, even, than getting your number retired . . ."

"This hot dog's cold," Jimmy said.

The afternoon was raw. The beer was flat, and Jimmy did not want a sip; he picked up and pounded his glove. Robert did not know the names of the latest Yankee stalwarts; nothing, it seemed, was at stake. They discussed the designated hitter rule. The men across the aisle were drinking gin.

"It's too cold," Jimmy said.

"We'll get another."

"No. I mean, just sitting here."

"It's only the sixth inning," Robert said. "Maybe the sun will come out."

"It won't. It's boring."

Men dropped flies. They struck out repeatedly. In the last half of the seventh inning, Jimmy said, "I want to go."

"Let's stay till it's over."

"Just *this* game, OK?"

"All right," Robert said. "We can go."

He gathered his papers and cup. There were peanut shells at his feet, and sandwich leavings, and a discarded scarf. The batter bunted on a third strike pitch. The ball went foul. A woman to his left threw back her head, revealing a mouth full of silver. A traffic helicopter banked and wheeled.

His skill was a surveyor's skill, his habit that of witness. He could identify snippets of speech, the overheard fragment, the volitional veiled glance. He knew, in a room, who was sleeping with whom, or wanted to; his talent was control. Reviewers praised his tact, his chilly noticing eye. They did so, however, in terms as measured as his own—and this had come to worry Robert; his work had been at best a moderate success. Like Roland's pal in the palace, he said, he was waiting for the call. The call would be a clarion; it would come from a reverberating distant horn; it would crack the very sinews of his throat. "Moderation in all things" was the advice a doctor gives, and an insurance agent. It did not work for art. He dreamed of a great summons, an immoderate subject, the panic that is Pan's penetrating entry, a cry. Meantime, he built his small books. They were shapely and succinct. He was neither stupid nor lazy, and he wanted once to write a story or a novel that was larger than its author, that would demonstrate craft anchored, not adrift. With increasing bitterness, he doubted that he would.

On his way back he stopped in Weston for a drink. His friends the Hartogs had purchased a farm—a white sprawl of buildings with lawn tractors and the neighbor's hay in what was once a barn. They had made a sauna of the chicken house. Robert arrived at four-thirty. The afternoon was hot. Pieter Hartog was recovering from hepatitis; he told Robert it had been the strangest thing. One day he was feeling fine, smoking, boozing: business as usual. And the next day he had liver trouble, hating the taste of bourbon, nauseated by smoke. He supposed it was a clam. He would like to claim the needle, or something fashionably short of AIDS—but it must have been a clam. Pieter laughed. You know how mussels can be full of grime and shit, he said, how one sandy mussel can ruin the broth—well, that must have been what did it in his case. And he didn't find it funny even now. One of the first things that goes when you're sick—Pieter took his arm, avuncular—is a sense of humor. You keep just about everything else. You notice the nurses, for instance. But you fail to find things funny that had been uproarious before.

It hadn't been that simple for Leslie either, Pieter said; she took it on the chin. She probably thought he was banging some junkie, some infectious number at the office. They were going to the Yucatan next week. Uxmal and Chichén-Itzá, those would be the tickets: a tequila sunrise for breakfast and a margarita at lunch. He could have shown her Cancún. He would have taken her to Cozumel, or Puerto Vallarta, but they're on the beaten track and mostly she wants to get off.

Tommy Hartog was back for the weekend, from his boarding school in Montana. "Wears his old man out," said Pieter. "Wish I'd had that arm . . ."

"If you'd care to catch, sir?" Tommy asked.

"I'd like that," Robert said.

The men had rum and tonics on the porch. Tommy swung on a suspended tractor tire; the tree it was tied to was dead. After some time he approached with three mitts. He threw the ball and caught it in one hand, repeatedly.

"Batter up," said Pieter. "I'll get the fungo bat."

They ascended to the meadow. A fire siren sounded to the west.

His mitt was stiff. He pounded it, remembering those hours spent with neat's-foot oil and rags, the saddle soap and liniment and sweat-absorbent leather that meant Saturday mornings, or summer, or practice after school. He had played second base. Tommy threw the hardball, and he caught it in the webbing of his glove. Then he threw to Pieter, and Pieter to Tommy, and Tommy tagged imaginary runners and threw them out at the plate. As Robert's sureness returned, and he put some force behind the throw, Pieter seemed to flag. He complained about the sun. Tommy, however, grew bright in the declining light, and his throw snapped into Robert's pocket with a satisfying whomp. Robert fired back. The boy caught the return throw, returned it, and soon the two of them exclusively played catch.

He was sweating now, elated, at the outer limit of his arm. He shagged flies and gauged the bounce of grounders with an accuracy that surprised him. Pieter, watching, picking his teeth with whip grass, cheered. They retreated the length of the meadow, and the man and boy were intent now, competitors. Then something happened to him that had not happened in years: a release in action, a sudden setting free, a grace that caused him to run faster and throw harder and catch the baseball more securely than he could run, throw or catch. He was winded soon but continued; his hair grew wet with sweat. Then Tommy laid down his glove. Robert called, "I've had enough," and theatrically spread-eagled, falling backward in the grass. There was a white slice of moon. The following weekend, he promised himself, he would see his son.

In October he drove to Vermont. He had been invited to the second annual "Apple Harvest Festival" reading Monday night. Robert could foresee it all: the praise, his counterfeited modesty, the question period, the deserted hall his host would tell him was an impressive turnout for this place. They would pay enough to cover his expenses in Newfane, and he would spend the night before the reading with the woman married to his editor; she had called him ten days earlier to say she would be free.

There was much weekend traffic heading south. There were many DETOUR and NO SHOULDER signs. Melissa had arrived before him at the inn. She was drinking sherry in the lounge.

"I'm sorry," Robert said.

"Don't be." She stood.

"Leaf-peepers. I hate them," he said. "We're leaf-peepers also, of course."

There was no one at the desk. She kissed him on the cheek. "Hello."

"Hello."

"I'm starting to unwind," she said. "It took all afternoon."

"Have you registered?"

"Yes." She gave him that half-grimace of complicity he had first noticed six months before. "You should see the bathroom, baby. Copper. They've got a copper sink."

He smiled. He looked around him at the inn, the empty vestibule, the tiles and beaming and plaster that represented "rustic charm"; he had been more weary than he knew. There were magazines on a table: *Country Living*, *Art in America*, *Vanity Fair*, *Yankee*, *Newsweek*, *Vogue*.

"I'm glad we're here," he said.

"Happy anniversary."

He checked his watch, the date.

"One hundred days," she said. "Since the last time we promised not to meet this way again." She lifted the glass to her lips and tongued the sherry. "Your health."

They ate at a lodge down the road. Melissa wore a white silk dress, a strand of pearls; her hair was coiled. The whole effect—the rouge, the rings, the cigarette holder—seemed an incongruity: a woman on a mountain slope but wearing three-inch heels. The food was pretentious. They drank two bottles of wine. The waiter blandished them, flourishing the saltshaker and peppermill and ashtrays as though these were objects of value. He kissed his fingertips and then the air; he ignited the duck and said, "Aaah!" He asked, repeatedly, if everything were to their satisfaction; Robert nodded.

"Is something wrong?" she asked.

"No. Why?"

"You've been, oh, distant. Somewhere else. I haven't seen you since the snails."

"I'm here."

"Yes."

"You look lovely."

"Thank you," said Melissa. "But that isn't what I meant."

He brought himself back to attention. "What did you mean?"

"Just that you seem preoccupied." She buttered bread. "Is something wrong about tonight?"

"No. You're the one with commitments, remember?"

"My sociable hermit," she said.

Her form of flattery was to repeat his own previous opinion; he had used the phrase "sociable hermit" the last time they met. He was not by nature convivial; his work required this. He suffered fools gladly, he told her, as long as they bought books.

"It killed the cat," she said. "I know. I don't mean to crowd you."

"You're not. If I knew what was bothering me . . ."

The waiter wheeled the dessert cart to their table. There were lemon mousse and chocolate mousse and strawberry tarts and cakes and the house specialty, a charlotte Malakoff. Robert ordered charlotte Malakoff. As he tasted the first forkful, the candle on their table guttered out.

She also had been busy: her schedule was insane. She crisscrossed New England, she said, leaving Tim and Sally with the housekeeper at home. She was working her way up the Corporate Ladder, but it felt like Child-Life Swings. Had he ever noticed the way they space the rungs? The bottom rungs of a Child-Life ladder are spaced close together, easy to climb; as you get higher, however, the spaces are farther apart. So you keep small children off the top where falling's risky; she had made it, this year, to middle management of the Division of Design.

At the table next to them a man announced, "I'm living in Ottawa now. My father's in New York. I see him every month."

Her dress had ridden up along the thigh. He dropped his hand there and squeezed. It felt like a revision of his furtive gropings when in school: the knees' articulation slick in pantyhose.

"Let's go," Melissa said. "If it's all right with you."

"All right." He put down his fork.

"This coffee's rotten."

He folded his napkin, then rolled it. She continued her complaint. He, Robert, couldn't know what it meant to marry young and sleep with a beautiful boy until he turned away from you and chose his own beautiful boys. He was off in Hollywood, making deals, making it with tennis players in the clubhouse shower; she had accused him of that. She had driven him into the closet, then out of the closet and to the West Coast. His paperback line was shoddy, failing, he wasn't there for the kids. . . .

Someone opened a door in the hall; wind entered. He paid. They moved outside. Their breath was white smoke, visible, and Melissa shivered. "What happened to summer?" she asked.

"You know what they say"—he tried the old joke—"about weather in Vermont. It's nine months of winter and three of poor sledding."

She laughed. She took his arm. A sadness that he could not name was with him, however, and would not be dispelled. It clung to him as she did when they went back to their room, took off their clothes and went to bed.

It was a compound of time passing, drunkenness, dissatisfaction, flesh. It took him in its mouth and opened its long legs to him and sang his name in darkness and whimpered in the sheets. It was ardent, acrobatic, and it whispered that it could not let him leave. It said he was married to silence, wedded to failure forever. It breathed beside him through the night and woke and showered and had coffee and croissants and grape jelly from the vine behind the inn. Melissa too was with him, but she drove back to her husband in White Plains.

Palinurus

WHEN THE NOVELIST George Chapman asked Enoch for a favor, Enoch said, of course. He had been doing so for years and saw no reason to stop. It was a pattern between them. When Chapman required money, Enoch wrote the check; when Chapman needed a place to retreat to, he used Enoch's house in Vermont. In smaller ways also—the phone calls at two in the morning, the jerry can of gas when Chapman's car ran dry, the protective caution with which he fielded questions (from interviewers, ex-wives, creditors) as to the writer's whereabouts—Enoch made himself of use. "My buddy," Chapman called him. "My sidekick. My rod and my staff."

This last allusion was typical. Chapman knew the Bible and liked thinking he had servants; he was too busy, he claimed, to clean up "that mess, my life." It was other people's business to pick up the pieces and balance accounts. He focused wholly on work.

The nicknames were typical also. Chapman liked to label things and make them over by naming. "Any fool," he said, "can call a spade a spade. The artist calls it 'hoe.'" For the two years he wrote *Virgil*, he referred to Enoch as "my pal Palinurus"—that faithful foredoomed helmsman who was sacrificed at sea. "*Te petens Palinure*," he would mumble, squinting, as if the horizon were water. Chapman himself did not swim. *Virgil*, with its homespun folksy wisdom, its startling transformation of Dido into rock star and Aeneas to her bodyguard, was made into a movie; Chapman coauthored the script.

While at work on the story "Quixote at Home," he insisted on calling the younger man "Sancho." "My faithful retainer," he said. In fact Enoch was tall and thin, whereas Chapman in his forties acquired a pronounced potbelly. But the truth behind appearances, the novelist would say, "is what we're after, isn't it; that's why I dream for a living. It explains my mournful countenance, the nightmares, the bad teeth."

"Bad teeth?" Enoch asked. "I didn't know your teeth were bad."

"Pitted. Carious. Noisome." Chapman lit his pipe. "Like your hair, pal. Falling out."

"Have you seen a dentist?"

"Every week."

They kept track of each other. Chapman needed acolytes, and Enoch gladly served. With the notion of a memoir or critical biography, he took notes. He kept a journal labeled C and recorded his reactions to the novelist during, then after, a visit. He organized their correspondence in much the same manner, by year. He had a dozen folders and he kept them by his desk.

Enoch felt in the presence of greatness. If some of it rubbed off on him, so much the better, he thought; if not, the mere proximity sufficed. Chapman flattered him in person, and this could be more gratifying than praise behind the back. Over time Enoch acquired some of his mentor's habits—the love of sour pickles and Stilton, the bottles of beer before sleep. To have heard the conversation, to have read the drafts of manuscript, to have suggested changes and to see those changes made: such would be his reward. He remembered Yeats's phrase about how hard it is, when your own work has come to nothing, to "be secret and exult." "Of all things known," Yeats wrote, "that is most difficult."

Enoch was a writer too. At forty-four he was the author of two novels and a monograph on Conrad. This last remained in print. His career had little of the reach and bright trajectory of Chapman's, nor the success. He taught.

He was an only child. His father died when he was young, his mother died on April 7, 1988. He had been teaching at Middlebury College—his marriage a failure, his wife remaining with her carpenter in Thetford, his sons Ricky and Allan being raised by a stranger, with chickens. If there were any comfort in his mother's rapid illness, it was how he kept from her his own impending divorce. Dying, she had asked him if he were as happy in his marriage as she had been in hers. This was the one lie Enoch could remember telling; he stroked her thin hair, the irradiated stubble, smoothing the skin at her temples. He told her, softly, yes.

She had not believed him, he knew. Earlier, she would have pressed and questioned him—eliciting from his hesitation, the half-evasive half-inventions and the way he changed the subject—that Rita had moved up the valley and was not coming home. But, dying, his mother was tired; the pain made her aloof. She wanted her boy to be settled; she settled for Enoch's white lie.

"What I want from you," said Chapman, "is something you should think about."

It was midnight; they were drinking. They were sitting on the porch.

"What I want is a favor."

"All right."

"I've got this mess of manuscript." He waved his arm inclusively at the porch rail, the elm stump, the cars in the yard. "Those books. All those cardboard boxes. You should be my executor."

"Your what?"

"In case something happens. In case you outlive me, you bastard."

"Well, since you put it that way"—Enoch rocked back again, tilting, savoring the warm night breeze—"since you put it with such, such *delicacy*. The actuarial tables . . ."

"I'm not kidding," Chapman said.

Then Enoch stopped rocking and, sober, said yes, it would be an honor. It would not, he hoped, come to pass.

His ice cubes had melted. He turned to his guest. It had been a difficult spring. "Have you been working?" Chapman asked, and he had no answer. What Enoch read was stale and flat; what he wrote was unprofitable.

In the protective darkness, rocking, he continued his complaint. Even the boys annoyed him. Their jostling, daylong rumble, the racketing clatter and fuss from their room, the hours he spent managing the house (Rita off at Country Things, selling quilts and draping hoops with sweaters and meeting her carpenter for coffee, he came to learn, and hanging the SORRY, WE'RE CLOSED sign in the window while she opened her legs to him on the camp bed by the delivery entrance), the weekly round of shopping, cooking, the flutter in his thighs when he spent more than minutes rototilling what would not be a garden—all this aggrieved him. He smoked. He weathered May, then June. For the final two weeks of his marriage, as if in opposition, the sun shone every day.

"I used to think," said Chapman, "that we carried it all with us. All that baggage in our heads. Old lovers, our parents, the taste of applesauce, our fourth grade teacher's maiden aunt's lisp"—he raised his glass—"the watermark in stationery, telephone calls, old books. But we don't. We lose it, it passes. All that's lovely passes."

"Have another?" Enoch asked.

There were constellations, but he could not name their names.

The writer shook his head. "It's time to quit. To get some sleep."

"I'm glad you came, George. Really."

Chapman was solicitous, and this did seem strange.

"She picked the hell of a time to leave you, didn't she? Rita, I mean."

"We left each other."

"Yes?"

They slept till noon. The grass required mowing, but Enoch could not face it. He sat on the porch instead, rocking, drinking coffee. Chapman was to give a reading in Detroit, then Salt Lake City, then Denver. His novel *Spindrift* had appeared; the first printing had sold out. "A magic, sprawling book," the advertisements proclaimed. "This is vintage Chapman: a literary event!"

Enoch drove him to Burlington Airport, and they shook hands formally. They would see each other soon, they promised, they would go fishing together.

"So we go off headlong, hurtling to eternity," Chapman said. He did not appear to be joking. He wore his cowboy hat. He carried his typewriter with him, as always, and his black leather suitcase, its handles reinforced by string. The last view Enoch had of him was distant, at the Northwest gate; he was standing by the counter, threadbare, plump, smoking an unlit pipe, raising his hand—not waving it—in the hieratic gesture of farewell.

When he died in Denver it was, somehow, not a shock. The car that hit him went out of control; the driver collapsed and plowed into the taxi station by the Brown Palace Hotel. The driver, Clarence Hovey, died on impact too. The coroner reported this. The writer had been pinioned (facing the other direction, lighting his pipe, protecting it) and crushed—though Chapman's companion and publicist, Ms. Margot Zimmerman, escaped unharmed. It was, she told the newspapers, a bolt from the blue, a total devastation; they had been going to lunch.

Enoch attended the funeral. Avoiding the airport, he drove. Chapman had been born and raised outside of Philadelphia; he was buried in the graveyard where his parents had a plot. A sister was buried there also. The day grew hot. On August 22, he would have been fifty years old. There were mourners Enoch recognized, and many that he failed to; the coffin stayed shut. To his surprised relief, when he introduced himself to Chapman's lawyer, the man knew his name. "You're the executor, right?" he said. "The literary executor. He asked me to include you."

"When?"

"Include you in the will, I mean. Last month."

So Chapman must have made the choice before his trip to Enoch's house and their drunken discussion on the front porch. How like him, Enoch thought—to come to a decision and then ask as if for a favor what in fact was prearranged. He must have known, of course, that his host would accept. He might have taken for granted that the offer would be flattering: "*Te petens Palinure.*"

On the way home he fought sleep. He drove his Subaru station wagon—silver, rusting, six years old. Its backseat disgorged candy and Walkman batteries and Kleenex and socks. He would have left it with Rita, but she had the carpenter's truck. The carpenter's house was passive solar; it backed into a hill. Its windows were unpainted and green with hanging plants. Enoch wanted to be able to collect his sons in something they would recognize; therefore he kept the car.

The Subaru provided him with the illusion of family; parked, it still could seem as if Ricky and Allan might come bounding from the IGA or Fox Village Movie House or renovated Grange Hall where they went for child-care on the mornings that he taught. Those final months, he had done all the driving. Rita had had it, she said. She was tired of being the homemaker, the perfect provider, the one with MOM'S TAXI stuck to the bumper; let Enoch make arrangements for a change. Now she was staying put. Now his muffler needed fixing, and the tailgate rattled, and he had to hold the steering wheel to keep from veering left.

A year passed. He took a leave of absence from teaching; with his mother's legacy, he could afford two years. He grew a beard. His old sense of entitlement had faded; he could not bring himself to fight for custody, acclaim. The divorce went through uncontested; he saw little of his sons. He buried himself in Chapman's papers—the unfinished drafts, the sketches, the letters and journals and libretti and eleven versions of a play.

There had been a flurry of sympathy after the accident; admirers wrote to condole. There were telephone calls and visits from doctoral candidates working on *Virgil* or the early novels or the three books of short stories. Rumor reached him also. Chapman was a suicide; he had been dying of AIDS. Margot Zimmerman was his new mistress; her husband had driven the car. He had left a million dollars or, alternatively, a million-dollar debt. He had known he was going to die; he had had premonitions all that week.

There was an article in *People*; there were television interviews and a speculative essay in *The New Republic*, comparing Chapman's fate to that of his great predecessors: D. H. Lawrence, Thomas Wolfe. A piece in the *TriQuarterly* compared him to both Hart and Stephen Crane. There was talk about a musical based on *Sharon's Speedboat*—the last, unfinished play. *Spindrift* ascended the best-seller list, remaining there ten weeks. There were letters sent, in care of Chapman's publisher, asking Enoch for a photograph or lock of hair or clothing scrap or page of manuscript, and it was at times unclear to him if they meant Chapman's manuscript or his, Enoch's, own.

Jonathan Alton called often. Six years before, they had been introduced by Chapman in New York. The party was in honor of the publication of *Virgil*, and there were many people drinking white wine and Perrier. Chapman appeared amused; he stoked his pipe. "This guy's writing my biography," he said. "Imagine that."

Alton was a sallow man with a ridge of scar tissue under his chin; he had been Chapman's colleague when they taught together at Rochester. Then Chapman got famous and quit. "I couldn't wait," he said to Enoch later. "I had to write best sellers to get out of bloody Rochester, *comprende*?"

Alton, however, remained. At the funeral, wearing a black three-piece suit and bow tie, he commiserated with Enoch as if they were old friends. Repeatedly, he blew his nose. "It's up to us now, isn't it?" he said. "It's really up to us."

"What is?"

"We've got to see it through."

The biographer proved indefatigable. He wanted clarification on the whereabouts of manuscripts, the various drafts and their dates. His interest in detail (where had Chapman been on June 27, 1979; what was he wearing and what did he say when the divorce from Caroline, his second wife, was settled; who had been at the party, then gone fishing in the Chesapeake in 1980?) seemed to Enoch pointless—or at least beside the point. At the funeral he'd copied out, then fretted over the accurate spelling of names inscribed in the Memorial Book. He'd noted the starting time of the service, its duration, and who had tears in their eyes. It took him longer to research a text than Chapman had taken to write it; by 1989, he began on 1981. It was fortunate for Alton, Enoch thought, that his subject's production had—abruptly, irrevocably—ceased.

The calls grew plaintive, urgent. Alton made them, he would say, in order to keep Enoch up to date. "You're the executor. You ought to know." With the disconcerting habit of assuming their shared purpose, his letters outlined the book's progress. "I've blocked in Chapter IV. I can't seem to settle it, though. I'm having trouble with 'Homer,' the tone of his decision to locate the last scene in Darien. How much of this is unconscious association, and how much a bad joke? What do you think? I feel I've lost my bearings—there's just so much to do!"

On the anniversary of Chapman's death, Alton mourned: "My office is a shambles. The fifth chapter's killing me. I mean this literally. I wonder if you'd write a letter to my Chairman, stating you know me, and that you acknowledge the importance of this project. Only if you're comfortable saying it, of course."

Two weeks later things were worse. "In a manner of speaking," wrote Alton, "we're in the same boat, you and I. We've lost our captain, we're adrift." Enoch had an image—fleeting, fading—of a wave, the whelming rush of Chapman that had swept them off their feet.

The biographer's great fear was that he worked too slowly. Someone else would "scoop" him or might "steal a march." There were only so many publishers, only so much interest in a writer's life, and what would happen if some fast-talking journalist, say, some Chapman groupie got a contract; what would happen in that case to his chances of promotion, his own scholarly career? "The trouble is," said Alton, "George died before he authorized me. You know the way he used to be: the more the merrier."

"I didn't know that. No."

"Of course. It's just the way he was. You're lucky you got it in writing."

Still, Enoch felt a kind of kinship with the man. That dogged persistence, the systematic snail-paced accretion of data, the reverential caution with which the biographer verified fact—all this felt familiar. They spelled the same ghost. He could have predicted the call.

"How are you, Enoch?"

"Holding on." The day was waning brightly. "I was thinking of you."

"Oh? What were you thinking?"

"Nothing much. I just had the feeling you'd call."

"Did you get my article? The one from *Toho-Bohu*?"

"Yes."

"Do you dream about him every night?" Alton coughed. "There's so much wreckage in his wake."

"Do you ever think of—what was his name? That driver?"

"Hovey. Clarence Hovey. All the time."

Clarence Hovey is sixty-six years old. He drives a 1987 Oldsmobile Cutlass Supreme. It is black, with red interior trim. He is a retired C.P.A. who keeps his hand in doing tax returns and with the occasional consulting job; his doctors tell him he should ease up a little, relax. He has diabetes and must regulate his diet; he can't be at his desk all day or out in the woods by himself. He doesn't mind it, truth be told; he intends to take up carpentry and has improved his golf. This morning he puts on his golfing cardigan, his yellow pants, and turns on the TV to catch the local weather: *sunny, chance of evening showers, seasonably warm.* He drops candy in his pocket and puts on his Broncos cap. He plans to wash the car, then drive out to the Fairview Club to see what's up, what's doing, who's making up a foursome and could use a fourth. He turns off the TV while they describe a fire in Aurora, a "blaze of suspicious origin" with at least one woman dead. He has lived in Denver thirty years and watched the place get fancy, watched it through hard times and good and now hard times again. When he drives up to the Soft Cloth Wash, his is the third car in line; he wants the Red Star Special: undercarriage and hot wax. He's on his ninth wash—tenth one free—and the attendant takes six dollars, punches his card, says "Fine day."

He shuts off the radio. The aerial retracts. He puts the car in neutral, checks the windows, settles back. He feels the jolt beneath him when the track engages, watches soapy water drench his windshield, then his windows, then the slap of cloth like kelp on his hood, roof, windows, doors. Lights blink at him: first red and then amber, then green. He rests his right hand lightly on the steering wheel. It always makes him sleepy: the blue nylon brush advancing, the rollers, the jets of hot air. He shuts his eyes an instant within this charmed enclosure. It is, Clarence supposes, as good for the car as a bath for the body—an easy, mechanical passage out of darkness into light. When he emerges, blinking, the attendants wave him forward. He puts the car in drive again with something approaching reluctance; he cracks the window open half an inch. They perform their complicated dance with rags and take the red indicator clothespin off his windshield wiper, smiling, and pat him on the driver's door and disappear. He nods. He taps the horn.

It is 11:37. He feels fine. On impulse—because it would have been faster to circle than negotiate downtown—he follows the flow of traffic (thinking of his daughter's daughter, six years old and cute as a button, sending him that tape of her first piano recital, "Twinkle, twinkle, little star," and the audience applauding, and then she pipes up, "Grandpa, wish you could be here. When are you coming to visit?") and glides beneath the buildings' shade, and slowing down because he has to (a delivery van, a taxi stand by the Brown Palace, a lady in a Mustang changing lanes), Clarence sees the true dark rise before him, the tossing spume behind his eyes, the black beyond, and feels the sudden relinquishment, floating release, and reaches for what even as he touches it he knows he is too late to suck, the candy to counter the insulin shock, and turns toward the taxis and a fat man with a pipe.

"What I want to know," asked Chapman, "is how long you're planning to stay."

"Where?"

"In this house. This little palace with a porch."

"A man's home is his palace," Enoch said.

"You're spoiling yourself, *tonto*." Chapman gave his high, staccato laugh. "You're doing it for egotism—holding on for safety's sake."

"'The artist at risk,' correct? I've heard that line before."

"What I mean is," Chapman said, "you've constructed this elaborate system of domesticity. You're minding the store when they've taken the store, minding the barn though the horses are out. You're pretending you've got chickens when they've flown the coop."

"Last call. Ten minutes. The bar closes down."

"I'm trying to tell you," he said, "mortality's the subject. It's the only issue worthy of our serious attention. Death. And what you're doing, Enoch, is practicing avoidance; you're getting up and getting dressed and trundling off to work each day as if you were immortal, as if we wouldn't die."

Margot Zimmerman called too. She was putting back the pieces of her life. She felt that she knew Enoch like the brother that she never had, she very much looked forward to meeting him someday. She would like to tell him her side of the story; a note was in the mail. She had been working for George's publisher in sub rights, not publicity; the reporters got it wrong. She had first met Chapman in the office in New York. It didn't matter now. What mattered was the way he told her thank you when she asked if he'd like coffee; his face lit up, his whole expression changed. He was a famous author, fourteen years her senior, but you could tell from how he took the cup that she was the one bearing gifts. It wasn't the standard old man on the make, the artist in town for the night. He paid attention, let her know (not saying it, just smiling, staring, just burying his nose in what she brought him—coffee, two sugars, no cream) that he was needy, grateful, and that his need and gratitude were not just for the coffee but the fact of its existence: yes, and hers.

"You understand," she finished, "why I wasn't at the funeral. I simply couldn't face it. I think about him every day, I wake up feeling haunted. But it's water under the bridge. My husband has been wonderful. We're leaving for Switzerland tomorrow on what I suppose you'd call a second honeymoon." Her voice was breathy in his ear. "I wanted you to have the last thing George was working on that day in the hotel. It's the start of the sequel to *Spindrift*. The very beginning, I think."

Her letter arrived the next day. The envelope was white. It contained no language of her own, but only the note she had promised. The paper had been folded into eighths. He recognized the handwriting, the yellow foolscap Chapman liked, the wide margins, dark blue ink.

"*Though holding the tiller, I fell. Three nights I clutched it, tossing, from Detroit to Salt Lake City to this mile-high wind-swept plain. And I did not for I could not die at sea; Apollo forbade it, foretold I would land. That part of our shared craft I took will leave you with no helmsman, although you man the helm. I did not quit you willingly; I did not shut my eyes. The rock-rimmed shore draws near. This is the fate of all who value failure, who think it more distinguished than the easeful thing, success. Savages attacked me as I set foot on Italy, weighed down by these wet clothes. They are my winding sheets. Hero, if you love me, throw dirt upon this corpse.*"

"What you have to understand," Rita told him, leaving, "is not to be so serious. You used to take things lightly, Enoch. Look on the light side for once."

"You sound like a commercial."

"No."

"The good life," Enoch said. "Come on over for a thirty-second spot. This afternoon we'll do a promo for Bud Light."

"All this darkness in you. It wasn't there before."

"My mother never died before. My wife never left me before."

"I'm sorry, I really am sorry. You know that."

"Yes."

"But it's not what I'm talking about. I mean this anger, all of a sudden."

"Don't talk about it," Enoch said. "There's nothing left to say."

"The problem Chapman poses," Alton wrote, is how best to utilize what he in conversation would frequently refer to as 'free-floating myth.' By this he meant that mythic referents are everywhere about us and that to consider them too curiously is to kill the cat. At any rate that was his answer when I asked him, on the afternoon of April 7, 1983, why he had chosen the flight from Troy as the governing principle of *Virgil*, but then referred to *The Aeneid* in language at best inexact. Some decry his scholarship, others his rush into print. Few will deny, however, that the tale-telling energy so marked in Chapman's early prose derives its impetus in part from his reading of the classics when recovering, at fifteen, from a broken back. His fall from the ladder had at least this second consequence: immobilized, he read. What passionate escape for a young man in bed! What compensatory excess in the flights of fancy in that darkened upstairs bedroom in the house on Granger Street! School, for young George Chapman, was a chance to read.

"This was the lifelong wound and its accompanying bow. This was his forge, his crucible. Uncle Harald from Millerton Falls had attended college (the first member of the Chapman family to do so) and he gave George the Harvard Classics that summer, twenty-seven dog-eared volumes that were an introduction to what the writer later called his 'brave old world.' So it is possible to think of Aeneas as the young man propped on pillows, staring out the window and fantasizing escape, while his father in the living room drunkenly describes the plight of the worker at United Steel. It is possible to think of Dido as the girl on the street corner, waiting for a bus. At any rate some such reverie prefigures what became the fevered, fertile inventiveness of the work; Chapman himself described it as an 'adolescent's damp dream.'

"He was not wholly serious. He called all 'voyage' novels derivative of Gilgamesh, and said Palinurus's tiller is the ancients' oar. Such leaps of the imagination, it may be argued, characterize the autodidact no less than the invalid; they need not make too large a claim nor lay a heavy burden on the scholar's expertise. 'Do not understand me too quickly,' was one of Chapman's mottos, pinned above his work desk in the second Cambridge apartment. We have tried."

Enoch poured a beer and cut a wedge of cheese. He carried his meal to the porch. It was his accustomed place: a prow jutting out over grass. Clouds were building westerly, and their shadows on Red Mountain moved like water. The logging roads and power lines looked, from his vantage in the valley, like rocks on a far shore.

It grew dark. He held out a piece of Stilton, but there was only air. Whatever had so trammeled him had slipped its moorings, drifted loose. Whatever kept him in its thrall had lasted one full year.

He shut his eyes and pictured—corporeal, this final time—his dead friend in the chair. Chapman was declaiming, reciting W. E. Henley's "Invictus." He wanted to warn Enoch of the dangers inhering in pride. His teeth were brown. "'I am the master of my fate,'" he intoned, "'the captain of my soul.' What unbelievable nonsense. 'Head bloody but unbowed.'

What you have to understand is the reason they believed him—old, crippled, crazy Henley—is because of meter. It's because his amazing sentimentality was expressed in rhyme."

Translucent, Chapman rocked. "'I am the captain of my soul,'" he said again. "Ridiculous. That's probably what the third mate on the Exxon tanker thought when he ran aground and spilled oil in Alaska and wrecked the fisheries. While his master slept it off belowdecks, the boozy captain, Full Speed Astern! When your work has come to nothing, be noisy about it, pal." His voice grew distant, as if conferring release. "The prince of wanderers, whale-roaded, the casual familiar . . ."

Enoch ate. In the morning he would drive to Thetford and go swimming with his sons. They have learned to dive. Rita would be canning; she stands there wreathed in steam. She would be wearing the apron he gave her, and the carpenter would enter from his workroom, forearms white with sawdust. The carpenter would put his hands on Rita's hips and say, "It smells of berries, here," and shavings from his overalls would flutter to the floor. They hold each other, leaning, in the fragrant steam.

"What I want from you," said Chapman, "is to act as my executor."

"And what does that mean, really?"

"Nothing. Keeping track."

"I'm not sure I'm so good at that."

"I trust you," Chapman said.

"'For counting overmuch on a calm world, Palinurus, you must lie naked on some unknown shore.'"

The moon appeared. It would be a proper burial. They stretched.

The Brass Ring

VASTATION—THAT WAS the word in his head. He had used it once before, when young, and his father's friend complained. "You mean *de*vastation, don't you? Why don't you write what you mean?"

"But it's a word."

"Vastation?"

"Yes. It's what Catholics say, I think, when they can't locate God. When they can't find Him anywhere. It's the absolute absence of God."

"Except you're Jewish," said Meyer Rosen. "Jews have no right to that word."

"It's in the language, isn't it? The dictionary." Frederick Hasenclever raised his voice. "You don't have to be a Catholic to use a dictionary."

"*I* don't use one when I'm reading." Meyer Rosen nodded. "Devastation's what you mean. That's why you don't sell many copies of your books."

They were standing in the living room of the Rosen apartment, by the jade plant and the Kathe Kollwitz, across from the self-portrait by Kokoschka. Kokoschka's gaze was baleful; his eyes appeared half-closed. It was hot. The party was in honor of Frederick's father's sixtieth birthday, and his relatives were eating shrimp and drinking Campari and soda and white wine and exclaiming at the view of the East River from this height—how traffic on the Triboro was crawling, how the skyline changed each year, how well he, Fred, was looking, without that awful beard he wore for his book jacket picture, and did he want to look like a rabbi, and how was he liking New Hampshire, what courses did he teach?

There were aunts and cousins and business partners and his younger brother, Arnold; there was cold roast beef and turkey and beef salad and pâté. "The thing I'm proudest of," his father said—when it came time to offer a toast—"is friendship. Is my family and friends. Is the memory of my beloved wife Lilo, and how wonderful you were to us last year." Briefly he faltered, halted. "Is how much a friend my sons remain to me, and matter to each other, and I don't say I've deserved it but will try. Your friendship, Meyer and Ilse, who made this occasion, everyone"—he raised his glass—"there's nothing you could ask I wouldn't give you. Gladly. The suit off my back."

"That's because it's worn out," Rosen called. He was the host; the guests laughed. He was an investment banker, with a collection of Nolde watercolors in the bedroom; he and Hans Hasenclever had been friends since their shared childhood in Berlin. He wore a blue monogrammed shirt and a dark blue foulard and was taking a proprietary interest in young Freddy's progress; he wanted to know the marketing strategies for this new novel; just because you use the word "vastation" doesn't mean you shouldn't sell . . .

"I thought you said," said Frederick, "that *was* the reason."

"One of them. The other is the sales force, the way they choose to market."

"It does my heart good," said his father, nearing, "to see the two of you like this. Conferring together, the business man and the artist. It meant so much to your mother"—he squeezed Frederick's cheek—"that we should stay in touch. That's what they mean by *present*. To see you here this way."

"I have to leave, Dad. Soon. First thing in the morning, I teach."

"You hear that?" Rosen chortled. "All those shiksa horse-girls in the hills. Our Freddy is spreading the word. Our Freddy is filling their heads. Go with God," he said. "And then may God help you. 'Vastation.'"

For twenty-five years he did teach, moving to Northeastern and Amherst and finally Columbia. His father died. Arnold moved to the West Coast. Meyer Rosen, too, was dead—though Fred heard this only secondhand and somehow imagined the old man, a fatter, less placid Bernard Baruch dispensing strict opinion still from the park bench by the river. He smoked cigars, then a pipe. He married one of his students—an Episcopalian from St. Paul, whose paper on Fitzgerald had been suffused, he wrote on the margin, with an insider's insight. Sarah came to his office next morning. "Why did you say that?" she asked. "What exactly did you mean?" She fingered the fringe of her skirt.

Their marriage was childless; it lasted three years. She left him for a contractor from Minneapolis with whom she had gone sailing and played hockey as a girl. Colin had been waiting; he was her one true beau. Frederick, by contrast, with his "Jewish bonanzas of mouth-love," was simply not her scene. She had been reading *The Time of Her Time.* If she left now, Sarah told him, she could go with no hard feelings or regrets. She read Werner Erhard, too. She knew it would be painful, but they could let bygones be bygones, and there's no time like the present to start with the rest of your life.

Two years later he married again—this time a divorcee with three children of her own. Lavinia owned a fabric import firm and an apartment on Park Avenue into which he barely fit, with his additional records and bulky red Selectric, and his books. She liked the fact he worked at home and could answer the phone; she loved the way he got on with the kids. And he did enjoy the ritual of making lunch and helping with homework and meeting them for ice cream and then coffee and then cocktails while Lavinia was traveling; he stayed while she made buying trips to Bangkok and Bombay. Once he joined her, and his gleaming lacquered wife seemed scarcely less foreign to Frederick than the sari-swathed hostess at the Ashoka Hotel. He was, he realized piercingly, alone and far from home; he had flown across the world to join a woman in New Delhi of whose history he was as innocent as the woman handing him his key. When they divorced, in 1982, it was uncontested; he was fifty and bearded again and issueless, the author of six books.

His reputation, if small, felt nonetheless secure; he had twice been nominated for the American Book Award. He contributed to literary quarterlies and joined symposia and, having received grants himself, dispensed them for the National Endowment for the Arts or the Bush Foundation; it was a pleasure, he would say, to give other folks' money away. He lived on Claremont Avenue, in a Columbia-owned apartment, and watched with what he thought of as dispassion while his students grew famous and rich. Their pictures were in magazines, often—*People, Newsweek, Esquire, Time*—and he himself would sometimes be mentioned as having put the seal of his approval on their prose. He went to movies based on their books, or for which they wrote the screenplays, and their publishers sent him the glossy promotional packets that heralded success. They stared at him—the girls, the gifted boys—from supermarket racks. His own work appeared without fanfare, and sometimes he remembered Rosen's bluff conviction that the market could be rigged.

As he settled more and more into middle age (his morning bagel in the toaster oven, his decaffeinated blend from Zabar's, his baldness no longer a sorrow), Hasenclever asked himself if he had missed some turning, or failed to face some challenge; his most recent novel was titled *The Brass Ring*. The book was about a German-Jewish refugee who changes his last name in order to succeed. He does so, in the advertising business, but then discovers that his lack of honesty has barred him from promotion; the owner of the agency is an old German Jew. The two of them engage in discussions, wrote the reviewer for *The Nation*, "bordering on the Talmudic. These authenticity *mavens* have a sideline in TV. What seems at stake in Hasenclever's work is the quiddity of things, the suchness of gesture as act. And his elusive hero is not quite the protagonist, nor even the old mogul Lehrman. We sense a shadowy third figure—the one who grabs the ring, the carousel horseman with prayer shawl and *payes*, the groping compassionate self . . ."

Was there mockery in this? What in heaven's name, he asked himself, did the reviewer mean by "quiddity of things"? What shadowy "elusive hero" could he have created, and what sort of "devotional author"—a tag from the review in *Newsday*—has no faith in God? That a writer is his own worst critic may be conventional wisdom, but it is nonetheless wrong. Hasenclever knew himself; he was fifty-six years old, farsighted, and there was nothing to see.

In New York for an audition, Arnold came down with the flu. It was January 3. He had flown in from Seattle and felt "punk" all through the flight, as if the pressure in the cabin were calibrated wrong; he went straight to the hotel. He took aspirin, drank scotch. When he tried to stand, his feet hurt so badly he could not stay on his feet. He tried to dominate the pain and distract himself by walking in the hall. Then he kept his feet above his head. He stood on his head; he took cold and scalding baths. His knees felt as though they were crushed. He took a taxi to the Emergency Room of the nearest hospital and was barely conscious by the time he arrived. They saved his life. He pieced all this together, later, lying in Intensive Care unable to breathe, speak or move. He had what was variously described as acute idiopathic polyneuritis and Landry's ascending paralysis and Guillain-Barré syndrome. He could move his eyelids; that was all. He conveyed his needs by blinking while the nurse held up a chart. It could take him half an hour to spell "Right elbow," for instance, or "Rub foot."

The prognosis was uncertain; those who did not die at once had a chance of full recovery. The recuperation period could last up to two years. After three weeks of Intensive Care, he was transferred to the Institute for Rehabilitation Medicine, the "Rusk." He would improve. Hasenclever learned the news from Arnold's third wife; her voice was reedy, high. Ginger was calling from Phoenix; she and Arnold had been separated for six months. She was living with a systems analyst for an engineering firm in Phoenix; he gave her a sense of security that Arnold never gave. "He wants to see you," Ginger said. "He's ready for company now."

"Yes."

"I called. I was up there just last weekend."

"I'm sorry. I was out of town."

"Don't worry. He's insured."

"Will he know me?" Hasenclever coiled the cord. "Why didn't I know this before?"

"He has trouble focusing. He didn't want to worry you. He's lost a lot of weight."

"Is there something I can do for him? Bring, I mean?"

"Chocolate. You mustn't be shocked."

He tried to imagine a catheter, a tracheostomy, a view dictated by the pillow's placement at the neck.

"And now he's being wonderful. He's got his sweet tooth back." Her voice changed pitch, increased. "His eyes, Fred, it's astonishing. They positively shine."

The cord was black.

"He wanted me to let you know. He didn't want a visit when it was so terrible. He's getting better now."

"Of course."

"I was named as the person to contact, but you're the next of kin."

He pressed his nose. He closed one eye and saw only the flat of his hand. They had played tennis together. They ate and gesticulated and collected each other at airports with a shared assumption of mobility so common as to go unnoticed until gone.

It had had, to begin with, the flavor of dream. There was a night nurse whose right arm he focused on: the puckering flesh at the elbow, the bracelets and wrist. Arnold saw the glucose bottle, its transparent teat. He did not know the date or time or, absolutely, where he lay; he had seven doctors. They announced their number to him, as if there were safety in numbers and he would be reassured. At first he watched them with relief; they could help him, he was certain, they knew what was wrong and the procedures by which he could and would be cured. They succeeded each other, conferring; they stood at the foot of his bed.

Often there were students also—deferential, intense, wielding clipboards. They turned him cautiously. They raised his feet and rotated his arm and sponged him down and asked him, if he understood, to signify by blinking. He blinked. This was an involuntary mechanism as well as voluntary, however, and sometimes when he blinked they asked him to please blink again while they consulted the chart. The danger of not blinking is that you go blind.

His tongue felt huge. It filled his mouth. Had he been able to spit he would have spit; there was spittle on his tongue. He practiced swallowing. There were motel beds that jiggled for a quarter; they were called Magic Fingers, and the bed would hum and purr. He supposed it was for sex. He had never tried out Magic Fingers with a partner, but he shoved three quarters in once somewhere in Iowa and jiggled on the green chenille bedspread, feeling like a salesman. That was how his body felt in this unmoving bed, as if not merely a finger or forearm or foot had fallen asleep but all of him, the bone beneath his stretched skin protuberant, the blood too thin to clot. He closed his eyes. He would get better, they assured him, it was only a question of how much and when; you look at the big picture, that's the point. The point is you're recuperating and you're young and healthy, look at those stroke victims, for example, I wouldn't want to name names. Alfred Anderson had no left side to speak of and would not regain it; Porfirio in the bed beside him was a double amputee. Count your lucky stars. That was what the nurses said: count your lucky stars, your blessings, plan for the future, think how much worse off you could be. So he tried to imagine how he could be worse and what much worse would be.

Faces neared him: mouths like fish, making sucking motions at the air—chins with powder or pockmarks or hair. It was as if he held a camera, held it steady on the shoulder or a tripod, focusing on what swam into his vision indiscriminately—the venal, over-scrupulous, the saccharine, concerned. "Your face looks like a monkey's ass"—he spelled this to an X-ray technician, or thought he did, or wanted to: the pouches of her cheeks, the plucked line of her eyebrows and the parallelepiped of birthmarks at her neck. They were not unkind, were kindly; they meant well. They arrived and asked him, "How ya' doin', Arnie? How's the boy?" When he still was unable to speak, they sent in a psychiatrist. "This is a stressful period for you," the man pronounced. "It's difficult, we understand that, a time for anxiety, right? I know you can't discuss it yet, but sometime you'll want to discuss it. Remember I'm ready to listen, OK? OK." The man patted his sheet. He rose, limitlessly satisfied, and promised, "I'll be back."

For some time where he lay he entertained himself : he could have spoken if he chose. This was a charade he played. He did not choose. He had lost everything but memory, an infant at forty-eight, beginning. Elected silence, he blinked at the medical students: I'm an actor, I'm playing a monk. They studied their clipboards and coughed.

Room 504 had five beds. A nurse was lifting Arnold's leg. She lowered it and covered it with sheets. His face was bright. He needed a shave. The flush on his cheeks made it appear as if he had been exercising or out in the sun. He turned his head. He could do that. "Well, well," he said. "Look who's here. About time, schmuck." His voice was a rough whisper. There was a tube in his throat; another tube curved down toward his mouth.

"I'm Susan," said the nurse. "We haven't met."

"I'm his brother, Frederick. Hello."

"This is a good time," she said. "I was just finishing."

"Bye-bye," said Arnold. He said it audibly. "See you tomorrow."

"Same time, same station. If you don't stand me up."

"I wouldn't do that."

"One day you will," Susan said. "I'll be coming here to work and you'll be in the Bahamas."

"I'd take you with me, darling."

"They all say that." She took an armful of linen from a chair by the bed. She blew a kiss and moved away. Hasenclever sat.

"She's wonderful," said Arnold. "Everyone's been wonderful."

He loosened his tie. "That's impressive."

"Wonderful. They had to turn me every six hours. Maybe more often—I lose track of time. But I never lost the knowledge of how wonderful they were." His eyes glistened; he did seem grateful. "Tell me everything," he said.

"I brought you chocolate. Ginger told me to fatten you up."

"For the kill," said Arnold. "That must be what she means."

He slipped two Toblerone bars out of his jacket pocket. His brother had blue eyes.

"That's wonderful," said Arnold. "Perfect."

"Would you like some?"

"No. Not now." Infinitesimally, he shifted his head. "Put it in the drawer over there."

Then there was silence between them. Hasenclever heard a television behind a curtain in the room. Someone muttered, sleeping; a wheelchair hummed past. Arnold demonstrated the workings of the tube beside his mouth. He sucked and spat at it, and the television turned on. He made sucking motions, and the channel switched. So did the volume and contrast control. Then he spat decisively and the machine went blank.

"Tell me when you're tired. I don't want to tire you out."

"Five minutes."

"As long as you want."

"I knew I wouldn't get the part. There's nothing for me in New York. *Gornisht.* I don't even know why I came."

The blue intensity of Arnold's gaze had slackened. His speech slurred. Hasenclever said, "I'm going now," and he did not object. "Come back," he said. "You can watch me work my automatic reader. It turns the page. It does everything but tell me what to read."

"Take care of yourself."

"Yes."

"Not to worry." He patted the bed. "You'll be doing Errol Flynn remakes. You'll be turning cartwheels . . ."

Arnold made no answer. Hasenclever left. Two women in wheelchairs had come face to face by the first nurses' station; they could not negotiate the turn. They backed away from each other, then forward, like bumper cars at Playland or a county fair. A travel poster for Biarritz hung in the waiting room, as did a poster of *Sesame Street*'s Big Bird. He pressed the elevator button repeatedly, waiting. By the Gift Shoppe he breathed freely and waved at the policeman. A one-armed violin player, his bow held in his mouth, took money in a hat.

One evening the writer had cocktails with a colleague. Her husband was a doctor; medical books lined the shelf. While she went to replenish the cheese and nuts, he pulled a volume at random—turning to the index, then Chapter 56. Barry G. W. Arnason observed in a footnote, on page 1110: "Other commonly encountered designations for this entity in the English and American literature include idiopathic polyneuritis, acute febrile polyneuritis, infective polyneuritis, postinfectious polyneuritis, acute toxic polyneuritis, acute polyneuritis with facial diplegia, acute infectious neuronitis, polyneuritis, mononeuronitis, radiculoneuritis, polyradiculo-neuritis, myeloradiculoneuritis, myeloradiculitis, Guillain-Barré syndrome, Guillain-Barré-Strohl syndrome, and Landry Guillain-Barré syndrome."

Frederic went often to the Rusk. Wanting air, he told the cab to let him off on Thirty-fourth street and Second Avenue. Then he walked. Weekend fathers stood in line for that day's double feature, or—as spring progressed—bought hot dogs and pretzels at a Sabrett's. Inside, the elevator might disgorge a bald black legless woman laughing. "The phone," the woman told him. "I got to use the *phone*." On the second floor a man with a walker would enter; he made a *Brrr* sound repeatedly, spraying. Porfirio cried out in Spanish, sleeping; he beat at the bed with his fists. A green cart made delivery of what looked like fruit.

Arnold gained weight. He covered his mouth while he ate. He could eat salami, but he had trouble with crackers. He could open jars and cans, and he cut out coupons and stirred Jell-O in physical therapy; he drank from a wineglass because of the stem. He had periodic spasms of exhaustion—but his progress was surprising, week by month. He had purely focused on working his way back to health. Frederick admired this resolve.

Still, there did seem something fretful about the way he exercised and ate, as if his comfort and wellbeing were of universal interest. He hoped to pass unnoticed in the street. But he also expected to be made much of, fussed over; he wanted to be left alone and also wanted pampering. He was happy, hearing music—Gershwin, early Mozart, the Goldberg Variations. Frederick purchased a Walkman, and brought tapes. Arnold sat in the wheelchair leafing through books: the autobiography of Alec Guinness, photographs of Burma or by Margaret Bourke-White. He studied faces intently but seemed unwilling to read. His eyes were weak, he said. The animal exuberance about him, once, had gone.

"My artistic children," their father used to say. "My writer and my actor. Thanks heaven you won't starve." Arnold liked performing, even in high school, and studied jazz dancing and how to stage fights. He had been a gymnast—tight, springy muscled, strong on the parallel bars. Frederick, the studious brother, had not known what to make of this dervish—Arnold on the diving board or parapet, while he did not like diving and feared heights. Laurence Olivier, according to Arnold, said an actor requires physical strength; it is the first tool of the trade.

He went to Juilliard and LAMDA and joined repertory companies in Chicago, San Francisco, and Seattle; he never did play Romeo or Hamlet, and now he was missing Macbeth. That was how he measured age; he hadn't given up quite yet on Prospero or Lear. Not that he played Shakespeare much, but Shakespeare wrote a part for every age of actor; you could measure your life by his parts. Meantime, Arnold worked. He did the odd commercial and the sidekick in a series that ran for eighteen episodes; *Billy and the D.A.* had been the name of the show. Once Hasenclever, late at night, saw him on TV. His brother was being a drunk. He said "Melancholy baby," often to the pianist; he rolled his eyes and tugged at his collar and slurred, "Play me one for the road. One more time."

The maimed were everywhere about the Rusk, pitching themselves at the traffic or bravely up on skateboards or sunning in wheelchairs in doorways. He saw his brother routinely; the policemen in the lobby knew Hasenclever's name. Arnold improved. Visiting hours were late, and often there were others in the room—though not often there for him. Arnold's neighbors came from Puerto Rico and had large families. Their daughters played canasta every day. Porfirio who had no legs was excellent at cards; he had worked as a croupier.

At times the men met in the hall. "Are they crowding you?" asked Frederick. His brother shook his head. "The first thing you get rid of is the need for privacy. That goes so quickly you wouldn't believe it."

"What next?"

"Pride."

"You should be proud of yourself."

Arnold smiled. He used a wheelchair now that he could guide by buttons. "It's slow."

"'Slow but steady wins the race.'"

He ceased smiling. The play of attitude across his face seemed somehow volitional, as if he prepared himself to frown, then frowned. The elevator opened. A woman on a hospital bed lifted her right hand. She did not move her head. The linoleum was marbled, mottled: red and black.

"You're getting better."

"Yes."

"Remember what Dad used to say? '*Wenn man eine Operation durchgemacht hat, dann braucht man eine bischene Erholung.*'"

"I don't remember, no."

"After an operation, it takes time to recover."

"Now tell me how much I've grown," Arnold said. "Since the last time you visited, tell me how grown-up I seem."

"I'm sorry."

"Don't be."

"Are you in pain?"

He shook his head. When they first brought him to his bed, he fell asleep in comfort; when he woke the pain was gone. He had felt nothing else, except in the "procedures"—the nasogastric tube replacement, lumbar puncture, EMG. What he felt was shock, drugged puzzlement, a disembodied floating that was like relief.

"How long will they keep you?"

"Here?"

"Yes."

"I've got to figure out," said Arnold, "where to go to next. And when I stop improving, that's when I get sprung."

A black orderly with an anchor on his forearm cuffed the wheelchair. "Hey," he said. "How goes it?"

"It goes."

Hasenclever rolled his wrist so he could check his watch: six-sixteen.

"It's boring," Arnold said. "You can't imagine how boring this is. I can beat an egg by now. And I'm sanding wood. They change the sandpaper each week, so it takes more strength. I position checkers on a checkerboard."

"Do you swim?"

311

"A little. Mostly in the pool I practice how to walk. And then there's the tilt table. They've got me at ninety degrees."

The note of pride and the exacting accuracy were familiar; he seemed truly on the mend. The Puerto Ricans laughed. They crowded to the elevator, bearing pineapples. "I'll take you," Frederick said. "If you want a place to stay when you get out of here, you come with me."

Arnold turned his wheelchair. His room was the fourth on the right. "It's kind of you."

The writer stood. He adjusted his sleeve. Each gesture felt adroit to him, the coordination fluent to the point of mockery. "I mean it. You can stay."

Deracination, he told his students, is the commonplace condition of contemporary man. It is the rule, not exception, in our mobile time. How many of us live where our parents' parents lived and have no need to improvise an answer to the question "Where do you come from, where's home?" The executive and migrant worker are alike in this. Voluntary exile is a subtle, sapping thing. The tree dissevered from the root can take a transplant, possibly, but the root system must be handled with some care.

By April, using crutches, Arnold managed stairs. There were none in the apartment. There were hallway runners, however, and the doorsill to the bathroom was pronounced. Hasenclever studied the rooms closely to see how his brother might fit. He prepared what used to be the maid's room and was now a storage closet. The apartment faced a corner: south and east.

Experts from the hospital arrived on May 15—in order to evaluate facilities, they said. A brother and sister, Koreans, they came from the suburbs of Seoul. "This is a most nice apartment," they chorused, shedding coats. He tried to examine the space with their eyes, to see what they, measuring, saw. They told him that the patient would be ambulatory but would require handle insets in the shower stall. Arnold could arrange his transfer from the wheelchair with a transfer board; he had practiced getting into and out of cars. They had a sample kitchen in the first floor of the Institute, as well as a model living room and bedroom and dinette and bath.

The rollaway bed was too low. It should be set on blocks. The passage to the kitchen would be difficult to manage, and Hasenclever should remember that the patient would have difficulty lifting food from the refrigerator shelf. This would not continue. His provisions should be stored—the juice half-poured, the cereal measured, the berries within easy reach—on the bottom shelf. "The juice half-poured?" he questioned them, and they nodded, smiling; we mean half a glass.

Frederick agreed. His guests accepted tea. Only while they measured the kitchen table's height did he start to say that such precaution seemed excessive; Arnold had a life elsewhere, and would leave. But as they left him, bowing, nodding, it came clear to him the stay would be indefinite. He would be his brother's keeper, he told the Koreans. They laughed.

He was working on a book about Brazil. "Brazil" became a country of the mind. It was a nation ruled by a provisional junta, but the junta did want unity, so there was perfect union—if provisional, if fleeting—in city and in country, for the elderly and youthful, male and female, rich and poor. Such distinctions fell away. The artisan—the man in a wineshop, fresh from his potter's wheel or lathe, come to dispute at noon—might also be a senator or scholar or a priest. Here flourished just such a union of the political, artistic and religious life as Yeats dreamed in *A Vision* might have obtained in Byzance. Yet you can't go back to Constantinople—so Hasenclever's hero sang. We've changed its name. We call it, now, Brazil.

I thought they call it Istanbul, said his antagonist; on my map that's how it's spelled. The traveler flourished his atlas, explaining. Here's the White Sea, Vastation, and here the Despond Slough. Leander swam the Hellespont, using something like the breast stroke, to gain his promised land. O ye of little faith, said Hasenclever's hero; though you close your eyes it is not night, that you fail to hear a waterfall does not render the waterfall silent. The citizens of our republic listen for a music that is not a marching band.

I admire such a passion, said the girl. Indeed, it feels exciting—here she squeezed his hand—but I don't know how to swim yet and don't trust the vasty deep. She ran her fingertips lingeringly down the skin graft on his forearm where the numbers had been burned. Trust it, says the artisan, and pours unwatered wine.

He bought balloons and streamers. He festooned the entrance foyer, as if for a child's birthday, crisscrossing crepe at the center. It formed a canopy. The colors were pastel: yellow, orange, white, and green. He cut the letters

WELCOME out of colored paper, draping the sign from the crepe. He bought noisemakers and leis and conical paper hats and Taittinger champagne. He bought more cheese and salami than they could possibly eat.

Hasenclever worked in what he recognized as a frenzy of avoidance, rolling back the rugs. He diced onions and hard-boiled eggs for caviar; he put two bottles of the Taittinger on ice. He cut lemon into wedges, placed the caviar and sour cream in bowls, unwrapped the melba toast. When Arnold arrived he was waiting. The buzzer announced him. He went to the door. An attendant stood behind the wheelchair. They both were wearing raincoats, and Arnold had a lap rug also. Its pattern was tartan, its colors green and black. His cheeks were red. He had been recently shaved. There were indentations at his temples; his lower lip slanted, his eyes seemed half-shut.

"We made it," the attendant said. "I'm Bob."

"You made it," the writer repeated, and Arnold said, "Hello."

The balloons were an embarrassment. The crepe was in the way. He wheeled toward the WELCOME sign and stopped before it, staring.

Bob said he was heading out and Arnie was a trouper and ought to take it slow. You ought to seen him leaving—all those nurses kissing him, that candy he left at the desk. Hasenclever gave him twenty dollars, and Bob straightened his cap and withdrew.

The chandelier was on a rheostat. He increased the light.

"You know what Susan asked me? 'How many assholes have you met—twenty, twenty-five?'" Arnold's voice was low. "I said I used to meet that many every morning, I must have known ten thousand in my life. And she said, 'Guess what, every one of those assholes can walk.'"

He shook himself out of his coat. Frederick retrieved it. "Are you hungry?"

"No."

"Let's go into the living room," he said.

The carpet that he thought of as too thin was an encumbrance. He steered his brother to the coffee table, angling widely past the couch. Then Arnold transferred to the couch. He rearranged his feet. Arnold was crying, he saw, had been crying since arrival, making sounds in his throat as if a bone were caught there. Hasenclever bent above him, but he shook his head. He fled to get the caviar, the salami and champagne. In the kitchen, too, time telescoped. He saw his parents everywhere. Lilo stood in the kitchen, complaining about the fashion in which Hans cracked eggs; he was spilling the egg yolk over the bowl rim and careless of the shell. "It's good for the digestion," Hans proclaimed. "You don't want too much egg yolk. You use too much salt."

Repeatedly the writer asked himself if he had failed them, how he failed; what was Arnold doing somewhere else and therefore unprotected? Could he have protected him; could it have been helped? A baby passes by a stove and reaches for the kettle and is scarred for life; a second's hesitation at the crossroads and the train keeps coming and the driver dies. Lavinia's children were grown. They sent him birthday cards. Between them, the brothers had married five times. He made his way back to the living room, balancing the tray. Arnold had recovered. A blue balloon by the window inched past the sill, then fell.

Yet Hasenclever had been spared; his life was a constant such sparing. Others died. They crossed the street or crossed a supermarket's second aisle or a line they had been warned against by someone with a cross-hatched scope who lay in a duck blind or tower. They were blown up while waiting for tickets or buying magazines.

His parents' generation died in Bergen-Belsen or Dachau. They died in Auschwitz and Sachsenhausen and Munich and Berlin. His generation died of myocardial infarction or lung cancer or on New Year's Eve in Saugatuck and Valentine's Day in Nashville, skidding; they died behind the wheels of Corvairs, Rivieras, Datsuns, convertibles, jeeps. They died by their own hands. They placed their heads in ovens or jumped at an on-rushing subway train or jumped from the Golden Gate Bridge. They died by misadventure with the toaster; they crashed in airplanes and buses and Boston Whalers and on the jetty at low tide. They used cyanide carelessly, attempting to fumigate bees. They misused the shotgun or leaf mulcher or linseed oil or heroin or ladder or the station wagon on ice.

Meyer Rosen joined the party. He approved of the champagne. Hasenclever opened the champagne, not popping the cork but releasing it. Then he poured. "Go with God," said Rosen. "Didn't I tell you to travel? You need a dictionary, though. '*Entschuldigen Sie mich, mein Herr, wie kommt man zum Post*'? Excuse me, sir, where is the post office?" Ginger was doing the rhumba, or perhaps the tango; he could not be certain, since she practiced in the hall.

Their mother brought a dish of mussels with a separate bowl for broth;

the broth had parsley floating in it, and a fleck of parsley appeared on her thumbnail. He remembered how she diced the scallions and the garlic and the parsley, the feel of the cutting board afterward sluiced down with lemon, the buttery brine in their cups. He could taste and see and feel and smell and even hear them; they were a tactile presence, a part of him inalienably, the marrow of his bone and pith of his eyebrow and muscle, ligature, and teeth.

Everything

THE LONG, LOOPING syntax of things, the way they wind together then unwind, the feel of the light in your mouth, the sound you make while touching it, the slant of the sunshine precisely the angle it arrived at yesterday, only not *now*, not through the same set of trees or at the equivalent instant, not this minute of the watch he fails to wear—yet keeping watch—not needing radium strapped to a wrist, the reminder (as if anyone needed reminding how time itself is circular and deadly not least because dull, the measure of man's metronomic regularity—this man's, at any rate, who soon enough would be patted and fed and prepared) of our dutiful segmenting declension, the habit of a hierarchy, compassed degrees: fifty-nine to sixty, twelve subordinate to one—and the sun where it was once and would be routinely, as if fifty-nine and sixty are and should be parallel, as if it matters, is of consequence, the sun and dial and generation rising but to fall, his brothers dead or dying or coopted or corrupt, his actual cousin doing just fine, thank you, a C.P.A. south of Glens Falls; it's not what we'd planned for, this split-level, says Georgy—Martin cannot help it, thinks of him as Georgy still, would introduce him even now as Georgy, even at seventy-eight, if ever they might meet once more or furnish introductions—but Georgy worked for General Electric in Fort Edward, and retired there, and the likelihood of such a meeting now again is slim; it's not so bad, he used to say, good benefits, time off for good behavior, he liked to go hunting and sailing, they have this camp on Lake George (and Bindy, George's second wife, never failed to make a joke of it, a point that she points out by laughing, lifting her arms, her chin, the single dimple on her right cheek creasing, George bought this place before we married so they named the lake here after him, they're sweet to put it on the map and put up all those signposts so even after too many Manhattans we can't lose our way. How many, he asked, is too many; she lifted her hands to him then, two, six, who's counting, you can find us in the dark), and long ago he, Martin, had done so and sat on the rock outcrop while his cousin snored within, and watched the slate-gray water beneath its mist-sleeve, rising, thinking how the Indians had split that surface earlier, deer swimming in front of them, startled, the inlet not too wide to ford—imagining what deer must feel, wet panic, the waterlogged forelegs unable to leap, the long, snouting hollow birch behind it implacably, hissing, no camouflage in water where your head remains outstretched like his own above the rocker pillow, pinioned, and then the bow-and-hatchet man, the shadow, the uplifted arm, the stench of mortality nearing—he shut his eyes and saw not his housekeeper but Bindy, pulling her negligee over her knees, crossing her hands there, smoking, flicking the ash at the water, asking him is something wrong, is there something we or anyone can do?

He told her, or tries to, about regularity, our brothers corrupted as three-day drowned game: you can make the same turn ninety times, coming out of the same driveway; you could make it nine hundred, nine thousand times, can make it till the brake pads fail while sun slants through the frost rime that you failed to bother wiping, till the road goes slick and a pickup with a driver fiddling with the radio, his right hand at the dial and left hand just touching the wheel, his sleep this past night troubled, his daughter not back until three (and though he'd waited in the living room, watching football from the coast, nodding off, dozing with the long day done and what the hell's the point, it's now or later, sooner or never, giving her time and rope and falling asleep at the two-minute break, waking as she tiptoed past, the screen a blue haze only, ready to tell her the things that she does, the way she worries him, her mother too—yet something in the way she walks, some aspect of her high-hipped gait, the care she takes to let him sleep, the way she pushes the knob in gently, and the blue glare contracting till blank, the streetlamp light in her disarrayed hair, some attribute of beauty that he has not seen in her before and knows will not remain, will tarnish from this newly minted precious thing, this

coinage called womanhood—something of that stayed his hand and held
his tongue and kept him in the armchair while she tiptoed up the stairs),
and therefore he broods now, dialing, inattentive, and does not notice the
car nosing out, the intersection that had been a driveway entrance only,
threatless, abandoned or at least unoccupied, the way what was habitual
now shifts. And if that is the case for a driveway, how much more true
of highways and the crossroads of a nation, the inside lane on I-80 by
Moline when diesel rigs explode—the air is wet, he drops his head as if
to dive, as if the wind were liquid, he can hear as clearly as if clicking
stones across that inlet, as if Bindy spelled it out, I'm dying of boredom, of
your good cousin, of life beside that snuffling hulk and Hudson Falls and
Glens Falls and Fort Edward and the Library Committee, stripping with
a single gesture, arms out, and diving splay-footed into the lake, the length
of her swirling, submerged; I dare you, Bindy offers, what's wrong with it
anyhow, why not, he's sleeping, and anyhow he'll never know, and anyhow
he wouldn't mind, and what did you come here for otherwise, why?—the
start of the visit, the knee raised, the instep, the startled beginning again.

"Martin, it's too cold out here."

He straightened.

"You have to come in."

He blinked. He licked his teeth—the uppers, left to right.

"They'll be coming for the photographs in half an hour. That nice man
from the interview. You were sleeping. You messed up your hair."

Mrs. Thompson's voice, he thought, might have been gentle once. Now
it sounded like mosquitoes in his ear.

"We've got to get you ready. We'd better come in from the porch."

Is there a word, he asked himself, for many mosquitoes at the same
time? Are they a cluster, gaggle, pride; would mosquitoes be a swarm?

"Up we go now, Martin. Easy does it. Up."

Strange, he thought, that she should call him Martin whereas he, her
employer, her elder, spoke of her as Mrs. Thompson and did not think of
her as Kate. She had been his housekeeper for eleven years.

"*That's* better. In we go."

The maple leaves cascaded where he watched. There had been an early
snow. The birch were finished, and the beech, and the oak tree at the
driveway's edge stood sere and bare and brown. He must remember, later,

to check the variorum on "bare ruin'd choirs"; what did "choirs" mean, and what sort of church allowed birds? "Where late the sweet birds sang," made sense, but "choirs" was a puzzle, music merely; he'd puzzle it out.

And she was right, his chittering chorus, his shrew: it had been growing cold. He lifted his arms, rolled his neck. She collected his blanket and mug. She steered him to the door. The newel-post and railings needed paint. His rocker, weightless, abandoned, rocked. "What time is it?" he asked.

"Three-thirty. Almost four. That nice young man's coming at four."

If it had been a woman, she would have been less eager—more protective, more solicitous, more watchful of his privacy. If it had been a pretty woman—and most journalists have flair, at least, and television women have a scrubbed gleam about them, and the young girls writing now are not, he knows, uneager—then heaven help the visitor. Mrs. Thompson would be dusting. Mrs. Thompson would be fluffing up the pillows and making significant noises and pointing to her watch. The last one, she'd thrown out. The girl had brought all Martin's books for him to sign—a selection anyway, a baker's goodly dozen—and she told him they were wonderful and meant everything to her, and always had, and sat beside him on the couch with no bra and pert little nipples and so much perfume he had sneezed, her red hair flicking his shoulder as he bent to write. "You're cold," said Mrs. Thompson. "You must be tired, Martin. Maybe we can send them with suitable inscriptions when he's feeling better."

"But I drove here all the way from Portsmouth," said the girl.

'Then you can drive right back. Just leave me your address and postage."

"I'm all right now," he said. "I'm fine. Why don't you bring us a drink?"

Sniffing, she had gone to make the tea, and he had had ten minutes and reached for the redhead and she drew back from him, shocked—pretending shock, he was certain, playing hard to get, playing for time. "We don't have much of it," he said, and fell on her bare legs, and squeezed. He was a strong man still, and heavy, and she lay beneath him, rigid, while he told her of King David and Abishag the Shunammite and how the old king needed warming and what he would require. "Don't," she said. "Please don't." That was one of the things he required, the wriggling protestation, the heart beating under his fist, and it would have worked, was working, her hair in his right hand, her knee at his left, when Mrs. Thompson came back in—to ask, she told him later, if their guest took milk and sugar—and cried, "Oh no, oh not again," and the girl jackknifed beneath him and stood and that was that. Mrs. Thompson had bundled her out. Then she had bundled him up. Then she had bundled him into the daybed in the library. Prepositions are as various as women, he had written, their minute alterations of language—"up, out, into, in, around"—their manipulative meaning like the skeined tune and tone of the skin.

Martin Peterson, the novelist, had been "promising" and then was "accomplished" and now was "distinguished"; this year marked half a century since his first book appeared. There were citations, celebrations, a *Festchrift* from his publisher, a renewed campaign to win the Nobel Prize. It wasn't his idea. He didn't have much hope. He had earned what he won and given good weight and been translated into more languages—he lost count at seventeen—than a normal man might speak. Once, in Singapore, he had taken an airport taxi and complimented the driver on his excellent command of English. "I speak nineteen languages," the driver had announced. He remarked this without undue pride. It turned out he spoke English and eighteen Malay dialects; inflection is what matters, the taxi driver said.

Martin and his third wife stayed in the Raffles Hotel. The manager received them. He was waiting on the steps. There are too few serious people these days, he said; the businessmen all stay in something recent, something modern; they have not even heard of Somerset Maugham and don't even know why they should. We are honored that you're with us, sir, he said.

He had traveled with Margit, the year before she left. She had had enough, she said, of his needy preening; she needed a life of her own. She wanted to have children with a husband, not a husband too arrested to have children in his life. "Your phrases turn less nicely than your ankles," he had said. "You should save your mouth for what it's good at." But that evening, in the Raffles, she was pure compliance. He could remember the hooded look she gave him as she stepped into the shower long after he forgot the details of divorce; he could remember the small of her back, but not the name of the lawyer or who settled for what; he remembered the rum and the fish and the long-fluked fan and palm trees in the courtyard and the pool. She had been more beautiful than anyone, but her small hands were not beautiful; he rinsed them free of soap.

And it was like this often now, a half-remembered turn of phrase, the echo of another's work he thought of as his own—the detail that, enlarging, fills the frame. He remembered someone's teeth and someone else's laughter, this one's habit of clearing his throat, that necklace on a bureau—its rumpled glinting, the purple scarf, the gold watch and mother-of-pearl cuff links from his father, the fragment from the Greek anthology he used as an epigraph once. "'In my nineteenth year,'" he recited, "'the darkness drew me down. And ah the sweet sun!'"

Then there was the epitaph for a sailor lost at sea. "'This gravestone lies if it says that it marks the place of my burial.'" That was all. That was it in its entirety. He remembered, for instance, a diner—the blue Formica counter, the white coffee mug and sugar doughnut and the napkin dispenser and ashtray and saltshaker in a perfect parallelogram when he rearranged the mug—remembered how the waitress had strawberry marks on her forearm, how she knew the customer beside him and was saying, "What I think is, if she doesn't want to rollerskate that's fine; why pay for all them lessons and them broken teeth, why make her do something she's too scared to do?"—remembered how the man at his right smiled, nodding, dipping his cruller in milk—but could not for the life of him imagine why he had gone to the diner or what he was doing there or when.

Bindy would be dead perhaps and certainly not swimming. George would weigh two hundred pounds. He had used them in his book about the love affair with that Peruvian who married someone else and rented out canoes. While Mrs. Thompson readied him—the washcloth at his neck, his mouth, the brush, the shirt button, the cuffs—he remembered his heart's darling, the lilt of her laughter, the falling of her arms.

At four o'clock the car arrived. He could hear it in the driveway, then the engine closing down. The boy had sandy hair. He wore blue jeans and a leather vest and a blue shirt with white collar—like a stockbroker slumming or a doctor on vacation. Hauling stiff black boxes and cameras and shoulder bags and a tripod, he made several trips from the car. Martin watched this from the couch. He moved confidently, easily; his boots were cowboy boots. He was whistling, adept at the work. Mrs. Thompson, too, enjoyed it; she held the screen door open while he carried in the lights.

Then she introduced him. "Martin, you remember Peter."

"No."

The boy advanced. "It's good to see you, sir." He held out his hand.

"We've met?"

"Last Thursday, sir, remember? And you invited me back."

"I don't remember. No."

"Well anyway, I'm here," the boy said breezily, and started connecting the lights.

"What's he here for?" Martin asked.

"'The usual.' To bother you. That's what you said last week."

Mrs. Thompson giggled. "I told you he has brass. He asked me if you want to look like Frost or Hemingway this time. He says he can do either."

"Get me a podium," the writer said. "Give me a president first."

"Excuse me, sir?" said Peter—rolling the hooked rug away, setting the tripod in place.

"Get me a podium, and then I'll look like Frost." It came to him, however, that the boy would have worn diapers at the Kennedy inaugural—or maybe was not even born. "All right." He glared at Mrs. Thompson where she held the electrical cord. "How long does this vaudeville take?"

"It's important, Martin. It's the cover photograph."

"One word is worth a thousand pictures. You know I say that, always." He never had said this before. He was feeling ornery, did not like how his housekeeper had organized the session, how she and the boy were in league.

"I couldn't agree with you more." The boy was being charming. "I did read your trilogy, sir, as you suggested last Thursday. It's wonderful. I loved it."

He doubted this. "What was their name?"

"Sir?"

"The woman in the second book—the one who gets pregnant—what's she called?"

"Ariel, of course," said Mrs. Thompson. "Everyone knows that."

"He didn't."

"Ariel," the boy said. "I love what you did with her. Smile."

So then they settled into what he did know and could do, and Martin sat there smiling and then serious, looking straight ahead, then left, then right, then down and at his books. He allowed himself to drift. The way the light falls glancingly across an upraised palm, his father's love of marmalade, the thick-cut bitter taste of it on toast, wisteria by the garage, systole and diastole, this improbable adherence to the surface of the earth, so that falling one falls down and dying by water drifts up; his mother's ring embedded in the flesh behind the knuckle, her tennis racket in its press, his dream of Margit early on, the way she would enfold him, so passionate, so pleasing, the smell of brie on biscuits and the taste of shrimp—we do not leave this easily, not cease the circuit's spasm, the pain at the knee when one kneels, the tang of apples in the autumn, woodsmoke, ceremony, hillocks, the horn, the split-leaf maple flaming, dog snuffling at a groundhog's hole, that gathering tightness prior to sex. He shut his eyes, then opened them. The shuddering release, the phone left unanswered, and doorbell, the taste of prosciutto on melon, rain on a tent flap, the first sight of the Parthenon, or Stonehenge, or the World Trade Center, the second subject of the first movement of the Schubert Quintet in C major—the feel of her hand in his, gripping, convulsive, her bed a harbor where he beached: he blinked. There are bills to pay and objects to acquire and the long diurnal round of meals and sleep and argument and manners and disease; there is music, oxygen, barbed and chicken wire. What seemed unimportant becomes important, critical; he would rectify the slave trade, violated borders and dispossessed peoples and forced labor camps and drug addiction and penury and sickness and starvation in the four dark corners of the earth.

"I'm afraid he's not himself. I told you he gets tired."

"Fifteen more minutes," said Peter. "That's all I need." He changed film.

"Are you awake?" she asked. Martin made no answer. Mrs. Thompson neared him, looming. "Would you like tea?"

He let his mouth hang down.

"Since the operation," she confided. "He just hasn't been himself."

"How long ago was that?" asked the photographer. He was back behind the tripod. He was adjusting the lights.

"It's not the operation, really. That was a success. It's what happened to him afterward."

"What happened," Martin said, "is he allowed his housekeeper to talk too much. Yes, tea."

She colored; she patted her hair. She made for the kitchen, retreating.

"I did read those novels," Peter said. "Her husband's name was Sam. Her sister was called Marjorie. You dedicated them to someone called Yvonne."

"Yvonne." That had been his first wife. She died, he learned, last month.

She came to Martin nightly and he covered her with kisses: he woke rigid, drenched in sweat. The smell of her stayed on his hands. He hesitated to wash. He needed her far more than he had recognized, or told her, more than he had known. This lack of knowledge on her part tormented him. He told her nightly, as she faded, while he woke. She rose from the pillow. Her arms were damp, her ribs pronounced. He needed her to scold him for survival. She would be a crone, she had warned him, one of those women with no extra flesh and breakable needle-point bones. What are needle-point bones? he would ask—incurious, needing only to keep her in conversation. Her hand had been translucent, lifting.

He pictured her in Mexico and Point Barrow and Versailles; she had told him of these places and the way they made her feel. He followed her. He admired her street slang in Cuernavaca, the brilliant glance of her big-irised eyes. She squeezed herself against him while he slept. She could describe the ice rime on a field of snow at Christmas, or the "honey bucket" they used for plumbing in Alaska. She returned. Always she appeared before him, legs scissoring his, an intervening presence where he walked. She wanted competence, space for herself; she wanted the vistas of Point Barrow in midwinter, with only a seal at the edge of her vision and maybe one conical cloud. She could last forever on one box of crackers and a pound of tea; she needed him, wanting him tonguing her collarbone and there, darling, there in the small of my back.

He had picked a four-leaf clover for her by the barn. He bent and, in a single motion, collected and offered it up. She had never found a four-leaf clover and was gratified. A white-tailed deer leaped past them, bounding for the tamaracks. "It's perfect," said Yvonne. Once when they were thirsty on the beach a man approached them, saying, "I've got a headache. I shouldn't drink this. Here"—and offered them a bottle of white wine. Once while they were making love a bee settled on her arching neck; by the time he reached to brush it off, she had been stung. He reconstructed that. Of such stuff were his memories made.

By the time the tea would cool sufficiently to drink, she had arrived. He could not keep her out. Yvonne lay on the beach or stood by the car or studied a cluster of leaves. Her shadow fell across the picket fence. She inhabited the bathroom mirror or the faucet or the butter dish; she left her fingerprints. He wanted to powder the room. There was a dust that fingerprint experts used, and usage would show everywhere; there would be thumbprints on the walls and floors and cabinets and towels. Her palm would be emblazoned on the icebox door. It adhered to his knee and arm and shoulders. Her flesh had flaked minutely and drifted by the sink.

"What I like about it," Peter said, "is how you make them history. Historical convergence is what I noticed there."

He roused. He licked his teeth.

"That's what you were saying, right? In the interview, I mean, last Thursday. About the way the past gets present, since the present is 'no country for old men.' And if I understand you, that's why we're always young. How we stay in touch with history."

"Something like that," Martin said.

"What you said was—I checked the transcript—'It doesn't help the body but it mightily comforts the mind.'"

Mrs. Thompson brought them tea. "Are we finished?"—he turned toward her, querulous. "How long does this go on?"

"Do you need?"—she tilted her head to the hall.

"Yes."

"Excuse us," she told Peter. "We're off to the little boys' room."

He remembered going with his sisters and his father for the Christmas tree. They would make a journey of it, jostling for position; they would drape a dropcloth in the open flatbed of the truck. "You want that tree to rest easy, don't you?" their father would ask. "You wouldn't want it to scratch." He and his sisters would nod. They could have cut a tree behind the house or from the fence line by the overpass—but they went every year to Ned Fellers's farm.

Ned Fellers knew the family, he liked to say, since back before the Flood. He had a yellow moustache. His hair was white, and what colored his moustache was nicotine; his teeth were brown. He had difficulty seeing when they pulled into the driveway. Dogs surrounded them. He would fumble with the door latch, then step into the mild December air as if it were true winter, shivery, wearing gloves; he carried a hatchet and saws. Ned would invite them in for tea, but he and his sisters would fidget so their father said, maybe later when we've cut the thing, all right? "I'll put the kettle on," said Ned. "You don't want to keep them waiting."

Then they would trek to the ridge. It was important not to spot the tree too soon. He never could distinguish between Scotch and white pine,

Fletcher fir or Douglas or balsam or spruce. Fellers planted stands of each, and their father would always say, well, what do we want this tree to be, what kind this year, how big? In the corner of his eye Martin saw the one he wanted, knowing by its contour just how perfectly the tree would fit, how the others would agree, would say his choice was beautiful, this is the perfect one. Sometimes, however, the perfect one would prove on closer scrutiny to have an imperfection—a bend in the trunk, a clutch of missing branches where it had been crowded by the next pine in the row.

At some point while they wandered their father would say, this is far enough in, we don't want to drag it a mile. Then they would double back, assessing and discussing and finally determining—at that point where impatience took over, where desire overmastered caution—which tree to cut. They would take turns with the saw. They each could take five strokes. He had been the youngest, and therefore he went first. Their father took the original cut, establishing the point where Martin continued, and the angle, and he would guide his hand.

When the season was over they took out the tree. This too was ritual. There would be days after New Year's when the needles fell in clusters to the carpet underneath, and their mother said, we don't want to burn down the house. Wouldn't you say, Martin, it's getting to be time? At length he would agree. He and his sisters would dismantle all they'd hung judiciously, taking hours to arrange: the balls, the ornaments, the popcorn and gingerbread men. Their father cut the strings with which he had steadied the tree. It tilted. They carried it out of the house.

Birds eat the dying needles, Ned Fellers had explained: you stand a pine tree in the snow and if there's nothing else around a sparrow can live off the sap. It's nice to know a tree keeps being useful once it's cut. Martin picked off what tinsel he could. They carried it toward the brush pile by the fence.

Then, in the weak slanting light, the lawn came alive with silver—strands of tinsel that blew free. They lodged in the flagstone paving. They worked their way to the fence. They lifted in the breeze and winked at him, as if the whole garden were precious, dew lasting all the bright day. His mother told him to pick up that trash, but he left the tinsel alone.

What he meant to tell the boy was not convergence, *confluence*, was how time is a trickle that feels like a river to swimmers, and then it trickles out. Man cannot step in the same stream twice. Except he, Martin, was doing just that, was chewing the past like a cud. While Peter packed and was dismissed and said he'd send the proofs along, or maybe bring them by if Mr. Peterson felt up to it, he tried to formulate a phrase about the son as father, Peter and Peterson, the way they mirrored each other, child and man, how orthograph and autograph and author graphically linked.

But it made no sense, made nonsense, and he was too tired. He wanted his dinner in peace. This was the time of day he loved, the lengthening shadows, the low brilliant light. Mrs. Thompson would turn on the television news. They were blowing up the tankers in the Gulf. They were hoping that prosperity would trickle down. They were knaves and fools in Washington, and all the more lamentable for meaning what they said.

It came to Martin, suddenly, there had been pigeons in Hagia Sofia; they roosted in the eaves and swooped and ululated and shat with impunity there. So that kind of church did host birds. Those particular bare ruined choirs made a museum now. Margit had worn her slate-blue suit, and they stayed in the Pera Palas. He remembered the barman—brown, compact, wiping the counter carefully—saying with great satisfaction, "Brandy, I have." Their shared history, he saw, could be plotted by hotels—the grand relics of the grander past where Martin felt at home. She gripped the bedpost rattlingly and rose on her knees in the bed. They had reached Istanbul the night before some sacred feast, and streets were clogged with sheep. All night he heard the sounds of bleating, the muezzin at his window. In the morning there had been no sheep, and the gutters ran with blood.

The housekeeper brought him his scotch. She had added water, and no ice. "He's a pleasant fellow," he said to Mrs. Thompson, placatory. "You were right." There were floaters in his eyes. The window framed a photograph. The meadow appeared to sprout snow. He thought of those two-dollar paperweights you shake to make a squall. A hut on a hillside would find itself buried, a green tree go white. The deer would look like reindeer till the flakes settled again. Yet the shift in seasons altered nothing else; the glass would not grow cold as it registered winter, the hunter did not shiver or take off his coat with the thaw. Such systems were protected, a synthetic storm.

Then the telephone began. They called about the prize—the Pulitzer? the National Book Critics Circle?—and wanted to know his opinion of this year's recipient. "Never heard of it," he said. "But Mr. Peterson," they protested, "you're in the jacket copy. You're credited with having sponsored this novel when nobody would publish it."

"Nonsense."

"So you feel justice has been served?"

"Don't quote me," Martin said.

"You *don't* feel justice has been served?"

"*Servus.*" He hung up.

They called about the reading in his honor at the Library of Congress, and if he could attend. Mrs. Thompson told them he would try. The documentary about him was being shown that Saturday; they called for his opinion. He told them he was pleased, extremely pleased; in every particular, really, it improved on the original. The house they showed, for instance, was so much more appropriate than the one he had really been born in. He loved it all, them all.

Mrs. Thompson brought his dinner. She was a jolly old soul. He tasted what she set before him, but it had no taste. He invited her to join him. She would eat no lean. She used remote control to turn on the TV. There were girls in bikinis, on water skis, and a ship's captain with gold braid on his uniform. There were happy couples promenading, and a black man with a trumpet.

"What are we eating?" he asked.

"Grilled cheese," she said. "And tuna."

"Is there celery?"

"Pickles."

A blonde, glistening with the pleasure of a swim, emerged to smile at the new member of the crew. She shook her hair, exuding packaged animality. Then there was an advertisement for Maxipads, and one for cereal, and one that took him some time to decipher: a brunette looking out of a window, getting dressed, descending to a car which snouted up into the alley where she lived. Men stared at her, and then the driver glided off, and Martin asked, "What are we watching?"

"Nothing. An advertisement."

"Tomorrow I'm planning to work."

She looked at him.

"I don't suppose you take dictation."

"No."

"What was her name—the one who did? The one who took dictation?"

"Irene. She'll be here tomorrow, Martin. Tomorrow's the morning she comes."

"That's good." He ate a pickle. "That'll be fine."

"You have a pile of mail."

"I'm writing tomorrow. Not letters." He shifted his potato chips. He did not want them near the pickle juice.

"Your women," Mrs. Thompson said. "The ones who take such care of you, who always have—Irene, for instance. You forgot she takes dictation." She pressed a button; the TV went blank.

"I wouldn't forget *you*."

She sniffed. "And there's the night nurse coining soon. Mrs. Mirabelli."

He was the messenger again, the emissary, the one with the white flag. "It's only that I want to work."

"Go right ahead," she said. "Don't let me interrupt you. I'll finish the dishes. You work."

So then he settled down to write, the language inching up the shale like water in a tidal pool, filling slowly where he sat, the voice in the well of the throat, the story of his second wife, the story of apprenticeship, the way she hurtled home from market, so gladly, so dark-eyed, her arms full of fruit—the hard first spate of study, night classes, the old men telling stories, the cordwood he cut (and remembered walking, years ago, past men with retrievers and hunting gear. They were drinking by a duck-blind, wearing orange caps. There were half a dozen of them, bearded, overweight. One of them wore waders. He hailed Martin, asking, "Hey buddy, which way's town?" Another said, "What town is it?" as if this were a joke. They laughed and slapped each other's backs. They burbled hilariously, repeating, "You call that a *town*?" Teal beat overhead. They wheeled and shot and stumbled, while the dogs tore in circles. He continued, feeling what he felt again now: himself the target, leaving . . .), then sound enlarging into shape, a paragraph, a page, a chapter, library, Alexandria in flames—contending, however, contending with water. He dove.

The scotch was unblended, Glenlivet. He swallowed cautiously, sipping. But ah, the sudden soaring lilt of it, those words by which he lived, the astonishing regalia of his titles on the shelf: and how had he come to this pass? There had been some injury, some consequential rupture, some way in which he lost what he had worked so long to find—the sheaf of script with which he started in his nineteenth year, the notebooks, the letters, the light on the page that the pond at midday, refracting, might cast, and endurance—his mother, his father, the pattering trill of gossip, rain on the windows on Sunday, the decanters on the sideboard and the lilac by the door, his wives, his friends and professors and sisters and critics and associates and place of my burial and editor at Scribner's, all death-undone, so many, their strange eventful history, the raindrop that falls farthest on the pane . . .

What was difficult to tell was if he dreamed or wrote them, those men and women huddled in the corners of the room. He had been in such rooms, often. He was unimpressed. He had described them enough. They edged toward the canapés and eyed each other joylessly and spoke of book contracts and paperback sales and foreign sales and auction floors, the ways of the publishing world. It had been his trade. He made a living from books. But it was strange to Martin still that art should be a business, that there was profit in it as well as certain loss. The ballyhoo, the overpraise, the cultivated jockeying, venality, the fool's gold blurbed as real—or, conversely, true talent ignored—this subsided near him, lately, and went dim. There was a stuffed polar bear in the Explorers Club. There was a boy on the porch. He could not hear what they were saying—who was in, who out, who promoted, who bypassed, who wielded the tin gavel in which parliament of fowls. He did not try to hear. "The parliament," for instance: had he written that, or meant to; was it a short story or the tipped cap to Chaucer—the bard he'd named his Newfoundland in honor of, beloved, one hundred fifty pounds of panting slavish sweetness, the noble black head, the pink tongue? So when he thought of Chaucer now he thought not so much of pilgrimage or Canterbury as a pet. He was writing his memoirs. He completed the third volume while they lounged about the pool.

Martin had discomfort but no pain. He shifted in his seat. The light was fading, westerly; he watched. The point of entry is the center of a circle. The circles are concentric, and at the pond's perimeter they double back, contracting.

"Have we been being gloomy?"

"No."

"Your nose." She gave him her handkerchief. He used it. "That's better."

"How are your children?" He lifted his head. "They'll be coming east for Christmas, am I right?"

"Why, yes, they will." She studied him. He would not cry. "How nice of you to remember."

"And little Kate? The youngest? Jane's daughter, isn't it?"

"She's wonderful." Now Mrs. Thompson grew expansive. "She's a hellion, that one. She whistles through her teeth. She's got her front teeth missing, and she points her finger there and gives me this enormous smile and says, 'Gammer, my gap!'"

He shook his head to clear it. "I want to go back to the porch."

She checked her watch. They compromised. "Just for a little?"

"A little."

"Don't you love the weather, though? Don't you wish it was always like this?"

"I do," he admitted. She opened the door. She helped him through. The rocker had his blanket. "I'll sit here just a little."

"Tomorrow we do letters," Mrs. Thompson said.

Correspondence: he mocked it, it bored him, was boring, was pat, no more than a comes-around goes-around tag line remaining with him nevertheless to come around and go around and fail to fade, no matter how he sat quiescent, how the swallows flashed fluttering by, and now the bats—recurrence: this momentary certainty that everything suspended falls, that motion accretes inertia, inertia motion, and all things inflated collapse—from the balloon, the tire, from the bullfrog's calling, the rubbery pneumatic flesh of its throat distended to croak, then convulsing, *glut glut*, from the way his own flesh grew tumescent, emitted, collapsed, from the way the economy inflated, the black band of blood pressure circling an arm—everything examples it, the trees are an instruction, rain, the hospital bill, the credit system, the heat engendered by decay, and everything is circular that once argued causality, the arc, the sudden shattering (that time he was thrown from a horse, that time he missed the second step on the staircase descended habitually, these months, that time the maroon Dodge pickup with the tailgate rusted out, the right front fender painted green, boxing gloves slung from its mirror, swerved to avoid him and skidded and went down the embankment by the driveway where he'd braked; when he got out and went to help and clambered down the frozen slope he heard Sinatra crooning "Autumn in New York" on the truck radio; it's nothing, the man said, my daughter, that sumbitch, the ice, just give me a hand with this winch—the jolt of rearrangement, Bindy near him at a party, presenting cheese, whispering, how could you do it, how, why to me, why last night you bastard, what did you mean?—the way the veil of what we call propriety is rendered transparent by need, the surface of the pond by trout, the air by dum-dum bullets, so when will I see you? I need to discuss it, we have to . . .), remembering that, time he waited on the tree stand three days into the season and a man and woman walked into the clearing underneath, holding hands, he dark-haired, she blond, she wearing leather boots and silver fur and with no coy preliminary or any of the actions of seduction leaned against a maple trunk and raised her coat and raised the dress while her lover dropped his pants, she wearing nothing underneath, he jockey shorts, then entered her, her long legs taut, the two of them absorbed beneath him, not looking up, not around, not saying anything while Martin watched with what even then he recognized as an aroused dispassion this buck and mating shudder and slap of flesh on flesh, all of it so quickly done that he barely saw what he was seeing before they straightened, steadied each other, replaced their clothing with a negligent attentiveness and, holding hands, walked off; it is diversion, all of it, a way to pass the time, to move from fifty-nine to sixty, twelve to one, not serious the looping components of subject and object, clause upon clause—and if even such diversion might depend or signify, might produce a child or marriage or gonorrhea or divorce, her ass as pert beneath him as the white-tailed deer, retreating (the silver box, the apple tree, the trusty oak, sans teeth, the days of courting . . .), then why not break the pattern, smile at this night nurse who's taking his pulse, Mrs. Thompson departing, materialized, and what he did not manage but might again, again.

REPRISE

AND OTHER STORIES

For ELENA, as Ever

Contents

Aubade

THEY ARE DRIVING, as they often do, to the beach at Lobsterville; it is the middle of June. "Up-Island" this gray morning, little traffic shares the road; the fog has not yet lifted and the sun is not yet warm. Just after dawn, it rained.

They drive with the top down. His car is an Impala convertible, on extended loan; his indulgent mother had been planning to trade in the Chevrolet for a newer model, but gave it to her son instead as an eighteenth birthday present. Divorced, she can be turn by turn extravagant or chary of expense.

He washes and waxes the car's chassis often, but the dirt roads of Martha's Vineyard leave a film of dust on fenders and doors; small branches scratch the trunk. In later years he'll understand both how lucky he had been to drive the white convertible and how it could be bettered once he had the wherewithal to buy cars himself. In time to come he will own an Alfa Romeo, a second-hand Jaguar, and a vintage Porsche. But he is nineteen now, just having completed his sophomore year in college, and the girl at his side is, she says, in love with him. They use the back seat to fuck.

They have done so already this morning; it is eleven o'clock. The air feels cold for swimming, but they plan to take a walk. Her family rents a house above Menemsha harbor, and has been doing so since 1952. They live in Manhattan year-round. It is 1961. Her father, a corporate lawyer, flies up for weekends when he can, and spends the month of August playing golf and tennis and surfcasting from the beach. He rarely catches anything of sufficient size to keep.

The boy wants to be an actor. He has a confident stage presence and can remember his lines; his voice is strong and he is, she tells him, beautiful to look at. What this beauty consists of he is unsure—wishing he were taller, wishing his muscles more pronounced and his nose less large. But the general effect is good, and the desire to be someone else—to mime and be a mummer, as his drama teacher puts it—has been, all his conscious life, strong. In college, he has joined the Drama Club and plays secondary leads—Hotspur in *Henry IV, Part I*, for instance, or Mercutio in *Romeo and Juliet*. Last October he played Mitch in *A Streetcar Named Desire*, and the play's director singled him out for praise.

She too has dreams of performance. In childhood and early adolescence, till her hips grew wide and breasts pronounced, she had hoped to be a ballerina; then she studied Modern Dance. There are certain people—hard to know why—on whom attention stays fixed while on stage, and this girl is one of them. Not particularly so in private, where she tends to be self-effacing, but put her in a spotlight and all eyes are riveted; she has a wide smile and a focused energy at odds with the person now sitting beside him and putting her hand on his knee. After graduation she will relinquish the study of dance and turn to work in television; of this she will make a career.

The fog is lifting, lessening, and the air grows mild. They approach a small shingled house at the side of the road, with two rusted pumps beside it. The gasoline pumps have long since been disabled, but the screen door has an OPEN sign, and she tells him, "Stop!"

"What for?" he asks.

"It's almost never open."

"So?"

"The food's wonderful. Her brownies are the *best!* You have to taste them."

He brakes. There is a gravel parking space, with an old Oldsmobile parked at the far edge, and he pulls up alongside. A small painted sign reads FOOD; underbrush and scrub oak hug the curb.

"You're sure?" he asks.

"I want to, yes."

He isn't hungry at this hour and looks forward to the beach. But his girlfriend knows the Vineyard—its secret paths and special haunts—and he wants to please her, so he kills the engine and they stand and stretch and briefly kiss, she nuzzling his cheek afterwards, and walk to the cottage's door. Pine trees cluster wetly just beyond the roof.

"Hansel and Gretel," he says.

"Come in and meet the witch."

The screen door has swollen, so it requires effort to lift it from the lintel where it catches, squeaking. He forces the thing ajar. Once he succeeds, she enters and he follows her inside. The room is dark—one small lamp on a table—and empty.

"Hello, hello?" she calls.

It is, clearly, a room intended for the preparation and then purchase of a meal. A counter runs the length of it, and there are four stools. The stool-stands could use polishing, and the red leather seats have faded and cracked. He twirls one; it squeaks, creaks. There is a black-and-white photograph of an Indian chief in full regalia—wearing a headdress, holding a tomahawk—on the slope of plunging dunes. There is a photograph of fishing boats and men unfurling nets.

Behind the counter, on the kitchen side, he can make out appliances: a stove with four gas burners, a discolored Kelvinator, and a rusted toaster and sink. There are wood cabinets with peeling yellow paint along the wall, and a blackboard with items listed in chalk: Hot Dog: $.35, Hamburger, $.50, Coffee, $.20, Brownie, $.10. Even in 1961, these prices are outmoded, and he turns to her, smiling, and says, "What a deal!"

She puts her finger to her lips. They stand there a moment, in silence, and she calls again, "Hello?" He finds a bell on a string cord and jarringly rings it. As the echo dies away, they hear a shuffling from within and slow footsteps approaching; then a door he has not noticed scrapes open from the right rear corner of the kitchen.

"Good morning," says the girl.

The woman who enters is ancient. Bent and white-haired, wearing an apron, she peers at them unspeaking, and rubs her outstretched hands. It is as though they interrupted some private undertaking, some labor she engages in they cannot comprehend. She is short and stout and, it would appear, half-blind; her eyes are light blue, clouded, and they do not focus. Her cheeks are pink.

"Good morning," the boy echoes, but she does not speak.

Respectful, the girl inquires: "Are you serving food this morning?"
She nods.

"Could we buy a brownie?"

Again, she nods.

Surprising himself, he asks if he can also have a hamburger, and the
woman tells him, "Yes."

They are, he understands, the first customers this Thursday; the battered two-tone Oldsmobile in the parking area no doubt belongs to the
proprietor and not another client. They stand in the small space behind
the barstools, uncertain whether to sit. She has taken out a pad of yellow
paper, with a pencil clipped to it, and writes *Brownie, Hamburger,* then
asks—in a low whispering mutter—"Anything to drink?"

"A Coca-Cola, if you have it," says the girl.

Nodding, she adds, *Coca-Cola* to the list and turns to him, expectant,
but he says, "Just water, please."

Meticulously, the woman prices the three items and adds them up and
tells him, "That'll be seventy cents."

He produces a dollar and she stuffs it in the pocket of her apron, then
extracts a quarter and a nickel from a beaded change-purse and says, her
voice half-audible, "Coming right up."

"We're glad you're open," says the girl. "I told him you make the *best*
brownies."

He looks at his companion. She smiles at him, shrugging, sharing the
heat of their recent encounter and fingering her ponytail.

"Fine day," he offers.

"Sit."

What follows is a test. Rapt, they watch the woman labor in a silence
neither of them breaks. Ten years later he will joke about it; thirty years
later still picture it, and when he in turn becomes an old person he will
remember it clearly: the step-by-step procedure he and his girlfriend
witness while the woman cooks. First, she scrapes the griddle and wipes
down the spatula; there is no grease. She washes the spatula nevertheless
and, striking three matches till one of them flares, turns on the gas. She
does not switch on the light. Slowly, she takes a pad of butter and sets it
to sizzle on the warming metal surface, then removes a hamburger patty
from the refrigerator's second shelf, where it has been prepared and sits

between wax paper sheets. Next she pours a glass of water and places it in front of him, then adds paper napkins and tin cutlery to the countertop, then salt and pepper shakers, all this with hands that shake. It takes far longer in the doing than describing; by the time she has completed preparations for the hamburger—extracting a bun which she butters, finding a jar of mustard and a jar of ketchup—the griddle has burned and gone dry. If "short-order cook" is the name for this method of cooking, the deliberation of her step-by-step procedure is anything but "short." The word must be recalibrated to mean something slow and focused; each stage of her labor takes time.

Above the sink there is a clock; he watches it. Ten minutes pass, then twelve. Fourteen minutes pass.

The Coca-Cola arrives. So does a church-key and glass. Her fingers are knotted and swollen with what he will later identify as severe arthritis; the knuckles compel his attention, as do the broken nails. He offers to open the soda, but the girl puts her hand on his wrist. They watch while the cook positions the bottle, and then the church-key, then lifts. She does this twice, a third time until the cap comes free. Unsteadily, she pours.

Meanwhile, the hamburger heats. "My brownie?" asks the girl.

"Coming right up."

As if prompted by the question, their host turns towards a baker's bin and, fumbling, opens it and retrieves a chocolate wedge. On the top are crumbled nuts. This she places on a blue-rimmed china plate and carries to the counter and carefully positions by the glass of water, then removes and centers it in front of the girl's stool instead.

They are trying not to smile. They dare not look at each other, and he clears his throat. "Will it rain this afternoon?" he asks.

The cook makes no answer. She gives them her back and attends to the brown lump of meat, lifting it with the spatula and dropping it on the bun. Turning, she brings him his hamburger, next goes to fetch a pickle and adds that to the plate. When the whole has been assembled, she steps back again and, sighing, commences to scrub down the griddle, then wipes the surface of the counter and the sink.

They eat.

"Delicious," says the girl, and offers him a bite.

"Delicious," he agrees.

The woman ignores them. She removes a sheet of paper towel from a roll at the side of the cupboard and folds it into a square. This she does with what he now can recognize as habitual deliberation; she polishes the faucet and, having rubbed it dry and clean, discards the used soiled towel in a yellow plastic garbage can with a swinging lid. There is, he notices, a coil of flypaper by the single window, and it is black with flies.

He wants to leave. He eats his hamburger quickly, then the dill pickle, then empties his glass. He thinks all this should have some meaning and be somehow important, but the girl is focusing so hard on the crumbs in front of her that he dares not break their silence for fear they both will laugh. They are, he thinks, in harmony; they have a perfect understanding of the great good luck they share. They have their lives before them, an endlessly opening vista, a beckoning array of plans to make, trips to take.

"Thank you," says the girl.

She makes no answer.

"Thank you," he repeats.

Watching his companion swallow, he puts his hand on her wrist. The boy feels stirred by desire and remembers making love that morning where he parked his car. There is a grove behind her house where the Impala's rocking motion cannot be seen from the road. In her bedroom that night they will have sex again—less furtively this time, since her mother will have gone to Vineyard Haven, sharing a meal with a friend. She says she will love him forever and ever, and he promises the same.

He will spend the summer idling, doing yard-work for the rich. He will improve his tennis game and read *Madame Bovary* and, later, *War and Peace*. But the old woman wiping down the cutlery has helped him see the world might be a small one, and progress through it slow. She *is*, he tells himself, a witch; she has magicked him with ketchup and a pickle and the hypnotic rituals of labor: the preparation and the presentation of a meal.

In "Hansel and Gretel" the young couple survives. They emerge from the cottage and follow crumbs back through the forest to the safe haven they call home; the crone who had imprisoned them gets pitched into the oven and caught in the trap of her own devising. The children in this fairy tale do not, however, live happily ever after.

The end.

Two-Part Invention

I

THEY LIVE IN Hyde Park, on 50th Street, in a refurbished row house with a garden at the rear. Their son is three years old. He had noticed how the boy enjoyed stuffed pets but was frightened of an actual animal, shrinking back if they encounter dogs playing in the park. So he acquired a Golden Retriever, telling his wife Timmy shouldn't be scared, and anyhow a big barking dog will help ensure their safety and won't be a bad thing.

Their new puppy is exuberant, but easy to house-break and train. Their son likes to scratch his ears and give out doggie-treats.

"I want him to be careful," says his wife.

"Not of retrievers. They're sweetness itself!"

"But what if he gets bitten by mistake?"

"Darling . . ."

"It could happen!"

She is rarely this anxious or fearful; he wonders if her caution masks some additional concern. She had difficulty getting pregnant—three miscarriages—and can have no second child. They have been married seven years, and he watches her gaze wander when they go to concerts or parties, as if she needs to ratify her sensual allure. Her face is often recognized, her body ogled nightly on the television news while she crosses or splays out her legs. Now her thirty-fifth birthday approaches, and the milestone worries her; it's the beginning, she says, of the end.

He too assesses graduate students, and the younger faculty wives. For the years of their marriage he has stayed faithful, rejecting what might be on offer and honoring his vows. Yet uncertainty has entered in, and he thinks about the expression, "the seven-year itch"; is this restlessness what the phrase means? His candidacy for promotion at the University of Chicago also feels uncertain, though his Department Chair assures him that the odds of acquiring tenure are good, and his forthcoming book on Feydeau and Antonin Artaud will, the Chair is confident, "make a splash."

Pleased with the phrase, the chairman repeats it: "make a splash." Attempting a response, he pictures the two playwrights diving—cannonballing, really—into a pool. Feydeau would no doubt sport a bathing costume appropriate to time and place, but Artaud (that haunted, saintly face, that stick-thin frame) would jump in fully clothed. Or, perhaps, naked and pale. In any case the matter of security—will they be able to stay together in Chicago or must he, next year, enter the job market and be prepared to leave Hyde Park?—is a large if largely silent question, and he tries not to ask it. "Seize the day," he tells himself, quoting the title of a novel by a local author, and plays with his puppy and son.

This October afternoon, they return from the neighborhood park. The sky is growing overcast; the wind is strong. When he and Timothy come through the door, his wife is lying on the couch, a bottle of red wine beside her on the coffee table, and she does not rise.

"Hello," he says.

"Hello."

"Mommy, there were flying tigers!"

"Monarch butterflies, I think he means. With what look like tiger-stripes."

"Did you enjoy yourselves?" she asks, not making it a question, and he studies her more closely and sees the bottle has been emptied though her glass remains half-full.

"Are you all right?"

"I'm fine," she says. "I don't have to go to work. It's Saturday, in case you haven't noticed . . ."

"Good."

"Why do you ask?"

"No reason. Politeness." He unzips his son's jacket, then his own. "I just wondered . . ."

"The great diplomat. The mannerly inquisitor." She says this with undisguised venom, and he tries to quiet her with the French warning, "*Dans la présence des enfants.*"

But Timmy has gone to the corner to play with his fire-truck and ambulance and pays them no attention. The puppy falls asleep. His wife sits up, unsteadily, balancing herself with cushions and crossing her arms on her chest. "What are you saying? Suggesting?"

"Your French is good enough," he says.

"I can translate it, don't worry. 'In the presence of the children.' Child. But what are you trying to say?"

"Has something happened?"

"Why?"

"I just wondered." He sits beside her on the couch and reaches for her hand. Always, in their arguments, he's the one to make the first concession, but he does not know what bothers her or which grievance to address.

"Happened?"

"Since we went to the park just now. Something to upset you?"

"Or not happened, maybe. Something's always not happening here."

"We saw the Hutchesons," he offers. "They were doing circus tricks. On the jungle gym, both mother and daughter. They say hello."

"That's nice. What was she wearing?"

"Who?"

"Ellen Hutcheson, of course. The gay divorcée. The one whose ass you so admire."

He tries to keep calm. "It's a little early, isn't it, for you to play the hanging judge? And a little late for you to be judgmental."

"What a fine turn of phrase." She scans the ceiling. "Did you read it somewhere? Or is that in your book?"

"Thank you for asking."

"Well, is it? Your fine turn of speech?"

"About a hanging judge? If you're asking seriously, it isn't in my manuscript. That's not what Artaud means by 'Theatre of Cruelty.' And not what Feydeau meant by 'bedroom farce.'"

"So what was she wearing?"

"Ellen? Some sort of jumpsuit. I don't remember," he lies.

Now Timothy stands and comes to them. "Mommy?"

"Yes, my little prince?"

"Can we have psketti tonight?"

He calls spaghetti "psketti," and the mispronunciation is endearing, as is his dropped "t" in "Frooloops," and his way of saying "chris-miss" when they see an ornamental pine. He loves their son and loved his wife and is doing what he can to make the past tense present, to fall again under her spell.

"Yes," she says. "It's just what I was planning."

"And broccoli, of course."

"Do I have to?" the boy asks.

"Have to what?"

"Eat broccoli?"

He nods. "Your mother's the soft touch. Me, I'm the big bad vegetable man."

"Susie did a cartwheel," says Tim. "And she fell and hurt her head. She went whoof! *Wahoo!*"

"Did she cry?"

"Mm-hmn. But then her mommy picked her up. And rocked her till she stopped. Daddy did too."

She looks at him. "Did Daddy help?"

"She stopped crying anyhow," he says.

"The great comforter . . ."

Again, the anger in his wife's voice warns him; again he wants to shield their son, who stands behind the couch. Of a sudden, heavily, it rains. He says, "We got home just in time," and his wife says, "Yes, just in time," and drains her glass. He tries to mask the memory: the warm yieldingness of Ellen's breasts, the smell of her skin, and how she brushed against his body while he consoled her crying daughter. Your circus act is over, he told inconsolable Susie Hutcheson, but was a great success.

The divorce goes smoothly; his wife receives the house. As far as such things go, he feels, the two of them stay civil. Both parents want to keep Timothy safe, to protect him from crass legal wrangling and recrimination; they try to act as if nothing has changed. And, in a certain sense, this is true; he still comes by to walk the dog; he coaches his son's baseball team when the boy grows old enough for baseball, playing second base and learning to switch-hit. As his chairman had predicted, he does receive tenure and, two years thereafter, a full professorship. His career at the

University of Chicago is minor but respectable, and in 1992 he in turn becomes Department Chair, dealing with curriculum change and personnel decisions and the problem of declining enrollment and a growing disenchantment—which he largely succeeds in keeping private—with the field. In conference or at symposia, he laments, as do his colleagues, the marginalization of language and literature, the general collapse of standards at the undergraduate level, and the fall-off in funding for graduate degrees.

His second marriage succeeds. He continues to delight in Ellen's presence, her physical responsiveness, the bounty of her breasts. To the best of his ability, he acts as a surrogate father for Susie, although she holds aloof. As time goes by, he watches while his son goes off to and then graduates from college, while his stepdaughter joins a commune and earns money waiting tables, while his first wife remarries and, after a dozen years, dies. Her husband had been a commercial pilot, flying for American Airlines; he also owned a private plane which crashes on the shore of Lake Huron, up by Sault St. Marie. There had been sleet, and engine failure, and the pilot tried but failed to land his Cessna safely; he managed to come within sight of the locks but crashed just short of a landing strip that might have saved them. The couple died on impact and not in the ensuing fire, the coroner declares.

He and Timothy attend the funeral, which is a large affair. There are family members and business associates and colleagues of his ex-wife from the television station; media coverage of the accident means strangers also attend the service, since her face was widely known. She had been co-anchor of the local CBS-affiliate for the Chicago evening news, and many come to mourn "the untimely passing"—as one eulogist describes it—of "our steadying hand and TV's bright light."

He finds himself remembering his first wife's legs, her anger, the way she looked in the hospital bed when delivering their baby. He thinks of her inventive soups, her pleasure in cuisine. He thinks of sex those late mornings when Tim was at school and she had not yet left for work to prepare the nightly broadcast. Their son—now a head taller than he— stares straight ahead, controlling himself, or trying to; he is in his final year of Law School and has put on weight. Although the professor attempts to pay attention, his attention wanders; he thinks about their long-dead dog, his hip dysplasia and incorrigible sweetness and, towards the end, his drooping head and great drooling tongue. He thinks about his wife again, the rancorous slow failure of desire, the divorce. He wishes Ellen were with them, but she has stayed in bed for three days, felled by the flu and leveled—absolutely leveled, as she puts it—by a bug.

"We'll miss you," he had said.

"No you won't, you're better off without me. Without all these sneezles and wheezles."

"I wish I didn't have to go."

Her logic was inarguable. "You're Timothy's father. He needs you there."

"Not so you'd notice ..."

"All right," she said, "*I* need you there."

"Why?"

"To make certain she's buried," said Ellen. "To make sure it's finally over."

This had shocked him. It was as though she viewed their marriage as a private Feydeau farce, with slammed doors and locked closets and lovers underneath the couch, with the serio-comic business of fidelity, infidelity, credulity, incredulity and all the rest of it: maids in aprons, men in top-hats, and children with whistles and whips.

"I didn't know you were jealous. "

"I'm not."

"It's you I left her for, remember."

"I remember," Ellen said.

"It's over now, don't worry."

"But every time we watch the news and she's up there smiling—talking about the mayor or the latest scandal with police—every time I see her it isn't over, really."

"You're using the wrong tense," he said.

"So sorry, professor. My syntax is garbled: I do know she's dead."

"*De mortis nihil nisi bonum.*"

"What's that supposed to mean?"

"'Of the dead, say nothing bad.'"

"I can translate it, honey, I understand the line. Everybody does. But why do you use Latin when you could just as well speak English? Always you say something in some other language when you're scared to talk ..."

She had been right, of course, she's always right, and his is a helpless allegiance not to his first wife's memory but the fact of their shared youth: when he was young, when they were young and everything seemed possible and no one yet had fallen ill or failed.

"Can I get you anything?"

She turned her face to the wall.

"*Carpe Diem*."

In a small voice, Ellen said, "There you go again."

"Yes. When we come back from the service, I'll tell you all about it."

"Do."

"And tonight you'll see us on TV. The front-row mourners. The son and ex-husband."

"Can't wait," said Ellen. "Wear your red tie."

"Amen."

II

A professor of theatre history and a widower, retired, he has moved to what was once their summer home on Cape Cod. His wife has been dead for four years. The place is full of memories—glad echoes of Ellen's laughter or the tone she took when inquisitive, a slant of light while sun gilds the harbor and they share their morning coffee on the deck. Having grown used to solitude, he shops and cooks his meals and finishes the crossword puzzle without his wife's assistance. Her raincoat still hangs on a peg by the stairs; her cosmetics crowd the shelf.

He has always been a private man, although used to speaking in public, and has settled into isolation with—or so he tells himself—ease. There are half-remembered snatches of song, her gardening gloves and the straw hat she wore, a set of dishes she cherished and insisted on washing by hand. He is lonely, yes, but not alone; Ellen's presence fills the house.

His son has moved to the west coast, and raises a family there. From time to time he wishes he could watch his grandchildren growing, but the distance is—or so he likes to put it—"only one of geography," and the twins call him once a week for a video chat and FaceTime. Watching their blurred hyperactive images, seeing them perform a dance or sing a song from *The Wizard of Oz*, he feels he knows enough about their personalities to predict with some assurance what their interests will consist of and where their talents reside. He himself attended Yale and hopes that Ben or Nancy—or, perhaps, the two of them together—will do so in their turn.

They are nine years old, however; it is too soon to predict. At seventy-five he doubts he will attend their college graduations, but this too is hard to predict. What comes will come, he tells himself, and is beyond his power to influence or forestall. The future does not much concern him; what he dwells on is the past.

His step-daughter and he are estranged. She too is a westerner; she and her partner belong to a woman's collective in Portland. Although he tries to make amends for what he thinks of as her troubled youth, Susan is having none of it; at her mother's funeral she told him childhood was a misery, and when she joined the circus—not as an acrobat but publicist, with a focus on local media outlets—it was to turn her back on bourgeois attitudes and the assumption of ownership. She sports elaborate nose piercings, and her arms have been emblazoned with tattoos.

At times he thinks he should return to Paris, where once he studied "the irrational" in theatre, from Artaud to Genet. Later, he had written on Racine, Corneille, and Voltaire. The eighteen-hundreds were a period in which it had seemed possible that reason could prevail. But even in his daydreams of the Seine and the Sorbonne, he knows relocation is impractical; his doctors and lawyer and accountant all work within a thirty-minute radius of where he lives, and his French is rusty. He would not be welcome abroad.

So he contents himself with puttering about the house, arranging and then rearranging shelves. Like most men with large libraries, he has a personal system for cataloging books: the ones he keeps or plans to donate to the Wellfleet library, the ones he wrote, the ones he still wants to read. Most days he does not make his bed, just pulling up the sheets and blankets and then reversing the process when he takes a nap or reads himself to sleep. Most evenings he will eat at home, having poured a cocktail or two glasses of red wine. Ten years ago he and his wife installed a first-rate audio system, and often he listens to music: the Beethoven sonatas and Bach cantatas she loved. That he needs to find a project is, he thinks, clear, but he wants it to be worthy of his skills.

This self-protective self-regard is new. His was a small reputation, if solid, and his lectures had been well-attended and, when published, praised. He has a few friends on the Cape, and from time to time entertains them, or is entertained. But when he joins them in a restaurant or at a cocktail party he's shocked by their bent backs and white or thin or absent hair, and the illusion of continued youth is simpler to maintain alone. He shaves every two or three days but otherwise avoids the mirror; it shows him an old man he would prefer not to see.

On Father's Day his son in San Diego sends a gift certificate from a nursery in Orleans. Tim has become a partner in a law firm, and the gift is generous: one thousand dollars' worth of plantings—for shrubs and trees and perennials—delivery included. It had been, he senses, his daughter-in-law's idea; she is the attentive one, and her belief in "family" is strong. That they should live three thousand miles apart, on separate coasts, is something she laments and urges him to change, but the professor feels no need to uproot himself and make California home.

Also included has been the cost of planting, and the "expert advice of our staff." This is the phrase the gift-coupon proclaims, and when he calls to inquire if they are open on Monday—when the traffic is less bothersome and Route 6 less crowded—the woman at "Cultivate Your Garden" suggests he should come down. "Ask for Maisie," she tells him.

He does.

Maisie is a short, plump woman in late middle age; her hair has been hennaed bright red. She tends the cash register in a building stocked with garden tools, bird houses and bird-feeders and bags of fertilizer and grass seed. There are wooden carved orioles and cardinals and calendars of birds and welcome mats that say "Humus, Sweet Humus" or "Dew Drop Inn." A plastic owl presides over a rack of seeds. One whole wall proclaims itself "Organic," and there are gloves and bug-sprays and rabbit-repellents and a sign that reads: "Nature is (y)our friend!"

"How may we help you?" she asks.

"I live in Wellfleet."

"Yes?"

"Looking down over the harbor."

"That's nice," says Maisie, shutting the register and appraising him more closely.

"And it's sandy soil."

She smiles. Her teeth are dentures, protruding. "Most of the cape is sandy ..."

"But I have this gift certificate ..."

He offers it, and when she scans the amount she grows more respectful and calls him by his name. "You're here for advice, am I right?"

"And to buy things."

"Welcome to the nursery. We'll do our best, sir, I promise. You haven't been here before?"

"I think my wife used to," he says. "Be a customer, I mean."

"Let's see if we have you in our system."

"System?"

Consulting the gift certificate, she types in his name on a computer, then asks for and enters his telephone number and Ellen's name, but finds nothing listed and says, apologetically, "We updated two years ago. Maybe it was before that?"

He nods. "She was the gardener."

"You'll want advice from one of our consultants," says Maisie. "Wayne, do you have a minute?"

A man with a green shirt and matching pants approaches, smiling. He is tall and muscular; his forearms—the sleeves are rolled up—show coiled yellow hair. He wears calf-high rubber boots; his name has been stitched on his shirt. They shake hands, and when they do so the professor winces; Wayne did not mean to hurt him, but his grip is strong.

The two men move outside. The gardener discourses on the plants and trees and shrubs for sale, and which would seem appropriate for, as he puts it, "your needs." He has, the professor wants to say, no "needs"; he has a thousand dollars to spend, and can distinguish between an azalea and a rhododendron, a tulip and a rose. But that's about the extent of his horticultural knowledge, and the reason he has come to "Cultivate Your Garden" is to deploy some other someone's expertise, not to demonstrate his own.

They continue down the rows. In the June sun—Wayne dons a wide-brimmed battered straw hat—they walk past pots of conifers and ornamental trees. Some feature berries or blossoms, some will grow large, some furnish ground cover or require extensive watering. In each instance the salesman consults a clipboard he carries and reads off the Latin as well as colloquial name—pronouncing the former with relish—before he announces the price.

The professor is slow to decide, aware of his own ignorance and untutored taste. There are other customers and additional "consultants" in the middle distance. Some push shopping carts. At this early stage of the summer, business is brisk. The client says he wants a yard with minimal tending, not fussy plants or ones that need a lot of water. The gardener nods, taking notes. Pulling a plastic water bottle from his pocket, he drinks.

Then, standing by the overhang of the greenhouse in welcome shade, smiling, in his sing-song high-pitched voice Wayne talks. He embarks on what sounds like a pre-arranged speech, and does so at length. You might want to know our purpose, our *mission*, he says, and what we plan to do. It's the age-old question, isn't it: "Where am I going and where do I come from and what am I doing while here?" Wayne says he was born and raised in Utah and had never seen the water, but when he was twenty-three he drove east on his honeymoon, since his wife's family settled in Chatham way back when, and she wanted to see where they were buried in the early 1800s and they never left. *We* never left, I mean to say, her people went out west and stayed, but the two of us came back. We fell in love with water, he continues, which is a precious resource; the aquifers are overused, they're being drained and polluted, and so he understands totally, totally, why all planting should be local and each species uninvasive, and though he himself, if he may say so, is an example of the adaptation of the species—why should a Mormon from the desert feel so much at home in New England?—it's better to stay cognizant of what best flourishes where. Furthermore he applies this, he might as well call it, *philosophy* to the rearing of families also: we're God's creatures, aren't we, says Wayne, and it doesn't matter if we're animal or mineral or—he waves his thick arm—vegetable, we all deserve to grow.

A site-visit, the salesman concludes, would be useful. "Will tomorrow suit?"

"Why not?"

"I'm up your way anyhow tomorrow afternoon. There's a lady in Wellfleet I read to."

"Read to?"

He spreads his hands. "She's blind."

"That's good of you."

Wayne's face is red; his neck glistens with sweat. His voice is mild and breathy, ill paired with a man of such muscle and bulk. "I wouldn't say that," he says. "It's just a service."

"Still ..."

Then he says something unexpected. "Home visits like the ones I make—I do them every day. This afternoon it's Eastham and a quadriplegic. What Christians call 'an act of charity.' And Jewish people call a *mitzvah*. For me, it's a proud service to perform."

It grows hot in the noon sun. Church bells ring. The gardener elaborates his story, discoursing on the benefits of service, the way value given is value received, describing why he and his bride on their honeymoon chose this particular part of the Cape, and don't tire of it, ever, just the smell invigorates.

The professor sniffs.

"Can you *smell* it?" Wayne prompts him. "The sea? The everlasting ocean and, just down the road, the bay ..."

On Route 6, a car radio blares, its beat loud. A backhoe labors past, its bucket filled with mulch. Wayne talks about his own tin ear yet abiding love of music, how all their children sing in the choir and every single one of them plays an instrument—the piano, the fiddle, the flute, and the harp—at home.

"We have seven little ones." Wiping his face with the palm of his hand, he leaves a dirt-smear on his cheek. "But four come from Addis Ababa. We went to an orphanage there. The wife and I home-school them, which is—you'll understand—a *mitzvah*, although I won't pretend the day has minutes or hours enough, so it isn't a burden to read to a blind lady, and I'd be happy—honored, really—to pass by your garden tomorrow and see what's best to plant."

"You'd be welcome."

"Four o'clock? Expect me, sir."

"I will."

The professor understands he has been a customer and the salesman's chatter practiced. Against his better judgment, however, he finds himself impressed. There is something persuasive about Wayne's seeming-sweetness and daily round of assistance and missionary zeal. To serve with such enthusiasm is to have a calling, and it does feel rare.

Yet part of the encounter rankles, and he tries to put his finger on what troubles him. Is it the reference to old established families in Chatham, the assumption of his Jewishness and use of the word *mitzvah*, the trip to Ethiopia in order to adopt? Is it the incongruity of the gardener's size and dirt-soiled clothes with his gentle tending of orphans and old ladies; is it the smell of his sweat? Is it, perhaps, that he himself feels added to the list of charitable visits—an additional soul to redeem?

He has grown weary, listening, and standing in bright heat. They confirm a site visit for four o'clock tomorrow and, having repeated his address and said goodbye to Maisie who is passing through the courtyard with an empty watering can and holding a pot of New Zealand Impatiens, the professor leaves.

"Goodbye," says Wayne. "My blessings on your plot of ground."

"Till tomorrow, then."

"Amen."

Ring Around the Rosy

Rosalie Smithson turned eighty-five. All such occasions were honored by the family, but this one carried special weight, the first that she would celebrate without her husband at her side. Jack had died in June. They had been married for sixty-one years, and by now the Smithson clan—five children, nine grandchildren, two great-grandchildren and counting—bulked large. There were assorted in-laws also, and in Philip's case a redheaded girlfriend who would—or so he had assured his mother—become his second wife.

They gathered at the house. It was September 27th, and the leaves were turning; as Margaret observed to Alice, there was "a chill in the air." This far north the fall came early; maple leaves were on the lawn, and the summer people had by and large gone home. Around Lake Sunapee in August there might be nose-to-nose traffic, and the roar of motorboats precluded easy conversation; today the late arrivals could park cars in the road.

Jackson Jr. had done so; he always came late. "But that's all right," his mother said. "You can set your clock by him. Except you have to set it an hour or two early; that way he comes on time." She had, it seemed to strangers, a special fondness for Jackson—but then she had a special fondness also for his brother Philip and for the three girls: Margaret, Alice, and baby Jane. This was the birth order—two sons, and then three daughters, with fifteen years between them, so Jackson and Jane almost seemed to belong to separate generations. By the time the final child was born, the oldest wanted to be left alone and on his adolescent own; the middle siblings too were busy with their own pursuits, so Rosalie and her youngest formed a tribe within the tribe.

Jane was beautiful. The others in the family were fit, and in their ways attractive, but Jane was a head-turner and had been so since the start. As a baby, her profuse blonde curls would elicit praise from passersby; as a teenager her legs and breasts were the envy of her cohort, and by the time she met and married Jonathan she'd left a trail of suitors in her wake. This was all the more compelling since she did not seem to notice, as though she took beauty for granted and set little store by it, spending less time in front of the mirror than either of her sisters and wearing hand-me-downs without complaint: a Cinderella who was certain to attract her prince.

Margaret and Alice were not, of course, step-sisters; neither were they wicked, but it was hard to consider the Smithson clan without an overlay of fairy-tale. They seemed, to strangers, notable and an occasion for envy. The house on the lake—with its wide pine floors and peeling white paint on the clapboards, its dark green shutters and four brick chimneys and slate roof from a nearby quarry—seemed the very definition of New England's storied sturdiness. It had been built to last.

The family name was an old one: Smithsons landed in America just after the ships bearing Pilgrims, and though their fortunes had declined there was some money left. Jack's ancestors owned textile mills, and two of them represented New Hampshire in Congress. His grandfather had been a general in what would later on be called The Civil War. Although the mills went bankrupt and the Smithsons' social prominence declined, they felt themselves—without ever quite insisting on it—entitled to respect. In town hall their complaints were heard; and their suggestions listened to; at concerts they sat in a row of named brass-plated seats. Proper consideration was what Rosalie Amelia *née* Hatch Smithson expected, in church or at the bank. Her manners were as gracious and old-fashioned as the word *consideration* itself.

By now she was legally blind. The children had hired a driver to ferry their mother on errands, or deliver her to Providence and Boston where they lived. Outlier Jane and Jonathan and their two sons had moved to Colorado, but the other four siblings were settled within easy driving distance of Lake Sunapee, and made the journey often. It was the homestead, the family manse, the place where they stored high school and college diplomas, old photograph albums and sweaters and skis. It was where they'd learned to sail, to drive, to plant gardens and catch fish and shoot.

Jane called her mother daily, to inquire how Rosalie was feeling and to hear her voice. Always, the talk seemed inconsequential; always it meant a great deal. They discussed the plans they'd made, the meals they'd had or were planning to eat, the weather, the grandchildren, health. "How are you feeling?" Jane would ask, and her mother would answer "Tip-top."

"I'm glad to hear it. Really?"

"How are *you* feeling, sweetheart?" Rosalie felt closest to her final child, for Jane had been a late surprise, the result of a romantic hike she and Jack took one spring day at dusk.

"Fine. Getting ready to pack up the boys. It seems so far away—college."

"I miss you."

"I miss *you*. We all do, mom."

Then Rosalie would list her complaints: the trouble with the kitchen door, the trouble with sciatica, the apple cider that went sour after just one week. But her list of concerns was never a long one, and Jane paid attention. When the women bade farewell, they said "Love," and kissed the air.

Mid-afternoon the family arrived. The morning had been wet and gray, but soon the west wind brought its fabled clarity, and the house and lawns were bathed in light; whitecaps furled like liquid banners on the lake. The five children and four in-laws and Philip's redheaded girlfriend, the grandchildren, (two sets of twins, one of them identical and one fraternal) and Oliver, the toddler, and the girls Maisie and Clara—but not Irene, who was in Aix-en-Provence on her junior year fall semester, or Garrett, now in India—came in. "Hello, hell-*o*" they called to each other. "Let the wild rumpus begin!"

Their father had been born here, as had his father before. What admiring strangers might label "antiques" were, to the Smithsons' way of thinking, just tables and bureaus and chairs. The floors were strewn with Persian carpets, no matter how faded or worn. Rosalie had trouble walking; her ankles—which her husband once described as "achingly thin," intending a compliment—both had broken. She had taken two serious falls and used a cane or walker and an ancient wooden wheelchair to navigate the house. She slept behind the kitchen now, in what had been the maid's room, and therefore avoided the stairs.

Jackson drove a pick-up truck and Alice and Philip had Subarus. Margaret's husband, Michael, drove a Lexus hybrid; Jonathan and Jane had rented a car at the airport, collecting their two sons and spending the night in Amherst. Maisie and Clara arrived together in Clara's Morris Minor. By five o'clock the rooms were full of traffic and laughter and shouting, the ruckus of arrival and who would claim which space. The children used their childhood rooms, the grandchildren slept in the attic—long since converted into a kind of dormitory—and the in-laws and redheaded girlfriend made do with pull-out sofas or narrow trundle beds. Jackson, Philip, Margaret, and Alice were feeling both happy and solemn to have gathered once more at the house. Here was where they planned to celebrate and where they had the subject of their mother's future to discuss.

"How *are* you, Mom?" they asked in turn.

"I can't complain."

"Of course you can," said Jackson, who had inherited his father's blunt declarative speech, as well as his prognathous jaw and light blue eyes. "Complain away."

"It's your birthday," Philip said. "And you're entitled."

"Tell us what's been bothering you. If there's anything bothering you," said Alice.

They turned to their mother, expectant. Unfocused, she smiled at the room. Each piece of furniture or oil portrait on the stairwell wall retained its chosen place. A caretaker couple—Bill and Alice Lawrence—would stop by daily to cook and clean up, and she was rarely lonely for anyone but Jack. The last of her Golden Retrievers—Mr. Chips the Third—had been put down by the vet two years before, and she'd not had the heart or energy to raise another puppy. Still, his leash and collar hung on a nail by the door.

"I'm glad you've come," said Rosalie. "I'm so grateful everybody's here."

"To absent friends," said Philip, and they all knew whom he meant.

"Complain away," Jackson repeated. "You're entitled, mom." He raised his whiskey glass.

"It isn't fair. It's not the way"—Alice turned to her third husband, Tom—"these stories are supposed to end."

"How? 'Happily ever after?'" Jane inquired. "Is that how it's supposed to be?"

Jonathan put his hand on hers, and his elegant consort subsided.

"My stars, but what's the point of it?" asked Rosalie of those gathered together in the large living room. "Let's not everybody get their knickers in a twist . . ."

The wallpaper had faded but the patterned yellow roses climbing on white trellises gleamed in the last light.

"The point of what?" asked Jackson.

"Complaining." Again, their mother smiled at the room. "There's nothing to be done."

"That's what we want to talk about," said Alice. It was her cue, though she and Margaret and her brothers had expected it to take longer to perform their intervention; they had planned to raise the subject only after cake and ice cream. "We need to discuss what to do."

Now it was Margaret's turn. "You've taken two falls and the house is too big. You can't spend the winter alone."

"Why not?"

"You've never done so," Philip said. "There were always two of you."

"Don't remind me," said the birthday girl. She was wearing a conical hat and a paper necklace proclaiming *85 & Counting*. "Does anybody think I need to be reminded?"

Jane offered consolation. "We miss him too. Of course we do. It's hard to be here in the house without Dad at the head of the table."

"It is," the others chorused, and their mother said, again, "There's nothing to be done."

"You're wrong," said Jackson Jr.

"Excuse me?"

"There's something we've been discussing. Something we think you should do."

The grandchildren were enlisted. Kate and Kyle, the fraternal twins, had turned fourteen, and they declared without prompting how much they *wished* their mee-ma would come live nearer them. Elizabeth, sixteen, pitched in. "Please, oh *please*," she said. The children, said their parents, all love it here in summertime, but it's too isolated in winter, and remember how last year the furnace broke and took three days to be repaired? None of us want to think about you living alone at the end of this long driveway, iced in, and relying on the town to plow you out. It was one thing to be here with Dad, the two of you together, but it's very different not to have a second person in the house if anything goes wrong. And in a house this old, of course, something always does go wrong . . .

Over lamb stew and green beans and boiled potatoes and salad and cheese they each adduced their reasons, but Rosalie was adamant. Emptying her glass of white wine she looked around the table. "I'm touched by your concern," she said, "but to my way of thinking this is where I've lived my life and where I want to die."

"We're not talking death," said Jackson.

"Nobody believes you'll die," said Philip. "Death's not what we're talking about."

"Just that we don't think," Margaret persisted, "you ought to be here by yourself. It's not"—she hunted the word—"appropriate, *convenient*, and we can't always guarantee we'll be in a position to help."

Jane disagreed. "Let's not talk about convenience. Whatever feels best for you, mom."

"Miss Goody two-shoes." Jackson turned on her. "*You're* not the one who gets the call in Denver, or wherever."

"Colorado Springs," she said.

"I don't need reminding, I've been there, remember? The Garden of the Gods. All those gigantic rocks, and the Air Force Academy, all those college-kids and dyed-in-the-wool conservatives inhabiting their separate worlds, the Republicans and radicals, and you and Jonathan decamped to your treehouse where you can see for miles and miles, but not what's going on or going down right *here*."

Jonathan Herwitz was Jewish, and though none of the Smithsons declared as much, he and his wife seemed somehow therefore alien. This was what Jackson meant by "separate worlds" and what he couldn't quite forgive: the sheep strayed from the fold. Though Jane herself did not convert, they sent their sons to Temple, and both Daniel and Evan had been bar-mitzvahed. Further, Jonathan's work for the space industry was too highly classified for their brother-in-law to discuss.

It rankled. "Why should he be keeping secrets?" Margaret asked Alice. "Why are they so secretive?"

"You don't want to know," said Alice. "Or, anyhow, that's what I tell myself. I couldn't care less what he's doing or about his lordship's self-importance. Our Johnny-come-lately," she sniffed.

By this she meant, in truth, that his parents had been refugees from

Lithuania, and she did not trust his expertise or his security clearance, which felt like an affront. A wedge had been driven between the three sisters by this Jewish stranger and how he beguiled Jane and took her away. Their life in Colorado was not easy to forgive.

Yet the Smithson clan abided by rules, and two of their rules were: *No one gets up angry from the dinner table* and *Nobody drives home drunk*. It fell to the mother to keep the peace.

"I'll think about it," Rosalie said.

"Please do," the family chorused, and sang "Happy Birthday" and cut the birthday cake.

For the next weeks she thought about it, or, rather, attempted to have an opinion on the topic her children had raised. She knew what they were asking, and as the days grew shorter and the nights grew colder their proposal made some sense. Her caretaker couple brought groceries, and at her urging might remain for tea, or even a game of canasta, but her company was Judy Woodruff on the nightly news, and then a series of dark-haired men and women whose rapid rate of utterance was difficult to follow. These commentators seemed to Rosalie outraged, incensed at what was happening in Washington; they repeated on a nightly basis that President Trump's behavior was little short of scandalous; the rules of good behavior and truth-telling and plain common decency had been broken, perhaps irrevocably, and would be hard, perhaps impossible, in her lifetime to restore.

This troubled her. If there was anything to be thankful for in the awful new reality of her husband's absence, it was that he escaped from this, had never known and would not know how far his dear republic (or, for that matter, his dear Republican Party) had fallen from its once-high standard of comity and trust. There was a term, she knew, from the Roman playwright Plautus, *Miles Gloriosus*, and she retained sufficient Latin to know it meant, "Braggart Warrior," for that was who Trump was. He could not be trusted, she knew. He had no sense of comity or probity or any of the qualities that Jack so valued all his life, and stood for at the bank. The President boasted that not paying taxes showed the world how smart he was; he cheated people routinely, sued when they complained. He was a liar and philanderer who had been married three times, then cheated on each of his wives. These women suffered at his hands, though no doubt they also grew rich. His children all were crooks, but when Rosalie found herself thinking about the President and his children and braggadocio and crookedness, she knew she was changing the subject from the one her own children proposed: where to weather the winter now soon to arrive and in what manner to live.

She loved her house. She wore it like an old frayed cardigan or shawl thrown down on the living room couch. Without the slightest hesitation, she knew which knife was in the drawer and where her knife-block was on the counter. She knew which plate would be required for her evening repast and where the *Anthology of Roman Plays* or the book on the care and feeding of goats had been positioned on the study shelf—although with her now-failing eyesight she could no longer read. The Lawrences would do so at her urging, sounding out articles in the local paper or telling her which envelopes were personal and required a response.

Often she listened to audiobooks, headphones disarranging her hair. When Jack had first invited her to meet and visit with his family, and they drove up to Sunapee on a bright May morning, she understood on the instant, somehow, that this was where she'd live her life and where she hoped to die. It had not been explicit—*This is where I'll live my life and where I hope to die*—but long years later, looking back, Rosalie knew she had known.

Therefore through the month of October, and then for the month of November, she tried to imagine departure. The trees went bare, the frost grew thick, the furnace hummed continually and the first snows fell. She listened to music in the daytime and watched, at night, the nightly news; she mourned the loss of an old birch tree by the water's edge that came crashing down one afternoon with no apparent warning. When Ed Lawrence cut it up, however, he said the root structure was too shallow, and she should thank her lucky stars the tree fell away from and not onto the roof of the house.

She did; she thanked her lucky stars and did not tell the children about the fallen birch. Though she no longer prayed at night, Rosalie beguiled herself with memories: Jackson on the riding mower, learning to steer on his proud father's lap, Margaret and Alice in the school chorus singing "Oklahoma," Philip in the Boston Whaler in a life-preserver twice his size, and Jane wearing tights and ballet slippers in her ballet class. The family played checkers; the family played basketball and chess.

In her own childhood there had been a game she taught her children and, thereafter, grandchildren: "Ring Around the Rosy." In the dance and song each player circled, holding hands and chanting till the final line: "Ashes, Ashes, all fall down!" Jack's death had been an easy one, and that too was a blessing; one afternoon she asked him if he'd mind going up to the road for the mail, and when he made no answer she repeated the request; then, when she tried to rouse him from his nap it had not been a nap.

"Darling?"

He did not snore, not breathe.

"Jackson? *Jack?*"

He remained in his chair.

She had called the Lawrences and then called 911. It was too late. When the people from the Funeral Home arrived, she watched them lift him—that large man—as though he were weightless, then straighten his stiffening legs. They closed Jack's open eyes. They arranged him on a stretcher, then covered him with a dark green sheet. The French doors had been open, since it was a warm spring day, and those were the doors they elected to use. She watched them—two dark bulky shapes—convey the body carefully into the open air.

It would be hard to leave. She had retained her husband's chair but did not sit in it; it still bulked by the fireplace, with its upholstered armrests and horsehair pillow and tattered brocade; it was his favorite piece of furniture and empty ever since June.

On Thanksgiving the clan reassembled. Jane and Jonathan again flew in from Denver, collecting their twins, and the rest of them (absent Irene and Garrett, who remained abroad) drove to the house. Rosalie had made arrangements with the local caterers—a couple down from Montreal who provided what they called *Bistro Bis*—to cook for the family party. But the children would not hear of it—or, rather, they accepted only side dishes and *hors d'oeuvres variées*, since from time out of mind they themselves had helped their mother make the meal. Alice brought pies and Margaret carried in a set of vegan dishes for her children who were now vegan, and Philip brought two smoked turkeys from a farm outside of Lexington he swore raised the best turkeys in New England. His redheaded girlfriend, however, was no longer part of the party. When she inquired, of Philip, why the girl (what *was* her name? Rosalie attempted to remember, and could not) was elsewhere, he shrugged and said, "You know."

She did not know. The table had been set with china and silver and linen napkins and crystal glasses, as had always been the case. She placed Oliver the two year old in his high-chair at the far end of the dining table, with his mother next to him; the others took their seats on a "first-come-first serve" basis, since she no longer provided place-cards or managed a seating arrangement. In her husband's absence, and as the oldest person at the feast, she tried but could not bring herself to offer the first toast.

"Happy Thanksgiving," said Jane.

"Happy Thanksgiving to all of us," said Jackson Jr.

Jack's chair remained unoccupied, and when Philip said, "To absent friends," the others raised their glasses in the direction of the fireplace and pronounced, in unison, "Rest in Peace."

"We have so much to be thankful for," said Margaret.

"It was his favorite holiday, always."

"Yes," said Rosalie. "Your father disliked the way the world gets gussied up for Christmas and for Easter, even the Fourth of July and, lately, Halloween. But this one's not commercial, it's still a family occasion, and we're all of us—well, most of us—together."

"So, mom," said Jackson, "let's get to the point. We've found a place in Providence we think you'll enjoy for the winter. It's got a lovely dining room and you could have a small apartment where you can have your furniture and come and go whenever you want. Also, it's just around the corner from us, full of retired Brown professors, not a mile away from Benefit Street . . ."

"What are you suggesting?"

"We talked about it," Philip said. "You can't stay here this winter, remember?"

"I remember. But did I agree?"

"She never said she'd leave," said Jane. "She said she'd think about it."

Swallowing, Rosalie understood how little she could understand what her children and grandchildren wanted. There had been a time, perhaps, when what mattered to the Smithson clan had mattered elsewhere also, but now was no longer that time. The nation's fate was nothing she could conjure with beyond her own small part in it; the family's behavior was no longer hers to control. Now what she hoped for, only, was to keep the peace. Yet peace was hard to keep.

"I'd like to come back on Sunday," said Jackson. "And I'll do the packing and we'll settle you in Providence at your new winter home. They call it Patchin' Place."

"Isn't that where e. e. cummings lived?" asked Elizabeth, who had read the poet in tenth grade, the year before.

"Yup," said her mother, Margaret. "But more than one place can have the same name, Lizzie, and the Patchin' Place he lived in was New York. In Greenwich Village . . ."

"His people lived not far from here," mused Rosalie. "On Silver Lake. They had a place they called 'Joy Farm.' I believe that he was happy there."

"Who?"

"Edward Estlin Cummings. He called himself e. e."

"So," asked Philip. "Can we call it settled?"

Alice said, "I think you'll enjoy it there, mom."

But that night it was not settled, and she could not fall asleep. She understood that her children and grandchildren wished the best for her, but their idea of what she needed was not her own. She was willing to continue, not as yet ready for change. This "Patch Inn Place," or whatever it was, would be full of chatty strangers, the old and bald and palsied she would need to learn to recognize and, at mealtimes, greet. Rosalie knew Providence, a little, and two of the family lived there, but it had never been home.

In the watches of the night she told herself, or tried to, that her husband would abide with her wherever she traveled, yet when she tried to picture Jack beside her in a new strange place he evanesced. She reached out to take his arm, but he was incorporeal, and she could not hold it or hold onto it, half-dreaming. What she held instead were knotted bedsheets and a pillow, so that when she roused she roused to solitude, the ticking clock, the curtains rubbing up against the windowpane and rustling in the puffs of heat the furnace labored noisily to send.

Her cheeks were wet. Her heart, she felt, would crack. What does it mean, she asked herself, to have a heart that cracks, and why should she be feeling sorry for herself when so many of her children and grandchildren were doing what they could to make her feel less sorry and alone? In her dream she had been sailing in Jack's cat-boat, and they had packed a picnic and the sun was bright on the dark lake and he had proposed to her by putting a ring on her finger while she was holding the tiller. She did not need to tell him "Yes" because he could see by the tears in her eyes that she was thinking, *Yes, Yes, Yes,* but she told him anyhow, and he said "That's my girl."

In the morning, early, she wheeled herself into the kitchen in order to make coffee, but the coffee was brewing already, and she knew that who was brewing it must be her daughter Jane.

"Hi, Mom," said her visitor, "how did you sleep?"

"You're up early," Rosalie answered, not wanting to admit that she had had a difficult night, and Jane said, "Not so early; it's two hours later here."

"But doesn't that mean," she wanted to ask, "that six o'clock is four o'clock? What are you doing at four o'clock?"

She refrained from asking this, however, since possibly she'd got it wrong, and Denver was two hours later so that six o'clock was eight o'clock and well past time to be wakeful. In any case, in either case, her daughter was wearing a terrycloth robe and the coffee-aroma was strong.

"Are you ready for breakfast?" Jane asked.

"By all means . . . ."

Yet she felt uncertain, a little, since it was clear her darling had trouble sleeping too and was wide awake. Rosalie remembered now; it was two hours earlier in Colorado, not later, and therefore, to a traveler, the time of six o'clock was four o'clock not eight. Jane poured hot coffee in her chosen cup and, without asking, added just the right amount of cream and the two lumps of sugar Rosalie preferred. The girl was radiant this morning with her own essential radiance, and she pared and sliced an apple and also quartered a pear. They ate the fruit. The two of them sat unspeaking at the kitchen table, the way they'd done long years before, when Jane had been the only child remaining in the house: a companionable silence like the one they used to share. Then, when they could hear the sounds of others stirring in the rooms above, her daughter took her hand and said, "Come back with us."

"What?"

"Come back with us."

"Who's us?"

"With me and Jonathan. To Colorado Springs."

"Excuse me?"

"The boys are both in college and it's lonely in the house. We'll drop Danny and Evan at school, then fly home. There's heaps of room."

"I'll think about it," she started to say, but that had been her evasion when others in the family had asked her to move to Patchin' Place. Then Rosalie had played for time, had—what was the word?—*temporized.* This invitation was different, however: this was her youngest, her darling, who wanted to take care of her in Colorado in her own family's home. "Isn't it too much to ask of Jonathan?"

"He would be happy if you came, Mom. We want you with us. We've discussed this."

"You mean it?"

"Yes. I wouldn't ask you otherwise."

"But what about the others? Their plan, I mean, to move me to Providence?"

"They won't be happy," Jane said. "When I proposed Colorado, they were dead set against letting you live that far away. We may have to keep it a secret."

Rosalie savored her coffee—sweet, not too hot—and, swallowing, tasted the reward of it: thick pleasure in her throat.

Her children filled the kitchen. There was traffic and laughter and shouting, as had been the case before, but now she had a secret, a plan shared with Jane and silent Jonathan, not something to discuss. Jackson and Judy and the kids had packed already, and stowed their bags in the pick-up, and he said he'd be back on Sunday morning to collect Rosalie's luggage and personal effects. Philip too was quick to go, explaining he had a business lunch with his senior partner in Cambridge. "What kind of man schedules a business meeting the day after Thanksgiving?" he asked, but did not await an answer. "I'll tell you. A *sadist*, that's who."

Margaret and Alice and their husbands and children and grand-children departed turn by turn. By noon the house was empty, except for Jane and Jonathan and their two sons. Now Jane commenced to pack her mother's things, reminding her it could be cold in Colorado also and asking which dresses and sweaters and datebooks and necklaces and medicines she wished to bring along. Daniel and Evan deposited her suitcases and walker in the rental car's large trunk and the three men fastened the shutters and made sure the fireplace ash was cold and turned off the hot water and turned the furnace down.

"The Lawrences will do this," Rosalie protested, and Jane said, "Yes, but I gave them the weekend off after Thanksgiving, and we don't want to disturb them or have anyone sound the alarm."

"You make it seem so . . . so *clandestine*."

"It took some doing, mom, but Jonathan got you a ticket to fly with us—not all that easy this weekend. He found out who to call."

"I'm grateful," said Rosalie.

"No, you needn't be. But I do need to be certain this is what you want to do. Because there'll be hard feelings . . ."

"I can't imagine why."

But later, in the car, riding in the passenger seat up front with Jonathan, while Jane and the twins sat behind her, she *could* imagine why. She had decamped without a word of warning to her other progeny, and even though they'd urged Rosalie to leave the manse they had not wanted her in Colorado, all those miles away. The children should be glad, she told herself, their mother would live in a private house and not some sort of Patchin' Place with the name of a New York City alley it would in no way resemble. "Such an adventure," she breathed. The Cummings family, she knew, had summered on Silver Lake, and Jack in his youth had known the old poet and said he had been quarrelsome and an anti-Semite. This was not something she wished to discuss with Jane and Jonathan, however, for if she was their captive she would be a willing captive and happy to escape.

As happened to her often now, Rosalie half-closed her eyes and felt her husband at her side, approving what she decided to do and coming along for the ride. He rested his hand on her arm. He said, though in silence, "Good girl, it's just the trick."

The boys were both freshmen at Amherst, and as they barreled down the Interstate she tried to ask them questions. She tried to remember which questions to ask. What did they like and dislike about their time in college; what subjects were they studying or would they plan to major in; when would they have to choose? Did the school prefer to keep twins separate, or did they have a policy allowing the pair to stay together in a shared dormitory space; what were their roommates' names? How did it feel to be, for the first time, living far away from home; had they made any new friends?

Daniel and Evan answered politely, but she could not hear their answers since the car's heater hummed. Nor, to be wholly truthful, was Rosalie certain she'd inquired out loud as to courses and the names of their roommates and friends; she might have been thinking not voicing these questions, for the voice in her head was not easy to hear, a whisper like that of the heater or windshield wipers slapping back and forth and forth and back in the sudden squall of rain. Jane too was difficult to hear, a voice in her ear asking how do you feel, and telling her the flight would be a long one, since they had to change planes in Chicago, but they'd all be home by midnight and her bed had been prepared. The passenger—she was not, she reassured herself, a prisoner, a captive—allowed herself to drift, a little, and to close her eyes, because the car was warm and the hum of the roadway beneath her was somehow both busy and tranquil, a *ratatat-tat* of the tires on potholes and bumps. The wipers too were busy yet tranquil, and Jonathan was a good driver, and she told him so, or thought she did, and he smiled and nodded "Thank you," or so she believed, turning the heater down. The fairy tale had ended; the happy dream was done.

Still, her son-in-law's dark sharp-nosed profile was a comfort; so was Jane's hand at her neck. So were the twins behind her, and the music they were playing on what they called their iPods, and the dark verge of the road. It would be, she understood, a challenge, since Jackson, Philip, Margaret, and Alice would feel disregarded and even, possibly, aggrieved. On Sunday when Jackson Jr. returned to the house she would not be waiting for him; she would instead be sharing fruit and coffee, perhaps a breakfast biscuit—it would be two hours earlier—with her devoted daughter, not strangers in an Old Age Home. She would have to explain to the others how she hadn't meant to hurt or deny or deceive them but after due consideration could not accept their plan.

The day was growing dark. Soon enough it would be dark enough for headlights to be needed and Rosalie closed her eyes. She would not die in her home. She dreamed this wheeled conveyance was the Lincoln Continental she bought for Jack for his forty-ninth birthday, when he became Bank President.

"You shouldn't have," he said.

"Oh, darling, you deserve it."

"No one deserves a car like this," he said, running his hand along the fenders and down the gleaming grill. Yet she had been certain her husband was happy—elated, even—and grateful for the gift. He very much deserved the car, along with every honor accrued in his life; a modest man who folded himself to the seat by her side with neither fuss nor bother, coming gladly along for the ride. On their anniversary he always gave her roses, saying "A posy for my Rosie," and with as many roses as the years they had been married: first a single bud, then two then ten, then twenty-five and counting until the final year and sixty-first red rose. She knew and had known she was drifting, was letting the present be part of the past, since almost everything was past for her—including, Rosalie was sure, the future, the house perched on a rock outcropping with its sliding doors and plate-glass windows and a distant down-facing vista of the Garden of the Gods, where the great boulders loomed.

She woke when the boys clattered off. Jane explained that they were late for the plane, or not so much late as on a tight schedule, and therefore they would bid farewell to Daniel and Evan down here at the dormitory door. She did; she bade farewell.

Orpheus and Eurydice

I

His father was both powerful and rich. He had made a fortune in the music business, back when it was possible to be a "player" in the music world, and men like Sting and Elton John relied on him for counsel. The women were harder to work with, since his father slept with them, although crossover stars like Joni Mitchell and Patti Smith could side-step his romancing and nonetheless succeed. In any case, he told his son, he preferred the softer ones: the moving mattress of their bodies should never be rail-thin.

His mother was an absent presence—often away at a luxury spa or, later, Zen retreat. She was statuesque and blonde, like his father's young companions, but as she aged she grew less careful about her hair and neck. They lived in Beverly Hills. She had also been a singer, which is how his parents met, but did not pursue a career.

"What matters," she told Stephen, "is what's *inside* you, darling, and that music you've been hearing is what you need to listen to, no matter how much noise the world *outside* is making. Shut it out."

He was an only child. But he was rarely lonely, since the household had maids and cooks and gardeners, and often his father's P.A. would spend hours in the studio, dealing with contracts and bills and making telephone calls. Stephen liked to lie down on the carpeted floor, listening to arguments and tracking spoken rhythm: da *dum*, da *dumdumdum*. Before he had the words for them he made up nonsense-songs. Long before his fingers spanned an octave he would spread them on the piano, pounding: *tum*, ta, *tumtumtum*. It made his mother proud.

In school he was a solitary, hearing the music inside his own head and not what the teachers were saying. They would talk about addition and subtraction and later on, The Civil War, or the slogan, "Westward, Ho." But Stephen was hearing Cat Stevens or, later on, Chopin. The melodies and harmonies he listened to compelled him more than speech. It was as though the world he entered was a world of sound not sight, and the ukulele, the guitar, the piano he played gave utterance to language in a way mere language failed to; he could hear it much more clearly than what his teachers said.

For it was *sang*, not *said* throughout his youth; he was always humming, chanting, vocalizing, hearing himself making music and, out of sweet sounds, a tune. His mother made much of him when she was home, nodding and clapping her hands and tapping her heels to the beat. "My little Mozart," she cooed.

His father, less effusive, said, "You're bitten by it, aren't you?"

"What?"

"The bug."

"The bug?"

"That buzzing in your ear."

At times he wondered if in fact there was some sort of animal inside his head, a chirping chirruping presence that drowned out background noise. Or, perhaps, a bird or insect—an *earworm* is what they called it—with a repeated melody that spurred him into song. It was how he saw the world, and seeing was hearing for Stephen: *Da dum, da tumtumtum*.

By the time he turned thirteen he played both piano and guitar with what his teachers called astonishing talent; he had only to hear a melody once, and he would retain it. Too, he had perfect pitch. Stephen learned to read music, then write it, and his notations were clear. He sang in the shower and sauna and the echoing arch of his skull. His parents introduced him to musicians from the agency, and sometimes they let him join their sessions in the studio, nodding and moving their feet to the beat and, if they were women, stroking his cheek and his hair. He was "little Stevie Wonderful," they joked.

For tax purposes, his father moved to Monaco, saying he had had it up to here with Hollywood's idea of performance, and why not leave the rat race before the ship started to sink? He flew back several times a year but stayed for long stretches abroad. His parents' quarrels were therefore less frequent: a silence settled in. With the godlike paternal presence elsewhere, Stephen and his mother lived in the house alone.

In truth they were never wholly alone; she also had friends and companions and men to paint the stairwell and trim the cypress branches and bougainvillea bushes and regulate the swimming pool and take her to St. Barts or, later on, St. Kitts. There were singers from his father's stable who still came by, from time to time, and let him harmonize. By the age of seventeen, he knew that who he hoped to be was a person living with music, *in* music, *for* music, and who would give his life to it when he became a man.

There were distractions, of course: tennis and baseball and girls. There were cars to learn to drive and, in the case of his mother's Mercedes, wreck on a hillside, descending, but the air-bag protected him and he walked away.

All young people think themselves immortal and do not consider peril a harbinger of death. He brushed the accident off. When he closed his eyes he heard the high B-flat of the engine, and the steel drum of the hood collapsing: *pa-pa-pock*. But Stephen abandoned the red crumpled car with a sense of good fortune not trouble; he was a survivor, and his mother was less angry than relieved. Nobody had been hurt.

"I'm sorry, Mom," he said.

"*Sorry?* Is that what you're feeling?"

"I don't know how it happened, but it won't happen again."

And, as he seemed remorseful, his mother said, "Forget about it, darling, the main thing is you're safe."

Since there were sufficient funds, he did not take a job. Instead he spent hours every day with the guitar—a Favilla C-6, then a Martin, then a Fender Stratocaster—and the piano in his parents' living room. When he focused on its keyboard, the world looked black and white. There was much he did not understand or choose to study, but music—classical to start with, at the insistence of his teachers—was the shrine he worshiped at. Stephen listened to Segovia and Eric Clapton and Jimi Hendrix and Julian Bream; he carried their recordings everywhere and fell asleep seeing a sequence—a *processional*—of notes. He went with his mother to concerts, or to cafés and bars by himself. His tousled hair and bright blue eyes made an impression on strangers, as did the length of his fingers, and their agility and strength.

Then language entered in. He began to read the poets and, like a tuning fork, quiver to rhyme; he added Homer and Byron to the list of those he studied, and soon enough he *heard* the language of Dickinson and Ginsberg. Stephen paid attention to the troubadours, believing himself their disciple. It delighted him to know that, in the Province of Albi in the thirteenth century, every imaginable syllabic pattern had been, by the poets, deployed.

Bob Dylan understood this, and so did Leonard Cohen, a pair of "wand'ring minstrels" more authentic than that prince in "The Mikado," who in the operetta dons a costume and travels in disguise. That he could name these names—Homer and Cohen, Byron and Dylan, and the rest—became a form of tribute, and he began to write songs. His rhymes were rudimentary at first—*moon* and *June* and *croon* and *spoon* and, later, *fuck* and *suck*. But they were rhymes, in any case, and he shaped them into stanzas, and when he put the music and language together he felt he had a calling and the calling mattered.

It gave him a reason to live.

> As I walked out one morning
> Down the windswept street
> I thought of you, the dawning
> Glitter in your dark brown eyes, the sweet
> Anticipation of bright
> Daytime, day at night,
> And how the clocks and whistles and bells
> All rang and chimed together, shells
> In a necklace I strung from the sea
> To garland your neck with, to be
> Bedazzled by, ensorcelled by,
> To listen to the tide with you, as I
> Walked out one morning
> Down the windswept street.

She was taking a course on "Paradise Lost," and the Professor was a fiend for it, talking about hermeneutics and making them memorize ten lines a day. He called on them in class. He wore a bowtie, always, and striped shirts with turquoise cufflinks; the stripes' colors and the bowtie changed each session of their seminar. Claire could admire the lectures but found the poem a bore.

"There's no music in it," she complained to Stacey, but Stacey disagreed.

"What about 'with wand'ring steps and slow,'" her roommate asked. "Or 'adamantine chains cast down?'"

"What about them?"

"Don't you find them musical? Don't you admire the rhythm?"

She was willing to agree: once every hundred lines or so the blind bard hit his note. "But the weird politics," said Claire. "What about his politics?"

"Whose? Professor Archibald's?"

"No. Milton's."

They were having coffee after class, and there were buds on the fruit trees, and the grass had greened. It was April 21. The semester neared completion; her term paper was due in a week. They were sitting at an outside table on the edge of College Street.

Claire found it hard to focus on the poet's strategy or the poem's hermeneutics. She and Stacey shared a pair of doughnuts: one powdered and one glazed. Whether God was merciful or merciless did not engage her interest; religion just wasn't her thing.

In any case she liked to argue. "What about that line about Eve, 'And she for God in him'?"

"You can't blame Milton," Stacey said.

"I can blame him," she maintained. "All that forced subservience. All that, 'Yes, massa, No, massa. Whatever you want from me, massa.'"

"You're not serious," her roommate said.

"No. Yes, yes I am."

"We have to remember the reason he wrote. And put those lines in context. It's the seventeenth century, for God's sake."

"You're a disciple, aren't you?"

"Of?"

"Professor Archibald's."

"I like his ties," said Stacey. "And his goatee. I adore the way he adores the poem and calls us 'Miltonists.'"

A boy walked by, wearing sandals and a Los Angeles Angels cap and carrying a guitar. He was tall and thin and beautiful, and when he turned to smile at her his eyes were the bluest eyes Claire ever saw. They stared at each other, unspeaking, and she put down her coffee cup while the boy tipped his cap and walked on.

Her neck went hot, her fingers cold. The cup rattled in its saucer, and the napkin's doughnut-crumbs spilled out onto the table. Something was happening to her, *had* happened to her when he smiled, and later they would joke about it and call it "lust at first sight."

After he rounded the corner, and Claire regained her breath at last, she told her roommate that now she understood it. The poem had made sense.

"What are you talking about?" Stacey asked, and she said, pointing, "'God in him.'"

"You can't be serious."

"I've never been *more* serious. Not ever in my life."

Her life so far, Claire understood, had been unimportant—a childhood and girlhood and young womanhood that mostly was predictable. It had been a maypole dance. Her parents had stayed married and her elder brother and two sisters all were married now as well, and everybody lived in Richmond and expected her to come back home once she was finished with college. Then she would hitch her wagon to the star of someone familiar—a doctor or lawyer or in any case the son of a doctor or lawyer or perhaps a local businessman as long as the party in question was the C.E.O. It was as though the track she ran on was her high-school's oval track: a circuit with white lines and red clay she was supposed to practice on and then remain inside the lane and handle and pass the baton . . .

She wasn't being fair, she knew, but it didn't matter. She would turn twenty-one in a week. Her senior year had been a bore, a series of small freedoms—the chance to share a bottle, for example, or a bed or a joint. In the matter of personal freedom, she had been branching out. The bourbon and branch water that was her father's favorite drink—except on Derby Day when he drank two Mint Juleps—now seemed to her unoriginal, and as an act of rebellion she ordered Cosmopolitans or, in the heat, a Mai-Tai.

But it was difficult to tell when such freedoms turned to duty, and the unexpected behaviors became expected. She was tired in advance of staying in her parents' world; she wanted something new. There was little new under the Charlottesville sun, and what made Claire so restless was how it all seemed foreordained: a job, an engagement, a marriage, and 2.3 children by the time that she turned thirty. There would be a house and garden and white wooden picket fence.

For no reason she could make sense of, the course on Milton mirrored and prefigured this; "man's disobedience, and the fall" of Eve and Adam was just an old sad story with a foreseeable ending, one she wanted to avoid. During her senior year she'd tried on clothes and attitudes that would have shocked her parents, but even such rebellion seemed a little too predictable, like the choice of a Mai-Tai. The track was oval, always, and the lines had been carefully drawn. The lane that Claire was running on was the same width—neither wider nor more narrow—as the lane on either side. At night she dreamed of something new: an underworld, a landscape she'd not known . . .

So, sitting in the coffee shop and watching the boy with the guitar walk past—his long lingering gaze that rested on her, his hair in a tangle and jeans that needed patching—she sensed she'd heard a summons and that she could be free. It made her feel newly special, a renegade within the clan and mistress of her fate. She tried to explain this to Stacey, but Stacey was having none of it and said, "We're not talking original sin."

"We're talking *Eden*," Claire declared, "and what it means to live in it."

"Without a fig leaf?"

"Right."

As if he'd heard her—*heard* her—the boy had turned around. He came walking back and stopped in front of their table and, staring at Claire, eyes unblinking, asked, "Can I join you?"

Wordless, she pointed to a third metal chair. Stacey said, "I'm late for chorus practice. Take my place."

He sat.

> My tongue
> Is young
> My strings are tightly
> Tautly
> Strung
> And my guitar strap hung
> Across my shoulders,

Just so, in the Lydian scale.
Yet all song molders
And is stale
Without you as its subject, love.
The colors
Of this technicolor
And famous overcoat pale.

They slept together that night. A breaking wave of feeling had flung Claire far from shore. The wave was steep and deep. This was not something she had done before—sex with a near-stranger—and it felt both dangerous and safe. She could not bring him to her room, or ask Stacey to remain away, but Stephen had been staying in a guesthouse on the property of one of his mother's old friends. She followed him down the winding path and stood for a moment, collecting herself, before she stepped inside.

The cottage sat at the rear of a garden already in bloom, and the fragrance of blossoms was strong. Fruit trees had begun to flower: cherry and apple and pear. The moon was full. The air was warm. The place was furnished with a table, two chairs and an easel—did it also serve as a painting studio, she wondered?—and a king-size bed.

On that bed they lay down wordless, and it was as though they knew each other, had known each other's desires and needs from the beginning. There was neither hesitation nor uncertainty; there was neither pride nor shame. Of all the men she'd known—and, in truth, there were not many—he was the most familiar, an extension of her body in the space they shared. Of all the women he had known—and, in truth, there had been many—she was the one he marveled at, a fantasy now fact. Theirs was a dream made flesh.

He told her his life's story, and she told him her life's story, and they reveled in the great good luck that brought them here together. Next morning Stephen played his guitar for her, and sang; his voice was strong yet sweet. He played the recorder too. She made them tea and—sitting naked, cross-legged on the bed—said all she ever wanted was to stay with him and travel wherever he went. He would never leave, he said. He had nowhere to go to that required his attendance and nothing to do that couldn't wait; he'd wait for her, he said.

In this fashion their courtship proceeded. She wrote her term paper on

"Paradise Lost," but the true topic of the essay was, she joked with Stacey, "Paradise Regained." Claire finished out her senior year and graduated in a bright haze of inattention; all that mattered was her love of Stephen, and his love for her. That it was "love" she did not doubt, no matter how sudden or strangely arrived; there was nothing in her life before that matched this passion, or even approached it. She felt herself reborn.

Or not so much reborn as born; the life ahead was life with Stephen at its center, and they decided to get married because the condition of marriage meant a more perfect union. It did not matter, they agreed, and would not change the truth of things; they had been wedded, *welded* together the instant he walked past her table.

But it might make a difference to the outside world. They wanted to announce it: the world should know they could not be dissevered and were joined together henceforth forever and ever. Unlike their own fathers and mothers—who all made concessions in marriage—they would brook no compromise. They would countenance no distance or stay a night apart.

Claire and Stephen drove to Richmond where she introduced him to her family in the large brick whitewashed antebellum house. He had some trouble remembering names—who was married to whom and whose child was who—but everyone was on their best behavior and made the suitor welcome. At two in the morning, with the rest of the family sleeping, he tiptoed barefoot down the hall and joined her in her canopied bed. The good manners of established gentry won out over uncertainty, and Stephen received her father's blessing and was offered a cigar.

Then they flew from Richmond, via Dulles, to LAX where Claire met his parents. In this case also the elders were guarded but cordial, and Stephen's mother said to him, "I hope she's as radiant *inside* as out." This was the distinction she had made before about his commitment to music.

He told his mother, *Yes.*

His father had arrived from Monte Carlo. In the kitchen he told Stephen, "She's a piece."

"A *piece?*"

"A peach is what I meant to say. Didn't I say that? A real Georgia peach."

"She's from Virginia, Dad. It's not the same."

"Close enough," his father said. "You've got yourself a beauty. And she makes you happy, doesn't she?"

"She does."

"Then you've got my blessing, kiddo." His father poured out two portions of brandy and raised his snifter, winking. "Bottoms up."

> Long ago and far away
> But in my memory
> It feels, still, like today
> For who can know
> How long ago
> I saw you standing there
> Upon the winding stair
> But wasn't sure
> If you were then ascending
> Or descending.
> Still, the memory is pure
> And clear,
> As is the image of your
> Body, your face,
> Your central place
> In the exhibition space
> Of objects I hold dear.

The engagement was a brief one, and the wedding small. She did not want to wait, Claire said, for the ritual and fuss of a formal ceremony because she felt married already and had no need of bridal gowns or vows or tossed bouquets. Stacey served as witness. Her two sisters and her sister-in-law threw a reception afterwards at the Jefferson Hotel. Stephen—ever the solitary—did not want a best man or ushers, although his mother did fly east and his father sent a case of Dom Perignon champagne. At evening's end he brought out his guitar and played for the assembled company a song he'd written for her: "Wedding Dawn."

It was a simple chord progression, in the key of C. He plucked it: 1-4-5-1. The melody took flight from and was a variation of the Quaker hymn, "Amazing Grace." "You must not be angry with this planet," Stephen sang. He knelt before her at the final chord, and kissed her outstretched hand.

She could not believe her good luck. Before he had a following, she followed where he had led. She went with him to coffee shops and bars and concert houses; she sat in the front row or back row and watched and listened while his audience expanded. It was as though a waiting world knew this was someone special when Stephen walked onstage. The pause while the performer gathered himself and tuned strings softly, gauging pitch, was always a pause when Claire held her breath; the audience too held its breath. There was a sheen about him—sheen *was* the word, she told herself—and the surrounding air felt charged.

He smiled at her, then dropped his head and began to play. The young bride was enthralled. Before he settled on a sequence for performance, she could always tell—by the tilt of his head or a chord-progression—which song he would choose next. He began with standard repertoire—ballads and blues and folk tunes—and followed with songs of his own. Stephen closed his set with their signature, always: the wedding hymn and its last word, *enthralled.*

Each day they reveled in the prospect of the night to come; each night they marveled at the pleasures of the day gone by. As in public, so in private: he understood her moves, and she knew his, in a fashion that required no instruction. It was as though they'd been disseevered in their childhoods but henceforth would cleave together as though a single being and not twain.

The very formality of such a description seemed apt, an old—even archaic—way of being in the world. The two of them defied arithmetic; together they were greater than the sum of their separate parts. Twain *was* the word for it, a twine by which they were fastened, for it was as though their bodies had been twinned.

For the first years they were ebullient, happy in ways neither chose to describe: glutted and sated by love. *La-la-la*, he hummed, while practicing his melodies, and *Ho-ho-ho*, and *Ha.* They were young and wealthy and comely and hopeful, and the world—whatever that expression meant— was their oyster.

"What *does* it mean?" Claire asked.

"What does what mean?"

"That expression: the world is our oyster . . ."

He put his hand on hers, then moved it to her knee, then up her thigh. "I've got a gig tomorrow," Stephen said. "You'll come with me?"

"Where?"

"D.C."

"Wherever. You know that," she said.

He pushed his hand up higher, and she lay back on the bed.

II

Such a state of things could not of course continue. The time came when she required female company, the pleasure of previous friendship. Stacey was finishing Business School at UVA and juggling offers from consultants—rival organizations based in Dallas that specialized in health care management and shopping malls. She couldn't decide, she admitted, and in either case it was a stepping stone; she didn't think she'd stay there long and had no desire to call Dallas home, but there would be travel involved. She needed Claire's advice.

The two of them had lunch together in what used to be their hangout, but now the clientele seemed young and loud and boorish; by contrast, they were women of the world.

"I'm happy you could make it. You look radiant," said Stacey, "so *settled* and sure of your place . . ."

"What did you want to talk about?"

"I have a question."

"Ask away."

Then Stacey launched into a speech about uncertainty, the way she'd been planning to live out her life and the direction she'd been taking, and the midnight recognition—or, more exactly, fear—that the things she hoped and planned to do were not what she now wanted. Except she didn't truly know what or who she wanted. There'd been a succession of men but none of them were serious or lasting, which is one of the reasons she needed to ask, how did you understand so quickly that real romance had come? And how did Stephen know? It seems like the stuff of ancient alliance, of fairy tales or fable—remember our course in Milton? Remember how you used to say you needed to take the road not taken and set out on your own? So can you tell me what you saw and how you knew you knew?

Claire had no easy answer. "It just happened," she said. "You were there."

"Yes. But I had chorus practice."

"Which is why you left."

"Not really. It's just there were such sparks between you, such—what can I call it?—electricity, I thought I would be burned."

"Was it so obvious?"

"Yes."

Claire blushed. She talked about her husband's career, the recording contract he'd signed, the bookings next month in New York and Nashville and Detroit. Success had been starting to come. But because his father always dealt with famous people—they'd been in the house throughout his childhood—Stephen seemed unchanged by it, *unfazed* was maybe the right word. Success seeks its own level, just the way that failure does, and because he had been born to money the money he was making did not make that much difference. "His head is where his head was when we met."

"His heart too?" Stacey asked.

"Let me explain," Claire said. Out of old habit she tried to be useful, to offer an opinion and even—since she had been asked for it—advice. "It's mostly been a mystery, but there are things I know. In a way he *has* been born to it—the music, I mean, not money—so sometimes I feel I'm just listening in, it's almost like eavesdropping, really. Stephen believes that what he's doing is the only thing worth doing, and there was never any doubt about his music making. It's been his ambition from the start.

"And I believe"—she spread her hands—"that same lack of doubt is what he felt the day we met. It's certainly the way *I* felt, not like a choice I was making, not as if I had a choice . . ."

"But I do," her friend said. "These jobs are apples and oranges; I don't know which one to accept."

At the next table an old man was reading a book. He did so with focused attention, tapping on the Formica surface and adjusting his glasses and frowning as he turned the page. He had thin white hair tied back in a ponytail and a thick white moustache. Claire tried to read the title of the orange text he held, but could not manage it; she watched him mouth the words. Poetry? History? A book about carpentry or travel or gardening or faith? She was distracted, watching him, and tried to bring herself back to the subject of Stacey's dilemma. They both were twenty-three. The question, *Where am I going and what am I doing* is one we all—well, everyone but Stephen—must ask ourselves somewhere along the way. It shouldn't worry you, she said; just throw the dice and see.

Most of the other customers were still in college, shouting, laughing. It was hard to concentrate. There was salsa music blaring from the speakers on the wall. She wanted to be certain her friend understood what she was saying, or trying to say, or hoping to: choice isn't always what it seems to be, a rational decision. And it isn't so surprising that the future looks unclear. You wait and wait and suddenly the real thing comes along. As far as Claire herself was concerned, the two consulting companies—one in health care management and one in shopping malls—are not all that different from one another; it's the consulting that counts. She had never been to Dallas or, for that matter, Houston—not to mention Austin or San Antonio or El Paso or anywhere in Texas—but it seemed somehow unimportant and at any rate irrelevant: you're starting out, and where you start is less important than where you plan to go . . .

They finished their entrées. They drank their sweet tea. They kissed and went their separate ways—Stacey to Dallas for a second round of interviews, and she to her one darling's side.

"I missed you."

"I missed *you*."

"How was lunch? How's Stacey?"

"Not all that much fun. Juggling job-offers . . ."

"She's our fairy godmother. She's why we met that afternoon, or anyway the reason you were there."

"I know, and I don't mean to be ungrateful. It's just I couldn't wait to be back, to hold you . . ."

"Why wait?" Stephen opened his arms.

> Apollo taught me.
> The god of music taught me
> How to tune and pluck the lyre.
> And yet I call him, "Liar,"
> Since what he calls concord
> Is discord
> And will not charm birds from trees.

Please
Understand it was not
Ever my intention, not
My invention but that of the god
Of music himself, an odd
Creature with nothing
He wants or hopes for or can propose but harmony:
A song to sing.
A chance to bring you back.

The King of Thrace, my father,
And the Muse Calliope, my mother,
Turn by turn desire and attack
Each other.
Swearing they would rather
Listen to than read
These lines, to heed
This need
I have to sing to you,
About you, *of* you, *for* you, *through* you
Who
Are gone. Surprise
It is that, listening,
Apollo heard my plea,
And granted me
The chance to have my lover live again
To join me when
We dead arise.

In New York he played across the street from The Bitter End. The Sweet
Start's room was full. The spotlight focused on Stephen, and there were
gnats and dust-motes in the air. She had accompanied him, as always, to
rehearsal, where he checked the lighting and sound-levels and walked
around the room and told her where to sit. He needed to know, he told
her, where exactly she would be sitting before he felt ready to sing. They
waited together in the dressing alcove with its mirror and counter and
two folding metal chairs, sharing a sandwich and a glass of orange juice

and hot water with lemon and honey for his throat. Then, five minutes before his performance, she left for her selected place in the rear of the room, first kissing her husband goodbye.

Claire said, as always, "Break a leg." Leaving, she asked herself, as always, why the expression meant, "Good luck." Did it mean you would elicit sympathy or be sent back from the front in war and the injury would therefore save your life; did it mean you crossed the "leg line" on stage that signaled you were ready to perform? "Break a leg" did not, on the face of it, sound like something to wish for a friend, but it did mean "Good luck."

Good luck had been his, hers, theirs. In any case, Claire told Stephen, she hoped that he would break a leg, and he smiled and nodded at her, encased in inward-facing solitude before he walked out to begin.

He began. There had been conversation, laughter, the rattle of ice in glasses, the scraping of chairs on the floor. Then came attentive silence and the hush of expectation while the artist gathered himself and the audience readied themselves. He adjusted his tuning, unsmiling, bending his curl-covered head. She held her breath. As he commenced his first series of chords Claire knew it would bring what he hoped for: a hymn to the bright light of music.

> O Muse, be with me as I go
> Wherever I go,
> Whenever I go,
> I want you to know,
> I need to know
> You come too.

Yet there was darkness, also, in the performer's hesitation, a syncopated tension while he played the bridge. Stephen's chord-changes were agile and his vocal register large; he sang with eyes wide open and then with both eyes closed. His melodies were intricate, the key shifting from major to minor. He could modulate from bass to tenor in a single phrase.

Now what had been an empty space filled instead with song. Hard-edged yet supple, his voice charmed birds from trees. It woke the bear from hibernation and weaned the suckling stoat. He sang as if, one critic wrote, possessed. The music was his, and only his, though there were echoes of other tunes and lyrics and the line of descent was, to listeners, clear: take Harry Chapin, Gordon Lightfoot and Paul Simon, as another critic wrote, and put them in a cocktail shaker and shake and mix and pour. Here was a lineage, a third critic wrote, of Child's Ballads and the blues, tempered by innovation.

> I need you
> I miss you
> I will always miss and need you
> But what have you done
> To my life?

At 2 A.M. the after-performance party started. Claire had not wanted to go, had been wary and fretful, even fearful, but Stephen needed some time to relax and space to spread his arms out, dancing; there were friends from L.A. who had come to New York and were renting a loft on Grand Street and who had drink and dope in quantity and wanted to connect again, to celebrate in the old way.

Remember me, Stevie, they said, and clapped him on the back. They said, Brother, you're a *star*! You're *it*, you're fucking *it*!

The noise was loud, the smoke was thick, and after two glasses of wine Claire knew she would rather be elsewhere, be back in their hotel.

"I'm not up for this," she said. "I need to go to sleep."

"Let's go."

"No. Stay, you were wonderful."

"I'll come with you."

"But you deserve a party. I'll see you soon."

He kissed her on the cheek, then throat, then lips. "I'm happy to be hanging out," he admitted. "I do need some unwinding, I'm still feeling tight as a spring."

"I know you are, baby. If I'm asleep when you come back, wake me. OK?"

"You're sure?"

"I'm sure."

He took her down to the street. After some minutes, a taxi approached. He raised his arm and the taxi stopped and he opened the door for her and gave the driver—a gray-bearded Sikh in a turban—the name of their hotel. Then Stephen handed the man twenty dollars and waved and turned on his heel, returning to the party, and she settled in for the ride, yawning, half-closing her eyes.

In a haze of weariness Claire spread her legs and leaned back. Much later they would ask each other if it was the force of old habit or a premonition, some sort of foreknowledge—*she'd been wary and fretful, even fearful*—that caused her to reach for the seatbelt above her right shoulder and find the slot beneath her left hip and insert the metal prong and probe for the connector until she heard it click. This was the action that saved her, because she survived the accident and thereafter was only half-dead.

At the intersection of 14th Street and Broadway, a Hummer driven by a drunk ignored the red light and, accelerating, slammed into the cab. The car's left front door pinioned its driver where he sat; the steering wheel impaled him. His thick beard was matted with blood.

The driver of the Hummer also died, although not instantly. It would take eleven minutes before the ambulance arrived and police cleared the intersection and the medical technicians administered to and then delivered the car's owner to the Emergency Entrance at Bellevue—by which time it was too late.

He had had a heart attack, which might have occasioned his jumping the light—not the alcohol in his system, nor the trace amounts of cocaine. The coroner's report could not determine with full precision whether the massive coronary had preceded by ten seconds or been coincident with or a result of the crash. In either case, in any case, the lethal conjunction of metal on metal was sufficient to destroy the man: five-foot nine, 173 pounds and, according to his driver's license, forty-three years old. The Sikh was fifty-eight, five-foot seven, 211 pounds, and the two accident victims, once identified, lay side by side in the morgue.

But Claire was not killed in the crash. Miraculously, the doctors said—although they did not use the word "miraculously," since it does not belong to medical parlance—she lived. It was not a scarless, woundless survival like that of her husband when, years before, he totaled his mother's Mercedes on an S-curve in Topanga Canyon. Then, in youthful invincibility, he had simply walked away.

In her case, however, it was unclear for days and weeks to come if Claire would emerge from the coma or walk without a limp. Both legs were broken—*Break a leg*, Stephen reminded himself, was what she'd said to him—and there were lacerations on her arms and upper body from the shattered glass. Her left wrist was broken too. Shielding herself, she had raised her left arm to ward off destruction; at her elbow there was a swelling the size of a balloon. All down her torso spread bruises and contusions, a blue and green and purple testimonial to the seat-belt's protective restraint. She had been sitting, belted in, on the right rear seat of the taxi and not on the driver's side which bore the brunt of the impact.

Therefore her injuries, although massive and life-threatening, did not in the end prove lethal. Her condition was critical but—post-operative, and after six days in the Intensive Care Unit—stable. What most concerned the doctors was her skull. The acute subdural hematoma occasioned when her head snapped back had caused Claire to lose consciousness, and that lack of consciousness was normal to begin with, the doctors said to Stephen, because the patient would not remember what had happened or how, and in this case the lack of memory would be a benison. Again, the surgeon did not use a word like "benison"—but it had been a kind of blessing and would allow the patient slowly, slowly over time, to heal.

She did not heal. Time passed. The promised blessing leaked away and instead became a curse. They had performed a craniotomy and a burr hole procedure, draining blood out of the brain and waiting for the swelling to reduce. It only slowly reduced. The patient lay as if embalmed—unmoving, pale, her breathing barely visible or audible, her toes and fingers inert. From time to time she twitched them, but the brief body-spasms did not signify alertness. Her vital signs were monitored in a blue beeping rectangle above her by the bed. She did not need a tracheostomy or a ventilator but did require feeding from an intravenous tube. She also had a tube for urine and a collection bag.

At intervals Claire moved her lips, as if to formulate language, but no sound emerged from her except the soft sound of her breath. Her head moved on the pillow, but barely, imperceptibly, and her husband who sat watching tried to conjure up her consciousness, if any, and make sense of what behind her shut unmoving eyes she might be able to see.

Stephen pictured the accident over and over, rehearsing the instant the vehicles collided, the sound of their engines, the shriek of the metal and glass. It was cacophony, an unstrung bow, a pair of cymbals clashing, dragging over piano keys. He had not been beside her but played the scene over and over, imagining what she had seen and heard and whether she'd had time to be afraid. He pictured the corner, the ambulance and then the emergency medical technicians, twisted wreckage on the street. He could not forgive himself for letting her leave the party alone, for being elsewhere when the taxi crashed, for not learning for an hour till his cellphone rang and someone in the Emergency Room apologized for waking him, although he still was wide awake and surrounded by a noisy clutch of revelers, of sycophants, and only beginning to think of departure. There had been a long-legged girl at his side with no bra and a snake tattooed on her upper right arm and neck who had been coming on to him and made it clear that she was primed for sex and willing, if he wanted to use the back bedroom, to show him the rest of her snake tattoo, but he was working out a way to tell her he was married, happily married, and the offer wasn't something he was ready to accept. She was tall but not as tall as he, and he bent to tell her, "Not tonight," when the voice on the cellphone said his wife was on the operating table and gave the hospital's address and Stephen said "Thank you"—absurd to say "Thank you!"—and fled.

Later he would learn the name of the taxi driver—his address in Queens, the number of his siblings and ages of his wife and children— and the name of the dead driver of the Hummer who had caused the crash. He would learn to deal with surgeons and hospital administrators and the members of Claire's family who came and grieved and were supportive, except for Claire's inconsolable father, who said, "My girl was healthy when you married her, and now look, just look at what's become of her, you self-centered son of a bitch . . ." then the physical therapists and occupational therapists and insurance adjustors and insurance agents and attorneys for the suit brought by the dead Sikh's family and by his own father's company attorney who reminded him that the medical and therapeutic costs might well amount to millions and could be open-ended, not to mention the loss of his wife's potential earning power and the high cost of mental stress and the loss of his own earning power because he would not leave.

He canceled all his bookings and stayed—with the permission of ward personnel—beside her every day. The hospital staff came and went. He had journeyed to the alien landscape of the medical establishment: Emergency Rooms and Intensive Care Units and Step-Down and Trauma Centers and a shared then private room. Although such surroundings were at first foreign to Stephen, they soon enough grew familiar. He could not imagine a new life without her—his lithe dark-haired dark-eyed intelligent soft-spoken darling—and did not try.

> It was easy
> Once, so easy
> You
> Who
> Had been so supple and
> Pliant a partner, so
> Sweet. Defiant now, so
> Bitter and angry and
> Demanding and—
> Replete
> With—what's the word?—
> Defeat.

Each plan he made he abandoned; each night he waited for day. At his request, the nursing staff positioned a reclining chair by the hospital bed where Claire lay. He slept next to her bed. This held true as well for the Rehabilitation Center to which she was, once stabilized, removed. Parallel, unspeaking, the husband and wife lay side by side together. Each time her vitals were taken and checked—blood pressure, temperature, oxygen levels—Stephen watched. When her eyes opened wetly—she was not crying, said the nurse, but only maintaining a degree of moisture in order to avoid exposure keratopathy—he took it as a sign.

"Don't give up hope," one young doctor said, "the body can always surprise us. The brain's power of regeneration—we know too little about this—is not something we can predict. It happens in a second and takes a long time to fix."

He did not give up hope. He read to her, he spoke to her, he sang to her, but always with the same result of no result. For weeks there was no change. The constancy was silence and a kind of deathly pallor, since her skin was drained of color. Claire had had no weight to lose, but she did lose weight. The bed sores came and went. The shaved head grew back hair. He tried to tell himself her face remained the same, for it retained its old plasticity when he kissed her cheek.

Each day he waited for night. When she moved her lips or shifted her position perceptibly in bed, he tried to take some comfort in the fact of her mobility, or at least a kind of comfort in the prospect of mobility, but all was silence except her stertorous intake of breath.

It's unoriginal to think
That this and only this
And this
Is what it takes to rise,
And then again to sink,
To have what seemed like the peaceable skies
Open up not in the guise
Of benevolent
But malevolent
Deities thundering down in the blink
Of an eye, of eyes
Shut now that were wide
Open only a moment ago.

"Where there's a will there's a way."
"Let's take it a day at a time,"
The doctors and therapists say.
Except
Their platitudes I can't obey,
Their attitudes I'm
Supposed to accept.

How difficult it is to sing.
There's nothing, no thing
To bring
To the table except:

I loved you
I love you
I will always love you.
Please come back to life.
To my life.

When Claire moved at last, and moaned, and spoke, he was uncertain if she moved or spoke, since she had been silent so long. But then she shaped Stephen's name in the air and stretched her lips into a smile and he knew himself again.

III

Recovery commenced. She would have to learn everything, the doctors said to Stephen, from speaking to eating and walking; think of how an infant starts to speak and eat and walk. The progress will be slow, they said, but there *will* be progress, the worst part's behind you now. The patient just has to be patient, they said, and you have to be very patient as well and not expect too much too fast: look straight ahead and not behind you, OK?

She learned how to use a bedpan and began to use a fork and spoon when he carried in and sliced up her food. After three months in the rehabilitation program, and with medical permission, Stephen took her to his parent's house in California. The flight was long but uneventful; they traveled with a wheelchair and a nurse. Claire had been sedated, and she slept much of the way.

They settled in. Since his father stayed in Monaco and his mother was often elsewhere, the pair had the run of the place. The word "run," however, did not apply to Claire; her first steps were halting and slow. A physical therapist arrived at the gate in Beverly Hills three times a week. Tanya was thin and strong, with cropped brown hair, and came from the Ukraine.

His wife used a walker to start with, and he watched her arms and legs tremble while she practiced her slow *left* foot, *right* foot wobbling advance, lips tight and tautly frowning. She looked at him imploringly, but Stephen had been trained to offer no assistance, to make her reach the door or bench or coffee table by herself. When she did reach the door or bench or coffee table on her own, he would applaud and kiss her on the cheek.

Then came crutches; then a cane. They went to Cedars-Sinai for an assessment every month. The doctors were guarded but hopeful and urged him to take it one day at a time. Look at the big picture, they said; the vital signs are good. There's still some risk of bleeding in the brain—a cerebral aneurysm—but locomotion improves. The corticosteroids have helped. Her youth and previous good health and strength will aid in convalescence; there's light at the end of the tunnel, the visiting nurses declared. Where there's a will there's a way.

He knew these sentiments were shopworn and meant merely to encourage him, but was grateful nevertheless. Tanya too would nod approval and say, *Again, again*. The time came, in late November, when Claire walked without assistance, her legs supple, and they agreed the Thanksgiving holiday was an occasion for thanks.

> It is my subject.
> It has always been my subject.
> You.
> You have always been my subject,
> Long before I knew you,
> Long before I touched you.
> For I have always loved you,
> As I will always love you.
> Therefore it's natural and easy, both,
> To make of our garments one cloth.

He understood that what he wrote was a pastiche. The rhymes were facile and the scansion inexact. The words that once came readily—emerging from song like a bird from its nest or bud from stem—were difficult to conjure now, forbidding in their aspect. There was nothing he wanted to say. *Pa-pa-pock!*

Still, Stephen attempted to work. While he hunted for ways to write about sorrow, his metrical patterns grew dense. He had renounced his music while Claire lay in a coma; now he heard melodies once more, although distant and discordant: a noise that had been silence while she lay unmoving. *Wei-la-la. Tum tum.*

At length he restrung his abandoned guitar, and as his wife continued to heal he began to sing again. In the exercise room of the pool house, under the unvarying skies and in the constant heat he tried his old familiar chord-changes and rhymes and progressions. His grief and guilt at her near-death might somehow, he hoped, bring her back.

"Your wife making excellent progress," said Tanya, "but please understand there's more to do, Mr. Stephen, and work is never quick."

"I understand," he said.

"Do you really? It's not—how do you say this in America?—a walk in the green park."

He did not correct her. He liked to watch her hands on Claire, the adjustments she made to alignment. The therapist chanted, "Two, and four, and six, and eight, and *good*!" when they performed their repetitions of knee-bends or sit-ups or stretches. Tanya was thirty-seven and the mother of twins; she showed them photographs of her daughters on a seesaw or dressed in frills for Christmas, holding candles, smiling at the camera and showing their missing front teeth. Her husband worked in a supermarket loading bay and hoped to be an actor. After her tenth session—with a beguiling mix of indirectness and directness—Tanya asked if maybe her husband could come to the house and meet your people personally, since if the parents is as nice as you they in person maybe will offer Jorgi help.

"My father's retired and has no office," said Stephen. "He doesn't come here much."

"But he must has *friends*," she protested. "Everybodies in this business is everybody's friend."

"What is he good at, your Jorgi? What does he hope and plan to do?"

"Oh, everythings," she said.

The trainer and patient worked effortfully together, and camaraderie burgeoned between them; at the end of every hour they drank their bottled waters and discussed what would come next. He never knew which Tanya would emerge from these discussions—the subservient or the imperious one, the one who made quiet suggestions or gave hard-to-follow orders. When at length he and Claire ventured alone past their gate to the street, he found himself gauging the potholes and cracked risers in the pavement where tree-roots had displaced the plane of poured cement. What once had seemed a level place to stroll became instead a gauntlet of heights and sudden drop-offs, a perilous path through dark woods.

His mother returned from St. Kitts. She had used sunblock to cover her arms and face and neck and legs, but had neglected her ankles, and they were swollen and red. She complained about this loudly, but did not seem concerned about Claire. When Stephen reminded her that his wife had escaped from a near-fatal crash, his mother said, "We all have our crosses to carry, don't we? Remember that phrase at your wedding? 'In sickness and in health.'"

"I never said that," he said. "It wasn't part of our service."

"It should have been," she said.

"'For better or worse.' *That* part I mean."

"It's terrible how much I itch. Maybe I'm allergic. Or some insect bit me that's only at home in the tropics." She pointed. "This is a new kind of rash, more like shingles than a bite."

"You're not listening."

"Of course I am, Stevie, I hear you. But I don't want you to whine."

"We get more sympathy from Tanya."

"Why should I be impressed," his mother asked, "that a woman you pay to be useful to Claire is sympathetic to her? *Acts* sympathetic is more likely. What's so special about that?"

"You're not sympathetic?"

"I am. But I'm in a kind of torment too. These ankles. Just *look* at them, Stevie. They've swollen right out of my shoes."

In Claire's presence, however, his mother was kind. She brought tea and strawberries and dry white wine. Stressing the value of Zen practice, she praised discipline in gesture and the control of breath. She preached the virtue of meditation, the life of the body as part of the mind. During the hot afternoons, while Stephen worked on his songs, the two women sat cross-legged beneath umbrellas by the pool.

They did jigsaw puzzles together, and played childhood board games: Monopoly, Chinese Checkers, and Clue. Claire's dexterity increased. She could manipulate the jigsaw shapes, putting them into their rightful place, and her choice of words at Scrabble—*wither* and *whither* and *zither*—enlarged.

"She's beautiful," his mother said. "If anything, more lovely than before the crash—so pale and pure and calm. And peaceful too, I think."

"She's coming back," he said.

And this was true. It was as though Claire woke from deep drugged sleep and was herself once more. Her skin grew clear. Her hips and lips and breasts and cheeks looked again sculpted and full. Stephen watched as she began to eat and walk and dress and talk with fluency, as though the accident and coma no longer needed to define her. She worked hard every day.

The return was not easy or steady, however, and sometimes he found her weeping in the pillowed chair or staring at the ceiling in what seemed a wakeful sleep. The jigsaw puzzles lost their charm, and Monopoly and Clue were children's games she no longer wanted to play. Those times he tried to comfort her, to tell her it would be all right, her answering smile was an effort, he knew; her hand when he pressed it was cold.

Step by step Claire tried to ascend to a place where she would again feel welcome and at ease among the living. But her husband and his mother and Tanya made it difficult even while trying to help. They did not understand, they could not know what she was afraid of: her soles on fire, her toes on ice, her ankles so wobbly and weak.

For the first time in their marriage, she felt distant from her consort. He walked ahead of her down ill-paved streets bordered by mansions with hedges and walls. His long loping stride was a reproach no matter how he slowed it, and she feared Stephen's impatience, his yearning to break free.

"Are you all right?" he'd ask. "Is there anything I can do for you?"

She shook her head. Her auburn hair had grown out thickly, and discoloration from the bruising and her swellings all had gone.

"You're sure?"

"I'm sure," Claire said.

It would be, he told his mother, hard; it would be, Stephen said to Tanya, a miracle of diligence, and she said, "What is *diligence*, please?"

Claire dreamed. She dreamed herself in a valley of shadows and gray moss-draped trees, with Stephen up ahead of her, both near and far away. The road through hell was a dark avenue, with shuttered storefronts, people sleeping under scaffolds, and a string of "Keep Out" signs and yellow tape. There were policemen blowing whistles, and many sirens wailing. On both sides of the alley, dumpsters reeked. There were abandoned cars on either side, or maybe horse-drawn carriages, or hay-carts with dead bodies piled like logs upon the hay. From the quick and dead alike all eyes were trained upon her, unblinking, paying close attention to the way she walked and talked.

Baleful was the word to describe the gaze of those who stared, who said, "Let's just check your vitals, dearie," and poked and probed and pricked. She tried to tell them, "No, please don't," but what she said was noiseless and they paid no attention, taking out their needles and blood pressure sleeves and tongue depressors with professional dispassion, as though they did not hear her or, hearing, choose to abide by her wishes. She had no volition, no will of her own:

Two and *Four* and *Six* and *Eight*!

But what was worse was how she felt about her husband on the path they trod: estranged. He was attentive, of course, and doing what he knew how to do, yet it was as though the seamlessness they shared before had come apart at the seams. He tried to help; he failed. Stephen did not know and could not know, no matter how she hinted at it, that his loving kindness lost its power to compel her. She was dependent on him, yes, but could not forgive him, really, for sending her home from the party alone and putting her into a taxi while he went back upstairs. She had almost died on Broadway while he hooked up at a dance.

Claire knew she was being unfair. She tried not to be unfair. He had come to her side as soon as he could, and stayed with her through thick and thin when it was mostly thin. But fairness had nothing to do with the way she felt: so angry and alone. His blithe mobility was painful, as were his attempts at melody intended to beguile. She would not be beguiled.

"*It's not my fault,*" she wanted to scream, and—since there had to be some blame attached to the horror that befell her—it had to be his fault. Claire could not blame the taxi driver or the drunk at the wheel of the Hummer, because they both were dead. She was the sole survivor of the accident, although it felt as if, for all practical purposes, she too died at the intersection, belted in and dangling there among the shards of glass. She felt survivor's guilt.

Now nobody—not Stephen, not even Stephen, most especially not Stephen—could understand, or hope to know, what it had felt like pinioned there before she blanked out and forgot. The world that was so welcome once had grown unwelcome, foreign; what had been benign was malign.

"How are you feeling?" her husband asked each morning.

"Fine. I'm fine."

"You mean that?"

"No."

"Is there some way to make it better?"

"No."

"Something I can do for you?"

She shook her head. She could do that. She said, "Leave me alone."

And so the marriage faltered and, like Eve in that old poem she took "wandering steps and slow." Her early light-filled nakedness by the side of her companion instead felt clothed in darkness; the space between them grew. "The world was all before" Claire, maybe, but it did not look like Eden and it did not feel like Paradise regained. What she once took for granted was no longer hers to take.

This continued for some time. The path she followed Stephen on was full of rocks and brambles, and her feet—she could at least feel them—were tender, so she placed her feet with care. When she reached out her arms to brush the low-hanging branches and cobwebs aside, the effort made her weary, and though she was only twenty-five she felt like an old woman or, what was the word for it? *Crone.*

Once or twice he made a gesture that might have led to making love—the act they'd shared so happily and often—but she said she was not ready yet and he would have to wait. Her physical self, she tried to say, was still strapped to the gurney and hospital bed, and Stephen said he understood and did not want to press himself upon her until she wanted him to take her again in his arms.

"To fuck, you mean," said Claire.

"That's one way of putting it, yes."

"It's what you mean, isn't it?"

"Yes."

"I can suck you off. Or jerk you off. Or get you off however you want it. But don't touch *me*, OK?"

"You never used to talk this way."

"Get used to it," she said.

IV

The time that followed tested both of them, but in different ways. She tried to deal with anger, her sense of having been abandoned and left on the altar of Stephen's career. His reputation flourished while she lay ill and abed, half-dead.

At her mother-in-law's suggestion, Claire sought help. Yet the therapists and councilors and analysts she spoke to all were useless. For weeks and months she talked and kept a record of her dreams and fears, but though "Time is the great healer," as one therapist assured her, the woman's glib assurance did not help. Claire's physical health had been restored; her mental well-being had gone.

For Stephen it was difficult in other ways. He could not understand, in truth, what had gone so wrong. Everywhere were women who would open up their arms to him except for this one woman who had been his eager partner. Claire was clothed, it seemed to him, in stiff white funereal garments; she was more dead than alive.

So he maintained his distance, and she maintained her distance, and what had been a unity became instead a separation. They shared a bedroom in Beverly Hills but did not share a bed. They walked together through the streets but seldom hand in hand. He told himself that, once emerged, his darling would return to him as gladsome and exuberant as had been the case before. She told herself that, once escaped, she would be free from all constraint and able to behave again as did the girl in Charlottesville who saw him on the street.

Yet this was not to be. He stayed home each night but began to think about gatherings elsewhere in the city; he remembered his blithe rambling youth and how rarely—unless choosing to—he had slept alone. While driving or at traffic lights he could not keep from noticing the legs and breasts and buttocks of girls who passed in front of him, sipping coffee out of paper cups or adjusting their headphones and swiveling hips and snapping painted fingers to the beat. Los Angeles was full of nymphs and sirens gamboling down the pavement or crossing at a traffic light while Stephen waited for the sign to turn from red to green.

Therefore he had a new stanza:

> You be the paper and I'll be the pen.
> You tell me where and I'll tell you when
> We start again
> And now will no longer mean then.

Her dreams were tumultuous things. She saw the Sikh, the driver of the Hummer, their bodies prone on marble slabs that in fact she never saw but could not cease imagining. Her father in his anger, her mother in her sorrow, her sisters and her brother and their partners and children and classmates and the professor with his bowtie all gathered to mourn her and stood by the bier. But why would it be called a bier and did that mean they were drinking not wine or ale or vodka but *beer*, and was it a tailgate party with, on the tailgate, a coffin and who was cheering on which team and what sport did they play? Claire knew herself suspended in a kind of wakeful wide-eyed sleep, a willed suspension of the business, the *busyness* of life, neither absent nor present, the blood vessels and nerve-endings and ganglia and capillaries and brain cells inside her head not yet entirely healed or receptive but getting there, *getting there*, yes. What did it mean, she asked herself, that she would follow Stephen to the ends of the earth if the earth was a circle, a sphere? If the path they followed had no end but doubled back upon itself, why was he leading her on?

He led her on. In the early mornings, sitting by the pool or at the kitchen table, he would reach across and take her hand, and she would answer his pressure by squeezing his fingers and smiling, or attempting to. They went walking every day. Theirs was no longer a warring silence but there was little to say.

One afternoon in September they met Tanya's family, having invited them for tea. Tanya's husband was short and muscular, with a shaved head and goatee. It was as though he'd dressed himself for the role of Russian gangster, but he was gentle with his daughters and did not announce himself as an actor or ask for any favors. He spoke of his job in the loading bay; he lifted boxes *Down, down, down*, then *up*. The visit was a pleasant one, with Stephen's mother behaving well and Tanya telling everyone how *proud* she was for Claire.

His mother remained in the house but on a diet of protein shakes she called a fast, and he and Claire therefore consumed their meals alone. One Friday in December, returning from their neighborhood walk, Stephen saw a town car pulled up in front of their driveway gate, and his father stepping out.

His father looked old, travel-weary. Yet he remained upright and trim, sporting the trademark gap-toothed grin that made him still seem youthful. His leonine mane had gone white.

"You kids," he said. "You kids."

"Hel-*lo*," said Stephen. "We hadn't expected you, Dad."

The driver extracted two bags from the trunk, then tipped his cap and returned to his seat and started the engine again. His father handed over a hundred dollar bill and made a hand-fluttering gesture: "Keep the change."

"Very kind of you, sir."

"No problem." Then, turning to Stephen, he asked. "Your mother didn't tell you I was coming?"

"No. But I'm glad to see you. *We're* glad to see you. Welcome back."

"She's getting forgetful, isn't she? Or is she maybe being wishful?"

"Wishful?"

"Right. She hoped I wasn't coming, and if she didn't mention it I wouldn't come on home. The old ostrich principle: 'Bury your head in the sand' and tell yourself no danger approaches. 'What you don't know can't hurt you.'" He raised his shoulders, shrugging. "Well, anyhow, I'm here."

"It's excellent to see you."

"Been way too long. Been what feels like forever; how long *has* it been?"

"Since we moved here after rehabilitation. After the hospital. The accident."

"'Time flies when you're having fun,'" his father said. "I don't mean that, obviously, it's only an expression. I meant it's been too long."

"Or not."

"Not?"

"Not having fun. Time also crawls."

"My son the songwriter." His father addressed the hot afternoon air. "He's grown up, hasn't he?"

Through all of this Claire stood unspeaking, gazing at her father-in-law as if they had not met before, as though he were a stranger.

"Don't I get a kiss?" he asked.

Obedient, she stepped forward, and he enfolded her. The limousine drove off. Stephen collected his father's luggage and the three of them passed through the wrought iron gate and walked up the brick entrance path.

As they approached it, the front door opened, and his mother appeared in the foyer, clothed entirely in white. Wearing a garment that could serve either as an evening gown or dressing gown or nightgown—draped tunic-like from her shoulders and reaching her white-sandaled feet—she looked to her son like a goddess again, and he was moved to see her so: resplendent, looking down upon the three of them while they ascended the steps.

His mother stood unsmiling. She wore lipstick, eye-shadow, and rouge. "Welcome home."

"You look wonderful," her husband said.

"He always was a flatterer," she said to Claire. "It's part of his world-famous charm."

"But what if I mean it?"

"What?"

"That you look wonderful. A sight for sore eyes."

"Put your glasses back on," said his mother.

"My eyes are going, I admit it. But this much I can see."

"What did I tell you?" Again, she turned to Claire: "It's what he says to ladies everywhere. Our conquering hero returns."

"Can we stop this, please," said Stephen. "Dad just arrived. Can we be happy just once?"

"He's right," his father said. "I bring the olive branch."

> Your lips have been botoxed.
> Your skin has been detoxed,
> You act like you've outfoxed
> Time.

> Welcome home
> Welcome back
> I'm happy to hang up your coat on the rack,
> Your old coat and your nothing-left-to-lose
> Insouciance, your dusty shoes:
> I'm
> Happy to see you here: home.

In the days that followed they did indeed behave like family, the parents and the younger couple gathering for meals and having conversations—discussing the weather, the chance of rain, the headlines, war, the eclipse of the moon. *The New York Times* and *The Los Angeles Tribune* were tossed in plastic wrappers, early, over the protective fence; the housekeeper carried them in.

His parents' marriage was a mystery to Stephen, not something that made sense. So often apart, or with other companions, they seemed content again. They told jokes and played gin rummy and took long swims in the pool. Their version of fidelity was not the one he had with Claire or could imagine having: it was an "open marriage" and not the closed charmed circle he and his partner once shared.

Yet in ways he came to recognize, his parents had fashioned a truce. After every separation they rejoined each other happily, as though the reunion were planned. His mother settled down while her husband settled in. Even their arguments seemed staged, a ritual procedure and prelude to agreement.

On the third day, his father took Stephen aside. "What's going on?" he asked.

"How do you mean, Dad?"

"You know what I mean. Or *not* going on. What's going down with your wife?"

"Claire?"

"I know her name. I'm asking a serious question. What's wrong with the two of you?"

"She had an accident, remember? She's in recovery. *We're* in recovery."

"Tell me something I don't know. Your mother and I had an accident too. It's called marriage."

"Very funny."

"I'm not joking, Stevie. Something's not right with her."

"No."

"No you agree or no you don't agree?"

"She's taking time—*we're* taking time—to get over it. Healing."

"Are you together?"

"Yes, of course."

"You know what I mean, what I'm asking. Are you *together*?"

"What are you asking, exactly? Do we enjoy shared nuptial bliss? Conjugal relations?"

"Don't get cute with me, I'm asking a serious question."

"Do I inquire about you and Mom? Do I ask about your—what's the right word for it?—sex-life?"

"No, and you don't have to. And it's none of your damn business. You used to be a player, Stevie, and you used to sing."

"I will again."

"Do you promise me?"

"Yes."

"I'm in your camp," his father said. "You understand that, don't you? I've always been in your camp."

Stacey paid a visit. She was in Los Angeles, attending a convention, and she called and asked if she could come for a drink. "I know it's last minute," she said, "but it turns out I've got the afternoon free."

Stephen said, "Of course, come on by," and gave her their address. Claire was excited to see her old roommate and prepared to make her welcome. His parents were in Malibu, having a late lunch with friends.

"What a spread," said Stacey, once she'd been buzzed in. She had called an Uber and pulled up at the gate.

"It's not much, but we call it home," he joked. He had changed out of his shorts.

Indeed, the house was palatial: a three-story central structure with two two-story wings. The exterior was stucco, painted yellow, and with dark green shutters and a mansard roof. Climbing yellow trellised roses flanked the entrance arch. A set of six French doors opened to the colonnade that gave out on the pool.

The floors were tiled, the banisters were marble, and a matched pair of chandeliers dangled, sparkling, from silver-plated chains. There was a grandfather clock by the door, its pendulum and numbers faced in gold. A key protruded from the clock-face, which needed to be wound. A row of platinum records from his father's days as a producer hung side by side in the hall.

"It's been too long," said Claire.

"Been *way* too long," her roommate said, and embraced them each in turn. She was wearing a business suit; her hair was cut short and curled. Her three-inch heels were red, her white silk shirt unbuttoned to her cleavage, and everything about her seemed both harsh and soft.

"You look wonderful," said Claire.

"You too. You two."

To Stephen's surprise, the woman pressed herself against him and tongued his open mouth. "Hello, stranger," Stacey said. Then, smiling and wiping her lips, she stepped back and curtseyed. "At your service, sir."

What did she mean, he wondered; was this a proposition? He offered her a gin and tonic and a plate of pre-cut fruit. Claire drank, as usual, tea. They caught up on Stacey's work, her consulting opportunities, the nation's politics. They spoke about their families and the suicide last week of Stacey's cousin; they discussed her rapid marriage and even more rapid divorce. "You married Mr. Right," she said to her old confidante. "But I got Mr. Wrong."

Their visitor was, Stephen, recognized, stoned. Her voice fluted unsteadily, her diction slurred, and more than once she reached out—as if to stabilize her balance—for his arm. Jiggling her heels, Stacey kicked off her shoes and sat back, crossing her legs. Her legs were tan. She embarked upon a speech about her life since Charlottesville, how it all felt very long ago: water far under the bridge.

Everything has changed, she said, but nothing *really* changes. She had been at the Convention Center, now, for two whole days and was learning nothing new and wishing she'd not bothered except for seeing *you*, you two, and how it makes *me* feel. The way it makes me feel, she said, is time stands still yet anyhow flies; do you remember what we used to say about a clock being right twice a day?

"Well, *that's* exactly how this feels today, as if I got it right this time, this second time around for me, and could I have another gin and tonic, please? Except leave out the tonic, it only gets in the way."

Claire smiled. In the sunlit library, she seemed herself again. The women interrupted each other and finished each other's sentences and laughed at the same time. Stephen felt excluded yet content to sit back and listen while his wife reverted to gossip and a high-pitched giggle which he had not heard for months. It was as though her old companion's visit had erased the years gone by: the accident—which she referred to only in passing—and its long aftermath. The two women ignored him except for the way, leaning forward, Stacey placed a hot hand on his hand.

At seven o'clock, she said I'd best be getting back. "You wouldn't want to drive me, would you?"—she looked at Stephen archly—"I'm staying at The Standard and, as you maybe noticed, I could use a lift."

He said he'd call a car. "I can't leave Claire," he said.

"I wasn't suggesting you ought to." She laughed. "'It never entered my mind.'"

His parents returned and said "Hello, how are you?" and Stacey embraced Claire, then Stephen, probing his mouth with her tongue again, then touched his cheek and left.

Yet what could be more vulgar than the chase
He daily undertakes for someone like his heart's
Own darling, gold hair hammered to ringlets,
Gold skin raised where they beat her,
Each welt worth principalities,
And follows therefore anyone with "Follow me"
Printed backwards on her sandals,
Enticing him with signatures
In dust.

What do I mean by saying, "Stay,"
What do I really mean?
My queen grows old,
And cold.

Husband and wife lay together. Stacey had departed and, having greeted his parents, Claire said she was tired and needed to lie down. He joined her in the bedroom and took off his clothes. Naked, he was planning to remind her of that first day in Charlottesville when he had been walking by and they met each other. It was as though no time had passed and nothing between them was lost.

She had been wearing green. They loved each other still. They had done so from the start. Stephen was feeling hopeful, spurred on by his parents' reconciliation and the discussion with his father and, earlier that evening, by Stacey's physical suggestiveness; he was planning to propose, next year, a trip to Greece. They were home, were almost home. They were there, were almost there.

As he approached, however, Claire shifted on the pillow. Her head ached. It had never ached this much before; it was the fiercest of headaches and she felt she would throw up. The pain increased. Her body arced. It convulsed.

She could not speak. She saw Stephen doubly, and yet her vision dimmed. She watched while the bulk of him neared. She tried to tell him how it felt to feel so far removed that everything she saw she saw as through a scrim. She tried to tell him that the pain was all-encompassing, impossible, unbearable. When Stephen moved to comfort her she saw a brightness exploding, a flash behind her eyes that resolved itself as lightning, then a thunderclap behind it that she could not hear. Claire was dead.

A dog in the distance was howling; another barked and barked.

It was—Stephen consulted his watch—9:21. He lay beside her on the bed for what felt like eternity but was perhaps three minutes, trying to match his breath to hers, except they did not match. He switched off the bedside lamp. All he had done, he tried to say, was turn back at the pathway's end in order to tell her, "We're home," and point towards the door.

He said these words out loud. Yet the door was receding, was endlessly elsewhere, not something he or they could reach. The lights beyond the bedroom wall were flickering and fading while nighttime fog rolled in. The portico and pool house and the pool grew invisible, unattainable.

What the surgeon feared, he later learned, was what in fact had happened: a rupture in the brain. The cerebral aneurysm could not have been prevented, the doctors told him later, it could only have been monitored and was being monitored and medicated and they should perhaps have operated but there were dangers attendant on any such operation and they did not elect to perform one since the condition had stabilized and did not seem a mortal threat.

It was, however, mortal. This time she did not wake. It was 9:26. His wife was so completely still he waited, listening for breath the way he'd done while Claire lay in a coma, and her chest would rise and fall.

It did not rise or fall. He took her pulse, or tried to, but there was no pulse, no breath. Her hand went cold. He had learned enough in their hospital stay to know her vital signs had flatlined; she would not again revive. All that he hoped for, planned for, was to no avail. They would not begin again or travel together to Greece.

Stephen continued to breathe. It was not her fault, he tried to say; it never was her fault. Neither was it his. Where did she go, he wondered, and could he follow Claire again? Might he bring her back to the bright world through which they once had wandered?

He knew the answer: "No." He could not charm birds from trees. He would wake no bear from hibernation or wean the suckling stoat. Claire lay stiffening beside him while he waited for the dawn and rigor mortis to set in. It was 9:31. He had dared a backwards look and now his wife was dead.

V

It took him some time to accept this. Stephen could not retrieve her. His parents were of no help to him; neither were the doctors or his followers and friends. He was twenty-eight years old. a singer with a literary bent and sufficient funding so he did not need to sing. There was no music he wanted to make and nothing left to celebrate. His run-on-lines and verbal play were somehow both modern and ancient; in the act of breaking them he'd honored time-bound rules. Yet the poets he had studied and the lyrics he had written seemed unimportant or, if not unimportant, utterly beside the point.

The point was Claire was gone. There was nothing remaining to say. Death had become his subject, but there was nothing about it to sing. Now Stephen lived with silence as once he'd lived with song. His sense of vocation had failed.

> *Wei-la-la, weilala, weilala*
> Why did I let you leave?
> How do I let you know
> That you are with me where I go?
> Darling, we must not grieve.
> For you are with me,
> Always with me,
> *Wei-la-la,*
> And I with you
> Although you seem to be
> So distant, near, you
> Lie unchanging,
> Changed.

He moved east, as far away as possible from the coast where Claire had died and back to the city where last she'd been fully herself. He had believed in her recovery, the prospect of renewal. Yet the trail they walked so carefully had ended on a cliff. Or, if not a cliff, a cave with no second exit to find, a lead line where the string dissolved, a dark thick wood through which there was no crumb-strewn path. There were no concerts to give.

He left his instruments behind, his books behind, because he did not wish to be reminded of the instruments he'd played and books he'd read while his wife remained alive. He took an apartment on Riverside Drive and walked along the river, seeing tugs and ferries on the Hudson and steering clear of the bicycle lane where riders clattered past. He bought sandwiches from vendors and fed the ravening pigeons with crusts of sandwich-bread. Repeatedly he consulted his watch and registered the time: 11:11, 11:14, 11:26, 11:31. Time had stopped for Stephen, yet his watch ticked remorselessly on.

He waited for a sign. He sat on weathered wooden benches—with their knife-cut initials and metal commemorative plaques and stains from bird-droppings and food—and watched joggers jogging by either rapidly or slowly; he studied old people with their handlers and nannies wheeling toddlers and talking on cellphones with friends. Couples walked past hand in hand; children threw Frisbees and balls. All such evidence of life troubled and distracted him; he surveyed the lives of others for hours every day.

His own life had come to a halt. There was no consolation to offer, no song he wanted to sing. His innocence had drained away, and—watching the toddlers and joggers and pigeons hunting crumbs on the grass—Stephen told himself that, if he were to start once more, he would do so with no language and without a tune.

His parents stayed in touch. His mother said, "You did everything you could."

His father said, "I don't mean to be flippant, and you know I'm on your team. But there *are* other fish in the sea."

"What are you trying to tell me, Dad?"

"It's only an expression: there are other fish to fry. I mean you'll get over it."

"I won't."

"You will. It's how we're put together, Stevie, what we do."

Both his mother's reassurance and his father's worldly counsel were beside the point; the point was Claire was dead. She had been half-dead in the hospital and now was wholly dead. The difference was a beating heart and one that had stopped beating. The difference was he was alone who for years had had a partner; although he should have been prepared, he felt unprepared.

In this new circumstance Stephen asked himself new questions. Was he being punished, he wondered, for some sort of transgression he simply failed to foresee? What had he done or failed to do that brought him to this pass? His great good luck and privilege had been, in an instant, revoked.

This made it hard to sleep. Always there was yellow tape and a police car with its siren and an ambulance arriving and the harbingers of loss on either side while he reconstructed the scene. Always there were IV tubes and monitors above her bed and bedpans to empty and rinse. As if through a form of contagion, Claire's death undid him also, and he found nothing now to celebrate. His world had turned to ash.

> I loved you
> I love you
> I will always love you.
> Please come back to life.
> To my life.

Stephen walked the streets of Manhattan in a daze of inattention, passing shuttered storefronts and vendors with gloves and hats and umbrellas for sale. The homeless slept beneath the slats of scaffolding outside. They lay on discarded mattresses and under plastic bags.

He walked in rain and heavy weather and through a heat-wave in June. He walked to and from the George Washington Bridge, imagining how it might feel to throw himself from the span's commanding height. He wondered if he could bring himself to do so, climbing the wire fence intended to contain him, then jumping, leaping, falling free, and if the fall would prove fatal or if he would surface and swim.

These were idle fantasies, of course, but he imagined himself in the river, singing *Claire, Claire, Claire*, and being swept out past the harbor to the sea. *You, ewe, yew.* One afternoon in September Stacey texted to say she'd heard he had moved east and she too was in the city and wondered if he'd care to get together for a drink.

It was 6:17. She couldn't stop thinking, she told him—when, on an impulse, he called back—about the death of her dear friend, her *best and boon companion.* Those were the words she used and repeated when they met. She was staying at the Hotel Surrey and he came up to her room. She had a bottle of red wine waiting, uncorked, and poured them each a glass. She was only in town for the evening, she said, and it had been a long day. He had not shaved or changed his shirt but Stacey was in full regalia: a floor-length skirt, a sleeveless silk top, a necklace of intertwined vines.

"I'm *inconsolable*. Aren't you?" she asked.

"It isn't easy."

"No. I've been trying to console myself. Have you?"

They clicked their glasses and drank. Then, as she had done when visiting the two of them the day Claire died, she pressed herself against him and kissed him open-mouthed. He tried not to be but was aroused; he kissed her back.

"To the memory of our best friend," said Stacey, and filled his glass again. "My sweet best dearest friend."

They drank. In the ensuing silence, she studied him.

"We need to do this, don't we?"

He made no answer.

"You know what *I* think," Stacey said. "I've been thinking and thinking about it."

"What?"

"We need to bring her back. We should console each other. Just this once we need to try to bring her back."

And so they slept together. She bit and scratched him and was passionate, but Stephen stayed aloof. It was 8:13. When they were finished, Stacey asked, "What are you thinking? Tell me what you're thinking," and he told her, "Nothing. I'm just happy to be here."

"True?"

"True," he lied.

"You're elsewhere, aren't you?"

"Elsewhere?"

She put her hand on his chest. Her fingernails were pink. "I've wanted to do this," she confessed, "for forever, just about, and now we've gone and done it but it doesn't bring her back."

"No."

"What are you going to do?" Stacey asked.

"I don't know," Stephen said.

> They call it timeless, dateless death;
> They name him a fell messenger.
> They say time is a wheel

Which must continue turning
With the loss of rate according
To the loss of friction,
And another word for the laws of friction
Is life.

Each plan he made he abandoned; each day he waited for night. He continued to walk in the park and take a seat on benches and watch the boats and birds. He asked himself if what he felt was what others also felt, or if he and his partner had been somehow set apart. His love of Claire—so absolute since that first time they saw each other, so unquestioning and foreordained—seemed more and more unreal. Or, if not unreal, implausible, as if in an old story where a man and woman meet, and by some necromancy a fatal spell is cast.

It is a shared spell. It is both curse and blessing; it is a love-draught swallowed, an arrow impaling two strangers shot from the same single bow. Often there are obstacles—a warring faction, a marriage or oath of fealty elsewhere—but the obstacles are nothing in the face of strong shared passion, and nothing matters but love. Such love may cause catastrophe, a suicide, a war between nations; it can cause a king to abdicate or queen to yield her throne. It can cause joy or heartbreak in the several versions of the story; it provides a happy ending or, more often, not. But what it *is* is irrevocable, and that remained the case for Stephen and had been the case for Claire.

This did not set him free. Ridiculous, he told himself: I'm living in an old sad story composed by troubadours. Love is a blessing yet curse. It lingers for better or worse. It makes for third-rate verse. The men and women he once studied had used up all the rhymes. He could remember singing to Claire, singing for her in their courtship year, when the world spread out before them like a map of trips to take.

There had been lilies and roses abounding; there had been apples and pears. All omens had been glad. The garden bloomed and ripened and the crop was new. *You, ewe, yew.* Then he had written songs of *love*, blue skies *above*, the morning *dove*, and hand in *glove*, the bridal veil she *wove*.

One afternoon in October—although the skies were threatening—he took his usual place beneath Grant's Tomb and stared out at the river. It was 2:17. On an adjacent bench an old man was reading a book. He did so with focused attention, tapping on the wooden slats and adjusting his glasses and frowning as he turned the page. He had thin white hair tied back in a ponytail and a thick white moustache.

Stephen tried to read the title of the text his neighbor held, but could not manage it; he watched him mouth the words. Poetry? History? A book about carpentry or travel or gardening or faith? He was distracted, watching, and tried to bring himself back to the subject at hand. He was twenty-nine. It was 2:34.

Nearby there were tennis courts and women walking dogs. Leaves were falling, swirling, blowing past. His manager was urging him to cut another record, or at least consider it, or to book a session and rerelease old songs. His parents were suggesting that he come to California and live with them again. He asked himself how he had failed, *why* he had failed, *if* he had failed, and how and when and where to start anew.

> Why
> Should I sing of memory
> And not your near
> And actual presence now?
> How
> Is it possible you're gone
> So long ago and far away
> And would not stay:
> Gone, gone.

The god of music was displeased. It said to Stephen, "Stop this nonsense; stop pretending I'm immortal and that things don't change. Stop believing you have agency—that's what they call it nowadays—and can turn back the clock. You can't. It doesn't work that way, it never has and never will."

He walked along the river in the increasing wind. It had been growing dark. There were schoolgirls playing on a soccer field below him; they wore uniforms, waved hockey sticks, and they seemed to Stephen to be chanting—in loud unison—one of his songs. Storm clouds gathered; on the Hudson there were whitecaps and the threat of rain. He told himself that he could start again, perform again, and as he did so lightning struck and killed him on the instant. He sang *Claire, Claire, Claire* and *Claire*.

Quintet

THE BROTHERS TRY to keep the peace, but it is hard to do. All their lives they have been intimate but wary of each other, all through childhood shared a room. Now Andrew is forty and James thirty-seven, and since their father died this year they must divide the estate. Both men fear the prospect, and neither wife is willing to help; the women have long since stopped speaking to each other, and refuse to meet.

"Just once?" asks Andrew. "Can't you jump over your shadow?"

"No."

"Please. Is it so difficult?"

"I'm not an acrobat," says Jill. "I can't do a backflip. And don't want to try."

"Why not?"

"That bitch would cheer if I hurt myself. Jumping over my shadow, I mean. Your father was a sweetheart, but it's too much to ask."

James too has hoped for, if not the full cessation of hostilities, a truce. But Ariane remains implacable, her Gallic sense of honor at stake and her anger unassuaged. "I like *ton frère*," she tells her husband, "and while he is alone I wish always to accommodate him. But this is not something a reasonable person does. I refuse absolutely to be part of her ambition and her scheming ways. No good result will come of it, I warn you, *chéri. Je le jure*."

The women have been rivals, not for their husbands' affections but for their father-in-law's. The dead man was indiscriminate in his love of women or, as he used to put it, an all-embracing admirer of the fair sex. "Beautiful!" he would exclaim. "I need to take a photograph. I need to draw you, my lovely, I must preserve you in oil!"

Then he'd produce his Leica or his sketchbook, staring intently at the face and body of his visitor until they turned away or shed their clothes. "I adore you," he would whisper. "A goddess. An absolute vision in lace!"

Such admiration was omnivorous and, the boys knew, non-selective; there were always women by their father's side. After twenty years of suffering through his amorous adventures, their mother filed for divorce. The next year she succumbed to ovarian cancer, and the boys in youth and manhood watched a series of blondes and redheads and brunettes their father praised while painting and sooner or later made love to. "I need to explore you," he'd say. They were tall or short, ample or slender, keen-eyed or myopic; it didn't seem to matter to the artist. Always, he reached out an arm.

Over time that arm embraced the girls and women they in turn brought home; loudly, he commended this one's neck or that one's thigh. His romantic partners called him charming and suggested or declared that he was full of, to put it delicately, passionate enthusiasm: so *much* a ladies' man and *so* appreciative. Their wives would not, the brothers told themselves, have encouraged their father's advances, and not let him take them to bed. But perceptibly they brightened when flirting with the old roué, and perceptibly each bridled when the other one entered the room.

Near the end his reputation grew. His nudes became a calendar: arms and legs and breasts and backs and buttocks—never a face or distinguishing feature—that composed the sequence of a year. The twelve months displayed twelve separate models; the bodies were rendered in much the same way, but proportion and emphasis differed. Some of the figures were young, some old; April looked pregnant, and November was skeleton-thin. These were not "Miss April" or "Miss November" in the manner popularized years before by *Playboy*; rather they were studies—warts and all—of puckering tangible tactile female flesh.

The drawings were fashioned in chalk. The chalk was red, on gray paper, and it seemed as though the artist's model—whether plump or lean, big-breasted or pert—hid her face on purpose, abashed by the gaze of the witness and turning her face to the wall. This brazen display of modesty proved somehow doubly affecting—like Degas's pastels of women emerging from or entering a bath. But where the Impressionist master's nudes conveyed a kind of inwardness, a self-absorbed *Noli me Tangere*, the women of the calendar suggested to the viewer that each had been thoroughly touched.

Their father's landscapes and, later, abstract figure-scapes are hanging in private collections, and a 2002 self-portrait—done in blue and gray, with his horn-rimmed glasses emphasized, and a bottle of scotch by the easel—has been recently purchased by MOMA, though not as yet for display. Two additional self-portraits hang in museums in San Francisco, and one in New Orleans. He studied himself, thinks Andrew, and examined women often, but when did he see *me*? James wonders the same, but his pronoun is *us*.

They each retain an early portrait of their mother—dressed, not naked—and have had it framed.

The brothers meet for lunch. Afterwards they plan to dismantle their father's studio apartment on West 29th Street, and have chosen a bistro nearby. "Sans Souci" is modest yet pretentious, the walls festooned with photographs of Paris and performers such as Maurice Chevalier, Edith Piaf, Yves Montand, and Charles Aznavour. Tables occupy the pavement, but they tell the black-haired waitress they prefer to sit inside. They have not seen each other in three weeks.

"How have you been?" asks James.

"OK. And you?"

"OK. Thanks for asking; we're fine."

"Where are we?" Andrew inquires. "In this procedure, I mean."

"God knows," says James. "It's a busy time of year."

"You can say that again," Andrew says.

It is June 1. The studio lease comes due in July, and the men agree there's no point in renewal; instead, they must clean the place out. They have begun to do so, dealing with all but the art. Their father's clothes were worn and tattered and easy enough to donate to Goodwill; with the exception of a standing floor-length mirror and a mahogany cabinet—six drawers of unfinished work—his furniture was junk. The TV set was ten years old, the stereo system defunct. His catalogues and art-books went to the Art Students League of New York, where he taught for twenty years as an adjunct faculty member; the librarian assured them that certain texts would enhance their collection and others would be sold in order to enlarge the acquisition fund. Three scholarship students, under James's supervision, have boxed and removed the books.

Art galleries and juice bars dot the neighborhood; there are cigar shops also, and falafel stands. Andrew arrived ten minutes early and walked past the building where their father lived and worked; James has done the same. These initial forays did not coincide, however. Tenth Avenue is thick with trucks, the side streets clogged with delivery vans and double-parked cars and men selling paperback books. Outside the restaurant, a wild-haired woman begs, the sign at her neck reading, "HOMELESS and ABUSED!"

"Ariane sends—what's the word?—regrets."

"I didn't expect her," says Andrew. Politeness rules the day.

"No."

"Jill does too."

"Please give her my best," says James, not meaning it.

"I will."

A butcher shop and package store flank their father's door. His studio is a third-floor walk-up, with north-facing windows and a small bedroom and galley kitchen befitting a young person and not a white-haired bent-backed seventy-six year old with emphysema who collapsed on the second-floor landing and died before the EMT's arrived. The painter was wearing his old leather jacket, his blue jeans and a paisley scarf; whether he fell while ascending or descending is an unanswered question. James likes to believe he was coming back home and Andrew likes to think that he was headed out. But because of the way the body lay sprawled—knees curled and arms akimbo—they do not know if he was stepping up or down.

"Hot day," says Andrew.

"Yes. It might rain."

"I don't believe it. The forecasters always announce it might rain . . ."

"Well, someday they're bound to be right."

They smile. This is a reference to a movie they once saw together, an Australian film: *Breaker Morant*. The hero of the movie—a brave man, even reckless—has as his motto the phrase: "Live every day as if it's your last. And someday you're bound to be right."

"Live, eat and be merry," says Andrew.

His brother completes the bad joke: "For tomorrow we diet."

The men have inherited, if little else, their father's penchant for comic platitudes. He pronounced them often. "A painting a day keeps the doctor away," he would tell his children, squinting at an easel. Or, "Just remember Hokusai, the 'old man mad about painting.' He said that in his seventies he was beginning to understand landscape; for me it's the same thing. The valley of a clavicle, the absolute hill of a hip . . ."

His will is clear—an equal division to each of the sons—but there is not much money to divide. After having paid the legal fees and extant debts and the surprisingly high cost of an obituary notice, only a small sum remains. This they share. It was their father's wish to have no Memorial Service and to be cremated; his ashes repose in a box. James and Andrew plan to scatter them, but have not as yet decided when or where.

The bulk of the "estate" lies in oils, stacked or shelved or still on easels in the studio; after lunch they will begin the process of dismantling. Their principal remaining challenge, therefore, is the artist's archive: where to store it, how to sell it, which drawings to claim and preserve. Artists have, their father said, either too much success or too little; the hardest thing of all is just to keep on keeping on. He did keep working till the end; the self-portrait on his easel—a rainbow of dabbed stabs of color at the eyes and eyebrows—was, when he died, still wet.

"You're sure you don't want to go through his closet?" Andrew had inquired of his wife, and she told him, "Yes."

"Yes, you're sure or yes you'll come along."

"Not if she's there."

James asked Ariane the same question, and the answer was similar: "*Non.*"

Task-oriented, the older child produces his iPad with a list titled "To Do." He sets it between them while they scan the menu, deciding against the "Prix Fixe." The brothers order soup and a Salade Niçoise and a bottle of Sauvignon Blanc. The room is nearly empty; the staff wear black and white.

"How's things?" asks James.

"Fine," Andrew tells him. "You?"

"Getting ready for school's summer break. I tell you, I can't wait."

"They don't get any older, do they? Your students."

"Tenth grade is the pivot-point, it seems. Tenth grade is when you start to see who they might become as grown-ups. But nothing's been decided yet, and I spend the entire semester trying to persuade them that the Federalist papers matter. The Bill of Rights means what it says. All those dead white men who wrote the constitution were once alive, I remind them, and the fuss about *Hamilton* helps. These are the sort of kids whose parents bought them tickets, and who know the show's lyrics by heart."

"You must be a good teacher."

"Getting better. But I'm bored."

James teaches in a private school in Riverdale, where wealthy teenagers are groomed for Ivy League colleges. His subjects are American History and English, and his annual salary is roughly the equivalent of what the children's chauffeurs earn—a point he often makes when Ariane comes home with a new scarf or costly cut of meat. Andrew, on the other hand, works as a Hedge Fund manager and his Christmas bonus sufficed to finance the purchase, in February, of a summer home in Southampton. Jill has hired an Interior Decorator, and spends her days with color wheels and wallpaper samples and in the shops of Antique dealers who specialize in French provincial furniture. Each brother has a son and daughter, and when members of the family convene—which they do only rarely now—the children form what they have called "the cousins' club."

"To Dad," says Andrew, and they clink glasses.

"To the old bugger," says James.

"Do you ever ask yourself," asks Andrew, "what it would have felt like to have a—oh, I don't know—a normal childhood? A father who came home from work and dropped his briefcase in the hall and drank his waiting martini?"

"You've been watching a rerun of *Mad Men*."

Andrew nods. "But that doesn't mean I can't wonder about it. Imagine what it would have felt like if our parents loved each other. And had a good marriage instead of a circus."

"Every marriage is a circus," James declares. "Not a three-ring circus, maybe, but always at least two."

"What are you saying?"

"Mom loved him, I'm certain. Until she couldn't take it any longer. Always that third act under the tent, always a contender for his affections at night."

"What an elegant way to put it."

"Have you seen this?" James asks. He produces a spiral notebook of the sort their father used, its pages thick with pen and pencil drawings. The cover page, in large block letters, proclaims the one name: JILL. Carefully he hands it to his brother, who holds the book as if deciding whether or not to open it, then puts the object down. The bottle of wine and the pitcher of water and the notebook form a triangle on the red checked tablecloth.

"Where did you get this?" asks Andrew. "When?"

"From Dad's cabinet of curiosities. Last week when I was helping those kids from the Art Students' League pack up his books and catalogues. Right next to the sketchbook that says ARIANE."

From his briefcase he pulls an identical volume and sets it on the table also. "The sisters-in-law," he offers. "They make a matched pair."

The rectangular sketchbooks confront each other like a reproach. Their covers are thick mottled cardboard: yellow ochre. Now, with a fourth focal point, the objects on the table form a square.

Andrew empties his glass. "Have you looked at them?"

"It's hard not to," says his brother. "But I haven't studied them closely. He missed Ariana's mole—the one, I mean, on her lower back."

"I didn't know she had one."

"No, you wouldn't. But dad of course did."

"Dear Christ," says Andrew. "He never ever stopped, did he?"

"We could ask them if they want these . . ."

"Or want them destroyed."

"Do you?"

"Do I what?"

"Want to destroy them?"

The waitress clears their plates. She suggests a second bottle; they shake their heads and order espresso instead. The men share a reluctance to leaf through the sheets, to study what their father saw or look at what he drew. They wait for the coffee to come. What to make, they ask each other, of a life lived so selfishly that nonetheless felt devotional; what example has the painter set? How best to deal, they wonder, with their father's legacy: a shambling yet absolute focus, an inconsistent constancy?

After some moments, agreement is reached. Each takes the sketchbook with his own wife's name and positions it face upward where the leavings of the meal have been removed. The objects bulk on the now-rumpled cloth.

"Let's see what's here," Andrew says.

The first five studies of JILL are her ankles and toes—intimate viewings and carefully wrought. There are three or four versions on each of the pages, as though the draughtsman wished to rehearse his knowledge of anatomy and his proficiency with metatarsals, toenails, and the arch of an instep—all delineated with precision and crosshatched with fine pencil strokes. Then comes a calf and then knee. By the time the artist draws the expanse of upper thigh his strokes grow broad, and at the cleft of the model's spread legs he uses a thick yellow chalk. Andrew clears his throat. He wants to use the formal words: his wife's pudendum has been attentively studied, her labia incised with ink, and the coiled pubic hairs are rendered with care: tight spirals in a cluster. The slight roll of fat above her vulva feels familiar; so does the look of her navel and the line of her arched lower back. By the next drawing—the woman's buttocks raised and splayed, her hand between them, probing—his formality of language fades, and Andrew thinks, *Cunt, cunt.*

"Dear Christ," he says again.

"You didn't know?"

He shakes his head. "Did you?"

James hesitates. "I guessed, I think. Once I asked Ariane what she'd been doing at the studio—she came home late and a little disheveled—and she said she made some soup for Dad while he was noodling with his sketchbook. *Canoodling* I suppose would be more like it—whatever that word means. But when I pressed her she said nothing, implying it wasn't my business, and I should leave it alone."

"And?"

"Frankly, I was happy to. And did."

"Jill never told me."

"No."

"When did he do these drawings, do you think?"

"Six years ago, roughly; they're dated. October 12, 2016 is the sketchbook for Jill and November 1 for Ariane." James points. "Here. On the title page."

"So they overlapped?"

"A little, maybe. One went in as the other went out."

They sit back, surveying each other and each other's wives. Their dead father's hand hovers between them, fondling the demitasse cups. His is a palpable presence, a reminder of old venery. The long-legged high-breasted waitress, passing by their table, asks, "Is everything all-right, *Messieurs?*"

James answers in his fluent French that they have much enjoyed the meal but will sit a little longer. She brings a plate of macaroons, saying "*Compliments de la maison.*" Their father's paintbrush limns her, and the dead man licks his lips. Hips swiveling, she turns away, and Andrew asks: "Is that why they're so angry with each other?"

"Who?"

"Jill and Ariane."

"I thought you knew. Of course."

There are additional reasons. Ariane attended the Sorbonne; her parents are retired doctors, living in Aix-en-Provence. She has a deep-seated conviction that the culture of America is second-rate, and crass commercialism is the hallmark of the bourgeoisie. Her sister-in-law, for example, exemplifies this acquisitiveness, and she looks at Jill's possessions with a mixture of envy and scorn. The jewels are vulgar, she tells her husband, the apartment tastelessly furnished, and the house in Southampton—which she has no intention of seeing, and will not be invited to—sounds like a perfect horror of *nouveau riche* display.

"It's not so much," says Ariane, "that she is stupid—this I can forgive, it's how she was born and no fault of her own. But that she believes herself intelligent and her opinions should be listened to, this is insupportable. Ignorance! *Bêtises!*"

For her part, Jill is outraged by what she calls the unearned self-assurance of her French sister-in-law. Their mutual dislike has simmered for years and at the least provocation erupts into a boil. "I won't be condescended to," his wife insists to Andrew. "That high horse she rides, it's full of horse-shit, it's attitude, attitude, *attitude*, and I won't put up with it; what makes you think I should?"

Ariane is lean, intense, and only recently has given up on cigarettes; Jill is conscious of her weight and—even with a personal trainer and three sessions a week of Pilates—fights to keep it down. Ariane is dark, Jill pale; the former is an excellent cook, the latter pays a catering service to provide their meals. Ariane, a Democrat, is outraged by her recently acquired knowledge that Jill votes Republican. The women share a birthday—October 23—and somehow that too has become an affront.

The children are a further bone of contention: their manners, their mode of education, their need to wear glasses, their proficiency at the piano or agility in sports. This competitive rancor has poisoned the well, and only the dead painter's admiration had been a source of comfort and a provisional peace. He praised the two of them equally, or so it seemed, and told his sons how fortunate they were to have married such great beauties—a pair of blessed damozels he would love to draw.

He has done so with a vengeance. They lie splayed on the restaurant table like fresh cuts of meat. There are quick sketches, composite ones, with several studies crossed out. The final pages of each notebook contain finished full-length portraits: small-scale but exact. Their wives have been anatomized, both lying back on what the husbands recognize as their father's camp bed and both with their legs spread.

The detailing is careful; Jill's ample upper thighs, full breasts and outthrust elbow are crosshatched with a fine-nibbed pen that—no matter how rapidly the artist worked—would have taken time to complete. The visage too—unlike the blank or absent faces of the models in his calendar—is one that's fully drawn. The expression on Jill's face is one of pleased satiety, and Andrew cannot keep himself from wondering why his wife would have permitted or solicited this session: what was she doing while posed? When did his father paint her, how often, and why such an open display? The word has become a refrain in his head, and he cannot keep from repeating it: *cunt.*

Ariane, too, seems available on paper in a way that surprises her husband: the taut-wound caution gone, the hunger for sensation keen—though in his own experience she could prove distant and withholding in the act of sex. This figure, by contrast, seems wholly absorbed in pleasures of the flesh. Her eyes are glazed, half-shut above the avid-seeming invitation of her open mouth. Her hair curls in tendrils above a wet ear; her chin has been tilted, upturned. He cannot look at her the way a stranger might; he cannot see this pencil-and-ink study of a naked woman as a work of art. An objective viewer might perhaps find fault with or praise the portrait as accomplished; what James sees on the pages he leafs through is an act of infidelity: his wife on his dead father's bed.

"*À la prochaine,*" says the waitress, now tending the cash register, and James nods. They leave. The day has grown hotter, or perhaps it's the aftereffect of lunch with wine, but both men feel dizzy, a little. Turning the corner, Andrew stumbles and must steady himself on a trash receptacle. Two black teenagers approach them, singing, then pass by.

James produces a key to their father's apartment and opens the door and checks the mailbox—which contains, now, only third-class mail and circulars stuffed within. Slowly, Andrew going first, they climb the stairs and pause at the second-floor turnaround; bicycles and rollerblades occupy the landing where their father fell. Someone has been frying onions; somewhere, a radio blares.

Inside, they see his coffee cups and soup pots arrayed on hooks above the sink. His painter's smock and white straw hat still hang from pegs in the hall. The studio is airless, and Andrew cranks open a window, then they turn to face each other and the array of canvases piled three or four deep on the floor. There are a hundred or so such objects: two feet by three feet, as if in a series; there are larger canvases also, most of them facing the wall.

"OK?" asks James.

"OK."

They set to work. This means, they have agreed, they will separate what's finished from what was rejected by the artist or stored against future completion; they will catalogue what's complete and what remains to do. The finished paintings and the works-in-progress can be readily determined, since the latter are unsigned. Habitually, their father added his signature and date to a canvas only when he deemed it done.

The brothers know that what they scan has scant commercial value; the artist's two last dealers closed their galleries, and one of them is dead. It is in any case a world with which they're unfamiliar; in part, perhaps, as a reaction against their father's role in it they both have steered clear of the "art scene." His reputation, though solid, is small. Once or twice they met a critic or a curator who regaled them with some anecdote about parental misbehavior; and once or twice somebody asked if they were related to the painter, since the last name is unusual. But the task they face is private, not a public one, and no third party will supervise or second-guess decisions. James hopes to be finished by late afternoon; his brother knows it will take longer and is prepared to return.

Andrew takes out his iPad and commences to fashion a list. There are four categories: *Landscapes, Abstractions, Portraits, Nudes.* The fourth is the most populous, their father's focus in old age. The nudes are faceless, always, and always female; in the first hour, of the forty works they catalogue, sixteen are studies—begun or finished—of a woman's back or breast. Another four detail an ankle; two focus on a knee.

It ought to be, the brothers tell each other, a time for revelation; it ought to come clear finally whether the artist was major or minor—what sort of achievement and what sort of talent was his. Was his, they wonder, a noble pursuit or self-indulgence or just seductive skill? It would be nice, says James, if we spent more time together, but they both know this won't happen; once their task has been completed, they will go their separate ways.

For all they can see are the nudes. The women turn to face them, or turn their heads away. They line the artist's studio like prostitutes in a bordello painted by Lautrec—indifferent, filing their nails. In his landscapes and skyscapes and seascapes the brothers see the limbs of naked female bodies also; in his abstract compositions they discern, or think they do, the outline of arms, breasts, and legs. Where earlier the studio seemed only and entirely the place their father lived and worked, it now feels haunted, threatening, a place to flee.

At four o'clock, Andrew says, "I'm not sure I can handle this."

"No."

"It seems somehow intrusive. Or, what's the word, invasive . . ."

"Can't we hire someone?"

"Who?"

"Oh, anyone. One of those students who boxed up the books . . ."

They come to a large canvas that had been facing the wall. The brothers turn it face-forward: four feet high by six feet wide, and signed by the painter in the lower right-hand corner, then dated 12/17/16. Two life-sized naked women crowd the composition, though one lies left to right, the other right to left. The blonde lies above the brunette. This is not so much an opposition as a charged asymmetry; the plump one's head faces the lean one's feet, and they meet in the center, navel to navel, where they have joined hands. Flesh occupies the bulk of the canvas; there is only the dark outline of a bed, a rumpled sheet, and the wall behind them is a wash of blue. In the upper right-hand corner of the painting, a window opens out upon a world elsewhere.

As in their father's calendar drawings, the faces of the models are an ochre blur. The bodies, however, have been rendered with anatomical precision: painted in the manner of an Alex Katz, or the photorealism of mid-career Chuck Close. The arrangement itself—two naked women facing each other—suggests a Tibetan mandala and owes much to Matisse. The fluid circularity of their adjacent legs and arms evokes *La Danse*: a daisy-chain of reaching hands, of near-interchangeable limbs. Whatever else is true of the conception and composition, the canvas argues mastery: these models are present, are *here*.

Four people crowd the room. Even without distinguishing features, the two men recognize their wives; the painting might as well be titled JILL & ARIANE. Now what the artist saw is what their husbands see. The final studies in the sketchbooks they examined over lunch are studies for this full-size effort: a back-to-front adjacency of buttocks, bellies, legs. The women have been lovers, clearly, and are engaged in or preparing for—or, perhaps, in a brief respite from—the act of love.

Andrew looks at James; James looks away. "What do you make of this?" the older brother inquires.

There is silence between them. The silence extends. They want to ask:

1. Is this scene imagined or real?
2. When did the women consent to be drawn, and how often: why?
3. Did they come together willingly, by accident, or only after the fact?
4. Were the two women rivals; was a preference expressed for one over the other?
5. Did their father need to urge his models to remove their clothes?
6. Then to embrace?
7. Had the painter slept with them also?
8. Separately or together?
9. Did he want his sons to see this? Did he show it to strangers? Art dealers?
10. Could the canvas be sold? Hung in a gallery?
11. Disposed of in private? Shared?

12. How did he pleasure his models; what did they say to each other?

13. Had they been eating together? Drinking? Laughing? Enemies already?

14. Cajoled into, resistant to, or eager for the act?

15. Why have the women kept for all these years silent? Estranged?

16. Why, hands clasped across each other's sex, do they now refuse to shake hands?

17. Does art follow nature here?

18. Or the reverse?

19. Do their wives know this painting exists?

This is not twenty questions, however. The brothers say nothing for minutes. Then they leave.

Passacaglia and Fugue
in C-Minor

FOOD, CLOTHING, SHELTER, our teachers instructed us, are the three conditions of dignified survival. Man requires each. It's a comprehensive list and makes a kind of catch-all sense, but lately I've found myself questioning it; why not clean air, for instance, or any of the things we swear we live for—art, tactile alertness, God, love?

I make this latter list on purpose arbitrarily, to show how simple it must once have been. Some sociologist pulls at his beard, having disposed that morning of the problems of the Industrial Revolution, and over a glass of sherry with his cousin he coins the phrase. "Food, clothing, shelter. That's all a person needs."

His cousin disturbs him; he has not seen her in years. The faint smell of musk envelops her, them; she stands six inches too close. Her auburn hair is perfectly pinned but gives the impression of disarray anyhow, as if restraint might come undone.

He does not know her well. Her marriage is less than it should be, it seems, and she has journeyed to this seaside town in order to consult with him on what course it's wisest to chart. Her breast heaves when she says this, and therefore he focuses on the eyelet lace at her throat.

There is an amber pin also.

"Food, clothing and shelter," he repeats—struggling to maintain composure, not sure why the phrase should satisfy him but knowing it worth repeating, and he'll use it in committee the next day. It simplifies things somehow and keeps incoherence back. His cousin has a beauty mark on her left cheek.

I imagine it that way this morning—the pedant backing and filling, the passionate woman imploring his aid. So he remarks upon the usefulness of lodging while she tempts him to bed. The sound of the bay on the shingle down at the foot of the garden is soft, then loud, then soft. At the end of the evening the pair make a civilized parting; he helps her into her cloak. Or, by unspoken agreement, she follows him upstairs: propriety be damned . . .

But perhaps the woman's not his cousin, not already married, and he throws himself on his knees before her and says, "I offer you lifelong protection. Be mine forever, my dearest, and with the Good Lord's help we'll be content." The whole thing feels Victorian, so stuffed with cubby-holing certainties: he *has* to be on bended knee and she above him, trembling, her hand on his shoulder, rings glinting in the lamplight. There has been music playing—Bach—from the Victrola by the garden-facing window. There's a half-filled decanter, silk in her skirt and his cravat; there's intricate plaster ornamentation above their juxtaposed heads.

What else might one require to flesh the scene more fully? There's art, tactile alertness, God, and the civilizing possibility of love; we have, in short, meat, rags, and roof.

B's wife and daughter have departed; he will join them the next day. "Like speculators," he told his wife. "House-flippers, that's what we've been. We've fixed this place up perfectly. In order to leave."

"We'll come back," she said. "Darling, I promise."

"I don't think you mean that."

She made no answer; she was pasting labels on the packing crates. Her handwriting was black, and bold; he could see across the kitchen's width how she assorted their things.

"Possessions," she said. "So many things we thought we needed but never used one single time. Yogurt makers, pasta makers, meat grinders, meat slicers, two Cuisinarts. Whatever were we thinking of?"

"Food." B. stared at the silo, through the pantry windows he'd had reglazed that fall.

"We didn't starve," she said. "And we never used that yogurt maker."

"So why bother packing it?"

She looked at him. "How do you mean?"

"I mean, why pack up all this stuff? There won't be room in the apartment kitchen; we don't have to take it all with us."

She unrolled the packing tape, then cut it raspingly. "This is for storage," she said.

Andrew Corrigan was never at home on the land. But in ways that other men might fight to overcome shyness, or a pattern of speech that keeps them from promotion, he forced himself to muster at least the appearance of ease. Terrified of heights, he learned enough about rock-climbing to mask that fear from others if never from himself. Though he thought of horses as threatful and capricious, he nonetheless seemed calm in the saddle when riding. Each time he felled a tree he imagined in advance how the trunk might pinion him; his two cycle engines would sputter, then stick. He remembered how Curt Simmons lost his toe to a lawn-mower blade, and how the left-hander's pitching career was hampered by the accident; each time he started the machine, Andrew did a jig-step of avoidance.

His feet would blister easily. What looked like white water to him was a trickle to enthusiasts; what seemed a ten-acre meadow to mow would be, to a farmer's practiced eye, three and a half, maybe four. Deer-hunting, he half-hoped to miss, and when he went out skiing he would pray for poor conditions so it would not be shameful to quit. Skeet-shooting, he might claim a headache, and he said he went fly-fishing for the solitude and beauty, not the catch.

But reputations are rarely made by those with the ability to judge, and Andrew had some small repute as a sportsman and outdoorsman in the circles where he moved. He could tell the sugar maple from the split-leaf maple, after all, and could tell a Dunham boot-tread from a Frye. He ordered clothes from Abercrombie & Fitch and spoke with knowledge and assurance of the way to string a bow; he took his Eddie Bauer down-bag where he went on weekend visits, and said he preferred it to sheets. Sleep on a pine-bough bed, he proclaimed: it's better than foam rubber; what finer canopy can any of us ask for than the open sky?

"All right?"

"We maybe can work something out."

"Call it a deal then?"

"I imagine . . ." Roy begins, but lets his voice trail off.

B. waits. "Yes?"

"We maybe could work something out."

"I'll be leaving soon."

Roy nods.

"Tomorrow, in fact."

"I heard that."

"So what I mean is, Roy, it would give me satisfaction—be a load off my mind, so to speak—if I knew this thing was settled."

Roy ponders, lights his pipe. In the interval that follows, B. wonders if perhaps he pressed too much, or has been over-urgent in his displayed hope for help.

"'Course you would," says Roy.

"So?"

"So like I said," he says. He stops; his match gutters out. "These things take time."

"You know the place. You know it better than I do."

"Wouldn't say that," Roy says.

"The fence is good."

"I grant you . . ."

"We fixed the barn last summer. That crosstie. It'll hold."

"Mm-mn."

"You've worked it all these years," says B.

Now Roy says nothing. B. decides he too will wait; they puff in silence, contrapuntal.

I suppose I could go on inventing instances, but neither the Victorians nor Andrew are germane. This fable deals with psychic need, the love of rootedness when all else seems to shift. Our hero is a man of early middle age who spent his childhood traveling, since his father was Vice-President of an import-export firm. Whether the commodity was bristle, piassava, artificial Christmas trees or fur, there always seemed to be some need to visit the country of origin, set up an office and send B. to school. Then, just as young B. grew acclimatized, having acquired friends or learned the rudiments of a new language and earned entry into some new group, the family would be transplanted again.

B's brother took it better. Younger by three years, he appeared to want only his relatives' protective circle; he had no trouble sleeping and seemed to welcome change. But B. was reading books about the pioneers. For him the family circle was like a group of covered wagons, nosed together to ward off assault; his night-light was a campfire and his dreams were full of Indians who pillaged their supplies. After his father's fatal heart attack, when the widow and sons returned to America, B. had lived more than half his life abroad.

It's not uncommon: children of a foreign-service family—or the army, or multinational corporations—get used to travel as the norm. He had food and clothing in abundance; he had money to invest. So the first portion he paid out from his portion of inheritance was earmarked for a home where he himself might set down roots; he hunted through New England for six months. The house he chose, he realized with small surprise, was a brick colonial in imitation of the English house where he had been born. It had four chimneys and a stately entrance hall; he bought it on the spot.

Let's imagine for a moment that those Victorian cousins—who are they: total strangers? seasonal neighbors? creatures of our author's overheated fancy? the grandparents of my fiancée?—announce their betrothal next day. Subsequent to the exertions of the night. After having climbed the stairs (p 436). Is this the proper order or sequence in the narrative, and does it make a difference? What difference does it make?

Would the pair have willingly yielded to temptation, knowing already they would become husband and wife? Was this "consultation" the one that tipped the scale? What role did sherry play? Or melodic repetition in the composition by Bach? Who takes advantage of whom? But since this is not present tense, who *took* advantage of whom? Do they remember huddling in the summerhouse when he was twelve, she ten? And what then did they dare?

"Off, off, you lendings," as King Lear on the heath proclaims, but are we talking here about a playsuit, a jumpsuit, a pair of shorts, a skirt, and not, as the mad monarch intends, the clothes he wore at court? When they were "huddling in the summerhouse," was it predictive of the previous scene when she journeys to his seaside home for help?

Or was their youthful innocence intact? Do they recall the mouth she made, the lips that grazed each other's lips, his halting hand on her not-yet swelling breast? And what of their later romantic careers and subsequent erotic adventures together or apart? Do I need discuss them here? Would the lady have remained, if not *virga intacta*, chaste?

Now let's fast forward twenty years, or possibly thirty, or twenty-five; let's leave the summerhouse behind and return to the locale in our opening passage (p. 435) evoked. Is that beauty mark and smell of musk a statement of authorial intention, of his/her/our/their descriptive strategy, and did it persuade? And what of that suggestive—is it in fact suggestive?—amber pin pinned at her throat? Not to mention eyelet lace.

Have these two once been lovers, and will they become so again? Was she in fact already married and did her cousin the sociologist take advantage of their hot proximity or urge her to go home? Having called a cab. What was her marriage like, and was her soon-to-be-ex-husband an insufferable bore? Or perhaps, with this beauty, a beast? Would it be a horse and carriage he summons, a transom cab, car service, an Uber or Lyft? What is the relevant time-frame, and which word might best evoke it?

Let's substitute, for cab, the word *cabriolet*. Has he had his way that after-noon already with the kitchen maid—she with her back to him bent down across the sink or stove, her smock raised high, her arse exposed—or perhaps the thick-thighed red-haired hard-muscled gardener and is he therefore, if not entirely sated, doubtful of his readiness, unwashed, to start again?

I haven't got it right.

I can't *see* them, can't enter the room . . .

Let's establish additional context and content for the scene.

Take 2.

Would there have been others involved? Does the supplicant's second-cousin by marriage, Lady Margaret Cholmondoly, anticipate the matrimonial union heretofore predicted and has she encouraged it by offering to lend them for their honeymoon the gardener's cottage at Mull? That green island in the Inner Hebrides where, since 1562, Lady Margaret's people have retained a foothold or at least a toehold and much-shrunken manse. Where the rain raineth every day. (And have you noticed, reader, how once again our writer references Shakespeare, linking Lear to leer as well as royal court to courtship, "the lips that grazed each other's lips, his halting hand on her not-yet swelling breast?") Is this habit of quotation a good or bad idea? Does milady sanction their shared antics or, *per contra*, disapprove?

Would the couple need encouragement prior to such coupling; are their circumstances pinched? Sufficiently constrained, I mean, so they accept her generosity, or are they self-sufficient and gone to Venice instead? Booking the Gritti Palace or the Danieli or the Bauer-Grunwald or Hotel Excelsior because his own pockets are deep? Or are the pocketings hers?

Take 3.

Who therefore pays which piper, calls what tune? Should I have written, *fiscal* circumstances and, if only by sonorous association, *physical* circumstances, and is there in fact a useful link between the two terms or a mere accident of sound? *Lear* and *leer* and *court* and *court* might well prove acceptable, but *fiscal* and *physical* go too far. What do *clothing* and *shelter* in any case imply, and who will doff what where?

Take 4.

In order for this entry to have the ring of fictive fact, we need to give them food as well; they need to share a meal. Does she cook for him, he her? Do they go out to a restaurant or order room service instead? Are they in a hotel together—the Danieli, the Gritti?—-or a private home? His, hers? Has he had previous lovers, twelve or twenty-two? Or two hundred possibly, as did Frank Harris in *My Secret Life*, and is the risk of gonorrhea real? Or is our sociologist per contra a serious scholar, more used to port at High Table than dalliance in the alleyways and streets? And what of his partner, his soon-to-be but not-yet-in-depth described wife?

Auburn hair. A pin at the base of her throat. Eyelet lace. Five feet, four inches tall. One-hundred thirteen pounds. Is she a woman of the world or first venturing to enter it, as does a debutante, balling? Is that an acceptable pun? We have accepted "Lear" and "leer" but "debutante balling" is too far to stretch. And what of her silk skirt? The beauty mark on her left cheek? Let's say they meet not in Cornwall ("The sound of the bay on the shingle down at the foot of the garden is soft, then loud, then soft," p. 436) but, rather, in the Cotswolds, where there's no noise of the sea. In the village of Chipping Camden or—more authentically—Combe.

In England (as opposed to, say, America) one is never further from the water than seventy-five miles distant, so the sound of water lapping might well prove appropriate. Should I compare the sound of bedsprings to the sound of the shingle and tide? Or should I find some inland metaphor or simile—cows ruminant in unison or *like* the rustling of tree branches in a western wind? That the small rain down can rain. Strike that. ~~That the small rain down can rain.~~

The bed's mattress is horsehair, and firm. It will not retain their imprint. It has been worn thin by generation after generation, that great word of art and of life.

(This is under the assumption, reader, that her "imploring his aid," p. 436, contains as it were, an implicit agreement as to what that aid entails, and a bargain has been struck. Their encounter is no accident but by both of them carefully planned; it is, one might say, tat for tit. When he made her welcome, offering *Food, Clothing, Shelter*, he knew what reciprocity consisted of, consists of, would consist of, and when she would unpin her auburn hair. And will she be the one in the morning—her penmanship practiced, her spacing adept—to record for our posterity the italicized phrase in the previous sentence? I think so, yes. Why not? There's no real mystery here.)

Chipping Camden or, more authentically, Combe, would likely have a horsehair-stuffed mattress in each village home. For Combe is the less up to date of the two locales, not engulfed by tourists or today with a functioning picturesque pub. Therefore waterbeds and Posturepedics and the like would have no currency in that unfashionable place, where the residents still have a Vicar and bad teeth. Where pensioners still gather on the village green on Sunday and the postman knows each pensioner by name. With few cars, and none of them new.

But have the sheets been ironed, freshly laundered, or are they silk not cotton and are they pink not white?

This is the sort of observation that, as W. S. Gilbert puts it in "The Mikado," lends "corroborative detail, intended to give artistic verisimilitude to an otherwise bald and unconvincing narrative." But who gives a flying fuck? Who cares if sheets be pink or white or silk or patterned or Cottonelle, and with which thread count? What of Lady Margaret Cholmondoly and her offer of the house in Mull? Who cares if this transpires in Cornwall or the Cotswolds, in 1763 or 1897 or 1921? The "Victrola by the garden-facing window" referred to on p. 436 was not commercially available till 1925, so there's anachrony here. Would they have been playing Bach, his Passacaglia and fugue? When *was* the Victorian age, its dates I mean, and what was the age of the Queen's consort, Prince Albert, when to her enduring sorrow and after having sired nine children the dear man passed away? *Answer:* 49.

But is it not the function of each imaginative artist to leave room for imagination, to let his/her/their/our readership fill in the blanks? Let us therefore draw the curtain (silk or cotton, diaphanous or dark?) on the encounter here adduced, whether real or imagined, practiced or fumbling, amateurish or adept. The scene's dénouement need not concern us. Reader, I married him. Please turn the page.

"How long you think to be away?" asked Roy at last.

"Don't know. Can't tell. A year anyhow."

"You fixing to rent the place out?"

"No."

"Drain the pipes?"

"I'll do that," B. said. "Tomorrow when we leave. Or maybe I'll get back to check on it."

"What about 'lectricity?"

"I figured I'd turn it off. Why?"

"Electric fence," said Roy. "I use it off the barn."

B. did not know this bargaining system, and therefore he waited.

"You turn it off," continued Roy. "I'd have to string up new."

"We've got a separate box up there."

"But woven wire," Roy said. "That's better for the sheep. Better for me, anyways; I wouldn't have to be down here at all hours checking the line. You know, a wind comes up . . ."

"All right. I'll buy the stuff; you string it."

Roy lit his pipe.

"Anything else?" asked B.

"There's seed. Which field gets corn?"

"I leave it up to you," he said.

"The woodlot. Back behind Bailey's . . ."

"Whatever . . ."

"All right. Except that silo. It'll take some patching."

So they dickered the short afternoon, and by three o'clock he'd given the farmer free rein. It was what B. wanted anyhow: permission to depart. His house would be taken care of, emptied out; his land would flourish in his absence. It was November 18. The ground was not yet frozen, and Roy's tractor-tire therefore crimped it as he left.

There are three ways to see this, he thinks. Three ways to tell it, to read it.

The restaurant "Extebari" in the Axpe Valley near Durango in the north of Spain (Fire, Live Coal, Ember!) has a tasting menu, and it's a famous place. Famously expensive, too. In the various gastronomical lists of "the world's top ten destinations," Extebari is often included: everything local, everything grilled. Yet those fortunate enough to join the nightly banquet have—absent a declaration of allergies—no choice in what they eat. On the night of 14 October, 2017, the menu offers:

> Cracker & mushrooms (the latter a hot broth)
> Salt anchovy, toasted bread
> Butter (goat's milk)
> Buffalo Tomato and belly white tuna
> Mussels, marinière
> Pumpkin leaves and King Crab (the former rolled around the latter)
> Chlamys varia (these being squid)
> Prawn of Palamos
> Baby squid and its ink and caramelized onion
> Ceps and aubergine (these being mushrooms and eggplant, infused)
> Red sea bream and vegetables, the former divided at table and served
> Beef chop: ditto.
> Reduced milk ice cream with beetroot sauce
> Fig in almond cream
> Magnardise and cocoa, chocolate pastry and mousse

He won't even mention the wines. Which were pairings and delectable but too many now to describe. Or in detail to recall. Because, come the next morning, he had had the hell of a headache and couldn't remember the vintages or even the name of the driver who ferried them from their hotel for twenty Euros, then twenty Euros back. *Them* being our author, his uncomplaining wife, and the two "foodies" with whom they traveled and who had booked the seating five months in advance. The Axpe Valley near the coast was, as his knowledgeable friend explained, "in the middle of nowhere," and in any case they planned to drink and wouldn't want to find the place or, after drinking, return to the hotel in the deep dark. What *was* their driver's name?

The four of them commenced their journey by flying to Madrid. Thereafter they flew to San Sebastian and from San Sebastian drove to

Durango—the nearest town to the valley where they intended to eat. They had been on the road for a week. There were the usual muddles, · the usual excitements, but both couples traveled widely and there was little notable in their so-far excursions: talks, walks, fine museums and churches and views.

At two in the morning, he woke in pain and was violently ill. We use the term "violently" almost as a commonplace, a word conjoined to "ill" or "sick" in standard parlance and not meaning much. But on this night, it did mean much; he feared a heart attack. Softly, so as not to wake his sleeping wife, he got out of bed and groaned. She was a deep sleeper and did not hear him moaning. Keeping the bathroom door shut, he knelt before or sat on the toilet instead. He thought that he might die.

The ache in his chest traveled both up and down; he was shivering and sweating, cold and hot. His stomach felt caught in a vise. His throat was raw; both arms hurt. His knees protested too. "If I'm going to die," he told himself, "this is a hell of a place to do it in, and where's the nearest hospital, and do the EMT's speak English and who am I going to call?"

The pain, however, diminished. It was relieved by vomiting and diarrhea; after an hour or so in the bathroom he understood it had been food poisoning, not cardiac trouble, with which he was afflicted. This was a comfort of sorts. Queasily, and course by course, he reconstructed the meal. Was it the crab, the tuna, the sauce for the mushrooms or squid?

There had been other diners: Japanese and Italian couples and a table of men speaking Polish or Russian or Czech. Spanish music had been playing: guitars and castanets. One woman ate alone. He thought of their imperious waiter, the pretty girl who brought them bread, the boy who replenished their glasses of water and the chef and sous-chef who passed by wearing toques. He thought of the candles, the lanterns, the white linen cloths. Food portions were parceled out, plate after plate; the ballet of presentation had been expertly choreographed. This held equally true for the wines. They arrived with regularity and were discoursed upon and poured with a pedantic flourish and emphasis on provenance. The twelve-year-old Rioja, for example, came from the next set of hills. Though he had understood the meal would be excessive, he was unaware of overeating till the sixth or seventh course.

By then it was too late. He plowed on through the bream and beef and ice cream and the various sweets and dessert cordials with a sense of obligation. Obligatory, too, the praise, the language of informed consumption, the tasteful chatter as to what they sampled and its aftertaste. He was too old for this, he knew, ill-suited for lavish consumption or expenditure and half-naked on the bathroom floor. His head above the toilet bowl, his left hand on the handle, he waited for the tank to fill, then flush. *Misericordia, Misericordia; mea culpa, pater optime*: these were the words in his head.

He was not religious, not a Catholic, but prayer and repentance seemed the order of the night. He promised himself he would eat no such meal ever and never again. He rubbed his eyes; he yawned. He swore to himself there would be moderation, a stately progress through the years, however few or many might be left to him. Again he threw up, again groaned.

Tentative, he attempted to stand and, shivering, sweat pouring down, succeeded. From the tap he took a sip of water: lukewarm, iron-tinged. His was a life not unlike those of his associates: the time-share in Sanibel, the car repairs, the casual and not-so-casual infidelities, the decreasing interest in politics because things do not change. At some point in the pre-dawn dark, he heard laughter in the street. Young men and women—he assumed their youth—promenaded past the window of the *parador*, talking and flirting and singing while our hero held his head.

Let's take it from the top. In the soul's dark night, the body's ditto, while our nameless character bends above the toilet bowl, the snatch of song he overhears from the street is *La Cucaracha*, and it's sung off-key. What passes before him while he shuts his eyes are images of conquest: a driver's test passed, a first girl kissed, a salary trebled once he closed the deal on that shopping mall in Amarillo, Texas. Then come images of failure: the weight he gained, the hair he lost, the death of their twenty-two-year-old only child from a lethal cocktail of cocaine and applejack and crystal meth. The boy left no note behind.

His own youth passed before him, the nights when he too roamed the streets, the snatches of song and flirtation. He dried his face and hands. He knew that he would die. It was no longer an immediate concern, but partook of the long view. His insides had been hollowed out; he lay on the tile floor, convulsing, until the convulsiveness passed. We all are born to die.

I've just returned from northern Spain and the cave of Altamira. It ranks among the oldest of our species' sites. The dating is approximate, since our ancestors lived there for thousands of years, and the Upper Paleolithic Period was a lengthy one. But somewhere between thirty-five thousand and thirteen thousand years ago, Altamira sheltered tribesmen who sought relief from the weather and safe haven from assault. Here they built their fires underneath the rock-vault and cooked and ate and slept and honed their tools and tanned their hides and buried their young and old dead. Here they learned the rudiments of speech. Further, they made art.

Many years previous, and in the south of France, I visited Lascaux; the two are collateral cousins. Those who produced the paintings were no doubt unacquainted, and eons as well as miles intervene, but there's an overarching similarity of atmosphere in the two caves. They have the feel of temples, really, with polychrome walls and ceilings long before Michelangelo's Sistine Chapel or the work of Tintoretto in Venice or the murals of Rivera in Detroit. The visitor still stands in awe of human ingenuity and the enduring power of the artistic impulse—color and form displayed on rock since the seeming-beginning of time.

There are other places and cultures where much the same holds true. In India, Australia, Namibia—all over the globe, it would appear—*Homo Sapiens* emblazoned figures on cave walls. They drew bison and horses and wild boar and goats, with protuberant bellies and horns. The fissures and bulges and hollows in rock form part of the bodies portrayed. The animal kingdom predominates in Altamira, though in other countries a shaman or stick figure may also be seen on outcroppings of stone. These shapes are colored red and black and brown, ochre, sienna, and white. How the artist or artists managed to take perspective into account—the rocks are irregular, often cracked—is a mystery among mysteries, and to imagine lying on your back in the deep dark of such a cave, then blowing pigment upwards or painting with an upraised palm is to beggar the imagination. This is mastery.

We don't fully understand the purpose of these images, whether they were hunting aids or emblems of some sort of worship, whether they were in essence descriptive or prescriptive: a way of showing what the tribesmen saw or hoped to see. But the power of these renderings is undiminished, wholly present, and a first reaction to Altamira's discovery (in 1879) was that this was modern art, a hoax.

Once the caves were uncovered and explored, modernity did enter in. By this I mean the trickle and then stream and torrent of visitors, the bacteria on clothes and mud on shoes and the stale of tobacco and pollen and hot humid breath. In order to preserve the paintings from indiscriminate exposure, the governments of Spain and France (to take only the examples of Altamira and Lascaux) constructed replicas of the original halls. Now the visitor—unless particularly privileged and arranged for long in advance—must study imitations, not the thing itself. You join a line of fee-paying tourists and walk past display-cases and maps. As the depth and dark accretes, you peer upwards at the colored rock and, dimly at first and then with increasing acuity, learn to identify shapes. *Here's* a tusk and *there's* a hoof and *see* how the seam in the stone runs between them, suggesting a belly or back. Guides tell you what you're looking at and hold out their hands for a tip.

In the Dordogne I'd felt short-changed, a little, as if the lack of authenticity turned Lascaux into Disneyworld, a second-hand experience of the original site. The installation felt commercial and the crowd was large. This is one paradox of democracy: common access to a place—think of Jones Beach or the gallery housing the *Mona Lisa*—robs it of its singularity. But somehow in northern Spain (there are many other caves in the area of Altamira; size and centrality suggests it served as meeting-place) the same did not hold true. My wife and I were happy to take sanctuary in a hall replicating the one first occupied by bands of tribesmen: fifteen or thirty in a clan, and most of them short-lived.

They would have retreated for safety but settled near the mouth of the cave, where there was light and air. The average life-expectancy was less than thirty years; almost no one survived to fifty, and women were—because of the dangers of child-bearing—doubly at risk. Thomas Hobbes's description of life as "Nasty, brutish, and short" held true for *Homo Sapiens* then, as it does, alas, for many on the planet still today. There would have been, of course, neither electric light nor heat; those comforts of contemporary man. The carpeting we walked on and the shoes we wore to walk on it did not yet exist.

But what a place! Pablo Picasso famously said, "After Altamira, everything is decadence." What he meant, I think, is that art as play (or decoration or ornamentation or self-expression or exploration or prophecy or homage) is in every instance a subset of the original impulse: to render the world in color and shape so we may take our place in it. And it matters not a whit if what we're looking at is the original or its careful replica and modern imitation. I felt as moved in the presence of "false" Altamira as would have been the case, I think, had I gained entry to the "true"; the fifteen thousand years of what we label progress were irrelevant. We marvel now as then.

All this has set me to thinking: the child's beloved comfort-blanket, the totemic carving, the religious relic or the collector's prized painting belong to the same category: an object imbued with reverence, a still-point in the turning world. For those of us who think of art as a necessity, the looming head of a wild boar or belly of a pregnant horse transforms a wet cold cave into a sacred space.

What the hell is he talking about? Why is he writing this down? Why should I care, or anybody care, about C's night of groaning and shitting and puking in a four-star *parador* while his wife stays asleep? Who needs to read another line about expensive restaurants and fake caves maintained for tourists and the near or the long view? How do these parts make up a whole; what's nonfiction doing here?

The arc of the universe bends toward justice; so said the Reverend Martin Luther King not long before they shot him while he stood hoping for a breath of air on the balcony of the Lorraine Motel in Memphis, Tennessee. "The arc of the moral universe is long, but it bends towards justice."

(Yeah, right. If there were any justice I would not have been in Extebari, eating an infected mussel in its sauce. I would not have been without my consort, who died giving birth to our son. Thirty thousand years ago, on the wet floor of this cave. I would not have been subject to scurvy or bitten by vampire bats; I would not have been so hot and then cold and remorseful or nasty, brutish, and short.)

Imagine for a moment that the boy who died eight years ago is still alive, recovered, clean, and setting up a model train for his own son in the living room. There's Christmas music playing on the radio, there's the smell of standing ribs just extracted from the oven, there's a table set for twelve. It's a gathering of relatives and friends or what we call "the clan." Electric candles flicker in sequence; there's a white linen tablecloth with sprigs of holly and pine cones and a Christmas wreath clustered at the center of the table, green napkins at each dinner plate and the family silver gleaming, though (in order to avoid temptation or the risk of relapse) only water glasses adorn the table setting, and we serve no wine. My wife is an admirable cook. We're all so glad, so grateful, so fortunate that Don is with us once again, and the trains run on time.

Two of the guests look quizzical, uncertain; they can't tell if I'm being serious or sarcastic as to scheduled trains. I tell them I'm referring to the model version in the living room and not to Mussolini. We pass the potatoes, the carrots and squash; we thank whatever gods there be for our unconquerable souls. This is a reference (I feel further compelled to explain, since I am after all the host and what faces have been turned towards me are blank, polite, uncomprehending) to the poem "Invictus" by W. H. Henley, who proclaimed himself unconquerable, although covered by the dark from pole to pole. The roast beef—which I let Don carve, entrusting him with knives once more—is on the verge of overdone. I do wish there were wine.

The Brussel sprouts in garlic are, however, fine.

There are three ways to see this, he thinks. Three ways to tell it, to read it. I've just returned from northern Spain and the cave of Altamira. What *was* their driver's name? They had been on the road for a week. He thought of the candles, the lanterns, the white linen cloths.

For those of us who think of art as a necessity, the looming head of a wild boar or belly of a pregnant horse transforms a wet cold ancient cave into a sacred space. It ranks among the oldest of our species' sites. At the risk of repetition, we lift our forks in unison, *continuo*, and manage the refrain. We all are born to die.

But it might have been different; the formula for "dignified survival" might have been agreed to in committee by voice vote or a show of hands or even printed ballot. After a brief or lengthy discussion, the secretary of the meeting writes the triad down: *food, clothing, shelter*. There had been disagreement; now comes unanimity. We need no sociologist and his alluring cousin to ratify the wording, no love affair to flesh the phrasing out. We need no marriage plot. The gentlemen who constitute "The Society for the Betterment of Social and Living Conditions in Great Britain and the Colonies" pronounce themselves content . . .

After his original purchase, years pass. B. uses the place for summers, then for Christmas vacations also, and Thanksgiving, and soon gives up his city apartment and lives there all year round. Though it could never have been profitable as such, he calls the place a farm; the soil is rocky and the hills too steep for satisfactory plowing. The forty acres of meadow have been over-grazed. But he learns to love the chores of mowing, chopping, checking fence; Roy, the neighboring farmer, sets his Holstein heifers out to pasture on the land.

B. had not known what 'heifer' meant, or how to tell a Holstein from Hereford, and as he acquired farm-lore he preened himself on growth. Nor was it preening, merely; he found the barn as rich a place as, when an adolescent, he found the Turkish Bazaar. Here was a whole new way of life to enter, a separate system of values to learn. The sensory assault, the welter and smell of bodies while he helped Roy cart the feed, or crack the well-ice open of a February morning, the way the cats would wait their turn at milking-time for slops from the tin pail: all this delighted him.

As years went on he married, had a child. His daughter loved the sheep they kept, and ducks that clustered to her when she came to the pond with cracked corn. Since he did not farm for profit, he could take the losses equably. Slowly he reclaimed the fields that had returned to thicket, and his woodlots were harvested well. On crisp October evenings, when the moon came through the final leaves and lit him where he smoked his pipe (by the chunk-stove in the kitchen, or on the screen-porch with it warm enough to sit outside and hear the stream), B. took stock.

Like those members, years before, of the Society for the Betterment of Social and Living Conditions in Great Britain and the Colonies, who agreed to the phrase, "Food, Clothing, Shelter," he called himself content.

His wife was not, however, and he loved her, so they left. She needed neighbors, lights, and said she felt far safer with a chain and police lock in Manhattan than in their isolated home. Their child, too, needed playmates and had grown frightened of strangers; they needed films and galleries and dance recitals if they were not to "rusticate." The word itself had changed for her—from positive to negative, from an adventure in countrified living to keeping a country mouse-house.

His roof was slate from the nearby quarries, and under that were wooden sheets. The struts were pine, and he had wedged six inches of insulation between the rafters, then tarpaper and sheetrock and paint. Therefore the house was tight on top, and cleanly, with layered resistance to snow.

These are a series of versions of shelter. Yet B. relinquished his play-property with something akin to relief. He had proved that roots were vertical, that he could stay through winters when he had the means to flee. They left; they returned to New York. Only sometimes in the years to come he came to think of those first years as the pattern of comfort entirely; the house had seen two-hundred winters, and it saw him and would see others through.

Note the supple arrangement of English; how to "see him through" is apposite to "seeing through him," yet opposed. My cousin's auburn hair is a tent when she unpins it, and we huddle here as once I did when pinned behind a waterfall that was a brown cascade. Together, we visited Combe. Our mattress has been stuffed with horsehair, firm. Our mattress *had* been stuffed with horsehair, firm. It does not retain our imprint where we lie. Lay. Andrew Corrigan now lives in Nice and sends us postcards of the Dolomites, with red arrows pointing to his summertime encampment. They offered Roy a Cuisinart for his caretaking kindness; he refused.

The House

H E BOUGHT THE house in a day. He had to; there were other bidders, and the market had been "hot." He flew from the small town in Vermont, where he, his wife, and their two daughters were living, to the town in Michigan where he would start a new job. They had been living in a barn, a remodeled white clapboard structure with a wood stove in the center of what used to be a granary. Outside were meadows and then a steep slope. They had lived there the length of their marriage, and were reluctant to leave.

This job, however, was a promotion. The salary would double what he currently earned. And now that their daughters were going to school, the caliber of local education was an issue; their daughters were seven and four. William worked as the Director of Admissions for the Johnson State Campus of the University of Vermont, but the college was in trouble and the applicant pool small. Regional economy had stalled, and this offer of employment was too good to refuse. He would become an Associate Director of Admissions in a university with thousands of out-of-state applicants; his was to be a focus on the high schools of New England. He had attended Dartmouth, then received an M.B.A. from Harvard, and his credentials as an "easterner" were strong.

Alice, his wife, opposed change. It wasn't fear, she told him, it wasn't even anxiety, but they had been so happy in their backwater town in the mountains she found it hard to imagine a move would mean improvement. She liked the snow, the skiing, the hot summers and brisk autumns; she even liked mud season and the impassable roads. They had a dog, two cats, and chickens till the chickens were killed by a fox.

"'If we want things to stay the same,'" he told her, quoting a novel he admired, "'they will have to change.'"

William had turned thirty-nine; Alice would do so soon. They had been married eight years. On this particular journey, however, he made the offer of purchase by himself. He drove the hour into Burlington and then flew to Detroit and took a taxi to Ann Arbor and met the real estate agent, who had called to say, "This is what you're looking for. But it won't stay on the market long; you have to come and decide."

Two tickets would cost twice as much, and they had no babysitter on standby for the trip. Alice said, "I trust you, darling. Make up our mind."

The real estate agent was fat. She had black hair and a nervous twitch of her right eye and cheek; she had been in the business for years and sympathized with, or so she said, his desire for a house in town, the chance to walk to work. She had been born in Australia, a world away, and it had taken her two hours to commute from her own parents' farm near Adelaide to her first job in marketing. Therefore, she assured him, she understood the value of convenience. The point of a town like Ann Arbor, she said, is that you want to live in it and be near the center of action; why else would you move from Vermont?

On each of his previous visits, he had viewed several properties, and none of them were suitable: too small, too expensive, too grim. So when William came upon the white brick house with dark green shutters that evoked New England, he placed a bid that afternoon and hoped his wife would approve. The house was a center-hall colonial: a dining room on the north side, a living room on the south. It had three small bedrooms, two baths. There were wallpaper patterns he knew she would hate, and no bookshelves for their books.

But these things could be remedied, and the neighborhood was tree-lined and the school zone good. He promised her the place was just a stop-gap measure, something to live in while they continued to look. "It's not what we were dreaming of," he told Alice. "But a good place to start."

They lived there thirty years. They built bookshelves and did replace the wallpaper and, in time, repaired the roof. He came into a small inheritance and they paid off the mortgage and enlarged the footprint of the house.

They added a standalone two-car garage and converted the original attached garage into a family room and porch. What first had seemed provisional began to feel like permanence. The neighbors all were affable, and sometimes when he walked the dog it took a full twenty minutes to circle the street. If other men were raking leaves, or getting into or out of their cars, they engaged in conversations about weather and the football game that Saturday and local politics. He learned to welcome small talk and contrasted it in memory with the silence he had known before: Vermont reserve.

The dog died, and so did the cats. The girls grew up and left for college and were graduated turn by turn. They found work in New York and Providence, and then found men to marry and began separate lives. Once they themselves had families, both girls grew sentimental, hoarding letters and poems and paintings by their children, attentive to scraps of the past. In album after album they preserved the year's activities: a camping trip, a trip to France, a first tooth lost or letter written to Santa, a complicated drawing of an alligator or prince. But their own childhoods had no power to compel them, and the boxes in the Ann Arbor attic (of diaries, school essays, yearbooks, diplomas, photographs, and postcards) were things they told their parents they were prepared to ditch.

"Ditch?" William asked. "You mean just toss them?" and his daughters said, "Why not?"

By then he had become Director of Admissions at the University of Michigan, and he read the essays in which applicants extolled their parents' values or wrote how much they admired an uncle who'd helped launch "Doctors without Borders" or a program in sub-Saharan Africa that established freshwater wells. He came to terms with his own children's independence, or tried to, telling Alice their self-sufficiency and distance were proof of how well they were raised.

"That they don't need us is a compliment," he argued. "It's a way of saying, 'Dad and Mom, we're OK on our own.'"

"That's not the point."

"No?"

"Let me try to explain this," she said. Her hair was white, her body wide, but in his mind's eye she remained the quicksilver creature he'd married, the girl from Smith with, as he liked to put it, standards. "You're very good at denial. Or not so much denial as not noticing. You don't seem to notice, do you, that everybody else's children pay them respectful attention.

Other people's children come to visit and remember their parents' wedding anniversaries and call to offer help if help is needed . . ."

"It isn't," William said.

"But some day it will be. And we don't dare to ask."

"They'll help us when we need them to."

"Let's sell the house," she said. "Let's retire and then start again."

He watched her. "I'm not the retiring type."

"That's not what I'm talking about . . ."

"What *are* you talking about?"

Alice took his hand. "You've done a great job at the office, Billy, but they want you to step down. They might not say so, but they do. They'll throw a farewell party and we'll get a retirement package and can move some somewhere where we don't know everybody at the tailgate party every Saturday."

"I thought you liked it here."

"I do. I did. But that was then and this is now and time to start again."

Their real estate agent had died. Therefore they met with younger agents and chose as a representative a blond divorcée with a black convertible and a high chittering laugh. She assured them the sale would be rapid, that the real estate market was once again "hot"; all they as owners needed to do was clean the house of bric-a-brac and leave the rest to her.

"What do you mean by bric-a-brac?" Alice asked. "I understand the word, of course, but how do we define it here?"

"Our life," said William. "She means, I think, the markers of our life."

"Mostly photographs," the agent said. "Family photographs. Too many knickknacks and personal pictures. You know, memorabilia, the sort of thing that reminds a prospective buyer someone else is living here, and doesn't let them imagine themselves as owners of the house."

It was February 10. Outside, snow drifted down.

"The bookshelves too?" Alice had a degree in Library Science and was proud of their collection. "Should we remove the books?"

They were standing in the living room. He touched her wrist.

"Well, some of them. We call it, 'staging,'" the agent explained. "We'll bring in bright pillows and take down a few of these paintings"—she pointed at the stairwell, still festooned with children's art—"and suddenly it looks like new. We'll do some touch-up work."

"Who pays for it?" he could not keep from asking.

"I do." She gave her practiced giggle. "It's standard procedure these days. We'll set a date for photographs next week, for a day when the sun's shining. Do you know the latest thing?"

"No," William said. "What's the latest?"

"Drones! We'll have a drone take aerial photographs to point out how near to the center of town you guys are living, with the Arboretum only a short walk away."

"Location, location, location," said Alice.

"Correct. It's a cliché, of course, but like most clichés it has some logic behind it. Don't worry. The house will sell like hotcakes, I promise. It has oodles of old world charm."

"You understand," he told her, "we're not certain yet we want to sell. We don't really know where we're going instead. Or what we plan to do."

"Downsizing, am I right? There's all these co-ops and condos downtown. They're selling like—I said this already, didn't I?—hotcakes."

"And when should it go on the market?" asked Alice.

He watched his wife.

"The end of April, maybe. Certainly by May." Again, the agent giggled. "Spring's the season for Ann Arbor. By July the market's dead."

"That's when I retire."

She turned to him. "And can move with a clear conscience, am I right?"

So they dismantled what they'd lived with, boxing photographs for storage, and old tax records and art. He culled the bookshelves carefully, making space on the stacked shelves. They took used shoes and clothing to the Thrift Shop; they took worn towels and blankets to the A.S.P.C.A. for bedding, they took suitcases and duffel bags to the Homeless Shelter, as their agent had advised.

Day after day they stripped the place and readied it for purchase. They took extra chairs and tables and china to the Treasure Mart for resale; they gave away records and CDs and paperbacks. They hauled broken radios and televisions and cans of paint to what was now termed "Recycle Ann Arbor" and had once been the town dump. Their kitchen counters stood empty; the fireplace mantle was bare.

As March wore on, moreover, he warmed to the procedure. William filled carloads each day. Every time he emptied out a closet or a storage bin he felt he'd done something of value. When he himself could not lift objects—a ping-pong table no longer in use, a Barcalounger or upholstered couch—he arranged with *Habitat for Humanity* to haul the stuff away.

Alice became a whirlwind of activity; she boxed cartons of food for Food Gatherers and cleaned cabinets and drawers with a fixed intensity, saying, "It's spring cleaning. Except maybe for the last thirty springs, we haven't done this properly. Look at these 'Sell By' dates, Billy, the drugs are useless and the food could kill us. These cans have been here for years."

"It hasn't hurt us, has it?"

"No. But now it's time."

The nights were difficult; he could not fall asleep. Images recurred. He saw their daughters coming out of school and running on fat legs forward when they spotted him; he saw them growing tall and lean and twirling, in high school, batons. He saw them learning how to drive and cook and asking for help with trigonometry and standing on fold-out stepstools to place ornaments on the higher branches of the Christmas tree. There was no sequence to such scenes, no logic of chronology; they would be two years old, then twelve, then six, then twenty-three. It was as though he'd come unmoored in time and drifted through it rudderless, as though the "family album"—for this was what he called it when Alice asked him what was wrong—had been wrested from its resting place and consigned to trash. She, too, became a palimpsest: a series of women he married: middle-aged, then young, then old. Her hair was gray, then black, then white.

"It's hard," he said.

"Of course it's hard."

"And I'm not sure I'm up to this."

"It won't get any easier. It's now or never," said Alice.

Where, he wondered, had she gained such certainty; why did she insist on departure? They had nowhere in particular to go. He was turning seventy and ready to retire, but unsure of the next move.

William thought of where their daughters lived and if they would be welcome in their neighborhoods and what would the grandchildren make of it if they lived nearby. He considered distant countries—Italy, New Zealand—and if it made sense to settle there, or maybe to rent. He remembered the small town of Johnson, where they had been happy, and wondered if it would be wise to return. They googled "Retirement Communities" in Connecticut and Massachusetts and North Carolina, and decided they were not yet ready for a "managed life style"; that would be, they agreed, not the next but final stage.

In the watches of the night, while his wife lay sleeping, William rehearsed the lost past. What their agent had described as clutter were layers of lived life. That his had been uneventful was, he'd long since decided, a gift. He prepared the children's breakfasts and their lunchboxes for school. He cheered them on at soccer and field hockey and in high school productions of *The Miracle Worker* and *The Diary of Anne Frank* and *The Pirates of Penzance*. He attended graduations and, later on, commencements, and tried to remember the names of their third-grade teachers and the names of their first boyfriends' parents and their roommates and their majors at Cornell and Brown. Reliving their daughters' childhoods, then adolescence, then young womanhood, he lay awake and asked himself why things were doomed to change. That was the word, he told himself, doom, and cajoled sleep by repeating it: *doom di doom-doom-di-doom.*

He had had a successful career. At the office, he had supervised the transition from typewritten individual essays to online common applications; he created a network of alumni interviewers all across the country, and the University of Michigan refined its admission protocols and broadened its out-of-state and international applicant pool. He walked the fine contested line between state-based enrollment and special dispensation to the children of alumni and the children of major donors and politicians and minority applicants and athletes; the matter of quotas and "weighted candidacy" had been adjudicated in court.

All this had absorbed him, and William was good at the work. In the decades of his tenure, the applicant numbers enlarged three-fold and the rate of acceptance increased. Yet what he retained of the years of travel and speech-making and meetings with staff and twice-yearly staff retreats were his daughters in his office on the days school had been canceled, coloring coloring books.

"This is an old people's house," said Alice. "The bathroom's too small for millennials. And the kitchen's a disgrace."

"You cooked there."

"Making do. That's what I did at dinnertime. Made do."

Where, he wondered, had this new bitterness come from; what made her so ready to leave? She who had resisted change now embraced it, or appeared to. His memories were happy ones, rose-tinged by nostalgia, and always when he thought of nights by the fire or drinks on the porch he thought of them with pleasure. What he remembered, always, were the sounds of laughter and gossip from his daughters' rooms.

"I'm seeing the house," said Alice, "through other people's eyes."

"And?"

"And what they see is two old people living in a space that needs to be updated."

"I don't want an 'entertainment wall,'" he protested. "A hot tub or sauna or, what's the word? Jacuzzi."

"But maybe a sink or bathtub that drains without clogging? And toilets that properly flush?"

"Marble counters. Granite counters. Whatever it is that's fashionable this week will be out of fashion next year."

"I don't need a discussion of living habits, Billy. I'm trying to tell you what's what . . ."

"There's never been a time," he told her, "in the history of the human condition when we expect so many square feet per person. Or want them. This house is plenty big enough."

"For us."

But he was in his lecture-mode. "Even Versailles. Or Buckingham Palace. Of course they're huge houses: tens, maybe hundreds of thousands of square feet. But if you add the three-hundred people who lived belowstairs, then divide it up per capita, each human being—even the King, even the Queen and her ladies-in-waiting—had less space to call their own than every damn millennial believes to be their birthright."

"I hear you," said his wife. "You don't have to make a speech."

"Four people lived in this space for years," he finished. "And were glad to do so."

"Then why don't they ever come back?"

To this he had no answer. "You're right. Let's sell. We'll leave."

The house went on the market in May. The real estate agent was, or so she said, sympathetic. "It's a stressful time," she said. "Selling a home is like losing a loved one, it's famously hard on the people who sell."

"You can say that again," said Alice.

"To watch a stranger traipsing through, am I right or am I right? And 'specially if, like the two of you, you've lived here a very long time; what, thirty years? Thirty years plus? Why don't you take a trip or visit your children or something; why don't you treat yourselves to a vacation and just get out of town? And leave the rest to me."

But William wanted to *be* there, to see what new potential owners saw. He wanted to know which cars they drove and how many minutes they took for a house-tour and if they approved of the plantings and what the agent labeled "curb appeal." He needed to know their professions, ages, the number of children or if they were childless and whether they already lived in Ann Arbor or came from out of town. He tried to imagine how the house could continue without his wife in the kitchen or himself in the living room building a fire—crossways so as to contain the draft and making certain the logs and the kindling were dry.

Except that Alice forbade it, he would have parked across the way or down the street and watched each time an agent came and dealt with the lock-box where the keys were stowed, then ushered a customer in. He asked himself if he would welcome change—a new paint-color or bathroom, a new master-bedroom wing and kitchen—or preferred the house intact.

"You're having abandonment issues."

"Who, me?"

"Yes," she said. "You."

"*I'm* not the one who's been feeling abandoned. Who complains about our daughters and says they should be here to help."

"That's not what we're discussing."

"No?"

"This wanting to lurk in the bushes like some, oh I don't know, Peeping Tom. To see who's next in line."

But it wasn't a new life he wanted to spy on; it was his own old. He saw his hair when thick, not thin; he saw himself upright, not bent. He wanted to go back in time. He saw the children on weekends, watching *The Smurfs* and *Eight is Enough* and then a series of teenage comedies he couldn't quite keep straight: who was friends with whom or having relationship problems or needing to find a new job. He saw his dog grow halt and lame and finally unable to walk with him in the Arboretum, along familiar trails. He saw their preening cats. He heard guests in the dining room, the conversation loud; he saw candles guttering, the bottles of wine on the sideboard and the after-dinner drinks. He weeded the garden; he mowed the lawn until he himself grew weary and hired a service instead.

These memories were clear but failed to signify; it was as though he listened in on conversation in a foreign language, or watched mute speakers move their lips in a pantomime of speech. Sheep-counting, he called it when Alice asked him how he'd slept.

"Well enough," he told her. "Thanks for asking. You?"

"I slept just fine. But you were dreaming, Billy, you were talking in your sleep!"

"I was? Not so I remember."

"That's why it's called a dream."

"Do you think," he ventured, "we're making a mistake?"

"What, by selling the house? Putting it up for sale?"

He nodded.

"I thought *I'd* be the one with the second-thoughts, sweetheart. I never thought you'd feel this way."

"Well, guess again."

"This isn't a game and I don't feel like guessing. Why don't you tell me what you want?"

"I want," he told her, "everything to stay the same. Even though it has to change."

Alice was washing dishes. She scrubbed and rinsed them carefully, then placed them in the dishwasher. "Well, guess what, things don't stay the same, and it's us who have to change."

"When did you get so—so decisive?"

She was wearing her blue apron with the design of crossed spoons and knives. "I'm not. I'm heartsick about this. But you haven't given me the chance to say, 'It's a mistake.'"

"I haven't?"

"No, I don't expect you to." She circled her thumb on the rim of a glass, testing it for cracks. "And it isn't a mistake . . ."

"We don't have to sell."

"Let's be realistic," she said. "In case you haven't noticed the place has grown beyond us. We're only living in three rooms; the others are gathering dust."

"Let's just block them off. Let's put in a woodstove and put on our snowshoes and pretend we're young again"

She took his hand. "Exactly. Let's pretend."

There were two bids, then three, then four, and then a bidding war. "Not really a war, a skirmish," said their blonde agent, giggling, "but I've asked them to write letters presenting their case and their reasons to buy. One is a cash offer but all are creditworthy and they're coming in, all of them, at just about the same price. I asked for 'best and final offer,' so we can't go back again or start another round. You two will have to choose."

"On what basis?" William asked.

"Just, oh I don't know, how you feel about it. Who you want to replace you. To live here when you're gone."

The letters arrived. The first of them was, Alice said, functionally illiterate; she couldn't bear to sell the house to someone who wrote: "We XOXOX your place and high-5 about it's being ours!"

A second woman wrote, "This street was where my mother lived, across the way from the Jacksons, and it would be a dream come true for her to come back home again along with my husband and I! She turns ninety-six in June. We've driven and walked down this same street forever! We love the new garage!"

A third was elegantly hand-lettered, on embossed stationery, and said the prospective purchasers had been a couple for twenty years and now were legally married by the State of Michigan and would of course pay cash and preserve the "amenities"—that was the word the writer used—of the charming living room and walnut-paneled den.

A fourth described at length the nature of his research in subatomic particles and his wife's in music theory and their son's work as a Park Ranger and their daughter's recent marriage to a lawyer in Detroit. "We're ready to downsize," claimed the writer. "But the family still needs a family home!"

As he parsed the letters, William felt as though he were again in his office reading application essays, making choices based on syntax and sincerity but doing so, now, in the dark. He could not imagine the house owned by strangers and did not want to try. He could not select whom to pick. When one of the potential buyers praised the cat door in the kitchen, saying she loved cats and had two Siamese, he told Alice, "I can't bear this. Let's let our girls decide."

She was sitting at the kitchen table, shelling peas. Adjusting her glasses, she looked up at him. "Excuse me?"

"Let's send them a copy of each of the letters. Let's ask them what to do."

"Remember that old TV show, *The Price is Right*?"

"Yes, what was his name, the MC?"

"I don't remember."

"Bill Cullen. That was his name, I think."

"You make a guess, is how it worked. And if your guess comes closest to the actual asking price, the merchandise belongs to you. The car, the stove, the cruise . . ."

"They're making the same guess," he said. "All our potential purchasers are 10k above the listing."

"So?"

"It isn't an auction; we can't start again or wait for the gavel to drop."

"I know." She placed the letters on the kitchen table, facing down. She shuffled them back and forth, swirling. Each of the letter writers made a case for purchase, and each was a petition.

Alice looked at him. "You pick."

He closed his eyes. He did.

The Letters

Do drop me some sort of line.

SARAH MILLER TAUGHT English at The University of Iowa. Having graduated from the Iowa Writers' Workshop, she was assigned three sections of Freshman Composition per semester. Others of her cohort received the offer too. It was, she knew, provisional, and when her parents called the job a "plum," she said it felt more like a "prune." In 1982, when she first entered a classroom at and as the head of it, she was twenty-six years old.

Her students, undergraduates, could not enroll in the curriculum of the Writers' Workshop. There a young writer might grow famous, and the faculty—famous already—were drunks. Not all of them, of course, and not all of them flamboyantly so, but the early 1980's were years of self-indulgence, and often Sarah found herself in the company of men and women who recited poetry in bars. Or those who, playing pool, would bet on the size of a visiting author's print-run; the loser had to purchase the next round.

Dark-haired, dark-eyed and willowy, she enjoyed her time with the affable drunks but went home, routinely, alone. Although born and raised in Manhattan, she came to like Iowa City: the heavy snows in winter, the walks by the river in spring. A Ph.D. candidate in Political Science lived in the same apartment building, one flight up, and the two of them had an affair. She and Eric drove to the Amana colonies and to the birthplace of Herbert Hoover; they spent weekends together, grilling salmon on the barbecue or hunting for morels. Once they drove to Hannibal, Missouri, and explored Injun Joe's cave. The couple agreed, however, not to opt for a long-term commitment, and when Eric went to Arizona for an entry-level job at Tempe, she stayed on alone.

Every third semester, instead of Composition, she taught a Creative Writing Class in Prose Fiction. This she preferred. In 1984, she published an appreciation of John Cheever in *The Iowa Review* and a short story in *Ploughshares*; her appointment was renewed. In the watches of the night, or at her writing desk each morning, it seemed as though her own career might be gathering momentum, but the novel she was working on had stalled. And, since Sarah was conscientious, the teaching took most of her time.

In her fiction workshop in the spring of 1985 there were twenty students; one of them stood out. His name was Angus Waterston, and he was barrel-chested, with masses of black curls. He was, she learned, a junior, and majoring in History. She could not place his accent, but when he came to her office to discuss his second effort he explained he hailed from Maine, a small town northeast of Augusta; his mother's family was French-Canadian. The majority of those who took the class were—or so it seemed to Sarah—talentless and dull; this boy was an exception. His fictions were knowing, his language alive, and she found his descriptions (of slaughtering chickens and cutting and marketing Christmas trees, of being set upon by hard-fisted uncles and first having sex in a hay-mow) vivid. She told him so, and gave him an A for the course.

That summer she received a letter.

Dear Professor Miller:

I hope you won't mind—why should you?—my telling you how much our class this last semester meant and means to me. It was lively and exciting and informative and informed and I know this sentence takes too long but what the hey. I'm working on my story now about the motorcyclist and a penguin and the pail of fish; it's getting better, I think. And I just wanted to wish you Happy Birthday when it arrives on August 27; did you know that Lyndon Johnson and Theodore Dreiser share that day?

Toodles. And oodles of thanks.

His scrawl was loopy, ornamental, and he left the letter unsigned. It both pleased and disturbed her. How had he learned the date of her birthday; why did he get in touch? She was flattered, of course, by Angus's praise, but she kept apart from her students and had no desire to eradicate that distance or read his work again. A penguin and a pail of fish did not ignite her interest, and she was working hard that summer on her own novel-in-progress, forcing herself to add page after page to *Counterfeit: A Love Story*. It was not going well. On her birthday she received a postcard from him, saying, in block letters, MANY HAPPY RETURNS. This card was signed; the image on the postcard-front was the famous photograph of a wide-eyed forward-facing, severe Charles Baudelaire.

Sarah did not answer. She was sleeping with a classmate from her own time at the Writers' Workshop, who had won a contest for a debut collection of poems and was going on the market in the fall. In October she received, again, a letter from Angus describing his own labors and discoursing—this time at length—on how much her encouragement mattered, and how he had been wrangling with the metafictional para-meters of narrative. That was his phrase—"the metafictional parameters of narrative"—and she found herself oddly moved by it: this clumsy boy obsessed with style, trying to wrest an original tale from his fleet-if-flat-footed excursions into storytelling, and his admiration for experimental authors she'd included in the syllabus: Coover, Gass, and Barth.

The letter was lengthy, handwritten. That night she showed it to her lover, and he said, "Wow" and joked that they should try to expand their own metafictional parameters and use, if she agreed to it, ankle-ties; he had a pair in his bag. He reached his orgasm quickly, but she found herself focused on Angus Waterston, thinking about his combination of experience and innocence, his copycatting fictions in the mode of Barthelme or Nabokov. What interested Sarah was the strange amalgam of his down-home plotted action and the elaborate diction deployed. His complicated rhetoric seemed compellingly at odds with the rural venue: the uncle with a bottle and belt used as a whipping strap, the first girlfriend with a milking pail she carried to the barn.

She wrote him back. The return address on Angus's missive was a dormitory room, and she imagined him—surrounded by books and wea-ring his thick glasses—sitting cross-legged on the floor. He had touched a nerve in her, a memory of what it felt like years before to be possessed by fiction's possibilities and forcing a phrase into form. "Sometime if you want a coffee," Sarah offered, "I'd be glad to meet and talk."

Dear Ms. Miller:

I don't drink coffee. I don't need to see you again. What I want and need is the idea of witness, the notion of a hovering muse so generous over my shoulder, the audience incarnate I dream of that for the moment and perhaps for an extended period takes and has taken your shape. Don't worry; this isn't personal, there's no tactile reality envisioned or involved, only the desire on your 'umble servant's part to make of this nothingness, language, a living breathing entity that will outlast breath. My very own golem in prose. It's what we talked about, remember, when we were reading Malamud: the side-long glance of the pigeon-kicker, the overheard snatches of speech. What I want and plan to do is build a structure out of semblan-ces, *re*-semblances, so that a brother and doomed wanderer is also the prodigal son. As to the philosophers I've studied—Foucault, Derrida, Barthes, et. al.—I've come to recognize that all of it is no-thingness, *le grand néant*, and as to the pursuit of French literature and history it's sufficient to say, *Je m'en fiche*. You've made me see, and for this I'm in your perpetual debt, that the oxymoronic beauty of English lies in its very ugliness. Or, as my high school teacher said, when trying to be witty, "Rearrange the following words into a well-known phrase or sentence. 'Off fuck.'"

He went on in this vein. He wrote about his hope to couple rural par-lance with the extravagance of courtly praise, the yin of the demotic and yang of mandarin. The six-page letter, handwritten—she asked herself if his use of "oxymoronic" had colored her reading?—was both fascinating and dull. Angus was, if nothing else, ambitious, and she kept his letters in a folder next to the folder containing her notes for class.

Things continued as before. She felt discouraged, a little, but also a little encouraged by the fact of publication; Chapter 2 of *Counterfeit* appeared in *Epoch*, a magazine where she had known the Fiction Editor from their old workshop days. The long slow business of completing her novel was—

again she thought of Angus—both fascinating and dull. It seemed to her that somewhere just beyond the reach of consciousness a narrative awaited, one needing to be told. But what it was was unclear.

Her poet-companion received a job offer from Vanderbilt, and the night before he left—promising to stay in touch—they celebrated avidly, drinking and sleeping together as if in the first stage of courtship. They made plans to get together for the Christmas holidays, to maybe go to Mexico or France. Yet she knew their goodbye was goodbye.

"I'll miss you very much," he said.

"I'll miss *you*," Sarah agreed.

He hummed the tune from "Leaving on a Jet Plane," John Denver's composition. His voice was quavery, off-key, but she joined him in the chorus: "Oh, babe, I hate to go." Peter, Paul, and Mary also had recorded the song, and she tried to sound like Mary Travers: deep-voiced and throaty, aggrieved. In the morning, after orange juice and waffles and a final session together in bed, he drove south.

Two years later, Sarah too departed, going home. Her novel found an agent and the agent found a publisher; it was a heady time. *Counterfeit: A Love Story* earned respectful if small review attention, selling three thousand copies. Soon, it disappeared from bookstore shelves, and her hopeful energy flagged. But she had, after all, completed and published a book, and her parents—retired now, and removed to Florida—were proud. New York City felt familiar, as Iowa City had not. She was pleased to be back in Manhattan, living on Broadway near her old undergraduate haunts at Barnard and going to jazz clubs and restaurants and plays and museums and bars. Her second novel failed to sustain her interest, however, and she gave it up.

That autumn, hunting work, Sarah found a job in the publicity department of a downtown publisher who, a year later, was acquired by a larger publisher, Simon & Schuster, and had its staff reduced. She survived the first round of layoffs, contenting herself with desk-duties and the occasional road-trip, accompanying celebrity authors and setting up print interviews and radio and television appearances. On her thirty-third birthday Sarah gave herself a party and, after the celebration, took stock; she had no permanent partner or job and her dream of a career as writer had gone dim.

The next day she heard again from Angus, who acknowledged her birthday routinely, using it as an occasion to be back in touch. Again, she was surprised and slightly troubled by the fact of his seeming-devotion and how he'd found her address at the office, although not her home address. He wrote two or three times yearly, always in longhand and using black ink, and always discoursing on art.

Ms. Miller:

Salutations. Greetings and salutations; many happy returns of the day. It's been two months since I wrote you, and the nice news won't be news to you; Simon & Schuster—your very own publishing house—has bought my book. There was what they are calling an auction (or an imitation of it, anyhow, four editors jostling for position and bidding against one another, so I like to imagine them at a kind of Sotheby's or Christie's not selling pictures or cattle but the space-time empyrean-continuum of language, waggling their fingers and raising their hands and offering and counter-offering, until my agent—blessings on her mortal soul!—called out "Sold. Hold. Enough!" In truth I told her to favor your house, on the off-chance we might meet again, which now becomes a likelihood, a crossroads (my mother calls it *carrefour* and I like the resonance with *care for*) in the intersecting weave and warp of the public and the private life, this business we share.

You mustn't worry, and I mean it, that I'm poaching on her ladyship's terrain. *Counterfactual: A Story of Hate.* Howzat for a title betimes? It was you, my dear Ms. Miller, who made me see the difference if not the distinction ("a dimple of a ditch that a small frog can straddle," so writes Nabokov, or words to that effect), as to the gulf perceived and proclaimed by C. P. Snow between science and the humanities. Or was it *Sense and Sensibility*, a census, con-sensus, *che faro senza Eurydice*, as that other author from the hinterland centuries ago averred—and as long as I'm putting in my two cents worth by way of speculation, have you noticed in the novels of Jane Austen how there's never, and I mean *never*, a scene between two or more men alone? Not that she didn't write about them or the private interactions of the less fair if stronger sex, but always as recounted after-the-fact by a male witness, since she didn't truly trust herself to know and therefore record the chitchatting badinage of men without women, to throw Hemingway's title into the stew. Let them severally boil.

What I'm trying to explain to you—well, not explain, you never needed explanation from your 'umble servant—but express to you is the way I seem suddenly out in the world, the world of cocktail parties though you know I never drink. In any case my doctors say the cocktail of drugs they prescribe for me (the downers, the uppers, the six large and little pills ending in *zine*) would, when conjoined to alcohol, be a problem, a bummer, a grave—note the term, please— mistake. So I stand like a cigar-store Indian, erect and wooden and silent while the tourbillion around me froths. That's the word for it, isn't it, *froths.* The weightless set of bubbles billowing above the surface of what one might hope instead to be an enduring and even a deep draught. Draft.

Now she was truly unsettled. She tracked Angus Waterston's contract down, and the advance was twenty times what she herself had earned. His novel, *Sexing the Chicken,* was generating excitement and had been sold to six countries already; a preemptive bid by Universal Pictures for film rights had been signed. Pre-publication notices—from *PW, Kirkus,* and *Library Journal*—all were rapturous. "A crucial young talent!" they claimed. "A fresh voice from Down East!" The author had indeed, she learned, asked for her to be part of his publicity team, and the three-week debut tour was scheduled to start in Iowa City on August 27.

Sarah resigned.

In the next years his reputation soared. Angus became a major landmark on the literary map. His collection of short stories, *Arguments with Famous Men,* and his second novel, *Dust,* both made the *New York Times* best-seller list, and *Dust,* weighing in at eight-hundred pages, was a con- tender for the National Book Award. The movie of *Sexing the Chicken* attained cult-classic status almost the day it appeared. His mass of curly hair (now braided in a pigtail) was intaglioed on T-shirts, and his essays on marriage and baseball and having a baby were much-anthologized. He continued to send Sarah letters, but they grew less personal and urgent, as well as more controlled. It was as though his ritual observance of her birthday had become only a dutiful habit; in 1994, when his August missive failed to arrive, she took it as a sign.

He wrote in September, however, apologizing profusely for having missed the birthday date; he had been on tour in Australia, and the incessant travel and the time-zones had disoriented him.

> Note (Angus wrote) how "orientation" and "the Orient" are somehow conjoined as ideas, and how limited if seemingly limitless is our terminology for what's strange. What's strange is how that class of ours remains a lodestar in my filament—whoops, I meant to write "lone star in my firmament," no, "loadstar in my fundament"—and did you know that one of the presenting symptoms of tertiary syphilis is hopeless and hapless helpless sonority, the continual usage of puns? Not that I have it, the clap, I mean, the sound of one hand clapping, which is what I heard this afternoon at the bookstore in Perth. Please accept my apologies, lady; next year, I promise, I'll be writing right on time! I hope you're well, well at work.

By then her star, never all that bright, had faded. What once had seemed to Sarah a professional engagement became, in time, a personal withdrawal. Let others write fiction, she said to herself; she no longer shared their ambition. Since Angus claimed, in interviews, that Sarah Miller was his mentor—the Athena to his wandering Greek—she took a kind of second-hand pride in his increasing fame. There was a little envy, a little jealousy involved, but mostly she resigned herself to being on the margins of the literary life. It was a life she did not yearn for or still could be excited by; one novel would suffice.

Instead, she became a serious cook and joined a downtown collaborative; one Saturday, when it was her turn at the register, she met the man she would marry. He bought three loaves of bread. His name was Arthur Williams, and she did not fail to notice that the initials of his monogram—though she only learned, months later, that he in fact used monograms—were those of Angus's too. He was lean and blond and movie-star handsome, and he came from Rhode Island, a state his distant ancestor had founded. Roger Williams was a dissident who believed in religious freedom, and went out into what was then the wilderness and—unlike those who settled Massachusetts—proved generous when he encountered indigenous tribes. According to the legend, Roger Williams in the 1600s rode up-country in his voyage of discovery not on a mule but bull.

Arthur worked in advertising, as a designer for TV ads. His specialty was food presentation, which was why he patronized Sarah's co-op and engaged her on the subject of *boules* and *pain de campagne*. Theirs was an instant attraction, an easy camaraderie, and the wedding was a large one, in Watch Hill. Her parents—elderly now and, she feared, too easily impressed by Arthur's pedigree—flew up from Florida. At the wedding dinner, her mother fell asleep.

She and Arthur joked about it, promising each other that for all the years and years to come, they would remain awake. The couple honeymooned in Mexico and, shortly thereafter, took a business trip to food markets in France. Fleetingly, in the Dordogne, while sampling the paté and truffles and rillettes on offer, Sarah remembered her intention, years before, to travel to the South of France with her poet-lover. Things felt more solid now, and real. On their second anniversary, Anthony Williams was born.

She settled into motherhood with ease. Much else in her life had seemed problematic, but the birth and feeding, then weaning of her son, went smoothly; so did his learning to walk and talk. The business of toilet training; of teaching him to use a fork, of instructing him in letters and arithmetic and manners: all the tasks of tending to her darling seemed natural to Sarah. The rest of the world was the rest of the world, and the only thing that mattered was her boy's well-being; his happiness was hers. Through the years of Tony's childhood and early adolescence, she felt she knew his every move and attitude and mood ...

Her parents died. Her husband's mother and father did too. They sold the family manse on Watch Hill and with the proceeds bought a brick faux-Tudor in Rye, on Long Island Sound, from which Arthur commuted to work. To her surprise, their son—now a sophomore at Brown—said his grandparents' house was the only one he'd ever thought of as home, and that summer he went wandering through Ireland and Wales and Scotland and disappeared from view. He had been, she learned from his roommates and the authorities in Providence, arrested twice for drugs. He had been using, then dealing, and he was caught shoplifting watches and an iPad from the campus store. Twice, he was involved in street-fights, and his nose was broken and earlobe torn. She and Arthur had known none of this and chastised themselves for having failed to notice signals Tony sent: what the therapist she went to called a cry for help.

August 26
Dear Prof.

Did you know that Miller Williams is a pretty damn good poet, at least Bill Clinton thought so, which is why he was named laureate, so in his honor I will call you Dear Ms. Miller-Williams, though in truth I have no notion of the moniker you choose. Or why you are no longer writing, which is why I'm doing so for both. Both of us, I mean. Am I correct in the assumption that you renounced—to use great Beckett's word—our shared profession some years back? Or perhaps are keeping powder dry? At any rate I see no trace of you in the various journals that bulk by the door, the endless array of *les feuilles mortes*, which is what Verlaine called those downward-fluttering leaves that sent him yon and hither in the wind. Chasing after his bonny companion, little Arthur. Crazy randy deregulated-in-the-senses Arthur. Rimbaud, I mean, not your husband of course, the prodigy who also gave it up, though in his case perhaps because of malaria or gangrene or opium; *on sait pas*. These fragments I have shored against my ruination, which in the eyes of the world is success, and I wanted to ask you—directly, directly—what caused you to lay down the metaphoric quill pen and actual typewriter, then word processor, and why?

Because it tempts me too. This silence in surrounding noise, this peace that passeth understanding which perhaps you understood. Remember in the early days when I used to describe you as that nice muse over my shoulder, perched there so smilingly and with such generous approval? Well, professor, you've done gone. Gone elsewhere, silent, mute. And I know I oughtn't mind or care because, lord knows, there are substitutes, a processional of candidates for the job of Calliope, talkative muse. Yet for reasons I don't fully understand or, understanding, can render in prose, the class in 1985 was Edenic for your 'umble servant, and since then it's been only autumn. The fall out of Eden, I mean.

Our paths have failed to crisscross, now, for thirty years. Which is how you wanted it, clearly, and I don't disagree. But it seems to me, as it must have to you, that silence and renunciation, *abdication, absence, aphasia*, is the cleansed form of speech. I join you in it, ma'am. Do drop me some sort of line.

Sarah was frantic, hunting their son. She hounded the authorities and fruitlessly flew to Scotland and put up a reward for information that would provide a lead. There was no information and there were no leads. To start with, Arthur humored her, saying it was just a phase for Tony, a wanderlust that would play itself out. In part she believed this, or tried to. He would, she was certain, return. He would make his way safely back home. Yet as the weeks and months went by, while no word came, she learned to live with—if not accept, never accept, never ever accept—the possibility of loss. She would not believe that her beautiful boy (so curly-headed, bright-eyed) had been harmed in ways beyond her remedy, or that he was hostage to some controlling chemical demon from which he could not be freed. Captors or kidnappers or dealers might be approachable; release could be negotiated and a ransom paid.

There were, however, no captors she heard from—only this ongoing silence, only this absolute absence. When the telephone rang or mail arrived she ran to it, expectant, but there were merely telemarketers or work-related conference calls for Arthur or invitations or bills. This went on for two years. She grew accustomed—not resigned, never resigned, never ever resigned—to the void in which Anthony wandered, which had become her void.

On the day of her sixtieth birthday, August 27, 2016, Sarah again received a postcard with the photograph of Baudelaire, the one Angus sent her long before—that baleful glare caught by Nadar—but this time the block-letter legend read: *N'IMPORTE OÚ, HORS DE CE MONDE.*

Dear Angus:

~~I owe you an explanation. I have something I do need to say. Or to write except it isn't easy . . . .~~

~~Dear dear Angus:~~

~~Apologies for my long silence; I'm no longer in the writer's trade~~

~~and never really felt at ease with a position of authority, though it~~
~~was fine to talk about and teach the work of others. When you . . .~~

Mr. Waterston:

~~Forgive me, please. I've been meaning to write and answer your~~
~~letters, but speech after long silence--the title of a poem, if I re-~~
~~member correctly, by Yeats---doesn't come all that easily or readily~~
~~now, because we haven't been in touch for years, and I don't know~~
~~how to start~~
~~Angus~~
~~Dear Angus Waterston:~~
~~Dear Mr. Waterston:~~
~~Many thanks for the postcards and letters.~~
Oh useless, useless, useless; I had something I did want to say.

Their neighbor Alison De Witt owned a farm northeast of Windhoek, in Namibia. A divorcée, embittered—her husband was a plastic surgeon who decamped with his assistant—Alison was tall and pale and used a cane. This was, she said, because a polo pony shattered her knee in the years she played polo, and though they had replaced the knee it gave her trouble, walking. Her people had been Afrikaans, and in the 1940s her grandfather purchased thirty thousand hectares in the desert of Namibia. The land became a game preserve and family retreat.

It had been, said Alison, a small investment at the time; the land was worthless then and not worth all that much now. But it had been her childhood hideaway in summer, a place of happy memories, and she went back whenever she could. Given the state of things and the prospect of government-sponsored land confiscation, there might not be many more chances; she was flying home this fall.

With her habitual declarative abruptness, Alison told Sarah that the colors of the countryside—the sand and rock and high wide sky—were not to be believed or missed, and she and Arthur should come for a visit. She herself was going in September and would make them welcome and conduct a private tour.

They were drinking gin and tonic in the Williams' living room. There had been a thunderstorm, and the humidity abated, but the women stayed inside. Alison had brought a photograph album and showed pictures of the Sossesvlei dunes, a white rhino at a riverbank, the bones and wrecked ships scattered all down the Skeleton Coast. Two cousins lived in Windhoek and managed the family farm, keeping the waterholes open and culling by killing the herd. They ate and sold the meat. There were giraffes and springbok and oryx and zebras and eland in abundance; there were windmills to generate power and barbed wire fences and dogs.

"You've never seen anything like it," she said. "'God was angry when he made this place'—so goes the Bushman saying. It will enlarge your mind."

There was implicit reproach in the statement, or at least a condescension: why should Sarah need her mind "enlarged" and what was her neighbor suggesting? What was so narrow about her horizon, and why should a springbok or reebok be required to furnish perspective? She felt resentful, a little, but also a little excited; it would be good to see "the land God made in anger," and from the back of a jeep. It had been years since she ventured any distance from what Alison called the "comfort zone," and, because Sarah was restless, she told their neighbor "Yes."

In October she and Arthur took the trip, flying overnight to Schiphol airport, and after several hours emplaning again and flying through the night from Amsterdam to Johannesburg and then north to Windhoek, sleepless and embattled and losing track of time. On arrival she felt dizzy, dazed by the long wrangle of forms to fill out, the declarations at customs, a customs agent pawing gravely through her suitcase, the porters sitting on barrows, the robed women on the floor. At length, when they were finished with the process of arrival, the driver Alison had sent strode forward through the waiting crowd, collecting and wielding their luggage like shields. "My name, sir and lady, is Harris," he said. "It is my honor to serve."

"We thank you," Arthur said.

They changed money. They used the airport restrooms and bought large bars of chocolate and a bag of nuts. When finally they walked out into open air they were assailed by beggars, men and children shouting, the reek of gasoline. Harris drove an old Land-Rover, brown and mud-bespattered, with a pair of auxiliary tires on the roof rack; he had parked the vehicle just beyond the airport entrance at a pull-out in the sand. A beggar sat cross-legged beside it, holding up his hand. Harris shooed the man away. Then, unlocking the Land Rover with a key tied to his belt-loop, he ushered them to the car's rear seat with elaborate courtesy, patting the fabric and asking if the gentleman and lady might desire Coca-Cola, or perhaps an Orange Squash? A wooden cane with a thick metal handle lay across his seat.

They drove. They made their way through the outskirts of the city and then villages and unfenced land where the road was hard-packed dirt. They passed abandoned cars and rusted farm machinery and termite mounds and, by the roadside, high-piled trash. The sky was a bright blue. Two hours north of Windhoek, at an intersection marked by a white wooden cross, they made a sharp right turn and, shifting gears, Harris nodding and smiling and pointing ahead, took a narrow track towards a gate. In a blur of exhaustion Sarah watched the driver clamber down to open it, then advance the Land Rover, then stop again to secure the gate behind them, then take a curving uphill drive to a clearing with several huts and a house. The house was green, with a red roof, and there was a dark verandah from which their hostess emerged, smiling, waving, saying *Wilkommen*, Welcome, and holding out her hand.

"You must be tired," Alison said, "and it's important you rest. I'm very happy you're here!"

"We're grateful," Sarah said.

They were ushered to their quarters and told to unpack and wash and take their time before the cocktail hour, which was five o'clock. Arthur lay back on their camp-bed and fell, on the instant, asleep.

She, however, could not sleep. She heard dogs barking, the raw caw of birds, the shouts of workers in the compound and the Land Rover starting up again and being driven off. Her husband lay snoring beside her. Sarah closed her eyes and saw herself somehow afloat on the ceiling, bumping up against the ceiling tiles and suspended near the fan. There were mourners at a funeral, but whose she could not tell. Troubled, she stood up again and, shoeless, padded to the window to identify the noise beyond and see what she could see.

A dead oryx hung outside, flayed and being butchered; two men with knives and saws were at work on the carcass, and a toothless woman in a turban smiled at her, collecting offal and dropping it into a pail. A pair of Rhodesian Ridgebacks lay at the woman's feet, snouts quivering, attentive. A legless child propelled itself on a cart across the clearing. A portable radio played. There were trees in flower and plants she could not name. She had indeed, Sarah recognized, obeyed the postcard's stern injunction and traveled "Anywhere out of this world." The smell of death was on her hands and, in her mouth, the taste of rot; she could see and hear and feel it. It would not dissipate. It stayed with her through Alison's tour of the compound and then through drinks and dinner and all through the night.

The next day, on the internet, she read of Angus's suicide. He had hung himself from a crossbeam in the haymow of the barn converted to a studio, where he kept his writing desk. It was one of three outbuildings on the property he and his wife and children lived in in New Mexico, twenty miles north of Las Cruces.

The obituary was long. *Excellent Fancy*, Waterston's second collection of essays, had received the National Book Critics Circle Award, and there were drumbeats rolling for his unfinished novel, *Professor*. But there were rumors, also, of worsening depression, his withdrawal from the publishing scene and speaking occasions and the apparatus of fame. There were photographs of Angus in his childhood near Augusta, then his first publicity photo, with a fishing rod and tackle box and, over his shoulder, a net. There was a photo of him staring at the camera while wearing a tuxedo at the annual PEN dinner at Cipriani's, his glasses perched low on his nose. On his work-table, the article said, there had been hundreds of pages—drafts of articles and stories, the crossword puzzle and the novel he was working on and doodles he drew then crossed out—but no suicide note or statement of intent.

She and Arthur discussed the news. "I can't believe it," Sarah said, "I just can't believe it . . ."

"No."

"First Tony and now . . ."

Arthur put his hand on hers. "They're not the same."

"Why not? How not?"

"Because suicide's a different thing."

"I felt so sick," said Sarah. "I felt like I was dying."

"When?"

"When we arrived here. Yesterday, when we arrived."

"Why didn't you tell me?"

"You were sleeping, darling. You were so peaceful and sleeping it off. But something felt terribly wrong, a kind of premonition . . ."

"We don't know Tony's dead," he said. "He wouldn't be a suicide."

"Are you so sure?"

He shook his head. "You should take a shower. It will make you feel better; a shower will help."

"What makes you think there's help? What makes you such an optimist?" She turned on him. "There fucking isn't any help: Angus is dead. He killed himself. They're dead, I'm certain."

"We don't really know that."

"Dream on."

When the couple flew back home to Rye, it was without surprise she found a letter waiting, in Waterston's black scrawl. It had been sent—Sarah checked the date—the day before he hung himself, and therefore the writer would have known she would not read it while he remained alive. He sent, she later learned, a dozen such letters and postcards to family and editors and to his agent and friends; they amounted to a kind of testimonial, circling around the same idea and saying the same thing. He had planned this last will and testament, clearly; he knew what he wanted to say:

October 13, 2017

Lost wax. I'm using the lost wax method, which *ma mère* called *cire perdue*. You shape a figure out of wax or clay—they did this as far back as 6000 years ago in the Indus Valley, then a tad later in Israel, then Europe till the eighteenth century—and make a mold and pour in molten metal and the wax melts and runs out. Hey presto what's left is the image itself, the shape and simulacrum rendered permanent, not malleable, and that's how I intend to be impressed upon your memory, the pendant man, *de*-pendent man, the hanging man, the participial phrase dangling uselessly two feet above the floor. This carapace of language reconfigured as stiff shell.

Fast forward with me, friend. Imagine for a moment that the man who dies tomorrow is still alive, recovered, clean, and at work upon a memory—a *me*-moir—of childhood, adolescence, tumescent college days, that classy class I took with you when the world was young. With its pencils and papers and the yellow sheets your acolyte full-filled with observation: the window, the gray metal chairs, the book shelf and blackboard and chalk. The nape of the neck of the girl to my left, the smell of the guy's armpit at my right. We were all so certain once, remember? that the page we blackened out of blankness would become a proclamation and resound throughout the kingdom: *Hear Ye, Hear Ye*, wide and far. How it used to matter that my name was Ozymandias and you the King of Kings. Well, let me be more accurate: the Queen of Kings and Kings. A ring-giver to heroes, bestrider of thrones, a dominator of whales. The one who told me, and I listened, that the life of art is long.

But I've passed the halfway mark by now, or, rather, half a century: fifty-one-and-counting: fifty-two-and three! Counting up and counting down. My hair is streaked with gray, my cheeks are wattled, bloat, and I find myself contented by, or at any rate unresistant to and acquiescent in (note those lovely prepositions, Prof.) the formulaic usage, *my hair streaked with gray*, my shoulders slumped, for it no longer matters that I find the just word in just spring. And when I do at length stumble-bumble upon it, I'm so very grateful that I wanted you to know. For once in every once in a while and at the risk of repetition I do in fact stumble-bumble upon it and sing hallelujah or at least shout ray-hooray, *Eureka*, on this final day. Lost wax. Where twelve low words were wont to creep in one slow line. Cut, cut.

And ten low words oft creep in one slow line.

Poor dwarfish Pope. Poor rich cloven-footed Byron. Poor dyspeptic Dr. Johnson with his ankles ballooned by the gout. These are my boon companions and all of them are dead. Outside it's eighty-two degrees and unremitting light, that baleful glare from the crest of the hills, the wind stirring nothing but dust. I think of us in early spring, the world before us beckoning in all its languid glory, lying back and offering itself wetly: *I'm yours, I'm yours. Take, take.* But I've consumed my goodly portion and must now pass the plate.

Goodbye.

At sixty-five Arthur retired. His skills had grown outmoded, and his technological competence did not match his younger colleagues'; he would, he told Sarah, lose his job if he did not relinquish it. They put the house up for sale. When clearing out the attic, she came upon her folder of Angus's letters—stored in a steamer-trunk along with Anthony's high-school diploma and college application essay and postcards from camp. Rereading, she decided that Waterston's statements had biographical as well as autobiographical value and should be preserved.

She Xeroxed them and, with a yellow highlighter on her copy, noted the sentence:

> There was what they are calling an auction (or an imitation of it, anyhow, four editors jostling for position and bidding against-one another, so I like to imagine them at a kind of Sotheby's or Christie's not selling pictures or cattle but the space-time empyrean-continuum of language, waggling their fingers and raising their hands and offering and counter-offering, until my agent—blessings on her mortal soul!—called out "Sold. Hold. Enough!"

Only now did Sarah recognize that these last words were an echo of Macbeth's last speech when challenging Macduff. It was the warrior's battle-cry, a premonition of soon-to-come death, and she was, again, astonished at her student's self-awareness—or, perhaps, just his blithe willingness to quote. She still had some connections to the world of publishing and found out where to consign the letters—thirty-four of them—and a dozen postcards and the signed first edition of *Sexing the Chicken*, with its coy inscription: *Ma Muse, Tu m'amuse*. The market for Waterston memorabilia was, she was informed, strong.

It had been years since Tony's disappearance; his parents had given up hope. They dismantled his bedroom and donated his books and clothes and cracked guitar. The house sold rapidly, and they moved back to Manhattan and a two-bedroom co-op with a view of the Hudson and, to the north, The George Washington Bridge. To Sarah Miller's astonishment, her dead student's letters and postcards and autographed books earned, after commission, one-hundred thousand dollars. They were purchased not by a library or public institution but by a private collector, a major admirer of Waterston who had been his contemporary in college. When she tried to learn the purchaser's name, she was told that a condition of the sale was anonymity. But the seller was informed the buyer lived in Iowa City; he and Angus shared—this was as much as the auction house was willing and permitted to disclose—a creative writing class in 1985. Their paths had thereafter diverged.

She could, she knew, contact the university registrar's office and call up her old roster and do a little research and find out who was who. But all this seemed beside the point; the man who bought Waterston's letters was buying them for his own reasons; his reasons were not hers.

Our paths have failed to criss-cross, now, for thirty years. Which is how you wanted it, clearly, and I don't disagree. But it seems to me, as it must have to you, that silence and renunciation, *abdication, absence, aphasia*, is the cleansed form of speech. I join you in it, ma'am.

She tried to remember the class. She pictured the room, the twenty students, the squared-off circle of their desks, their faces and bodies and clothes. She tried to remember their names. Sarah saw herself exhorting her charges to learn to see then say then write what mattered and excise the rest. She felt, as once she had when working on *Counterfeit: A Love Story*, that somewhere just beyond the reach of consciousness, a narrative awaited.

But it was all a blank.

The Twins

HARRY AND GRETA were twins. He was—or so their parents told them—older by nine minutes, and therefore when they argued he claimed to be older and wiser, the one whose opinions took precedence and to whom she should defer. She laughed at him, of course; she had spent her young life laughing, and when he said, "Just listen to me," she said she'd heard it before.

They lived in Sausalito, with a distant view of the Bay. Their parents had been "hippies" when the term did not require quotes and it was still possible to buy a shingled cottage for what is a pittance today. The young couple owned a sandal shop, where they sold sandals and leather bags and wallets and headbands and belts. They also planted a large garden in the hillside weeds. There was always marijuana, and sometimes a plateful of "shrooms," which was what their father called peyote, and friends who came by with tequila and sat cross-legged on the porch at night discussing politics. "Everything's political," their mother liked to say. "What they're teaching you in school is only one person's opinion; you should make up your own mind."

"Your minds," their father said.

The twins' childhood was a happy one, with forays down to Stinson Beach and excursions up to Inverness and Point Reyes National Seashore, where they saw herds of deer. Once, they saw a bear. The local school was progressive and their course of study fruitful; they learned arithmetic and French and were each other's rivals in the sixth-grade spelling bee. Harry spelled "polygamous" and Greta got it wrong; then she spelled "polyandry" correctly but he thought it had an "i." Later, they studied American history and how to draw buildings and roads in perspective; at home they learned about food preparation—the best way to peel garlic, to pare an orange—and how to throw ceramic pots and build, out of cedar scraps, shelves. Their parents were supportive and called them "small persons" or "little people" and, on the rare occasions when they lost their tempers, apologized for having, as they put it, "gone ballistic."

"It's that time of month," their mother said, and their father said, "This masculine hegemony thing. I've got to get over it, *got* to get past it, and you should pay me no mind."

Their parents died in a crash. On a switchback on Mt. Tamalpais, coming down from the crest of the mountain on their ancient Harley, Paul and Jane were killed. There had been fog and an oncoming truck, but no blame attached to the driver; their father swerved to avoid him and hit a tree instead. The children were in school. It was 1991. In later years, Harry would wonder if their parents had been wasted, or had only been unlucky, and Greta said one way of looking at it is they died on impact, still holding on to each other, and we're the ones who've been unlucky; Mom and Dad lived their lives to the full, and then it was suddenly over, *kerblam.*

"You're joking," Harry said.

"*Kerplatt!* I've never been more serious. Not ever in my life."

"If you're not joking, you're crazy." He kissed her on the neck.

He embraced his sister often. They were engaged, they told each other, in a war against convention; they were following the path their parents took. Because of a life insurance policy their mother, on a whim, had purchased five years earlier, there were available funds. The twins inherited the house in Sausalito, and did not need to work. Blue-eyed and tall and sandy-haired, they were beguiling to look at, and Greta's breasts grew large. At school she was approached by boys with cars and electric guitars, but she always came home to her brother, saying Sebastian was a dork and Alan a prick and the girl across the street—skinny Wilhemina—a cunt.

"What's wrong with her," asked Harry, and she said, "Don't make me tell you," and he said, "Why not?"

They were each other's confidantes, each other's second selves. It's not uncommon with twins. No one else could make them quite so pleased or angry; no one else had known their secrets since they first discovered secrets, or could understand entirely what made them glad or sad. They had a private language, or so it seemed to strangers, and a set of signals that kept the world at bay. A curl of the lip, for example, or twice blinked right eye could signify they wanted to get out of here and please just let's go home; a certain kind of laugh could mean, "This isn't funny," or, "Kiss my neck again."

When their parents died on the mountain, the children were fourteen. After the funeral, their mother's younger sister, Harriet, moved in to manage things. In truth she was the one who needed managing; she'd been divorced and drank too much and couldn't remember to turn off the stove. She made large pots of stew to last the week and emptied the pantry of wine. Turn by turn she slept with old family friends: the ones who still dropped by with tequila and, for old times' sake, sat on the porch. Then, when the overnight or week-long relationship soured, she complained the men were losers and Sausalito a dump.

"It's a dead-end town," she maintained. "Stuck in a time-warp, if you want my opinion."

"We don't," Greta wanted to say.

"Mom loved it here," said Harry

"And Dad did too!"

"*We* love it here."

"It's just my opinion," said their aunt. "OK?"

Harriet felt chary of the twins. They were polite and evasive and aloof. Harry had been named for her, and Greta took after her long-legged dead sister, but they proved hard to control. In her role as legal guardian, she dealt with real estate taxes and paid for repairs to the plumbing and flooring and, when it leaked, the roof. She sold the sandal shop and made arrangements with a local bank to invest the savings from the life insurance settlement and the sale of "Leathers and Such." Yet there was something in her niece and nephew's privacy she could never truly penetrate; they were happier without her, and she knew it, and the three of them maintained a warring peace.

When Harry and Greta turned eighteen, they told their aunt (who wanted to, who'd been complaining of the fog) she could leave town. That autumn she had taken up with a real estate developer from San Diego, and was glad to go.

"I'll miss you kids," said Harriet, half-meaning it, and they chorused, "We'll miss *you*."

"Take care of each other," she said. "And call if you need me."

"We will."

And so they lived alone. The first time they slept together, taking each other's virginity, they had been seventeen. On that shared birthday night (their aunt away in Belvedere, at a dinner party) they decided it was time to try what all their friends were discussing in school—the subject on everybody's mind, or so it seemed—and found it no big deal. Sex was only an extension of the intimacy they'd long enjoyed, their habit of lying together on the camp-bed or the bunk-bed or in sleeping bags.

"Get off of me," said Greta, when her brother had finished inside her, and Harry said, "OK."

This went on for some time. The young people read a story about a brother and sister who felt superior to society around them. In *The Blood of the Walsungs* by Thomas Mann, the German couple was convinced of their own excellence: no one could measure up who did not possess their lineage. Therefore, incest was appropriate; a way of remaining allied and intact and keeping the family pure; it was like making love in a mirror, to a mirror, or jackknifing into a pool . . .

Harry and Greta felt the same way. Sex was a source of comfort, a form of consolation, and they assured each other that theirs was a secret to keep. When Aunt Harriet was in the house, she helped with their homework and taught them to drive, but she was often elsewhere or on a brief "business trip." Those nights they would fall into bed, or make love at dawn, and it felt as though the birds beyond the window were signaling their praise. They were each other's intimates, each other's mirror image, and the pleasure they took in and gave to each other was shared. *Chirrup, chirrup,* and *hoo-hoo hoo* went the chorus from low-hanging branches, and when she said, "Get off of me," her brother said "OK."

A familiarity and ease with sex is visible to strangers, almost as though the initiate has shifted shape with knowledge, and Greta and Harry were soon sought after by others in classrooms and bars. They were young and comely and athletic, and men and women noticed, but they rejected all advances and felt, or so they assured each other, happier alone.

"Alone together," Greta said.

"Just the two of us," he said.

What they did at home was sacrosanct and no one else's business; in the absence of their parents they needed no one else. With Harriet elsewhere, they did not bother with clothes, and could sing loudly or shout. The constraints of "good behavior" were not ones they felt hampered by; there were no adults in the house to monitor their nakedness, and the twins felt free.

"It's natural," said Harry.

"Human nature," she agreed.

That Halloween, the two attended a costume party just outside of town. They dressed up as Castor or Pollux and Clytemnestra or Helen, the fatal twins whose father, Zeus, had come down to earth in the guise of a swan and impregnated Leda with his godlike seed. They carried a sandwich board with the four names and asked their friends and parents' friends to guess which one was which. From a laurel tree in the garden, they fashioned laurel wreaths. He wore a bedsheet as toga and she see-through negligée, with a body stocking beneath. Two of Leda's four children, they explained, were crucial to Greek history and central to the Trojan War and its grim aftermath; the others went to heaven on the spot.

"Who is whose partner?" they asked.

"Castor and Clytemnestra?"

"Helen and Pollux?"

"Guess again," said Harry.

"Clytemnestra and Pollux?"

"Castor and Helen? 'The face that launched a thousand ships'?"

"You got it wrong," said Greta.

Then they danced away.

The hosts of the party felt puzzled. What did names from Greek mythology have to do with a pair of parentless children, no matter how alluring or how self-assured? What did an ancient fairy tale have to do with orphaned teenagers, and why be asked to decide? For a time there were suspicions, a sense of something not quite right, and people wondered privately if the twins were in some sort of trouble or had somehow transgressed. Yet the talk of taboo is conducted in code, and it's difficult to think of incest as something that happens next door. So their friends' suspicions faded or were never fully formulated, and things went on as before. Always, when they finished, Greta said, "Get off of me," and Harry said, "OK."

In the fall of 1995, the pair enrolled in San Francisco State University, meeting other young people to date. Though the Harley had been totaled in the crash on Tamalpais, their parents' Saab Convertible still worked. They drove to school together, taking turns as passenger or driver, and together they went home. Her chosen course of study was Art History, and he majored in Theatre Studies; both learned much. Once back in Sausalito, they studied in the No Name Bar, where strangers would inquire if they were identical twins.

"Not identical" said Harry. "Identical have to be same-sex and come from just one egg."

And Greta would say, smiling, using her French, "*Vive la différence!*"

Romance was in the air those years, and both enjoyed flirtation; but something would always go wrong. There were disappointments, always, in a new potential partner, some sort of fault to find. The girls he drank tea with were shallow, the boys she drank beer with were dull. Whether in or out of school, sister and brother felt something was missing: a sundering, a severance if they spent time apart. And always on the weekends they remained together in the house where they were born and their mother and father had lived.

They purchased matching rings. They wore the same blue jeans and boots. They cut their hair in similar fashion—his hair long, hers close-cropped—and traded caps and scarves. Harry stood two inches taller, but when Greta wore high heels and they kissed each other she did not need to raise her head nor he to lower his.

As time wore on the couple grew inventive: oral sex and anal sex and costumes and bondage and drugs. They masturbated each other, or in front of each other, or at the same time. Still, the affair stayed innocent, or felt that way: as if they lay together in their mother's womb. Their father had taken a photograph, when the two first shared a cradle, of bodies intertwined. This photograph—yellowing and poorly framed—hung in their parents' bedroom, the one the twins now occupied: infants lying nose to nose and arm to arm.

I want, I want, I want.

I wanted.

I will want.

I want.

They had no need to speak of this; it was their secret, their pact. It was a way of keeping the family alive. "These are the ties that bind," joked Greta, when she tied her brother loosely to the bedposts, and straddled him, using two of the old belts from Leathers and Such. Then, when his turn came to be on top, she repeated her mantra, "Get off!"

There was a pregnancy scare. Twice, she missed her period, and began to feel queasy and dizzy; her stomach cramps grew painful and she woke sweating at night. They asked each other what to do, and whether to call Harriet, who had promised to be useful if they were in trouble.

"Am I the father?" Harry asked.

"You know you are. There hasn't been anyone else. No one else, not ever."

So he thought he'd better be the one to take action and find help. He called Harriet in San Diego—or, rather, the small town just to the north where Harriet now lived. Her real estate developer had failed her, going back to his wife, but there was a retired investment banker in Rancho Santa Fe. The two of them played golf together and raised orchids and were flying to Hawaii in the morning, she told Harry when he called.

"Hello?"

"It's Harry."

"Long time, no talk to," she said.

He could hear a barking dog. "Is that your dog, or something going on outside?" The bark was loud.

"Ransom? He's ours. Peter says the vet bills and the cost of adoption were a king's ransom, so that's what we call him."

"What kind of place is Rancho Santa Fe? Is it a working ranch?"

"No. We're going to Maui, but just for a week."

"I've never been . . ."

"We'll take you the next time. Both of you. I miss you kids. How's tricks?"

"They're fine. We're fine."

"You don't sound it . . ."

"No?"

"Come off it, Harry, I know you, I can hear it in your voice. You only call when there's trouble, not to ask about a dog."

"Bingo," he said.

"So what's up?"

He was preparing to confess and ask his aunt for her adult advice; he would tell her that his sister had a lover, and had gotten pregnant. They needed to locate a clinic; Greta needed help. Her lover was a married man who was a practicing Catholic and did not believe in abortion. Harry had worked out the story; he coughed and cleared his throat.

"It's Greta," he began. "She's having—what do you call it?—female trouble. Female troubles."

Then his sister emerged from the bathroom. Her hair uncombed, her lipstick smudged, she looked as though she'd been crying, but the tears were the tears of relief. She wore no bra and her nipples were visible through her white nightgown; he could see them where they strained against the silk.

Pointing to the telephone, he mouthed, "It's Harriet."

Greta waved him off.

"She'll help us," he whispered.

"I'm bleeding." She fingered her crotch. "Don't tell her a thing, not anything. We're OK."

Harriet hung up the phone and walked to the screen door and let Ransom out. He treed a squirrel, barking, while she lit a cigarette. When her nephew made his lame excuse and ended the call quickly, she knew he had been intending to talk till Greta silenced him. She had watched them, after all, while the twins were growing up, and she had heard in the tone of his voice that he was nervous, worried, and something had gone wrong. She tried to imagine what could have gone wrong. She pictured the kids in the kitchen, in the garden, in the bedroom, and that was when she knew.

Her sister had named her the twins' legal guardian; the children were her charge. But Harriet had suitcases to pack for Maui, and Ransom to take to the kennel in Solana Beach, where he had stayed before. Tomorrow morning's car for the airport was scheduled at six, and the last thing she wanted or needed was to get involved again with Harry and Greta, their wanton ways. She put the twins out of her mind, or tried to. She packed. She left instructions for the maid as to which flowers needed watering and when they would return. She arranged to halt delivery of the newspapers and mail. She could not stop thinking, however, of what Harry was asking, or starting to ask, and thought of her dead sister, Jane, and how Jane would have answered and what she might have done.

They had been three years apart. She wore her sister's hand-me-downs and inherited the tricycle when Jane got a two-wheeler, and pedaled behind her furiously, trying to catch up. She never did. Jane was always ahead of her, always around the corner or at the top of the hill. Jane was the one who learned to play the recorder; she was the first to be arrested at the Alameda County Courthouse, with her support of the Black Panthers and her "Free Huey Newton!" sign. She was the one who went to jail for trespassing and came home with black men sporting Afros and wore T-shirts saying "Off the Pigs!" and "Make Love, not War!"

Their parents were frantic but tried not to show it and instead tried, as Jane urged, to "stay cool." Their father was in advertising and the family lived on Nob Hill. When finally Jane came to the house with a boy from Colorado who had attended Berkeley but did not wear dreadlocks or carry a gun, they sanctioned the marriage gladly. It was a formal affair. Paul's mother and father were doctors, and they too were relieved. As a wedding gift, the four adults bought and deeded the young couple the house in Sausalito. There Jane and Paul lived happily, or so it seemed, and after five years Jane got pregnant with twins. "You never do anything by half measures, do you?" she could remember joking, and her sister replied, "Don't be jealous," and Harriet said, "I'm not."

Her brother-in-law was a painter, or wanted to be a painter, and he built a shed behind the house he called his studio and filled with oil paintings of clouds. He also bought a potter's wheel, and the children played with clay. Together Jane and Paul were disciples of Timothy Leary; they believed in his slogan, "Turn on, tune in, drop out" and were a pair of poster children for the counterculture, even in their thirties, even turning forty in the Ronald Reagan years. They were peaceable and affable and musical and kind, tending their garden and selling leather articles until the accident, which left the children bereft.

Harriet too was bereft. For the twins' sake she tried not to show it, as her parents had done earlier when Jane tested their resolve. She tried to be, if not a role model, at least a responsible adult in the empty echoing house. She herself had been divorced from her mistake of a husband, with nowhere else to be or go, so she moved to Sausalito and watched over her young charges, joining their reindeer games. She attempted to keep things in order, but always when she closed her eyes she saw her older sister disappearing on a bicycle around the corner or over the top of a hill.

Peter's timeshare in Maui was right on the water, and he loved it there. Harriet looked forward to the trip; she liked the food and liked to dance by the fire at night and liked to lie out in the sun. Idly now she asked herself if she should let him go ahead and join him later, having gone to see the twins and, using her key, let herself into the house; she would find out what was happening and what the trouble was. She corrected herself: *is.* She would tell them to come clean. She pictured their bedrooms and beds. "Fess' up," she heard herself saying, "What's going down with you two?"

But that would mean a ticket-change and the hassle of changed schedules and flying to San Francisco and then Hawaii by herself; whatever had been going on had gone on now for years. It could wait. The dog was snouting at the door, whining, scratching, trying to come in. Harriet finished her cigarette and stubbed it out in the sink. She told herself that, once returned, she would fly north and drive to Sausalito; she would talk to Harry and Greta and get to the bottom of things.

"We maybe ought to stop," he said.

"Stop what?"

"You know, I don't need to tell you."

"No."

"No, what?"

"You don't need to tell me."

"But what did you mean just now by 'No'? 'No, we shouldn't stop'?"

"What do you think?" asked Greta.

"I want what you want," he said

"Did you think the baby would be perfect?"

"Or in trouble. You know what they say about, oh, inbreeding . . ."

"It would have been perfect," she said.

"It would have had your nose," he tried to joke. "My coloring. Our eyes and teeth and hair."

"Why wouldn't it be perfect? *The Blood of the Walsungs*, remember?"

"Bad blood. Bad genes . . ."

"Two rights don't make a wrong," said Greta. "How could our baby be—have been, I mean—anything other than perfect?"

"Stop using that word, 'perfect.' It's *perfectly* irrelevant."

"I don't want to stop."

"I don't, really, either."

"I've been bleeding. I'm not getting pregnant."

"I should have used a condom."

"I won't get pregnant."

"No."

"I wouldn't get pregnant."

"It's my fault. It was all my fault!"

"Well, here's your punishment." She dropped her hand to Harry's lap.

"What are you doing?" He stiffened.

"I want what you want," she repeated.

"Yes."

"I want you to fuck me." Greta let her nightgown fall and put on her porn-star expression and dropped her voice to a whisper. "Fuck me hard."

Things continued as before. The homes and houseboats in Sausalito grew chic; the real estate values increased. The town filled with up-scale commuters who worked in San Francisco or Oakland and came home to Jacuzzis and backyard barbecues and gin. The twins' house on the hill seemed, by comparison, shabby, and the trust-fund from the accident no longer paid all the bills. Yet Greta and Harry scraped by.

The two of them took part-time jobs: she working in a gallery, he in a theatre company. The theatre was non-equity and therefore Harry helped with building sets and sometimes, as an understudy, got to play a part. In her job as a receptionist, Greta encountered well-dressed strangers who lingered by the desk and asked for her opinion as to what was on the walls. Attractive and unmarried, both were approached by those who hoped to know them better and to draw them out. Sometimes the offer of friendship and courtship was same-sex, not heterosexual, but the twins' response was always the same. "I've got a partner," they said. "I'm involved with someone else."

More and more routinely, he fucked her in the ass. She wanted it that way, she said, not because of the risk of pregnancy but because it made her feel as if she were inside him too, and there was no difference in who penetrated whom. "I want what you want," he told her always, when she got on her knees and offered him her back. She purchased and greased a dildo, using it on Harry, and when he said "Get off me," Greta said, "OK."

They cooked for each other and slept with each other as if they were a married couple, as their mother and father had done years before. They read the same books often, taking turns with who went first. In the mornings, often, it turned out they'd had the same dream. Cultivating their hillside garden, they planted herbs and tomatoes and eggplant and lettuce and beans. Sometimes when Harry watched his sister—tall and lithe and lovely—he wondered what it would be like to see her as a stranger might: an object of desire. Sometimes when she watched her brother—tall and smoothly muscled—Greta asked herself if other women saw him also as the perfect chevalier.

On September 12, 2007, the twins turned thirty years old. The gallery she worked in had been sold and then, by its new owner, closed; his theatre company also shut down. George Bush was in his seventh year as president, and the wars in Iraq and Afghanistan were failing or had failed. The national mood was embittered; the economic bubble soon would burst. Brother and sister told each other they should celebrate in any case, and, remembering their old masquerade as twins out of mythology, decided to travel to Greece. They had not been abroad before, and Athens, the place where democracy and Western art began, seemed like the right port of call.

By now they had been lovers for nearly half their lives, and, although they seemed unmarked by age, they were no longer young. Harry had thickened, a little, and Greta's breasts began to droop. Yet a certain bodily ripeness looks all the more inviting; men and women still paid the pair court, or tried to till rebuffed. The twins knew each other's thoughts. They had grown tired, they said without saying, of dealing with anyone else. So when they flew to Athens—a long flight, and a wearying one—they did so as husband and wife.

In California there might have been some risk attached, but there was small danger in Greece. They had the same name, after all, the same home address, and wore the same paired rings. In their first hotel, a Pensione in the Plaka with a view of the Acropolis, they booked a single room with a window looking out on the site, and with a double bed. The clerk who took their passports took this as a matter of course.

It was a splendid trip. They visited the Parthenon and the theatre at Epidaurus and the museums and tavernas that made the city famous; next they rented a Peugeot and made their way to Delphi and then the Mani peninsula, passing Corinth and Olympia and seaside towns like Gytheio and Napflion and, finally, Monemvasia, where they remained three days. In each of the hotels they registered as man and wife and took a single room. When they came down to breakfast, they did so hand in hand. This seemed natural, appropriate, and they told each other over drinks—she liked retsina wine, he preferred ouzo and water—they were glad to share this timeless place, and felt they both belonged.

Entertainers from the restaurant came to their waterfront table, smiling, bowing, plucking their bouzoukis and harmonizing loudly. Harry and Greta tipped them, then waved the musicians away. Old women in black and old men wearing cardigans promenaded past. When a flower girl approached, he purchased a bouquet and gave it to his sister-wife. The breeze was fresh, the sky blue. Local olives and the fresh-caught fish seemed somehow both ancient and new.

"Are you happy?" Harry asked.

"You know the answer."

"Yes."

"I'm happy," Greta said. "I wish we could stay here forever."

"Like Paris and Helen . . ."

"Which didn't work out all that well."

"It was Gytheio where they hid out. That promontory by the lighthouse. The place they first made love . . ."

Her expression darkened. "That's what I meant by trouble."

"Why can't we?"

"What?"

"Stay here forever?"

"We can't."

"Why not?"

"No spikka da language, Harry."

"I'm not joking. The hermaphrodite we saw in Athens, the one lying down on the white marble slab; he/she seemed so happy. Fulfilled. So much at ease."

"It's a statue," Greta said.

Her brother changed the subject. He talked about the fishing boats beneath them in the harbor, the men spreading nets on the sand. He talked about where they would drive tomorrow, and what was left to see in Monemvasia, and how, in *Richard III*, the Duke of Clarence had been "drowned in a butt of Malmsey wine." The local wine, he told her—he had been reading the guidebook—was a kind of sherry or sweet white retsina, and the Elizabethans called it "Malmsey" since they could or would not pronounce the Greek word. Harry went on in this fashion, avoiding the topics of Paris and Helen and the statue of the hermaphrodite lying wreathed to itself, marmoreal. He lifted his glass and touched hers. But something in his face, she saw, partook of disappointment, as though the dream of Attic grace he harbored had—in the cold wind of her reaction—been blown away.

"Don't be angry with me," Greta said.

"No."

"It's, just, I don't think we can stay here. It isn't a matter of money, or our tickets home next week. What would we do in the morning?"

"Take two aspirin."

She completed the line. "And call me in the morning . . ."

Mirthlessly, they laughed. In truth the seaside towns were empty and abandoned by the local young, who had escaped to Athens or left Greece altogether. In truth they had no reason to be eating fish and potatoes and peas or sitting by this harbor in the increasing dark. The charade of playing man and wife had somehow come between the twins, as if the actuality had grown more distant and less possible while they were acting it out. In the Mani peninsula they might escape from censure; in Sausalito, not. When they made love that evening in their narrow bed—the rusted metal bedposts, the blankets that reeked of ammonia and the badly stained Flokati rug where, Harry joked, the ghost of Agamemnon lay—it was as though they bade farewell to a shared future.

"Get off me," Greta said.

Returned, they did try to break free. He met a woman called Heather in the Farmer's Market; she was selling marigolds and honey and eggs from her family's farm. Her hair was thick and long. She was happy to converse with him and happy to sell him a half dozen eggs and, later, in the meadow, take his hand. She was less tall than his sister, and her limbs less supple, but he made himself participate in the shared seduction and they went to a motel. When she shrugged off her clothes and opened her legs he felt a drowning sensation, as though the pool he dove into with Greta had grown suddenly threatful, and strange. The noises Heather made, the way she thrashed beneath him, the hair in her armpits and smell of her sweat all seemed alien, unwelcome, and when they parted that evening he did so with relief.

For Greta, things went better. A man in the No Name Bar was sipping cappuccino beside her on the bench, and on impulse she asked him the make of the car he had parked so carefully and noisily in front of the plate-glass window.

"I'm glad you noticed," the man said, and told her it was a 1991 Porsche 968. He explained it was a beauty to drive but a pain in the ass to have serviced, and by the time he finished his discourse on the excellence of handling and the pleasure of performance he had offered someday to take her out "for a spin."

"Is that a metaphor?" she asked.

Then, when he looked uncertain, Greta recited the first words of the poem by e. e. cummings about a virgin car: "She, being brand new . . ."

"'And consequently a little stiff . . .'" He pleased her by knowing the poem's next phrase, and said he'd always liked the line, but his Porsche was an old model, a collector's item. There was nothing to break in.

They introduced themselves. His name was Paul. Greta said that was her father's name, and maybe that was why she found him sympathetic. She said she came here often, and he said he'd just now moved to town and only recently discovered the No Name Bar. They continued talking, discussing the car and the poem and weather, and Greta said, surprising herself, "No time like the present. Why wait for you to call before we take a 'spin'?"

Paul agreed. He was, it turned out, thirty-eight and a freelance writer. A script he wrote for Universal Pictures had been green-lighted recently, and, feeling flush, he'd bought the car.

"What kind of script?" she inquired, and he said, "The usual. Blood and gore and vampires and sex."

"You're joking, right?" she asked him, and he told her "No."

Without her having noticed, quite, Paul had driven them up Mt. Tamalpais, into the increasing fog, and when she shivered and explained that this was where her parents died, he was sweet about it, truly, and they parked in a turn-out that was supposed to be a Scenic View. Because of the fog she saw nothing, and no one else could see them. Greta closed her eyes. His hand on her was heavy, but his lips were pleasing, and since the body of the car was small there was no way to withdraw from him, and she did not want to. He pushed her seat all the way down. The sex was cramped, uncomfortable—she heard cars and trucks on the switchbacks—but now someone other than her brother had been inside her, thrusting, and when he pulled out she was happy it happened and ready to see him again.

Paul called the next afternoon. "I'm going out of town," he said, "for a table reading in L.A. But it was great to meet you."

"*Meet* me?"

"Well, a little more than that. I was trying to sound like e. e. cummings."

"You didn't," Greta said. "But I accept the reference."

"Can we get together when I get back? They want me at the studio; I'm flying down tomorrow."

"What's a 'table reading?'"

"Of my script. My *Buffy the Vampire Slayer* reborn. We'll see what it sounds like, what needs to be done."

"Good luck with it. And, yes, let's meet. But maybe not in your car."

"I hear you," he said. "And I'll call."

He did not call. The days and weeks went by, and it was hard for Greta, a memory to store against the shoals of her confusion; for the first time since her seventeenth birthday there had been another lover, and she did think about Paul. Once a full month passed, however, she came to terms with silence and the process of forgetting and hoped he would not call. She wondered if this was a form of betrayal, and whom she was betraying, and wondered if her brother was feeling the same way.

The two of them discussed it. Keeping no secrets from each other, they were clear about the pleasures and displeasures of what felt like infidelity, a reaching out to someone new. Harry told her of his afternoon with Heather and his disappointment. He described the smell of Heather's skin and the appendix scar beneath her navel as exciting and repellent, both; she told him Paul was circumcised and it had been a surprise. He asked if she planned to continue and she asked if he planned to continue, and they agreed they'd try again and if it worked, then fine, and if it didn't work it also would be fine. Harry confessed there was an actress from his old theatre company who, coincidentally, had called out of the blue that morning and asked if he wanted to audition for a role in *Hedda Gabler*; she said a man who owned a Richard Diebenkorn she'd known from her gallery days had called to ask what to do with the painting, and hoped for her advice . . .

"There's only one problem."

"What?"

"I only want you."

"I only want *you*," Greta said.

"It isn't all that complicated. They knew about it as far back as 'Song of Solomon.' He called his beloved, 'My sister, my spouse.'"

"Way back when, they understood . . ."

Harry put his hand on hers. "Let's not bother with an actress or an art collector. Let's just be us, OK?"

"My brother, my spouse," Greta said

Through the Obama years the pair remained inseparable, living in Sausalito and taking trips together and joining advocacy groups: Habitat for Humanity and Save the Children and local organizations in support of same-sex marriage and legalized marijuana. They were glad when Jerry Brown, a man their parents might have known, returned as California's governor; they much preferred him to his predecessor, the muscle-bound ex-movie star. They reread Thomas Mann's *The Blood of the Walsungs*, in a new translation, and found it as compelling as they had when young. Most evenings they remained at home, listening to music or watching television, and after a bottle of wine closing the shutters of their tree-protected retreat and falling into bed.

From time to time the twins pursued romantic adventures with others; these did not end well. And as their social circle shrank they left Sausalito less, complaining about the traffic in San Francisco or on the Golden Gate Bridge. No longer in the flush of youth or blush of first encounter, they had grown jaded, a little, and could not help comparing new "players"—it was the word they used—with their second selves at home. They slept together, back to belly, like a pair of turtledoves or a pair of spoons. They were used to each other, at ease with each other, and wondered if the Platonic ideal—a shadow-self—had come to be embodied in their love.

Yet sometimes they were angry with each other.

"How are you feeling?" Harry asked.

"Fine. And you?'

"Thank you for asking. I'm fine."

"Why do you ask?"

"I just wondered."

"What exactly? Wondered what?"

"If you're telling me everything?"

"Is this some sort of inquisition?"

"No."

"Can we change the subject? Can't we change the subject?"

"If you insist."

"Let's talk about the weather."

"Hot, it's very hot today."

"Not as hot as yesterday."

"What are you so angry at? What have I done?"

"I thought we were changing the subject."

"We were. But not to the weather."

"Let's try again, OK?"

"OK. Who do you like in the World Series?"

"Come off it. That isn't a question."

"Yes, it is. Who do you like in the World Series? I'm just asking."

"Well, stop it."

"You don't have a team? A preference?"

"I'd rather talk about the weather."

"So, do you maybe think it'll rain?"

"Could be. We need it, that's for sure."

"See, it's not so difficult. We can agree when we try to."

"Agree on what?"

"'Mine, O Thou Lord of Life, send my roots rain . . .'"

"Who said that?"

"*Wrote*, not said it."

"Well, who?"

"Gerard Manley Hopkins."

"Who?"

"The Jesuit poet. Great Jesuit poet. In one of his 'Terrible Sonnets' . . ."

"Every night I pinch myself. I say my brother's a scholar. Isn't that wonderful, I ask myself?"

"Well, is it wonderful?"

"Don't be ridiculous. You're not a scholar. You simply have a memory for other people's language, the way most actors do."

"There are worse things."

"Such as?"

"Such as not knowing who you like in the World Series. Or refusing to pray for the rain."

"Which everybody knows we need."

"Guess what? I'm changing the rules of our game. You can still play, if you want to. But it's not one-liners anymore, it's an extended opinion. Or perhaps a declaration, an open-ended announcement, and it goes beyond two sentences to actually say what you actually mean."

"No, I don't agree, I didn't agree to a change of the rules."

"I love you."

"I love *you*. But sometimes . . ."

"Sometimes, always, what's the difference?"

"If I have to tell you, darling, you wouldn't understand."

Harry earned a bit-part in a television series set in Marin County and featuring a husband and wife detective team who were modeled on the old TV and movie couple, Nick and Nora Charles. They solved problems—teenager disappearances, bank robberies, suspicious deaths—up and down the picturesque coast; their home base was Bolinas. Each episode began with the detectives in their house on the Mesa, mixing a martini and settling down to read or eat when they were interrupted because their cellphones rang. Harry played the police dispatcher who was always in the opening scene, sitting at the station desk and informing the couple of trouble, but then not seen again.

Greta did indeed have a brief dalliance with the man who bought the Diebenkorn, and this resulted in an offer to serve as a consultant on his other purchases. She had, he said, the instinct for it, and her advice was good. She told him not to buy a Basquiat that turned out to be a forgery, and he was grateful to her and asked how she'd known.

"It just smelled fishy," Greta said. She wrinkled up her nose and sniffed. "You can *smell* the handwriting. I know it makes no sense, but that's the sense it makes."

Her sense of authenticity, honed by research and experience, felt nonetheless innate. She *knew*, she said, the fingerprints of artists she had studied, and it was easy to distinguish the real thing from the fake. Her lover asked, did that include him, and she did not answer, and he changed the subject to an Ellsworth Kelly he'd been looking at with an eye to purchase, and she said, "Go ahead."

Their jobs sufficed to keep them in funds, but were undemanding. From time to time the pair needed to travel in different directions, so they bought a second vehicle, a used Subaru. The Saab broke down routinely, but they kept it running for errands close to home. Harry did summer stock one season in a nearby circus-tent, and Greta guest-curated an Abstract Expressionist show for a new gallery in Oakland. When the twins turned thirty-five they told each other, marveling, that now they had been lovers for more than half their lives.

"Imagine if we'd married. Somebody else, I mean," she said. "If I were someone else's wife, and you had a wife of your own . . ."

"Why would I want to do that?"

"Why not? It's how most people live."

"We're not most people, darling."

"Tell me about it," she said.

"I'm happy this way," he declared. "As a—what would you call it?—confirmed bachelor. It's who I am."

"You can say that again."

He tried their old joke, repeating himself. "It's who I am.'"

"And I am your sister, your spouse."

Harriet turned seventy the year the twins turned forty, and they flew to Los Angeles in order to sing "Happy Birthday." She was living, now, in Hancock Park, on Muirfield Place. Three years before—after her liaison with Peter from Rancho Santa Fe ended—she moved in with and finally married a lawyer who had specialized and made his reputation in environmental law. In Los Angeles the stakes and fees were high, and he and his firm prospered.

Alistair was seventy-eight, stooped and inattentive, but his eyes still twinkled and his white hair stayed trim. He had three children, eight grandchildren, and a great-great-grandchild living in Las Vegas. The pre-nuptial agreement with Harriet had been carefully composed; she would receive an allowance of ten thousand dollars per month for the rest of her life, plus household expenses and the right of residence in but not ownership of the stone and stucco gatekeeper's cottage by the property's rear wall.

This was, she said, fine by her. She needed nothing else. Harriet had aged, of course, but remained the tart-tongued cigarette-smoking expensively free spirit she had been before. Where others of her circle swore by plastic surgery, she kept what she called her "fault lines" and liked to call attention to, by complaining about and pointing out, her network of varicose veins. Her limit now, she liked to say, was one bottle of wine and three cigarettes per day. She had no children of her own but maintained a cordial contact with her niece and nephew, sending birthday cards and checks.

At the La Brea Bakery, they bought their aunt an elaborate cake: carrots and walnuts and coffee cream icing, with a pink confectioner's rose. Then, following the GPS, they arrived at Muirfield Place. The property had a brick wall and high wrought iron gates at the driveway; they buzzed and were let in.

Harriet came to the door. "Long time, no see."

"You're looking well," said Greta.

"She means it," Harry said.

"You don't have to be polite, you two. I'm an old bag, a hag."

"Not so I noticed," they in unison protested.

Their aunt introduced them to Alistair, her husband, who shook hands and said how glad he was to meet them and withdrew. Then she led them through the garden to her remodeled bungalow back behind the mansion, where a tray of fruit and pot of tea stood waiting.

"The sun isn't over the yard-arm," she said. "So I made tea in case you guys are now teetotalers. Hah! I never thought of it like that: *tea* totalers, get it?"

They sat. Greta had bought candles, and they sang "Happy Birthday" and produced the birthday cake. They said again how well she looked, and she said, "Why shouldn't I? I do Pilates twice a week, and there's a masseuse who comes to the house. Alistair requires her. He thinks she's cute; he's right."

"It's a beautiful place," Harry said. He pointed to the flowerbeds, the garden walls and marble nymphs and elegant espaliered vines. Across the pool rose the main building, a brick mock-Tudor with a slate roof and four chimneys where Harriet spent the bulk of her time with her new husband. But she escaped from it, she said, when Alistair had a business meeting or company that bored her, as he did today.

"Besides, I want to talk to you. How's things in Sausalito, kids?"

"You'd recognize the house," said Greta. "Nothing changes all that much . . ."

"No? Is that good news?"

"We think so," Harry said.

"I'm too old," said their aunt, "to beat around the bush these days. I love you two but you're not children any longer, are you, and I've got questions to ask. Private questions, personal ones, nothing hubby needs to hear or know about ..."

"OK."

Her gaze was piercing, level-eyed. "Is there anyone else in your life? Your lives?"

They shook their heads.

"Why not?"

"We have each other," said Harry.

"And you," Greta added, smiling.

She studied them. "It's what I wanted to ask you about ..."

"Yes?"

"Yes?"

"Why a pair of kids so good to look at have never found other—oh, what would you call them?—partners, companions to be with, why you don't ever get involved with anybody else? Aren't other people good enough?"

Harry drank his tea. "What exactly are you asking us?"

"You know what I'm asking," she said.

"No, I'm not sure."

"You know what I'm saying," she said.

"Do you want an explanation?" Greta asked. "Or a confession, maybe?"

"Sweetheart, I'm too old to need an explanation. And I don't want confessions from you either. Unless, that is, you've got something to confess."

Then there was silence between them. Harriet sat back and waited; the twins looked down at their feet. They felt themselves fifteen again, being chastised or confronted by the adult in the room. They had no need to say aloud what they both were wondering: should we tell her finally? Unspeaking, they agreed to it: yes, *yes*.

He put his hand on Greta's arm. She took her brother's hand in hers.

"Is that my answer?" Harriet asked.

"It is."

Surprising them, their hostess did not seem surprised. She talked about the time that Harry called to tell her Greta was in trouble, and how she'd told herself—when was it, twenty years ago?—that something should be done about their situation, but had flown to Hawaii instead.

"I thought you'd grow out of it," Harriet mused. "I told myself you'd get over it."

"Why would we want to do that?"

"Most people do."

"We're not most people," Greta said, surprised by her own vehemence and repeating what she said to Harry after reaching orgasm at the count of ten. When she was nearly ready, and he was nearly ready, she liked to urge, "Let's come together," and they synchronized their rhythm and took turns counting down. Varying the intervals between the numbers, thrusting, he'd say, "*One*," and she'd breathe "*Two*," then he'd count "*Three*" and she'd say "*Four*" until together they cried, "*Ten!*" When they both had climaxed and she said, "Get off of me," he always said, "OK."

"I understand that," Harriet said. "You're special, you two have always been special. And when you came into my life I understood, or thought I did, that family is family and blood is thicker than water. That old cliché. I'm making a speech now, aren't I, I don't usually make speeches, but maybe it's the sight of you two not getting any younger, *I'm* not getting any younger, that makes me want to settle up and call a spade a spade."

"Your second cliché," Harry started to say, but held his tongue.

"So what I mean to tell you is, just be careful, kids. Your business is your business, not mine, and I don't mean to sound like a schoolmarm or, god help us, a Republican, but you're in my will and I want you to live, hah, happily ever after. The way your parents didn't but I need you two to do. You understand I'm asking, no, telling you, be careful, OK?"

"OK," they said in unison, and kissed her on the cheek.

Harriet presented a plate of nuts, olives, and cheese. Next, opening a second bottle of Pinot Grigio, she regaled them with stories about her husband, his devotion to clean water and investments in clean energy and his regimen of walking three miles every morning on the treadmill in the basement while he listened to the news. Because of Alistair's increasing deafness, and even with the world's best hearing aids (at least that's what they ought to be, given how much they cost and how many times he had had them replaced) he played NPR at deafening levels for anyone else, and that—combined with the racket of the treadmill and his heavy breathing and the maid who mopped the floors all day and the gardeners shouting at each other in Spanish with their mowers and blowers and weed-whackers—made her relieved to have this little hideaway (she raised her arm, evoking it: the kitchenette and bedroom and the screened-in-porch) to retreat to, where she could be alone: a person needs privacy sometimes . . .

"We feel that way too," said Greta.

"Alone together," Harry said.

Their aunt was not convinced. "This business of somebody else—strangers? I wonder if you're missing something?"

"What do you think we're missing? This?" Greta waved her hand. She was feeling argumentative and trying not to argue. The trappings of wealth and privilege—the hot tub steaming by the pool, the pool-man now testing the water with his thermometer and adding chemicals and cleaning it with nets—had no power to compel her. She wanted Harry, only Harry, and knew that he felt the same way. He was her perfect mate, her mirrored second self . . .

"I love you," said their aunt.

Returned to Sausalito, they took stock. They were forty years old and societal outlaws except that society (with, now, the exception of Harriet) did not understand they were breaking its rules. Yet those rules were subject to change. Issues of sexual identity and sexual politics had altered, and it was no longer dangerous or even notable to call oneself a lesbian or "bi." Same-sex marriages and openly gay soldiers or television personalities had become a commonplace; the "new normal" was what had seemed abnormal only a few years before. Transvestites and transgender couples sat in restaurants and coffee shops and went walking unmolested down the Berkeley streets.

Therefore when they went outside together—as had been the case in Greece—they did so arm in arm or holding hands. That siblings should be intimate was unremarkable, and all the more so in the case of twins. Was there any reason, Greta asked, their own enduring liaison needed to stay hidden; why not declare themselves in public as, in private, they had done with Harriet?

The question of fidelity was one they tried to answer; what did it mean to stay faithful, and to whom were they both pledged? Which standard of behavior or system of morality had the two of them transgressed? Since they believed themselves paired halves of a shared single whole, how could they be unfaithful? Was it self-love or the love of company that kept them bound to each other and, from all others, aloof; was it pride or a kind of humility that kept them together alone?

His small career in television and hers in the art world faltered; they no longer turned heads where they walked. Their brief affairs and one-night stands were over, and they knew nothing of what lay ahead. What had they accomplished or failed to accomplish, and why? What were they doing, or failing to do, with their lives?

"I've been reading Plato," Harry said. "'The Cave.'"

"Oh?"

"Re-reading him . . ."

"Does it hold up: 'the cave,' I mean?"

"All that stuff about spelunking."

She looked at him, quizzical. "What are you talking about?"

"The three fates. The ones who card and spin and cut."

"Clotho, Lachesis, Atropos?"

He clapped. He was playing to an audience, although they were alone. Addressing the imagined camera, Harry said, "It's my sister, folks, my spouse. The one who answers twenty questions and who knows the answer, always. Who knows the names of the three Fates. Give her a hand!"

"But why reread him, Harry? I'm serious. Wasn't that first time enough?"

"The great philosopher was probably in love with Socrates. And certainly and often with a bunch of other students. Remember the Platonic 'Dialogues?' All those conversations while they ply each other with olives and wine; all that heavy breathing over the definition of truth."

"But didn't Plato say the true purpose of philosophy is the preparation for death? And therefore . . ."

He took his sister's arm.

Greta had a dream. In the dream her parents were alive, and young, although since she was just a girl they seemed large and old. She was six, maybe seven or five. She and Harry and her parents were playing by the water's edge, on Stinson Beach, and they were having a picnic; she could remember bananas and chicken and what she liked but could not keep control of: a bag of buttered popcorn in her hand. The gulls were greedy for popcorn, and they clustered above her cawingly, and took turns swooping down at her to peck at the kernels of corn. She covered her head with her towel. It had grains of sand, and pebbles, and the grit of sand and pebbles got in her hair and eyes. In the dream her mother held her, and her words were soothing—I've got you, don't worry—though for reasons Greta could not follow her mother was speaking in French. "*Je t'embrasse*," her mother said, and also, "*Je m'en fiche*."

Her father was making a speech. He was discoursing, as he often did, on the lure and danger of capitalism, and she could read his lips but did not need to listen since she'd heard the speech before. His bathing suit was wet from where he'd waded in the water, but he must not have swum because there was a line across the fabric—a blue nylon suit, with pockets—where it was wet, then dry. The line was the line of his crotch. It bulged above his hairy legs, and she did not like to look at them and closed her eyes again in order to shut out the sight. This had the effect of making her hear but not see him, and he too was speaking in French.

As dreams do, this one cut through space and time, and now she was with Harry on the point at Gytheio where, according to the story, Paris and beautiful Helen lay together their first night. The lighthouse on the promontory had been boarded up. Rusted wire and old bottles and plastic containers and algae and kelp and food-scraps beat against the rocky shore of what Homer used to call the "wine-dark sea." In the dream she could hear herself asking, what if the wine were white, not red, why wouldn't it be called the "wine-bright sea" instead? She and Harry now were lovers, and they sat at a restaurant where their plates kept getting filled with lamb and peas and fish and rice, for no matter how much she protested the smiling mustachioed waiter filled her plate again.

He would not take no for an answer, and she understood at last that when the Greeks say, "No," they do so by nodding their heads up and down and clicking their tongues and saying something like "*Ochi*" or "*Okki*," but when she shook her head he must have thought she had been saying, "Yes."

Greta was seeing Robert Rauschenberg and Robert Indiana and Robert Motherwell—not seeing *them*, exactly, but seeing what they painted, and the paintings kept displacing one another like a deck of shuffled cards. She was sitting at her desk in the gallery's foyer, with catalogues of the three Roberts and their recent work, but she wasn't wearing anything below the desk's white marble surface, and she worried that the customers would complain or at any rate remark upon her nudity and laugh. What would become of her, she wondered, if she failed to sell a painting, and who would understand or shout that she, the emperor's idiot daughter, wasn't wearing clothes?

It was Harry, of course, who first noticed, and Harry who came to the rescue and gathered her up in his arms. He placed her in his waiting boat, at the stern holding the tiller, the white wooden craft gently rocking, and handed her a sheet with which to cover her nakedness. "Take this," he said, "and this." He was openhanded in his generosity and gave her the popcorn she'd thrown to the gulls and crows at the start of her dream, and therefore nothing was lost.

Long years before, and as a result of their pregnancy scare, the twins agreed to birth control; they discussed the forms of contraception: condoms, pills, an I.U.D. In the end, and having considered the options, Harry chose a vasectomy and signed up to have it performed. Greta sucked him off, that morning, in order, she said, to remember the taste; then, at the appointed time, they drove to the clinic together. On the paperwork he listed her as his emergency contact and wrote down their telephone number.

"This isn't an emergency," his sister said, and kissed him on the neck.

It proved to be a simpler procedure than they both had feared. When Harry woke from anesthesia, hers was the first face he saw. "I did this for you," he tried to tell her, and Greta added, "You did it for us." They had no need, however, to say these things aloud, and he fell, again, asleep.

Thereafter the sex felt risk-free. As with any long-term couple, the landscape of the body, from toe to ear and ankle to collarbone, had been closely mapped. They knew each other's moves. They could not have a child, of course, but neither of them wanted one: a creature to raise in this dangerous world and to put in peril. What they were doing together might be, by others, considered profane, but to them it seemed sacred and right. "I do this for you, you do that for me; we do it to each other!" This had been their understanding from the start.

At forty-one, however, Greta found herself wanting a child. It was, she knew, the biological clock, and though she tried to ignore it she heard its tick-tick-tock. On the street she stared at babies; at night she dreamed about them and in the morning mourned the fact of being barren. Harry could not be the father, and she wanted no other partner, yet the procedure of sperm banks put her, as she told him, "off her feed."

"You're not a cow," said Harry, "you don't have to use that expression."

"I feel like a cow. I look like a cow."

"Don't be ridiculous."

"Look at these udders!" She lifted her breasts. "I'm an old lady, Harry."

"You're beautiful," he said.

But she was having none of it. "Don't lie to me. Don't condescend. I want to get pregnant before it's too late. I need to, we need to have children."

"The blood of the Walsungs?"

"Correct."

"Were you thinking of an anonymous donor?"

"No. Someone we know," Greta said.

The next day, in what seemed like more than mere coincidence, she ran into the man with the Porsche: Paul. She had been buying groceries and standing at the checkout line, and she looked up and saw the customer in the next aisle was somebody she recognized. It was—Greta did the arithmetic—a full decade since she'd seen him, and he'd grown older and grayer and had lost some of his hair. He was wearing a red and black checked shirt and tan leather jacket and staring at her, quizzical, half-smiling. When they both had paid and wheeled their shopping carts to the exit vestibule, he said, "It's been a while."

"How have you been?" asked Greta.

"Fine. I'm glad to see you. You look wonderful, you haven't changed."

She did not return the compliment. "Do you still have that car?"

"You mean, my e. e. cummings-mobile?" He smiled and shook his head. "No, it's no longer eco-friendly. And it kept on breaking down. I drive a Tesla now."

"Does that mean your movie worked?"

"It means I'm still writing for Universal. Under contract, anyhow. And, no, they didn't shoot the thing and no, to answer your question, I don't mind."

"That wasn't my question," she said.

A fat woman on a motorized cart idled loudly by. She was staring up at them, steering, and they waited till she piloted herself through the glass doors. When there was silence again, Paul spoke: "Look, I know I didn't call. One time I tried to and hung up instead, but that's the right expression, isn't it, for the way I behaved back then, *hung up*? So next time I tried to call I couldn't find your number and"—he spread his hands—"couldn't track you down because you never told me your last name. I still don't know it, do I? Greta, Greta *what*?"

Late afternoon sun had emerged from the clouds, and wind created wavelets on the bay.

"I'm better now," Paul finished. "And I apologize for telling you I'd be in touch and then not following through."

She asked herself, and did not know the answer, if she wanted him to go away or stay. She remembered his hot bulk above her in the seat, and how he had been sensitive about her parents' death.

"Apology accepted," Greta said.

He pointed out and walked her past his own gleaming car and steadied her cart while she opened the Subaru's trunk. Carefully, she positioned the groceries between a pile of blankets and the wicker picnic basket she routinely stored there, with its bottle of water and napkins. Leaning down and arranging the bags, she was conscious of him watching her, assessing the curve of her back and breathing just above her neck.

"Are you still living with your brother?"

"I'm surprised you remember . . ."

"Well, are you?"

"Yes."

"That's a relief," Paul said. "That means you don't have someone else."

"No. We don't."

"That's a relief," he repeated.

It was mid-August, and hot. "And you?"

"I was married, didn't I tell you? And, to put it mildly, not seeing eye to eye with the lady and in the process of getting divorced. That happened many years ago, and it's water under the Golden Gate Bridge but it's one of the reasons I was, oh, skittish about our afternoon together, not ready to repeat it just then, but if you give me your number I won't lose it this time through."

"How can I be sure?" she could not keep from asking.

"Give me your number." He pulled out his cellphone and went to Contacts. "This time I promise I'll call."

When Paul asked her to dinner, Greta told him "Yes." She had discussed this with her brother, and told him what she planned to do, and how much she wanted a child. Adoption did not interest her, and the authorities in any case were against single-parent adoption, so she needed her eggs fertilized before it was too late. Harry made her promise to lay her cards on the table and not mislead Paul or string him along. That was the phrase he used, "string him along," and Greta said, "Of course not. I'm doing this for us."

But the night with her suitor proved complicated in ways she hadn't planned. He was talkative and courtly and insisted on driving to a restaurant in Tiburon where she'd not been before. The waiters all were dressed in black, the tablecloths were yellow, and the view of the harbor—its lights twinkling, the moon a silver sliver in a sky replete with stars—looked like a stage-set arranged for her private enjoyment.

Greta drank too much wine. Paul talked about his college years, his years in advertising and his dream of a great novel, the great American novel he was certain he was born to write, and then the dawning recognition that this was not to be, or anyhow was not his calling. Television had instead provided an income; he talked about the business of collective authorship, the scripts and writers' rooms and hospital shows and conspiracy dramas once he settled in L.A.

"When we first"—Paul gestured, raising his glass—"met and spent that afternoon on Tamalpais, I was trying to escape and, let me be honest, trying to escape from both my work and marriage, except it didn't pan out. It's done so now, at least the part about marriage succeeded—I've been divorced these last eight years—but I still earn a living in the writers' room and am less self-deluded. Less ambitious too. I know what I can do, what I can't," and while he rambled on, attempting to impress her, she studied his fingers and mouth.

"I wouldn't be here," Greta said, declaring herself, "if I hadn't wanted to see you."

"I'm very glad. Me too."

"And you know what I mean by *see* you," she said.

It was two weeks past her period, mid-month. They drove back to his house. He was living in a Condo complex just beyond the harbor, with a walkway by the water where life preservers hung on poles as a design motif, and the railings were draped with fishnets. The attached houses were sided in pine, the units indistinguishable, but he parked the Tesla in front of his door, and when he opened it to let her through he was excited, clearly, and fumbled with his keys. It was not so much an assignation as a kind of service call, and Greta planned, as Harry had urged, to "lay her cards on the table." But the idea of anything laid out on the table seemed overly suggestive, a second-rate joke, and when he said, "I'm glad you're here" she said, "I'm glad I came."

They sat. They made small talk and drank. She started to explain to him the reason for her visit, the hope she had of getting pregnant, but it seemed unfair somehow and businesslike and even a little unkind. She wondered if Paul would be flattered to know she had selected him, but since she had no intention of seeing him again, and certainly not as the father of her as-yet-unborn child, she thought it made more sense to let him keep his innocence, his ignorance intact. It was appropriate, she told herself, to let him play the role of—what was the word for it?—*stud*. She liked him, a little, and liked how he blushed when she reached for his belt and unbuckled it and then unzipped his pants. They were sitting in his living room (a stack of books, a poster of a Toreador, an elaborate sound-system and shelves of CDs) and he suggested they should go upstairs where at least this time around he had a bed.

All through the sex she thought, "I'm doing this for us, for *us*." She was doing this, she told herself, not for herself and Harry but their unborn child, in order that a child be born, and doing this to guarantee that the father be—what was the word?—*appropriate*, in terms of age and looks and sanity. But age and looks and sanity were not what she was thinking of when Paul and she were making love, and she was urging him, "Come on, come *on*," and telling him not to pull out because she wanted him inside her and it would be all right. She was thinking instead of how strange this all felt, how a camera on the ceiling, if there were a camera on the ceiling, would catch the two of them naked, entwined, and how she was holding his shoulders and pounding the small of his back. "Come on, come on," chanted Greta, while he was plunging, convulsing, and when at last he had his orgasm and lay sweating, breathing heavily, asking "Was it good for you?" and making a joke of it, smiling, she said, "Yes," and stroked his cock.

"I've given up smoking," he said, "but now's when we should have a smoke and talk . . ."

"Can you come again? Do you want to?"

"Do you want me to?"

He was thickening, hardening, and she pulled him back inside her and breathed, "Yes."

That month she missed her period and it was exciting, but she kept her hopes and fears private. Harry did not press her, and—for the first time in their history—Greta stayed silent, not sharing her own thoughts with him or saying how she felt. The second month was harder, a slow processional of days and nights; each time Paul called she made an excuse: she was setting up a gallery show, she was traveling to see her aunt, she was sick with strep throat and the flu, until he got the message and stopped. Six weeks after their night together, when she missed her second period, she began to think perhaps her plan had worked. It was, she knew, improbable that at her age she should get pregnant on the first attempt, but it had nonetheless happened. She felt, she told Harry, at ease in her skin; she felt the time had come for her to be a mother and to have a child. Twice, Greta tested herself, and the results were positive; then she went to the clinic for confirmation: a baby was bulking inside.

By the end of the third month her stomach had distended, and she marveled loudly at the fact of pregnancy. "Believe it," she told Harry. "Our little princess. Or prince!"

"You'll be a terrific mother."

"And you a father, darling."

He spread his hands and hummed the tune from Carousel. "'My boy Bill, I will see he's not named after me . . .' My boy Paul, I meant to say."

"I'm serious," she said. "You'll be our child's father. You know that, don't you?"

"No."

"Not technically, maybe, but in all the ways that matter."

"Oh?"

The twins prepared a nursery. They painted what had been their childhood bedroom yellow and painted the wooden floor blue. They bought calico curtains and sanded down and varnished their old cradle and put Teddy Bears on shelves. At this point, however, they halted the process, since they were feeling superstitious and did not want to push their luck or make everything ready too soon. Over tea they planned in detail the ways they'd raise and teach their child, the songs to sing and books to read and walks to take together. They remembered their parents' saying, "Small persons" or "Little people," and started to talk about names.

Yet distance had opened between them. The sense of separation the two once felt in company now came to occupy their solitude as well. And it felt different, somehow, than their arguments before. Had it begun, Greta wondered, when she decided to get pregnant by and with another man? Her brother seemed competitive in ways she failed to understand, shadow-boxing with a shadowy male presence in his mind; he grilled her on Paul's furnishings, his house, his car, the jokes he made, the way he'd been in bed. He wondered if his rival knew she was having a baby, or if Paul had other children, or if he'd lay claim to the child. He asked her if she meant it when she said she'd finished with her sometime-lover; he wondered if in private she was nursing happy memories of the night of her baby's conception. How could Harry be angry or jealous, she asked herself, how could he forget how she'd wanted his child and believed it would be perfect? She tried to repeat what he anyhow knew, that he was her brother, her spouse.

Harry had a dream. He was standing at his father's side, on the hill above their home. They were planting lettuce and harvesting spring peas. His father had been showing him the way to prune tomato vines, the way to snip or cut or peel away or simply pinch the plant beneath the branching junction where there was only greenery. "That way," said his father, "you don't waste all this sunshine on stuff that isn't edible; you want—the word is chlorophyll—to be working for the tomato itself and not its leaves, *comprende?*"

"Chlorophyll," he pronounced.

"That's it. It's nature's way of growing things for us to eat."

His father was godlike and they were in Eden and the sun was hot. Harry was sweating, was seven years old, maybe six. They had built a scarecrow. Their father nailed the lumber together so one arm pointed out, one up, and he and Greta dressed the thing: a skirt, a flannel shirt, old coal for its eyes and corn-silk for its hair and a battered straw hat on the circle of wood their father had cut for a head.

In his dream the scarecrow spoke, but what it said was unintelligible: a cawing, a clucking, a high-pitched mutter that became a scream. The gloves on its hands were rabbit-fur and then they were suddenly rabbits and shitting and the garden blazed around him so he ran for the black hose. Greta was a woman now and dressed in bra and panties and lying back on their parents' shared bed. "Come on, come on," she told him and opened up her arms to him, and then she opened her legs. "Chlorophyll" he heard himself saying, and his sister put a finger to her lips.

I have always loved you.

I will always love you.

I love you.

Now get the hell out of my life.

He stood on stage. He was reciting from *Hamlet*, but knew he did not know the lines, and when he said, "Soft thee, the fair Ophelia," he put his finger to his lips in imitation of Greta's gesture while she floated merrily, merrily down the stream. He did not want a child, he tried to tell her, and did not want children, had never wanted children, had always only wanted her and did not like the way she floated, as had mad Ophelia, down the stream. With a clarity he thought he'd lost, and a fixed focus of attention, Harry positioned himself on the river's near bank and reached out his hand to her, holding a branch, until she grasped the other end and he reeled her in. The mud-soaked garments fell from her, the lunacy fell away also, and she was his clever sister who had studied art and made a living selling paintings and was all he hoped for in life.

This was better, this was a good deal better than the bloated belly-swollen figure bobbing in the shallows, in the weeds and reeds. This was what he'd always hoped for and as a child imagined: the two of them transfigured, wheeling upward through the sky. What astonished him, he understood, was that even in the act of dreaming he knew that he was dreaming and would never be an actor with the part of Hamlet or obliged to pull his partner from a death-dealing stream. For she was his sister, his spouse.

The distance grew. They slept in the same bed, as before, but when she moved towards her twin and signaled she was ready for sex he turned away. When she offered to make coffee he said, "Not now, no thank you," as though she were a waitress and not his life-long confidante who knew how much milk he would take in his cup, and whether he used sugar. Harry no longer rested his hand on her knee or smacked his lips appreciatively when she tried on a new sweater; he told her he was going out but not where he was going then started up the Mazda he now drove in place of the Saab.

"Will you be back for dinner?" Greta asked, and he said, "Why not?"

She watched him go. The weather had turned cloudy and, over the bay, rain threatened. Once her brother was no longer visible, she went to the kitchen and telephoned her doctor for the results of the plasma protein screening and the Alpha-fetoprotein screening; she had received an email that the results were in. Doctor Pescak had advised against amniocentesis, since there were risks attached.

It was November 10th. While the office phone offered its pre-recorded announcement Press One, press Two, you're number Three in the line to be answered—Greta crossed her fingers and, preparing herself, shut her eyes. Because of her age and long-term infertility, she felt half-terrified of what would be revealed.

When finally her turn arrived, the nurse asked her name and date of birth and for the last four digits of her Social Security Number. With this information registered, the woman asked if she was sitting down, then said she was carrying twins. Everything was A-OK, the embryos both were healthy—one male, one female—and Greta said, "Oh wonderful, oh thank you, I can't wait to tell my partner! I'm a twin myself, you know."

Elated, she hung up the phone, turning to Harry to share the good news. Her brother was not there. She understood, of course, he had simply gone off on an errand and would be home in an hour. Yet somehow his absence surprised her, as if he should have been waiting also for the verdict of the call. She had called the clinic in his absence, but that should not have mattered; he should have stayed at her side. Greta walked into the nursery that was their childhood bedroom, then into the master bedroom she now shared with her brother, then out to the screened porch. He occupied none of those spaces, and she tried not to take his absence as a sign.

The nurse had said, "Congratulations!" and she answered, "Thanks!"

"It's a great thing, isn't it, but you'd best start getting ready! There's twice as much to do—you know this, don't you—when a person is carrying twins."

"I understand. I will get ready, I promise."

"Good luck!"

Greta felt both glad and frightened, as if their history and that of their parents would now be enacted again. The wheel had come full circle and was spinning in a pre-cut groove; she would replicate her mother's role and be the mother of twins. She would protect the two lives burgeoning inside her, and try to feel two heart-beats and four feet. When Harry returned from wherever he'd been, she could not wait to tell him and rushed out to the Mazda and leaned into his window and said, "Guess what?"

"What?"

"We're having *two* babies!"

"You're having two babies," he said.

She would never forget the look on his face: his mouth set in pure opposition, eyes blank.

"We're having twins," Greta repeated. "A girl and boy!"

"I'm not a part of this."

"Of course you are. Of *course* you are."

"If you say so," Harry said.

"I say so."

"Fine."

She heard, in her voice, hysteria. "Why aren't you happy, you son of a bitch? Why won't you back me up on this?"

He turned off the engine and opened the door. He stood and stretched and said, "I've got your back. I want what you want, remember? But get off of me, OK?"

Over the next months she was careful, and her brother too was careful, and the breach between them healed. It did not wholly disappear, but the sundering, the severance was gone. Her second trimester went well. They completed the layette. On Saturday, March 17, the pair drove to Bolinas, where Harry showed Greta the house the D.P. photographed for his TV show. It sat on the grid of the Mesa, clad in redwood from the time when it had been habitual to build with redwood siding. Bolinas was a private place, and did not welcome strangers; only the establishing shot had used the actual house. There were few road-signs and no tourist traffic, and the twins agreed their parents—who had chosen Sausalito once—would now prefer it here. Had their parents lived, they asked themselves, would anything—would everything—have changed?

They walked the streets of the village, past Smiley's Saloon and down Wharf Road and shared a cup of chowder and a dozen oysters from a food-truck in the square. It was two-thirty in the afternoon, gray and raw with gusts of rain. They talked about their trip to Greece and agreed it would be fine someday, when it again seemed feasible, to return to the

Mani peninsula and this time visit the islands as well. They imagined their lithe children splashing happily in the Aegean sea.

"No spikka da language, remember?" said Greta, and he laughed and said the twins would both be fluent in Greek.

A motorcyclist approached. His muffler had been perforated and made loud growling sounds. He was weaving slowly, lazily, and came close enough so they could see he wore no helmet and his belly spilled over his pants. He had a white beard and white wisps of hair that fluttered in the winter wind; he looked, they told each other, joking, like a Santa Claus no longer occupied with Christmas-season labors, and therefore out for a spin. He passed the twins and made for the harbor, then executed a wide circling turn and, sputtering, drove back.

This is what Harry saw:

The man on the motorcycle rode up the hill. It was not so much a hill as gentle rise, and he drove unsteadily, weaving, gunning the engine then tamping it down. There was gravel on the roadway; there were two trucks parked in front of Smiley's Saloon, and a car nosed out from the space between them. It was, he saw, a Saab 9000 not unlike the one his parents owned, which years before he'd sold for scrap because it wasn't drivable and would have cost more to repair than replace. The Saab was a convertible, the driver a young woman wearing white. Its plates were California plates, its right front fender sprung. All this he saw the way one sees without attending to the details of a scene passing by outside a train window, or while walking down a city street; he noticed a shorebird wheeling up from the sea and a glint of orange in the window of the bar.

What he did not see until too late (and would it, Harry asked himself, have made any difference had he been watching more closely; would his reflexes and reaction-time have been sufficient to alter the sequence of things; what would have happened had he stood on the verge of the curb with Greta on his left-hand side instead of at his right, or if they were walking more quickly or slowly or had paused a moment to try to identify the high wheeling bird, or crossed the road, or been still on the Mesa, or finishing lunch, or waving to and even perhaps conversing with the driver of the Saab 9000, so the woman at the wheel would have paused and not presented a seeming-obstacle to the fat man on the motorcycle, now swerving to avoid her car, and lifting his hand in a sort of salute intended to warn or wave them away) was the cyclist's spinning tires and the spitting gravel and the skid.

He knocked Greta off her feet. It was a glancing blow only, a side-swipe with the handlebar. She hesitated while falling, as if choosing whether to fall. The rider himself did not lose his balance or crash his Yamasaki, which had been painted—every inch of it—with emblems of the zodiac and skulls and crossbones and rainbows, and which came to a clattering stop. The Saab continued on.

"Are you all right, man?" the cyclist said, and Harry said, "Of course not, no, *of course* she's not all right."

Greta lay bleeding beneath him. The blood was on her arm. Her eyes were open, her mouth too, and there was grit in her hair. He bent to pick his sister up and then remembered not to move a person in an accident, for fear of broken bones or internal injury.

Looking up, she tried to smile.

He asked her if she thought she could stand, and Greta answered, "Yes."

"You maybe shouldn't, though. You shouldn't move . . ."

Unsteadily, she built herself back to her feet. He helped her, held her, brushed her off.

She said, "It's OK, I'm OK."

"Is there a hospital?" asked Harry—of no one really, not the air, and not the motorcyclist who said again, "I'm sorry, man," and, having ascertained to his apparent satisfaction that Greta was uninjured, said, "Goddamn this road, I'm sorry, man," and started up his stalled machine and waved at them and left.

In years to come Harry remembered with a perfect clarity the driver's torn black pants, his black tattoos, his shoes. He remembered how the man wore a bead necklace and a Mickey Mouse Watch and took out a red handkerchief and loudly blew his nose. He would recall how he had failed to take the license plate number of the Yamasaki, or its owner's name, was thinking only and instead of how their parents also had a motorcycle accident, and the wheel had come full circle, spinning, but their parents' crash had killed them and Greta had survived . . .

"Let's go *home*," she was saying, repeating.

"Are you sure? We could maybe find a clinic. Or a doctor's office . . ."

"I want to go home, Harry."

"OK. I'll get the car."

It was parked two streets away. He ran to it and started the engine and made a U-turn to where she stood and helped her in and buckled her seatbelt as though she were a child. Greta was white and shaken but kept saying, "Let's go home." They drove out of Bolinas and past Stinson Beach and the turn-off for Muir Woods and pulled into their driveway, and only when he stopped the car did Harry understand his sister was in shock.

"Are you all right?" he asked again.

She repeated, nodding, "Yes."

But she was not all right. Greta sat unblinking, staring at the windshield as though some deity had savaged her, its great wings battering, its handlebar a weapon. She was alive but stunned. His sister was, he saw, profusely bleeding and pressing both hands to her stomach; he called 911, and the EMTs came quickly, but it was too late. They took her, Harry following, to Greenbrae and Marin General Hospital, but could not keep her from losing the twins. Though the accident itself was clear to him, all this was confusion: the ambulance lights, the siren, the high-speed arrival at the Emergency Entrance, the gurney where she lay. He too, he came to understand, had been in shock. And in the aftermath—that night, that week, for the rest of his life—he could not fully reconstruct the sequence of events; they crowded in upon each other and bled into each other like the herky-jerky action of a reel-to-reel black-and-white movie: the bearded man on the motorcycle, his handlebar a truncheon, the woman in the Saab 9000, his sister lying in the road, the bloody mass that would have been twins, his own relief at the fact of her survival and relative indifference to the loss of what she carried, his guilt at not having wanted the children, or not the way that Greta did, their parents, their vanished future and the past that fused together seamlessly each time he shut his eyes.

Harriet flew north. She did so at her nephew's urging; he had called for help. She flew up the coast and landed in San Francisco and drove the old familiar roads in traffic out to the Golden Gate Bridge, then crossed the bay and made her way through Sausalito to the hill now clotted with houses where her charges lived. The place had fallen into disrepair: weeds in the yard and under the porch, a shutter hanging slantways with missing wooden slats, a window crisscrossed with strips of tape. She reminded herself that her own retirement cottage was a million-dollar structure in the garden of a mansion worth ten times as much, and she should not compare the apple of Muirfield Place to the orange of this rundown shack her sister once called home.

Harry met her at the door. "Hello."

She stared up at him, wordless.

"Thank you for coming. How was the flight?"

"How is she?"

"On the mend, I think. I hope. Except she's very very sad." He pointed down the hallway to where his sister lay.

"I need to use the bathroom first. All this traffic, all that driving."

"We're grateful to you. It's been a hard time for Greta. For us."

Harriet made no answer and, while sitting on the toilet, wondered what she ought to ask and what else she needed to know. The last time she had seen the twins, she warned them to be careful, and they had kissed her smilingly and waltzed away. Now they had not been careful, and trouble had indeed arrived, and her niece and nephew were three times the age they'd been the day their parents died.

Harriet sighed. Harry had told her on the phone that the children Greta carried would not have been his children; this made things both better and worse. She wiped herself and washed her hands and looked around the dingy space—the threadbare towels, the peeling paint, the spots on the mirror and window—and thought how many years ago she'd lived here with the twins. It all felt very distant, dim; she splashed water on her face and dried her hands and went to the bedroom where Greta waited and, seeing her, was shocked.

The girl was white. Her cheeks were drained of color, her hair dank, her blue eyes red with weeping. When she struggled up on the pillow, her body looked bloated and bruised. The lissome child she'd cared for years ago was a middle-aged woman, or nearly, and one who needed a bath. Where once she'd been a thing of beauty, now the truth of Greta's circumstance was disappointment and loss ...

"What happened to you, darling?"

"A motorcycle."

"I can see that. I know that." Harriet sat.

"Just like mommy and daddy."

"Except they rode the motorcycle. And you didn't die."

"My babies did," said Greta. "My babies didn't make it. Never made it."

"No. Are you in pain?"

"Two lives snuffed out, *kerblam.*" She spread her hands. "I survived the first accident too. Well, I wasn't with them, I was at school, so was Harry, and I remember when the principal called us both into his office and said, 'I've got bad news for you, terrible news.' You know the rest of the story, but now it's come around again and what they told me in the hospital—well, no, not the hospital, not even the hospital because it happened in the ambulance and the EMTs were talking—was also bad news, terrible news, and I know you think I'm making no sense, I know I sound, oh, peculiar, but I can't stop thinking how both my parents and children are gone, all four of them, every single one of them, exactly the same way. What is it about me, I wonder, I feel as though I'm cursed. I've been thinking and thinking about it: an engine of destruction. Or not so much cursed as a curse. *Kerplatt...*"

Harriet put out her hand. Her outburst over, Greta shifted forward in the bed. The two of them sat silently, hands clasped and their heads near.

Harry coughed. He had been standing in the bedroom door. "Can I get you anything?"

"No."

"You're sure? You must be hungry. Thirsty."

"Not for birthday cake," said Harriet.

"Excuse me?"

"That's what you brought, remember? Two years ago, the last time I saw you. When you came down to L.A ..."

"I remember," Harry said. "You told us you were worried, and we should be careful."

"Yes."

He took a seat at the foot of the bed. "How's Alistair?"

Her niece was weeping noiselessly.

"He's well. He sends his best."

"Please tell him hello for us."

"I will."

But it was not their visit to Los Angeles Harriet was thinking of; it was her own old sojourn in this house. Jane and Paul were newly dead, and she had moved into the master bedroom, where the invalid now lay. Then she had tried to watch over the twins, and none of what happened had happened already, with everything still in the future that had become the past. There had been tequila; there had been—what was his name?—Matt Anderson with the shoulder-length black curls and the trips he took on LSD and invited her to take with him, except she had refused. She did remember sleeping with Matt in the hammock, a Pawley's Island hammock strung behind the potting shed, and how hard it was to maintain a rhythm and how, afterwards, there had been welts and rope-burns down her back . . .

"It's all right," Greta said. "I'll be all right, aunt, won't I?"

"Of course you will," she said.

"I'll get through this, won't I?" Her voice was high. "Promise?"

"I promise."

"You know, I'm good at spotting birds, I can identify their markings. And I find four-leaf clovers without half-trying—my brother will tell you—when we're out in the garden or even just taking a walk and looking down. But I've never been OK with stars, I can't recognize the constellations, no matter how they're pointed out or who tries to show me. The Milky Way I maybe can manage, and sometimes the Big Dipper, but Orion the Mighty Hunter and Cassiopeia the Crab and Ursa Major and the rest—oh, I know I'm blabbering but I can't *see* them, not Castor and Pollux, not ever, they're up there somewhere, I'm completely sure of it, but I just can't see, can't see! It's why I'm being punished because I broke the rules."

"Don't think that way," said Harry. "It isn't any use."

"I can't help it," Greta said.

"You can," said Harriet. "You will. You must."

"I can," the girl repeated. "I will. I must . . ."

Harriet stayed in the house four days and nights, through Greta's speeches and her silences. She settled in the nursery that had been prepared for twins, with its blue and yellow floors and walls and shelves of teddy bears. Knowing she was bound to fail, she tried to be a parent; knowing they were adults, she tried nonetheless to be again their guardian. The sounds of distant traffic and the sound of wind persisted, as did the patient's grief.

"My babies died," said Greta. She studied her spread hands. "My babies didn't make it."

"No."

The girl spoke about the hope she'd had, the dream she'd had of being a mother, the wet mass oozing out of her that would have been her twins.

She counted, on her fingers, months; there would have been only two left. In two more months, she would have had children, but this was not to be. Like a painting by Botticelli that becomes instead, said Greta, a scene from Hieronymus Bosch. She herself was cursed, she said, for going against nature, and what she meant by that was going against her devotion to Harry and sleeping with another man and trying for a family that was not her proper family; she should have slept with a swan.

"Excuse me?"

"The old story. The one where topless towers fall . . ."

"You've got to stop thinking and talking like this," Harry said. "It's nonsense, it's making no sense."

"I can't help it."

"Yes you can."

The morning fog was thick, and cold, and burned away by noon. On the third day, Greta left her bed and washed her face and even put on lipstick and sat at the kitchen table for a meal. Harry cooked. He made pasta with tomatoes preserved from the garden, and basil, and artichokes bought from a roadside vendor, and they drank a bottle of Chianti and watched the sun go down. It was as though the three of them had come to terms with their shared fate; the twins talked about what would have happened if they'd not gone to Bolinas, if the fetuses had lived. Greta spoke of crime and punishment, and Harry told her that the accident was only that, an accident, and she mustn't blame herself for standing in a road. What came to pass was not her fault, and there was no point trying to alter the pattern of things.

"I'm not trying to alter a pattern," she said. "I just wish I'd been anywhere else."

"But what I need to tell you"—Harry took his sister's hand—"is I somehow always knew that nothing good would come of this, and we were going to be punished for, oh, I don't know, our luck in life, our luck in love, our sense of being singled out and special with each other. We weren't that special, really, we were a pair of orphans who got inside each other's heads, each other's bodies too. Because we *did* feel singled out, two halves of a shared whole. But all this time I think I was waiting for something to happen, some judgment to be handed down or punishment pronounced. And now, gentlewoman of the jury"—he pointed to his aunt—"a verdict has been reached."

"What verdict?" Harriet asked.

He spoke about the years they'd been each other's second selves. He spoke about his fear of change, his hope that when the children came their life would not be changed. He confessed he had been jealous, not so much of the man who fathered her twins, but of the fact of them, the prospect of them, the way he'd known without really knowing that their family circle was broken, ruptured, and her attention would from that point on be elsewhere-focused . . .

Sobbing, Greta told their aunt her brother was the only thing she'd ever wanted, and when she thought she needed more she'd overreached. "I deserve to be punished," she said. Harry said again this was unfair, and she shouldn't blame herself, and he should have been on the side of the road where the motorcyclist crashed.

"You believe that?" the girl asked.

"Cross my heart and hope to die." He mimed the childhood gesture, right hand lifted to his chest.

She tried to laugh.

"I'm older and wiser, remember? I'm older by nine minutes."

She laughed.

"And what I need to explain," Harry said, "is all I ever wanted is for you to be all right. For us to be together and, oh, safe from harm, the way we used to make each other feel. And I know these months I failed you, failed to want exactly what you wanted and need to beg forgiveness, although I know you'll tell me there's nothing to forgive. But I've been thinking and thinking about it—just the way you say you have—and mine is a different opinion. My way of thinking about punishment is different from yours for once, and that's what I need to explain.

"It isn't fate, it wasn't. Don't think about it as a curse, or some sort of verdict; the handlebar that knocked you down was only that, a handlebar, and it wasn't pronouncing a judgment, it wasn't volitional, Greta, it was some weirdo skidding out of control on a patch of roadside gravel. So every day of every week, and every minute of each day we're all of us at risk. See, aunt"—he turned to Harriet—"she's not the only one who needs to tell you finally that we got it wrong. Wrong to think we were protected, wrong to think we could escape . . ."

When Harriet flew south again, it was with the twins' assurance that the worst was past.

Yet the dynamic between them had shifted; there were interludes of rage. They read each other's gestures; they understood intention; they heard tonic and dominant, both. They did not speak of grief, or loss, but grief and loss persisted.

"Let's try to be honest," said Greta.

"All right."

"Do you want to stay together? To stay, in our own way, married?"

"I do. I do."

"Don't joke with me, you son of a bitch."

"Was I joking?"

"And don't fuck that blonde, all right?"

"Which blonde?"

"The one that you're fucking."

"There are so many. Give me a name."

"I don't know it, I just see her hair."

"Where?"

"On the back seat. Where you fuck her."

"You're being ridiculous."

"Am I?"

"Full of—oh, I don't know—fantasy. Paranoia."

"'Help, the paranoiacs are after me.'"

"Very funny."

"No, it's not."

"I'm leaving. I've got an appointment."

"Oh, with who?'

"With whom?"

"Whom, then? With fucking whom?"

"Does it matter? I'll be back."

"Which car are you taking?"

"The Subaru."

"The one with the back seat?"

"Come off it."

"Come on it, you mean."

"I can't stand this."

"Join the club. Let's change the subject."

"What are you so angry at? What have I done?"

"I thought we were changing the subject."

"OK. Who do you like in the Super Bowl?"

"What?"

"'Who do you like in the Super Bowl?' I'm just asking."

"Well, stop it."

"You don't have a team? A preference?"

"I'd rather talk about the weather."

"So, do you maybe think it'll rain?"

"Could be. We need it, that's for sure."

"See, it's not so difficult. We can agree when we try to."

"I just wondered."

"What exactly? Wondered what?"

"If you're telling me everything?"

"What a question."

"Well, are you?"

"Telling you everything?"

"Yes."

In years to come they would remain each other's second selves. No longer young or venturesome, they settled into middle-age with something akin to relief. The story of their lives, they knew, was unremarkable: an early loss, a later one, a set of small profits between. When Harry watched his sister now, he saw a round-shouldered woman whose hair was streaked with gray; when Greta studied her brother, she saw a man gone bald. What they had tried and hoped to do was inhabit a world without danger or risk; in this, the twins had failed.

They lived modestly and quietly, attracting small attention, and when Harriet died at eighty-three came into an inheritance. With money from their aunt's bequest, they purchased a new Prius and a Lexus hybrid SUV. They had the house reroofed. The garden continued to yield. Neighbors on the hillside came and went. They asked each other if another trip to Greece, or a trip to Paris or Kyoto, would be welcome, and agreed they were not ready for a distant voyage or a new adventure but preferred to stay at home.

At night, sometimes, lying side by side, they read each other stories. There was the story of *Hansel and Gretel*, the tale of *Sleeping Beauty* and the one about three little pigs. There was *The Blood of the Walsungs* and *The Iliad* and *Odyssey*, with its history of carnage and kingdoms won and lost.

They would fall asleep together, and wake with the bedside table light still burning, or when birds announced the dawn. They lived this way for the rest of their lives and died at home, at peace.

Old Age

THEY ASKED HIM to stop sailing, or at least to stop going out solo, which he was willing to do. They asked him to stop driving, or at least not to go for long drives by himself, and to this he also agreed. When they asked him, however, to have a helpmeet in the house, Sam told them, "No. Not yet."

"Helpmeet" was the word his children used, and it puzzled him. Did "meet" mean "mate"; was it "mete" that some other someone should help? Was it a contraction for "meeting the help"; were "meat and potatoes" involved? "Mete" means "appropriate," he told his son, and it wouldn't be appropriate—or would it?—to find a new mate. "Your mother made me promise," he lied, "I'd have no other woman here. It was my deathbed promise to her, and I intend to keep it."

She had asked for no such thing. Instead, Elyzabeth had often said she couldn't bear the thought of him doing the shopping and cooking and cleaning alone, not to mention folding sheets or using the washing machine. "You're hopeless, darling," she would say, "you'd be completely hopeless, and I can't imagine you trying for hospital corners or learning to make a soubise."

"What's a soubise?" he asked.

"My point exactly," Elyzabeth said. "You don't really want to know."

This was true. He had relied on her so long and so entirely that "hospital corners" meant nothing to Sam, and although he could have looked it up he did not want or need to know the recipe for "soubise."

When in the final months she was hospitalized he watched her nurses changing sheets—the expert way they stripped and then remade the bed, with the patient rolled from side to side—and knew he could not manage it; he was hopeless, *helpless, hapless*, in the face of grief.

They had been married for fifty-three years. For all his adult life, it seemed, he and Elyzabeth shared a life, and it was *life* not *lives* they shared. To continue on without her was not something he prepared for or had in any way planned. The Rhodes 19 could remain at the dock, the Subaru in the garage, but what Sam could not manage was living alone in the too-large empty house. This was the puzzle he lived with and now had to learn how to solve.

His daughters were in California, half the world away. It wasn't half the world, of course, it was the other American coast, but the distance felt unbridgeable and the world his daughters occupied was not one he understood or could call his own. They called him once a week, in tandem, as though they'd agreed beforehand which one would reach out on which day. It was Sheila who first said, "Helpmeet." Next afternoon Marianne echoed the word, and therefore he knew they'd discussed it and told them both, "Not yet. The cleaning lady shows up every week. I don't need in-house help."

His son Michael lived nearby, on the border of Rhode Island. They saw each other often, over lunch. But Michael was a lawyer, up to his eyeballs in depositions and lawsuits, not to mention the collapse of his own marriage and the ongoing disagreement as to their troubled daughter, Sally. Insurance had run out. Michael's soon-to-be ex-wife was adamant that Sally—who twice had tried to kill herself—should stay in Silver Hill Hospital until (a million dollars later, Michael said) she maybe could be cured.

"There's no guarantee," his son complained. "There's only the guarantee she will stay safe."

"Then it's worth it."

"Right."

The two of them met regularly at Joe's Diner in New Bedford, an Italian pizza-joint with excellent chili and fries. The window had an American Flag and a large metal hanging spoon next to a sign with its owner's name in neon, *Joe*. The walls had photographs of movie stars Sam did not recognize and signed publicity photos of Perry Como and Carl Yastrzemski and Joe DiMaggio. The place was always full at noon and always, by one-thirty, empty; he and his son shared a booth.

Sally had been Sam's particular darling, the one of their four grandchildren to whom he felt the closest. Elyzabeth felt the same way. All through childhood they cosseted her, all through her adolescence found ways to support her decisions: the nose-rings, the tattoos. "It's only a phase," he told his son, "remember when she wore—what do they call them?—dreadlocks, and wouldn't take a bath?"

Michael shrugged and spread his hands.

"And when she went to live in New Mexico, on that reservation?"

"I do," said Michael. "What does that have to do with anything?"

"She's gone her own way, always."

"Dad, she cut her *wrists!*"

"It's a cry for help, is all I'm saying. And Silver Hill can help."

"That's why I'm paying," said his son.

"If I can be useful, I'd like to . . ."

"It's kind of you. We'll manage."

So he found himself imagining his twenty-six-year-old granddaughter, wrists bandaged where she sliced them, staring at the floor. He could not bring himself to visit Silver Hill, the place in New Canaan where Sally was lodged. He had seen photographs—the large white buildings, the walkways and lawns—and knew it was not likely she'd be staring at a floor. But this was how he pictured her, her dark eyes blank, her black hair shorn, wrists manacled with tape.

"Manage? Is that what you're doing?"

"Not really, no, I admit. But it's the best we can do . . ."

It was not an argument between them; it was, Sam offered, only disagreement. He put down his fork. When Michael said, "She tried again, she got our attention this time through," he told his son, "You should have paid it earlier. Attention, I mean."

"What are you trying to tell me?"

"The girl has always needed it. Attention. She's been asking to be *noticed* since she first learned to walk."

This was, he knew, not helpful, and Sally needed help. In his time Sam had known trouble, but never not wanted to live. An uncle had committed suicide, leaping out the third-floor window when they came to take him off to Buchenwald or Dachau or wherever the Nazis would have slaughtered him if he hadn't jumped. The "suicide gene" in a family can be inherited, he knew, like hair color or a propensity for heart disease. But an uncle who had killed himself in Hitler's Munich was not, Sam felt, predictive; it would not be a trait to pass on.

His darling had not known. Elyzabeth had been too ill, too far gone into dementia and her final inwardness to recognize what Sally did, or was trying to do. This was a good thing. If there were any comfort in the loss of his wife's consciousness, it was how she failed to understand their son's divorce proceedings and granddaughter's misery and how the things she took for granted were no longer there to take . . .

Sally arrived at Elyzabeth's bedside but had had nothing to say. It was the final week. His granddaughter stood unspeaking, jiggling her left leg and patting the sheet and understanding—so it seemed to Sam—what oblivion would look like by the example of that figure on the bed. By the time she tried to kill herself a second time, his wife was dead.

"Why not have her come and live with me?"

"You don't mean it, Dad."

"I do."

"Be careful what you wish for . . ."

"I'm being careful. I'd have—what's the word, a *helpmeet*?—another person in the house."

He was assailed by memory. They were standing in the kitchen, by the sink. He remembered this because Sally was wearing her grandmother's apron, and it did not fit. On Elyzabeth the garment's hem rode just above her knees, but the girl wore it down to her ankles; she had been nine, perhaps ten. Her socks were white, her sneakers red; the neck-straps dangled down above her not-yet breasts.

"I have dark thoughts"

"What do you mean," he had asked her. "'Dark thoughts'?"

"You know."

"I don't know, no. Tell me."

"It's not important."

"Yes it is. It is, to me . . ."

Sally turned away. He had been washing dishes, and she liked to help him dry them; he would pass her the plates and glasses one by one. The girl was scrupulous, fearful of dropping a fork or plate or coffee cup, and she placed each towel-dried object on the kitchen table. Her parents were in the living room, their voices low, and he could not hear what they discussed. There had been water-droplets on the wood.

Sam could remember his question: "Don't you want to tell me?"

"What?"

"What 'dark thoughts' you've been having?"

"No."

"I could help you, maybe. If I understood the problem . . ."

"No."

"But not if I don't understand what's bothering you . . ."

"It's OK."

He finished washing and rinsed out his sponge and brush. "Are you happy?" Sam inquired.

"Why?"

"I need to know."

"Why do you ask?

"Because your happiness concerns me. I want you to be happy."

"Why?"

"Glad to be alive is another way of putting it. I don't want you to have any, what did you call them? dark thoughts. Doubts."

She turned to him, her brown eyes opaque in her as-yet unblemished face. "What's happiness, grandpa? Can you explain it?"

"Being neither too young nor too old."

They stood a moment together in silence. Elyzabeth was sleeping, taking her "post-prandial nap," which is what she liked to call it, snoring lightly on the couch in the bay window at the kitchen's south-facing wall. Her head thrown back, she watched them, or appeared to watch them, except her eyes were shut.

"Will I have children?"

"Someday if you want to. Maybe."

"And will *they* have children?"

"Yes, it could happen."

"So I'd be a grandparent too?"

"If you and then your child want children. Yes."

"And will I have freckles?" Sally pointed to his hand.

"Those aren't freckles, darling. They're called liver spots."

"What's that?"

"The spots you get when you grow old."

"I'm not sure I want children," she said.

Now Sam was eighty-two. He had long ago retired from his job in the accounting firm of which he was a partner, and the nest-egg he acquired there enlarged. It could, he joked, fill the fork of a tree. It was not so much a bird's nest as a squirrel's nest chock-full of IPO's and stocks and bonds he had—*haha!*—squirreled away.

"You call it crazy but I call it nuts," he would say.

All his life he'd had the habit of bad jokes and puns and verbal play, and it pleased him to make such pronouncements. Sam knew, of course, that others did not find them funny; his wit had just a single member of the audience: himself. Elyzabeth had asked her husband, not always gently, to stop it, but he could not stop considering such words as "helpmeet" or "squirrely" and did not want to try.

Most things, these years, he no longer wanted to try. There were games he did not play—golf, backgammon, water polo—that never had been "in his wheelhouse." But what is a "wheelhouse," he wondered, and did that have to do with steering a passenger liner or train? Was it the wheel of a mill? Did it also mean he would never go snorkeling or sky-diving or to the island of Malta, which he and Elyzabeth once planned to see?

It would not happen now. Such actions and adventures were the business of younger men, and he was neither young nor middle-aged but old. He went to revivals of plays. Knowing the lines of *Death of a Salesman* or the songs of *South Pacific* made it more entertaining, somehow, than trying to follow the lines of a new song or play.

"I'll draw them for you," Sally said.

"What?"

"Dark thoughts."

"I'm not sure I know what you're talking about."

"Just watch," she said, and bent over the page.

An ogre emerged, a tree-trunk in flames, a rifle with bullets that sped at a target, a dog lying—dead?—in a street. She drew with a Sharpie, in quick fluent strokes, and seemed to know, when starting, how the image would look when complete.

"Is that dog sleeping?"

"No."

This also he remembered; she had been twelve or thirteen. She had come to stay with him, with *them*, when Michael and his now-ex-wife Diana had gone to Paris, briefly, for what Michael called a renewal of vows. So Sally was dropped off at her grandparents' house, her backpack stuffed with school books and action figures from a show he'd heard of but not seen about a family of superheroes striving to save a doomed world.

"You'll die."

"Yes. Everybody does."

"But not so soon."

"I hope it won't be soon, my darling."

"No. But how do you know?"

"I don't know, really. There are always accidents, always unexpected things, but it's a reasonable guess. Or maybe a good bet."

"Does anybody live forever?"

"Only in memory maybe."

"But *forever*?"

"No."

His three other grandchildren—two boys, one girl—remained in California, and they too had lives of their own. They were thirty-two and thirty-one and twenty-seven. Often, Sam marveled that he somehow had attained an age to have such grown-up progeny: married or with same-sex partners and careers. One was a grade-school teacher, one an engineer. One had joined the world of finance and was working in Silicon Valley and making, so Marianne told him proudly, a fortune doing God knows what for God knew whom.

This was not the same as what he'd done—punching a time-clock in a firm of C.P.A.s—and the risk-reward quotient was higher, yet the field was in essence the same. He rarely saw his daughters' families, but they were not estranged. He understood, or thought he did, his three other grandchildren's ways.

Only the youngest, Sally—with her fist raised in memory of "Black Power" and her refusal to follow the rules of middle-class comportment— was a renegade. Only she behaved as though the world she came from was a world to leave behind. As time wore on, and she grew up through adolescence and young womanhood—or, as she insisted on describing it, *personhood*—she seemed more and more a separate creature, not someone who sprang from his loins.

Admittedly, there'd been a generation between the acts of generation, yet a line of descent could be drawn. Grandchildren take after grandparents, they say, and not the children in between, but Sam could find no trace of himself or his wife in this slogan-brandishing nose-pierced girl, not even when she told him she mourned the Nez Perce. That tribe had been betrayed by government, she told him, and their history was one of shame and subjugation; she would not countenance inequity, suppression and bigotry and murder or let it happen again. In later years, when the rallying cry, "Black Power" became, instead, "Black Lives Matter," she said, "It's not getting better but worse."

In some sense he admired her principled stand. Her father was a lawyer and her mother a real-estate agent, and they stood—so she declared to Sam—for everything Sally despised. They'd been co-opted by the system into becoming a part of the system, and she herself would never let this happen and would—did he remember the 1960s?—fight the good fight over again.

He did, he told her, he remembered Bobby Seale and the Weathermen and Woodstock and the rest of it, but if you ask me what has been co-opted it's the liberal or radical resistance you so much admire from the 60s and the 70s. It's all sloganeering now. It's advertising jingles, not a revolution; the things we stood for then are not so very different from what you want today. There's nothing new under the sun.

"Talk about slogans," she said.

His house in Padanaram was a rambling, shingled structure, built for a ship's captain in the mid-nineteenth century. It had eyebrow windows and a wraparound porch and a lawn sloping down to the harbor. He still mowed the lawn by himself. Sitting on the riding mower, bouncing and jiggling and cutting long swathes, he liked to remember how things had been—how often he'd done this before. The weeds and grass grew and were mowed exactly in the pattern he was used to, and the tide rose and receded as it had always done.

Because he repeated such actions, Sam liked to think things stayed the same. The cleaning lady, every Wednesday, did laundry and vacuumed and swept. His bed still had hospital corners, and the sheets were taut. Elyzabeth lived on in memory if not in physical fact.

"Do you mean it?" Michael asked.

"Mean what?"

"What you said two weeks ago. About making Sally welcome and living in the house?"

They were having lunch at Joe's. This time they shared a pizza with chicken and onions and olives and a Caesar Salad; they each drank Diet Coke.

"Of course I did. Of course I do."

"Because the folks at Silver Hill are saying—suggesting—she could be released. But they recommend supervision, and the last person she would accept is yours truly. Or Diana. Who's off at a retreat somewhere unreachable . . ."

"Do you know where?"

"Not really. Not any longer, I'm not supposed to ask. A mountain range or desert sanctuary somewhere where there aren't any cellphones. Which she wouldn't answer anyhow . . ."

"So Sally has improved?"

"It's wonderful how quickly they decide a patient has improved once the insurance runs out. It's the best treatment option, Dad: just fail to pay."

He did not like to hear this. He did not want to think his son could be dismissive—so angry at his ex-wife and their daughter that he would endanger or put the girl at risk. Not *girl*, he reminded himself, but a twenty-six-year-old patient who qualified as adult on her own recognizance, a danger to none but herself.

They ordered key lime pie and coffee. Joe's had been emptying out. Outside, it started to rain.

"Do you think she'd *want* to live with me?"

"Of course she would. You're the only member of the family she's willing to live with; so she told me when I asked. She'd still see her doctor in New Canaan, but we can arrange for a driver. In order to continue with her therapy she doesn't have much choice."

"What a nice way to put it."

"Two birds with one stone . . ."

"You mean, I keep an eye on her and she keeps one on me?"

"More coffee?" Michael asked.

When they bought the house, in 1973, it had been their first home. He and

Elyzabeth were married, and they had had Michael already, but where they lived before were apartments and, once, a rental property in Watertown with a leaky roof. They had not known about the roof when they signed the rental agreement, and Sam could remember returning from work one early evening in a rainstorm and finding his young wife in boots, with pails to catch the downpour in the baby's bedroom and a mop for puddles on the floor. Michael's crib had plaster in it, and was drenched. Luckily, if you could call it luck, she told him, she had been nursing the baby when the ceiling fell. Their landlord said "Sorry," but deferred the repair-work for weeks, saying he'd had trouble with his work-crew since the foreman was arrested for assault and battery, so they couldn't be relied on for a fix.

Elyzabeth had been pregnant again, with the child who would be Sheila, and on impulse —though it wasn't really impulsive, was something they had talked about—Sam broke the lease. They bought the house in Padanaram for more than they could then afford, and over time restored it and lived there ever since. His office was in Westport, not ten miles away, and he learned to use the back roads—with their stands of trees and high stone walls—when driving back and forth to work; he loved the morning light, the evening light, the spring flowers after snow. It was where they raised their children till the children went to college and began their separate lives. Michael remained on the east coast; Marianne and Sheila both moved west.

Years passed. His daughter-in-law, Diana, acquired a real-estate license and specialized in residential properties, the farmhouses and converted barns and cottages spread out along the shore. Often she would stop by for a coffee or a cocktail and tell him how smart he'd been to buy this old house when it was still affordable, at the bottom of the market, and not way out of reach the way it would be now. "You're sitting on a bundle," said Diana, and he said, "Yes, but it's a nest-egg I don't want to hatch."

Diana gave her practiced laugh. She and Michael had seemed happy and then did not seem happy and were warring partners while their daughter raged. When Sally finished high school she did not go to college but instead spent what her parents called a "gap-year" studying dance and yoga and making puppets at the Bread and Puppet Theater in Vermont. This was, Sam thought, a waste of time, but she told him it was more important than attending freshman mixers and going to cheerleading classes, which is what she called the curriculum at UVM; it's not, she said, important to me to learn how to become a card-carrying member of your society. Don't take this personally, grandpa, but I want something new.

"We all do," Sam declared.

"Yeah, right."

"Except 'There's nothing new under the sun.'"

"I've heard that before," Sally said. "I'm not trying to be rude, but you use that line so often it makes me believe you believe it."

He stared at her.

"What about docking-stations in space? Or computers and A.I.D.S. and the Genome project?"

"I'm not," Sam said, "talking about technology. Or new diseases and inventions. Of course there've been advances—but most don't count. I'm talking about the *heart*."

"It's why we build our puppets. Papier-mâché and wood: making an object of fat fascists we carry through the streets. These things don't change."

"My point exactly, darling."

"I'm leaving," Sally told him. "And it will be our secret. Don't tell my parents, please."

He did not tell her parents, so it was in fact their secret. He'd known she was planning to go. This troubled him in later years but only in the abstract; he could not have stopped her, Sam believed, and therefore did not try. Elyzabeth had known it too, and gave the girl her blessing; "We're here for you," she said.

Sally was nineteen. When she left the Bread and Puppet Theater and traveled to a commune in Wisconsin she came to them to say goodbye and promised she'd be careful. He gave her two-hundred dollars: all he could find in the house. She had always been a strong-willed girl, he repeated to Michael at lunch.

Again, it was raining. Leaves blew past. He ordered a cheese omelet and, to begin with, a cup of pea soup. There was a new waitress who asked him to repeat his order and then, serving, spilled the soup. She apologized profusely, and Sam said it wasn't important, but the girl insisted on wiping down the table and bringing a replacement bowl not cup. This too she set down on his placemat with an amount of spillage, but he told her to leave it alone. Sally had always known her own mind, though her mind had not always been clear.

"Tell me about it," said Michael. "That time she had her teeth pulled out in solidarity with—oh, you know, homeless people, veterans ..."

Sam finished his coffee. He put down his cup.

"I ask myself, I often ask myself"—Michael played with the saltshaker—"if we could have done something different. If there'd been any other way to deal with it."

"*Que sera sera*," said Sam.

"Don't Doris Day me, please. And don't pull out that bromide about 'the best of all possible worlds.'"

"All right."

"It isn't *all right*, Dad. I need you to see: this won't be easy."

"I've got nothing else to do," he said. "Or nothing that I want to do."

"If it doesn't work out we can always change plans. I'm collecting her tomorrow; you can always change your mind."

"Why would I want to do that?"

"We'll drive straight to the house," Michael said.

When the diagnosis came he had been unsurprised. Elyzabeth had grown forgetful, leaving the oven burner on and asking him what time it was while looking at the clock. They had lived together so long it took him longer than it should have to notice the change; you look at yourself in the mirror, he knew, and only after years and years do you come to understand the face in the mirror is new because old. She was, he thought, still beautiful but her hair was white not brown, her straight back had grown stooped. Her pert breasts drooped.

None of this mattered to Sam, because he too was bent and slow, but what did matter was the way she dropped her coffee cup and did not seem to recognize it lay broken on the floor. Or the way the book she tried to read, lips moving soundlessly, was something she held upside down. Or the way she smiled at him, unfocussed, and repeated the same sentence, trailing off. When finally the doctor said, "The best we can do, I'm afraid, is slow the progress of decline," he found himself repeating the phrase, "progress of decline" and wondering if it made sense or was a contradiction. We begin to die, he told himself, the moment we are born.

When Sally arrived he was shocked. Michael had collected her and called to tell his father they were in the car and should be there by two o'clock but not to wait for lunch. Michael drove a BMW sedan—black, polished to a fare-thee-well—and the car pulled up so silently he had not been prepared. He was in the bathroom, shaving with his electric razor, and therefore did not hear.

The doorbell rang repeatedly, and by the time he reached the door they had deposited her suitcases and backpack on the entrance porch. They were checking their cellphones, unspeaking, frowning, looking not at each other but down.

Sally had gained weight. Her clothes that once hung loosely now were tight. Her long hair had been cropped. Her neck was dark with blue tattoos, except for the red anchor incised below her chin. That first instant at the door he waited for some sign from her that she was happy to be back with him: released from Silver Hill and out again in the world.

It did not come.

"We're glad to be here," said his son. "It's what Sally told me earlier."

"I did?"

"Don't you remember?" Michael hung up his coat on the coatrack in the vestibule. The rack was polished oak, six-pronged, and it held Sam's hats. The visitor too removed her coat, as if she had been prompted, and draped it from a hook. She was her father's height, and both of them looked down at him.

"An easy trip?" Sam managed.

His granddaughter nodded. "Yes."

"Are you hungry?"

"No."

He cast about for something to say. "Tired, you must be tired,"

"No."

"There was a lot of construction," said Michael. "Route 7 is a nightmare."

"It's everywhere," said Sally. "The nightmare."

"Excuse me?"

"Construction, I mean. So many workmen."

"Yes?"

"So many trucks!"

"Well, *somebody's* working," he offered.

"And everywhere those plastic cones . . ."

"It's called progress," Michael said.

In the silence that followed, Sam tried to imagine what he might say that could possibly be useful. Should he talk about the nation's infrastructure and the cost of building and then repairing roads? Was it worth discussing how this country once had built Interstate highways and now was letting them crumble; would Dwight David Eisenhower—who created the project of the Interstate system—approve? Could the then-president imagine how we'd pave an area the size of France but then fail to maintain it, with potholes, sinkholes everywhere, so now again it's slow and dangerous to drive? Should he talk about the Founding Fathers and how they never pictured the automobile, no matter how forward-facing men like Benjamin Franklin and Thomas Jefferson had been at the time? He knew, of course, that Jefferson and Franklin had feet of clay all the way to their necks and should not be forgiven their sexist behavior and attitudes on slavery, but traffic congestion back in the eighteenth century meant rutted roads for horseback riders and the occasional carriage and mud after rain and not the sort of trouble she and Michael had encountered on their way through Providence—strange name for a city, isn't it? Should he mention how the Mafia had come to dominate the city and control its commerce and then discuss the uneasy alliance between self-proclaimed progressives and the entrenched establishment to root out corruption; was Sally of his opinion that the Providence she drove through was an improvement on the Providence of years gone by, or was it more of the same?

Sam said none of this. Father and son went into the kitchen. She carried her bags to the room the cleaning lady, Serafina, had prepared. It was on the second floor, down the hallway from the master bedroom where he and Elyzabeth slept. Michael raised his eyebrows, then spread his hands—palms out—and said, "Thank you, Dad."

"For what?"

"For making her welcome. Us welcome."

"Don't mention it."

"I need to. This'll take some getting used to. She'll take some time to get used to this place."

"She's known it all her life," Sam said.

"I know. But it isn't the same."

Sally appeared in the doorway. "What are you talking about?"

"Nothing important," Sam said.

"You're talking, I know it, about the way to *handle* me. To deal with a crazy, correct?"

"No."

"Goodbye, Dad," Sally said.

So they were left alone. His "helpmeet" did not seem unhappy, sleeping for hours and hours every day. Sam searched for the old spark in her, the old oppositional fervor, but could find no trace of it; instead, she stared unblinking at the kitchen or dining or living room wall. The Thorazine, he came to understand, had dulled the edge of anger. This held true as well for Sally's other medications, the cocktail she swallowed at night.

In truth he was untroubled by the silence in the house; he had grown used to silence in the last years with his wife. Time passed. The cleaning lady came and went, bringing supplies and groceries for which he reimbursed her, and making up the beds. Serafina wore ear buds and listened to loud music while she worked, but all he could hear was the rhythmic percussing: *ta-pock*. Her English was not good.

His granddaughter too used headphones, listening to music that Sam was unable to hear. He did not dare to ask, directly, why she'd tried to kill herself—or if it had felt different when she tried a second time. She would talk about it when she chose, he told himself; the rest could wait. Failed suicides were, he understood, a "cry for help," and by taking her in and making her welcome he was, he hoped, offering help

In answer to his question every morning, Sally told him she slept well. Then she asked him how *he* slept. When Sam offered to make dinner, she said she wasn't hungry, although he said he had been learning how to cook. "I do this rice and onions thing. It's called *soubise*."

"No thanks."

He tried not to feel rebuffed. When he offered to take the girl out for a meal, she said she wasn't ready yet for anything not cafeteria-style.

"Is that the way you ate in Silver Hill?'

"And with a spoon."

"A spoon?"

"Well, after I'd behaved myself they gave me plastic knives. The forks were dangerous."

"Why?"

She pointed to her eyes. He could not tell if she were serious or trying to frighten or warn him, so he asked a second question: "Are you allowed to drink?"

"*Allowed to drink?*" His granddaughter repeated what had been his question with such a flat inflection it seemed to him an echo not response.

"Why not?" he said. "I have a scotch most nights. A glass of single-malt."

"I know you do. You and grandma did."

"Join me?" he prodded. "Are you allowed?"

"Your call." She had been chewing peppermints; she kept them in the pocket of her denim shirt. "You're the dealer."

"I'm trying not to be."

"Are we discussing something here?"

"Yes. Do you want a Lagavulin and do you want it neat?"

The smell of her peppermint candy was strong. "Excuse me?"

"That's the name of my scotch," Sam explained. "I have a sixteen-year old Lagavulin, and it's very special. I save this bottle for special occasions."

"And is it?"

"Is it what?"

"A special occasion," she said.

Sam's crew had been Elyzabeth, but he could manage the Rhodes 19 alone, and if the tide and wind were right he liked to spend the morning out by himself on the bay. Those hours were hours he thought about nothing, and they passed rapidly by.

When she was fourteen, however, Sally asked if he would teach her, and he showed her how to set and trim the sails. She learned to hold the tiller and when to shout, "Ready, about!" She liked to raise the jib and use the jam-cleat and the centerboard and tack back and forth repeatedly on the open water; they were, they liked to say, shipmates. But when, one fine September Saturday, he suggested they go sailing, his granddaughter asked, "What for?"

"Just for a couple of hours. To get some air."

"Where would we go?"

"You name it. Narragansett. Nantucket. Nowhere. Somewhere that starts with an 'N.'"

"Ha, ha," she said, but did not laugh.

"Naushon?"

"I don't think you understand." With her fixed stare Sally studied him. "I've got no—what would you call it?—*destination*. No place I want or hope to get to and no place I need to be."

"Tell me about it," he said.

She did. In a monotone she said she was grateful and knew he meant well—Sam was shocked to hear her say, *mean well* so condescendingly—but you should try to understand I need to stay off the water, because it would be easy, wouldn't it? to put stones or bricks in the pocket of this jacket and simply roll across the gunwale of the Rhodes 19 and sink. "*Down, down, down,* and *down.* It's deep enough. At any rate, in any case, the pleasure of immersion, *sub*mersion, *drowning*—maybe in a bathtub, since you wouldn't want to make a mess—is something to think about, or the simplicity of bridges, a guardrail I could jump."

His granddaughter spoke, for the first time since her return to Padanaram, at length. She asked if he remembered when she'd run away before, and what she said to him and to Elyzabeth about the need for air. "I wouldn't try to swim," she said, "I'd not come up for air. Not many people in America have what I have and what you're giving me: food and lead-free water to drink, a roof above my head. But what have I done to deserve it; what did I ever do?"

Sally raised her red-striped wrists and held them at her ears. Again, she stared at him unblinkingly; he forced himself to look. He remembered her young face in the window of the Greyhound bus, the way she'd waved at him, departing, and had mouthed *Goodbye.* "There are," she said, "almost eight billion people on our planet, and why should one more matter, or in this case one less? What *difference* does it make? Most of us just keep on living because survival is an instinct—except for maybe lemmings, which humans maybe also are—and not because our lives are worth it, worth continuing I mean.

"Well, guess what, grandpa, hundreds of millions are starving and hundreds of millions don't have clothes and hundreds of millions have houses that are bombed or destroyed by fire or water or never were stable enough to call home in the first place; why *would* they want to live? Why *wouldn't* they want to kill themselves or, maybe, someone else? Why wouldn't they say, in Afghanistan or Somalia or Haiti or in Donald Trump's America now—it's his country, isn't it?—that women and children should be enslaved and turned into whores and soldiers or both and the hell with the idea of progress, the illusion of democracy; why wouldn't they make us wear protective scarves and a belt of bombs?

"I know you think I'm being crazy, sounding crazy, thinking I'm just saying shit to hear myself say it and not being serious—*serious*—enough. Well, to me there's nothing much more serious than what's happening out there, *not* happening out there, and you don't see any part of it in this protected place. You haven't seen how crazy things are getting, grandpa, and how many men with guns are ready to use them against us, *you*, well maybe not you, you're too old and will die anyhow, they tell themselves, but I don't want you to die."

This declaration finished, Sally subsided. He asked if she'd made any friends in Silver Hill, and she answered, "No." Gingerly, he asked if she'd had friends before, and who they were, and Sally said "You wouldn't want to know." When he persisted she said, "Harry and Harriet, Tom and Thomasina, not to mention Precious and Quan and Rosaria and Dick-Dick and Blackhawk and Mama Teresa; is that enough or do you need me to continue?"

"Yes" he said.

"Yes, what?"

"I need you to continue."

She looked at him, surprised. "You mean it?"

Sam nodded. "I need you to live."

They stayed together all fall. These days he ate less often at Joe's, since he did not like to leave the house, but when the woman he'd hired took Sally down to Silver Hill for her outpatient therapy session, he did drive to New Bedford and met his son for lunch.

"How is she?" Michael asked.

"Why don't you come over and see for yourself?"

"Would she want that?"

Sam studied the menu.

"Would she *accept* it, I mean?"

The wide-hipped waitress who had spilled his soup approached and, holding her pad and pencil, said, "Long time no see."

"It's been a while," said Sam.

"Are we ready to order yet, hon?"

"I'm not your *hon*," he wanted to say, "I don't need you to call me that." Instead he ordered chili and a side of fries.

"The same." Michael had grown a moustache, and it needed trimming. "With a dish of coleslaw on the side."

When they were alone again, his son continued, "The truth is, Dad, I'm nervous about seeing her and setting her off again somehow: bringing up old arguments. I don't know how it happened, or really *when* it happened, but I became part of the enemy in Sally's mind—we both did, Diana and me. Do you think it was maybe the drugs?"

Sam shook his head. "It's seven years ago by now. The day she left. I was busy with your mother."

"Right. And I'm not blaming you. But you knew about it, didn't you?"

They stared at each other in silence. "Knew about what?"

"That time when she finally quit. When you and Mom put Sally on the Greyhound Bus. I know about the cash you offered, the escape valve you provided, the way you helped her leave. I ought to sue."

Sam felt his skin grow hot. "You're joking, right?"

"Mostly I spend my time dealing with lawsuits and easements and riparian rights and squabbles over access and eminent domain. So I know about real estate, property issues, and who owns what, or wants to, or deserves to. Guess what? It doesn't help with children, it doesn't let me know which way to turn or what the law suggests."

"It isn't a matter of *law*," he said. "It's about how to behave."

"I know that," Michael said. "And yes I was joking and no I won't sue. But sometimes I wonder if maybe you and Mom quite understood what you were doing, *enabling*, and how we maybe weren't that wrong to try to hold the line."

"It isn't a question of right or wrong. It's a question of wanting to live."

"Here's your ice tea," said the waitress. "Bottoms up."

He could remember making love with his young wife, in the days when they first lived in Padanaram and the children were at school. He would walk them to the corner where the school bus would collect them, and raise his arm to Cecil Bugsby, who piloted the bus. Then, in the morning sunlight and before he drove to work, he would return to the house unbuttoning his shirt or, if the weather turned and he had worn a jacket, shrugging himself free and kicking off his shoes as he came through the door. Elyzabeth would be upstairs already, having cleaned the breakfast dishes and poured a second cup of coffee: one for herself, one for him.

He liked his coffee black. He liked it hot. She would have used the microwave to heat his coffee to a near-boil, while she added sugar and milk to her cup. Their cups were matched containers: conical, heavy, wide-handled. Her cup was yellow, his blue. He would take a sip, surveying her where she lay in the east-facing window, underneath the covers and smiling up at him. The moment before he shucked his pants and underpants and joined her in her nakedness was always a moment Sam savored, always a preliminary surge of pleasure. He could feel himself stiffen, aroused. The certainty that she would welcome and embrace him, already warm, already wet, was an excitement also.

"Come here," she would whisper. "Come in."

He mourned his old agility, their antics in the bed. He mourned the way Elyzabeth would get up afterwards, wearing only her terry-cloth robe, and, stepping lightly down to the kitchen, wave him off to work. He mourned the pleasure of returning, at day's end, with a day's labor done, to a house full of chatter and laughter, the children at the table and a pot of soup steaming or a casserole or pork roast or roast beef or leg of lamb on the sideboard waiting to be sliced.

He would, he decided, change his will. He would leave the house to Sally and hope she would accept it. He thought that he might kill himself to make the point of pointlessness and encourage her to live. The three grandchildren in California could share, in equal measure, the rest of his estate. He would compose a letter to Marianne and Sheila, saying he planned to travel west and see them over Christmas. This would register his intentions and a plan for the near future and thereby mislead the insurance adjustors when they looked at his old life insurance policies, hoping to avoid a pay-out. If they challenged his decision, his son, he knew, would sue.

Sam entertained these fantasies; they would miss him, would they not? They would mourn his resolute good humor, his bad jokes. He would take himself out on the Rhodes 19 and, when he was sufficiently distant from shore, roll overboard and—wearing shoes but not a life-preserver—sink. He had nothing left to live for and hoped they would live on.

Reprise

A S A WRITER, he has always had a fondness for the elderly. The action of his debut novel begins with the line, "She was old." Some thirty books and fifty years later, his protagonist lies dying on the opening page and will expire at tale's end. "The Long Sonata of the Dead," as one critic described it, is—he understands this now—his personal music and theme. The men and women he portrays have, since his youth, been old.

Now Alan is elderly as well and could be the central figure in one of his own stories, stretched out on the camp-bed or daybed or hospital bed or taking a nap on the couch. His friends are ailing or have died; his first and second wife expired within weeks of one another, as if in agreement, for once. Alive, they had been oppositional: water and oil, yin and yang. But now they are conjoined in death and seem somehow to have fashioned an alliance: Remember us, we are forgetting you.

This echoes a phrase from "Under Milkwood," Dylan Thomas's play for voices. There was an original cast recording, put out by Caedmon Records, which once he knew by heart. *Remember me, I am forgetting you*, says a character in *Under Milkwood*, speaking from her grave. More and more he finds himself reciting lines he loved when young; they sound a refrain in his head. The real and the invented worlds are not easy to keep separate, a semi-permeable membrane though which the language leaks.

Alan looks at himself in the mirror; a querulous person looks back. He sticks out his tongue and says, "Aah." He is seventy-nine years old. The voices he remembers and the voices he imagined seem interchangeable:

did he *write* that, did he *read* it, did he overhear it in the dentist's office or waiting for a bus? Who gave him what advice when he had been a student; what advice did he provide in turn to those who studied with him? "Let us leave these morbid matters," as Samuel Beckett somewhere writes, "and get on with the fact of my dying." Or words to that effect. What he hears in the echoing arch of his skull is what he once read or wrote down.

They are driving, as they often do, to the beach at Lobsterville; it is the middle of June. "Up-Island" this gray morning, little traffic shares the road; the fog has not yet lifted and the sun is not yet warm. Just after dawn, it rained.

They drive with the top down. His car is an Impala convertible, on extended loan; his indulgent mother had been planning to trade in the Chevrolet for a newer model, but gave it to her son instead as an eighteenth birthday present. Divorced, she can be turn by turn extravagant or chary of expense.

He washes and waxes the car's chassis often, but the dirt roads of Martha's Vineyard leave a film of dust on fenders and doors; small branches scratch the trunk. In later years he'll understand both how lucky he had been to drive the white convertible and how it could be bettered once he had the wherewithal to buy cars himself. In time to come he will own an Alfa Romeo, a second-hand Jaguar and a vintage Porsche. But he is nineteen now, just having completed his sophomore year in college, and the girl at his side is, she says, in love with him. They use the back seat to fuck.

The telephone rings.

Alan picks it up, expectant, but it is a robocall that tells him he's been pre-approved for a vacation cruise from Miami.

"Hello, my name is Carrie," says the voice on the recording, and she is pleased to offer him an upgrade on our trips.

"Thank you very much," he says.

"Press *One*."

He does, and the caller describes the delights of the cruise, the amenities of his cabin and the excellence of service and the gourmet-quality food. The cruise ship boasts a saltwater pool, a freshwater pool, and an updated gym. There are four separate dates of departure this month, and a cabin is reserved for him, its bargain price guaranteed.

"Press *Two*" the voice declares

"No thank you," he says to the phone. Staring out the window at the opposite apartment, Alan hangs up. He had expected a call from his nurse, whose appointment is for two o'clock and who telephones on arrival, since the building's intercom has broken and he must buzz her in. From windshield wipers on the cars, and splayed-out umbrellas on the street below, he can determine it rains.

He would, he decided, change his will.

The promised blessing leaked away and became, instead, a curse.

Often there are obstacles—a warring faction, a marriage or oath of fealty elsewhere—but the obstacles are nothing in the face of strong shared passion, and nothing matters but love.

Again the telephone rings. This time it is his visiting nurse, informing him she stands downstairs, and he tells her: "Come on up."

Like many other authors, Alan feels his work is undervalued and, in recent years, passed by. He had been "promising" when young; now—on those rare occasions when his writing is alluded to—he is described as "distinguished." This seems to him a synonym for "dull." What happened to that hoped-for inclusion in the Library of America, his nomination, once, for the National Book Award in Fiction, his dream of a Pulitzer Prize? Year by year the spotlight shines on younger writers, and he cannot bring himself to read their books or even remember their names. He tries to; he knows he should be interested, but the ambition to stay *au courant* with the world of publishing has dimmed.

His small career in television and hers in the art world faltered; they no longer turned heads where they walked. Their brief affairs and one-night stands were over, and they knew nothing of what lay ahead. What had they accomplished or failed to accomplish, and why? What were they doing, or failing to do, with their lives?

Still, Alan retains some renown. The living room bookcase (his titles arranged in chronological order of publication, and a second shelf with magazine articles and paperback and foreign editions) bulks large. The movie made from *Darkling Plain*, his fable of the Vietnam War, garnered an Oscar for "Best Adapted Screenplay" and made him, briefly, rich. Or, if not rich, sufficiently flush to purchase this co-op apartment with its ten-foot ceilings and a second bedroom that he uses for a study. The bathroom and kitchen are small and in need of renovation, but the bedroom has a distant view of Central Park. He lives in the four rooms alone.

He sang in the shower and sauna and the echoing arch of his skull
He could modulate from bass to tenor in a single phrase.

She settled into motherhood with ease. Much else in her life had seemed problematic, but the birth and feeding, then weaning of her son, went smoothly; so did his learning to walk and talk. The business of toilet training; of teaching him to use a fork, of instructing him in letters and arithmetic and manners: all the tasks of tending to her darling seemed natural to Alice. The rest of the world was the rest of the world, and the only thing that mattered was her boy's well-being; his happiness was hers.

From time to time Alan travels, a little, but no longer to promote his work or attend a conference at which he's asked to speak. He reads the *New York Times* each morning, but less attentively; he goes to dinner parties or restaurants with retired editors and colleagues from his teaching years at The New School. Such excursions are, however, infrequent; his social circle has contracted and—as he likes to put it—"One of the things you can't do in old age is to make old friends." New friends, perhaps, but this requires an effort he no longer seems able to make.

"Able" is not, he tells himself, precisely the word; the more exact word is "willing." Lately he has grown unwilling to enter conversation in the way that was habitual once, or to engage in flirtation. The surest way to fascinate a person is, he knows, to ask them to describe themselves; the surest way to be a bore is to change the subject and talk about yourself. At the rare gathering he now attends, he stands near a window nursing a drink and tries to make sense of the chatter and buzz, but cannot keep up with the topic at hand and does not try to, really; the names have passed him by.

That all this is predictable makes it only a little less painful: he loves many of the dead but, of the living, few.

I want, I want, I want.
I wanted.
I will want.
I want.

The doorbell rings. Mary stands in the vestibule, wearing a raincoat and transparent plastic hat from which moisture drips. She is sturdy and red-cheeked and Irish and works for the agency he hired to care for his wife in her long losing battle with cancer: a battle lost three years ago.

"Good afternoon."

"What's good about it?" Alan asks.

"I'm sorry I'm a little late. The bus took forever . . ."

"I meant the weather. All this rain . . ."

"Not a problem," she says, and hangs her coat in the hallway closet, dripping, then removes the plastic safeguards from her shoes.

Note the supple arrangement of English; how to "see him through" is apposite to "seeing through him," yet opposed.

Would the pair have willingly yielded to temptation and had they known already they would become husband and wife?

Would it be a horse and carriage he summons, a transom cab, car service, an Uber or Lyft?

Unlike the cleaning woman, who comes every other Wednesday, Mary is taciturn, efficient, and a welcome distraction from what he still describes as his job: the blackening of a blank page. At nine o'clock each morning, after a cup of coffee and a bran muffin topped with marmalade, he sits at his desk and attempts to write, but his verbal extrusions are paltry and slow and, often as not, he deletes them. Recently, some major artists in their eighties—Alice Munro, for example, or Philip Roth before his death—announced their withdrawal from fiction, and Alan envies their self-discipline and knowledge. But it's not the same for him; he continues to dream of inspired production: a collection of short stories or a novella that will ratify achievement and lay claim to fame. This causes him to try and try again, as the old adage would have it, but even in the writing he knows he won't succeed.

At times he thinks he should return to Paris, where once he studied "the irrational" in theatre, from Artaud to Genet. Later, he had written on Racine, Corneille, and Voltaire. The eighteen-hundreds were a period in which it had seemed possible that reason could prevail. But even in his daydreams of the Seine and the Sorbonne, he knows relocation is impractical; his doctors and lawyer and accountant all work within a thirty-minute radius of where he lives, and his French is rusty. He would not be welcome abroad.

"How do we feel?" asks the nurse.

"All right."

"All right or good?"

"All right."

"Let's take your blood pressure," she says.

Alan offers her his arm. The procedure is familiar, as are her registered notations of his temperature and pulse. Mary comes to visit every Thursday afternoon and sorts his medications and confirms that his pacemaker functions correctly and deals with his complaints. He knows her name, of course, and that she wears a yellow wig and travels from Astoria, but all else is a mystery: is she a wife, a mother, a lapsed Catholic or credulous; how many other patients does she attend to each week?

"Good. 158 over 84."

"Is that really good?"

"Well, better." She consults his chart. "When was your last cup of coffee?"

"This morning, at breakfast."

"And your last trip to the bathroom?"

"Just after lunch," he says. "Why?"

"We need to cut down on the sugar."

"Yes?"

"And alcohol. No more than two drinks a day."

What then, sang Plato's Ghost? What then? This is a line from a poem by Yeats, and although he recites it often, Alan cannot remember the name of the poem or when he first encountered it or why it so much moved him and remains now in his head. His foreign sales have disappeared; his books are out of print. The story he's been working on is, he knows, derivative and will not be published. While Mary updates his medical record, he rolls down and buttons his sleeve.

B's wife and daughter have departed; he will join them the next day. "Like speculators," he told his wife. "House-flippers, that's what we've been. We've fixed this place up perfectly. In order to leave."

"We'll come back," she said. "Darling, I promise."

"I don't think you mean that."

She made no answer; she was pasting labels on the packing crates. Her handwriting was black, and bold; he could see across the kitchen's width how she assorted their things.

"Possessions," she said. "So many things we thought we needed but never used one single time. Yogurt makers, pasta makers, meat grinders, meat slicers, two Cuisinarts. Whatever were we thinking of?"

"Food." B. stared at the silo, through the pantry windows he'd had reglazed that fall.

"We didn't starve," she said. "And we never used that yogurt maker."

"So why bother packing it?"

She looked at him. "How do you mean?"

"I mean, why pack up all this stuff? There won't be room in the apartment kitchen; we don't have to take it all with us."

She unrolled the packing tape, then cut it raspingly. "This is for storage," she said."

Alan's younger brother, Sebastian, is a "talking head" who appears with regularity on television talk shows, commenting on the political scene. This occasions some confusion, since the two men look alike. They have the same receding hairline and gaunt cheeks and beaked nose. Respectful strangers say how glad they are to meet him, how completely they agree with what he said on MSNBC the night before, but not that they have read his novels or short stories. He has learned to accept, without correction, the misdirected praise. Once, Sebastian told him that a girl of twenty-five flattered him shamelessly, shamefully, for the story "Rocking Horse" that had been assigned to her M.F.A. workshop in Minneapolis, and the brothers had agreed that turnabout is fair play.

Whatever the phrase means. Does it suggest some sort of dance, a *do-si-do*, or that Alan should be willing to yield pride of place? To have made a living from the work of words is something to be grateful for and not to second-guess. That he still quickens to language is something he still celebrates, and turnabout is fair play. *Getting and spending we lay waste our days*: this pronouncement from William Wordsworth also remains in his head. But his brother's eminence can rankle, and from time to time he wearies of being mistaken for another author of the same name; the language he lays claim to is not always or only his own.

Oh, useless, useless, useless; I had something I did want to say.

She was old, Orsetta Procopirios. That had been the actual sentence of the opening scene of his first book. It dealt with a grandmother and buried treasure on a Greek island—which one, Alan tries to remember, then does: *Rhodes*. She died in the opening chapter, and then there were family squabbles, and the question of who inherited what became a bone of plot-contention. The matter of inheritance, indeed, has been a theme of his for years, since he and his brother had been raised with the prospect of a sizable bequest: a promise that stayed undelivered and never came to pass. The family fortune is gone, the revocable trust revoked.

It transpired that their father had "mortgaged the back forty," which was how he put it when on his deathbed he admitted this, though the mortgage had nothing to do with land and much to do with failed business ventures and the attentive scrutiny of the I.R.S. Their father squandered his own father's money on foolish investments and cars.

It had all been well-intentioned and had all been a mistake. "I know you won't hold it against me," the dying man declared to his sons. "I did it out of love. I wanted the best for you boys."

Alan has written of this often, although at first obliquely: their father the fish in the card-game, the wish-fulfiller and inadvertent con-man, the emperor of bad deals. There had been the condo complex in Jamaica, the construction of a golf course in the north of Wales; there had been the "Ma and Pa" delicatessen in Dobbs Ferry with products grown only by small producers, locally. The condo complex was under-insured and blew down in a hurricane; the golf course on the coast of Wales ran into local opposition and afoul of zoning laws. For lack of sufficient patronage, the delicatessen failed. There had been the import license for artificial Christmas trees, the early twentieth century—dated but not signed—oil painting of Tahiti their father was convinced had been an undiscovered Gauguin and would fetch millions at auction. There were Broadway shows he lost his shirt on, (or, as he liked to put it, not his shirt but cufflinks) and a packaging system for furniture that needed assembly on site.

None of these projects were foolish; all of them were flawed. Their mother had been cautious but her husband overrode her and spent her inheritance too. He had been perennially hopeful, perpetually optimistic, but the devil's in the details and he got the details wrong. *Admittedly, there'd been a generation between the acts of generation, yet a line of descent could be drawn.* When their father died at ninety-seven he owned seven "classic" cars—dented and rusted and sheltering mice in a barn outside of Guilford—and nothing else of value to bequeath.

The brothers try to keep the peace, but it is hard to do. All their lives they have been intimate but wary of each other, all through childhood shared a room. Now Andrew is forty and James thirty-seven, and since their father died this year they must divide the estate. Both men fear the prospect, and neither wife is willing to help; the women have long since stopped speaking to each other, and refuse to meet.

"Just once?" asks Andrew. "Can't you jump over your shadow?"

"No."

"Please. Is it so difficult?"

"I'm not an acrobat," says Jill. "I can't do a back-flip. And don't want to try."

"Why not?"

"That bitch would cheer if I hurt myself. Jumping over my shadow, I mean. Your father was a sweetheart, but it's too much to ask."

James too has hoped for, if not the full cessation of hostilities, a truce. But Ariane remains implacable, her Gallic sense of honor at stake and her anger unassuaged. "I like ton frère," she tells her husband, "and while he is alone I wish always to accommodate him. But this is not something a reasonable person does. I refuse absolutely to be part of her ambition and her scheming ways. No good result will come of it, I warn you, chéri. Je le jure."

"I'll see you next Thursday," says Mary.

He nods, then hands her her payment in cash.

"Don't hesitate to call," she says, "if you need anything."

"Anything?"

"Not a problem."

"Really? Anything?"

The nurse closes her duffel and shrugs herself into her still-wet coat. "You got it."

Alan wants to make a joke of it, to ask her for a hot pastrami sandwich or a blow job or an opinion on Wordsworth's "Lyrical Ballads." But he knows these are not proper subjects to discuss or things to ask, and that he must restrain himself.

There are three ways to see this, he thinks. Three ways to tell it, to read it.

"Take care," he says. "See you next week."

They asked him to stop driving, or at least not to go for long drives by himself, and to this he also agreed.

The scene's dénouement need not concern us.

Mary leaves. Alan waits for her to walk down the hallway and ring for and enter the elevator before he closes his own door. Alone again, he goes to the window and watches the weather below. The rain looks more serious now. Since he has no immediate need to go out, this storm does not concern him, but the rain seems strong and blowing sideways and the dog-walkers in parkas and those who struggle with umbrellas bend against the wind. The book he is reading is mannered and flawed; the book he is writing has failed. What stretches before him is unscheduled time; what stretches behind him is gone.

They live in Hyde Park, on 50th Street, in a refurbished row house with a garden at the rear. Their son is three years old. He had noticed how the boy enjoyed stuffed pets but was frightened of an actual animal, shrinking back if they encounter dogs playing in the park. So he acquired a Golden Retriever, telling his wife Timmy shouldn't be scared, and anyhow a big barking dog will help insure their safety and won't be a bad thing.

Their new puppy is exuberant, but easy to house-break and train. Their son likes to scratch his ears and give out doggie-treats.

"I want him to be careful," says his wife.

"Not of retrievers. They're sweetness itself!"

"But what if he gets bitten by mistake?"

"Darling . . ."

"It could happen!"

She is rarely this anxious or fearful; he wonders if her caution masks some additional concern. She had difficulty getting pregnant—three miscarriages—and can have no second child. They have been married seven years, and he watches her gaze wander when they go to concerts or parties, as if she needs to ratify her sensual allure. Her face is often recognized, her body ogled nightly on the television news while she crosses or splays out her legs. Now her thirty-fifth birthday approaches, and the milestone worries her; it's the beginning, she says, of the end.

At four o'clock on this gray day the light is fading, failing, and he switches on the standing lamp and settles down to read. He will have dinner with his brother and his brother's wife, at an Italian restaurant they go to with some frequency and where, as "regulars," they are seated near the window. Too, the owner stops by their table to bring them a complimentary plate of antipasto and inquire, of Sebastian, how the children and grandchildren fare.

Alan takes pleasure in the routine, the small talk and family talk, and he likes to watch the other diners and conjure up their stories: who is married, who has a same-sex partner or is having an affair. If a pair at the next table do not converse while eating, he wonders if they know each other only a little or well. If a pretty woman passes by—this happens with some frequency—he admires her hair or her legs. The heavy book he is holding fails to retain his attention, and he finds himself reading the same passage twice and drifting into sleep.

Her children filled the kitchen. There was traffic and laughter and shouting, as had been the case before, but now she had a secret, a plan shared with Jane and silent Jonathan, not something to discuss. Jackson and Judy and the kids had packed already, and stowed their bags in the pick-up, and he said he'd be back on Sunday morning to help with Rosalie's luggage. Philip too was quick to go, explaining he had a business lunch with his senior partner in Cambridge. "What kind of man schedules a business meeting the day after Thanksgiving?" he asked, but did not await an answer. "I'll tell you. A sadist, that's who."

Alan has, he knows, some hours before he must prepare himself to exit the apartment; he hopes the rain will end. He tells himself to find a weather forecast, or listen to the radio and the prediction on the hour as to when the rain will end. He considers the matter of weather, and whether or not a forecast makes a difference, and is accurate, and if it constitutes the sort of knowledge on which he might act and how it might affect his behavior—or if, in fact, a foreknowledge of rain *would* alter his behavior. He considers the distinction between knowledge for its own sake and knowledge that engenders action and the question of altered behavior either in the long run (global warming!) or the short run (what sort of hat and coat should he wear?) and if it makes any difference as to what Kant called the categorical imperative; how an individual response, if universal, would matter in terms of the planet, and man's future as a species, and how scientists predict that even in nuclear winter the cockroaches will thrive.

Remember me. I am forgetting you.

But it was difficult to tell when such freedoms turned to duty, and the unexpected became expected behavior.

When in the final months she was hospitalized he watched her nurses changing sheets—the expert way they stripped and then remade the bed, with the patient rolled from side to side—and knew he could not manage it; he was hopeless, helpless, hapless, *in the face of grief.*

With the part of his conscious mind not yet adrift, he knows that he is dreaming, day-dreaming while it is turning dark outside and the novel he holds in his slackening grip *is fading, failing* like the light where he sits in the chair.

"How are you feeling?"

"Fine. And you?"

"Thank you for asking. I'm fine."

"You're sure?"

"Why do you ask?"

"I just wondered."

"What exactly? Wondered what?"

"If you're telling me everything?"

"What a question."

"Let's try to be honest."

"All right."

"Well, are you?"

"Telling you everything?"

"Yes."

When he wakes it is full dark outside, and he must get ready to go. Alan stands and stretches and steps to the window to look at the weather beyond. The sidewalk gleams, and there are puddles, but the rain has stopped.

Do drop me some sort of line.

In his dream there had been music, and also perturbation; old arguments rehearsed, old love affairs gone wrong. Could he use, he asks himself, just such an argument in the scene he has been writing and to which he will, in the morning, return; does it make sense to add scenes? Or would it be better to cut? The particularities of his wakeful dream (his first wife in a raincoat, her long hair blown behind her, a Boston Whaler somehow in a harbor and a dog yapping from the dock) do not in fact concern him, but the feel of it remains: the sense of possibility, of hope conjoined to loss.

These fragments I have shored against my ruination, which in the eyes of the world is success, and I wanted to ask you—directly, directly—what caused you to lay down the metaphoric quill pen and actual typewriter, then word processor, and why?

His first wife had been tall and thin, his second was—to use a word of which Bellow was fond—*zaftig*. His second wife (whom at first he does not recognize, because she is swathed in a poncho and hood) steps down into the boat. It dips a little, rocking, then steadies as she sits. She is his heart's one darling, but the cancer has, after years of remission, returned. The breeze is fresh, the water green; waves break against the dock. He has peopled his books with a fictional crew, and they strain at the oarlocks and sweat. Others pull the starter-cord of their two-cycle outboard motor while it sputters into life.

Her cheeks were wet. Her heart, she felt, would crack. What does it mean, she asked herself, to have a heart that cracks, and why should she be feeling sorry for herself when so many of her children and grandchildren were doing what they could to make her feel less sorry and alone? In her dream she had been sailing in Jack's cat-boat, and they had packed a picnic and the sun was bright on the dark lake and he had proposed to her by putting a ring on her finger while she was holding the tiller. She did not need to tell him "Yes" because he could see by the tears in her eyes that she was thinking, Yes, Yes, Yes, *but she told him anyhow, and he said "That's my girl."*

Alan goes to the bathroom, unbuckling his belt, then drops his pants and stands at the toilet and pees. In his dream there was the promise of sex, but it had evaded him, eluded him, and he remembers the phrase from *The Tempest*, "I cried to dream again." That had been the music, *that* had been the feel of it, and his throat constricts as though he is about to weep; he sticks out his tongue and says, "Aah."

The Trattoria where he will meet his family is two streets down and around the corner; he will walk. It is neither too cold nor too wet outside, and he could use the air. Sebastian's wife, Carla, was born in Arezzo and speaks English with a strong accent, although she has inhabited New York for thirty years. She is judgmental on matters Italian when transported to America—particularly its cuisine—but she approves of this restaurant, and Alan looks forward to liver and onions prepared the Roman way. *We all are born to die.*

He wrote of the power of darkness, the kingdom of the Underworld, the King he must petition to let his wife come back.

She would talk about it when she chose, he told himself; the rest could wait.

The telephone rings. Again it is a robocall, but this woman is named

Shirley and she offers to consolidate his debt. His credit rating, she tells him, is fine, but his credit cards could profit from consolidation, and while she tells him that her company has saved millions of people millions of dollars and he could be the next to profit from their savings plan, he cradles the receiver. Alan rubs his eyes. Then he drops his right hand to his cheek and rubs at the soft stubble and decides he ought to shave. His dream stays palpable, vivid, and he cannot shake it: the boat bobbing just beyond the pier and just beyond his reach.

He bought the house in a day. He had to; there were other bidders, and the market had been "hot." He flew from the small town in Vermont, where he, his wife, and their two daughters were living, to the town in Michigan where he would start a new job. They had been living in a barn: a remodeled white clapboard structure with a wood stove in the center of what used to be a granary. Outside were meadows and then a steep slope. They had lived there the length of their marriage, and were reluctant to leave.

This job, however, was a promotion. The salary would double the salary he earned. And now that their daughters were going to school, the caliber of local education was an issue; their daughters were seven and four. William worked as the Director of Admissions for the Johnson State Campus of the University of Vermont, but the college was in trouble and the applicant pool small. Regional economy had stalled, and this offer of employment was too good to refuse. He would become an Associate Director of Admissions in a university with thousands of out-of-state applicants; his was to be a focus on the high schools of New England. He had attended Dartmouth, then received an M.B.A. from Harvard, and his credentials as an "easterner" were strong.

Alice, his wife, opposed change. It wasn't fear, she told him, it wasn't even anxiety, but they had been so happy in their backwater town in the mountains that she found it hard to imagine a move would mean improvement. She liked the snow, the skiing, the hot summers and brisk autumns; she even liked mud season and the impassable roads. They had a dog, two cats, and chickens till the chickens were killed by a fox.

"If we want things to stay the same,'" he told her, quoting a novel he admired, "they will have to change."'

In the street he cannot keep himself from watching other walkers: the clothes they wear, the shoes they use, the handbags and the hats. He conjures up their histories, their naked selves, their hopes. They are restaurateurs from the north of Spain or English teachers or hedge fund advisers or Admissions officers in a Midwestern university; they have bad teeth or leukemia or have just returned from a tryst. They are short order cooks or prostitutes or receptionists in advertising firms; they are hoping to buy an apartment or get married or have children or go to a hockey game tonight.

The men and women in the street are talking on cellphones, or to each other, and he believes it his duty to describe them; he cannot keep himself from fleshing out the lives of those he passes, and who pass him by. They are his subjects, every one of them, but each will fade away. His gait is slow, an old man's pace, and at seven o'clock there's a hurry and bustle, a getting and spending he no longer joins or enjoys.

Imagine for a moment that the boy who died eight years ago is still alive, recovered, clean, and setting up a model train for his own son in the living room. There's Christmas music playing on the radio, there's the smell of standing ribs just extracted from the oven, there's a table set for twelve.

In the morning, he assures himself, the story he is working on will be complete. It is not a mess, not really, it needs only to be pruned. Or, instead, expanded. He has forgotten nothing, or nothing of importance: the last name of a nurse, perhaps, or the Platonic dialogue he read in the course he took his sophomore year in college: Great Books. That he has not composed one is, he knows, the case. But there is the prospect of liver and onions and a Barolo he particularly fancies, of which he will drink a third glass.

Artists have, their father said, either too much success or too little, the hardest thing of all is just to keep on keeping on.

His brother's wife reminds him, or so he likes to tell her, of Claudia Cardinale, the beauty from *The Leopard*, in the scene where she was flirting with a youthful Alain Delon. If he were young enough, and strong enough, or skilled enough, he would restore the Mercedes convertible now languishing in a barn outside of Guilford, but he is neither young nor skilled nor strong enough and their father's collection of automobiles will be—the brothers have agreed—put up for sale next month.

It will, he knows, yield little, and certainly not a large profit; like all of their father's investments, this one was a mistake. After a sufficient amount of neglect and inexpert restoration of a "classic car," the chassis and motor and rusted drive-shaft can be salvaged only for parts, but the red 1969 Mercedes Benz 290-SL with 37,435 actual miles is nonetheless a temptation, a temptation to resist.

There are many such. There are the siren songs of envy, the comforts of pity and pride. There is the self-deception of a backwards look: the present, the pluperfect and the past. At the wet northwest corner of 83rd St. and Columbus Avenue, Alan stands beneath green scaffolding and awaits the traffic signal's change so he can cross without risk. Briefly, he shuts his eyes.

Author's Note

These three books belong together. The first two collections of stories were published long ago: *About My Table, and Other Stories* in 1983, and *The Writers' Trade, and Other Stories* in 1990. The first contained nine stories about men in early midlife crisis, whose personal lives were central to the action but whose careers were tangential. I mean by this that I focused, as the title suggests, on what was going on at home and not in the law office or operating room or on the concert stage. The second contained nine stories about the world of writing. They focused on the professional rather more than the personal life—from that of a debut novelist to that of an old author whose active career is behind him. They were, I thought, companion-texts, and the eighteen brief fictions have been left unchanged.

The third part of this book, *Reprise and Other Stories*, contains more recent work—eleven tales of varying length, with the middle story, "Passacaglia and Fugue in C-Minor," itself a kind of fugue. Most of the stories here are written in third person; two of them have female protagonists and two approach the length of a novella. At a certain stage in one's career, one begins to recognize pattern, and the act of composition is writ large in the final piece, "Reprise." Let it stand as a collective title for the whole.

I did something of the same before, with Dalkey Archive Press, in *Sherbrookes*, 2011. There I took three novels—*Possession* (1977), *Sherbrookes* (1978), and *Stillness* (1980)—and combined them into one; the trilogy became a single volume. But that entailed revision, a stitching and unstitching, and in the case of the first two components of this collection I thought it wiser to leave well enough alone. Too, it seems to me that there's a through-line in the diction here; the young pup and old dog bark from the same single throat. These collected stories, therefore, contain the sum and substance of my work within the genre, and I hope they give the reader some of the pleasure in reading that they gave me, over all these years, to write.

The late John O'Brien (1945-2020) first proposed the idea of this collection. I'm very grateful to his memory and for the work of his successors at Dalkey Archive Press, Will Evans and Chad Post. Linda Stack Nelson and James Webster of Deep Vellum have maintained the standard of attentive excellence with which I've long associated this publishing endeavor, and I'm honored to be part of it. My agent, Gail Hochman, continues in her role as indispensable steward of what is by now a large body of work. And I want to thank and celebrate, as always, the dedicatee of this volume: Elena.

NICHOLAS DELBANCO is a British-born American who received his BA from Harvard and his MA from Columbia University. An editor and author of more than thirty books, Delbanco has received numerous awards—among them a Guggenheim Fellowship and two Writing Fellowships from the National Endowment for the Arts. He is the Robert Frost Distinguished University Professor of English Emeritus at the University of Michigan, where he served as Director of the MFA program in Creative Writing and of the Hopwood Awards.